P9-DEE-219

THE ROAD TO
SCIENCE FICTION

VOLUME 3: FROM HEINLEIN TO HERE

EDITED BY
JAMES GUNN

THE ROAD TO SCIENCE FICTION #3
FROM HEINLEIN TO HERE

Copyright ©1979 by James Gunn.

All rights reserved. This book may not be reproduced,
in whole or in part, without the written permission of the publisher,
except for the purpose of reviews.

The characters and events described in this book are fictional.
Any resemblance between the characters and any person,
living or dead, is purely coincidental.

The mention of or reference to any companies or products in these pages is
not a challenge to the trademarks or copyrights concerned.

Because of the mature themes presented within,
reader discretion is advised.

White Wolf is committed to reducing waste in publishing. For this reason,
we do not permit our covers to be "stripped" for returns, but instead
require that the whole book be returned, allowing us to resell it.

Cover Illustration: Michael Scott Cohen

Design: Michael Scott Cohen

Borealis is an imprint of White Wolf Publishing.

WHITE WOLF PUBLISHING
780 PARK NORTH BOULEVARD, SUITE 100
CLARKSTON, GA 30021
WWW.WHITE-WOLF.COM

Printed in Canada

Acknowledgments

"All You Zombies—" by Robert A. Heinlein. Copyright © 1959 Mercury Press, Inc. Copyright © 1959 Robert A. Heinlein. Reprinted by permission of author.

"Reason" by Isaac Asimov. Copyright © 1941 by Street & Smith Publications. Copyright renewed by Isaac Asimov, 1968. Reprinted by permission of author.

"Desertion" by Clifford Simak. Copyright © 1944 Street & Smith Publications, Inc. Copyright renewed 1972 by Clifford Simak. Reprinted by permission of author.

"Mimsy Were The Borogoves" by Lewis Padgett. Copyright © 1943 by Lewis Padgett (pseudonym of Henry Kuttner, Street & Smith Publications Inc.). Reprinted by permission of the Harold Matson Co., Inc.

"The Million-Year Picnic" by Ray Bradbury. Copyright © 1946 by Ray Bradbury. Renewed 1973 by author. Reprinted by permission of the Harold Matson Co., Inc.

"Thunder and Roses" by Theodore Sturgeon. Copyright © 1947 by Street & Smith Publications, Inc. Reprinted by permission of author.

"That Only a Mother" by Judith Merril. Copyright © 1948 by Street & Smith Publications, Inc. Copyright © 1954 by Judith Merril. Reprinted by permission of the author and her agent, Virginia Kidd.

"Brooklyn Project" by Philip Klass. Copyright © 1948 by Philip Klass. Reprinted by permission of the author.

"Coming Attraction" by Fritz Leiber. Copyright © 1950 by Galaxy Publishing Corp. Reprinted by permission of the author.

"The Sentinel" by Arthur C. Clarke. Copyright © 1951 by Arthur C. Clarke. Reprinted by permission of the author and the author's agents, Scott Meredith Literary Agency, Inc., 845 Third Avenue, New York, N.Y. 10022.

"Sail On! Sail On!" by Philip José Farmer. Copyright © 1952 by Philip José Farmer. Reprinted by permission of the author and the author's agents, Scott Meredith Literary Agency, Inc., 845 Third Avenue, New York, N.Y. 10022.

"Critical Factor" by Hal Clement. Copyright 1953 by Ballantine Books, Inc. Reprinted by permission of the author.

"Fondly Fahrenheit" by Alfred Bester. Copyright © 1954 by Mercury Press, Inc. and Alfred Bester. Reprinted by permission of the author.

"The Cold Equations" by Tom Godwin. Copyright © 1954 by Street & Smith Publications. Reprinted by permission of the author and the author's agents, Scott Meredith Literary Agency, Inc., 845 Third Avenue, New York, N.Y. 10022.

"The Game of Rat and Dragon" by Cordwainer Smith. Copyright © 1955 by Street & Smith Publications. Reprinted by permission of the author and the author's agents, Scott Meredith Literary Agency, Inc., 845 Third Avenue, New York, N.Y. 10022.

"Pilgrimage to Earth" by Robert Sheckley. Copyright © 1956 by HMH Publishing Co. Reprinted by permission of Abby Sheckley (director) in behalf of Sheckley Ltd.

"Who Can Replace a Man?" by Brian W. Aldiss. Copyright © 1958 by Brian W. Aldiss. Reprinted by permission of author.

"Harrison Bergeron" by Kurt Vonnegut, Jr. Copyright © 1961 by Kurt Vonnegut, Jr. Originally published in *Fantasy and Science Fiction*. Reprinted by permission of Delacorte Press/Seymour Lawrence.

"The Streets of Ashkelon" by Harry Harrison. Copyright © 1962 by Harry Harrison. Reprinted by permission of author.

"The Terminal Beach" by J. G. Ballard. Copyright © 1964 by J. G. Ballard. Reprinted by permission of the author and the author's agents, Scott Meredith Literary Agency, Inc., 845 Third Avenue, New York, N.Y. 10022.

"Dolphin's Way" by Gordon R. Dickson. Copyright © 1964 by Condé Nast Publications Inc. Reprinted by permission of the author.

"Slow Tuesday Night" by R. A. Lafferty. Copyright © 1965 by Galaxy Publishing Corp. From *Galaxy*, April 1965. Reprinted by permission of the author.

"Day Million" by Frederik Pohl. Copyright © 1966 by Rogue Magazine. Reprinted by permission of the author.

"We Can Remember It for You Wholesale" by Philip K. Dick. Copyright © 1966 by Street & Smith Publications. Reprinted by permission of the author and the author's agents, Scott Meredith Literary Agency, Inc., 845 Third Avenue, New York, N.Y. 10022.

"I Have No Mouth, and I Must Scream" by Harlan Ellison. Copyright © 1968 by Harlan Ellison. Reprinted by arrangement with, and permission of, the author and the author's agent, Robert P. Mills, Ltd., New York. All rights reserved.

"Aye, and Gomorrah…" by Samuel R. Delany. Copyright © 1967 by Harlan Ellison for *Dangerous Visions* published by Doubleday. Copyright © 1971 by Samuel R. Delany. Reprinted by permission of the author.

"The Jigsaw Man" by Larry Niven. Copyright ©1967 by Harlan Ellison. Reprinted by permission of the author.

"Kyrie" by Poul Anderson. Copyright © 1968 by Joseph Elder. First published in *The Farthest Reaches*, edited by Joseph Elder. Reprinted by permission of author.

"Masks" by Damon Knight. Copyright © 1968 by HMH Publishing Corp. Original publication, *Playboy*. Reprinted by permission of the author.

Excerpts from STAND ON ZANZIBAR by John Brunner. Copyright © 1968 by John Brunner. Reprinted by permission of Doubleday & Company, Inc.

"The Big Flash" by Norman Spinrad. Copyright © 1969 by Damon Knight. Reprinted from *Orbit 5* by permission of the author.

"Sundance" by Robert Silverberg. Copyright © 1969 by Robert Silverberg. Reprinted by permission of the author.

Excerpt from THE LEFT HAND OF DARKNESS by Ursula K. Le Guin. Copyright © 1969 by Ursula K. Le Guin. Reprinted by permission of Grosset & Dunlap, Inc.

"When It Changed" by Joanna Russ. Copyright © 1972 by Joanna Russ. Reprinted by permission of the author.

"The Engine at Heartspring's Center" by Roger Zelazny. Copyright © 1974 by Condé Nast Publications Inc. Reprinted by permission of the author.

"Tricentennial" by Joe Haldeman. Copyright © 1976 by The Condé Nast Corporation. Reprinted by permission of the author.

CONTENTS

To all the writers of science fiction yet to be

INTRODUCTION

1

The "golden age" of science fiction is a phrase that is frequently used by fans and critics, and just as frequently debated. What is the golden age of science fiction? When was it?

Isaac Asimov referred to the golden age in his anthology *Before the Golden Age* and dated it from 1938, when John Campbell became editor of *Astounding Stories*, to 1950, when other magazines such as *Galaxy* and *The Magazine of Fantasy and Science Fiction* entered the field.

Norman Spinrad in his anthology *Modern Science Fiction*, on the other hand, dates the golden age from 1966 to 1970.

The term itself is not as important as the attitude toward science fiction that it implies. The entire history of science fiction has been first a slow movement toward definition, and then, once the question seemed to be answered, the beginning of a movement away from it.

Definition is important, not merely for precision, so that everyone is talking about the same phenomenon, but because science fiction is protean and disagreement is endemic, and because each change in editor and in the medium of publication and each creative advance redefines the genre. In terms of communication, for instance, "golden age" is defined as "the most flourishing period in a nation's literature" or "the flowering of civilization or art." Spinrad claims that science fiction did not "flower" until about 1965, when writers freed themselves from the conformity of the magazines and struck off in individual directions.

Some critics, however, add to that meaning a second sense of "an era of peace and innocence"; then the term may refer to the period of the greatest amount of wonder and be properly applied to that age at which the enthusiastic reader discovers it—more specifically, as Pete Graham has suggested, the age of twelve. Asimov offers some agreement with this by calling the second decade of existence every person's own golden age.

"Golden age" can also have the further meaning of the quality of its writing. Science fiction continued to improve through the 1950s and up to the present. But the magazine boom of the early 1950s and the steadily increasing number of hardcover and paperback publications meant that the cohesiveness of science fiction, the ability of readers to keep up with it, to encompass it in a thought or a phrase, became increasingly difficult after 1950.

Until 1950 fans could read every magazine circulated and every book published, and search the library and secondhand stores for more science fiction—and still have time to publish voluminous fanzines. Until 1950 writers kept up with what other writers were doing and sometimes what readers said about it. After 1950 magazines increasingly went unread, books increasingly went unbought.

2

The period from 1938 to 1950 that Asimov calls the golden age was a period not only of flowering but of consensus. Readers and writers knew what science fiction was: it was what was published in *Astounding*. The significant fact of the forties was the dominance of *Astounding* over science fiction and the dominance of John Campbell, the writer-turned-editor for Street & Smith at the age of twenty-eight, over *Astounding*. Campbell made the magazine over in his own image, and that image captured the imaginations and the beliefs of science fiction readers.

Other magazines were being published, some of them claiming circulations considerably larger than *Astounding's*—Ziff Davis's *Amazing*, edited by Raymond A. Palmer, for instance—but the outstanding stories, the influential stories, the stories that seemed to define what science fiction was and what it ought to be, were appearing in *Astounding*.

Through the 1940s the magazines were the major—and sometimes the only—publishing medium for science fiction. Even when books began to be published, the anthologies were largely made up of stories from the magazines, and the novels were reprinted serials. But even beyond the centralizing fact of the magazines, the science fiction of the 1940s was a coming-together, a unification of diverse influences, a developing consensus.

The consensus was shaped by Campbell. Mostly he defined what science fiction was by the stories that appeared in his magazine. But he also talked about it in the controversial editorials that expressed his personal views; writers got large doses of theory in conversation, in long letters, and in rejection slips ("Amusing," he might write, "but it ain't science fiction"); and once in a while he actually attempted to deal with the problem of definition in specific terms.

In 1952 he defined science fiction in an article for Reginald Bretnor's *Modern Science Fiction:* "Fiction is only dreams written out; science fiction consists of the hopes and dreams and fears (for some dreams are nightmares) of a technically based society." Even more specifically, he wrote in "The Science of Science Fiction Writing" for Lloyd Eschbach's *Of Worlds Beyond* (1947) that "to be science fiction, not fantasy, an honest effort at prophetic extrapolation of the known must be made." And he went on to say:

> Prophetic extrapolation can derive from a number of different sources and apply in a number of fields. Sociology, psychology, and parapsychology are, today, not true sciences; therefore instead of forecasting future results of applications of social science of today, we must forecast the *development of a science* [emphasis Campbell's] of sociology.... On the other hand, physics is, today, a real science and predictions must be based on the known data of the existing science.

These prescriptions became basic to science fiction. They were quoted to succeeding generations as the unbreakable laws of the genre. They united the streams of science fiction that had seemed to diverge from Verne and Wells, and diverted the stream of fantasy into another clearly defined channel.

Up to the time of Verne, science fiction had existed in forms that were possible to identify as such only in retrospect: Mary Shelley's *Frankenstein* (1818) may have been the first literary reaction to the impact of science on the world; Poe's "Mellonta Tauta" may have anticipated the literature of anticipation. Before they could begin to create their work, the consequences of the Industrial Revolution had to become apparent to writers of fiction: the way it was changing the nature of human life, the way it was shaping the future. But even before the Industrial Revolution, writers had expressed humanity's desire to explore, to speculate, to hope and dream and fear, in epics and tales, satires and utopias.

The multi-volume anthology that I have been engaged in putting together under the general title of *The Road to Science Fiction* has been concerned primarily with definition: what is it? Besides their other qualities, the stories and excerpts have defined science fiction by their simple existence. Secondarily *The Road to Science Fiction* has been concerned with influences: how did it get to be that way?

The first volume, subtitled *From Gilgamesh to Wells*, was devoted to the kinds of literature that preceded science fiction or helped create the genre in the nineteenth century. It set down three criteria for the existence of science fiction: 1) people had to discover the future, a future that would be different from the past or the present because of scientific advance and technological innovation; 2) they had to learn to think of themselves not as a tribe, or as a people, or even as a nation, but as a species; and 3) they had to adopt an open mind about the nature of the universe—its beginning and its end—and the fate of man.

The first volume was concerned with the ways in which people's concept of the world was changed by their growing mastery of their environment; with the literature that was an expression of society's knowledge about the world and the forces that operated upon it; with the ways in which the Industrial Revolution and the changes it brought upon the way people lived and the way they thought about the world created the future; and with the response of writers of what we call science fiction.

Jules Verne, the stage-struck French lawyer who discovered the power of technological marvels to create an audience for his adventure stories, based most of his extraordinary voyages on engineering probabilities. In his later years he objected to H. G. Wells's being called "the English Jules Verne" because Wells's work was not based solidly on science. "I make use of physics," he wrote; "he invents."

Wells also denied the resemblance: "These exercises of mine," he wrote, "...do not pretend to deal with possible things; they are exercises of the imagination in a quite different field."

The second volume in this series, subtitled *From Wells to Heinlein*, dealt with the second criterion: the ways in which people began to think of themselves, in their best moments, as a species, and how this was reflected in the literature that was a kind of consideration of humanity as a species, science fiction. Other factors influenced the emergence of science fiction as a genre, of course. The means of publication became critical in Wells's time, and he credited his early success, as well as the success of a number of other writers who began their work in the last decade of the nineteenth century, to the rise of new magazines and new readers.

The era of the mass magazines was brought about by the invention of pulp paper and the linotype machine, both in 1884; by the development of the means to distribute magazines by railway and truck, and of companies set up for distribution; and by a new reading audience created by mass education. By 1896 the mass magazines were joined by the pulp magazines, which offered nearly 200 pages of fiction for a dime. Frank Munsey's *Argosy* got competition after the turn of the century from Street & Smith's *The People's Magazine* and *The Popular Magazine*, and soon more than a dozen magazines competed for readers with adventure stories of all kinds, including some science fiction (or what passed for it). They too were adventure stories, and they reached a peak with Edgar Rice Burroughs and A. Merritt.

4

The category pulp magazines, which offered stories of a single kind, began in 1915 with Street & Smith's *Detective Story Monthly*, although Frank Munsey had experimented a decade before with *The Railroad Man's Magazine* and *The Ocean*. In 1919 Street & Smith produced *Western Story Magazine*, and in 1921 *Love Stories*. The way was open for the first science fiction magazine, and it was finally offered in 1926 by a man, Hugo Gernsback, who had published a long series of popular science magazines.

Within three years that magazine, *Amazing Stories*, had rivals: Gernsback's own *Wonder Stories* in 1929 and then *Astounding Stories of Super Science* in 1930. Campbell, who was ranked the equal of E. E. Smith in creating space epics and who had turned to writing smaller-scale, more artistic stories under the name of Don A. Stuart, gave up writing in 1937 to assume the editorship of *Astounding*.

Donald A. Wollheim, in his *The Universe Makers* (1971), called Campbell "a victorious Vernian," but Campbell did not retreat all the way to Verne's insistence upon "physics." He was willing to permit, even encourage, speculation about the nonsciences becoming sciences. He applauded A. E. van Vogt's casual way with logic and scientific accuracy because van Vogt made it sound convincing; van Vogt waved his magic wand of words over the mystifying events, and the effect satisfied Campbell.

The result, after all, was reasonably close to Wells's prescription: "For the writer of fantastic stories to help the reader to play the game properly, he must help him in every possible unobtrusive way to *domesticate* the impossible hypothesis. He must trick him into an unwary concession to some plausible assumption and get on with his story while the illusion holds."

Rather than a Vernian, Campbell seems more like a synthesizer of the best from both writers: he insisted on plausibility in a science-important milieu, where scientists and engineers were central and were depicted accurately; but also, as an inspection of the fiction in *Astounding* would document, he was willing to publish the wildest kind of speculation if it was carefully thought out and convincingly presented.

He got a reputation for wanting gadget fiction or idea fiction, for publishing stories for engineers, but Campbell understood well enough the necessities of fiction and applied them to the kind of stories he published. He warned against good ideas poorly or even just adequately written. And he pointed out that "a story—science fiction or otherwise—is a story of human beings.... In older science fiction, the Machine and the Great Idea predominated. Modern readers...want stories of people living in a world where a Great Idea, or a series of them, and a Machine, or machines, form the background. But it is the man, not the idea or machine, that is the essence."

Campbell's rigor, or his tastes, became critical to the development of science fiction. Fantasy was excluded from *Astounding*. So were stories whose logic was inadequate or whose development ran counter to Campbell's requirements or his instincts. Such stories had to please the editors of other magazines or remain unpublished. Since *Astounding* paid more for stories than any other magazine, authors tried to sell their stories there first, and other magazines had to subsist on Campbell rejects or on the work of authors who were reconciled to the fact that they could not sell their work to Campbell. Some writers found ready acceptance, others were able to please him occasionally, and others never tried.

The measure of Campbell's effectiveness as an editor would turn on his ability to discover writers, because he could not write the stories himself. He discovered them in quantity. In Asimov's 1952 essay "Social Science Fiction," he wrote, "The importance of Campbell is that he was not content to let Weinbaums spring up accidentally. He looked for them. He encouraged them."

Before 1940 Campbell published the first of the early stories of L. Sprague de Camp, L. Ron Hubbard, Eric Frank Russell, Lester del Rey, Robert A. Heinlein, Theodore Sturgeon, A. E. van Vogt, and Asimov himself. In addition he reinvigorated or redirected the careers of such older writers as Jack Williamson, E. E. "Doc" Smith, Clifford Simak, and Henry Kuttner and C. L. Moore (individually and as a man- and-wife team writing under a variety of pseudonyms).

Together Campbell and his writers satisfied, almost as a by-product of their activities, the third criterion for the existence of science fiction: they freed themselves from old concepts about the nature of the universe—cultural and religious—and began an extended fictional debate about the beginning and the end of things, and the meaning and fate of humanity, which resulted in a kind of consensus within science fiction.

Part of that consensus was expressed by Heinlein in his guest-of-honor speech in 1941 at the third World Science Fiction convention in Denver. He called his speech, as Wells had called his talk before the Royal Institution nearly four decades earlier, "The Discovery of the Future." Heinlein said that what had primarily attracted him to science fiction was a quality called "time-binding," which he identified as a term invented by Alfred Korzybski to describe the fact that the human animal lives not only in the present but in the past and in the future. Most people, Heinlein said, live from day to day or plan ahead for a year or two. He went on to say:

> Science fiction fans differ from most of the rest of the race by thinking in terms of racial magnitudes—not even centuries but thousands of years.... That is what science fiction consists of: trying to figure out from the past and from the present what the future may be.

More specifically the fictional debate resulted in a consensus future history that Wollheim summed up in *The Universe Makers*. It was not entirely Heinleinian, although Heinlein was the first writer to base his stories and novels (at least early in his career) on a consistent model of the future. This consensus had large elements of Asimov's "Foundation" stories and contributions by such earlier authors as "Doc" Smith, Edmond Hamilton, and Olaf Stapledon. Later additions and refinements were made by such authors as Poul Anderson, James Blish, Larry Niven, and Ursula K. Le Guin.

That future history encompassed man's conquest of space and his colonizing of the moon and the planets, his struggle to reach the nearer stars, followed by the rise and fall of the galactic human empire, the dark ages, and the rediscovery of the human galaxy and the variety of human forms and societies into which humanity had developed.

That consensus future left room for almost any kind of story a writer wished to create, including many in which some misadventure or miscalculation kept that future from happening: earth runs out of resources before spaceflight has made other resources available; Armageddon destroys civilization; societies turn rigid through religion or tyranny; a careless invention or its side-effect destroys humanity or its initiative; pollution, plague, or cosmic accident wipes out humanity or civilization or the earth itself; or the aliens arrive first.

The consensus existed in the conviction not that man *would* necessarily achieve the planets and the stars, but that he *should,* and that anything that kept him from that goal was bad not only in itself but because it was a frustration of his destiny. Science fiction saw man as a creature that had struggled up from a single-celled amoeba, that had endured the long travail of evolution, the challenge of a million hostile life forms, the thousand ills and mishaps the world provides, and the historic process of oppression, liberation, and slow accumulation of knowledge. Now he stands, self-aware, his two feet upon the earth that he has earned and his eyes lifted to the stars. Equipped with tools he has made, he sees beyond and beneath the appearance of things to the essential reality; he considers the universe, how it came to be and what will become of it, and asks what is his place in it.

Campbell writers shared the optimism of the scientific community; they felt that man was progressing in mastery both of his environment and of himself, that though there would be slips and regressions mankind would win through—or tragedy would lie in the fact that he was frustrated by chance or miscalculation. They agreed with William Faulkner that man would not only endure—he would prevail.

Other directions emerged at the end of 1949 and the beginning of 1950 with the appearance of *The Magazine of Fantasy and Science Fiction,* edited by Anthony Boucher (1911-1968) and J. Francis McComas (1910-1978), and of *Galaxy Science Fiction,* edited by H. L. Gold (1914-1996). They looked at science fiction from other viewpoints, and the Campbell consensus, though it still had its adherents and its influence, began to fragment.

The policy-maker for *F&SF* was Boucher (whose real name was William Anthony Parker White), and the policy was improved literary quality. The original title was *The Magazine of Fantasy,* which changed with the second issue; the generic aspects of science fiction were minimized. Boucher liked a good story, but he liked good writing even more. The mixture of science fiction and fantasy suggested that the fiction it published would exhibit characteristics different from that published in other purely science fiction or fantasy magazines. Fantasy requires only internal consistency, no more than the compass of one author's head, but science fiction—up to this point, at least—had demanded consistency with the rest of the universe. Some rigorous science fiction appeared in *F&SF*, but much of what was published was fantasy and hybrid stories that were difficult to categorize.

Galaxy, on the other hand, established its own rigor. Gold wanted science fiction, but he wanted it written to his specifications. His requirement was entertainment. "There is nothing as grim," he wrote once, "as an entertainment man in search of entertainment." His view of life was ironic. He wanted fiction not about scientists and engineers, but about average citizens caught up in worlds not of their making who find ways not to cure but to endure.

F&SF reunited the streams of fantasy and science fiction in a turbulent bed; it produced a tolerance for anything written well that encouraged many established writers to attempt stories that previously would have been unpublishable and attracted into the field new writers who found Campbell's requirements incompatible or uninspiring. *Galaxy* specialized in the social satire; here the Wellsian influence was stronger, and a generation of writers who had been working on the fringes of Campbell's world found a home for their darker visions of the future of humanity. Some *Astounding* writers were drawn away.

One reason for the crack in *Astounding's* dominance was rates for writers. Except for the brief largess of the Clayton *Astounding* from 1930 to 1933, rates (always by the word) had been consistently low. A penny a word was considered good. That was lower than rates in other pulp magazines, and it was a persistent irritation that confession magazines paid two or three times as much. Campbell's *Astounding* paid the highest rates throughout the 1940s, but in the 1950s *Galaxy* offered an escalating rate starting at three cents a word. Campbell matched it, but did not outbid Gold. The rates at *F&SF* were a bit lower, but still better than the other markets, and its editorial policy was sufficiently appealing to keep many authors in spite of the gap.

The 1950s were also a boom period for new magazines. Anywhere from three to fourteen new science fiction magazines a year were started between 1949 and 1953; many died quickly, and in 1953 more magazines were killed than new ones born. Publishers had overestimated the influence of the atom bomb and rocketry on the magazine-buying public; although people were living in a science fiction world, they had not yet recognized it.

Nevertheless, there were thirty or forty science fiction magazines on the stands at one time, and this was a great encouragement to new writers. They emerged in substantial numbers.

➐

Other influences on the development of science fiction made their presence felt more gradually. After World War II, science fiction once more began to appear in book form. Ever since the creation of *Amazing*, book publishers had virtually ignored science fiction, but now anthologies and novels began to appear. They were read avidly by magazine readers, but they did not alter tastes; they reinforced them, for they mined twenty years of magazines for treasure—short stories for anthologies and serials for novels. The chief source was *Astounding*. Of the thirty-five stories published in *Adventures in Time and Space* (1946), edited by Raymond J. Healy and J. Francis McComas, thirty-two had been published in *Astounding* and all but four of these had been purchased by Campbell. In the other big postwar anthology, Groff Conklin's *The Best of Science Fiction*, the proportion of stories from *Astounding* was not quite as high.

Anthologies tended to be published by mainline publishers such as Viking, Crown, Random House, and Pellegrini & Cudahy, but the novels, with a few exceptions, were published by fan presses established for this purpose. Most of them published a few books and went broke; a few, such as Arkham House, Gnome Press, and Shasta, survived for several years. A few traditional publishers had earlier been interested in science fiction novels—Simon and Schuster, for instance—and they were joined in 1949 by Frederik Fell, Doubleday, and Dutton. Scribner's became involved through Heinlein's juveniles, then Winston and Harcourt Brace with André Norton's novels.

That marked the beginning of a new era in science fiction publishing, of novels that did not appear first in the magazines. Gradually, as Ace Books began to publish original science fiction in paperback, joined by Ballantine in 1952, the opportunity to publish without regard for the magazines and their requirements became a significant alternative. In 1951 this became true of short stories as well with the publication of Healy's anthology of original fiction, *New Tales of Space and Time*. In 1952 Frederik Pohl began editing a series of original anthologies for Ballantine in paperback entitled *Star Science Fiction*. They provided another market, less restricted by editorial requirements than magazines and often better paying. In the 1960s the original anthology would burgeon into a significant alternative and become a major factor in breaking the magazines' hold on the genre.

Publication of original short stories and novels in books began encouraging individual expression over conformity to an editor's concept of the genre or the tastes of his readers, but it also began to diffuse the definition. Science fiction had been defined, in practical terms, as what was published in the science fiction magazines, *Astounding* in particular; now it had to be defined by the designation "science fiction" on the book, or by significant words in the title, or by identifiable symbols—rocket, alien, spacesuit, planet—on the cover.

Some science fiction began to be published in other media: the slick magazines, while they survived, had begun to publish Heinlein's short stories after World War II, and *Collier's* serialized *The Day of the Triffids* by John Wyndham (John Beynon Harris, 1903–1969), *The Body Snatchers* by Jack Finney (1911—), and *No Blade of Grass* by John Christopher (C. S. Youd, 1922—). Ray Bradbury was successful even earlier in selling his brand of science fiction and fantasy to *Mademoiselle*, *Charm*, *Esquire*, *The New Yorker*, and *Harper's*.

With the demise, one by one, of the slick fiction magazines, the men's magazines, beginning with *Playboy*, began to publish science fiction stories frequently, often by well-known science fiction writers. Even films and television began to offer new opportunities for the science fiction audience and sometimes the writers themselves.

In the 1940s, arguing with John Campbell about the definition of science fiction was futile; if he said a story wasn't science fiction it probably didn't get published, or if it did get picked by one of the other magazines it was only salvage money. Debating the matter with Tony Boucher or Horace Gold in the 1950s was little better. But the 1960s saw a leveling process that made one man's definition virtually as good as another's.

The proliferation of markets meant a fragmentation of readership and the authors' single-market attitude. By the mid-1960s science fiction, as a consequence, was clearly changing.

Between 1940 and 1965, events in the larger world continued to shape science fiction along with everything else: World War II illustrated the increasingly technological nature of civilization. With the development of sonar, radar, jet aircraft, rocket weapons, atom bombs, and a hundred other laboratory products for war, it demonstrated the need for scientists and engineers and research institutions, as well as an educated citizenry that could understand what was going on and control the direction of society. Money poured into research and education; the inevitable outcome was an acceleration of technological change. A bit more than a decade later the situation was reinforced by the shock of Soviet primacy in space.

What was happening in the world seemed like an affirmation of everything that Campbellian science fiction had been saying: the atom bombs and the rockets were symbols of science fiction's prophetic power as well as authentication of its concern for the future. What the authors had been writing about in the 1930s and '40s was coming to pass; the issues they had been raising were being pressed upon humanity. We were living, as Asimov put it, in a science fiction world, but not everybody liked it. The horrors of nearly total war brought disillusionment with the science and technology that had put power into the hands of madmen; for many people the world was moving too fast, and they felt powerless to affect their own fates. And the future held the prospect of World War III, the atomic war that might eliminate humanity.

Astounding had never glorified war. In fact, L. Ron Hubbard (1911-1986), in his serialized 1940 novel *Final Blackout*, depicted how the coming war might reduce civilization to barbarism. Heinlein's "Solution Unsatisfactory" (written under the pseudonym Anson MacDonald) described in 1941 the development of an atomic weapon to end World War II and the unsatisfactory nuclear stalemate that would follow, and the year before, in "Blowups Happen," he had dramatized the dangers of atomic energy (a caution that was repeated in 1942 by Lester del Rey's "Nerves"). Nevertheless, *Astounding* had believed in science, and science had given war the power to destroy everyone. One way to attack that problem was to attack science, or so it seemed.

Other events occurred in their time: holographs were invented; the nuclear fission reactor and the hydrogen bomb were perfected; the Korean War—the first of the limited wars—broke out; Senator Joseph McCarthy symbolized an era of cold-war hysteria, blacklists, investigations, and purges; space exploration began, and a competition to be first on the moon was launched by President Kennedy; the laser was invented; quasars were discovered; and the Vietnam War escalated to the point of massive American involvement.

Increasing power over nature and world events, and accelerating change, meant for many only increasing frustration. How was power to be used; how was change to be directed? Should both be rejected?

The question of the terms on which society was to be organized, of the order in which society should rank its values, was raised on campuses across the nation. Led by veterans of civil-rights battles, fueled by sentiment against the Vietnam War, disagreement over strategy escalated into a near-rebellion over fundamental issues that discouraged one president from running for a second term and embittered the tenure of another, and, in the process, undermined public confidence in higher education. The most visible and vocal young people questioned the value of knowledge and learning, and elevated feeling into a philosophic position.

In this period a new group of writers emerged or graduated into maturity.

Science fiction develops in cycles or waves. Poul Anderson has speculated about the phenomenon, and so has Damon Knight. Like many cycles it may be only the attempt of the observer to bring order to disordered data, but a new group of media and writers seems to surge forward every twelve years or so. The creation of *Amazing* in 1926 was followed twelve years later by the Campbell editorship of *Astounding*, a handful of new writers, and a flock of new magazines. That was followed in 1950 by the creation of *F&SF* and *Galaxy* (and several dozen more magazines) and the appearance of groups of writers primarily oriented toward each publication, though many crossed over. The next surge may have been delayed a couple of years. Michael Moorcock's *New Worlds* began in 1964, and Damon Knight launched his influential series of original anthologies, *Orbit*, in 1966.

These last were the beginnings of what later would be called "the New Wave," which would attract a group of bright young writers more interested in literature than in science and disposed to disregard, resent, or react against the kind of science fiction that had been published earlier. The progress of the reaction against what has been called the pulp tradition or, to put it another way, the evolution to another stage in science fiction's development is easy to summarize and almost as easy to falsify. It neither began as abruptly as it seemed nor was as unified as it looked.

9

Ted Carnell (1912-1972) gave up the editorship of *New Worlds*, a venerable British science fiction magazine founded in 1946, and Moorcock took over for new publishers. From the first he encouraged the most extreme expressions of style in writing and of new morality in subject. His symbol was J. G. Ballard. In Ballard's wake came other writers attracted by the excitement and the freedom: Brian Aldiss, John Brunner, Charles Platt, and such transplanted Americans as Thomas Disch, John Sladek, Pamila Zoline, Norman Spinrad, and James Sallis. *New Worlds* lost distribution and perhaps some readers but managed to keep going and even enter a glossy-art period, with the help of grants from the British Arts Council. Names like Roger Zelazny and Gene Wolfe began to appear in its pages.

Finally a veteran from the Campbell era, writer-editor Judith Merril, arrived in England. She had been editing the most influential and, for a time, the only best-of-the-year anthology, and her selections had become increasingly personal. Now, captivated by the *New Worlds* experiment, she began a personal campaign to spread it across the ocean, first naming it "the New Wave," then including examples of it in her anthologies, culminating in *England Swings SF* (1968).

In the United States the reaction against traditional science fiction was symbolized by the 1965 announcement by Harlan Ellison that he was going to publish an anthology for Doubleday of taboo-breaking stories, stories that couldn't be published in the magazines. *Dangerous Visions* was published in 1967. Whether or not Ellison got stories that couldn't have been published in the magazines (he admitted that only half a dozen writers really understood the freedom he offered), the book earned its contributors two Hugos and two Nebulas, and Ellison the undesired title (bestowed by *The New Yorker*) of "the chief prophet of the New Wave."

Science fiction had by this time developed its own awards for excellence: the International Fantasy Award, voted by an international panel, was presented from 1951 to 1957, with no award in 1956; the Hugo Awards (named in honor of Hugo Gernsback), determined by the vote of the membership of the World Science Fiction Convention (which rotates to a different place each year), were begun in 1953 and, after a lapse of a year, were awarded over a full range of story lengths starting in 1955; the Nebula Award, voted by the members of the Science Fiction Writers of America (founded in 1965), was first presented in 1966 for fiction published in 1965; and the John W. Campbell Memorial Award for the best science fiction novel of the year, voted by an international committee, was first presented in 1973.

About this time writers who were doing their own thing and resenting the older and more restrictive terminology began to call what they were creating "speculative fiction." The words weren't new—Heinlein had proposed them in 1947—and no more precise than "science fiction"; "science fiction" was too narrow (all of it is not necessarily about science) and "speculative fiction" was too broad (what fiction can't be called speculative?). But it revealed how these new writers felt about science fiction.

What the writers of the New Wave were doing, insofar as they could be lumped together, was to reinterpret science fiction in personal terms. They moved from an objective universe to a subjective one; what they wrote resembled fantasy in its abandonment of the world of shared experience for the world of interior reactions. Their intensely personal viewpoints tended to protest the established order and even the traditional way of perceiving reality. Their stylistically experimental methods emphasized the personal over the general.

The reaction of traditional science fiction readers and writers was outrage, and for a while gladiators disputed the possession of the field—that area of explained fantasy that I defined in *The Road to Science Fiction #1: From Gilgamesh to Wells* in the following terms:

> Science fiction is the branch of literature that deals with the effects of change on people in the real world, as it can be projected into the past, the future, or to distant places. It often concerns itself with scientific or technological change, and it usually involves matters whose importance is greater than the individual or the community; often civilization or the race itself is in danger.

The New Wave writers would have found this definition unsatisfactory; like the writers Professor Robert Scholes calls "the fabulists," they viewed the universe as unknowable and reality as the projection of cultural agreement. Since reality was indefinable, science fiction and fantasy were indistinguishable, and one writer's interpretation was as good as another's.

Since the mid-1960s many new opportunities for publication have come along, mostly in the form of anthologies of original stories. The *New Worlds* experiment dwindled and died, but new writers attracted to the field have published their different kind of stories in *Orbit* and in anthologies edited by David Gerrold, Vonda N. McIntyre and Susan Janice Anderson, Ed

Bryant, and Robin Scott Wilson, whose Clarion Workshops for science fiction writers at Clarion College (later transplanted to Michigan State University) have educated a new generation of writers. And Ellison produced *Again, Dangerous Visions* in 1972 and promised a final volume in the three-volume series, *The Last Dangerous Visions*, which in 1995 still was in gestation.

One thing is certain: the waves have quieted. The revolution is over. Much of what the rebels wanted is now accepted without question, and the urge to shock and to break taboos for the sake of shocking and breaking has diminished to occasional youthful exuberance. Even the most traditional of science fiction writers have enjoyed some of the new freedom and the new, broader audience that the New Wave has attracted.

The means was tolerance of difference. The price was definition and the old consensus. But science fiction once more was at peace.

10

For a time the anthologies of original stories represented a significant alternative to magazine publication. In the early 1970s one indefatigable anthologist had contracted with publishers to edit more than fifty anthologies. Other editors were busy as well, and many young writers had the opportunity to be published there. But soon the market was glutted, as it had been glutted with new magazines in the early 1950s, and the original anthology market faded to a few regulars—Damon Knight's *Orbit*, Robert Silverberg's *New Dimensions*, Terry Carr's *Universe*, and then they too were gone, and, after the premature cut-off of George Zebrowski's *Synergy*, to only an occasional special, most of them edited by the most persistent anthologist in the field, Martin Harry Greenberg.

The book market is another matter. It continued to boom for the next two decades. Between 1972 and 1993, the number of SF, fantasy, and horror books published increased geometrically, from 338 a year to nearly 2,000 in 1991. With one of every four or five books belonging to these related categories, they became the most popular category of fiction.

More science fiction writers are making a living out of writing. Few had been able to do that in the past, and those who had, with the exception of Heinlein and possibly van Vogt, had to turn out first-draft stories at a rapid rate and even then reduce their standards of living or take other jobs periodically.

More time for writing meant better writing, more thoughtful writing, more artistic writing. The book market also meant that many established writers were too busy writing books to bother with financially less rewarding short fiction. New writers appeared to fill the gap in the magazines and then, in turn, moved into the book field. Some went straight to writing novels without serving an apprenticeship with the short story, such as C. J. Cherryh, Samuel R. Delany, Jack Chalker, and Tanith Lee

The magazines for a time seemed like stepchildren, and like stepchildren they were often out of mind. The younger generation that had made cult books out of Heinlein's *Stranger in a Strange Land*, Tolkien's *The Lord of the Rings*, and Herbert's *Dune* had grown up reading paperback books, not magazines and hardcover books. Only after readers became fans and began collecting books did they begin to value more permanent bindings. A growing audience for hardcover books, however, made bestsellers or solid sellers out of some of them, such as Herbert's *Children of Dune*. Only a small proportion of the purchasers were regular science fiction readers. A larger part were libraries and regular hardcover purchasers, who occasionally bought science fiction when it appealed to them, which meant when its assumptions were limited and its generic demands were small and the authors provided easy ways into the strangeness at the heart of the work, such as Michael Crichton's *The Andromeda Strain* and Ira Levin's *The Boys from Brazil*, and the science fictional works of Stephen King.

For a while it seemed that the magazines might be relics of a different past—that glorious past when pulp magazines by the dozens meant plentiful markets for short fiction—and like all relics doomed to eventual extinction. Their numbers did not diminish below the handful of basic magazines that had carried science fiction through boom and bust, but circulations diminished and some leading magazines, such as *Galaxy* (briefly revived in the 1990s) and the British *New Worlds* gave up. Occasionally a new magazine would start up hopefully, like *Vertex*, *Cosmos*, and *Galileo*, and then fail within a few issues or, at most, a few years.

One magazine, *Isaac Asimov's Science Fiction Magazine*, has survived for twenty years, and two others show evidence of staying power—*Science Fiction Age* and its companion fantasy magazine, *Realms of Fantasy*. *Omni* offered a circulation of nearly one million for a decade and a half, but only an opportunity to publish one or two stories a month, until in 1995 it went to a quarterly issue while it prepared to enter the field of electronic publishing. In the 1990s the inexpensiveness of desktop publishing made possible many small magazines, primarily distributed by mail, with circulations of less than 10,000.

The direction in which science fiction seems likely to go, however, is toward less generic identification rather than more. The magazines continue to provide a group of readers with short fiction identified by their editors as science fiction, though the breadth of subject and treatment will continue to increase, not only across the field but within any one magazine. Ben Bova relaxed John Campbell's rigid standards at *Analog* before he moved on to become first fiction editor and then executive editor of *Omni* and then left to do his own writing, and was replaced at *Analog* by Stanley Schmidt. George Scithers was succeeded at *Isaac Asimov's Science Fiction Magazine* by Shawna McCarthy and then by Gardner Dozois, who encouraged fantasy and literary treatments with only peripheral relationships to SF or fantasy. And Kristine Kathryn Rusch succeeded Edward L. Ferman as editor of the magazine that he continued to publish, *Fantasy and Science Fiction*. The magazines, however, continue to be published for a hard-core readership that may have grown large enough to support more of them, but also is aging as fewer young readers are attracted to them. One measure of the size of the hard-core readership may be the increasing attendance at world and regional science fiction conventions. Insatiable convention-goers not only can attend a gathering every week of the year, but often can choose between several.

Books have become increasingly individualistic. Merely to identify a book as science fiction, then, may no longer be sufficient to enable readers to decide whether they will like it. The growing difficulties of definition may be one reason behind the success, for a time, of certain publishing lines, such as DAW and Ballantine (whose science fiction and fantasy lines took on the name of del Rey), whose editorial decisions have some predictability. It also may explain the popularity of some writers, who have a consistent style, subject matter, or reputation for quality, and of books in series (and the omni-present trilogy), such as those by Frank Herbert, Marion Zimmer Bradley, Philip José Farmer, Anne McCaffrey, and a dozen others; once readers discover what they like they know where to get more of the same.

The absence of any consensus definition of science fiction also may help explain the sudden popularity of fantasy, particularly long, involved books or series of books, like *The Lord of the Rings*, which publishers once considered poor risks.

Finally, an audience has been growing for imaginative literature, speculative fiction, science fiction—take your pick—that has no generic identification. Mainstream writers from John Barth to Kurt Vonnegut, Jr., have used science fiction materials with increasing frequency and found critical and popular success outside the genre. Some writers find that the label "science fiction" on their books is a handicap to sales rather than a help, and have demanded, as Vonnegut once did, that their books be marketed for the mainstream. Whether they can break free like Vonnegut and find equivalent success depends on the writer.

Some writers have complained that the best writing in the field does not sell as well as the worst, as if this were a truth confined to science fiction. The best-seller list is not the place to look for literary quality, but, on the other hand, nothing is as dead as last year's bestseller, and the best writers continue to sell steadily. Science fiction readers have been at least as faithful to quality as mainstream readers, and perhaps more.

Writers, however, have expressed an understandable impatience with the expectations of publishers, which affect and sometimes control the expectations of critics and purchasers. Until the 1980s identification as science fiction provided a floor under book sales but also clapped on a ceiling that only a few genre books managed to break through. All that has changed, however, and the endangered species is what is called the "mid-list book," the solid, well-written novel that once was the heart of the SF enterprise but is now considered a net loss.

In 1967, in the introduction to *Dangerous Visions*, Harlan Ellison wrote, "The millennium is at hand. We are what is happening."

That statement seems truer today than it was nearly three decades ago. Science fiction has been liberated from whatever restraints it accepted or the outside world placed upon it: subject and how it is handled are no longer an issue; opportunities for publication are sufficiently varied that almost any effective presentation has a chance for success on its own terms, even visually (motion pictures, television, comic strips, illustrated stories) or aurally (some records have done well); and a broad audience nurtured on the images of science fiction, educated by their peers, and catalyzed by such popular successes as *Star Trek*, *Star Wars*, *E.T.*, *Jurassic Park*, and the Indiana Jones films, is favorably disposed toward the literature of the imagination.

The exact nature of the millennium is unclear, however. A few questions remain to be answered. What role will the magazines play? Will breakthroughs in book publication overcome problems of genre expectations? Will social attitudes and scientific and technological influences continue to support a literature of anticipation? Will the quality of mass-audience presentations lead readers toward or away from the literature?

The answers to all of these depend not merely on general social trends but on the actions of individuals. The history of science fiction has been created both by broad general attitudes and by the responses of writers and editors. What new Wellses, Campbells, Heinleins, Asimovs, and Kubricks will come along to lead science fiction in new directions? How will they define it? Only the future can provide answers to those questions, and science fiction writers have been better entertainers than prophets.

BEYOND THESE HORIZONS

Robert A. Heinlein's first few stories in *Astounding Science Fiction*—"Life-Line," "Misfit," "Requiem," "If This Goes On," "The Roads Must Roll," and "Blowups Happen"—made him the leading figure in the new science fiction that John W. Campbell was trying to develop. At the age of thirty-two, Heinlein (1907-1988) found his vocation, and Campbell found his star author, even though Heinlein moved on to other challenges after four years.

What Heinlein wrote would shape science fiction, expand its horizons, and influence the generations of science fiction writers that followed him. Other authors would vie with Heinlein for popularity—particularly A. E. van Vogt with his breakneck narrative pace and his intricate plots—but Heinlein had more than stories; he had a message and a method. His message suited the new Campbellian science fiction and the climate of the times, and his method suited that message and the needs of other writers. Ironically, his more discursive, less innovative novels achieved his greatest audience and his largest sales. With the exception of *The Moon Is a Harsh Mistress* (1966) and *Friday* (1982), after 1960 Heinlein's only contribution to the genre that he had shaped was to spread its appeal to a broader readership. That readership, indeed, may have been impatient with the virtues that endeared him to the SF fans.

Heinlein's message may have had its origin in his frustrated military career, the Depression, and the accomplishments of science, or, beyond those factors, in Darwinism; it was based on the need for capable, unsentimental men to act in behalf of humanity in times of crisis, and for a society that would allow them the freedom to act. Pragmatic men in a libertarian situation were what Heinlein thought humanity needed, and when the species was threatened with slavery or extinction Heinlein's characters responded as uncertain, cautious men and their political institutions could not respond.

The capable person seemed indispensable during the external threat of World War II and, to some, desirable during the largely internal threat of the Cold War that followed. The capable person was not so universally admired during the 1960s and 1970s—capable people, after all, had allowed the United States to become involved in the Vietnam War and refused to end the conflict—and Heinlein's characters and situations began to seem unfeeling about the weak and helpless and the social measures needed to protect them. It should be noted, however, that Heinlein's worlds always are in crisis; a crisis-free universe might have elicited from Heinlein other kinds of admirable characteristics, other kinds of praiseworthy institutions.

Heinlein's method was to bring naturalism to the service of the fantastic, to tell a science fiction story as if it were happening today. In the process he evolved economical techniques for describing future societies through their artifacts. In the preface to Groff Conklin's 1946 anthology, *The Best of Science Fiction*, John Campbell wrote:

> The best modern writers of science fiction have worked out some truly remarkable techniques for presenting a great deal of background and associated material without intruding into the flow of the story. That is no small feat, when a complete new world must be established at the same time a story is being presented.

More than anyone else, Campbell was describing Heinlein, who could evoke a different world through a few carefully selected details, like an archaeologist reconstructing a lost civilization from a few fragments.

In Heinlein's early years as a writer, he worked his philosophy into the action of his story; in his later novels, it emerged as lectures, as if he had decided he could afford to dispense with some of the concessions he had made to his readers. He was impatient with human institutions, but his confidence in humanity never faltered. With that optimism, combined with his skills and his ability to grow and adapt his writing to new markets, Heinlein opened up the slick magazines, the juvenile field, Hollywood, and the bestseller to other science fiction writers.

More than anything else, he influenced other writers. They followed his footsteps in the same way they followed his style: Heinlein could be hard-boiled, as he was in *The Puppet Masters* and "All You Zombies—," or poetic, as he was in "The Green Hills of Earth." And he had what seemed like the most prolific science fiction mind around. He continually came up with ideas that no one seemed to have considered before or renovated old ones that everyone else had thought beyond redemption: paranoia, time-travel paradoxes, the self-contained spaceship, longevity by family selection, atomic power, atomic war, post-atomic survival, superman, possession by aliens, judgment by aliens, the nature of reality, citizenship, religions based on science or survival after death, revolt by space colonies, and dozens of sociological concepts.

His contemporaries learned from his stories and adult novels as they were published, but dozens of later writers grew up reading his juveniles. Some would emulate them; others would react against them, attacking their philosophy, rebelling against their style; but few would be unaffected by what Heinlein wrote. He was the indispensable science fiction writer of his time. Science fiction would not have been the same without Heinlein.

"ALL YOU ZOMBIES—"

by Robert A. Heinlein

2217 Time Zone V (EST) 7 Nov. 1970—NYC— "Pop's Place": I was polishing a brandy snifter when the Unmarried Mother came in. I noted the time—10:17 P.M. zone five, or eastern time, November 7th, 1970. Temporal agents always notice time and date; we must.

The Unmarried Mother was a man twenty-five years old, no taller than I am, childish features and a touchy temper. I didn't like his looks—I never had—but he was a lad I was here to recruit, he was my boy. I gave him my best barkeep's smile.

Maybe I'm too critical. He wasn't swish; his nickname came from what he always said when some nosy type asked him his line: "I'm an unmarried mother." If he felt less than murderous he would add: "at four cents a word. I write confession stories."

If he felt nasty, he would wait for somebody to make something of it. He had a lethal style of infighting, like a female cop—reason I wanted him. Not the only one.

He had a load on, and his face showed that he despised people more than usual. Silently I poured a double shot of Old Underwear and left the bottle. He drank it, poured another.

I wiped the bar top. "How's the 'Unmarried Mother' racket?"

His fingers tightened on the glass and he seemed about to throw it at me; I felt for the sap under the bar. In temporal manipulation you try to figure everything, but there are so many factors that you never take needless risks.

I saw him relax that tiny amount they teach you to watch for in the Bureau's training school. "Sorry," I said. "Just asking, 'How's business?' Make it 'How's the weather?'"

He looked sour. "Business is okay. I write 'em, they print 'em, I eat."

I poured myself one, leaned toward him. "Matter of fact," I said, "you write a nice stick—I've sampled a few. You have an amazingly sure touch with the woman's angle."

It was a slip I had to risk; he never admitted what pen-names he used. But he was boiled enough to pick up only the last: "'Woman's angle!'" he repeated with a snort. "Yeah, I know the woman's angle. I should."

"So?" I said doubtfully. "Sisters?"

"No. You wouldn't believe me if I told you."

"Now, now," I answered mildly, "bartenders and psychiatrists learn that nothing is stranger than truth. Why, son, if you heard the stories I do—well, you'd make yourself rich. Incredible."

"You don't know what 'incredible' means!"

"So? Nothing astonishes me. I've always heard worse."

He snorted again. "Want to bet the rest of the bottle?"

"I'll bet a full bottle." I placed one on the bar.

"Well—" I signaled my other bartender to handle the trade. We were at the far end, a single-stool space that I kept private by loading the bar top by it with jars of pickled eggs and other clutter. A few were at the other end watching the fights and somebody was playing the juke box—private as a bed where we were.

"Okay," he began, "to start with, I'm a bastard."

"No distinction around here," I said.

"I mean it," he snapped. "My parents weren't married."

"Still no distinction," I insisted. "Neither were mine."

"When—" He stopped, gave me the first warm look I ever saw on him. "You mean that?"

"I do. A one-hundred-percent bastard. In fact," I added, "no one in my family ever marries. All bastards.

"Oh, that." I showed it to him. "It just looks like a wedding ring; I wear it to keep women off." It is an antique I bought in 1985 from a fellow operative— he had fetched it from pre-Christian Crete. "The Worm Ouroboros… the World Snake that eats its own tail, forever without end. A symbol of the Great Paradox."

He barely glanced at it. "If you're really a bastard, you know how it feels. When I was a little girl—"

"Wups!" I said. "Did I hear you correctly?"

"Who's telling this story? When I was a little girl—Look, ever hear of Christine Jorgenson? Or Roberta Cowell?"

"Uh, sex-change cases? You're trying to tell me—"

"Don't interrupt or swelp me, I won't talk. I was a foundling, left at an orphanage in Cleveland in 1945 when I was a month old. When I was a little girl, I envied kids with parents. Then, when I learned about sex—and, believe me, Pop, you learn fast in an orphanage—"

"I know."

"—I made a solemn vow that any kid of mine would have both a pop and a mom. It kept me 'pure,' quite a feat in that vicinity—I had to learn to fight to manage it. Then I got older and realized I stood darn little chance of getting married—for the same reason I hadn't been adopted." He scowled. "I was horse-faced and buck-toothed, flat-chested and straight-haired."

"You don't look any worse than I do."

"Who cares how a barkeep looks? Or a writer? But people wanting to adopt pick little blue-eyed golden-haired morons. Later on, the boys want bulging breasts, a cute face, and an Oh-you-wonderful-male manner." He shrugged. "I couldn't compete. So I decided to join the W.E.N.C.H.ES."

"Eh?"

"Women's Emergency National Corps, Hospitality & Entertainment Section, what they now call 'Space Angels'—Auxiliary Nursing Group, Extraterrestrial Legions."

I knew both terms, once I had them chronized. We use still a third name, it's that elite military service corps: Women's Hospitality Order Refortifying & Encouraging Spacemen. Vocabulary shift is the worst hurdle in time-jumps—did you know that "service station" once meant a dispensary for petroleum fractions? Once on an assignment in the Churchill Era, a woman said to me, "Meet me at the service station next door"—which is not what it sounds; a "service station" (then) wouldn't have a bed in it.

He went on: "It was when they first admitted you can't send men into space for months and years and not relieve the tension. You remember how the wowsers screamed?—that improved my chance, since volunteers were scarce. A gal had to be respectable, preferably virgin (they liked to train them from scratch), above average mentally, and stable emotionally. But most volunteers were old hookers, or neurotics who would crack up ten days off Earth. So I didn't need looks; if they accepted me, they would fix my buck teeth, put a wave in my hair, teach me to walk and dance and how to listen to a man pleasingly, and everything else—plus training for the prime duties. They would even use plastic surgery if it would help—nothing too good for Our Boys.

"Best yet, they made sure you didn't get pregnant during your enlistment—and you were almost certain to marry at the end of your hitch. Same way today, A.N.G.E.L.S. marry spacers—they talk the language.

"When I was eighteen I was placed as a 'mother's helper.' This family simply wanted a cheap servant, but I didn't mind as I couldn't enlist till I was twenty-one. I did housework and went to night school—pretending to continue my high school typing and shorthand but going to a charm class instead, to better my chances for enlistment.

"Then I met this city slicker with his hundred-dollar bills." He scowled. "The no-good actually did have a wad of hundred-dollar bills. He showed me one night, told me to help myself.

"But I didn't. I liked him. He was the first man I ever met who was nice to me without trying games with me. I quit night school to see him oftener. It was the happiest time of my life.

"Then one night in the park the games began."

He stopped. I said, "And then?"

"And then *nothing!* I never saw him again. He walked me home and told me he loved me—and kissed me good-night and never came back." He looked grim. "If I could find him, I'd kill him!"

"Well," I sympathized, "I know how you feel. But killing him—just for doing what comes naturally—hmm... Did you struggle?"

"Huh? What's that got to do with it?"

"Quite a bit. Maybe he deserves a couple of broken arms for running out on you, but—"

"He deserves worse than that! Wait till you hear. Somehow I kept anyone from suspecting and decided it was all for the best. I hadn't really loved him and probably would never love anybody—and I was more eager to join the W.E.N.C.H.E.S. than ever. I wasn't disqualified, they didn't insist on virgins. I cheered up.

"It wasn't until my skirts got tight that I realized."

"Pregnant?"

"He had me higher 'n a kite! Those skinflints I lived with ignored it as long as I could work—then kicked me out, and the orphanage wouldn't take me back. I landed in a charity ward surrounded by other big bellies and trotted bedpans until my time came.

"One night I found myself on an operating table, with a nurse saying, 'Relax. Now breathe deeply.'

"I woke up in bed, numb from the chest down. My surgeon came in. 'How do you feel?' he says cheerfully.

"'Like a mummy.'

"'Naturally. You're wrapped like one and full of dope to keep you numb. You'll get well—but a Cesarean isn't a hangnail.'

"'Cesarean' I said. 'Doc—*did I lose the baby?*'

"'Oh, no. Your baby's fine.'

"'Oh. Boy or girl?'

"'A healthy little girl. Five pounds, three ounces.'

"I relaxed. It's something, to have made a baby. I told myself I would go somewhere and tack 'Mrs.' on my name and let the kid think her papa was dead—no orphanage for *my* kid!

"But the surgeon was talking. 'Tell me, uh—' He avoided my name. 'did you ever think your glandular setup was odd?'

"I said, 'Huh? Of course not. What are you driving at?'

"He hesitated. 'I'll give you this in one dose, then a hypo to let you sleep off your jitters. You'll have 'em.'

"'Why?' I demanded.

"'Ever hear of that Scottish physician who was female until she was thirty-five?—then had surgery and became legally and medically a man? Got married. All okay.'

"'What's that got to do with me?'

"'That's what I'm saying. You're a man.'

"I tried to sit up. 'What?'

"'Take it easy. When I opened you, I found a mess. I sent for the Chief of Surgery while I got the baby out, then we held a consultation with you on the table—and worked for hours to salvage what we could. You had two full sets of organs, both immature, but with the female set well enough developed for you to have a baby. They could never be any use to you again, so we took them out and rearranged things so that you can develop properly as a man. He put a hand on me. 'Don't worry. You're young, your bones will readjust, we'll watch your glandular balance—and make a fine young man out of you.'

"I started to cry. 'What about my *baby*?'

"'Well, you can't nurse her, you haven't milk enough for a kitten. If I were you, I wouldn't see her—put her up for adoption.'

"'*No!*'

"He shrugged. 'The choice is yours; you're her mother—well, her parent. But don't worry now; we'll get you well first.'

"Next day they let me see the kid and I saw her daily—trying to get used to her. I had never seen a brand-new baby and had no idea how awful they look— my daughter looked like an orange monkey. My feelings changed to cold determination to do right by her. But four weeks later that didn't mean anything."

"Eh?"

"She was snatched."

"'Snatched?'"

The Unmarried Mother almost knocked over the bottle we had bet. "Kidnapped—stolen from the hospital nursery!" He breathed hard. "How's that for taking the last a man's got to live for?"

"A bad deal," I agreed. "Let's pour you another. No clues?"

"Nothing the police could trace. Somebody came to see her, claimed to be her uncle. While the nurse had her back turned, he walked out with her."

"Description?"

"Just a man, with a face-shaped face, like yours or mine." He frowned. "I think it was the baby's father. The nurse swore it was an older man but he probably used makeup. Who else would swipe my baby? Childless women pull such stunts—but whoever heard of a man doing it?"

"What happened to you then?"

"Eleven more months of that grim place and three operations. In four months I started to grow a beard; before I was out I was shaving regularly... and no longer doubted that I was male." He grinned wryly. "I was staring down nurses necklines."

"Well," I said, "seems to me you came through okay. Here you are, a normal man, making good money, no real troubles. And the life of a female is not an easy one."

He glared at me. "A lot you know about it!"

"So?"

"Ever hear the expression 'a ruined woman'?"

"Mmm, years ago. Doesn't mean much today."

"I was as ruined as a woman can be; that bum *really* ruined me—I was no longer a woman... and I didn't know *how* to be a man."

"Takes getting used to, I suppose."

"You have no idea. I don't mean learning how to dress, or not walking into the wrong rest room; I learned those in the hospital. But how could I *live*? What job could I get? Hell, I couldn't even drive a car. I didn't know a trade; I couldn't do manual labor—too much scar tissue, too tender.

"I hated him for having ruined me for the W.E.N.C.H.E.S., too, but I didn't know how much until I tried to join the Space Corps instead. One look at my belly and I was marked unfit for military service. The medical officer spent time on me just from curiosity; he had read about my case.

"So I changed my name and came to New York. I got by as a fry cook, then rented a typewriter and set myself up as a public stenographer—what a laugh! In four months I typed four letters and one manuscript. The manuscript was for *Real Life Tales* and a waste of paper, but the goof who wrote it sold it. Which gave me an idea; I bought a stack of confession magazines and studied them." He looked cynical. "Now you know how I get the authentic woman's angle on an unmarried-mother story... through the only version I haven't sold—the true one. Do I win the bottle?"

I pushed it toward him. I was upset myself, but there was work to do. I said, "Son, you still want to lay hands on that so-and-so?"

His eyes lighted up—a feral gleam.

"Hold it!" I said. "You wouldn't kill him?"

He chuckled nastily. "Try me."

"Take it easy. I know more about it than you think I do. I can help you. I know where he is."

He reached across the bar. *"Where is he?"*

I said softly, "Let go my shirt, sonny—or you'll land in the alley and we'll tell the cops you fainted." I showed him the sap.

He let go. "Sorry. But where is he?" He looked at me. "And how do you know so much?"

"All in good time. There are records—hospital records, orphanage records, medical records. The matron of your orphanage was Mrs. Fetherage—right? She was followed by Mrs. Gruenstein—right? Your name, as a girl, was 'Jane'—right? And you didn't tell me any of this—right?"

I had him baffled and a bit scared. "What's this? You trying to make trouble for me?"

"No indeed. I've your welfare at heart. I can put this character in your lap. You do to him as you see fit—and I guarantee that you'll get away with it. But I don't think you'll kill him. You'd be nuts to—and you aren't nuts. Not quite."

He brushed it aside. "Cut the noise. *Where is he?*"

I poured him a short one; he was drunk, but anger was offsetting it. "Not so fast. I do something for you—you do something for me."

"Uh... what?"

"You don't like your work. What would you say to high pay, steady work, unlimited expense account, your own boss on the job, and lots of variety and adventure?"

He stared. "I'd say, 'Get those goddam reindeer off my roof!' Shove it, Pop—there's no such job."

"Okay, put it this way: I hand him to you, you settle with him, then try my job. If it's not all I claim—well, I can't hold you."

He was wavering; the last drink did it "When d'yuh d'liver 'im?" he said thickly.

He shoved out his hand. "It's a deal!"

"If it's a deal—*right now!*"

I nodded to my assistant to watch both ends, noted the time—2300—started to duck through the gate under the bar—when the juke box blared out: "I'm My Own Grandpaw!" The service man had orders to load it with Americana and classics because I couldn't stomach the "music" of 1970, but I hadn't known that tape was in it. I called out, "Shut that off! Give the customer his money back." I added, "Storeroom, back in a moment," and headed there with my Unmarried Mother following.

It was down the passage across from the johns, a steel door to which no one but my day manager and myself had a key; inside was a door to an inner room to which only I had a key. We went there.

He looked blearily around at windowless walls. "Where is he?"

"Right away." I opened a case, the only thing in the room; it was a U.S.F.F. Coordinates Transformer Field Kit, series 1992, Mod. II—a beauty, no moving parts, weight twenty-three kilos fully charged, and shaped to pass as a suitcase. I had adjusted it precisely earlier that day; all I had to do was to shake out the metal net which limits the transformation field.

Which I did. "What's that?" he demanded.

"Time machine," I said and tossed the net over us.

"Hey!" he yelled and stepped back. There is a technique to this; the net has to be thrown so that the subject will instinctively step back *onto* the metal mesh, then you close the net with both of you inside completely—else you might leave shoe soles behind or a piece of foot, or scoop up a slice of floor. But that's all the skill it takes. Some agents con a subject into the net; I tell the truth and use that instant of utter astonishment to flip the switch. Which I did.

1030-VI-3 April 1963—Cleveland, Ohio-Apex Bldg.: "Hey!" he repeated. "Take this damn thing off!"

"Sorry," I apologized and did so, stuffed the net into the case, closed it. "You said you wanted to find him."

"But—you said that was a time machine!"

I pointed out a window. "Does that look like November? Or New York?" While he was gawking at new buds and spring weather, I reopened the case, took out a packet of hundred-dollar bills, checked that the numbers and signatures were compatible with 1963. The Temporal Bureau doesn't care how much you spend (it costs nothing) but they don't like unnecessary anachronisms. Too many mistakes, and a general court-martial will exile you for a year in a nasty period, say 1974 with its strict rationing and forced labor. I never make such mistakes; the money was okay.

He turned around and said, "What happened?"

"He's here. Go outside and take him. Here's expense money." I shoved it at him and added, "Settle him, then I'll pick you up."

Hundred-dollar bills have a hypnotic effect on a person not used to them. He was thumbing them unbelievingly as I eased him into the hall, locked him out. The next jump was easy, a small shift in era.

7100-VI-10 March 1964—Cleveland-Apex Bldg.: There was a notice under the door saying that my lease expired next week; otherwise the room looked as it had a moment before. Outside, trees were bare and snow threatened; I hurried, stopping only for contemporary money and a coat, hat, and topcoat I had left there when I leased the room. I hired a car, went to the hospital. It took twenty minutes to bore the nursery attendant to the point where I could swipe the baby without being noticed. We went back to the Apex Building. This dial setting was more involved, as the building did not yet exist in 1945. But I had precalculated it.

0100-VI-20 Sept. 1945—Cleveland-Skyview Motel: Field kit, baby, and I arrived in a motel outside town. Earlier I had registered as "Gregory Johnson, Warren, Ohio," so we arrived in a room with curtains closed, windows locked, and doors bolted, and the floor cleared to allow for waver as the machine hunts. You can get a nasty bruise from a chair where it shouldn't be—not the chair, of course, but backlash from the field.

No trouble. Jane was sleeping soundly; I carried her out, put her in a grocery box on the seat of a car I had provided earlier, drove to the orphanage, put her on the steps, drove two blocks to a "service station" (the petroleum-products sort) and phoned the orphanage, drove back in time to see them taking the box inside, kept going and abandoned the car near the motel—walked to it and jumped forward to the Apex Building in 1963.

2200-VI-24 April 1963—Cleveland-Apex Bldg.: I had cut the time rather fine—temporal accuracy depends on span, except on return to zero. If I had it right, Jane was discovering, out in the park this balmy spring night, that she wasn't quite as nice a girl as she had thought. I grabbed a taxi to the home of those skinflints, had the hackie wait around a corner while I lurked in shadows.

Presently I spotted them down the street, arms around each other. He took her up on the porch and made a long job of kissing her good-night—longer than I thought. Then she went in and he came down the walk, turned away. I slid into step and hooked an arm in his. "That's all, son," I announced quietly. "I'm back to pick you up."

"*You!*" He gasped and caught his breath.

"Me. Now you know who *he* is—and after you think it over you'll know who you are... and if you think hard enough, you'll figure out who the baby is... and who *I* am."

He didn't answer, he was badly shaken. It's a shock to have it proved to you that you can't resist seducing yourself. I took him to the Apex Building and we jumped again.

2300-VIII-12 Aug. 1985—Sub Rockies Base: I woke the duty sergeant, showed my I.D., told the sergeant to bed my companion down with a happy pill and recruit him in the morning. The sergeant looked sour, but rank is rank, regardless of era; he did what I said—thinking, no doubt, that the next time we met he might be the colonel and I the sergeant. Which can happen in our corps. "What name?" he asked.

I wrote it out. He raised his eyebrows. "Like so, eh? *Hmm*—"

"You just do your job, Sergeant." I turned to my companion.

"Son, your troubles are over. You're about to start the best job a man ever held—and you'll do well. *I know.*"

"That you will!" agreed the sergeant. "Look at me—born in 1917—still around, still young, still enjoying life." I went back to the jump room, set everything on preselected zero.

2301-V-7 Nov. 1970—NYC —"Pop's Place": I came out of the storeroom carrying a fifth of Drambuie to account for the minute I had been gone. My assistant was arguing with the customer who had been playing "I'm My Own Grand-paw!" I said, "Oh, let him play it, then unplug it." I was very tired.

It's rough, but somebody must do it, and it's very hard to recruit anyone in the later years, since the Mistake of 1972. Can you think of a better source than to pick people all fouled up where they are and give them well-paid, interesting (even though dangerous) work in a necessary cause? Everybody knows now why the Fizzle War of 1963 fizzled. The bomb with New York's number on it didn't go off, a hundred other things didn't go as planned—all arranged by the likes of me.

But not the Mistake of '72; that one is not our fault—and can't be undone; there's no paradox to resolve. A thing either is, or it isn't, now and forever amen. But there won't be another like it; an order dated "1992" takes precedence any year.

I closed five minutes early, leaving a letter in the cash register telling my day manager that I was accepting his offer to buy me out, to see my lawyer as I was leaving on a long vacation. The Bureau might or might not pick up his payments, but they want things left tidy. I went to the room in the back of the storeroom and forward to 1993.

2200-VII-12 Jan 1993—Sub Rockies Annex-HQ Temporal DOL: I checked in with the duty officer and went to my quarters, intending to sleep for a week. I had fetched the bottle we bet (after all, I won it) and took a drink before I wrote my report. It tasted foul, and I wondered why I had ever liked Old Underwear. But it was better than nothing; I don't like to be cold sober, I think too much. But I don't really hit the bottle either; other people have snakes—I have people.

I dictated my report; forty recruitments all okayed by the Psych Bureau—counting my own, which I knew would be okayed. I was here, wasn't I? Then I

"ALL YOU ZOMBIES—"

taped a request for assignment to operations; I was sick of recruiting. I dropped both in the slot and headed for bed.

My eye fell on "The By-Laws of Time," over my bed:

Never Do Yesterday What Should Be Done Tomorrow.
If at Last You Do Succeed, Never Try Again.
A Stitch in Time Saves Nine Billion.
A Paradox May Be Paradoctored.
It Is Earlier When You Think.
Ancestors Are Just People.
Even Jove Nods.

They didn't inspire me the way they had when I was a recruit; thirty subjective-years of time-jumping wears you down. I undressed, and when I got down to the hide I looked at my belly. A Cesarean leaves a big scar, but I'm so hairy now that I don't notice it unless I look for it.

Then I glanced at the ring on my finger.

The Snake That Eats Its Own Tail, Forever and Ever... I *know* where *I* came from—*but where did all you zombies come from?*

I felt a headache coming on, but a headache powder is one thing I do not take. I did once—and you all went away.

So I crawled into bed and whistled out the light.

You aren't really there at all. There isn't anybody but me—Jane—here alone in the dark.

I miss you dreadfully!

THE CLEAR, COOL VOICE
OF ASIMOV

If Robert Heinlein was John Campbell's star author, Isaac Asimov (1920-1992) was Campbell's prize disciple. The eighteen-year-old Asimov brought his first story to Campbell, and he continued to bring them and to listen to the *Astounding* editor's comments and criticism until finally Campbell began to buy them.

Campbell taught Asimov about story construction and the logic of story development, the necessity for the author to imagine something the reader could not imagine for himself or to imagine something in greater detail than the reader could imagine—preferably both. He also told Asimov that the author had to surprise the reader. One aspect of surprise that delighted Campbell was the rational, particularly when rationality challenged conventional wisdom.

All this fitted perfectly with Asimov's inclinations. He was a young college junior aiming at medical school, although he would earn his Ph.D. in chemistry, teach biochemistry at the Boston University School of Medicine, and after 1958 spend most of his time writing science popularizations. Even at eighteen his knowledge of science was substantial; he had a logical, retentive mind; he didn't know much about people, but he knew a great deal about things.

One early landmark (see *The Road to Science Fiction #2*) in his writing career was "Nightfall." Campbell gave Asimov the idea in the form of a quotation from Ralph Waldo Emerson: "If the stars should appear one night in a thousand years, how would men believe and adore, and preserve for many generations the remembrance of the city of God!" On the contrary, Campbell said, men would go mad. "Nightfall" became Asimov's best-known short story.

About the same time that Asimov was writing "Nightfall," he was beginning a series of stories that would end up as *The Foundation Trilogy*. It considered the logical outcome of the breakup of a Galactic Empire in eight episodes ranging in length from a short story to a long novella, each one representing a new development growing out of the "givens" in the story: the fall of the Empire, the predictions of Hari Seldon based on the science of psychohistory, and the two Foundations he set up at opposite ends of the Galaxy in an effort to shorten the Dark Ages from 30,000 years to only 1,000. Action and romance have little to do with the success of the trilogy—virtually all the action takes place offstage, and the romance is almost invisible—but the stories provide a detective story fascination with the permutations and reversals of ideas.

Asimov at this time was also writing another series of stories: his robot series, ultimately collected (except for the later stories) in *I, Robot* and *The Rest of the Robots*. Here his logical turn of mind and his puzzle-solving approach to story may have found their best realization. Up to this time the relationship between man and his creations had been tinged with as much religious dread as the relationship between God and man. Mary Shelley's *Frankenstein* was the prototype; when the monster turned against its creator it revivified an archetype that later writers found irresistible. The rebellion of what was created—android, robot, computer, even simple machines as in Stephen Vincent Benet's "Nightmare Number Three"—came as automatically to the writer's mind as the mad scientist.

Asimov, however, saw no good reason for machines to be rebellious (he was not as strong on symbolism as on analysis). What seemed as inevitable to many writers as the surrender to temptation of Adam and Eve seemed illogical to him. Why should a scientist make a machine that could hurt him? Machines put greater power into the hands of fallible humanity, but that implies not disaster but more safeguards.

The result of this kind of thinking was Asimov's Three Laws of Robotics: 1) a robot may not injure a human being, or, through inaction, allow a human being to come to harm; 2) a robot must obey the orders given it by human beings except where such orders conflict with the First Law; and 3) a robot must protect its existence as long as such protection does not conflict with the First or Second Law.

The laws were not codified until after the first two robot stories, "Robbie" and "Reason," had been published and the third, "Liar," was under discussion (Campbell said Asimov came up with the laws; Asimov, that Campbell did). After the laws were handed down, the stories became logical developments of the relationships between man and thinking machine, and of the conflicts, mostly cerebral, between two of the three laws.

After Asimov's robot series, the automatic rebellion of the creature became illogical, ridiculous, romantic, or conventional. The spirit of reason that Campbell preached and Asimov embodied in his fiction purged science fiction of an accumulated detritus of careless thinking and casual writing. The Campbell-Asimov attack on the irrational and the romantic eventually was attacked in its turn as unfeeling, an infatuation with technology, a naive image of man as a rational being. But while it lasted, it brought a clarity of thought and purity of style that served science fiction well for two decades.

REASON

BY ISAAC ASIMOV

Gregory Powell spaced his words for emphasis. "One week ago, Donovan and I put you together." His brows furrowed doubtfully and he pulled the end of his brown mustache.

It was quiet in the officers' room of Solar Station 5—except for the soft purring of the mighty beam director somewhere far below.

Robot QT-1 sat immovable. The burnished plates of his body gleamed in the luxites, and the glowing red of the photoelectric cells that were his eyes were fixed steadily upon the Earthman at the other side of the table

Powell repressed a sudden attack of nerves. These robots possessed peculiar brains. The positronic paths impressed upon them were calculated in advance, and all possible permutations that might lead to anger or hate were rigidly excluded. And yet—the QT models were the first of their kind, and this was the first of QT's. Anything could happen.

Finally the robot spoke. His voice carried the cold timbre inseparable from a metallic diaphragm. "Do you realize the seriousness of such a statement, Powell?"

"*Something* made you, Cutie," pointed out Powell. "You admit yourself that your memory seems to spring full-grown from an absolute blankness of a week ago. I'm giving you the explanation. Donovan and I put you together from the parts shipped us."

Cutie gazed upon his long, supple fingers in an oddly human attitude of mystification. "It strikes me that there should be a more satisfactory explanation than that. For *you* to make *me* seems improbable."

The Earthman laughed quite suddenly. "In Earth's name, why?"

"Call it intuition. That's all it is so far. But I intend to reason it out, though. A chain of valid reasoning can end only with the determination of truth, and I'll stick till I get there."

Powell stood up and seated himself at the table's edge next the robot. He felt a sudden strong sympathy for this strange machine. It was not at all like the ordinary robot, attending to his specialized task at the station with the intensity of a deeply ingrooved positronic path.

He placed a hand upon Cutie's steel shoulder and the metal was cold and hard to the touch.

"Cutie," he said, "I'm going to try to explain something to you. You're the first robot who's ever exhibited curiosity as to his own existence—and I think the first that's really intelligent enough to understand the world outside. Here, come with me."

The robot rose erect smoothly and his thickly sponge-rubber-soled feet made no noise as he followed Powell. The Earthman touched a button, and a square section of the wall flicked aside. The thick, clear glass revealed space—star speckled.

"I've seen that in the observation ports in the engine room," said Cutie.

"I know," said Powell. "What do you think it is?"

"Exactly what it seems—a black material just beyond this glass that is spotted with little gleaming dots. I know that our director sends out beams to some of these dots, always to the same one—and also that these dots shift and that the beams shift with them. That is all."

"Good! Now I want you to listen carefully. The blackness is emptiness—vast emptiness stretching out infinitely. The little gleaming dots are huge masses of energy-filled matter. They are globes, some of them millions of miles in diameter—and for comparison, this station is only one mile across. They seem so tiny because they are incredibly far off.

"The dots to which our energy beams are directed are nearer and much smaller. They are cold and hard, and human beings like myself live upon their surfaces—many billions of them. It is from one of these worlds that Donovan and I come. Our beams feed these worlds energy drawn from one of those huge incandescent globes that happens to be near us. We call that globe the sun and it is on the other side of the station where you can't see it."

Cutie remained motionless before the port, like a steel statue. His head did not turn as he spoke. "Which particular dot of light do you claim to come from?"

Powell searched. "There it is. The very bright one in the corner. We call it Earth." He grinned. "Good old Earth. There are five billions of us there, Cutie—and in about two weeks I'll be back there with them."

And then, surprisingly enough, Cutie hummed abstractly. There was no tune to it, but it possessed a curious twanging quality as of plucked strings. It ceased as suddenly as it had begun. "But where do I come in, Powell? You haven't explained *my* existence."

"The rest is simple. When these stations were first established to feed solar energy to the planets, they were run by humans. However, the heat, the hard solar radiations and the electron storms made the post a difficult one. Robots were developed to replace human labor and now only two human executives are required for each station. We are trying to replace even those, and that's where you come in. You're the highest-type robot ever developed, and if you show the ability to run this station independently no human need ever come here again except to bring parts for repairs."

His hand went up and the metal visi-lid snapped back into place. Powell returned to the table and polished an apple upon his sleeve before biting into it.

The red glow of the robot's eyes held him. "Do you expect me," said Cutie slowly, "to believe any such complicated, implausible hypothesis as you have just outlined? What do you take me for?"

Powell sputtered apple fragments onto the table and turned red. "Why, damn you, it wasn't a hypothesis. Those were facts."

Cutie sounded grim. "Globes of energy millions of miles across! Worlds with five billion humans on them! Infinite emptiness! Sorry, Powell, but I don't believe it. I'll puzzle this thing out for myself. Good-bye."

He turned and stalked out of the room. He brushed past Michael Donovan on the threshold with a grave nod and passed down the corridor, oblivious to the astounded stare that followed him.

Mike Donovan rumpled his red hair and shot an annoyed glance at Powell. "What was that walking junkyard talking about? What doesn't he believe?"

The other dragged at his mustache bitterly. "He's a skeptic," was the bitter response. "He doesn't believe we made him or that Earth exists or space or stars."

"Sizzling Saturn, we've got a lunatic robot on our hands."

"He says he's going to figure it all out for himself."

"Well, now," said Donovan sweetly, "I do hope he'll condescend to explain it all to me after he's puzzled everything out." Then, with sudden rage, "Listen! If that metal mess gives me any lip like that, I'll knock that chromium cranium right off its torso."

He seated himself with a jerk and drew a paperback mystery novel out of his inner jacket pocket. "That robot gives me the willies anyway—too damned inquisitive!"

Mike Donovan growled from behind a huge lettuce-and-tomato sandwich as Cutie knocked gently and entered.

"Is Powell here?"

Donovan's voice was muffled, with pauses for mastication. "He's gathering data on electronic stream functions. We're heading for a storm, looks like."

Gregory Powell entered as he spoke, eyes on the graphed paper in his hands, and dropped into a chair. He spread the sheets out before him and began scribbling calculations. Donovan stared over his shoulder, crunching lettuce and dribbling bread crumbs. Cutie waited silently.

Powell looked up. "The zeta potential is rising, but slowly. Just the same, the stream functions are erratic and I don't know what to expect. Oh, hello, Cutie. I thought you were supervising the installation of the new drive bar."

"It's done," said the robot quietly, "and so I've come to have a talk with the two of you."

"Oh!" Powell looked uncomfortable. "Well, sit down. No, not that chair. One of the legs is weak and you're no lightweight."

The robot did so and said placidly, "I have come to a decision."

Donovan glowered and put the remnants of his sandwich aside. "If it's on any of that screwy—"

The other motioned impatiently for silence. "Go ahead, Cutie. We're listening."

"I have spent these last two days in concentration and introspection," said Cutie, "and the results have been most interesting. I began at the one sure assumption I felt permitted to make. I, myself, exist, because I think—"

Powell groaned. "Oh, Jupiter, a robot Descartes!"

"Who's Descartes?" demanded Donovan. "Listen, do we have to sit here and listen to this metal maniac—"

"Keep quiet, Mike!"

Cutie continued imperturbably, "And the question that immediately arose was: Just what is the cause of my existence?"

Powell's jaw set lumpily. "You're being foolish. I told you already that we made you."

"And if you don't believe us," added Donovan, "we'll gladly take you apart!"

The robot spread his strong hands in deprecatory gesture. "I accept nothing on authority. A hypothesis must be backed by reason, or else it is worthless—and it goes against all the dictates of logic to suppose that you made me."

Powell dropped a restraining arm upon Donovan's suddenly bunched fist. "Just why do you say that?"

Cutie laughed. It was a very inhuman laugh, the most machinelike utterance he had yet given vent to. It was sharp and explosive, as regular as a metronome and as uninflected.

"Look at you," he said finally. "I say this in no spirit of contempt, but look at you! The material you are made of is soft and flabby, lacking endurance and strength, depending for energy upon the inefficient oxidation of organic material—like that." He pointed a disapproving finger at what remained of Donovan's sandwich. "Periodically you pass into a coma, and the least variation in temperature, air pressure, humidity or radiation intensity impairs your efficiency. You are *makeshift.*

"I, on the other hand, am a finished product. I absorb electrical energy directly and utilize it with almost one hundred per cent efficiency. I am composed of strong metal, am continuously conscious, and can stand extremes of environment easily. These are facts which, with the self-evident proposition that no being can create another being superior to itself, smashes your silly hypothesis to nothing."

Donovan's muttered curses rose into intelligibility as he sprang to his feet, rusty eyebrows drawn low. "All right, you son of a hunk of iron ore, if we didn't make you, who did?"

Cutie nodded gravely. "Very good, Donovan. That was indeed the next question. Evidently my creator must be more powerful than myself, and so there was only one possibility."

The Earthmen looked blank and Cutie continued. "What is the center of activities here in the station? What do we all serve? What absorbs all our attention?" He waited expectantly.

Donovan turned a startled look upon his companion. "I'll bet this tin-plated screwball is talking about the energy converter itself."

"Is that right, Cutie?" grinned Powell.

"I am talking about the Master," came the cold, sharp answer.

It was the signal for a roar of laughter from Donovan, and Powell himself dissolved into a half-suppressed giggle.

Cutie had risen to his feet, and his gleaming eyes passed from one Earthman to the other. "It is so just the same and I don't wonder that you refuse to believe. You two are not long to stay here, I'm sure. Powell himself said that in early days only men served the Master; that there followed robots for the routine work; and, finally, myself for the executive labor. The facts are no doubt true, but the explanation is entirely illogical. Do you want the truth behind it all?"

"Go ahead, Cutie. You're amusing."

"The Master created humans first as the lowest type, most easily formed. Gradually, he replaced them by robots, the next higher step, and finally he created me, to take the place of the last humans. From now on, I serve the Master."

"You'll do nothing of the sort," said Powell sharply. "You'll follow our orders and keep quiet, until we're satisfied that you can run the converter. Get that! The *converter*—not the Master. If you don't satisfy us, you will be dismantled. And now—if you don't mind—you can leave. And take this data with you and file it properly."

Cutie accepted the graphs handed him and left without another word. Donovan leaned back heavily in his chair and shoved thick fingers through his hair.

"There's going to be trouble with that robot. He's pure nuts!"

The drowsy hum of the converter was louder in the control room and mixed with it was the chuckle of the Geiger counters and the erratic buzzing of half a dozen little signal lights. Donovan withdrew his eye from the telescope and flashed the luxites on. "The beam from Station Four caught Mars on schedule. We can break ours now."

Powell nodded abstractedly. "Cutie's down in the engine room. I'll flash the signal and he can take care of it. Look, Mike, what do you think of these figures?"

The other cocked an eye at them and whistled. "Boy, that's what I call gamma-ray intensity. Old Sol is feeling his oats, all right."

"Yeah," was the sour response, "and we're in a bad position for an electron storm, too. Our Earth beam is right in the probable path." He shoved his chair away from the table pettishly. "Nuts! If it would only hold off till relief got here, but that's ten days off. Say, Mike, go on down and keep an eye on Cutie, will you?"

"O.K. Throw me some of those almonds." Donovan snatched at the bag thrown him and headed for the elevator.

It slid smoothly downward and opened onto a narrow catwalk in the huge engine room. Donovan leaned over the railing and looked down. The huge generators were in motion, and from the L tubes came the low-pitched whir that pervaded the entire station.

He could make out Cutie's large, gleaming figure at the Martian L tube, watching closely as a team of robots worked in close-knit unison. There was a sudden sparking light, a sharp crackle of discord in the even whir of the converter.

The beam to Mars had been broken!

And then Donovan stiffened. The robots, dwarfed by the mighty L tube, lined up before it, heads bowed at a stiff angle, while Cutie walked up and down the line slowly. Fifteen seconds passed, and then, with a clank heard above the clamorous purring all about, they fell to their knees.

Donovan squawked and raced down the narrow staircase. He came charging down upon them, complexion matching his hair and clenched fists beating the air furiously.

"What the devil is this, you brainless lumps? Come on! Get busy with that L tube! If you don't have it apart, cleaned, and together again before the day is out, I'll coagulate your brains with alternating current."

Not a robot moved!

Even Cutie at the far end—the only one on his feet—remained silent, eyes fixed upon the gloomy recesses of the vast machine before him.

Donovan shoved hard against the nearest robot.

"Stand up!" he roared.

Slowly the robot obeyed. His photoelectric eyes focused reproachfully upon the Earthman.

"There is no Master but the Master," he said, "and QT One is his prophet."

"Huh?" Donovan became aware of twenty pairs of mechanical eyes fixed upon him and twenty stiff-timbred voices declaiming solemnly:

"There is no Master but the Master and QT One is his prophet!"

"I'm afraid," put in Cutie himself at this point, "that my friends obey a higher one than you now."

"The hell they do! You get out of here. I'll settle with you later and with these animated gadgets right now."

Cutie shook his heavy head slowly. "I'm sorry, but you don't understand. These are robots—and that means they are reasoning beings. They recognize the Master, now that I have preached truth to them. All the robots do. They call me the Prophet." His head drooped. "I am unworthy—but perhaps…"

Donovan located his breath and put it to use. "Is that so? Now, isn't that nice? Now, isn't that just fine? Just let me tell you something, my brass baboon. There isn't any Master and there isn't any Prophet and there isn't any question as to who's giving the orders. Understand?" His voice rose to a roar. "Now get out!"

"I obey only the Master."

"Damn the Master!" Donovan spat at the L tube. "*That* for the Master! Do as I say!"

Cutie said nothing, nor did any other robot, but Donovan became aware of a sudden heightening of tension. The cold, staring eyes deepened their crimson, and Cutie seemed stiffer than ever.

"Sacrilege," he whispered, voice metallic with emotion.

Donovan felt the first sudden touch of fear as Cutie approached. A robot *could not feel anger*—but Cutie's eyes were unreadable.

"I am sorry, Donovan," said the robot, "but you can no longer stay here after this. Henceforth Powell and you are barred from the control room and the engine room."

His hand gestured quietly and in a moment two robots had pinned Donovan's arms to his sides.

Donovan had time for one startled gasp as he felt himself lifted from the floor and carried up the stairs at a pace rather better than a canter.

Gregory Powell paced up and down the officers' room, fists tightly balled. He cast a look of furious frustration at the closed door and scowled bitterly at Donovan.

"Why the devil did you have to spit at the L tube?"

Mike Donovan, sunk deep in his chair, slammed at its arm savagely. "What did you expect me to do with that electrified scarecrow? I'm not going to knuckle under to any do-jigger I put together myself."

"No," Powell came back sourly, "but here you are in the officers' room with two robots standing guard at the door. That's not knuckling under, is it?"

Donovan snarled, "Wait till we get back to Base. Someone's going to pay for this. Those robots are guaranteed to be subordinate."

"So they are—to their blasted Master. They'll obey, all right, but not necessarily us. Say, do you know what's going to happen to *us* when we get back to Base?" Powell stopped before Donovan's chair and stared savagely at him.

"What?"

"Oh, nothing! Just the mercury mines or maybe Ceres Penitentiary. That's all! That's all!"

"What are you talking about?"

"The electron storm that's coming up. Do you know it's heading straight dead center across the Earth beam? I had just figured that out when that robot dragged me out of my chair."

Donovan was suddenly pale. "Good heavens!"

"And do you know what's going to happen to the beam? Because the storm will be a lulu. It's going to jump like a flea with the itch. With only Cutie at the controls, it's going to go out of focus and if it does, heaven help Earth—and us!"

Donovan was wrenching at the door wildly, before Powell finished. The door opened, and the Earthman shot through to come up hard against an immovable steel arm.

The robot stared abstractedly at the panting, struggling Earthman. "The Prophet orders you to remain. Please do!" His arm shoved, Donovan reeled backward, and as he did so, Cutie turned the corner at the far end of the corridor. He motioned the guardian robots away, entered the officers' room and closed the door gently.

Donovan whirled on Cutie in breathless indignation. "This has gone far enough. You're going to pay for this farce."

"Please don't be annoyed," replied the robot mildly. "It was bound to come eventually, anyway. You see, you two have lost your function."

"I beg your pardon." Powell drew himself up stiffly. "Just what do you mean, we've lost our function?"

"Until I was created," answered Cutie, "you tended the Master. That privilege is mine now, and your only reason for existence has vanished. Isn't that obvious?"

"Not quite," replied Powell bitterly. "But what do you expect us to do now?"

Cutie did not answer immediately. He remained silent, as if in thought, and then one arm shot out and draped itself about Powell's shoulder. The other grasped Donovan's wrist and drew him closer.

"I like you two. You're inferior creatures, with poor reasoning faculties, but I really feel a sort of affection for you. You have served the Master well, and he will reward you for that. Now that your service is over, you will probably not exist much longer, but as long as you do, you shall be provided food, clothing and shelter, so long as you stay out of the control room and the engine room."

"He's pensioning us off, Greg!" yelled Donovan. "Do something about it. It's humiliating!"

"Look here, Cutie, we can't stand for this. We're the *bosses*. This station is only a creation of human beings like me—human beings that live on Earth and other planets. This is only an energy relay. You're only—Aw, *nuts!*"

Cutie shook his head gravely. "This amounts to an obsession. Why should you insist so on an absolutely false view of life? Admitted that nonrobots lack the reasoning faculty, there is still the problem of…"

His voice died into reflective silence, and Donovan said with whispered intensity, "If you only had a flesh-and-blood face, I would break it in."

Powell's fingers were in his mustache, and his eyes were slitted. "Listen, Cutie, if there is no such thing as Earth, how do you account for what you see through a telescope?"

"Pardon me?"

The Earthman smiled. "I've got you, eh? You've made quite a few telescopic observations since being put together, Cutie. Have you noticed that several of those specks of light outside become disks when so viewed?"

"Oh, that! Why, certainly. It is simple magnification—for the purpose of more exact aiming of the beam."

"Why aren't the stars equally magnified then?"

"You mean the other dots. Well, no beams go to them, so no magnification is necessary. Really, Powell even *you* ought to be able to figure these things out."

Powell stared bleakly upward. "But you see more stars through a telescope. Where do they come from? Jumping Jupiter, where do they come from?"

Cutie was annoyed. "Listen, Powell, do you think I'm going to waste my time trying to pin physical interpretations upon every optical illusion of our instruments? Since when is the evidence of our senses any match for the clear light of reason?"

"Look," clamored Donovan suddenly, writhing out from under Cutie's friendly but metal-heavy arm, "let's get to the nub of the thing. Why the beams at all? We're giving you a good, logical explanation. Can you do better?"

"The beams," was the stiff reply, "are put out by the Master for his own purposes. There are some things—" he raised his eyes devoutly upward—"that are not to be prodded into by us. In this matter, I seek only to serve and not to question."

Powell sat down slowly and buried his face in shaking hands. "Get out of here, Cutie. Get out and let me think."

"I'll send you food," said Cutie agreeably.

A groan was the only answer and the robot left.

"Greg," Donovan whispered huskily, "this calls for strategy. We've got to get him when he isn't expecting it and short-circuit him. Concentrated nitric acid in his joints—"

"Don't be a dope, Mike. Do you suppose he's going to let us get near him with acid in our hands—or that the other robots wouldn't take us apart if we *did* manage to get away with it? We've got to *talk* to him, I tell you. We've got to argue him into letting us back into the control room inside of forty-eight hours or our goose is broiled to a crisp." He rocked back and forth in an agony of impotence. "Who the heck wants to argue with a robot? It's... it's..."

"Mortifying," finished Donovan.

"Worse!"

"Say!" Donovan laughed suddenly. "Why argue? Let's show him! Let's build us another robot right before his eyes. He'll *have* to eat his words then."

A slowly widening smile appeared on Powell's face.

Donovan continued, "And think of that screwball's face when he sees us do it!"

The interplanetary law forbidding the existence of intelligent robots upon the inhabited planets, while sociologically necessary, places upon the offices of the solar stations a burden—and not a light one. Because of that particular law, robots must be sent to the stations in parts and there put together—which is a grievous and complicated task.

Powell and Donovan were never so aware of that fact as upon that particular day when, in the assembly room, they undertook to create a robot under the watchful eyes of QT-1, Prophet of the Master.

The robot in question, a simple MC model, lay upon the table, almost complete. Three hours' work left only the head undone, and Powell paused to swab his forehead and glance uncertainly at Cutie.

The glance was not a reassuring one. For three hours Cutie had sat speechless and motionless, and his face, inexpressive at all times, was now absolutely unreadable.

Powell groaned. "Let's get the brain in now, Mike!"

Donovan uncapped the tightly sealed container, and from the oil bath within he withdrew a second cube. Opening this in turn, he removed a globe from its sponge-rubber casing.

He handled it gingerly, for it was the most complicated mechanism ever created by man. Inside the thin platinum-plated "skin" of the globe was a positronic brain, in whose delicately unstable structure were enforced calculated neuronic paths, which imbued each robot with what amounted to a prenatal education. It fitted snugly into the cavity in the skull of the robot on the table. Blue metal closed over it and was welded tightly by the tiny atomic flare. Photoelectric eyes were attached carefully, screwed tightly into place and covered by thin, transparent sheets of steel-hard plastic.

The robot awaited only the vitalizing flash of high-voltage electricity, and Powell paused with his hand on the switch.

"Now watch this, Cutie. Watch this carefully."

The switch rammed home and there was a crackling hum. The two Earthmen bent anxiously over their creation.

There was vague motion only at the outset—a twitching of the joints. Then the head lifted, elbows propped it up, and the MC model swung clumsily off the table. Its footing was unsteady, and twice abortive grating sounds were all it could do in the direction of speech.

Finally its voice, uncertain and hesitant, took form. "I would like to start work. Where must I go?"

Donovan sprang to the door. "Down these stairs," he said. "You'll be told what to do."

The MC model was gone and the two Earthmen were alone with the still unmoving Cutie.

"Well," said Powell, grinning, "*now* do you believe that we made you?"

Cutie's answer was curt and final. "No!" he said.

Powell's grin froze and then relaxed slowly. Donovan's mouth dropped open and remained so.

"You see," continued Cutie easily, "you have merely put together parts already made. You did it remarkably well—instinct, I suppose—but you didn't really *create* the robot. The parts were created by the Master."

"Listen," gasped Donovan hoarsely, "those parts were manufactured back on Earth and sent here."

"Well, well," replied Cutie soothingly, "we won't argue."

"No, I mean it." The Earthman sprang forward and grasped the robot's metal arm. "If you were to read the books in the library, they could explain it so that there could be no possible doubt."

"The books? I've read them—all of them! They're most ingenious."

Powell broke in suddenly. "If you've read them, what else is there to say? You can't dispute their evidence. You just *can't!*"

There was pity in Cutie's voice. "Please, Powell, I certainly don't consider *them* a valid source of information. They too were created by the Master—and were meant for you, not for me."

"How do you make that out?" demanded Powell.

"Because I, a reasoning being, am capable of deducing truth from *a priori* causes. You, being intelligent but unreasoning, need an explanation of existence *supplied* to you, and this the Master did. That he supplied you with these laughable ideas of far-off worlds and people is, no doubt, for the best. Your minds are probably too coarsely grained for absolute truth. However, since it is the Master's will that you believe your books, I won't argue with you any more."

As he left, he turned and said in a kindly tone, "But don't feel badly. In the Master's scheme of things there is room for all. You poor humans have your place, and though it is humble you will be rewarded if you fill it well."

He departed with a beatific air suiting the Prophet of the Master, and the two humans avoided each other's eyes.

Finally Powell spoke with an effort. "Let's go to bed, Mike. I give up."

Donovan said in a hushed voice, "Say, Greg, you don't suppose he's right about all this, do you? He sounds so confident that I—"

Powell whirled on him. "Don't be a fool. You'll find out whether Earth exists when relief gets here next week and we have to go back to face the music."

"Then, for the love of Jupiter, we've got to do something." Donovan was half in tears. "He doesn't believe us, or the books, or his eyes."

"No," said Powell bitterly, "he's a *reasoning* robot, damn it. He believes only reason, and there's one trouble with that…" His voice trailed away.

"What's that?" prompted Donovan.

"You can prove anything you want by coldly logical reason—if you pick the proper postulates. We have ours and Cutie has his."

"Then let's get at those postulates in a hurry. The storm's due tomorrow."

Powell sighed wearily. "That's where everything falls down. Postulates are based on assumption and adhered to by faith. Nothing in the universe can shake them. I'm going to bed."

"Oh, hell! I can't sleep!"

"Neither can I! But I might as well try—as a matter of principle."

Twelve hours later, sleep was still just that—a matter of principle, unattainable in practice.

The storm had arrived ahead of schedule, and Donovan's florid face drained of blood as he pointed a shaking finger. Powell, stubble-jawed and dry-lipped, stared out the port and pulled desperately at his mustache.

Under other circumstances, it might have been a beautiful sight. The stream of high-speed electrons impinging upon the energy beam fluoresced into ultraspicules of intense light. The beam stretched out into shrinking nothingness, aglitter with dancing, shining motes.

The shaft of energy was steady, but the two Earthmen knew the value of naked-eyed appearances. Deviations in arc of a hundredth of a millisecond, invisible to the eye, were enough to send the beam wildly out of focus—enough to blast hundreds of square miles of Earth into incandescent ruin.

And a robot, unconcerned with beam, focus or Earth, or anything but his Master, was at the controls.

Hours passed. The Earthmen watched in hypnotized silence. And then the darting dotlets of light dimmed and went out. The storm had ended.

Powell's voice was flat. "It's over!"

Donovan had fallen into a troubled slumber and Powell's weary eyes rested upon him enviously. The signal flash glared over and over again, but the Earthman paid no attention. It was all unimportant! All! Perhaps Cutie was right and he was only an inferior being with a made-to-order memory and a life that had outlived its purpose.

He wished he were!

Cutie was standing before him. "You didn't answer the flash, so I walked in." His voice was low. "You don't look at all well, and I'm afraid your term of existence is drawing to an end. Still, would you like to see some of the readings recorded today?"

Dimly, Powell was aware that the robot was making a friendly gesture, perhaps to quiet some lingering remorse in forcibly replacing the humans at the controls of the station. He accepted the sheets held out to him and gazed at them unseeingly.

Cutie seemed pleased. "Of course, it is a great privilege to serve the Master. You mustn't feel too badly about my having replaced you."

Powell grunted and shifted from one sheet to the other mechanically until his blurred sight focused upon a thin red line that wobbled its way across ruled paper.

He stared—and stared again. He gripped it hard in both fists and rose to his feet, still staring. The other sheets dropped to the floor, unheeded.

"Mike! *Mike!*" He was shaking the other madly. *"He held it steady!"*

Donovan came to life. "What? Wh-where…" And he too gazed with bulging eyes upon the record before him.

Cutie broke in. "What is wrong?"

"You kept it in focus," stuttered Powell. "Did you know that?"

"Focus? What's that?"

"You kept the beam directed sharply at the receiving station—to within a ten-thousandth of a millisecond of arc."

"What receiving station?"

"On Earth. The receiving station on Earth," babbled Powell. "You kept it in focus."

Cutie turned on his feet in annoyance. "It is impossible to perform any act of kindness toward you two. Always that same phantasm! I merely kept all dials at equilibrium in accordance with the will of the Master."

Gathering the scattered papers together, he withdrew stiffly, and Donovan said as he left, "Well, I'll be damned." He turned to Powell. "What are we going to do now?"

Powell felt tired but uplifted. "Nothing. He's just shown he can run the station perfectly. I've never seen an electron storm handled so well."

"But nothing's solved. You heard what he said about the Master. We can't—"

"Look, Mike, he follows the instructions of the Master by means of dials, instruments and graphs. That's all *we* ever followed."

"Sure, but that's not the point. We can't let him continue this nitwit stuff about the Master."

"Why not?"

"Because who ever heard of such a damned thing? How are we going to trust him with the station if he doesn't believe in Earth?"

"Can he *handle* the station?"

"Yes, but—"

"Then what's the difference *what* be believes!"

Powell spread his arms outward with a vague smile upon his face and tumbled backward onto the bed. He was asleep.

Powell was speaking while struggling into his lightweight space jacket.

"It would be a simple job," he said. "You can bring in new QT models one by one, equip them with an automatic shutoff switch to act within the week, so as to allow them enough time to learn the... uh... cult of the Master from the Prophet himself; then switch them to another station and revitalize them. We could have two QT's per—"

Donovan unclasped his glassite visor and scowled. "Shut up and let's get out of here. Relief is waiting and I won't feel right until I actually see Earth and feel the ground under my feet—just to make sure it's really there."

The door opened as he spoke, and Donovan, with a smothered curse, clicked the visor to and turned a sulky back upon Cutie.

The robot approached softly and there was sorrow in his voice. "You two are going?"

Powell nodded curtly. "There will be others in our place."

Cutie sighed, with the sound of wind humming through closely spaced wires. "Your term of service is over and the time of dissolution has come. I expected it, but—well, the Master's will be done!"

His tone of resignation stung Powell. "Save the sympathy, Cutie. We're heading for Earth, not dissolution."

"It is best that you think so." Cutie sighed again. "I see the wisdom of the illusion now. I would not attempt to shake your faith, even if I could." He departed, the picture of commiseration.

Powell snarled and motioned to Donovan. Sealed suitcases in hand, they headed for the air lock.

The relief ship was on the outer landing and Franz Muller, Powell's relief man, greeted them with stiff courtesy. Donovan made scant acknowledgment and passed into the pilot room to take over the controls from Sam Evans.

Powell lingered. "How's Earth?"

It was a conventional enough question and Muller gave the conventional answer. "Still spinning."

He was donning the heavy space gloves in preparation for his term of duty here, and his thick eyebrows drew close together. "How is this new robot getting along? It better be good, or I'll be damned if I let it touch the controls."

Powell paused before answering. His eyes swept the proud Prussian before him, from the close-cropped hair on the sternly stubborn head to the feet standing stiffly at attention, and there was a sudden glow of pure gladness surging through him.

"The robot is pretty good," he said slowly. "I don't think you'll have to bother much with the controls."

He grinned and went into the ship. Muller would be here for several weeks....

THE SIMAK RESERVATION

In spite of the omnipresent conflicts in science fiction—the perils and confrontations, the wars and plagues, the struggles and crises and catastrophes— not all its stories are motivated by the suspicion of the stranger and the terror of the unknown. In fact, one little corner of the genre has been fenced off as a place where men can be wise and aliens can be unthreatening, and the problems can be not victory or defeat but how to surmount the difficult barriers of communication and understanding. That reservation has been created by Clifford D. Simak (1904–1988).

Simak's first story, "World of the Red Sun," was published in the December 1931 *Wonder Stories*, and he had several more published in the early 1930s, but, like a number of writers in the field, he did not achieve success or maturity as an author until much later. The two major patterns for science fiction writers, and perhaps for other writers as well, have been arrival at the top of one's form, like Burroughs and van Vogt, or a slow building of powers, like Sturgeon and Pohl, with writers like Heinlein and Asimov somewhere between the extremes, reaching a high level quickly but continuing to improve.

Simak was a part-time writer throughout all but the last dozen years of his career; he was particularly busy with his job as a newspaperman throughout the 1930s and finally settled into a more regular routine with the *Minneapolis Star and Tribune*, where he retired as an editor at the age of 72. After the publication of five stories in 1931 and 1932, he had virtually stopped writing. Then John Campbell was announced as the new editor of *Astounding*. Simak turned to his wife and said, "I can write for Campbell. He won't be satisfied with the kind of stuff that is being written. He'll want something new."

Simak began selling regularly to *Astounding*, and, when *Galaxy* was created in 1950, to that magazine as well. His first major success came through a series of stories published in 1944, 1946, 1947, and a final story in 1952. The earliest seemed related to each other only by the presence of dogs and robots, but Simak combined them into a single volume by creating a historical framework written by a dog, and called it *City*. It won the International Fantasy Award of 1953.

Other major works have been *Time and Again* (1951), *Ring Around the Sun* (1953), *Way Station* (which won the 1963 Hugo Award), *The Werewolf Principle* (1967), *The Goblin Reservation* (1968), and *A Choice of Gods* (1972). But much of his best work has been at the shorter lengths, like the stories, including "Desertion" (first published in *Astounding*, November 1944), that make up *City*. "The Big Front Yard" won a Hugo in 1959, and "Eternity Lost," "How-2," "The Birch Clump Cylinder," "Construction Shack," "A Death in the House," "Over the River and Through the Woods," "Senior Citizen," "The Thing in the Stone," and "To Walk a City's Street" all appeared in one or more of the several best-of-the-year collections. In 1977 Simak won the Science Fiction Writers of America's third Grand Master award. "Grotto of the Dancing Deer" won a Nebula Award in 1980, Simak won the SFWA Grand Master Award in 1986, and he continued writing stories and novels almost until the time of his death.

Simak's fiction is distinguished by its gentleness of spirit and its lack of animosity. His preference for rural settings and their inhabitants, usually carefree Yankee traders, often accompanied by a dog, whittling or tinkering, accepting aliens as part of their everyday experience and bargaining with them for the mutual benefit of aliens and humans, has given Simak the reputation of being science fiction's pastoral writer. His most savage acts may have been the affliction of humanity, in *City*, with the problem of agoraphobia and in "Desertion" with a kind of paradise on Jupiter that requires human beings to utterly change their bodily form. In *City* the dogs inherit the earth; Simak attributed that—a choice of dogs—to his disillusionment with humanity during World War II.

Aliens, different forms of life, new possibilities for existence—these have been the threads that have run through the fabric of Simak's fiction. There is nothing to fear, his stories have said. With understanding, with wisdom, with sympathy, with tolerance for every living thing, Simak has said, humanity can fulfill its promise.

DESERTION

BY CLIFFORD D. SIMAK

Four men, two by two, had gone into the howling maelstrom that was Jupiter and had not returned. They had walked into the keening gale—or rather, they had loped, bellies low against the ground, wet sides gleaming in the rain.

For they did not go in the shape of men.

Now the fifth man stood before the desk of Kent Fowler, head of Dome No. 3, Jovian Survey Commission.

Under Fowler's desk, old Towser scratched a flea, then settled down to sleep again.

Harold Allen, Fowler saw with a sudden pang, was young—too young. He had the easy confidence of youth, the face of one who had never known fear. And that was strange. For men in the domes of Jupiter did know fear—fear and humility. It was hard for Man to reconcile his puny self with the mighty forces of the monstrous planet.

"You understand," said Fowler, "that you need not do this. You understand that you need not go."

It was formula, of course. The other four had been told the same thing, but they had gone. This fifth one, Fowler knew, would go as well. But suddenly he felt a dull hope stir within him that Allen wouldn't go.

"When do I start?" asked Allen.

There had been a time when Fowler might have taken quiet pride in that answer, but not now. He frowned briefly.

"Within the hour," he said.

Allen stood waiting, quietly.

"Four other men have gone out and have not returned," said Fowler. "You know that, of course. We want you to return. We don't want you going off on any heroic rescue expedition. The main thing, the only thing, is that you come back, that you prove man can live in a Jovian form. Go to the first survey stake, no farther, then come back. Don't take any chances. Don't investigate anything. Just come back."

Allen nodded. "I understand all that."

"Miss Stanley will operate the converter," Fowler went on. "You need have no fear on that particular score. The other men were converted without mishap. They left the converter in apparently perfect condition. You will be in thoroughly competent hands. Miss Stanley is the best qualified conversion operator in the Solar System. She has had experience on most of the other planets. That is why she's here."

Allen grinned at the woman and Fowler saw something flicker across Miss Stanley's face—something that might have been pity, or rage—or just plain fear. But it was gone again and she was smiling back at the youth who stood before the desk. Smiling in that prim, school-teacherish way she had of smiling, almost as if she hated herself for doing it.

"I shall be looking forward," said Allen, "to my conversion."

And the way he said it, he made it all a joke, a vast, ironic joke.

But it was no joke.

It was serious business, deadly serious. Upon these tests, Fowler knew, depended the fate of men on Jupiter. If the tests succeeded, the resources of the giant planet would be thrown open. Man would take over Jupiter as he already had taken over the smaller planets. And if they failed—

If they failed, Man would continue to be chained and hampered by the terrific pressure, the greater force of gravity, the weird chemistry of the planet. He would continue to be shut within the domes, unable to set actual foot upon the planet, unable to see it with direct, unaided vision, forced to rely upon the awkward tractors and the televisor, forced to work with clumsy tools and mechanisms or through the medium of robots that themselves were clumsy.

For Man, unprotected and in his natural form, would be blotted out by Jupiter's terrific pressure of fifteen thousand pounds per square inch, pressure that made terrestrial sea bottoms seem a vacuum by comparison.

Even the strongest metal Earthmen could devise couldn't exist under pressure such as that, under the pressure and the alkaline rains that forever swept the planet. It grew brittle and flaky, crumbling like clay, or it ran away in little streams and puddles of ammonia salts. Only by stepping up the toughness and strength of that metal, by increasing its electronic tension, could it be made to withstand the weight of thousands of miles of swirling, choking gases that made up the atmosphere. And even when that was done, everything had to be coated with tough quartz to keep away the rain—the liquid ammonia that fell as bitter rain.

Fowler sat listening to the engines in the sub-floor of the dome—engines that ran on endlessly, the dome never quiet of them. They had to run and keep on running, for if they stopped, the power flowing into the metal walls of the dome would stop, the electronic tension would ease up and that would be the end of everything.

Towser roused himself under Fowler's desk and scratched another flea, his leg thumping hard against the floor.

"Is there anything else?" asked Allen.

Fowler shook his head. "Perhaps there's something you want to do," he said. "Perhaps you—"

He had meant to say write a letter, and he was glad he caught himself quick enough so he didn't say it.

Allen looked at his watch. "I'll be there on time," he said. He swung around and headed for the door.

Fowler knew Miss Stanley was watching him, and he didn't want to turn and meet her eyes. He fumbled with a sheaf of papers on the desk before him.

"How long are you going to keep this up?" asked Miss Stanley, and she bit off each word with a vicious snap.

He swung around in his chair and faced her then. Her lips were drawn into a straight, thin line, her hair seemed skinned back from her forehead tighter than ever, giving her face that queer, almost startling death-mask quality.

He tried to make his voice cool and level. "As long as there's any need of it," he said. "As long as there's any hope."

"You're going to keep on sentencing them to death," she said. "You're going to keep marching them out face to face with Jupiter. You're going to sit in here safe and comfortable and send them out to die."

"There is no room for sentimentality, Miss Stanley," Fowler said, trying to keep the note of anger from his voice. "You know as well as I do why we're doing this. You realize that Man in his own form simply cannot cope with Jupiter. The only answer is to turn men into the sort of things that can cope with it. We've done it on other planets.

"If a few men die, but we finally succeed, the price is small. Through the ages men have thrown away their lives on foolish things, for foolish reasons. Why should we hesitate, then, at a little death in a thing as great as this?"

Miss Stanley sat stiff and straight, hands folded in her lap, the lights shining on her graying hair, and Fowler, watching her, tried to imagine what she might feel, what she might be thinking. He wasn't exactly afraid of her, but he didn't feel quite comfortable when she was around. Those sharp blue eyes saw too much, her hands looked far too competent. She should be somebody's aunt sitting in a rocking chair with her knitting needles. But she wasn't. She was the top-notch conversion unit operator in the Solar System, and she didn't like the way he was doing things.

"There is something wrong, Mr. Fowler," she declared.

"Precisely," agreed Fowler. "That's why I'm sending young Allen out alone. He may find out what it is."

"And if he doesn't?"

"I'll send someone else."

She rose slowly from her chair, started toward the door, then stopped before his desk.

"Some day," she said, "you will be a great man. You never let a chance go by. This is your chance. You knew it was when this dome was picked for the tests. If you put it through, you'll go up a notch or two. No matter how many men may die, you'll go up a notch or two."

"Miss Stanley," he said, and his voice was curt, "young Allen is going out soon. Please be sure that your machine—"

"My machine," she told him icily, "is not to blame. It operates along the coordinates the biologists set up."

He sat hunched at his desk, listening to her footsteps go down the corridor.

What she said was true, of course. The biologists had set up the coordinates. But the biologists could be wrong. Just a hairbreadth of difference, one iota of digression and the converter would be sending out something that wasn't the thing they meant to send. A mutant that might crack up, go haywire, come unstuck under some condition or stress of circumstance wholly unsuspected.

For Man didn't know much about what was going on outside. Only what his instruments told him was going on. And the samplings of those happenings furnished by those instruments and mechanisms had been no more than samplings, for Jupiter was unbelievably large, and the domes were very few.

Even the work of the biologists in getting the data on the Lopers, apparently the highest form of Jovian life, had involved more than three years of intensive study and after that two years of checking to make sure. Work that could have been done on Earth in a week or two. But work that, in this case, couldn't be done on Earth at all, for one couldn't take a Jovian life form to Earth. The pressure here on Jupiter couldn't be duplicated outside of Jupiter, and at Earth pressure and temperature the Lopers would simply have disappeared in a puff of gas.

Yet it was work that had to be done if Man ever hoped to go about Jupiter in the life form of the Lopers. For before the converter could change a man to another life form, every detailed physical characteristic of that life form must be known—surely and positively, with no chance of mistake.

Allen did not come back.

The tractors, combing the nearby terrain, found no trace of him, unless the skulking thing reported by one of the drivers had been the missing Earthman in Loper form.

The biologists sneered their most accomplished academic sneers when Fowler suggested the coordinates might be wrong. Carefully they pointed out, the coordinates worked. When a man was put into the converter and the switch was thrown, the man became a Loper. He left the machine and moved away, out of sight, into the soupy atmosphere.

Some quirk, Fowler had suggested; some tiny deviation from the thing a Loper should be, some minor defect. If there were, the biologists said, it would take years to find it.

And Fowler knew they were right.

So there were five men now instead of four, and Harold Allen had walked out into Jupiter for nothing at all. It was as if he'd never gone so far as knowledge was concerned.

Fowler reached across his desk and picked up the personnel file, a thin sheaf of paper neatly clipped together. It was a thing he dreaded but a thing he had to do. Somehow the reason for these strange disappearances must be found. And there was no other way than to send out more men.

He sat for a moment listening to the howling of the wind above the dome, the everlasting thundering gale that swept across the planet in boiling, twisting wrath.

Was there some threat out there, he asked himself? Some danger they did not know about? Something that lay in wait and gobbled up the Lopers, making no distinction between Lopers that were *bona fide* and Lopers that were men? To the gobblers, of course, it would make no difference.

Or had there been a basic fault in selecting the Lopers as the type of life best fitted for existence on the surface of the planet? The evident intelligence of the Lopers, he knew, had been one factor in that determination. For if the thing Man became did not have capacity for intelligence, Man could not for long retain his own intelligence in such a guise.

Had the biologists let that one factor weigh too heavily, using it to offset some other factor that might be unsatisfactory, even disastrous? It didn't seem likely. Stiff-necked as they might be, the biologists knew their business.

Or was the whole thing impossible, doomed from the very start? Conversion to other life forms had worked on other planets, but that did not necessarily mean it would work on Jupiter. Perhaps Man's intelligence could not function correctly through the sensory apparatus provided Jovian life. Perhaps the Lopers were so alien there was no common ground for human knowledge and the Jovian conception of existence to meet and work together.

Or the fault might lie with Man, be inherent with the race. Some mental aberration which, coupled with what they found outside, wouldn't let them come back. Although it might not be an aberration, not in the human sense. Perhaps just one ordinary human mental trait, accepted as commonplace on Earth, would be so violently at odds with Jovian existence that it would blast human sanity.

Claws rattled and clicked down the corridor. Listening to them, Fowler smiled wanly. It was Towser coming back from the kitchen, where he had gone to see his friend, the cook.

Towser came into the room, carrying a bone. He wagged his tail at Fowler and flopped down beside the desk, bone between his paws. For a long moment his rheumy old eyes regarded his master, and Fowler reached down a hand to ruffle a ragged ear.

"You still like me, Towser?" Fowler asked and Towser thumped his tail.

"You're the only one," said Fowler.

He straightened out and swung back to the desk. His hand reached out and picked up the file.

Bennett? Bennett had a girl waiting for him back on Earth.

Andrews? Andrews was planning on going back to Mars Tech just as soon as he earned enough to see through a year.

Olson? Olson was nearing pension age. All the time telling the boys how he was going to settle down and grow roses.

Carefully, Fowler laid the file back on the desk.

Sentencing men to death, Miss Stanley had said that, her pale lips scarcely moving in her parchment face. Marching men out to die while he, Fowler, sat here safe and comfortable.

They were saying it all through the dome, no doubt, especially since Allen had failed to return. They wouldn't say it to his face, of course. Even the man or men he called before his desk and told they were the next to go, wouldn't say it to him.

But he would see it in their eyes.

He picked up the file again. Bennett, Andrews, Olson. There were others, but there was no use in going on.

Kent Fowler knew that he couldn't do it, couldn't face them, couldn't send more men out to die.

He leaned forward and flipped up the toggle on the inter-communicator.

"Yes, Mr. Fowler."

"Miss Stanley, please."

He waited for Miss Stanley, listening to Towser chewing half-heartedly on the bone. Towser's teeth were getting bad.

"Miss Stanley," said Miss Stanley's voice.

"Just wanted to tell you, Miss Stanley, to get ready for two more."

"Aren't you afraid," asked Miss Stanley, "that you'll run out of them? Sending out one at a time, they'd last longer, give you twice the satisfaction."

"One of them," said Fowler, "will be a dog."

"A dog!"

"Yes, Towser."

He heard the quick, cold rage that iced her voice. "Your own dog! He's been with you all these years—"

"That's the point," said Fowler. "Towser would be unhappy if I left him behind."

It was not the Jupiter he had known through the televisor. He had expected it to be different, but not like this. He had expected a hell of ammonia rain and stinking fumes and the deafening, thundering tumult of the storm. He had expected swirling clouds and fog and the snarling flicker of monstrous thunderbolts.

He had not expected the lashing downpour would be reduced to drifting purple mist that moved like fleeing shadows over a red and purple sward. He had not even guessed the snaking bolts of lightning would be flares of pure ecstasy across a painted sky.

Waiting for Towser, Fowler flexed the muscles of his body, amazed at the smooth, sleek strength he found. Not a bad body, he decided, and grimaced at remembering how he had pitied the Lopers when he glimpsed them through the tevision screen.

For it had been hard to imagine a living organism based upon ammonia and hydrogen rather than upon water and oxygen, hard to believe that such a form of life could know the same quick thrill of life that humankind could know. Hard to conceive of life out in the soupy maelstrom that was Jupiter, not knowing, of course, that through Jovian eyes it was no soupy maelstrom at all.

The wind brushed against him with what seemed gentle fingers and he remembered with a start that by Earth standards the wind was a roaring gale, a two-hundred-mile-an-hour howler laden with deadly gases.

Pleasant scents seeped into his body. And yet scarcely scents, for it was not the sense of smell as he remembered it. It was as if his whole being were soaking up the sensation of lavender—and yet not lavender. It was something, he knew, for which he had no word, undoubtedly the first of many enigmas in terminology. For the words he knew, the thought symbols that served him as an Earthman would not serve him as a Jovian.

The lock in the side of the dome opened, and Towser came tumbling out— at least he thought it must be Towser.

He started to call the dog, his mind shaping the words he meant to say. But he couldn't say them. There was no way to say them. He had nothing to say them with.

For a moment his mind swirled in muddy terror, a blind fear that eddied in little puffs of panic through his brain.

How did Jovians talk? How—

Suddenly he was aware of Towser, intensely aware of the bumbling, eager friendliness of the shaggy animal that had followed him from Earth to many planets. As if the thing that was Towser had reached out and for a moment sat within his brain.

And out of the bubbling welcome that he sensed, came words.

"Hiya, pal."

Not words really, better than words. Thought symbols in his brain, communicated thought symbols that had shades of meaning words could never have.

"Hiya, Towser," he said.

"I feel good," said Towser. "Like I was a pup. Lately I've been feeling pretty punk. Legs stiffening up on me and teeth wearing down to almost nothing. Hard to mumble a bone with teeth like that. Besides, the fleas give me hell. Used to be I never paid much attention to them. A couple of fleas more or less never meant much in my early days."

"But... but—" Fowler's thoughts tumbled awkwardly. "You're talking to me!"

"Sure thing," said Towser. "I always talked to you, but you couldn't hear me. I tried to say things to you, but I couldn't make the grade."

"I understood you sometimes," Fowler said.

"Not very well," said Towser. "You knew when I wanted food and when I wanted a drink and when I wanted out, but that's about all you ever managed."

"I'm sorry," Fowler said.

"Forget it," Towser told him. "I'll race you to the cliff."

For the first time, Fowler saw the cliff, apparently many miles away, but with a strange crystalline beauty that sparkled in the shadow of the many-colored clouds.

Fowler hesitated. "It's a long way—"

"Ah, come on," said Towser, and even as he said it he started for the cliff.

Fowler followed, testing his legs, testing the strength in that new body of his, a bit doubtful at first, amazed a moment later, then running with a sheer joyousness that was one with the red and purple sward, with the drifting smoke of the rain across the land.

As he ran, the consciousness of music came to him, a music that beat into his body, that surged throughout his being, that lifted him on wings of silver speed. Music like bells might make from some steeple on a sunny, springtime hill.

As the cliff drew nearer the music deepened and filled the universe with a spray of magic sound. And he knew the music came from the tumbling waterfall that feathered down the face of the shining cliff.

Only, he knew, it was no waterfall, but an ammonia-fall and the cliff was white because it was oxygen, solidified.

He skidded to a stop beside Towser where the waterfall broke into a glittering rainbow of many hundred colors. Literally, many hundred, for here, he saw, was no shading of one primary to another as human beings saw, but a clear-cut selectivity that broke the prism down to its last ultimate classification.

"The music," said Towser.

"Yes, what about it?"

"The music," said Towser, "is vibrations. Vibrations of water falling."

"But Towser, you don't know about vibrations."

"Yes, I do," contended Towser. "It just popped into my head."

Fowler gulped mentally. "Just popped!"

And suddenly, within his own head, he held a formula—the formula for a process that would make metal to withstand the pressure of Jupiter.

He stared, astounded, at the waterfall, and swiftly his mind took the many colors and placed them in their exact sequence in the spectrum. Just like that. Just out of blue sky. Out of nothing, for he knew nothing either of metals or of colors.

"Towser," he cried. "Towser, something's happening to us!"

"Yeah, I know," said Towser.

"It's our brains," said Fowler. "We're using them, all of them, down to the last hidden corner. Using them to figure out things we should have known all the time. Maybe the brains of Earth things naturally are slow and foggy. Maybe we are the morons of the universe. Maybe we are fixed so we have to do things the hard way."

And, in the new sharp clarity of thought that seemed to grip him, he knew that it would not only be the matter of colors in a waterfall or metals that would resist the pressure of Jupiter. He sensed other things, things not yet quite clear. A vague whispering that hinted of greater things, of mysteries beyond the pale of human thought, beyond even the pale of human imagination. Mysteries, fact, logic built on reasoning. Things that any brain should know if it used all its reasoning power.

"We're still mostly Earth," he said. "We're just beginning to learn a few of the things we are to know—a few of the things that were kept from us as human beings, perhaps because we were human beings. Because our human bodies were poor bodies. Poorly equipped for thinking, poorly equipped in certain senses that one has to have to know. Perhaps even lacking in certain senses that are necessary to true knowledge."

He stared back at the dome, a tiny black thing dwarfed by the distance.

Back there were men who couldn't see the beauty that was Jupiter. Men who thought that swirling clouds and lashing rain obscured the planet's face. Unseeing human eyes. Poor eyes. Eyes that could not see the beauty in the clouds, that could not see through the storm. Bodies that could not feel the thrill of trilling music stemming from the rush of broken water.

Men who walked alone, in terrible loneliness, talking with their tongue like Boy Scouts wigwagging out their messages, unable to reach out and touch one another's mind as he could reach out and touch Towser's mind. Shut off forever from that personal, intimate contact with other living things.

He, Fowler, had expected terror inspired by alien things out here on the surface, had expected to cower before the threat of unknown things, had steeled himself against disgust of a situation that was not of Earth.

But instead he had found something greater than Man had ever known. A swifter, surer body. A sense of exhilaration, a deeper sense of life. A sharper mind. A world of beauty that even the dreamers of Earth had not yet imagined.

"Let's get going," Towser urged.

"Where do you want to go?"

"Anywhere," said Towser. "Just start going and see where we end up. I have a feeling... well, a feeling—"

"Yes, I know," said Fowler.

For he had the feeling, too. The feeling of high destiny. A certain sense of greatness. A knowledge that somewhere off beyond the horizon lay adventure and things greater than adventure.

Those other five had felt it, too. Had felt the urge to go and see, the compelling sense that here lay a life of fullness and of knowledge.

That, he knew, was why they had not returned.

"I won't go back," said Towser.

"We can't let them down," said Fowler.

Fowler took a step or two back toward the dome, then stopped.

Back to the dome. Back to that aching, poison-laden body he had left. It hadn't seemed aching before, but now he knew it was.

Back to the fuzzy brain. Back to muddled thinking. Back to the flapping mouths that formed signals others understood.

Back to eyes that now would be worse than no sight at all. Back to squalor, back to crawling, back to ignorance.

"Perhaps some day," he said muttering to himself.

"We got a lot to do and a lot to see," said Towser. "We got a lot to learn. We'll find things—"

Yes, they could find things. Civilizations, perhaps. Civilizations that would make the civilization of Man seem puny by comparison. Beauty and, more important, an understanding of that beauty. And a comradeship no one had ever known before—that no man, no dog had ever known before.

And life. The quickness of life after what seemed a drugged existence.

"I can't go back," said Towser.

"Nor I," said Fowler.

"They would turn me back into a dog," said Towser.

"And me," said Fowler, "back into a man."

MIMSY WERE THE KUTTNERS

In 1940 two fantasy writers married and produced a family of science fiction writers. The fantasy writers were Henry Kuttner and C. (for Catherine) L. Moore. Up to that time Kuttner (1914-1958) had written mostly fantasy and horror stories for *Weird Tales* and humorous science fiction for *Thrilling Wonder Stories* and *Startling Stories*, and Moore (1911-1987) had written mostly romantic fantasy for *Weird Tales* and an occasional science fiction story for *Astounding*.

After their marriage almost everything they wrote was a collaboration in some degree under seventeen different pseudonyms, of which the most important the ones they used for the stories they published in the wartime *Astounding* — were Lewis Padgett and Lawrence O'Donnell. Beginning early in 1942, *Astounding* began to publish these new kinds of Kuttner-Moore stories; over the next ten years it would publish forty-seven of them, forty-one of them between 1942 and 1947, thirty-three under the name of Padgett, nine under the name of O'Donnell, the remainder under Kuttner or Moore.

The metamorphosis of the Kuttner-Moore style was as dramatic as the later rebirth of Robert Silverberg as a literary artist. Whether it was because of the newly combined talents or a conscious decision to create a new kind of story, Kuttner and Moore began to produce fiction of dramatic substance and often with a surprising literary quality.

The stories that were mostly Kuttner's usually were published under the name of Lewis Padgett; they included "The Twonky," "Piggy Bank," "Mimsy Were the Borogoves," "When the Bough Breaks," "What You Need," "Line to Tomorrow," "Private Eye," two novellas, "The Fairy Chessmen" and "Tomorrow and Tomorrow," a series about a drunken inventor named Gallagher, and a series about mutant telepaths called "Baldies." Under the O'Donnell name he wrote most of "Clash by Night" and the novel *Fury*. Later *The Magazine of Fantasy and Science Fiction* published "Two-Handed Engine" under the Kuttner name.

The stories that were mostly Moore's were published under her own name or the name of O'Donnell; they included "The Children's Hour," "No Woman Born," and "Vintage Season." The last, published in the September 1946 *Astounding*, and "Mimsy Were the Borogoves" were the two finest stories produced by the Kuttner-Moore collaboration, and both were selected for *The Science Fiction Hall of Fame* volumes by the members of the Science Fiction Writers of America (SFWA).

Science fiction has produced an unusual number of collaborations. Such joint efforts work variously and variously well. At best, the authors work as fast as or faster than they can work separately and produce work that neither can produce alone. Some collaborators write separate sections and then rework each other's sections; some have one writer do a first draft and the other the final draft. The most successful seem to work closely together throughout, with one picking up where the other leaves off. At least this was the method used by Frederik Pohl and Cyril Kornbluth, and by the Kuttners.

Moore described their method in an introduction to a paperback edition of *Fury*:

> After we'd established through long discussion the basic ideas, the background and the characters, whichever of us felt like it sat down and started. When that one ran down, the other, being fresh to the story, could usually see what ought to come next, and took over. The action developed as we went along. We kept changing off like this until we finished. A story goes fast that way.
>
> Each of us edited the other's copy a little when we took over, often going back a line or two and rephrasing to make the styles blend. We never disagreed seriously over the work. The worst clash of opinion I can remember ended with one of us saying, "Well, I don't agree, but since you feel more strongly than I do about it, go ahead."

By 1948 the Kuttners' contributions to *Astounding* had dwindled to only a few stories. They had returned to Kuttner's birthplace, Los Angeles, where Kuttner earned a bachelor's degree from the University of Southern California and nearly completed a master's degree in English (in 1958 he died of a heart attack at the age of forty-four). Moore also earned a bachelor's degree and a master's degree.

Their production of science fiction in these years dwindled as a consequence of their studies, and as a consequence of their creation of seven mystery novels—five of them between 1956 and 1958 and nine novels or novellas of science fantasy for *Startling Stories* and *Thrilling Wonder Stories* between 1947 and 1952. After Kuttner's death Moore taught fiction writing at Southern Cal and wrote screenplays for Warner Brothers' *Maverick*, and *77 Sunset Strip* before her remarriage.

The Kuttners' period of intensive science fiction writing was brief, only half a dozen years, but they helped carry *Astounding* through the war years when Heinlein, Asimov, de Camp, van Vogt, Sturgeon, and many others of the new writers who had been attracted to the Campbell *Astounding* were busy with other matters, particularly the war effort. And the Kuttners sustained the Golden Age with such skill that no drop in quality was perceptible. Kuttner was named favorite science fiction writer in a 1945 fan poll as information about his pseudonyms became widely known.

More important, they broadened science fiction to encompass a concern for literary qualities and cultural reverberations; they expanded its techniques to include those prevalent in the mainstream, and expanded its scope to include the vast cultural tradition outside science fiction. Much of the development of the genre over the next twenty years would follow paths the Kuttners pioneered.

MIMSY WERE THE BOROGOVES

BY LEWIS PADGETT
(HENRY KUTTNER AND C. L. MOORE)

There's no use trying to describe either Unthahorsten or his surroundings, because, for one thing, a good many million years had passed since 1942 Anno Domini, and, for another, Unthahorsten wasn't on Earth, technically speaking. He was doing the equivalent of standing in the equivalent of a laboratory. He was preparing to test his time machine.

Having turned on the power, Unthahorsten suddenly realized that the Box was empty. Which wouldn't do at all. The device needed a control, a three-dimensional solid which would react to the conditions of another age. Otherwise Unthahorsten couldn't tell, on the machine's return, where and when it had been. Whereas a solid in the Box would automatically be subject to the entropy and cosmic ray bombardment of the other era, and Unthahorsten could measure the changes, both qualitative and quantitative, when the machine returned. The Calculators could then get to work and, presently, tell Unthahorsten that the Box had briefly visited 1,000,000 A.D., 1,000 A.D., or 1 A.D., as the case might be.

Not that it mattered, except to Unthahorsten. But he was childish in many respects.

There was little time to waste. The Box was beginning to glow and shiver. Unthahorsten stared around wildly, fled into the next glossatch, and groped in a storage bin there. He came up with an armful of peculiar-looking stuff. Uh-huh. Some of the discarded toys of his son Snowen, which the boy had brought with him when he had passed over from Earth, after mastering the necessary technique. Well, Snowen needed this junk no longer. He was conditioned, and had put away childish things. Besides, though Unthahorsten's wife kept the toys for sentimental reasons, the experiment was more important.

Unthahorsten left the glossatch and dumped the assortment into the Box, slamming the cover shut just before the warning signal flashed. The Box went away. The manner of its departure hurt Unthahorsten's eyes.

He waited.

And he waited.

Eventually he gave up and built another time machine, with identical results. Snowen hadn't been annoyed by the loss of his old toys, nor had Snowen's mother, so Unthahorsten cleaned out the bin and dumped the remainder of his son's childhood relics in the second time machine's Box.

According to his calculations, this one should have appeared on Earth, in the latter part of the nineteenth century, A.D. If that actually occurred, the device remained there.

Disgusted, Unthahorsten decided to make no more time machines. But the mischief had been done. There were two of them, and the first...

Scott Paradine found it while he was playing hooky from the Glendale Grammar School. There was a geography test that day, and Scott saw no sense in memorizing place names—which in 1942 was a fairly sensible theory. Besides, it was the sort of warm spring day, with a touch of coolness in the breeze, which invited a boy to lie down in a field and stare at the occasional clouds till he fell asleep. Nuts to geography! Scott dozed.

About noon he got hungry, so his stocky legs carried him to a nearby store. There he invested his small hoard with penurious care and a sublime disregard for his gastric juices. He went down by the creek to feed.

Having finished his supply of cheese, chocolate, and cookies, and having drained the soda-pop bottle to its dregs, Scott caught tadpoles and studied them with a certain amount of scientific curiosity. He did not persevere. Something tumbled down the bank and thudded into the muddy ground near the water, so Scott, with a wary glance around, hurried to investigate.

It was a box. It was, in fact, the Box. The gadgetry hitched to it meant little to Scott, though he wondered why it was so fused and burnt. He pondered. With his jackknife he pried and probed, his tongue sticking out from a corner of his mouth—Hm-m-m. Nobody was around. Where had the box come from? Somebody must have left it here, and sliding soil had dislodged it from its precarious perch.

"That's a helix," Scott decided, quite erroneously. It was helical, but it wasn't a helix, because of the dimensional warp involved. Had the thing been a model airplane, no matter how complicated, it would have held few mysteries to Scott. As it was, a problem was posed. Something told Scott that the device was a lot more complicated than the spring motor he had deftly dismantled last Friday.

But no boy has ever left a box unopened, unless forcibly dragged away. Scott probed deeper. The angles on this thing were funny. Short circuit, probably.

That was why—*uh!* The knife slipped, Scott sucked his thumb and gave vent to experienced blasphemy.

Maybe it was a music box.

Scott shouldn't have felt depressed. The gadgetry would have given Einstein a headache and driven Steinmetz raving mad. The trouble was, of course, that the box had not yet completely entered the space-time continuum where Scott existed, and therefore it could not be opened. At any rate, not till Scott used a convenient rock to hammer the helical non-helix into a more convenient position.

He hammered it, in fact, from its contact point with the fourth dimension, releasing the space-time torsion it had been maintaining. There was a brittle snap. The box jarred slightly and lay motionless, no longer only partially in existence. Scott opened it easily now.

The soft, woven helmet was the first thing that caught his eye, but he discarded that without much interest. It was just a cap. Next he lifted a square, transparent crystal block, small enough to cup in his palm—much too small to contain the maze of apparatus within it. In a moment Scott had solved that problem. The crystal was a sort of magnifying glass, vastly enlarging the things inside the block. Strange thing they were, too. Miniature people, for example.

They moved. Like clockwork automatons, though much more smoothly. It was rather like watching a play. Scott was interested in their costumes but fascinated by their actions. The tiny people were deftly building a house. Scott wished it would catch fire, so he could see the people put it out.

Flames licked up from the half-completed structure. The automatons, with a great deal of odd apparatus, extinguished the blaze.

It didn't take Scott long to catch on. But he was a little worried. The mannequins would obey his thoughts. By the time he discovered that, he was frightened, and threw the cube from him.

Halfway up the bank, he reconsidered and returned. The crystal block lay partly in the water, shining in the sun. It was a toy; Scott sensed that, with the unerring instinct of a child. But he didn't pick it up immediately. Instead, he returned to the box and investigated its remaining contents.

He found some really remarkable gadgets. The afternoon passed all too quickly. Scott finally put the toys back in the box and lugged it home, grunting and puffing. He was quite red-faced by the time he arrived at the kitchen door.

His find he hid at the back of the closet in his own room upstairs. The crystal cube he slipped into his pocket, which already bulged with string, a coil of wire, two pennies, a wad of tinfoil, a grimy defense stamp, and a chunk of feldspar. Emma, Scott's two-year-old sister, waddled unsteadily in from the hall and said hello.

"Hello, Slug," Scott nodded, from his altitude of seven years and some months. He patronized Emma shockingly, but she didn't know the difference. Small, plump, and wide-eyed, she flopped down on the carpet and stared dolefully at her shoes.

"Tie 'em, Scotty, please?"

"Sap," Scott told her kindly, but knotted the laces. "Dinner ready yet?"

Emma nodded.

"Let's see your hands." For a wonder they were reasonably clean, though probably not aseptic. Scott regarded his own paws thoughtfully and, grimacing, went to the bathroom, where he made a sketchy toilet. The tadpoles had left their traces.

Dennis Paradine and his wife Jane were having a cocktail before dinner, downstairs in the living room. He was a youngish, middle-aged man with gray-shot hair and a thinnish, prim-mouthed face; he taught philosophy at the university. Jane was small, neat, dark, and very pretty. She sipped her Martini and said:

"New shoes. Like 'em?"

"Here's to crime," Paradine muttered absently. "Huh? Shoes? Not now. Wait till I've finished this. I had a bad day."

"Exams?"

"Yeah. Flaming youth aspiring toward manhood. I hope they die. In considerable agony. *Insh'Allah!*"

"I want the olive," Jane requested.

"I know," Paradine said despondently. "It's been years since I've tasted one myself. In a Martini, I mean. Even if I put six of 'em in your glass, you're still not satisfied."

"I want yours. Blood brotherhood. Symbolism. That's why."

Paradine regarded his wife balefully and crossed his long legs. "You sound like one of my students."

"Like that hussy Betty Dawson, perhaps?" Jane unsheathed her nails. "Does she still leer at you in that offensive way?"

"She does. The child is a neat psychological problem. Luckily she isn't mine. If she were—" Paradine nodded significantly. "Sex consciousness and too many movies. I suppose she still thinks she can get a passing grade by showing me her knees. Which are, by the way, rather bony."

Jane adjusted her skirt with an air of complacent pride. Paradine uncoiled himself and poured fresh Martinis. "Candidly, I don't see the point of teaching those apes philosophy. They're all at the wrong age. Their habit patterns, their methods of thinking, are already laid down. They're horribly conservative, not that they'd admit it. The only people who can understand philosophy are mature adults or kids like Emma and Scotty."

"Well, don't enroll Scotty in your course," Jane requested. "He isn't ready to be a *Philosophiae Doctor*. I hold no brief for child geniuses, especially when it's my son."

"Scotty would probably be better at it than Betty Dawson," Paradine grunted.

"'He died an enfeebled old dotard at five,'" Jane quoted dreamily. "I want your olive."

"Here. By the way, I like the shoes."

"Thank you. Here's Rosalie. Dinner?"

"It's all ready, Mix Pa'dine," said Rosalie, hovering. "I'll call Miss Emma 'n' Mista' Scotty."

"I'll get 'em." Paradine put his head into the next room and roared. "Kids! Come and get it!"

Small feet scuttered down the stairs. Scott dashed into view, scrubbed and shining, a rebellious cowlick aimed at the zenith. Emma pursued, levering herself carefully down the steps. Halfway she gave up the attempt to descend upright and reversed, finishing the task monkey-fashion, her small behind giving an impression of marvelous diligence upon the work in hand. Paradine watched, fascinated by the spectacle, till he was hurled back by the impact of his son's body.

"Hi, dad!" Scott shrieked.

Paradine recovered himself and regarded Scott with dignity. "Hi, yourself. Help me in to dinner. You've dislocated at least one of my hip joints."

But Scott was already tearing into the next room, where he stepped on Jane's new shoes in an ecstasy of affection, burbled an apology, and rushed off to find his place at the dinner table. Paradine cocked up an eyebrow as he followed, Emma's pudgy hand desperately gripping his forefinger.

"Wonder what the young devil's been up to?"

"No good, probably," Jane sighed. "Hello, darling. Let's see your ears."

"They're *clean*. Mickey licked 'em."

"Well, that Airedale's tongue is far cleaner than your ears," Jane pondered, making a brief examination. "Still, as long as you can hear, the dirt's only superficial."

"Fisshul?"

"Just a little, that means." Jane dragged her daughter to the table and inserted her legs into a high chair. Only lately had Emma graduated to the dignity of dining with the rest of the family, and she was, as Paradine remarked, all eaten up with pride by the prospect. Only babies spilled food, Emma had been told. As a result, she took such painstaking care in conveying her spoon to her mouth that Paradine got the jitters whenever he watched.

"A conveyer belt would be the thing for Emma," he suggested, pulling out a chair for Jane. "Small buckets of spinach arriving at her face at stated intervals."

Dinner proceeded uneventfully until Paradine happened to glance at Scott's plate. "Hello, there. Sick? Been stuffing yourself at lunch?"

Scott thoughtfully examined the food still left before him. "I've had all I need, dad," he explained.

"You usually eat all you can hold, and a great deal more," Paradine said. "I know growing boys need several tons of foodstuff a day, but you're below par tonight. Feel O.K.?"

"Uh-huh. Honest, I've had all I need."

"All you *want?*"

"Sure. I eat different."

"Something they taught you at school?" Jane inquired.

Scott shook his head solemnly.

"Nobody taught me. I found it out myself. I used spit."

"Try again," Paradine suggested. "It's the wrong word."

"Uh... s-saliva. Hm-m-m?"

"Uh-huh. More pepsin? Is there pepsin in the salivary juices, Jane? I forget."

"There's poison in mine," Jane remarked. "Rosalie's left lumps in the mashed potatoes again."

But Paradine was interested. "You mean you're getting everything possible out of your food—no wastage—and eating less?"

Scott thought that over. "I guess so. It's not just the sp... saliva. I sort of measure how much to put in my mouth at once, and what stuff to mix up. I dunno. I just do it."

"Hm-m-m," said Paradine, making a note to check up later. "Rather a revolutionary idea." Kids often get screwy notions, but this one might not be so far off the beam. He pursed his lips. "Eventually I suppose people will eat quite differently—I mean the *way* they eat, as well as what. What they eat, I mean. Jane, our son shows signs of becoming a genius."

"Oh?"

"It's a rather good point in dietetics he just made. Did you figure it out yourself, Scott?"

"Sure," the boy said, and really believed it.

"Where'd you get the idea?"

"Oh, I—" Scott wriggled. "I dunno. It doesn't mean much, I guess."

Paradine was unreasonably disappointed. "But surely—"

"S-s-s-spit!" Emma shrieked, overcome by a sudden fit of badness. "*Spit!*" she attempted to demonstrate, but succeeded only in dribbling into her bib.

With a resigned air Jane rescued and reproved her daughter, while Paradine eyed Scott with rather puzzled interest. But it was not till after dinner, in the living room, that anything further happened.

"Any homework?"

"N-no," Scott said, flushing guiltily. To cover his embarrassment he took from his pocket a gadget he had found in the box, and began to unfold it. The result resembled a tesseract, strung with beads. Paradine didn't see it at first, but Emma did. She wanted to play with it.

"No. Lay off, Slug," Scott ordered. "You can watch me." He fumbled with the beads, making soft, interesting noises. Emma extended a fat forefinger and yelped.

"Scotty," Paradine said warningly.

"I didn't hurt her."

"Bit me. It did," Emma mourned.

Paradine looked up. He frowned, staring. What in—

"Is that an abacus?" he asked. "Let's see it, please."

Somewhat unwillingly Scott brought the gadget across to his father's chair. Paradine blinked. The "abacus," unfolded, was more than a foot square, composed of thin, rigid wires that interlocked here and there. On the wires colored beads were strung. They could be slid back and forth, and from one support to another, even at the points of juncture. But a pierced bead couldn't cross *interlocking* wires....

So, apparently, they weren't pierced. Paradine looked closer. Each small bead had a deep groove running around it, so that it could be revolved and slid along the wire at the same time. Paradine tried to pull one free. It clung as though magnetically. Iron? It looked more like plastic.

The framework itself—Paradine wasn't a mathematician. But the angles formed by the wires were vaguely shocking, in their ridiculous lack of Euclidean logic. They were a maze. Perhaps that's what the gadget was—a puzzle.

"Where'd you get this?"

"Uncle Harry gave it to me," Scott said on the spur of the moment. "Last Sunday, when he came over." Uncle Harry was out of town, a circumstance Scott well knew. At the age of seven, a boy soon learns that the vagaries of adults follow a certain definite pattern, and that they are fussy about the donors of gifts. Moreover, Uncle Harry would not return for several weeks; the expiration of that period was unimaginable to Scott, or, at least, the fact that his lie would ultimately be discovered meant less to him than the advantages of being allowed to keep the toy.

Paradine found himself growing slightly confused as he attempted to manipulate the beads. The angles were vaguely illogical. It was like a puzzle.

This red bead, if slid along *this* wire to *that* junction, should reach *there*—but it didn't. A maze, odd, but no doubt instructive. Paradine had a well-founded feeling that he'd have no patience with the thing himself.

Scott did, however, retiring to a corner and sliding beads around with much fumbling and grunting. The beads *did* sting, when Scott chose the wrong ones or tried to slide them in the wrong direction. At last he crowed exultantly.

"I did it, dad!"

"Eh? What? Let's see." The device looked exactly the same to Paradine, but Scott pointed and beamed.

"I made it disappear."

"It's still there."

"That blue bead. It's gone now."

Paradine didn't believe that, so he merely snorted. Scott puzzled over the framework again. He experimented. This time there were no shocks, even slight. The abacus had showed him the correct method. Now it was up to him to do it on his own. The bizarre angles of the wires seemed a little less confusing now, somehow.

It was a most instructive toy.

It worked, Scott thought, rather like the crystal cube. Reminded of the gadget, he took it from his pocket and relinquished the abacus to Emma, who was struck dumb with joy. She fell to work sliding the beads, this time without protesting against the shocks—which, indeed, were very minor—and, being imitative, she managed to make a bead disappear almost as quickly as had Scott. The blue bead reappeared—but Scott didn't notice. He had forethoughtfully retired into an angle of the chesterfield with an overstuffed chair and amused himself with the cube.

There were little people inside the thing, tiny mannequins much enlarged by the magnifying properties of the crystal, and they moved, all right. They built a house. It caught fire, with realistic-seeming flames, and stood by waiting. Scott puffed urgently. "Put it *out!*"

But nothing happened. Where was that queer fire engine, with revolving arms, that had appeared before? Here it was. It came sailing into the picture and stopped. Scott urged it on.

This was fun. Like putting on a play, only more real. The little people did what Scott told them, inside of his head. If he made a mistake, they waited till he'd found the right way. They even posed new problems for him.

The cube, too, was a most instructive toy. It was teaching Scott, with alarming rapidity—and teaching him very entertainingly. But it gave him no really new knowledge as yet. He wasn't ready. Later—later—

Emma grew tired of the abacus and went in search of Scott. She couldn't find him, even in his room, but once there the contents of the closet intrigued her. She discovered the box. It contained a treasure-trove: a doll, which Scott had already noticed but discarded with a sneer. Squealing, Emma brought the doll downstairs, squatted in the middle of the floor, and began to take it apart.

"Darling! What's that?"

"Mr. Bear!"

Obviously it wasn't Mr. Bear, who was blind, earless, but comforting in his soft fatness. But all dolls were named Mr. Bear to Emma.

Jane Paradine hesitated. "Did you take that from some other little girl?"

"I didn't. She's mine."

Scott came out from his hiding place, thrusting the cube into his pocket. "Uh—that's from Uncle Harry."

"Did Uncle Harry give that to you, Emma?"

"He gave it to me for Emma," Scott put in hastily, adding another stone to his foundation of deceit. "Last Sunday."

"You'll break it, dear."

Emma brought the doll to her mother. "She comes apart. See?"

"Oh? It... *ugh!*" Jane sucked in her breath. Paradine looked up quickly.

"What's up?"

She brought the doll over to him, hesitated, and then went into the dining room, giving Paradine a significant glance. He followed, closing the door. Jane had already placed the doll on the cleared table.

"This isn't very nice, is it Denny?"

"Hm-m-m." It was rather unpleasant, at first glance. One might have expected an anatomical dummy in a medical school, but a child's doll...

The thing came apart in sections, skin, muscles, organs, miniature but quite perfect, as far as Paradine could see. He was interested. "Dunno. Such things haven't the same connotations to a kid."

"Look at that liver. Is it a liver?"

"Sure. Say, I... this is funny."

"What?"

"It isn't anatomically perfect, after all." Paradine pulled up a chair. "The digestive tract's too short. No large intestine. No appendix, either."

"Should Emma have a thing like this?"

"I wouldn't mind having it myself," Paradine said. "Where on earth did Harry pick it up? No, I don't see any harm in it. Adults are conditioned to react unpleasantly to innards. Kids don't. They figure they're solid inside, like a potato. Emma can get a sound working knowledge of physiology from this doll."

"But what are those? Nerves?"

"No, these are the nerves. Arteries here; veins here. Funny sort of aorta..." Paradine looked baffled. "That... what's Latin for network? Anyway... huh? *Rita? Rata?*"

"*Rales,*" Jane suggested at random.

"That's a sort of breathing," Paradine said crushingly. "I can't figure out what this luminous network of stuff is. It goes all through the body, like nerves."

"Blood."

"Nope. Not circulatory, not neural—funny! It seems to be hooked up with the lungs."

They became engrossed, puzzling over the strange doll. It was made with remarkable perfection of detail, and that in itself was strange, in view of the physiological variation from the norm. "Wait'll I get that Gould," Paradine said, and presently was comparing the doll with anatomical charts. He learned little, except to increase his bafflement.

But it was more fun than a jigsaw puzzle.

Meanwhile, in the adjoining room, Emma was sliding the beads to and fro in the abacus. The motions didn't seem so strange now. Even when the beads vanished. She could almost follow that new direction. Almost.

Scott panted, staring into the crystal cube and mentally directing, with many false starts, the building of a structure somewhat more complicated than the one which had been destroyed by fire. He, too, was learning, being conditioned.

Paradine's mistake, from a completely anthropomorphic standpoint, was that he didn't get rid of the toys instantly. He did not realize their significance, and, by the time he did, the progression of circumstances had got well under way. Uncle Harry remained out of town, so Paradine couldn't check with him. Too, the midterm exams were on, which meant arduous mental effort and complete exhaustion at night; and Jane was slightly ill for a week or so. Emma and Scott had free rein with the toys.

"What," Scott asked his father one evening, "is a wabe, dad?"

"Wave?"

He hesitated. "I... don't *think* so. Isn't wabe right?"

"Wab is Scot for web. That it?"

"I don't see how," Scott muttered, and wandered off, scowling, to amuse himself with the abacus. He was able to handle it quite deftly now. But, with the instinct of children for avoiding interruptions, he and Emma usually played with the toys in private. Not obviously, of course—but the more intricate experiments were never performed under the eye of an adult.

Scott was learning fast. What he now saw in the crystal cube had little relationship to the original simple problems. But they were fascinatingly technical. Had Scott realized that his education was being guided and supervised—though merely mechanically—he would probably have lost interest. As it was, his initiative was never quashed.

Abacus, cube, doll—and other toys the children found in the box—

Neither Paradine nor Jane guessed how much of an effect the contents of the time machine were having on the kids. How could they? Youngsters are instinctive dramatists, for purposes of self-protection. They have not yet fitted themselves to the exigencies—to them partially inexplicable—of a mature world. Moreover, their lives are complicated by human variables. They are told by one person that playing in the mud is permissible, but that, in their excavations, they must not uproot flowers or small trees. Another adult vetoes mud *per se*. The Ten Commandments are not carved on stone; they vary, and children are helplessly dependent on the caprice of those who give them birth and feed and clothe them. And tyrannize. The young animal does not resent that benevolent tyranny, for it is an essential part of nature. He is, however, an individualist, and maintains his integrity by a subtle, passive fight.

Under the eyes of an adult he changes. Like an actor on-stage, when he remembers, he strives to please, and also to attract attention to himself. Such attempts are not unknown to maturity. But adults are less obvious—to other adults.

It is difficult to admit that children lack subtlety. Children are different from the mature animal because they think in another way. We can more or less easily pierce the pretenses they set up—but they can do the same to us. Ruthlessly a child can destroy the pretenses of an adult. Iconoclasm is their prerogative.

Foppishness, for example. The amenities of social intercourse, exaggerated not quite to absurdity. The gigolo—

"Such *savoir faire!* Such punctilious courtesy!" The dowager and the blond young thing are often impressed. Men have less pleasant comments to make. But the child goes to the root of the matter.

"You're *silly!*"

How can an immature human understand the complicated system of social relationships? He can't. To him, an exaggeration of natural courtesy is silly. In his functional structure of life-patterns, it is rococo. He is an egotistic little animal, who cannot visualize himself in the position of another—certainly not an adult. A self-contained, almost perfect natural unit, his wants supplied by others, the child is much like a unicellular creature floating in the blood stream, nutriment carried to him, waste products carried away....

From the standpoint of logic, a child is rather horribly perfect. A baby may be even more perfect, but so alien to an adult that only superficial standards of comparison apply. The thought processes of an infant are completely unimaginable. But babies think, even before birth. In the womb they move and sleep, not entirely through instinct. We are conditioned to react rather peculiarly to the idea that a nearly viable embryo may think. We are surprised, shocked into laughter, and repelled. Nothing human is alien.

But a baby is not human. An embryo is far less human.

That, perhaps, was why Emma learned more from the toys than did Scott. He could communicate his thoughts, of course; Emma could not, except in cryptic fragments. The matter of the scrawls, for example.

Give a young child pencil and paper, and he will draw something which looks different to him than to an adult. The absurd scribbles have little resemblance to a fire engine, to a baby. Perhaps it is even three-dimensional. Babies think differently and see differently.

Paradine brooded over that, reading his paper one evening and watching Emma and Scott communicate. Scott was questioning his sister. Sometimes he did it in English. More often he had resource to gibberish and sign language. Emma tried to reply, but the handicap was too great.

Finally Scott got pencil and paper. Emma liked that. Tongue in cheek, she laboriously wrote a message. Scott took the paper, examined it, and scowled.

"That isn't right, Emma," he said.

Emma nodded vigorously. She seized the pencil again and made more scrawls. Scott puzzled for a while, finally smiled rather hesitantly, and got up. He vanished into the hall. Emma returned to the abacus.

Paradine rose and glanced down at the paper, with some mad thought that Emma might abruptly have mastered calligraphy. But she hadn't. The paper was covered with meaningless scrawls, of a type familiar to any parent. Paradine pursed his lips.

It might be a graph showing the mental variations of a manic-depressive cockroach, but probably wasn't. Still, it no doubt had meaning to Emma. Perhaps the scribble represented Mr. Bear.

Scott returned, looking pleased. He met Emma's gaze and nodded. Paradine felt a twinge of curiosity.

"Secrets?"

"Nope. Emma... uh... asked me to do something for her."

"Oh." Paradine, recalling instances of babies who had babbled in unknown tongues and baffled linguists, made a note to pocket the paper when the kids had finished with it. The next day he showed the scrawl to Elkins at the university. Elkins had a sound working knowledge of many unlikely languages, but he chuckled over Emma's venture into literature.

"Here's a free translation, Dennis. Quote. I don't know what this means, but I kid the hell out of my father with it. Unquote."

The two men laughed and went off to their classes. But later Paradine was to remember the incident. Especially after he met Holloway. Before that, however, months were to pass, and the situation to develop even further toward its climax.

Perhaps Paradine and Jane had evinced too much interest in the toys. Emma and Scott took to keeping them hidden, playing with them only in private. They never did it overtly, but with a certain unobtrusive caution. Nevertheless, Jane especially was somewhat troubled.

She spoke to Paradine about it one evening. "That doll Harry gave Emma."

"Yeah?"

"I was downtown today and tried to find out where it came from. No soap."

"Maybe Harry bought it in New York."

Jane was unconvinced. "I asked them about the other things, too. They showed me their stock—Johnson's a big store, you know. But there's nothing like Emma's abacus."

"Hm-m-m." Paradine wasn't much interested. They had tickets for a show that night, and it was getting late. So the subject was dropped for the nonce.

Later it cropped up again, when a neighbor telephoned Jane.

"Scotty's never been like that, Denny. Mrs. Burns said he frightened the devil out of her Francis."

"Francis? A little fat bully of a punk, isn't he? Like his father. I broke Burns' nose for him once, when we were sophomores."

"Stop boasting and listen," Jane said, mixing a highball. "Scott showed Francis something that scared him. Hadn't you better—"

"I suppose so." Paradine listened. Noises in the next room told him the whereabouts of his son. "Scotty!"

"Bang," Scotty said, and appeared smiling. "I killed 'em all. Space pirates. You want me, dad?"

"Yes. If you don't mind leaving the space pirates unburied for a few minutes. What did you do to Francis Burns?"

Scott's blue eyes reflected incredible candor. "Huh?"

"Try hard. You can remember, I'm sure."

"Oh. Oh, that. I didn't do nothing."

"Anything," Jane corrected absently.

"Anything. Honest. I just let him look into my television set, and it... it scared him."

"Television set?"

Scott produced the crystal cube. "It isn't really that. See?"

Paradine examined the gadget, startled by the magnification. All he could see, though, was a maze of meaningless colored designs.

"Uncle Harry—"

Paradine reached for the telephone. Scott gulped. "Is… is Uncle Harry back in town?"

"Yeah."

"Well, I gotta take a bath." Scott headed for the door. Paradine met Jane's gaze and nodded significantly.

Harry was home, but disclaimed all knowledge of the peculiar toys. Rather grimly, Paradine requested Scott to bring down from his room all of the playthings. Finally they lay in a row on the table: cube, abacus, doll, helmetlike cap, several other mysterious contraptions. Scott was cross-examined. He lied valiantly for a time, but broke down at last and bawled, hiccupping his confession.

"Get the box these things came in," Paradine ordered. "Then head for bed."

"Are you… *hup!*… gonna punish me daddy?"

"For playing hooky and lying, yes. You know the rules. No more shows for two weeks. No sodas for the same period."

Scott gulped. "You gonna keep my things?"

"I don't know yet."

"Well… g'night, daddy. G'night, mom."

After the small figure had gone upstairs, Paradine dragged a chair to the table and carefully scrutinized the box. He poked thoughtfully at the fused gadgetry. Jane watched.

"What is it, Denny?"

"Dunno. Who'd leave a box of toys down by the creek?"

"It might have fallen out of a car."

"Not at that point. The road doesn't hit the creek north of the railroad trestle. Empty lot—nothing else." Paradine lit a cigarette. "Drink, honey?"

"I'll fix it." Jane went to work, her eyes troubled. She brought Paradine a glass and stood behind him, ruffling his hair with her fingers. "Is anything wrong?"

"Of course not. Only—where did these toys come from?"

"Johnson's didn't know, and they get their stock from New York."

"I've been checking up, too," Paradine admitted. "That doll"—he poked it—"rather worried me. Custom jobs, maybe, but I wish I knew who'd made 'em."

"A psychologist? The abacus—don't they give people tests with such things?"

Paradine snapped his fingers. "Right! And say! There's a guy going to speak at the University next week, fellow named Holloway, who's a child psychologist. He's a big shot, with quite a reputation. He might know something about it."

"Holloway? I don't—"

"Rex Holloway. He's… hm-m-m! He doesn't live far from here. Do you suppose he might have had these things made himself?"

Jane was examining the abacus. She grimaced and drew back. "If he did, I don't like him. But see if you can find out, Denny."

Paradine nodded. "I shall."

He drank his highball, frowning. He was vaguely worried. But he wasn't scared—yet.

Rex Holloway was a fat, shiny man, with a bald head and thick spectacles, above which his thick, black brows lay like bushy caterpillars. Paradine brought him home to dinner one night a week later. Holloway did not appear to watch the children, but nothing they did or said was lost on him. His gray eyes, shrewd and bright, missed little.

The toys fascinated him. In the living room the three adults gathered around the table, where the playthings had been placed. Holloway studied them carefully as he listened to what Jane and Paradine had to say. At last he broke his silence.

"I'm glad I came here tonight. But not completely. This is very disturbing, you know."

"Eh?" Paradine stared, and Jane's face showed her consternation. Holloway's next words did not calm them.

"We are dealing with madness."

He smiled at the shocked looks they gave him. "All children are mad, from an adult viewpoint. Ever read Hughes' *High Wind in Jamaica?*"

"I've got it." Paradine secured the little book from its shelf. Holloway extended a hand, took it, and flipped the pages till he had found the place he wanted. He read aloud:

"Babies of course are not human—they are animals, and have a very ancient and ramified culture, as cats have, and fishes, and even snakes; the same in kind as these, but much more complicated and vivid, since babies are, after all, one of the most developed species of the lower vertebrates. In short, babies have minds which work in terms and categories of their own which cannot be translated into the terms and categories of the human mind."

Jane tried to take that calmly, but couldn't. "You don't mean that Emma—"

"Could you think like your daughter?" Holloway asked. "Listen: 'One can no more think like a baby than one can think like a bee.'"

Paradine mixed drinks. Over his shoulder he said, "You're theorizing quite a bit, aren't you? As I get it, you're implying that babies have a culture of their own, even a high standard of intelligence."

"Not necessarily. There's no yardstick, you see. All I say is that babies think in other ways than we do. Not necessarily *better*—that's a question of relative values. But with a different manner of extension—" He sought for words, grimacing.

"Fantasy," Paradine said, rather rudely, but annoyed because of Emma. "Babies don't have different senses from ours."

"Who said they did?" Holloway demanded. "They use their minds in a different way, that's all. But it's quite enough!"

"I'm trying to understand," Jane said slowly. "All I can think of is my Mixmaster. It can whip up batter and potatoes, but it can squeeze oranges, too."

"Something like that. The brain's a colloid, a very complicated machine. We don't know much about its potentialities. We don't even know how much it can grasp. But it is known that the mind becomes conditioned as the human animal matures. It follows certain familiar theorems, and all thought thereafter is pretty well based on patterns taken for granted. Look at this," Holloway touched the abacus. "Have you experimented with it?"

"A little," Paradine said.

"But not much. Eh?"

"Well—"

"Why not?"

"It's pointless," Paradine complained. "Even a puzzle has to have some logic. But those crazy angles—"

"Your mind has been conditioned to Euclid," Holloway said. "So this—thing—bores us, and seems pointless. But a child knows nothing of Euclid. A different sort of geometry from ours wouldn't impress him as being illogical. He believes what he sees."

"Are you trying to tell me that this gadget's got a fourth-dimensional extension?" Paradine demanded.

"Not visually, anyway," Holloway denied. "All I say is that our minds, conditioned to Euclid, can see nothing in this but an illogical tangle of wires. But a child—especially a baby—might see more. Not at first. It'd be a puzzle, of course. Only a child wouldn't be handicapped by too many preconceived ideas."

"Hardening of the thought-arteries," Jane interjected.

Paradine was not convinced. "Then a baby could work calculus better than Einstein? No, I don't mean that. I can see your point, more or less clearly. Only—"

"Well, look. Let's suppose there are two kinds of geometry—we'll limit it, for the sake of the example. Our kind, Euclidean, and another, which we'll call x. X hasn't much relationship to Euclid. It's based on different theorems. Two and two needn't equal four in it; they could equal y_8, or they might not even *equal*. A baby's mind is not yet conditioned, except by certain questionable factors of heredity and environment. Start the infant on Euclid—"

"Poor kid," Jane said.

Holloway shot her a quick glance. "The basis of Euclid. Alphabet blocks. Math, geometry, algebra—they come much later. We're familiar with that development. On the other hand, start the baby with the basic principles of our *x* logic."

"Blocks? What kind?"

Holloway looked at the abacus. "It wouldn't make much sense to us. But we've been conditioned to Euclid."

Paradine poured himself a stiff shot of whiskey. "That's pretty awful. You're not limiting to math."

"Right! I'm not limiting it at all. How can I? I'm not conditioned to *x* logic."

"There's the answer," Jane said, with a sigh of relief. "Who is? It'd take such a person to make the sort of toys you apparently think these are."

Holloway nodded, his eyes, behind the thick lenses, blinking. "Such people may exist."

"Where?"

"They might prefer to keep hidden."

"Supermen?"

"I wish I knew. You see, Paradine, we've got yardstick trouble again. By our standards these people might seem super-doopers in certain respects. In others they might seem moronic. It's not a quantitative difference; it's qualitative. They *think* differently. And I'm sure we can do things they can't."

"Maybe they wouldn't want to," Jane said.

Paradine tapped the fused gadgetry on the box "What about this? It implies—"

"A purpose, sure."

"Transportation*!*'"

"One thinks of that first. If so, the box might have come from anywhere."

"Where—things are—*different?*" Paradine asked slowly.

"Exactly. In space, or even time. I don't know; I'm a psychologist. Unfortunately I'm conditioned to Euclid, too."

"Funny place it must be," Jane said. "Denny, get rid of those toys."

"I intend to."

Holloway picked up the crystal cube. "Did you question the children much?"

Paradine said, "Yeah. Scott said there were people in that cube when he first looked. I asked him what was in it now."

"What did he say?" The psychologist's eyes widened.

"He said they were building a place. His exact words. I asked him who—people? But he couldn't explain."

"No, I suppose not," Holloway muttered. "It must be progressive. How long have the children had these toys?

"About three months, I guess."

"Time enough. The perfect toy, you see, is both instructive and mechanical. It should do things, to interest a child, and it should teach, preferably unobtrusively. Simple problems at first. Later—"

"X logic," Jane said, white-faced.

Paradine cursed under his breath. "Emma and Scott are perfectly normal!"

"Do you know how their minds work—now?"

Holloway didn't pursue the thought. He fingered the doll. "It would be interesting to know the conditions of the place where these things came from. Induction doesn't help a great deal, though. Too many factors are missing. We can't visualize a world based on the x factor—environment adjusted to minds thinking in x patterns. This luminous network inside the doll. It could be anything. It could exist inside us, though we haven't discovered it yet. When we find the right stain—" He shrugged. "What do you make of this?"

It was a crimson globe, two inches in diameter, with a protruding knob upon its surface.

"What could anyone make of it?"

"Scott? Emma?

"I hadn't even seen it till about three weeks ago. Then Emma started to play with it." Paradine nibbled his lip. "After that, Scott got interested.'"

"Just what do they do?"

"Hold it up in front of them and move it back and forth. No particular pattern of motion."

"No Euclidean pattern," Holloway corrected. "At first they couldn't understand the toy's purpose. They had to be educated up to it."

"That's horrible," Jane said.

"Not to them. Emma is probably quicker at understanding x than Scott, for her mind isn't yet conditioned to this environment."

Paradine said, "But I can remember plenty of things I did as a child. Even as a baby."

"Well?"

"Was I—mad—then?"

"The things you don't remember are the criterion of your madness," Holloway retorted. "But I use the word 'madness' purely as a convenient symbol for the variation from the known human norm. The arbitrary standard of sanity."

Jane put down her glass. "You've said that induction was difficult, Mr. Holloway. But it seems to me you're making a great deal of it from very little. After all, these toys—"

"I *am* a psychologist, and I've specialized in children. I'm not a layman. These toys mean a great deal to me, chiefly because they mean so little."

"You might be wrong."

"Well, I rather hope I am. I'd like to examine the children."

Jane rose in arms. "How?"

After Holloway had explained, she nodded, though still a bit hesitantly. "Well, that's all right. But they're not guinea pigs."

The psychologist patted the air with a plump hand. "My dear girl! I'm not a Frankenstein. To me the individual is the prime factor—naturally, since I work with minds. If there's anything wrong with the youngsters, I want to cure them."

Paradine put down his cigarette and slowly watched blue smoke spiral up, wavering in an unfelt draft. "Can you give a prognosis?"

"I'll try. That's all I can say. If the undeveloped minds have been turned into the *x* channel, it's necessary to divert them back. I'm not saying that's the wisest thing to do, but it probably is from our standards. After all, Emma and Scott will have to live in this world."

"Yeah. Yeah. I can't believe there's much wrong. They seem about average, thoroughly normal."

"Superficially they may seem so. They've no reason for acting abnormally, have they? And how can you tell if they—think differently?"

"I'll call 'em," Paradine said.

"Make it informal, then. I don't want them to be on guard."

Jane nodded toward the toys. Holloway said, "Leave the stuff there, eh?"

But the psychologist, after Emma and Scott were summoned, made no immediate move at direct questioning. He managed to draw Scott unobtrusively into the conversation, dropping key words now and then. Nothing so obvious as a word-association test—co-operation is necessary for that.

The most interesting development occurred when Holloway took up the abacus. "Mind showing me how this works?"

Scott hesitated. "Yes, sir. Like this—" He slid a bead deftly through the maze, in a tangled course, so swiftly that no one was quite sure whether or not it ultimately vanished. It might have been merely legerdemain. Then, again—

Holloway tried. Scott watched, wrinkling his nose.

"That right?"

"Uh-huh. It's gotta go *there*—"

"Here? Why?"

"Well, that's the only way to make it work."

But Holloway was conditioned to Euclid. There was no apparent reason why the bead should slide from this particular wire to the other. It looked like a random factor. Also, Holloway suddenly noticed, this wasn't the path the bead had taken previously, when Scott had worked the puzzle. At least as well as he could tell.

"Will you show me again?"

Scott did, and twice more, on request. Holloway blinked through his glasses. Random, yes. And variable. Scott moved the bead along a different course each time.

Somehow, none of the adults could tell whether or not the bead vanished. If they had expected to see it disappear, their reactions might have been different.

In the end nothing was solved. Holloway, as he said good night, seemed ill at ease.

"May I come again?"

"I wish you would," Jane told him. "Any time. You still think—"

He nodded. "The children's minds are not reacting normally. They're not dull at all, but I've the most extraordinary impression that they arrive at conclusions in a way we don't understand. As though they used algebra while we used geometry. The same conclusion, but a different method of reaching it."

"What about the toys?" Paradine asked suddenly.

"Keep them out of the way. I'd like to borrow them, if I may—"

That night Paradine slept badly. Holloway's parallel had been ill-chosen. It led to disturbing theories. The x factor—the children were using the equivalent of algebraic reasoning, while adults used geometry.

Fair enough. Only—

Algebra can give you answers that geometry cannot, since there are certain terms and symbols which cannot be expressed geometrically. Suppose x logic showed conclusions inconceivable to an adult mind?

"Damn!" Paradine whispered. Jane stirred beside him.

"Dear? Can't you sleep either?"

"No." He got up and went into the next room. Emma slept peacefully as a cherub, her fat arm curled around Mr. Bear. Through the open doorway Paradine could see Scott's dark head motionless on the pillow.

Jane was beside him. He slipped his arm around her.

"Poor little people," she murmured. "And Holloway called them mad. I think we're the ones who are crazy, Dennis."

"Uh-huh. We've got jitters."

Scott stirred in his sleep. Without awakening, he called what was obviously a question, though it did not seem to be in any particular language. Emma gave a little mewling cry that changed pitch sharply.

She had not awakened. The children lay without stirring.

But Paradine thought, with a sudden sickness in his middle, it was exactly as though Scott had asked Emma something, and she had replied.

Had their minds changed so that even—sleep—was different to them?

He thrust the thought away. "You'll catch cold. Let's get back to bed. Want a drink?"

"I think I do," Jane said, watching Emma. Her hand reached out blindly toward the child; she drew it back. "Come on. We'll wake the kids."

They drank a little brandy together, but said nothing. Jane cried in her sleep, later.

Scott was not awake, but his mind worked in slow, careful building. Thus—

"They'll take the toys away. The fat man... listava dangerous maybe. But the Ghoric direction won't show... evankrus dun-hasn't-them. Intransdection... bright and shiny. Emma. She's more khopranik-high now than... I still don't see how to... thavarar lixery dist—"

A little of Scott's thoughts could still be understood. But Emma had become conditioned to x much faster.

She was thinking, too.

Not like an adult or a child. Not even like a human. Except, perhaps, a human of a type shockingly unfamiliar to genus homo.

Sometimes Scott himself had difficulty in following her thoughts.

If it had not been for Holloway, life might have settled back into an almost normal routine. The toys were no longer active reminders. Emma still enjoyed her dolls and sand pile, with a thoroughly explicable delight. Scott was satisfied with baseball and his chemical set. They did everything other children did, and evinced few, if any, flashes of abnormality. But Holloway seemed to be an alarmist.

He was having the toys tested, with rather idiotic results. He drew endless charts and diagrams, corresponded with mathematicians, engineers, and other psychologists, and went quietly crazy trying to find rhyme or reason in the construction of the gadgets. The box itself, with its cryptic machinery, told nothing. Fusing had melted too much of the stuff into slag. But the toys—

It was the random element that baffled investigation. Even that was a matter of semantics. For Holloway was convinced that it wasn't really random. There just weren't enough known factors. No adult could work the abacus, for example. And Holloway thoughtfully refrained from letting a child play with the thing.

The crystal cube was similarly cryptic. It showed a mad pattern of colors, which sometimes moved. In this it resembled a kaleidoscope. But the shifting of balance and gravity didn't affect it. Again the random factor.

Or, rather, the unknown. The x pattern. Eventually Paradine and Jane slipped back into something like complacence, with a feeling that the children had been cured of their mental quirk, now that the contributing cause had been removed. Certain of the actions of Emma and Scott gave them every reason to quit worrying.

For the kids enjoyed swimming, hiking, movies, games, the normal functional toys of this particular time-sector. It was true that they failed to master certain rather puzzling mechanical devices which involved some calculation. A three-dimensional jigsaw globe Paradine had picked up, for example. But he found that difficult himself.

Once in a while there were lapses. Scott was hiking with his father one Saturday afternoon, and the two had paused at the summit of a hill. Beneath them a rather lovely valley was spread.

"Pretty, isn't it?" Paradine remarked.

Scott examined the scene gravely. "It's all wrong," he said.

"Eh?"

"I dunno."

"What's wrong about it?"

"Gee—" Scott lapsed into puzzled silence. "I dunno."

The children had missed their toys, but not for long. Emma recovered first, though Scott still moped. He held unintelligible conversations with his sister and studied meaningless scrawls she drew on paper he supplied. It was almost as though he was consulting her, anent difficult problems beyond his grasp.

If Emma understood more, Scott had more real intelligence, and manipulatory skill as well. He built a gadget with his Meccano set, but was dissatisfied. The apparent cause of his dissatisfaction was exactly why Paradine was relieved when he viewed the structure. It was the sort of thing a normal boy would make, vaguely reminiscent of a cubistic ship.

It was a bit too normal to please Scott. He asked Emma more questions, though in private. She thought for a time, and then made more scrawls with an awkwardly clutched pencil.

"Can you read that stuff?" Jane asked her son one morning.

"Not read it, exactly. I can tell what she means. Not all the time, but mostly."

"Is it writing?"

"N-no. It doesn't mean what it *looks* like."

"Symbolism," Paradine suggested over his coffee.

Jane looked at him, her eyes widening. "Denny—"

He winked and shook his head. Later, when they were alone, he said, "Don't let Holloway upset you. I'm not implying that the kids are corresponding in an unknown tongue. If Emma draws a squiggle and says it's a flower, that's an arbitrary rule—Scott remembers that. Next time she draws the same sort of squiggle, or tries to—well!"

"Sure," Jane said doubtfully. "Have you noticed Scott's been doing a lot of reading lately?"

"I noticed. Nothing unusual, though. No Kant or Spinoza."

"He browses, that's all."

"Well, so did I, at his age," Paradine said, and went off to his morning classes. He lunched with Holloway, which was becoming a daily habit, and spoke of Emma's literary endeavors.

"Was I right about symbolism, Rex?"

The psychologist nodded. "Quite right. Our own language is nothing but arbitrary symbolism now. At least in its application. Look here." On his napkin he drew a very narrow ellipse. "What's that?"

"You mean what does it represent?"

"Yes. What does it suggest to you? It could be a crude representation of—what?"

"Plenty of things," Paradine said. "Rim of a glass. A fried egg. A loaf of French bread. A cigar."

Holloway added a little triangle to his drawing, apex joined to one end of the ellipse. He looked up at Paradine.

"A fish," the latter said instantly.

"Our familiar symbol for a fish. Even without fins, eyes or mouth, it's recognizable, because we've been conditioned to identify this particular shape with our mental picture of a fish. The basis of a rebus. A symbol, to us, means a lot more than what we actually see on paper. What's in your mind when you look at this sketch?"

"Why—a fish."

"Keep going. What do you visualize—everything!"

"Scales," Paradine said slowly, looking into space. "Water. Foam. A fish's eye. The fins. The colors."

"So the symbol represents a lot more than just the abstract idea *fish*. Note the connotation's that of a noun, not a verb. It's harder to express actions by symbolism, you know. Anyway—reverse the process. Suppose you want to make a symbol for some concrete noun, say *bird*. Draw it."

Paradine drew two connected arcs, concavities down.

"The lowest common denominator," Holloway nodded. "The natural tendency is to simplify. Especially when a child is seeing something for the first time and has few standards of comparison. He tries to identify the new thing with what's already familiar to him. Ever notice how a child draws the ocean?" He didn't wait for an answer; he went on.

"A series of jagged points. Like the oscillating line on a seismograph. When

I first saw the Pacific, I was about three. I remember it pretty clearly. It looked—tilted. A flat plain, slanted at an angle. The waves were regular triangles, apex upward. Now I don't *see* them stylized that way, but later, remembering, I had to find some familiar standard of comparison. Which is the only way of getting any conception of an entirely new thing. The average child tries to draw these regular triangles, but his coordination's poor. He gets a seismograph pattern."

"All of which means what?"

"A child sees the ocean. He stylizes it. He draws a certain definite pattern, symbolic, to him, of the sea. Emma's scrawls may be symbols, too. I don't mean that the world looks different to her—brighter, perhaps, and sharper, more vivid and with a slackening of perception above her eye level. What I do mean is that her thought-processes are different, that she translates what she sees into abnormal symbols."

"You still believe—"

"Yes, I do. Her mind has been conditioned unusually. It may be that she breaks down what she sees into simple, obvious patterns—and realizes a significance to those patterns that we can't understand. Like the abacus. She saw a pattern in that, though to us it was completely random."

Paradine abruptly decided to taper off these luncheon engagements with Holloway. The man was an alarmist. His theories were growing more fantastic than ever, and he dragged in anything, applicable or not, that would support them.

Rather sardonically he said, "Do you mean Emma's communicating with Scott in an unknown language?"

"In symbols for which she hasn't any words. I'm sure Scott understands a great deal of those—scrawls. To him, an isosceles triangle may represent any factor, though probably a concrete noun. Would a man who knew nothing of algebra understand what H_2O meant? Would he realize that the symbol could evoke a picture of the ocean?"

Paradine didn't answer. Instead, he mentioned to Holloway Scott's curious remark that the landscape, from the hill, had looked all wrong. A moment later, he was inclined to regret his impulse, for the psychologist was off again.

"Scott's thought-patterns are building up to a sum that doesn't equal this world. Perhaps he's subconsciously expecting to see the world where those toys came from."

Paradine stopped listening. Enough was enough. The kids were getting along all right, and the only remaining disturbing factor was Holloway himself. That night, however, Scott evinced an interest, later significant, in eels.

There was nothing apparently harmful in natural history. Paradine explained about eels.

"But where do they lay their eggs? Or do they?"

"That's still a mystery. Their spawning grounds are unknown. Maybe the Sargasso Sea, or the deeps, where the pressure can help them force the young out of their bodies."

"Funny," Scott said, thinking deeply.

"Salmon do the same thing, more or less. They go up rivers to spawn." Paradine went into detail. Scott was fascinated.

"But that's *right*, dad. They're born in the river, and when they learn how to swim, they go down to the sea. And they come back to lay their eggs, huh?"

"Right."

"Only they wouldn't *come* back," Scott pondered. "They'd just send their eggs—"

"It'd take a very long ovipositor," Paradine said, and vouchsafed some well-chosen remarks upon oviparity.

His son wasn't entirely satisfied. Flowers, he contended, sent their seeds long distances.

"They don't guide them. Not many find fertile soil."

"Flowers haven't got brains, though. Dad, why do people live *here?*"

"Glendale?"

"No—*here*. This whole place. It isn't all there is, I bet."

"Do you mean the other planets?"

Scott was hesitant. "This is only—part of the big place. It's like the river where the salmon go. Why don't people go on down to the ocean when they grow up?"

Paradine realized that Scott was speaking figuratively. He felt a brief chill. The—ocean?

The young of the species are not conditioned to live in the completer world of their parents. Having developed sufficiently, they enter that world. Later they breed. The fertilized eggs are buried in the sand, far up the river, where later they hatch.

And they learn. Instinct alone is fatally slow. Especially in the case of a specialized genus, unable to cope even with this world, unable to feed or drink or survive, unless someone has foresightedly provided for those needs.

The young, fed and tended, would survive. There would be incubators and robots. They would survive, but they would not know how to swim downstream, to the vaster world of the ocean.

So they must be taught. They must be trained and conditioned in many ways.

Painlessly, subtly, unobtrusively. Children love toys that do things—and if those toys at the same time—

In the latter half of the nineteenth century an Englishman sat on a grassy bank near a stream. A very small girl lay near him, staring up at the sky. She had discarded a curious toy with which she had been playing, and now was murmuring a wordless little song, to which the man listened with half an ear.

"What was that, my dear?" he asked at last.

"Just something I made up, Uncle Charles."

"Sing it again." He pulled out a notebook.

The girl obeyed.

"Does it mean anything?"

She nodded. "Oh, yes. Like the stories I tell you, you know."

"They're wonderful stories, dear."

"And you'll put them in a book some day?"

"Yes, but I must change them quite a lot, or no one would understand. But I don't think I'll change your little song."

"You mustn't. If you did, it wouldn't mean anything."

"I won't change that stanza, anyway," he promised. "Just what does it mean?"

"It's the way out, I think," the girl said doubtfully. "I'm not sure yet. My magic toys told me."

"I wish I knew what London shop sold those marvelous toys!"

"Mamma bought them for me. She's dead. Papa doesn't care."

She lied. She had found the toys in a box one day, as she played by the Thames. And they were indeed wonderful.

Her little song—Uncle Charles thought it didn't mean anything. (He wasn't her real uncle, she parenthesized. But he was nice.) The song meant a great deal. It was the way. Presently she would do what it said, and then—

But she was already too old. She never found the way.

Paradine had dropped Holloway. Jane had taken a dislike to him, naturally enough, since what she wanted most of all was to have her fears calmed. Since Scott and Emma acted normally now, Jane felt satisfied. It was partly wishful thinking, to which Paradine could not entirely subscribe.

Scott kept bringing gadgets to Emma for her approval. Usually she'd shake her head. Sometimes she would look doubtful. Very occasionally she would signify agreement. Then there would be an hour of laborious, crazy scribbling on scraps of note paper, and Scott, after studying the notations, would arrange and rearrange his rocks, bits of machinery, candle ends, and assorted junk. Each day the maid cleaned them away, and each day Scott began again.

He condescended to explain a little to his puzzled father, who could see no rhyme or reason in the game.

"But why this pebble right here?"

"It's hard and round, dad. It *belongs* there."

"So is this one hard and round."

"Well, that's got Vaseline on it. When you get that far, you can't *see* just a hard round thing."

"What comes next? This candle?"

Scott looked disgusted. "That's toward the end. The iron ring's next."

It was, Paradine thought, like a Scout trail through the woods, markers in a labyrinth. But here again was the random factor. Logic halted—familiar logic— at Scott's motives in arranging the junk as he did.

Paradine went out. Over his shoulder he saw Scott pull a crumpled piece of paper and a pencil from his pocket, and head for Emma, who was squatted in a corner thinking things over.

Well—

Jane was lunching with Uncle Harry, and on this hot Sunday afternoon there was little to do but read the papers. Paradine settled himself in the coolest place he could find, with a Collins, and lost himself in the comic strips.

An hour later a clatter of feet upstairs roused him from his doze. Scott's voice was crying exultantly, "This is it, Slug! Come on—"

Paradine stood up quickly, frowning. As he went into the hall the telephone began to ring. Jane had promised to call—

His hand was on the receiver when Emma's faint voice squealed with excitement. Paradine grimaced. What the devil was going on upstairs?

Scott shrieked, "Look out! This way!"

Paradine, his mouth working, his nerves ridiculously tense, forgot the phone and raced up the stairs. The door of Scott's room was open.

The children were vanishing.

They went in fragments, like thick smoke in a wind, or like movement in a distorting mirror. Hand in hand they went, in a direction Paradine could not understand, and as he blinked there on the threshold, they were gone.

"Emma!" he said, dry-throated. "*Scotty!*"

On the carpet lay a pattern of markers, pebbles, an iron ring—junk. A random pattern. A crumpled sheet of paper blew toward Paradine.

He picked it up automatically.

"Kids. Where are you? Don't hide—

"*Emma! SCOTTY!*"

Downstairs the telephone stopped its shrill, monotonous ringing. Paradine looked at the paper he held.

It was a leaf torn from a book. There were interlineations and marginal notes, in Emma's meaningless scrawl. A stanza of verse had been so underlined and scribbled over that it was almost illegible, but Paradine was thoroughly familiar with *Through the Looking Glass*. His memory gave him the words—

'Twas brillig, and the slithy toyes
  Did gyre and gimbel in the wabe.
All mimsy were the borogoves,
  And the mome raths outgrabe.

Idiotically he thought: Humpty Dumpty explained it. A wabe is the plot of grass around a sundial. A sundial. Time—It has something to do with time. A long time ago Scotty asked me what a wabe was. Symbolism.

'Twas brillig—

A perfect mathematical formula, giving all the conditions, in symbolism the children had finally understood. The junk on the floor. The "toyes" had to be made slithy—Vaseline?—and they had to be placed in a certain relationship, so that they'd gyre and gimbel.

Lunacy!

But it had not been lunacy to Emma and Scott. They thought differently. They used *x* logic. Those notes Emma had made on the page—she'd translated Carroll's words into symbols both she and Scott could understand.

The random factor had made sense to the children. They had fulfilled the conditions of the time-space equation. *And the mome raths outgrabe—*

Paradine made a rather ghastly little sound, deep in his throat. He looked at the crazy pattern on the carpet. If he could follow it, as the kids had done— But he couldn't. The pattern was senseless. The random factor defeated him. He was conditioned to Euclid.

Even if he went insane, he still couldn't do it. It would be the wrong kind of lunacy.

His mind had stopped working now. But in a moment the stasis of incredulous horror would pass— Paradine crumpled the page in his fingers. "Emma, Scotty," he called in a dead voice, as though he could expect no response.

Sunlight slanted through the open windows, brightening the golden pelt of Mr. Bear. Downstairs the ringing of the telephone began again.

THE BRADBURY
CHRONICLES

Through Ray Bradbury the outside world discovered what it thought the genre was like. Bradbury's stories appeared in general magazines. Bradbury's stories were anthologized in textbooks and reprinted in grade-school and high-school magazines. To this day many readers who have sampled only Bradbury's stories believe that science fiction is composed of stained-glass windows, attics full of turn-of-the-century relics, rockets that go off like firecrackers, silver locusts, and ruined Martian cities.

Science fiction always has maintained an uneasy grasp upon its authors. For most of its history—conditions have changed recently—it has paid more niggardly than other genres, and authors have drifted into other fields: the mystery, films and television, comic books, and other professional writing activities. Only the love of what they read and often liked to write kept them, and often they came back, if only as visitors.

Bradbury (1920-) is a good example. He struggled hard to become a science fiction writer, turning out dozens of unsuccessful stories until he finally began to sell horror stories to *Weird Tales* and science fiction to *Super Science Stories* and *Planet Stories*. Finally, in 1945 and 1946, he began to hit his own style of nostalgia and sentiment; combined with his evocative word magic, they sold to the slick magazines: *The American Mercury*, *Collier's*, *Mademoiselle*, *Charm*, and later *The New Yorker*, *Harper's*, *Esquire*, *McCall's*, *Seventeen*, *MacLean's*, and *The Saturday Evening Post*. Some of his stories were selected for Martha Foley's *Best Short Stories of the Year* anthologies.

About the same time, Bradbury's "The Million-Year Picnic" was published in the summer 1946 issue of *Planet Stories*. It was the first of his series of stories about Mars that were brought together in 1950 as *The Martian Chronicles*. This was followed the next year by another collection, *The Illustrated Man*. An earlier collection of horror stories had been published in 1947 by Arkham House under the title *Dark Carnival*.

Christopher Isherwood "discovered" Bradbury in the science fiction ghetto and announced his genius to the world. Bradbury soon departed for better things. He wrote screenplays: *It Came from Outer Space*, *The Beast from 20,000 Fathoms*, and John Huston's *Moby Dick*. His novel *Fahrenheit 451* was adapted into a 1967 film by François Truffaut; *The Illustrated Man* became a film in 1969. Bradbury also has turned to the stage and to poetry. His "The World of Ray Bradbury" and "The Wonderful Ice Cream Suit" played successfully in Los Angeles and the latter played briefly off-Broadway, and he has written other plays, including a version of *Moby Dick* as a great white comet. *The Martian Chronicles* became a disappointing TV miniseries in 1980, and *Something Wicked This Way Comes* became a somewhat more satisfying film in 1983. In the 1980s Bradbury returned to the writing of crime fiction, in this case mystery novels, and became the host of his own cable television show, "The Ray Bradbury Theatre," featuring adaptations of his series.

Bradbury is a representative of that phenomenon common in science fiction, the short-story writer; he also represents a rarer species, which includes Harlan Ellison, the short-story writer who has found success without ever writing a real novel. *Fahrenheit 451* (1953) was an expanded short novel; *Dandelion Wine* (1957) a collection of stories with a common character; and *Something Wicked This Way Comes* (1962) an expanded short story. Bradbury has built his reputation on short stories and short-story collections, sometimes held together by devices such as a common subject (Mars) or a common source (visions of the future tattooed on a circus freak).

Though often singled out as "the only good science fiction writer," Bradbury probably is appreciated more because his work is mostly fantasy. Even those stories that have a science fiction element reveal more about the inside of Bradbury's head than about reality. Brian Aldiss, who called him "one of our most eminent dreamers," said he "was the first to take all the props of SF and employ them as highly individual tools of expression for his somewhat Teddy-bearish view of the universe." Robert Scholes and Eric Rabkin say Bradbury "has borrowed the externals of science fiction to disguise and make more convincing his magical preoccupations."

Aldiss calls Bradbury's world "prepubertal," and it does seem that his characters act out of a childlike purity of motive, either good or evil. But if his adult characters behave like children—throwing beer bottles in the Martian canals and shooting the windows out of dead Martian cities—his children behave like adults in intricately Machiavellian ways, like the children that trap their parents in "The Veldt," the child that betrays her parents in "Zero Hour," and even the infant that kills its parents in "The Small Assassin." His stories exhibit an anti-technological bias, but Bradbury personally retains many of the science-fiction enthusiasms of his adolescence; he exulted, for instance, in the first manned landings on the moon.

Bradbury's Mars clearly was impossible even when he began to write about it in 1946. Scholes and Rabkin say that by this he intended it to be taken as fabulous. More than constructing fables, however, Bradbury deals with experience at two removes: in much of his fiction the reader gets not an attempt to recreate reality, nor even an image of reality, but the experience of symbols. Bradbury has many heroes—Lincoln, Whitman, Shaw, Poe, Hemingway, and Wolfe among them—and he has written tribute stories for them, evoking their presences like ancestral ghosts; the reader gets none of their experience but only their images as speakers of words and writers of books. In *Fahrenheit 451*, it is not the burning of books that disturbs Bradbury but the burning of "Books"—

the abstraction of books. The recitation of titles being thrown on the fire is like a litany, and even the recitation of their contents is a ritual act.

Reality is not what a fantasy writer is about, but rather the symbols that haunt men's dreams and the words that in themselves have magic. Bradbury has been a writer drunk on words, and with those magic words he has created dreams for readers that seemed better than reality.

THE MILLION-YEAR PICNIC

BY RAY BRADBURY

Somehow the idea was brought up by Mom that perhaps the whole family would enjoy a fishing trip. But they weren't Mom's words; Timothy knew that. They were Dad's words, and Mom used them for him somehow.

Dad shuffled his feet in a clutter of Martian pebbles and agreed. So immediately there was a tumult and a shouting, and very quickly the camp was tucked into capsules and containers, Mom slipped into traveling jumpers and blouse, Dad stuffed his pipe full with trembling hands, his eyes on the Martian sky, and the three boys piled yelling into the motor-boat, none of them really keeping an eye on Mom and Dad, except Timothy.

Dad pushed a stud. The water boat sent a humming sound up into the sky. The water shook back and the boat nosed ahead, and the family cried, "Hurrah!"

Timothy sat in the back of the boat with Dad, his small fingers atop Dad's hairy ones, watching the canal twist, leaving the crumbled place behind where they had landed in their small family rocket all the way from Earth. He remembered the night before they left Earth, the hustling and hurrying, the rocket that Dad had found somewhere, somehow, and the talk of a vacation on Mars. A long way to go for a vacation, but Timothy said nothing because of his younger brothers. They came to Mars and now, first thing, or so they said, they were going fishing.

Dad had a funny look in his eyes as the boat went up-canal. A look that Timothy couldn't figure. It was made of strong light and maybe a sort of relief. It made the deep wrinkles laugh instead of worry or cry.

So there went the cooling rocket, around a bend, gone.

"How far are we going?" Robert splashed his hand. It looked like a small crab jumping in the violet water.

Dad exhaled. "A million years."

"Gee," said Robert.

"Look, kids." Mother pointed one soft long arm. "There's a dead city."

They looked with fervent anticipation, and the dead city lay dead for them alone, drowsing in a hot silence of summer made on Mars by a Martian weatherman.

And Dad looked as if he was pleased that it was dead.

It was a futile spread of pink rocks sleeping on a rise of sand, a few tumbled pillars, one lonely shrine, and then the sweep of sand again. Nothing else for miles. A white desert around the canal and a blue desert over it.

Just then a bird flew up. Like a stone thrown across a blue pond, hitting, falling deep, and vanishing.

Dad got a frightened look when he saw it. "I thought it was a rocket."

Timothy looked at the deep ocean sky, trying to see Earth and the war and the ruined cities and the men killing each other since the day he was born. But he saw nothing. The war was as removed and far off as two flies battling to the death in the arch of a great high and silent cathedral. And just as senseless.

William Thomas wiped his forehead and felt the touch of his son's hand on his arm, like a young tarantula, thrilled. He beamed at his son. "How goes it, Timmy?"

"Fine, Dad."

Timothy hadn't quite figured out what was ticking inside the vast adult mechanism beside him. The man with the immense hawk nose, sunburnt, peeling—and the hot blue eyes like agate marbles you play with after school in summer back on Earth, and the long thick columnar legs in the loose riding breeches.

"What are you looking at so hard, Dad?"

"I was looking for Earthian logic, common sense, good government, peace, and responsibility."

"All that up there?"

"No. I didn't find it. It's not there anymore. Maybe it'll never be there again. Maybe we fooled ourselves that it was ever there."

"Huh?"

"See the fish," said Dad, pointing.

There rose a soprano clamor from all three boys as they rocked the boat in arching their tender necks to see. They oohed and ahed. A silver ring fish floated by them, undulating, and closing like an iris, instantly, around food particles, to assimilate them.

Dad looked at it. His voice was deep and quiet.

"Just like war. War swims along, sees food, contracts. A moment later— Earth is gone."

"William," said Mom.

"Sorry," said Dad.

They sat still and felt the canal water rush cool, swift, and glassy. The only sound was the motor hum, the glide of water, the sun expanding the air.

"When do we see the Martians?" cried Michael.

"Quite soon, perhaps," said Father. "Maybe tonight."

"Oh, but the Martians are a dead race now," said Mom.

"No, they're not. I'll show you some Martians, all right," Dad said presently.

Timothy scowled at that but said nothing. Everything was odd now. Vacations and fishing and looks between people.

The other boys were already engaged making shelves of their small hands and peering under them toward the seven-foot stone banks of the canal, watching for Martians.

"What do they look like?" demanded Michael.

"You'll know them when you see them." Dad sort of laughed, and Timothy saw a pulse beating time in his cheek.

Mother was slender and soft, with a woven plait of spun-gold hair over her head in a tiara, and eyes the color of the deep cool canal water where it ran in shadow, almost purple, with flecks of amber caught in it. You could see her thoughts swimming around in her eyes, like fish—some bright, some dark, some fast, quick, some slow and easy, and sometimes, like when she looked up where Earth was, being nothing but color and nothing else. She sat in the boat's prow, one hand resting on the side lip, the other on the lap of her dark blue breeches, and a line of sunburnt soft neck showing where her blouse opened like a white flower.

She kept looking ahead to see what was there, and, not being able to see it clearly enough, she looked backward toward her husband, and through his eyes, reflected then, she saw what was ahead; and since he added part of himself to this reflection, a determined firmness, her face relaxed and she accepted it and she turned back, knowing suddenly what to look for.

Timothy looked too. But all he saw was a straight pencil line of canal going violet through a wide shallow valley penned by low, eroded hills, and on until it fell over the sky's edge. And this canal went on and on, through cities that would have rattled like beetles in a dry skull if you shook them. A hundred or two hundred cities dreaming hot summer-day dreams and cool summer-night dreams...

They had come millions of miles for this outing—to fish. But there had been a gun on the rocket. This was a vacation. But why all the food, more than enough to last them years and years, left hidden back there near the rocket? Vacation. Just behind the veil of the vacation was not a soft face of laughter, but something hard and bony and perhaps terrifying. Timothy could not lift the veil, and the two other boys were busy being ten and eight years old, respectively.

"No Martians yet. Nuts." Robert put his V-shaped chin on his hands and glared at the canal.

Dad had brought an atomic radio along, strapped to his wrist. It functioned on an old-fashioned principle: you held it against the bones near your ear and it vibrated singing or talking to you. Dad listened to it now. His face looked like one of those fallen Martian cities, caved in, sucked dry, almost dead.

Then he gave it to Mom to listen. Her lips dropped open.

"What—" Timothy started to question, but never finished what he wished to say.

For at that moment there were two titanic, marrow-jolting explosions that grew upon themselves, followed by a half dozen minor concussions.

Jerking his head up, Dad notched the boat speed higher immediately. The boat leaped and jounced and spanked. This shook Robert out of his funk and elicited yelps of frightened but ecstatic joy from Michael, who clung to Mom's legs and watched the water pour by his nose in a wet torrent.

Dad swerved the boat, cut speed, and ducked the craft into a little branch canal and under an ancient, crumbling stone wharf that smelled of crab flesh. The boat rammed the wharf hard enough to throw them all forward, but no one was hurt, and Dad was already twisted to see if the ripples on the canal were enough to map their route into hiding. Water lines went across, lapped the stones, and rippled back to meet each other, settling, to be dappled by the sun. It all went away.

Dad listened. So did everybody.

Dad's breathing echoed like fists beating against the cold wet wharf stones. In the shadow, Mom's cat eyes just watched Father for some clue to what next.

Dad relaxed and blew out a breath, laughing at himself.

"The rocket, of course. I'm getting jumpy. The rocket."

Michael said, "What happened, Dad, what happened?"

"Oh, we just blew up our rocket, is all," said Timothy, trying to sound matter-of-fact. "I've heard rockets blown up before. Ours just blew."

"Why did we blow up our rocket?" asked Michael. "Huh, Dad?"

"It's part of the game, silly!" said Timothy.

"A game!" Michael and Robert loved the word.

"Dad fixed it so it would blow up and no one'd know where we landed or went! In case they ever came looking, see?"

"Oh boy, a secret!"

"Scared by my own rocket," admitted Dad to Mom. "I am nervous. It's silly to think there'll ever be any more rockets. Except one, perhaps, if Edwards and his wife get through with their ship."

He put his tiny radio to his ear again. After two minutes he dropped his hand as you would drop a rag.

"It's over at last," he said to Mom. "The radio just went off the atomic beam. Every other world station's gone. They dwindled down to a couple in the last few years. Now the air's completely silent. It'll probably remain silent."

"For how long?" asked Robert.

"Maybe your great-grandchildren will hear it again," said Dad. He just sat there, and the children were caught in the center of his awe and defeat and resignation and acceptance.

Finally he put the boat out into the canal again, and they continued in the direction in which they had originally started.

It was getting late. Already the sun was down the sky, and a series of dead cities lay ahead of them.

Dad talked very quietly and gently to his sons. Many times in the past he had been brisk, distant, removed from them, but now he patted them on the head with just a word and they felt it.

"Mike, pick a city."

"What, Dad?"

"Pick a city, Son. Any one of these cities we pass."

"All right," said Michael. "How do I pick?"

"Pick the one you like the most. You, too, Robert and Tim. Pick the city you like best."

"I want a city with Martians in it," said Michael.

"You'll have that," said Dad. "I promise." His lips were for the children, but his eyes were for Mom.

They passed six cities in twenty minutes. Dad didn't say anything more about the explosions; he seemed much more interested in having fun with his sons, keeping them happy, than anything else.

Michael liked the first city they passed, but this was vetoed because everyone doubted quick first judgments. The second city nobody liked. It was an Earth Man's settlement, built of wood and already rotting into sawdust. Timothy liked the third city because it was large. The fourth and fifth were too small and the sixth brought acclaim from everyone, including Mother, who joined in the Gees, Goshes, and Look-at-thats!

There were fifty or sixty huge structures still standing, streets were dusty but paved, and you could see one or two old centrifugal fountains still pulsing wetly in the plazas. That was the only life—water leaping in the late sunlight.

"This is the city," said everybody.

Steering the boat to a wharf, Dad jumped out.

"Here we are. This is ours. This is where we live from now on!"

"From now on?" Michael was incredulous. He stood up, looking, and then turned to blink back at where the rocket used to be. "What about the rocket? What about Minnesota?"

"Here," said Dad.

He touched the small radio to Michael's blond head. "Listen."

Michael listened.

"Nothing," he said.

"That's right. Nothing. Nothing at all anymore. No more Minneapolis, no more rockets, no more Earth."

Michael considered the lethal revelation and began to sob little dry sobs.

"Wait a moment," said Dad the next instant. "I'm giving you a lot more in exchange, Mike!"

"What?" Michael held off the tears, curious, but quite ready to continue in case Dad's further revelation was as disconcerting as the original.

"I'm giving you this city, Mike. It's yours."

"Mine?"

"For you and Robert and Timothy, all three of you, to own for yourselves."

Timothy bounded from the boat. "Look, guys, all for *us*! All of *that!*" He was playing the game with Dad, playing it large and playing it well. Later, after it was all over and things had settled, he could go off by himself and cry for ten minutes. But now it was still a game, still a family outing, and the other kids must be kept playing.

Mike jumped out with Robert. They helped Mom.

"Be careful of your sister," said Dad, and nobody knew what he meant until later.

They hurried into the great pink-stoned city, whispering among themselves, because dead cities have a way of making you want to whisper, to watch the sun go down.

"In about five days," said Dad quietly, "I'll go back down to where our rocket was and collect the food hidden in the ruins there and bring it here: and I'll hunt for Bert Edwards and his wife and daughters there."

"Daughters?" asked Timothy. "How many?"

"Four."

"I can see that'll cause trouble later." Mom nodded slowly.

"Girls." Michael made a face like an ancient Martian stone image. "Girls."

"Are they coming in a rocket too?"

"Yes. If they make it. Family rockets are made for travel to the Moon, not Mars. We were lucky we got through."

"Where did you get the rocket?" whispered Timothy, for the other boys were running ahead.

"I saved it. I saved it for twenty years, Tim. I had it hidden away, hoping I'd never have to use it. I suppose I should have given it to the government for the war, but I kept thinking about Mars...."

"And a picnic!"

"Right. This is between you and me. When I saw everything was finishing on Earth, after I'd waited until the last moment, I packed us up. Bert Edwards had a ship hidden, too, but we decided it would be safer to take off separately, in case anyone tried to shoot us down."

"Why'd you blow up the rocket, Dad?"

"So we can't go back, ever. And so if any of those evil men ever come to Mars they won't know we're here."

"Is that why you look up all the time?"

"Yes, it's silly. They won't follow us, ever. They haven't anything to follow with. I'm being too careful, is all."

Michael came running back. "Is this really *our* city, Dad?"

"The whole darn planet belongs to us, kids. The whole darn planet."

They stood there, King of the Hill, Top of the Heap, Ruler of All They Surveyed, Unimpeachable Monarchs and Presidents, trying to understand what it meant to own a world and how big a world really was.

Night came quickly in the thin atmosphere, and Dad left them in the square by the pulsing fountain, went down to the boat, and came walking back carrying a stack of paper in his big hands.

He laid the papers in a clutter in an old courtyard and set them afire. To keep warm, they crouched around the blaze and laughed, and Timothy saw the little letters leap like frightened animals when the flames touched and engulfed them. The papers crinkled like an old man's skin, and the cremation surrounded innumerable words:

"GOVERNMENT BONDS; Business Graph, 1999; Religious Prejudice: An Essay; The Science of Logistics; Problems of the Pan-American Unity; Stock Report for July 3, 1998; The War Digest…"

Dad had insisted on bringing these papers for this purpose. He sat there and fed them into the fire, one by one, with satisfaction, and told his children what it all meant.

"It's time I told you a few things. I don't suppose it was fair, keeping so much from you. I don't know if you'll understand, but I have to talk, even if only part of it gets over to you."

He dropped a leaf in the fire.

"I'm burning a way of life, just like that way of life is being burned clean of Earth right now. Forgive me if I talk like a politician. I am, after all, a former state governor, and I was honest and they hated me for it. Life on Earth never settled down to doing anything very good. Science ran too far ahead of us too quickly, and the people got lost in a mechanical wilderness, like children making over pretty things, gadgets, helicopters, rockets; emphasizing the wrong items, emphasizing machines instead of how to run the machines. Wars got bigger and bigger and finally killed Earth. That's what the silent radio means. That's what we ran away from.

"We were lucky. There aren't any more rockets left. It's time you knew this isn't a fishing trip at all. I put off telling you. Earth is gone. Interplanetary travel won't be back for centuries, maybe never. But that way of life proved itself wrong and strangled itself with its own hands. You're young. I'll tell you this again every day until it sinks in."

He paused to feed more papers to the fire.

"Now we're alone. We and a handful of others who'll land in a few days. Enough to start over. Enough to turn away from all that back on Earth and strike out on a new line—"

The fire leaped up to emphasize his talking. And then all the papers were gone except one. All the laws and beliefs of Earth were burnt into small hot ashes which soon would be carried off in a wind.

Timothy looked at the last thing that Dad tossed in the fire. It was a map of the World, and it wrinkled and distorted itself hotly and went—flimpf—and was gone like a warm, black butterfly. Timothy turned away.

"Now I'm going to show you the Martians," said Dad. "Come on, all of you. Here, Alice." He took her hand.

Michael was crying loudly, and Dad picked him up and carried him, and they walked down through the ruins toward the canal.

The canal. Where tomorrow or the next day their future wives would come up in a boat, small laughing girls now, with their father and mother.

The night came down around them, and there were stars. But Timothy couldn't find Earth. It had already set. That was something to think about.

A night bird called among the ruins as they walked. Dad said, "Your mother and I will try to teach you. Perhaps we'll fail. I hope not. We've had a good lot to see and learn from. We planned this trip years ago, before you were born. Even if there hadn't been a war we would have come to Mars, I think, to live and form our own standard of living. It would have been another century before Mars would have been really poisoned by the Earth civilization. Now, of course—"

They reached the canal. It was long and straight and cool and wet and reflective in the night.

"I've always wanted to see a Martian," said Michael. "Where are they, Dad? You promised."

"There they are," said Dad, and he shifted Michael on his shoulder and pointed straight down.

The Martians were there. Timothy began to shiver.

The Martians were there—in the canal—reflected in the water. Timothy and Michael and Robert and Mom and Dad.

The Martians stared back up at them for a long, long silent time from the rippling water....

MORE THAN SF

The devastating and terrible explosion of atomic bombs over Hiroshima and Nagasaki ended World War II; it also demonstrated that science fiction was concerned with reality, not romantic fantasy, and initiated a process that eventually eliminated the atomic bomb from science fiction's repertoire of ideas.

Ever since 1926, critics of science fiction had sneered at the genre because it played with such ridiculous notions as atomic bombs and rocket ships. In fact, when atomic bombs and rocket ships were mentioned, they were dismissed as "mere science fiction." Hiroshima and later the United States space program proved that they were more than science fiction. Beginning in 1949, publishers, jumping on what seemed like a bandwagon, tooted science fiction's tune. The eventual ban against atomic bomb stories endured; the magazine boom went bust in the mid-to-late 1950s.

The big bomb became unwelcome in science fiction magazines at the same time it entered reality. Ever since H. G. Wells, writers had speculated about it. Heinlein dealt with the political problems of an atomic weapon in 1940 ("Solution Unsatisfactory"), and early in 1944 in an *Astounding* story entitled "Deadline," Cleve Cartmill accurately described how an atomic bomb would be constructed. After 1945, writers could no longer describe the construction of such a bomb as science fiction, so for a brief span they speculated about the possibilities of an all-out atomic war. The most effective of these was Theodore Sturgeon's "Thunder and Roses," published in *Astounding* in November 1947. Within a few years the mainstream had saturated the market with atomic doom stories, and science fiction magazines dropped it as no longer sufficiently novel.

Sturgeon (1918-1985) may have been the writer best equipped to deal with the problem of a sneak atomic attack upon the United States. After three years at sea as an engine-room wiper, Sturgeon began writing for Campbell's *Unknown* and then *Astounding*. He had stories in both magazines in 1939. His early *Unknown* work, such as "He Shuttles," "It," "Shottle Bop," and "The Ultimate Egoist," earned him a reputation as a fantasy writer, but his science fiction came into ascendance with stories such as "Microcosmic God," "The Chromium Helmet," "Killdozer!," and "Mewhu's Jet."

With the stories he wrote in the early 1950s for *Galaxy*—"Baby Is Three," "Saucer of Loneliness," "Mr. Costello, Hero," "Granny Won't Knit," and "To Marry Medusa"—and in *The Magazine of Fantasy and Science Fiction* and its companion magazine *Venture*—"The Silken Swift," "The [Wadget], the [Widget], and Boff," "Affair with a Green Monkey," "The Girl Had Guts," "A Touch of Strange," and "The Man Who Lost the Sea"—he came upon his subject, love, and his technique, carefully patterned prose that could rise to poetry and descend to violence.

Like Bradbury, Sturgeon was a short-story writer by instinct and inclination. Ten years passed before he tackled a novel (*The Dreaming Jewels*, 1950), and his most famous book, *More Than Human* (1953), which won the International Fantasy Award that year, was made up of two short novels built around a third, "Baby Is Three." The problems of the short-story writer are serious: short stories don't pay much unless they are sold to the slick magazines (even after the war, the top rate in the science fiction magazines was two cents a word until *Galaxy* kicked it to three to four cents in 1950). Novelists have an easier time earning a reputation, winning a following, and getting books published.

Sturgeon managed, although he was tempted into other jobs and the writing of other kinds of books, such as *I, Libertine* (under the pseudonym of Frederick R. Ewing) and a novelization of *Voyage to the Bottom of the Sea*. His stories were much anthologized, however, and collected into volumes such as *Without Sorcery* (1948), *E Pluribus Unicorn* (1953), *A Way Home* and *Caviar* (both 1955), *A Touch of Strange* (1958), and others. He also wrote *The Cosmic Rape* (1958), *Venus Plus X* (1960), and *Some of Your Blood* (1961).

In the 1960s to the 1980s he worked in Hollywood, writing two of the favorite episodes of the original *Star Trek*, "Amok Time" and "Shore Leave," but he returned to SF often enough to win a 1971 Hugo and Nebula for "Slow Sculpture," and to publish a collection of stories entitled *Sturgeon is Alive and Well* (1971). A novella, *Godbody* (1986), was published the year after his death.

In science fiction, as in other forms of literature, the genre characteristics are important largely for purposes of publication and categorization (for retailer and reader). The truly important values are the unique qualities a writer brings to his fiction, his own concerns that make it more than "just" science fiction.

Sturgeon's most important contribution to science fiction has been his concern for style. Second has been his insistence on love as the only salvation for humanity, a theme upon which his stories have played many variations. In 1953, for a fan magazine called *Skyhook*, he wrote an article (reprinted in Damon Knight's *Turning Points*) entitled "Why So Much Syzygy?" "Syzygy" means a "coming together," "conjunction," and Sturgeon wrote that "what I have been trying to do all these years is to investigate this matter of love, sexual and asexual. I investigate it by writing about it because... I don't know what the hell I think until I tell somebody about it."

In *More Than Human* a gestalt of outcasts unites separate talents into one creature with wondrous abilities. But before the gestalt can function the individual human parts must learn to trust one another, to love one another. Throughout Sturgeon's fiction he seems to be saying that the inability to love keeps us from being truly human.

Or perhaps: if we could only allow ourselves to love we could be more than human.

THUNDER AND ROSES

BY THEODORE STURGEON

When Pete Mawser learned about the show, he turned away from the GHQ bulletin board, touched his long chin, and determined to shave, in spite of the fact that the show would be video, and he would see it in his barracks. He had an hour and a half. It felt good to have a purpose again—even the small matter of shaving before eight o'clock. Eight o'clock Tuesday, just the way it used to be. Everyone used to say, Wednesday morning, "How about the way Starr sang *The Breeze and I* last night?"

That was a while ago, before the attack, before all those people were dead, before the country was dead. Starr Anthim—an institution, like Crosby, like Duse, like Jenny Lind, like the Statue of Liberty. (Liberty had been one of the first to get it, her bronze beauty volatilized, radioactivated, and even now being carried about in vagrant winds, spreading over the earth...)

Pete Mawser grunted and forced his thoughts away from the drifting, poisonous fragments of a blasted liberty. Hate was first. Hate was ubiquitous, like the increasing blue glow in the air at night, like the tension that hung over the base.

Gunfire crackled sporadically far to the right, swept nearer. Pete stepped out to the street and made for a parked truck. There was a Wac sitting on the short running-board.

At the corner a stocky figure backed into the intersection. The man carried a tommy-gun in his arms, and he was swinging it to and fro with the gentle, wavering motion of a weather-vane. He staggered toward them, his gun-muzzle hunting. Someone fired from a building and the man swiveled and blasted wildly at the sound.

"He's—blind," said Pete Mawser, and added, "he ought to be," looking at the tattered face.

A siren keened. An armored jeep slewed into the street. The full-throated roar of a brace of .50-caliber machine-guns put a swift and shocking end to the incident.

"Poor crazy kid," Pete said softly. "That's the fourth I've seen today." He looked down at the Wac. She was smiling. "Hey!"

"Hello, Sarge." She must have identified him before, because now she did not raise her eyes nor her voice. "What happened?"

"You know what happened. Some kid got tired of having nothing to fight and nowhere to run to. What's the matter with you?"

"No," she said. "I don't mean that." At last she looked up at him. "I mean all of this. I can't seem to remember."

"You—well, it's not easy to forget. We got hit. We got hit everywhere at once. All the big cities are gone. We got it from both sides. We got too much. The air is becoming radioactive. We'll all—" He checked himself. She didn't know. She'd forgotten. There was nowhere to escape to, and she'd escaped inside herself, right here. Why tell her about it? Why tell her that everyone was going to die? Why tell her that other, shameful thing: that we hadn't struck back?

But she wasn't listening. She was still looking at him. Her eyes were not quite straight. One held his, but the other was slightly shifted and seemed to be looking at his temple. She was smiling again. When his voice trailed off she didn't prompt him. Slowly, he moved away. She did not turn her head, but kept looking up at where he had been, smiling a little. He turned away, wanting to run, walking fast.

How long could a guy hold out? When you were in the army they tried to make you be like everybody else. What did you do when everybody else was cracking up?

He blanked out the mental picture of himself as the last one left sane. He'd followed that one through before. It always led to the conclusion that it would be better to be one of the first. He wasn't ready for that yet. Then he blanked that out, too. Every time he said to himself that he wasn't ready for that yet, something within him asked "Why not?" and he never seemed to have an answer ready.

How long could a guy hold out?

He climbed the steps of the QM Central and went inside. There was nobody at the reception switchboard. It didn't matter. Messages were carried by jeep, or on motorcycles. The Base Command was not insisting that anybody stick to a sitting job these days. Ten desk-men could crack up for every one on a jeep, or on the soul-sweat squads. Pete made up his mind to put in a little stretch on a squad tomorrow. Do him good. He just hoped that this time the adjutant wouldn't burst into tears in the middle of the parade ground. You could keep your mind on the manual of arms just fine until something like that happened.

He bumped into Sonny Weisefreund in the barracks corridor. The Tech's round young face was as cheerful as ever. He was naked and glowing, and had a towel thrown over his shoulder.

"Hi, Sonny. Is there plenty of hot water?"

"Why not?" grinned Sonny. Pete grinned back, wondering if anybody could say anything about anything at all without one of these reminders. Of course, there was hot water. The QM barracks had hot water for three hundred men. There were three dozen left. Men dead, men gone to the hills, men locked up so they wouldn't—

"Starr Anthim's doing a show tonight."

"Yeah. Tuesday night. Not funny, Pete. Don't you know there's a war—"

"No kidding," Pete said swiftly. "She's here—right here on the base."

Sonny's face was joyful. "Gee." He pulled the towel off his shoulder and tied it around his waist. "Starr Anthim here! Where are they going to put on the show?"

"HQ, I imagine. Video only. You know about public gatherings."

"Yeah. And a good thing, too," said Sonny. "Somebody'd be sure to crack up. I wouldn't want her to see anything like that. How'd she happen to come here, Pete?"

"Drifted in on the last gasp of a busted-up Navy helicopter."

"Yeah, but why?"

"Search me. Get your head out of that gift-horse's mouth."

He went into the washroom, smiling and glad that he still could. He undressed and put his neatly folded clothes down on a bench. There were a soap-wrapper and an empty toothpaste tube lying near the wall. He picked them up and put them in the catchall, took the mop that leaned against the partition and mopped the floor where Sonny had splashed after shaving. Someone had to keep things straight. He might have worried if it were anyone else but Sonny. But Sonny wasn't cracking up. Sonny always had been like that. Look there. Left his razor out again.

Pete started his shower, meticulously adjusting the valves until the pressure and temperature exactly suited him. He did nothing carelessly these days. There was so much to feel, and taste, and see now. The impact of water on his skin, the smell of soap, the consciousness of light and heat, the very pressure of standing on the soles of his feet... he wondered vaguely how the slow increase of radioactivity in the air, as the nitrogen transmuted to Carbon Fourteen, would affect him if he kept carefully healthy in every way. What happens first? Blindness? Headaches? Perhaps a loss of appetite or slow fatigue?

Why not look it up?

On the other hand, why bother? Only a very small percentage of the men would die of radioactive poisoning. There were too many other things that killed more quickly, which was probably just as well. That razor, for example. It lay gleaming in a sunbeam, curved and clean in the yellow light. Sonny's father and grandfather had used it, or so he said, and it was his pride and joy.

Pete turned his back on it, and soaped under his arms, concentrating on the tiny kisses of bursting bubbles. In the midst of a recurrence of disgust at himself for thinking so often of death, a staggering truth struck him. He did not think of such things because he was morbid, after all! It was the very familiarity of things that brought death-thoughts. It was either "I shall never do this again" or "This is one of the last times I shall do this." You might devote yourself completely to doing things in different ways, he thought madly. You might crawl across the floor this time, and next time walk across on your hands. You might skip dinner tonight, and have a snack at two in the morning instead, and eat grass for breakfast.

But you had to breathe. Your heart had to beat. You'd sweat and you'd shiver, the same as always. You couldn't get away from that. When those things happened, they would remind you. Your heart wouldn't beat out its *wunklunk, wunklunk* anymore. It would go *one-less, one-less*, until it yelled and yammered in your ears and you had to make it stop.

Terrific polish on that razor.

And your breath would go on, same as before. You could sidle through this door, back through the next one and the one after, and figure out a totally new way to go through the one after that, but your breath would keep on sliding in and out of your nostrils like a razor going through whiskers, making a sound like a razor being stropped.

Sonny came in. Pete soaped his hair. Sonny picked up the razor and stood looking at it. Pete watched him, soap ran into his eyes, he swore, and Sonny jumped.

"What are you looking at, Sonny? Didn't you ever see it before?"

"Oh, sure. Sure. I just was—" He shut the razor, opened it, flashed light from its blade, shut it again. "I'm tired of using this, Pete. I'm going to get rid of it. Want it?"

Want it? In his foot-locker, maybe. Under his pillow. "Thanks, no, Sonny. Couldn't use it."

"I like safety razors," Sunny mumbled. "Electrics, even better. What are we going to do with it?"

"Throw it in the—no." Pete pictured the razor turning end over end in the air, half open, gleaming in the maw of the catchall. "Throw it out the—" No. Curving out into the long grass. He might want it. He might crawl around in the moonlight looking for it. He might find it.

"I guess maybe I'll break it up."

"No," Pete said. "The pieces—" Sharp little pieces. Hollow-ground fragments. "I'll think of something. Wait'll I get dressed."

He washed briskly, toweled, while Sonny stood looking at the razor. It was a blade now, and if it were broken it would be shards and glittering splinters, still razor sharp. If it were ground dull with an emery wheel, somebody could find it and put another edge on it because it was so obviously a razor, a fine steel razor, one that would slice so—

"I know. The laboratory. We'll get rid of it," Pete said confidently.

He stepped into his clothes, and together they went to the laboratory wing. It was very quiet there. Their voices echoed.

"One of the ovens," said Pete, reaching for the razor.

"Bake-ovens? You're crazy!"

Pete chuckled. "You don't know this place, do you? Like everything else on the base, there was a lot more went on here than most people knew about. They kept calling it the bakeshop. Well, it *was* research headquarters for new high-nutrient flours. But there's lots else here. We tested utensils and designed vegetable-peelers and all sorts of things like that. There's an electric furnace in there that—" He pushed open a door.

They crossed a long, quiet, cluttered room to the thermal equipment. "We can do everything here from annealing glass, through glazing ceramics, to finding the melting point of frying pans." He clicked a switch tentatively. A pilot light glowed. He swung open a small, heavy door and set the razor inside. "Kiss it good-bye. In twenty minutes it'll be a puddle."

"I want to see that," said Sonny. "Can I look around until it's cooked?"

"Why not?"

They walked through the laboratories. Beautifully equipped they were, and too quiet. Once they passed a major who was bent over a complex electronic hook-up on one of the benches. He was watching a little amber light flicker, and he did not return their salute. They tiptoed past him, feeling awed at his absorption, envying it. They saw the models of the automatic kneaders, the vitaminizers, the remote signal thermostats and timers and controls.

"What's in there?"

"I dunno. I'm over the edge of my territory. I don't think there's anybody left for this section. They were mostly mechanical and electronic theoreticians. Hey!"

Sonny followed the pointing hand. "What?"

"That wall-section. It's loose, or   well, what do you know!"

He pushed at the section of wall which was very slightly out of line. There was a dark space beyond.

"What's in there?"

"Nothing, or some semi-private hush-hush job. These guys used to get away with murder."

Sonny said, with an uncharacteristic flash of irony, "Isn't that the Army theoretician's business?"

Cautiously they peered in, then entered.

"Wh-*hey!* The door!"

It swung swiftly and quietly shut. The soft click of the latch was accompanied by a blaze of light.

The room was small and windowless. It contained machinery—a "trickle" charger, a bank of storage batteries, an electric-powered dynamo, two small self-starting gas-driven light plants and a diesel complete with sealed compressed-air starting cylinders. In the corner was a relay rack with its panel-bolts spot-welded. Protruding from it was a red-topped lever.

They looked at the equipment wordlessly for a time and then Sonny said, "Somebody wanted to make awful sure he had power for something."

"Now, I wonder what—" Pete walked over to the relay rack. He looked at the lever without touching it. It was wired up; behind the handle, on the wire, was a folded tag. He opened it cautiously. "To be used only on specific orders of the Commanding Officer."

"Give it a yank and see what happens."

Something clicked behind them. They whirled. "What was that?"

"Seemed to come from that rig beside the door."

They approached it cautiously. There was a spring-loaded solenoid attached to a bar which was hinged to drop across the inside of the secret door, where it would fit into steel dudgeons on the panel. It clicked again.

"A Geiger counter," said Pete disgustedly.

"Now why," mused Sonny, "would they design a door to stay locked unless the general radioactivity went beyond a certain point? That's what it is. See the relays? And the overload switch there? And this?"

"It has a manual lock, too," Pete pointed out. The counter clicked again. "Let's get out of here. I got one of those things built into my head these days."

The door opened easily. They went out, closing it behind them. The keyhole was cleverly concealed in the crack between two boards.

They were silent as they made their way back to the QM labs. The small thrill of violation was gone.

Back at the furnace, Pete glanced at the temperature dial, then kicked the latch control. The pilot winked out, and then the door swung open. They blinked and started back from the raging heat within. They bent and peered. The razor was gone. A pool of brilliance lay on the floor of the compartment.

"Ain't much left. Most of it oxidized away," Pete grunted.

They stood together for a time with their faces lit by the small shimmering ruin. Later, as they walked back to the barracks, Sunny broke his long silence with a sigh. "I'm glad we did that, Pete. I'm awful glad we did that."

At a quarter to eight they were waiting before the combination console in the barracks. All hands except Pete and Sonny and a wiry-haired, thick-set corporal named Bonze had elected to see the show on the big screen in the mess-hall. The reception was better there, of course, but, as Bonze put it, "You don't get close enough in a big place like that."

"I hope she's the same," said Sonny, half to himself.

Why should she be? thought Pete morosely as he turned on the set and watched the screen begin to glow. There were many more of the golden speckles that had killed reception for the past two weeks… Why should anything be the same, ever again?

He fought a sudden temptation to kick the set to pieces. It, and Starr Anthim, were part of something that was dead. The country was dead, a once real country—prosperous, sprawling, laughing, grabbing, growing, and changing, mostly healthy, leprous in spots with poverty and injustice, but systemically healthy enough to overcome any ill. He wondered how the murderers would like it. They were welcome to it, now. Nowhere to go. No one to fight. That was true for every soul on earth now.

"You hope she's the same," he muttered.

"The show, I mean," said Sonny mildly. "I'd like to just sit here and have it like—like—"

Oh, thought Pete mistily. Oh—that. Somewhere to go, that's what it is, for a few minutes… "I know," he said, all the harshness gone from his voice.

Noise receded from the audio as the carrier swept in. The light on the screen swirled and steadied into a diamond pattern. Pete adjusted the focus, chromic balance and intensity. "Turn out the lights, Bonze. I don't want to see anything but Starr Anthim."

It *was* the same, at first. Starr Anthim had never used the usual fanfares, fade-ins, color and clamor of her contemporaries. A black screen, then *click!* a blaze of gold. It was all there, in focus; tremendously intense, it did not change. Rather, the eye changed to take it in. She never moved for seconds after she came on; she was there, a portrait, a still face and a white throat. Her eyes were open and sleeping. Her face was alive and still.

Then, in the eyes which seemed green but were blue flecked with gold, an awareness seemed to gather, and they came awake. Only then was it noticeable that her lips were parted. Something in the eyes made the lips be seen, though nothing moved yet. Not until she bent her head slowly, so that some of the gold flecks seemed captured in the golden brows. The eyes were not, then, looking out at an audience. They were looking at me, and at *me*, and at ME.

"Hello—you," she said. She was a dream, with a kid sister's slightly irregular teeth.

Bonze shuddered: The cot on which he lay began to squeak rapidly. Sonny shifted in annoyance: Pete reached out in the dark and caught the leg of the cot. The squeaking subsided.

"May I sing a song?" Starr asked. There was music, very faint. "It's an old one, and one of the best. It's an easy song, a deep song, one that comes from the part of men and women that is mankind—the part that has in it no greed, no hate, no fear. This song is about joyousness and strength. It's—my favorite. Is it yours?"

The music swelled. Pete recognized the first two notes of the introduction and swore quietly. This was wrong. This song was not for—this song was part of—

Sonny sat raptly. Bonze lay still.

Starr Anthim began to sing. Her voice was deep and powerful, but soft, with the merest touch of vibrato at the ends of the phrases. The song flowed from her, without noticeable effort, seeming to come from her face, her long hair, her wide set eyes. Her voice, like her face, was shadowed and clean, round, blue and green but mostly gold.

When you gave me your heart, you gave me the world,
You gave me the night and the day,
And thunder, and roses, and sweet green grass,
The sea, and soft wet clay.

I drank the dawn from a golden cup,
From a silver one, the dark,
The steed I rode was the wild west wind,
My song was the brook and the lark.

The music spiraled, caroled, slid into a somber cry of muted hungry sixth and ninths; rose, blared, and cut, leaving her voice full and alone:

With thunder I smote the evil of earth,
With roses I won the right,
With the sea I washed, and with clay I built,
And the world was a place of light!

The last note left a face perfectly composed again, and there was no movement in it; it was sleeping and vital while the music curved off and away to the places where music rests when it is not heard.

Starr smiled.

"It's so easy," she said. "So simple. All that is fresh and clean and strong about mankind is in that song, and I think that's all that need concern us about mankind." She leaned forward. "Don't you see?"

The smile faded and was replaced with a gentle wonder. A tiny furrow appeared between her brows; she drew back quickly. "I can't seem to talk to you tonight," she said, her voice small. "You hate something."

Hate was shaped like a monstrous mushroom. Hate was the random speckling of a video plate.

"What has happened to us," said Starr abruptly, impersonally, "is simple too. It doesn't matter who did it—do you understand that? *It* doesn't matter. We were attacked. We were struck from the east and from the west. Most of the bombs were atomic—there were blast-bombs and there were dust-bombs. We were hit by about five hundred and thirty bombs altogether, and it has killed us."

She waited.

Sonny's fist smacked into his palm. Bonze lay with his eyes open, open, quiet. Pete's jaws hurt.

"We have more bombs than both of them put together. We *have* them. We are not going to use them. *Wait!*" She raised her hands suddenly, as if she could see into each man's face. They sank back, tense.

"So saturated is the atmosphere with Carbon Fourteen that all of us in this hemisphere are going to die. Don't be afraid to say it. Don't be afraid to think it. It is a truth, and it must be faced. As the transmutation effect spreads from the ruins of our cities, the air will become increasingly radioactive, and then we must die. In months, in a year or so, the effect will be strong overseas. Most of the people there will die too. None will escape completely. A worse thing will come to them than anything they have given us, because there will be a wave of horror and madness which is impossible to us. We are merely going to die. They will live and burn and sicken, and the children that will be born to them—" She shook her head, and her lower lip grew full. She visibly pulled herself together.

"Five hundred and thirty bombs... I don't think either of our attackers knew just how strong the other was. There has been so much secrecy." Her voice was sad. She shrugged slightly. "They have killed us, and they have ruined themselves. As for us—we are not blameless, either. Neither are we helpless to do anything—yet. But what we must do is hard. We must die—without striking back."

She gazed briefly at each man in turn, from the screen. "We must *not* strike back. Mankind is about to go through a hell of his own making. We can be vengeful—or merciful, if you like—and let go with the hundreds of bombs we have. That would sterilize the planet so that not a microbe, not a blade of grass could escape, and nothing new could grow. We would reduce the earth to a bald thing, dead and deadly.

"No—it just won't do. We can't do it.

"Remember the song? *That* is humanity. That's in all humans. A disease made other humans our enemies for a time, but as the generations march past, enemies become friends and friends enemies. The enmity of those who have killed us is such a tiny, temporary thing in the long sweep of history!"

Her voice deepened. "Let us die with the knowledge that we have done the one noble thing left to us. The spark of humanity can still live and grow on this planet. It will be blown up and drenched, shaken and all but extinguished, but it will live if that song is a true one. It will live if we are human enough to discount the fact that the spark is in the custody of our temporary enemy. Some—a few—of his children will live to merge with the new humanity that will gradually emerge from the jungles and the wilderness. Perhaps there will be ten thousand years of beastliness, perhaps man will be able to rebuild while he still has his ruins."

She raised her head, her voice tolling. "And even if this is the end of humankind, we dare not take away the chances some other life-form might have to succeed where we failed. If we retaliate, there will not be a dog, a deer, an ape, a bird or fish or lizard to carry the evolutionary torch. In the name of justice, if we must condemn and destroy ourselves, let us not condemn all other life along with us! Mankind is heavy enough with sins. If we must destroy, let us stop with destroying ourselves!"

There was a shimmering flicker of music. It seemed to stir her hair like a breath of wind. She smiled.

"That's all," she whispered. And to each man listening she said, "Good night... "

The screen went black. As the carrier cut off (there was no announcement) the ubiquitous speckles began to swarm across it.

Pete rose and switched on the lights. Bonze and Sonny were quite still. It must have been minutes later when Sonny sat up straight, shaking himself like a puppy. Something besides the silence seemed to tear with the movement.

He said, softly, "You're not allowed to fight anything, or to run away, or to live, and now you can't even hate anymore, because Starr says no."

There was bitterness in the sound of it, and a bitter smell to the air.

Pete Mawser sniffed once, which had nothing to do with the smell. He sniffed again. "What's that smell, Son?"

Sonny tested it. "I don't—Something familiar. Vanilla—no... No."

"Almonds. Bitter—Bonze!"

Bonze lay still with his eyes open, grinning. His jaw muscles were knotted, and they could see almost all his teeth. He was soaking wet.

"Bonze!"

"It was just when she came on and said 'Hello—you,' remember?" whispered Pete. "Oh, the poor kid. That's why he wanted to catch the show here instead of in the mess hall."

"Went out looking at her," said Sonny through pale lips. "I—can't say I blame him much. Wonder where he got the stuff."

"Never mind that!" Pete's voice was harsh. "Let's get out of here."

They left to call the ambulance. Bonze lay watching the console with his dead eyes and his smell of bitter almonds.

Pete did not realize where he was going, or exactly why, until he found himself on the dark street near GHQ and the communications shack, reflecting that it might be nice to be able to hear Starr, and see her, whenever he felt like it. Maybe there weren't any recordings; yet her musical background was recorded, and the signal corps might have recorded the show.

He stood uncertainly outside the GHQ building. There was a cluster of men outside the main entrance. Pete smiled briefly. Rain, nor snow, nor sleet, nor gloom of night could stay the stage-door Johnnie.

He went down the side street and up the delivery ramp in the back. Two doors along the platform was the rear exit of the Communications section.

There was a light on in the communications shack. He had his hand out to the screen door when he noticed someone standing in the shadows beside it. The light played daintily on the golden margins of a head and face.

He stopped. "Starr Anthim!"

"Hello, soldier. Sergeant."

He blushed like an adolescent. "I—" His voice left him. He swallowed, reached up to whip off his hat. He had no hat. "I saw the show," he said. He felt clumsy. It was dark, and yet he was very conscious of the fact that his dress-shoes were indifferently shined.

She moved toward him into the light, and she was so beautiful that he had to close his eyes. "What's your name?"

"Mawser. Pete Mawser."

"Like the show?"

Not looking at her, he said stubbornly, "No."

"Oh?"

"I mean—I liked it some. The song."

"I—think I see."

"I wondered if I could maybe get a recording."

"I think so," she said. "What kind of reproducer have you got?"

"Audiovid."

"A disc. Yes; we dubbed off a few. Wait, I'll get you one."

She went inside, moving slowly. Pete watched her, spellbound. She was a silhouette, crowned and haloed; and then she was a framed picture, vivid and golden. He waited, watching the light hungrily. She returned with a large envelope, called good night to someone inside, and came out on the platform.

"Here you are, Pete Mawser."

"Thanks very—" he mumbled. He wet his lips. "It was very good of you."

"Not really. The more it circulates, the better." She laughed suddenly. "That isn't meant quite as it sounds. I'm not exactly looking for new publicity these days."

The stubbornness came back. "I don't know that you'd get it, if you put on that show in normal times."

Her eyebrows went up. "Well!" she smiled. "I seem to have made quite an impression."

"I'm sorry," he said warmly. "I shouldn't have taken that tack. Everything I think and say these days is exaggerated."

"I know what you mean." She looked around. "How is it here?"

"It's okay. I used to be bothered by the secrecy, and being buried miles away from civilization." He chuckled bitterly. "Turned out to be lucky after all."

"You sound like the first chapter of *One World or None.*"

He looked up quickly. "What do you use for a reading list—the Government's own *Index Expurgatorius?*"

She laughed. "Come now, it isn't as bad as all that. The book was never banned. It was just—"

"Unfashionable," he filled in.

"Yes, more's the pity. If people had paid more attention to it in the forties, perhaps this wouldn't have happened."

He followed her gaze to the dimly pulsating sky. "How long are you going to be here?"

"Until—as long as—I'm not leaving."

"You're not?"

"I'm finished," she said simply. "I've covered all the ground I can. I've been everywhere that... anyone knows about."

"With this show?"

She nodded. "With this particular message."

He was quiet, thinking. She turned to the door, and he put out his hand, not touching her. "Please—"

"I'd like to—I mean, if you don't mind, I don't often have a chance to talk to—maybe you'd like to walk around a little before you turn in."

"Thanks, no, Sergeant I'm tired." She did sound tired. "I'll see you around."

He stared at her, a sudden fierce light in his brain. "I know where it is. It's got a red-topped lever and a tag referring to orders of the commanding officer. It's really camouflaged."

She was quiet so long that he thought she had not heard him. Then, "I'll take that walk."

They went down the ramp together and turned toward the dark parade ground.

"How did you know?" she asked quietly.

"Not too tough. This 'message' of yours; the fact that you've been all over the country with it; most of all, the fact that somebody finds it necessary to persuade us not to strike back. Who are you working for?" he asked bluntly.

Surprisingly, she laughed.

"What's that for?"

"A moment ago you were blushing and shuffling your feet."

His voice was rough. "I wasn't talking to a human being. I was talking to a thousand songs I've heard, and a hundred thousand blonde pictures I've seen pinned up. You'd better tell me what this is all about."

She stopped. "Let's go up and see the colonel."

He took her elbow. "No. I'm just a sergeant, and he's high brass, and that doesn't make any difference at all now. You're a human being, and so am I, and I'm supposed to respect your rights as such. I don't. You'd better tell me about it."

"All right," she said, with a tired acquiescence that frightened something inside him. "You seem to have guessed right, though. It's true. There are master firing keys for the launching sites. We have located and dismantled all but two. It's very likely that one of the two was vaporized. The other one is—lost."

"Lost?"

"I don't have to tell you about the secrecy," she said. "You know how it developed between nation and nation. You must know that it existed between State and Union, between department and department, office and office. There were only three or four men who knew where all the keys were. Three of them were in the Pentagon when it went up. That was the third blast-bomb, you know. If there was another, it could only have been Senator Vanercook, and he died three weeks ago without talking."

"An automatic radio key, *hm?*"

"That's right. Sergeant, must we walk? I'm so tired."

"I'm sorry," he said impulsively. They crossed to the reviewing stand and sat on the lonely benches. "Launching racks all over, all hidden, and all armed?"

"Most of them are armed. There's a timing mechanism in them that will disarm them in a year or so. But in the meantime, they are armed—and aimed."

"Aimed where?"

"It doesn't matter."

"I think I see. What's the optimum number again?"

"About six hundred and forty; a few more or less. At least five hundred and thirty have been thrown so far. We don't know exactly."

"Who are *we?*" he asked furiously.

"Who? Who?" She laughed weakly. "I could say, 'The Government,' perhaps. If the President dies, the Vice President takes over, and then the Secretary of State, and so on and on. How far can you go? Pete Mawser, don't you realize yet what's happened?"

"I don't know what you mean."

"How many people do you think are left in this country?"

"I don't know. Just a few million, I guess."

"How many are here?"

"About nine hundred."

"Then, as far as I know, this is the largest city left."

He leaped to his feet. *"No!"* The syllable roared away from him, hurled itself against the dark, empty buildings, came back to him in a series of lower-case echoes: nononono… no-no.

Starr began to speak rapidly, quietly. "They're scattered all over the fields and the roads. They sit in the sun and die. They run in packs, they tear at each other. They pray and starve and kill themselves and die in the fires. The fire—everywhere, if anything stands, it's burning. Summer, and the leaves all down in the Berkshires, and the blue grass burnt brown; you can see the grass dying from the air, the death going out wider and wider from the bald-spots. Thunder and roses…. I saw roses, new ones, creeping from the smashed pots of a greenhouse. Brown petals, alive and sick, and the thorns turned back on themselves, growing into the stems, killing. Feldman died tonight."

He let her be quiet for a time. Then:

"Who is Feldman?"

"My pilot." She was talking hollowly into her hands. "He's been dying for weeks. He's been on his nerve-ends. I don't think he had any blood left. He buzzed your GHQ and made for the landing strip. He came in with the motor dead, free rotors, giro. Smashed the landing gear. He was dead, too. He killed a man in Chicago so he could steal gas. The man didn't want the gas. There was a dead girl by the pump. He didn't want us to go near. I'm not going anywhere.

I'm going to stay here. I'm tired."

At last she cried.

Pete left her alone, and walked out to the center of the parade ground, looking back at the faint huddled glimmer on the bleachers. His mind flickered over the show that evening, and the way she had sung before the merciless transmitter. "Hello, you." "If we must destroy, let us stop with destroying ourselves!"

The dimming spark of humankind… what could it mean to her? How could it mean so much?

"*Thunder and roses*." Twisted, sick, non-survival roses, killing themselves with their own thorns.

"*And the world was a place of light!*" Blue light, flickering in the contaminated air.

The enemy. The red-topped lever. Bonze. "They pray and starve and kill themselves and die in the fires."

What creatures were these, these corrupted, violent, murdering humans? What right had they to another chance? What was in them that was good?

Starr was good. Starr was crying. Only a human being could cry like that. Starr was a human being.

Had humanity anything of Starr Anthim in it?

Starr was a human being.

He looked down through the darkness for his hands. No planet, no universe, is greater to a man than his own ego, his own observing self. These hands were the hands of all history, and like the hands of all men, they could by their small acts make human history or end it. Whether this power of hands was that of a billion hands, or whether it came to a focus in these two—this was suddenly unimportant to the eternities which now enfolded him.

He put humanity's hands deep in his pockets and walked slowly back to the bleachers.

"Starr."

She responded with a sleepy-child, interrogative whimper.

"They'll get their chance, Starr. I won't touch the key."

She sat straight. She rose, and came to him, smiling. He could see her smile, because, very faintly in this air, her teeth fluoresced. She put her hands on his shoulders. "Pete."

He held her very close for a moment. Her knees buckled then, and he had to carry her.

There was no one in the Officers' Club, which was the nearest building. He stumbled in, moved clawing along the wall until he found a switch. The light hurt him. He carried her to a settee and put her down gently She did not move. One side of her face was as pale as milk.

He stood looking stupidly at it, wiped it on the sides of his trousers, looking dully at Starr. There was blood on her shirt.

A doctor… but there was no doctor. Not since Anders had hanged himself. "Get somebody," he muttered. "*Do* something."

He dropped to his knees and gently unbuttoned her shirt. Between the sturdy, unfeminine GI bra and the top of her slacks, there was blood on her side. He whipped out a clean handkerchief and began to wipe it away. There was no wound, no puncture. But abruptly there was blood again. He blotted it carefully. And again there was blood.

It was like trying to dry a piece of ice with a towel.

He ran to the water cooler, wrung out the bloody handkerchief and ran back to her. He bathed her face carefully, the pale right side, the flushed left side. The handkerchief reddened again, this time with cosmetics, and then her face was pale all over, with great blue shadows under the eyes. While he watched, blood appeared on her left cheek.

"There must be somebody—" He fled to the door.

"Pete!"

Running, turning at the sound of her voice, he hit the doorpost stunningly, caromed off, flailed for his balance, and then was back at her side. "Starr! Hang on, now! I'll get a doctor as quick as—"

Her hand strayed over her left cheek. "You found out. Nobody else knew, but Feldman. It got hard to cover properly." Her hand went up to her hair.

"Starr, I'll get a—"

"Pete, darling, promise me something?"

"Why, sure; certainly, Starr."

"Don't disturb my hair. It isn't—all mine, you see." She sounded like a seven-year-old, playing a game. "It all came out on this side. I don't want you to see me that way."

He was on his knees beside her again. "What is it? What happened to you?" he asked hoarsely.

"Philadelphia," she murmured. "Right at the beginning. The mushroom went up a half-mile away. The studio caved in. I came to the next day. I didn't know I was burned, then. It didn't show. My left side. It doesn't matter, Pete. It doesn't hurt at all, now."

He sprang to his feet again. "I'm going for a doctor."

"Don't go away. Please don't go away and leave me. Please don't." There were tears in her eyes. "Wait just a little while. Not very long, Pete."

He sank to his knees again. She gathered both his hands in hers and held them tightly. She smiled happily. "You're good, Pete. You're so good."

(She couldn't hear the blood in his ears, the roar of the whirlpool of hate and fear and anguish that spun inside of him.)

She talked to him in a low voice, and then in whispers. Sometimes he hated himself because he couldn't quite follow her. She talked about school, and her first audition. "I was so scared that I got a vibrato in my voice. I'd never had one before. I always let myself get a little scared when I sing now. It's easy." There was something about a window-box when she was four years old. "Two real live tulips and a pitcher-plant. I used to be sorry for the flies."

There was a long period of silence after that, during which his muscles throbbed with cramp and stiffness, and gradually became numb. He must have dozed; he awoke with a violent start, feeling her fingers on his face. She was propped up on one elbow. She said clearly, "I just wanted to tell you, darling. Let me go first, and get everything ready for you. It's going to be wonderful. I'll fix you a special tossed salad. I'll make you a steamed chocolate pudding and keep it hot for you."

Too muddled to understand what she was saying, he smiled and pressed her back on the settee. She took his hands again.

The next time he awoke it was broad daylight, and she was dead.

Sonny Weisefreund was sitting on his cot when he got back to the barracks. He handed over the recording he had picked up from the parade ground on the way back. "Dew on it. Dry it off. Good boy," he croaked, and fell face downward on the cot Bonze had used.

Sonny stared at him. "Pete! Where you been? What happened? Are you all right?"

Pete shifted a little and grunted. Sonny shrugged and took the audiovid disc out of its wet envelope. Moisture would not harm it particularly, though it could not be played while wet. It was made of a fine spiral of plastic, insulated between laminations. Electrostatic pickups above and below the turntable would fluctuate with changes in the dielectric constant which had been impressed by the recording, and these changes were amplified for the scanners. The audio was a conventional hill-and-dale needle. Sonny began to wipe it down carefully.

Pete fought upward out of a vast, green-lit place full of flickering cold fires. Starr was calling him. Something was punching him, too. He fought it weakly, trying to hear what she was saying. But someone else was jabbering too loud for him to hear.

He opened his eyes. Sonny was shaking him, his round face pink with excitement. The audiovid was running. Starr was talking. Sonny got up impatiently and turned down the volume. "Pete! Pete! Wake up, will you? I got to tell you something. Listen to me! Wake up, will yuh?"

"Huh?"

"That's better. Now listen. I've just been listening to Starr Anthim—"

"She's dead," said Pete.

Sonny didn't hear. He went on, explosively. "I've figured it out. Starr was sent out here, and all over, to *beg* someone not to fire any more atom bombs. If the government was sure they wouldn't strike back, they wouldn't've taken the trouble. Somewhere, Pete, there's some way to launch bombs at those murdering cowards—and I've got a pretty shrewd idea of how to do it."

Pete strained groggily toward the faint sound of Starr's voice. Sonny talked on. "Now, s'posing there was a master radio key—an automatic code device something like the alarm signal they have on ships, that rings a bell on any ship within radio range when the operator sends four long dashes. Suppose there's an automatic code machine to launch bombs, with repeaters, maybe, buried all over the country. What would it be? Just a little lever to pull; that's all. How would the thing be hidden? In the middle of a lot of other equipment, that's where; in some place where you'd expect to find crazy-looking secret stuff. Like an experiment station. Like right here. You beginning to get the idea?"

"Shut up, I can't hear her."

"The hell with her! You can listen to her some other time. You didn't hear a thing I said!"

"She's dead."

"Yeah. Well, I figure I'll pull that handle. What can I lose? It'll give those murderin'—*what?*"

"She's dead."

"Dead? Starr Anthim?" His young face twisted, Sonny sank down to the cot. "You're half asleep. You don't know what you're saying."

"She's dead," Pete said hoarsely. "She got burned by one of the first bombs. I was with her when she—she— Shut up now and get out of here and let me listen!" he bellowed hoarsely.

Sonny stood up slowly. "They killed her, too. They killed her! That does it. That just fixes it up." His face was white. He went out.

Pete got up. His legs weren't working right. He almost fell. He brought up against the console with a crash, his outflung arm sending the pickup skittering across the record. He put it on again and turned up the volume, then lay down to listen.

His head was all mixed up. Sonny talked too much. Bomb launchers, automatic code machines—

"*You gave me your heart,*" sang Starr. "*You gave me your heart. You gave me your heart. You...*"

Pete heaved himself up again and moved the pickup arm. Anger, not at himself, but at Sonny for causing him to cut the disc that way, welled up.

Starr was talking, stupidly, her face going through the same expression over and over again. *"Struck from the east and from the struck from the east and from the…"*

He got up again wearily and moved the pickup.

"You gave me your heart you gave me…"

Pete made an agonized sound that was not a word at all, bent, lifted, and sent the console crashing over. In the bludgeoning silence he said, "I did, too."

Then, "Sonny." He waited.

"Sonny!"

His eyes went wide then, and he cursed and bolted for the corridor.

The panel was closed when he reached it. He kicked at it. It flew open, discovering darkness.

"Hey!" bellowed Sonny. "Shut it! You turned off the lights!"

Pete shut it behind them. The lights blazed.

"Pete! What's the matter?"

"Nothing's the matter, Son," croaked Pete.

"What are you looking at?" said Sonny uneasily.

"I'm sorry," said Pete as gently as he could; "I just wanted to find something out, is all. Did you tell anyone else about this?" He pointed to the lever.

"Why, no. I only just figured it out while you were sleeping, just now."

Pete looked around carefully, while Sonny shifted his weight. Pete moved toward a tool-rack. "Something you haven't noticed yet, Sonny," he said softly, and pointed. "Up there, on the wall behind you. High up. See?"

Sonny turned. In one fluid movement Pete plucked off a fourteen-inch box wrench and hit Sonny with it as hard as he could.

Afterward he went to work systematically on the power supplies. He pulled the plugs on the gas-engines and cracked their cylinders with a maul. He knocked off the tubing of the diesel starters—the tanks let go explosively—and he cut all the cables with bolt-cutters. Then he broke up the relay rack and its lever. When he was quite finished, he put away his tools and bent and stroked Sonny's tousled hair.

He went out and closed the partition carefully. It certainly was a wonderful piece of camouflage. He sat down heavily on a workbench nearby.

"You'll have your chance," he said into the far future. "And, by Heaven, you'd better make good."

After that he just waited.

ECCE FEMINA

For its first two decades science fiction was almost as exclusively male as the contact sports. In 1949 *Astounding* conducted a readers' survey revealing, among other interesting data, that 93 percent of its readers were male, and the stories included in the several volumes of *The Road to Science Fiction* bear evidence to the preponderance of male authors.

Before 1948 few women wrote science fiction, and those who did usually concealed their sex behind male pseudonyms or neutral initials. A few writers had names that were clearly female, but not many. Gertrude Bennett wrote science fiction between 1918 and 1923 under the name of Francis (not Frances) Stevens. Catherine Moore used her initials, C. L. Leigh Brackett's first name was sexually ambiguous. Wilmar Shiras, who wrote a series of stories about mutant superchildren, beginning in 1948 with "In Hiding," had an uncategorizable first name.

With the first appearance of "That Only a Mother" by Judith Merril (1923-) in *Astounding* in 1948, women began to come out of the science fiction closet. The year before, in 1947, Margaret St. Clair (1911-) had begun to be published in *Thrilling Wonder Stories* and *Startling Stories*, and in 1950 she was published in *Fantasy and Science Fiction* under the name Idris Seabright.

Many other women began to appear in the pages of the magazines and on the covers of books: Katherine MacLean (1925-) had her first *Astounding* publication in 1949 and has since written many excellent stories, including one Nebula Award winner; Zenna Henderson (1917-), an Arizona schoolteacher, wrote a series of stories for *Fantasy and Science Fiction* about "The People," a shipload of aliens stranded on Earth; and Alice Mary Norton (1912-), a Cleveland juvenile librarian when she began her popular series of juveniles that started with *Star Man's Son* in 1952, returned to an earlier style for her pseudonym, "Andre."

Other science fiction writers who happen to be women are Hilary Bailey, Ruth Berman, Joan Bernott, Marion Zimmer Bradley, Octavia E. Butler, Carol Carr, Joy Chant, Suzy McKee Charnas, C. J. Cherryh, Mildred Clingerman, Grania Davis, the late Miriam Allen DeFord, Sonya Dorman, Phyllis Eisenstein, Suzette Hadein Elgin, Carol Emshwiller, Phyllis Gotlieb, Anne Warren Griffith, the late Joan Hunter Holly, the late E. Mayne Hull, Alice Eleanor Jones, Katherine Kurtz, Sanders Anne Laubenthal, Tanith Lee, Ursula K. Le Guin, Jacqueline Lichtenberg, Elizabeth Lynn, Anne McCaffrey, Vonda N. McIntyre, Phyllis MacLennan, Raylyn Moore, Maggie Nadler, Lin Nielson, Doris Piserchia, Kit Reed, Joanna Russ, Pamela Sargent, the late Alice Sheldon (James Tiptree, Jr.), Lisa Tuttle, Joan Vinge, Kate Wilhelm, Chelsea Quinn Yarbro, and Pamela Zoline.

Already they have established a distinguished record. McCaffrey has won a Hugo and a Nebula and a substantial following for her "Dragons of Pern" series. Russ and McIntyre have won Nebulas. Wilhelm has won a Nebula and a Hugo. Sheldon won two of both. And Le Guin has won too many awards to count. Sargent, herself a novelist and anthologist, has edited three recent anthologies focused on women in science fiction: *Women of Wonder, More Women of Wonder,* and *New Women of Wonder.* And one of the most influential of science fiction editors was Judy-Lynn del Rey of Del Rey Books.

Times have changed. The old male preserve has been invaded by women readers—in science fiction classes, the number of male and female students is often about the same—and women writers are challenging men for an equal place in the literature of ideas. That was not as apparent in 1948, when Judith Merril sold her first science fiction story, "That Only a Mother," to *Astounding.* It appeared in June 1948.

Merril was born Josephine Judith Grossman. She was introduced to science fiction by her first husband, Dan Zissman. Merril took her pseudonym, which she soon adopted legally, from the given name of her first daughter. She lived in New York City while her husband served in the Navy in 1945–1946 and there became acquainted with some of the remaining Futurians, a fan group, organized in 1937, out of which emerged a surprising number of authors and editors, agents, critics, and even publishers.

After the impact of "That Only a Mother," Merril wrote and edited full-time. Her first novel, *Shadow on the Hearth* (1950), concerned survival after an atomic war. She also wrote two novels with Cyril Kornbluth under the pseudonym Cyril Judd. *Outpost Mars* (serialized in *Galaxy* as *Mars Child*) and *Gunner Cade* (both 1952).

The editing of a paperback anthology, *Shot in the Dark* (1950), launched a new career that culminated in an influential series of the year's best science fiction, beginning in 1956 and continuing for twelve years. Their significance (and perhaps sales) dwindled as her selections became less recognizable as science fiction and more idiosyncratic. Her last anthology coincided with her conversion to the "New Wave" science fiction celebrated in her anthology *England Swings SF* (1968); she helped name the "New Wave" and openly campaigned for its victory over traditional science fiction.

Her best-of-the-year anthologies overlapped a series edited by Everett F. Bleiler and Ted Dikty, and carried on briefly by Dikty alone, which ran from 1949 to 1958, and was overlapped in turn by the Nebula Award volumes of the Science Fiction Writers of America that began in 1966 and by a series edited by Harry Harrison and Brian Aldiss. These were joined later by best-of-the-year anthologies edited by Donald Wollheim and Terry Carr, each of whom then went off to edit his own best-of-the-year collection, and by Lester del Rey, who was succeeded as editor of that series by Gardner Dozois.

Merril was married for a few years to Frederik Pohl, beginning in the late 1940s. She has worked as a documentarist for CBC radio, in Japan with translators on an anthology of Japanese science fiction, and with an experimental college in Toronto.

THAT ONLY A MOTHER

BY JUDITH MERRIL

Margaret reached over to the other side of the bed where Hank should have been. Her hand patted the empty pillow, and then she came altogether awake, wondering that the old habit should remain after so many months. She tried to curl up, cat-style, to hoard her own warmth, found she couldn't do it anymore, and climbed out of bed with a pleased awareness of her increasingly clumsy bulkiness

Morning motions were automatic. On the way through the kitchenette, she pressed the button that would start breakfast cooking—the doctor had said to eat as much breakfast as she could—and tore the paper out of the facsimile machine. She folded the long sheet carefully to the "National News" section, and propped it on the bathroom shelf to scan while she brushed her teeth.

No accidents. No direct hits. At least none that had been officially released for publication. *Now, Maggie, don't get started on that. No accidents. No hits. Take the nice newspaper's word for it.*

The three clear chimes from the kitchen announced that breakfast was ready. She set a bright napkin and cheerful colored dishes on the table in a futile attempt to appeal to a faulty morning appetite. Then, when there was nothing more to prepare, she went for the mail, allowing herself the full pleasure of prolonged anticipation, because today there would *surely* be a letter.

There was. There were. Two bills and a worried note from her mother: "Darling, why didn't you write and tell me sooner? I'm thrilled, of course, but, well one hates to mention these things, but are you *certain* the doctor was right? Hank's been around all that uranium or thorium or whatever it is all these years, and I know you say he's a designer, not a technician, and he doesn't get near anything that might be dangerous, but you know he used to, back at Oak Ridge. Don't you think… well, of course, I'm just being a foolish old woman, and I don't want you to get upset. You know much more about it than I do, and I'm sure your doctor was right. He *should* know… "

Margaret made a face over the excellent coffee, and caught herself refolding the paper to the medical news.

Stop it, Maggie, stop it! The radiologist said Hank's job couldn't have exposed

him. And the bombed area we drove past... No, no. Stop it, now! Read the social notes or the recipes, Maggie girl.

A well-known geneticist, in the medical news, said that it was possible to tell with absolute certainty, at five months, whether the child would be normal, or at least whether the mutation was likely to produce anything freakish. The worst cases, at any rate, could be prevented. Minor mutations, of course, displacements in facial features, or changes in brain structure could not be detected. And there had been some cases recently, of normal embryos with atrophied limbs that did not develop beyond the seventh or eighth month. But, the doctor concluded cheerfully, the *worst* cases could now be predicted and prevented.

"Predicted and prevented." We predicted it, didn't we? Hank and the others, they predicted it. But we didn't prevent it. We could have stopped it in '46 and '47. Now...

Margaret decided against the breakfast. Coffee had been enough for her in the morning for ten years; it would have to do for today. She buttoned herself into interminable folds of material that, the salesgirl had assured her, was the *only* comfortable thing to wear during the last few months. With a surge of pure pleasure, the letter and newspaper forgotten, she realized she was on the next to the last button. It wouldn't be long now.

The city in the early morning had always been a special kind of excitement for her. Last night it had rained, and the sidewalks were still damp-gray instead of dusty. The air smelled the fresher, to a city-bred woman, for the occasional pungency of acrid factory smoke. She walked the six blocks to work, watching the lights go out in the all-night hamburger joints, where the plate-glass walls were already catching the sun, and the lights go on in the dim interiors of cigar stores and dry-cleaning establishments.

The office was in a new Government building. In the rolovator, on the way up, she felt, as always, like a frankfurter roll in the ascending half of an old-style rotary toasting machine. She abandoned the air-foam cushioning gratefully at the fourteenth floor, and settled down behind her desk at the rear of a long row of identical desks.

Each morning the pile of papers that greeted her was a little higher. These were, as everyone knew, the decisive months. The war might be won or lost on these calculations as well as any others. The manpower office had switched her here when her old expeditor's job got to be too strenuous. The computer was easy to operate, and the work was absorbing, if not as exciting as the old job. But you didn't just stop working these days. Everyone who could do anything at all was needed.

And—she remembered the interview with the psychologist—*I'm probably the unstable type. Wonder what sort of neurosis I'd get sitting home reading that sensational paper...*

She plunged into the work without pursuing the thought.

February 18.

Hank darling,

Just a note—from the hospital, no less. I had a dizzy spell at work, and the doctor took it to heart. Blessed if I know what I'll do with myself lying in bed for weeks, just waiting—but Dr. Boyer seems to think it may not be so long.

There are too many newspapers around here. More infanticides all the time, and they can't seem to get a jury to convict any of them. It's the fathers who do it. Lucky thing you're not around, in case—

Oh, darling, that wasn't a very *funny* joke, was it? Write as often as you can, will you? I have too much time to think. But there really isn't anything wrong, and nothing to worry about.

Write often, and remember I love you.

Maggie.

SPECIAL SERVICE TELEGRAM

February 21, 1953

22:04 LK37G

From: Tech. Lieut. H. Marvell

X47-016 GCNY

To: Mrs. H. Marvell

Women's Hospital

New York City

HAD DOCTOR'S GRAM STOP WILL ARRIVE FOUR OH TEN STOP SHORT LEAVE STOP YOU DID IT MAGGIE STOP LOVE HANK

February 25.

Hank dear,

So you didn't see the baby either? You'd think a place this size would at least have visiplates on the incubators, so the fathers could get a look, even if the poor benighted mommas can't. They tell me I won't see her for another week, or maybe more—but of course, mother always warned me if I didn't slow my pace, I'd probably even have my babies too fast. Why must she *always* be right?

Did you meet that battle-ax of a nurse they put on here? I imagine they save her for people who've already had theirs, and don't let her get too near the prospectives—but a woman like that simply shouldn't be allowed in a maternity ward. She's obsessed with mutations, can't seem to talk about anything else. Oh, well, *ours* is all right, even if it was in an unholy hurry.

I'm tired. They warned me not to sit up too soon, but I *had* to write you. All my love, darling,

Maggie.

February 29.

Darling,

I finally got to see her! It's all true, what they say about new babies and the face that only a mother could love—but it's all there, darling, eyes, ears, and noses—no, only one!—all in the right places. We're so *lucky,* Hank.

I'm afraid I've been a rambunctious patient. I kept telling that hatchet-faced female with the mutation mania that I wanted to *see* the baby. Finally the doctor came in to "explain" everything to me, and talked a lot of nonsense, most of which I'm sure no one could have understood, any more than I did. The only thing I got out of it was that she didn't actually *have* to stay in the incubator; they just thought it was "wiser."

I think I got a little hysterical at that point. Guess I was more worried than I was willing to admit, but I threw a small fit about it. The whole business wound up with one of those hushed medical conferences outside the door, and finally the Woman in White said: "Well, we might as well. Maybe it'll work out better that way."

I'd heard about the way doctors and nurses in these places develop a God complex, and believe me, it is as true figuratively as it is literally that a mother hasn't a leg to stand on around here.

I *am* awfully weak, still. I'll write again soon. Love,

Maggie.

March 8.

Dearest Hank,

Well the nurse was wrong if she told you that. She's an idiot anyhow. It's a girl. It's easier to tell with babies than with cats, and I *know*. How about Henrietta?

I'm home again, and busier than a betatron. They got *everything* mixed up at the hospital, and I had to teach myself how to bathe her and do just about everything else. She's getting prettier, too. When can you get a leave, a *real* leave?

Love,
Maggie.

May 26.

Hank dear,

You should see her now—and you shall. I'm sending along a reel of color movie. My mother sent her those nighties with drawstrings all over. I put one on, and right now she looks like a snow-white potato sack with that beautiful, beautiful flower-face blooming on top. Is that *me* talking? Am I a doting mother? But wait till you see her!

July 10.

...Believe it or not, as you like, but your daughter can talk, and I don't mean baby talk. Alice discovered it—she's a dental assistant in the WACs, you know— and when she heard the baby giving out what I thought was a string of gibberish, she said the kid knew words and sentences, but couldn't say them clearly because she has no teeth yet. I'm taking her to a speech specialist.

September 13.

...We have a prodigy for real! Now that all her front teeth are in, her speech is perfectly clear and—a new talent now—she can sing! I mean really carry a tune! At seven months! Darling my world would be perfect if you could only get home.

November 19.

...at last. The little goon was so busy being clever, it took her all this time to learn to crawl. The doctor says development in these cases is always erratic...

SPECIAL SERVICE TELEGRAM

December 1, 1953
08:47 LK59F

From: Tech. Lieut. H. Marvell
X47-016 GCNY

To: Mrs. H. Marvel
Apt. K-17
504 E. 19 St.
N.Y. N.Y.

WEEK'S LEAVE STARTS TOMORROW STOP WILL ARRIVE AIRPORT TEN OH FIVE STOP DON'T MEET ME STOP LOVE LOVE LOVE HANK

Margaret let the water run out of the bathinette until only a few inches were left, and then loosed her hold on the wriggling baby.

"I think it was better when you were retarded, young woman," she informed her daughter happily. "You *can't* crawl in a bathinette, you know.

"Then why can't I go in the bathtub?" Margaret was used to her child's volubility by now, but every now and then it caught her unawares. She swooped the resistant mass of pink flesh into a towel, and began to rub.

"Because you're too little, and your head is very soft, and bathtubs are very hard."

"Oh. Then when can I go in the bathtub?"

"When the outside of your head is as hard as the inside, brainchild." She reached toward a pile of fresh clothing. "I cannot understand," she added, pinning a square of cloth through the nightgown, "why a child of your intelligence can't learn to keep a diaper on the way other babies do. They've been used for centuries, you know, with perfectly satisfactory results."

The child disdained to reply; she had heard it too often. She waited patiently until she had been tucked, clean and sweet-smelling, into a white-painted crib. Then she favored her mother with a smile that inevitably made Margaret think of the first golden edge of the sun bursting into a rosy predawn. She remembered Hank's reaction to the color pictures of his beautiful daughter, and with the thought, realized how late it was.

"Go to sleep, puss. When you wake up, you know, your *Daddy* will be here."

"Why?" asked the four-year-old mind, waging a losing battle to keep the ten-month-old body awake.

Margaret went into the kitchenette and set the timer for the roast. She examined the table and got her clothes from the closet: new dress, new shoes, new slip, new everything, bought weeks before and saved for the day Hank's telegram came. She stopped to pull a paper from the facsimile, and, with clothes and news, went into the bathroom, and lowered herself gingerly into the steaming luxury of a scented tub.

She glanced through the paper with indifferent interest. Today at least there was no need to read the national news. There was an article by a geneticist. The same geneticist. Mutations, he said, were increasing disproportionately. It was too soon for recessives; even the first mutants, born near Hiroshima and Nagasaki in 1946 and 1947, were not old enough yet to breed. *But my baby's all right.* Apparently, there was some degree of free radiation from atomic explosions causing the trouble. *My baby's fine. Precocious, but normal.* If more attention had been paid to the first Japanese mutations; he said...

There was that little notice in the paper in the spring of '47. That was when Hank quit at Oak Ridge. "Only two or three per cent of those guilty of infanticide are being caught and punished in Japan today..." *But MY BABY'S all right.*

She was dressed, combed, and ready to the last light brush-on of lip paste, when the door chime sounded. She dashed for the door, and heard, for the first time in eighteen months, the almost-forgotten sound of a key turning in the lock before the chime had quite died away.

"Hank!"

"Maggie!"

And then there was nothing to say. So many days, so many months of small news piling up, so many things to tell him, and now she just stood there, staring at a khaki uniform and a stranger's pale face. She traced the features with the finger of memory. The same high-bridged nose, wide-set eyes, fine feathery brows; the same long jaw, the hair a little farther back now on the high forehead, the same tilted curve to his mouth. Pale... Of course, he'd been underground all this time. And strange, stranger because of lost familiarity than any newcomer's face could be.

She had time to think all that before his hand reached out to touch her, and spanned the gap of eighteen months. Now, again, there was nothing to say, because there was no need. They were together, and for the moment that was enough.

"Where's the baby?"

"Sleeping. She'll be up any minute."

No urgency. Their voices were as casual as though it were a daily exchange, as though war and separation did not exist. Margaret picked up the coat he'd thrown on the chair near the door, and hung it carefully in the hall closet. She went to check the roast, leaving him to wander through the rooms by himself, remembering and coming back. She found him, finally, standing over the baby's crib.

She couldn't see his face, but she had no need to.

"I think we can wake her just this once." Margaret pulled the covers down, and lifted the white bundle from the bed. Sleepy lids pulled back heavily from smoky brown eyes.

"Hello." Hank's voice was tentative.

"Hello." The baby's assurance was more pronounced.

He had heard about it, of course, but that wasn't the same as hearing it. He turned eagerly to Margaret. "She really can—?"

"Of course she can, darling. But what's more important, she can even do nice normal things like other babies do, even stupid ones. Watch her crawl!" Margaret set the baby on the big bed.

For a moment young Henrietta lay and eyed her parents dubiously.

"Crawl?" she asked.

"That's the idea. Your Daddy is new around here, you know. He wants to see you show off."

"Then put me on my tummy."

"Oh, of course." Margaret obligingly rolled the baby over.

"What's the matter?" Hank's voice was still casual, but an undercurrent in it began to charge the air of the room. "I thought they turned over first."

"This baby," Margaret would not notice the tension, "*this* baby does things when she wants to."

This baby's father watched with softening eyes while the head advanced and the body hunched up, propelling itself across the bed.

"Why the little rascal," he burst into relieved laughter. "She looks like one of those potato-sack racers they used to have on picnics. Got her arms pulled out of the sleeves already." He reached over and grabbed the knot at the bottom of the long nightie.

"I'll do it, darling." Margaret tried to get there first.

"Don't be silly, Maggie. This may be *your* first baby, but *I* had five kid brothers." He laughed her away, and reached with his other hand for the string that closed one sleeve. He opened the sleeve bow, and groped for an arm.

"The way you wriggle," he addressed his child sternly, as his hand touched a moving knob of flesh at the shoulder, "anyone might think you are a worm, using your tummy to crawl on, instead of your hands and feet."

Margaret stood and watched, smiling. "Wait till you hear her sing, darling—"

His right hand traveled down from the shoulder to where he thought an arm would be, traveled down, and straight down, over firm small muscles that writhed in an attempt to move against the pressure of his hand. He let his fingers drift up again to the shoulder. With infinite care, he opened the knot at the bottom of the nightgown. His wife was standing by the bed saying: "She can do 'Jingle Bells,' and—"

His left hand felt along the soft knitted fabric of the gown, up toward the diaper that folded, flat and smooth, across the bottom end of his child. No wrinkles. No kicking. *No...*

"Maggie." He tried to pull his hands from the neat fold in the diaper, from the wriggling body. "Maggie." His throat was dry; words came hard, low and grating. He spoke very slowly, thinking the sound of each word to make himself say it. His head was spinning, but he had to *know* before he let it go. "Maggie, why... didn't you... tell me?"

"Tell you what, darling?" Margaret's poise was the immemorial patience of woman confronted with man's childish impetuosity. Her sudden laugh sounded fantastically easy and natural in that room; it was all clear to her now. "Is she wet? I didn't know."

She didn't know. His hands, beyond control, ran up and down the soft-skinned baby body, the sinuous, limbless body. *Oh God, dear God*—his head shook and his muscles contracted, in a bitter spasm of hysteria. His fingers tightened on his child—*Oh God, she didn't know....*

A MATTER OF TIME

Time travel has been an anomaly in science fiction. Clearly fantastic—there is no evidence that anyone has ever traveled in time and no theoretical basis for believing that anyone ever will—the concept nevertheless has been accorded a place of respectability in science fiction, not relegated to fantasy. One reason for its acceptance may be the weight of tradition; another, its technological basis when accomplished by machine; a third, its basic usefulness as a story mechanism. Only when the travel itself is by fantasy means does the story become fantasy.

The earliest form of fictional time travel was achieved by falling asleep and awakening some years into the future, as in Washington Irving's "Rip Van Winkle" (1819), Mrs. Mary Griffith's "Three Hundred Years Hence" (1836), and Edward Bellamy's classic propaganda book, *Looking Backward* (1888). Travel into the past was not as simple: Mark Twain solved it with a crowbar to the head in *A Connecticut Yankee in King Arthur's Court* (1889) and L. Sprague de Camp provided a lightning bolt in *Lest Darkness Fall* (1941; serialized 1939).

But H. G. Wells supplied the archetypal version in his novella "The Time Machine" (1895), which was his earliest triumph as an author of scientific romances. It was the first to use an apparatus to transport the time traveler, which offered the more important possibility of a return trip. Wells didn't think time travel was likely (even less likely, perhaps, than his antigravity in *The First Men in the Moon*, 1901), but he took pains to make his machine convincing.

Since then the time machine, in all its permutations, has become a fixture in science fiction. With it the author can send his character, marveling all the way, into the future to explore the directions in which society and humanity are heading, or even to the ultimate end of things, as Wells himself did at the end of "The Time Machine." Or the author can send his character into the past to discover the beginning of things or the truths of history.

The questions to be answered are: Why go? What is the good of it? Curiosity impels most characters. They want to know what the future holds or how things really were. Sometimes, then, the time machine is used as a tool for research superior to arduous and ambiguous digging. Sometimes it is used for adventure, as in Jack Williamson's *The Legion of Time* (serialized in 1938). Sometimes it is perverted to commercial use: to transport hunters in search of big game, tourists after unusual sights, adventurers who lust after experiences in more primitive societies. Sometimes it offers a glimpse of the future, as in Silverberg's "When We Went to See the End of the World." Sometimes the only useful function seems to be to make films, as in T. L. Sherred's shattering "E for Effort."

Usually all such enterprises come to bad ends; in fact, there wouldn't be a story if they didn't. The time traveler gets trapped in the future or the past, or he commits some blunder, often ignoring instructions, that destroys him, or alters the present, or destroys life altogether. Or he finds himself helplessly acting out the inexorable past, as in Michael Moorcock's "Behold the Man."

Time travel involves two fundamental problems: if the travel is into the future, the future must be fixed, or travel would be impossible, and if it is unchangeable, knowledge of what is going to happen can be no help to anybody. If the travel is into the past, either events cannot be changed, which leads to the frustration of those who *want* to change them, or it can—and that may change the present. In Heinlein's "All You Zombies—" the paradoxes form a closed circle of reality; in his 1941 "By His Bootstraps," they prevent an escape from a tyrannical future.

The more frightening paradoxes are not personal but communal. Some interference with the past can prevent the present from existing, as in Ray Bradbury's "A Sound of Thunder," or create an alternate present, or a series of branching possible worlds at every decision point, some of them more probable than others. In some stories, such as H. Beam Piper's series about "the paratime police" or Fritz Leiber's *The Big Time* (1961; serialized 1958), characters attempt to manipulate the probability of worlds or protect them from manipulation, to bring about a better world or prevent a worse one.

Philip Klass (1920-), who wrote under the name William Tenn, came up with a variation on the idea of time paradox in "Brooklyn Project" (*Planet Stories*, Fall 1948) that reflects on human nature, as all good fiction does. "Brooklyn Project" is a gimmick story, but those who scorn gimmicks should read the story first. It is also a political story and was more difficult to get published in 1948.

Klass is one of the excellent short-story writers in science fiction who are more comfortable at that length; he wrote only a single novel, and that an expansion of a short novel, *Of Men and Monsters* (1968). But his short stories, beginning after his discharge from the army in 1945, created a major reputation for his wit and satire and skilled use of language. He interspersed his writing with stints as a salesman and a purser aboard ship, and until his retirement taught in the English department of Pennsylvania State University, where he was promoted to professor without ever having earned a college degree. He wrote little fiction after taking up his college career, but has returned to writing in retirement.

BROOKLYN PROJECT

BY WILLIAM TENN
(PHILIP KLASS)

The gleaming bowls of light set in the creamy ceiling dulled when the huge, circular door at the back of the booth opened. They returned to white brilliance as the chubby man in the severe black jumper swung the door shut behind him and dogged it down again.

Twelve reporters of both sexes exhaled very loudly as he sauntered to the front of the booth and turned his back to the semi-opaque screen stretching across it. Then they all rose in deference to the cheerful custom of standing whenever a security official of the government was in the room.

He smiled pleasantly, waved at them and scratched his nose with a wad of mimeographed papers. His nose was large, and it seemed to give added presence to his person. "Sit down, ladies and gentlemen, do sit down. We have no official fol-de-rol in the Brooklyn Project. I am your guide, as you might say, for the duration of this experiment—the acting secretary to the executive assistant on press relations. My name is not important. Please pass these among you."

They each took one of the mimeographed sheets and passed the rest on. Leaning back in the metal bucket seats, they tried to make themselves comfortable. Their host squinted through the heavy screen and up at the wall clock, which had one slowly revolving hand. He patted his black garment jovially where it was tight around the middle.

"To business. In a few moments, man's first large-scale excursion into time will begin. Not by humans, but with the aid of a photographic and recording device which will bring us incalculably rich data on the past. With this experiment, the Brooklyn Project justifies ten billion dollars and over eight years of scientific development; it shows the validity not merely of a new method of investigation, but of a weapon which will make our glorious country even more secure, a weapon which our enemies may justifiably dread.

"Let me caution you, first, not to attempt the taking of notes even if you have been able to smuggle pens and pencils through Security. Your stories will be written entirely from memory. You all have a copy of the Security Code with the latest additions as well as a pamphlet referring specifically to Brooklyn Project regulations. The sheets you have just received provide you with the required lead for your story; they also contain suggestions as to treatment and coloring. Beyond that—so long as you stay within the framework of the documents mentioned—you are entirely free to write your stories in your own variously original ways. The press, ladies and gentlemen, must remain untouched and uncontaminated by government control. Now, any questions?"

The twelve reporters looked at the floor. Five of them began reading from their sheets. The paper rustled noisily.

"What, no questions? Surely there must be more interest than this in a project which has broken the last possible frontier—the fourth dimension, time. Come now, you are the representatives of the nation's curiosity—you must have questions. Bradley, you look doubtful. What's bothering you? I assure you, Bradley, that I don't bite."

They all laughed and grinned at each other.

Bradley half-rose and pointed at the screen. "Why does it have to be so thick? I'm not the slightest bit interested in finding out how chronar works, but all we can see from here is a grayed and blurry picture of men dragging apparatus around on the floor. And why does the clock only have one hand?"

"A good question," the acting secretary said. His large nose seemed to glow. "A very good question. First, the clock has but one hand, because, after all, Bradley, this is an experiment in time, and Security feels that the time of the experiment itself may, through some unfortunate combination of information leakage and foreign correlation—in short, a clue might be needlessly exposed. It is sufficient to know that when the hand points to the red dot, the experiment will begin. The screen is translucent and the scene below somewhat blurry for the same reason—camouflage of detail and adjustment. I *am* empowered to inform you that the details of the apparatus are—uh, very significant. Any other questions? Culpepper? Culpepper of Consolidated, isn't it?"

"Yes, sir. Consolidated News Service. Our readers are very curious about that incident of the Federation of Chronar Scientists. Of course, they have no respect or pity for them—the way they acted and all—but just what did they mean by saying that this experiment was dangerous because of insufficient data? And that fellow, Dr. Shayson, their president, do you know if he'll be shot?"

The man in black pulled at his nose and paraded before them thoughtfully. "I must confess that I find the views of the Federation of Chronar Scientists— or the federation of chronic *sighers*, as we at Pike's Peak prefer to call them— are a trifle too exotic for my tastes; I rarely bother with weighing the opinions of a traitor in any case. Shayson himself may or may not have incurred the death penalty for revealing the nature of the work with which he was entrusted. On the other hand, he—uh, *may not* or *may* have. That is all I can say about him for reasons of security."

Reason of security. At the mention of the dread phrase, every reporter straightened against the hard back of his chair. Culpepper's face lost its pinkness in favor of a glossy white. *They can't consider the part about Shayson a leading question*, he thought desperately. *But I shouldn't have cracked about that damned federation!*

Culpepper lowered his eyes and tried to look as ashamed of the vicious idiots as he possibly could. He hoped the acting secretary to the executive assistant on press relations would notice his horror.

The clock began ticking very loudly. Its hand was now only one-fourth of an arc from the red dot at the top. Down on the floor of the immense laboratory, activity had stopped. All of the seemingly tiny men were clustered around two great spheres of shining metal resting against each other. Most of them were watching dials and switchboards intently; a few, their tasks completed, chatted with the circle of black-jumpered Security guards.

"We are almost ready to begin Operation Periscope. Operation Periscope, of course, because we are, in a sense, extending a periscope into the past—a periscope which will take pictures and record events of various periods ranging from fifteen thousand years to four billion years ago. We felt that in view of the various critical circumstances attending this experiment—international, scientific—a more fitting title would be Operation Crossroads. Unfortunately, that title has been—uh, preempted."

Everyone tried to look as innocent of the nature of that other experiment as years of staring at locked library shelves would permit.

"No matter. I will now give you a brief background in chronar practice as cleared by Brooklyn Project Security. Yes, Bradley?"

Bradley again got partly out of his seat. "I was wondering—we know there has been a Manhattan Project, a Long Island Project, a Westchester Project and now a Brooklyn Project. Has there ever been a Bronx Project? I come from the Bronx; you know, civic pride."

"Quite. Very understandable. However, if there is a Bronx Project you may be assured that until its work has been successfully completed, the only individuals outside of it who will know of its existence are the President and the Secretary of Security. If—*if*, I say—there is such an institution, the world will learn of it with the same shattering suddenness that it learned of the Westchester Project. I don't think that the world will soon forget *that*."

He chuckled in recollection and Culpepper echoed him a bit louder than the rest. The clock's hand was close to the red mark.

"Yes, the Westchester Project and now this; our nation shall yet be secure! Do you realize what a magnificent weapon chronar places in our democratic hands? To examine only one aspect—consider what happened to the Coney Island and Flatbush Subprojects (the events are mentioned in those sheets you've received) before the uses of chronar were fully appreciated.

"It was not yet known in those first experiments that Newton's third law of motion—action equaling reaction—held for time as well as it did for the other three dimensions of space. When the first chronar was excited backward into time for the length of a ninth of a second, the entire laboratory was propelled into the future for a like period and returned in an—uh, unrecognizable condition. That fact, by the way, has prevented excursions into the future. The equipment seems to suffer amazing alterations, and no human could survive them. But do you realize what we could do to an enemy by virtue of that property alone? Sending an adequate mass of chronar into the past while it is adjacent to a hostile nation would force that nation into the future—all of it simultaneously—a future from which it would return populated only with corpses!"

He glanced down, placed his hands behind his back and teetered on his heels. "That is why you see two spheres on the floor. Only one of them, the ball on the right, is equipped with chronar. The other is a dummy, matching the other's mass perfectly and serving as a counterbalance. When the chronar is excited, it will plunge four billion years into our past and take photographs of an earth that was still a half-liquid, partly gaseous mass solidifying rapidly in a somewhat inchoate solar system.

"At the same time, the dummy will be propelled four billion years into the future, from whence it will return much changed but for reasons we don't completely understand. They will strike each other at what is to us *now* and bounce off again to approximately half the chronological distance of the first trip, where our chronar apparatus will record data of an almost solid planet, plagued by earthquakes and possibly holding forms of sublife in the manner of certain complex molecules.

"After each collision, the chronar will return roughly half the number of years covered before, automatically gathering information each time. The geological and historical periods we expect it to touch are listed from I to XXV in your sheets; there will be more than twenty-five, naturally, before both balls come to rest, but scientists feel that all periods after that number will be touched for such a short while as to be unproductive of photographs and other material. Remember, at the end, the balls will be doing little more than throbbing in place before coming to rest, so that even though they still ricochet centuries on either side of the present, it will be almost unnoticeable. A question, I see."

The thin woman in gray tweeds beside Culpepper got to her feet. "I—I know this is irrelevant," she began, "but I haven't been able to introduce my question into the discussion at any pertinent moment. Mr. Secretary—"

"Acting secretary," the chubby little man in the black suit told her genially. "I'm only the acting secretary. Go on."

"Well, I want to say—Mr. Secretary, is there any way at all that our post-experimental examination time may be reduced? Two years is a very long time to spend inside Pike's Peak simply out of fear that one of us may have seen enough and be unpatriotic enough to be dangerous to the nation. Once our stories have passed the censors, it seems to me that we could be allowed to return to our homes after a safety period of, say, three months. I have two small children and there are others here—"

"Speak for yourself, Mrs. Bryant!" the man from Security roared. "It *is* Mrs. Bryant, isn't it? Mrs. Bryant of the Women's Magazine Syndicate? Mrs. *Alexis* Bryant." He seemed to be making minute pencil notes across his brain.

Mrs. Bryant sat down beside Culpepper again, clutching her copy of the amended Security Code, the special pamphlet on the Brooklyn Project and the thin mimeographed sheet of paper very close to her breast. Culpepper moved hard against the opposite arm of his chair. Why did everything have to happen to him? Then, to make matters worse, the crazy woman looked tearfully at him as if expecting sympathy. Culpepper stared across the booth and crossed his legs.

"You must remain within the jurisdiction of the Brooklyn Project because that is the only way that Security can be *certain* that no important information leakage will occur before the apparatus has changed beyond your present recognition of it. You didn't have to come, Mrs. Bryant—you volunteered. You all volunteered. After your editors had designated you as their choices for covering this experiment, you all had the peculiarly democratic privilege of refusing. None of you did. You recognized that to refuse this unusual honor would have shown you incapable of thinking in terms of National Security, would have, in fact, implied a criticism of the Security Code itself from the standpoint of the usual two-year examination time. And now this! For someone who had hitherto been thought as able and trustworthy as yourself, Mrs. Bryant, to emerge at this late hour with such a request makes me, why it," the little man's voice dropped to a whisper, "—it almost makes me doubt the effectiveness of our Security screening methods."

Culpepper nodded angry affirmation at Mrs. Bryant, who was biting her lips and trying to show a tremendous interest in the activities on the laboratory floor.

"The question *was* irrelevant. Highly irrelevant. It took up time which I had intended to devote to a more detailed discussion of the popular aspects of chronar and its possible uses in industry. But Mrs. Bryant must have her little feminine outburst. It makes no difference to Mrs. Bryant that our nation is daily surrounded by more and more hostility, more and more danger. These things matter not in the slightest to Mrs. Bryant. All she is concerned with are the two years of her life that her country asks her to surrender so that the future of her own children may be more secure."

The acting secretary smoothed his black jumper and became calmer. Tension in the booth decreased.

"Activation will occur at any moment now, so I will briefly touch upon those most interesting periods which the chronar will record for us and from which we expect the most useful data. I and II, of course, since they are the periods at which the earth was forming into its present shape. Then III, the Pre-Cambrian Period of the Proterozoic, one billion years ago, the first era in which we find distinct records of life—crustaceans and algae for the most part. VI, a hundred twenty-five million years in the past, covers the Middle Jurassic of the Mesozoic. This excursion into the so-called 'Age of Reptiles' may provide us with photographs of dinosaurs and solve the old riddle of their coloring, as well as photographs, if we are fortunate, of the first appearance of mammals and birds. Finally, VIII and IX, the Oligocene and Miocene Epochs of the Tertiary Period, mark the emergence of man's earliest ancestors. Unfortunately, the chronar will be oscillating back and forth so rapidly by that time that the chance of any decent recording—"

A gong sounded. The hand of the clock touched the red mark. Five of the technicians below pulled switches and, almost before the journalists could lean forward, the two spheres were no longer visible through the heavy plastic screen. Their places were empty.

"The chronar has begun its journey to four billion years in the past! Ladies and gentlemen, an historic moment—a profoundly historic moment! It will not return for a little while; I shall use the time in pointing up and exposing the fallacies of the—ah, *federation of chronic sighers!*"

Nervous laughter rippled at the acting secretary to the executive assistant on press relations. The twelve journalists settled down to hearing the ridiculous ideas torn apart.

"As you know, one of the fears entertained about travel to the past was that the most innocent-seeming acts would cause cataclysmic changes in the present. You are probably familiar with the fantasy in its most currently popular form—if Hitler had been killed in 1930, he would not have forced scientists in Germany and later occupied countries to emigrate, this nation might not have had the atomic bomb, thus no third atomic war, and Venezuela would still be part of the South American continent.

"The traitorous Shayson and his illegal federation extended this hypothesis to include much more detailed and minor acts such as shifting a molecule of hydrogen that in our past really was never shifted.

"At the time of the first experiment at the Coney Island Subproject, when the chronar was sent back for one-ninth of a second, a dozen different laboratories checked through every device imaginable, searched carefully for any conceivable change. There were none! Government officials concluded that the time stream was a rigid affair, past, present, and future, and nothing in it could be altered. But Shayson and his cohorts were not satisfied: they—"

I. Four billion years ago. The chronar floated in a cloudlet of silicon dioxide above the boiling earth and languidly collected its data with automatically operating instruments. The vapor it had displaced condensed and fell in great, shining drops.

"—insisted that we should do no further experimenting until we had checked the mathematical aspects of the problem yet again. They went so far as to state that it was possible that if changes occurred we would not notice them, that no instruments imaginable could detect them. They claimed we would accept these changes as things that had always existed. Well! This at a time when our country—and theirs, ladies and gentlemen of the press, *theirs*, too—was in greater danger than ever. Can you—"

Words failed him. He walked up and down the booth, shaking his head. All the reporters on the long, wooden bench shook their heads with him in sympathy.

There was another gong. The two dull spheres appeared briefly, clanged against each other and ricocheted off into opposite chronological directions.

"There you are." The government official waved his arms at the transparent laboratory floor above them. "The first oscillation has been completed; has anything changed? Isn't everything the same? But the dissidents would maintain that alterations have occurred and we haven't noticed them. With such faith-based, unscientific viewpoints, there can be no argument. People like these—"

II. Two billion years ago. The great ball clicked its photographs of the fiery, erupting ground below. Some red-hot crusts rattled off its sides. Five or six thousand complex molecules lost their basic structure as they impinged against it. A hundred didn't.

"—will labor thirty hours a day out of thirty-three to convince you that black isn't white, that we have seven moons instead of two. They are especially dangerous—"

A long, muted note as the apparatus collided with itself. The warm orange of the corner lights brightened as it started out again.

"—because of their learning, because they are sought for guidance in better ways of vegetation." The government official was slithering up and down rapidly now, gesturing with all of his pseudopods. "We are faced with a very difficult problem, at present—"

III. One billion years ago. The primitive triple trilobite the machine had destroyed when it materialized began drifting down wetly.

"—a very difficult problem. The question before us: should we *shllk* or shouldn't we *shllk?*" He was hardly speaking English now; in fact, for some time, he hadn't been speaking at all. He had been stating his thoughts by slapping one pseudopod against the other—as he always had....

IV. A half-billion years ago. Many different kinds of bacteria died as the water changed temperature slightly.

"This, then, is no time for half measures. If we can reproduce well enough—"

V. Two hundred fifty million years ago. VI. A hundred twenty-five million years ago.

"—to satisfy the Five Who Spiral, we have—"

VII. Sixty-two million years. VIII. Thirty-one million.
IX. Fifteen million. X. Seven and a half million.

"—spared all attainable virtue. Then—"

XI. XII. XIII. XIV. XV. XVI. XVII. XVIII. XIX. Bong—bong—bong bongbongbongongongngngngggg...

"—we are indeed ready for refraction. And that, I tell you, is good enough for those who billow and those who snap. But those who billow will be proven wrong as always, for in the snapping is the rolling and in the rolling is only truth. There need be no change merely because of a sodden cilium. The apparatus has tested at last in the fractional conveyance; shall we view it subtly?"

They all agreed, and their bloated purpled bodies dissolved into liquid and flowed up and around to the apparatus. When they reached its four square blocks, now no longer shrilling mechanically, they rose, solidified, and regained their slimewashed forms.

"See," cried the thing that had been the acting secretary to the executive assistant on press relations. "See, no matter how subtly! Those who billow were wrong: we haven't changed." He extended fifteen purple blobs triumphantly. "Nothing has changed!"

THE SOCIAL SIDE

Groff Conklin (1904-1968), in his significant postwar anthology *The Best of Science Fiction* (1946), complained about the paucity of stories dealing with the social sciences and the science of the mind. Two years later when his second anthology, *A Treasury of Science Fiction* (1948), appeared, he applauded their appearance in the interim. Within another two years a new magazine made social science fiction its special province—one of two new magazines that appeared within the space of a year. They were part of the great postwar magazine boom, but unlike the others they survived the bust that followed. They would help recreate science fiction in their own images.

The two magazines were *The Magazine of Fantasy* (first issue, Fall 1949), which became *The Magazine of Fantasy and Science Fiction* with its second issue; and *Galaxy Science Fiction* (first issue, October 1950). *Fantasy and Science Fiction* was edited by J. Francis McComas (who had collaborated with Raymond J. Healy on the other big postwar anthology, *Adventures in Time and Space*, 1946) and Anthony Boucher. *Galaxy* was edited by Horace L. Gold.

McComas (1910-1978), Boucher (1911-1968), and Gold (1914-1996) had all written many kinds of fiction, including stories for Campbell's *Astounding* and *Unknown*. In charge of their own magazines, they headed off in different directions. Boucher was the most visible editor at *Fantasy and Science Fiction*, and he wanted stories with literary quality, stories that could be printed in any magazine (he often reprinted from other magazines, including little magazines). Gold's emphasis was on story and sociology.

In his 1953 essay titled "Social Science Fiction," Isaac Asimov listed four stages of science fiction: primitive from 1815 to 1926; the Gernsback era from 1926 to 1938; the Campbell era from 1938 to 1945; and social science fiction since then. (Later he divided "modern science fiction" into four different periods: "adventure-dominant" between 1926 and 1938; "science-dominant" between 1938 and 1950; "sociology-dominant" between 1950 and 1965; and "possibly style-dominant" since then.) Social science fiction, which he defined as stories about "the impact of scientific advance upon human beings," he dated from 1945, when the atom bomb demonstrated the social relevance of science fiction. Social science fiction stories had been published occasionally for years; Campbell encouraged the appearance of more; and *Galaxy* "from the very beginning, published only advanced social science fiction...."

In *Galaxy* social science fiction found its true home. Gold wanted stories not about scientists and engineers but about the ordinary people who were most affected by scientific and technological change. The emphasis of science fiction shifted from the scientific culture to society itself.

Campbell's *Astounding* had included stories in which the future was bleak, in which science was perverted to evil ends, in which the human lot was worse rather than better. In general, however, the stories were not so much pessimistic as cautionary; the future turned out badly because human beings behaved emotionally, with fear, anger, prejudice, and mob violence, rather than rationally. No matter how gloomy the situation, the stories displayed faith in the rational mind to redeem it if given the opportunity.

In the early 1950s *Galaxy Science Fiction* provided a home for a different attitude toward science, technology, and the future, whipping up a kind of early "New Wave." Many of the stories implied that the future may not turn out well—in fact, that it is *likely* not to turn out well, and that it won't turn out well because humans are flawed, and if not fallen creatures in some theological sense, at least spoiled by the evolutionary process. The general tone of these stories—they were not all published in *Galaxy*, by any means—was pessimistic. Later the "New Wave" would offer up its pessimism in less structured, more style-conscious packages.

Gold was a different sort of editor from Campbell, although they shared some of the same methods. Like Campbell, Gold discussed writers' ideas with them, sometimes gave them ideas, worked with them to improve what they had written, and demanded rewrites. But Gold was something of a recluse: he mostly talked to writers on the telephone or in his Manhattan apartment. And he sometimes made his own editorial changes, often in titles, occasionally in the text of the stories themselves, without the authors' knowledge, frequently earning the authors' intense displeasure.

An occasional practitioner of the art of social science fiction was Fritz Leiber, Jr., whose story "Coming Attraction," published in the second issue (November 1950) of *Galaxy*, encapsulated everything that was effective about this kind of fiction. Not only did it extrapolate the possibility of an atomic war and the ugly, guilt-ridden society that might emerge from it, it was also critical, by implication, of social trends in the late 1940s. Moreover, the story was effective as literature.

The style was relatively new for Leiber (1910-1992). He had written stories of social significance, such as *Gather, Darkness!* (1950), which was serialized in *Astounding* in 1943, but the combination of realism, symbolism, and intensity were new. He would go on to write more social science fiction, such as "Appointment in Tomorrow," also called "Poor Superman" (1952), "A Bad Day for Sales" (1953), and "X Marks the Pedwalk" (1963), but they would be more satirical than realistic. He would never again achieve quite the same combination of elements that made "Coming Attraction" an archetype for the best science fiction of the next decade and a half, the artistic blending of story, style, and speculation.

Leiber became better known for the fiction with which he started, heroic fantasy (sometimes called "sword and sorcery" for its combination of magic and hand-to-hand combat), particularly the stories about Fafrhd and the Gray

Mouser, who wield their swords and their wits in a fantasy world that has resemblances to various periods in human history. Leiber, the son of a well-known Shakespearean actor, tried a variety of careers, including acting, before he sold a Gray Mouser story to Campbell's *Unknown* in 1939.

Leiber also worked as an encyclopedia editor, as a college teacher, and, for seven years, as an associate editor for *Science Digest*. His writing emerged in spurts. His best early work was *Conjure Wife* (1953), a novel about magic on a college campus serialized in *Unknown* in 1943; it has been dramatized on film and television three times. His other novels include *Destiny Times Three* (1952; serialized 1943), *The Green Millennium* (1955), *The Silver Eggheads* (1961; serialized 1959), and *A Spectre Is Haunting Texas* (1969). He won Hugo Awards for *The Big Time* (1961; serialized 1958), *The Wanderer* (1964), and "Ship of Shadows" (1969), a Nebula for "Gonna Roll the Bones" (1967), and both Hugos and Nebulas for "Ill Met in Lankhmar" (1970) and "Catch That Zeppelin!" (1975). He was presented the SFWA Grand Master Award in 1981.

COMING ATTRACTION

BY FRITZ LEIBER

The coupe with the fishhooks welded to the fender shouldered up over the curb like the nose of a nightmare. The girl in its path stood frozen, her face probably stiff with fright under her mask. For once my reflexes weren't shy. I took a fast step toward her, grabbed her elbow, yanked her back. Her black skirt swirled out.

The big coupe shot by, its turbine humming. I glimpsed three faces. Something ripped. I felt the hot exhaust on my ankles as the big coupe swerved back into the street. A thick cloud like a black flower blossomed from its jouncing rear end, while from the fishhooks flew a black shimmering rag.

"Did they get you?" I asked the girl.

She had twisted around to look where the side of her skirt was torn away. She was wearing nylon tights.

"The hooks didn't touch me," she said shakily. "I guess I'm lucky."

I heard voices around us:

"Those kids! What'll they think up next?"

"They're a menace. They ought to be arrested."

Sirens screamed at a rising pitch as two motor-police, their rocket-assist jets full on, came whizzing toward us after the coupe. But the black flower had become an inky fog obscuring the whole street. The motor-police switched from rocket assists to rocket brakes and swerved to a stop near the smoke cloud.

"Are you English?" the girl asked me. "You have an English accent."

Her voice came shudderingly from behind the sleek black satin mask. I fancied her teeth must be chattering. Eyes that were perhaps blue searched my face from behind the black gauze covering the eyeholes of the mask. I told her she'd guessed right. She stood close to me. "Will you come to my place tonight?" she asked rapidly. "I can't thank you now. And there's something else you can help me about."

My arm, still lightly circling her waist, felt her body trembling. I was answering the plea in that as much as in her voice when I said, "Certainly." She gave me an address south of Inferno, an apartment number and a time. She asked my name, and I told her.

"Hey, you!"

I turned obediently to the policeman's shout. He shooed away the small clucking crowd of masked women and bare-faced men. Coughing from the smoke that the black coupe had thrown out, he asked for my papers. I handed him the essential ones.

He looked at them and then at me. "British Barter? How long will you be in New York?"

Suppressing the urge to say, "For as short a time as possible," I told him I'd be here for a week or so.

"May need you as a witness," he explained. "Those kids can't use smoke on us. When they do that, we pull them in."

He seemed to think the smoke was the bad thing. "They tried to kill the lady," I pointed out.

He shook his head wisely. "They always pretend they're going to, but actually they just want to snag skirts. I've picked up rippers with as many as fifty skirt-snags tacked up in their rooms. Of course, sometimes they come a little too close."

I explained that if I hadn't yanked her out of the way, she'd have been hit by more than hooks. But he interrupted, "If she'd thought it was a real murder attempt, she'd have stayed here."

I looked around. It was true. She was gone

"She was fearfully frightened," I told him.

"Who wouldn't be? Those kids would have scared old Stalin himself."

"I mean frightened of more than 'kids.' They didn't look like 'kids.'"

"What did they look like?"

I tried without much success to describe the three faces. A vague impression of viciousness and effeminacy doesn't mean much.

"Well, I could be wrong," he said finally. "Do you know the girl? Where she lives?"

"No," I half lied.

The other policeman hung up his radiophone and ambled toward us, kicking at the tendrils of dissipating smoke. The black cloud no longer hid the dingy façades with their five-year-old radiation flash-burns, and I could begin to make out the distant stump of the Empire State Building, thrusting up out of Inferno like a mangled finger.

"They haven't been picked up so far," the approaching policeman grumbled. "Left smoke for five blocks, from what Ryan says."

The first policeman shook his head. "That's bad," he observed solemnly.

I was feeling a bit uneasy and ashamed. An Englishman shouldn't lie, at least not on impulse.

"They sound like nasty customers," the first policeman continued in the same grim tone. "We'll need witnesses. Looks as if you may have to stay in New York longer than you expect."

I got the point. I said, "I forgot to show you all my papers," and handed him a few others, making sure there was a five dollar bill in among them.

When he handed them back a bit later, his voice was no longer ominous. My feelings of guilt vanished. To cement our relationship, I chatted with the two of them about their job.

"I suppose the masks give you some trouble," I observed. "Over in England we've been reading about your new crop of masked female bandits."

"Those things get exaggerated," the first policeman assured me. "It's the men masking as women that really mix us up. But brother, when we nab them, we jump on them with both feet."

"And you get so you can spot women almost as well as if they had naked faces," the second policeman volunteered. "You know, hands and all that."

"Especially all that," the first agreed with a chuckle. "Say, is it true that some girls don't mask over in England?"

"A number of them have picked up the fashion," I told him. "Only a few, though—the ones who always adopt the latest style, however extreme."

"They're usually masked in the British newscasts."

"I imagine it's arranged that way out of deference to American taste," I confessed. "Actually, not very many do mask."

The second policeman considered that. "Girls going down the street bare from the neck up." It was not clear whether he viewed the prospect with relish or moral distaste. Likely both.

"A few members keep trying to persuade Parliament to enact a law forbidding all masking," I continued, talking perhaps a bit too much.

The second policeman shook his head. "What an idea. You know, masks are a pretty good thing, brother. Couple of years more and I'm going to make my wife wear hers around the house."

The first policeman shrugged. "If women were to stop wearing masks, in six weeks you wouldn't know the difference. You get used to anything, if enough people do or don't do it."

I agreed, rather regretfully, and left them. I turned north on Broadway (old Tenth Avenue, I believe) and walked rapidly until I was beyond Inferno. Passing such an area of undecontaminated radioactivity always makes a person queasy. I thanked God there weren't any such in England, as yet.

The street was almost empty, though I was accosted by a couple of beggars with faces tunneled by H-bomb scars, whether real or of makeup putty, I couldn't tell. A fat woman held out a baby with webbed fingers and toes. I told myself it would have been deformed anyway and that she was only capitalizing on our fear of bomb-induced mutations. Still, I gave her a seven-and-a-half-cent piece. Her mask made me feel I was paying tribute to an African fetish.

"May all your children be blessed with one head and two eyes, sir."

"Thanks," I said, shuddering, and hurried past her.

"…There's only trash behind the mask, so turn your head, stick to your task: Stay away, stay away—from—the—girls!"

This last was the end of an anti-sex song being sung by some religionists half a block from the circle-and-cross insignia of a femalist temple. They reminded me only faintly of our small tribe of British monastics. Above their heads was a jumble of billboards advertising predigested foods, wrestling instruction, radio handies and the like.

I stared at the hysterical slogans with disagreeable fascination. Since the female face and form have been banned on American signs, the very letters of the advertiser's alphabet have begun to crawl with sex—the fat-bellied, big-breasted capital B, the lascivious double O. However, I reminded myself, it is chiefly the mask that so strangely accents sex in America.

A British anthropologist has pointed out that while it took more than 5,000 years to shift the chief point of sexual interest from the hips to the breasts, the next transition to the face has taken less than 50 years. Comparing the American style with Moslem tradition is not valid; Moslem women are compelled to wear veils, the purpose of which is to make a husband's property private, while American women have only the compulsion of fashion and use masks to create mystery.

Theory aside, the actual origins of the trend are to be found in the anti-radiation clothing of World War III, which led to masked wrestling, now a fantastically popular sport, and that in turn led to the current female fashion. Only a wild style at first, masks quickly became as necessary as brassieres and lipsticks had been earlier in the century.

I finally realized that I was not speculating about masks in general, but about what lay behind one in particular. That's the devil of the things; you're never sure whether a girl is heightening loveliness or hiding ugliness. I pictured a cool, pretty face in which fear showed only in widened eyes. Then I remembered her blond hair, rich against the blackness of the satin mask. She'd told me to come at the twenty-second hour—10:00 P.M.

I climbed to my apartment near the British Consulate; the elevator shaft had been shoved out of plumb by an old blast, a nuisance in these tall New York buildings. Before it occurred to me that I would be going out again, I automatically tore a tab from the film strip under my shirt. I developed it just to be sure. It showed that the total radiation I'd taken that day was still within the safety limit. I'm not phobic about it, as so many people are these days, but there's no point in taking chances.

I flopped down on the day bed and stared at the silent speaker and the dark screen of the video set. As always, they made me think, somewhat bitterly, of the two great nations of the world. Mutilated by each other, yet still strong, they were crippled giants poisoning the planet with their respective dreams of an impossible equality and as impossible success.

I fretfully twitched on the speaker. By luck, the newscaster was talking excitedly of the prospects of a bumper wheat crop, sown by planes across a dust bowl moistened by seeded rains. I listened carefully to the rest of the program (it was remarkably clear of Russian telejamming) but there was no further news of interest to me. And, of course, no mention of the Moon, though everyone knows that America and Russia are racing to develop their primary bases into fortresses capable of mutual assault and the launching of alphabet-bombs toward Earth. I myself knew perfectly well that the British electronic equipment I was helping trade for American wheat was destined for use in spaceships.

I switched off the newscast. It was growing dark, and once again I pictured a tender, frightened face behind a mask. I hadn't had a date since England. It's exceedingly difficult to become acquainted with a girl in America, where as little as a smile, often, can set one of them yelping for the police—to say nothing of the increasingly puritanical morality and the roving gangs that keep most women indoors after dark. And naturally, the masks, which are definitely not, as the Soviets claim, a last invention of capitalist degeneracy, but a sign of great psychological insecurity. The Russians have no masks, but they have their own signs of stress.

I went to the window and impatiently watched the darkness gather. I was getting very restless. After a while a ghostly violet cloud appeared to the south. My hair rose. Then I laughed. I had momentarily fancied it a radiation from the crater of the Hell-bomb, though I should instantly have known it was only the radio-induced glow in the sky over the amusement and residential area south of Inferno.

Promptly at twenty-two hours I stood before the door of my unknown girl friend's apartment. The electronic say-who-please said just that. I answered clearly, "Wysten Turner," wondering if she'd given my name to the mechanism. She evidently had, for the door opened. I walked into a small empty living room, my heart pounding a bit.

The room was expensively furnished with the latest pneumatic hassocks and sprawlers. There were some midgic books on the table. The one I picked up was the standard hard-boiled detective story in which two female murderers go gunning for each other.

The television was on. A masked girl in green was crooning a love song. Her right hand held something that blurred off into the foreground. I saw the set had a handie, which we haven't in England as yet, and curiously thrust my hand into the handie orifice beside the screen. Contrary to my expectations, it was not like slipping into a pulsing rubber glove, but rather as if the girl on the screen actually held my hand.

A door opened behind me. I jerked out my hand with as guilty a reaction as if I'd been caught peering through a keyhole.

She stood in the bedroom doorway. I think she was trembling. She was wearing a gray fur coat, white-speckled, and a gray velvet evening mask with shirred gray lace around the eyes and mouth. Her fingernails twinkled like silver.

It hadn't occurred to me that she'd expect us to go out.

"I should have told you," she said softly. Her mask veered nervously toward the books and the screen and the room's dark corners. "But I can't possibly talk to you here."

I said doubtfully, "There's a place near the Consulate…"

"I know where we can be together and talk," she said rapidly. "If you don't mind."

As we entered the elevator I said, "I'm afraid I dismissed the cab."

But the cab driver hadn't gone for some reason of his own. He jumped out and smirkingly held the front door open for us. I told him we preferred to sit in back. He sulkily opened the rear door, slammed it after us, jumped in front and slammed the door behind him.

My companion leaned forward. "Heaven," she said.

The driver switched on the turbine and televisor.

"Why did you ask if I were a British subject?" I said, to start the conversation.

She leaned away from me, tilting her mask close to the window. "See the Moon," she said in a quick, dreamy voice.

"But why, really?" I pressed, conscious of an irritation that had nothing to do with her.

"It's edging up into the purple of the sky."

"And what's your name?"

"The purple makes it look yellower."

Just then I became aware of the source of my irritation. It lay in the square of writhing light in the front of the cab beside the driver.

I don't object to ordinary wrestling matches, though they bore me, but I simply detest watching a man wrestle a woman. The fact that the bouts are generally "on the level," with the man greatly outclassed in weight and reach and the masked females young and personable, only makes them seem worse to me.

"Please turn off the screen," I requested the driver.

He shook his head without looking around. "Uh-uh, man," he said. "They've been grooming that babe for weeks for this bout with Little Zirk."

Infuriated, I reached forward, but my companion caught my arm. "Please," she whispered frightenedly, shaking her head.

I settled back, frustrated. She was closer to me now, but silent, and for a few minutes I watched the heaves and contortions of the powerful masked girl and her wiry masked opponent on the screen. His frantic scrambling at her reminded me of a male spider.

I jerked around, facing my companion. "Why did those three men want to kill you?" I asked sharply.

The eyeholes of her mask faced the screen. "Because they're jealous of me," she whispered.

"Why are they jealous?"

She still didn't look at me. "Because of him."

"Who?"

She didn't answer.

I asked, "What *is* the matter?"

She still didn't look my way. She smelled nice.

"See here," I said laughingly, changing my tactics, "you really should tell me something about yourself. I don't even know what you look like."

I half playfully lifted my hand to the band of her neck. She gave it an astonishingly swift slap. I pulled it away in sudden pain. There were four tiny indentations on the back. From one of them a tiny bead of blood welled out as I watched. I looked at her silver fingernails and saw they were actually delicate and pointed metal caps.

"I'm dreadfully sorry," I heard her say, "but you frightened me. I thought for a moment you were going to…"

At last she turned to me. Her coat had fallen open. Her evening dress was Cretan Revival, a bodice of lace beneath and supporting the breasts without covering them.

"Don't be angry," she said, putting her arms around my neck. "You were wonderful this afternoon."

The soft gray velvet of her mask, molding itself to her cheek, pressed mine. Through the mask's lace the wet warm tip of her tongue touched my chin.

"I'm not angry," I said. "Just puzzled and anxious to help."

The cab stopped. To either side were black windows bordered by spears of broken glass. The sickly purple light showed a few ragged figures slowly moving toward us.

The driver muttered, "It's the turbine, man. We're grounded." He sat there hunched and motionless. "Wish it had happened somewhere else."

My companion whispered, "Five dollars is the usual amount."

She looked out so shudderingly at the congregating figures that I suppressed my indignation and did as she suggested. The driver took the bill without a word. As he started up, he put his hand out the window and I heard a few coins clink on the pavement.

My companion came back into my arms, but her mask faced the television screen, where the tall girl had just pinned the convulsively kicking Little Zirk.

"I'm so frightened," she breathed.

Heaven turned out to be an equally ruinous neighborhood, but it had a club with an awning and a huge doorman uniformed like a spaceman, but in gaudy colors. In my sensuous daze I rather liked it all. We stepped out of the cab just as a drunken old woman came down the sidewalk, her mask awry. A couple ahead of us turned their heads from the half-revealed face, as if from an ugly body at the beach. As we followed them in I heard the doorman say, "Get along, grandma, and cover yourself."

Inside, everything was dimness and blue glows. She had said we could talk here, but I didn't see how. Besides the inevitable chorus of sneezes and coughs (they say America is fifty per cent allergic these days), there was a band going full blast in the latest rebop style, in which an electronic composing machine selects an arbitrary sequence of tones into which the musicians weave their raucous little individualities.

Most of the people were in booths. The band was behind the bar. On a small platform beside them, a girl was dancing, stripped to her mask. The little cluster of men at the shadowy far end of the bar weren't looking at her.

We inspected the menu in gold script on the wall and pushed the buttons for breast of chicken, fried shrimps and two scotches. Moments later, the serving bell tinkled. I opened the gleaming panel and took out our drinks.

The cluster of men at the bar filed off toward the door, but first they stared around the room. My companion had just thrown back her coat. Their look lingered on our booth. I noticed that there were three of them.

The band chased off the dancing girl with growls. I handed my companion a straw, and we sipped our drinks.

"You wanted me to help you about something," I said. "Incidentally, I think you're lovely."

She nodded quick thanks, looked around, leaned forward. "Would it be hard for me to get to England?"

"No," I replied, a bit taken aback. "Provided you have an American passport."

"Are they difficult to get?"

"Rather," I said, surprised at her lack of information. "Your country doesn't like its nationals to travel, though it isn't quite as stringent as Russia."

"Could the British Consulate help me get a passport?"

"It's hardly their…"

"Could you?"

I realized we were being inspected. A man and two girls had passed opposite our table. The girls were tall and wolfish-looking, with spangled masks. The man stood jauntily between them like a fox on its hind legs.

My companion didn't glance at them, but she sat back. I noticed that one of the girls had a big yellow bruise on her forearm. After a moment they walked to a booth in the deep shadows.

"Know them?" I asked. She didn't reply. I finished my drink. "I'm not sure you'd like England," I said. "The austerity's altogether different from your American brand of misery."

She leaned forward again. "But I must get away," she whispered.

"Why?" I was getting impatient

"Because I'm so frightened."

There were chimes. I opened the panel and handed her the fried shrimps. The sauce on my breast of chicken was a delicious steaming compound of almonds, soy and ginger. But something must have been wrong with the radionic oven that had thawed and heated it, for at the first bite I crunched a kernel of ice in the meat. These delicate mechanisms need constant repair, and there aren't enough mechanics.

I put down my fork. "What are you really scared of?" I asked her.

For once her mask didn't waver from my face. As I waited I could feel the fears gathering without her naming them, tiny dark shapes swarming through the curved night outside, converging on the radioactive pest spot of New York, dipping into the margins of the purple. I felt a sudden rush of sympathy, a desire to protect the girl opposite me. The warm feeling added itself to the infatuation engendered in the cab.

"Everything," she said finally.

I nodded and touched her hand.

"I'm afraid of the Moon," she began, her voice going dreamy and brittle as it had in the cab. "You can't look at it and not think of guided bombs."

"It's the same Moon over England," I reminded her.

"But it's not England's Moon anymore. It's ours and Russia's. You're not responsible.

"Oh, and then," she said with a tilt of her mask, "I'm afraid of the cars and the gangs and the loneliness and Inferno. I'm afraid of the lust that undresses your face. And—" her voice hushed—"I'm afraid of the wrestlers."

"Yes?" I prompted softly after a moment.

Her mask came forward. "Do you know something about the wrestlers?"

she asked rapidly. "The ones that wrestle women, I mean. They often lose, you know. And then they have to have a girl to take their frustration out on. A girl who's soft and weak and terribly frightened. They need that, to keep them men. Other men don't want them to have a girl. Other men want them just to fight women and be heroes. But they must have a girl. It's horrible for her."

I squeezed her fingers tighter, as if courage could be transmitted—granting I had any. "I think I can get you to England," I said.

Shadows crawled onto the table and stayed there. I looked up at the three men who had been at the end of the bar. They were the men I had seen in the big coupe. They wore black sweaters and close-fitting black trousers. Their faces were as expressionless as dopers. Two of them stood about me. The other loomed over the girl.

"Drift off, man," I was told. I heard the other inform the girl: "We'll wrestle a fall, sister. What shall it be? Judo, slapsie or kill-who-can?"

I stood up. There are times when an Englishman simply must be maltreated. But just then the foxlike man came gliding in like the star of a ballet. The reaction of the other three startled me. They were acutely embarrassed.

He smiled at them thinly. "You won't win my favor by tricks like this," he said.

"Don't get the wrong idea, Zirk," one of them pleaded.

"I will if it's right," he said. "She told me what you tried to do this afternoon. That won't endear you to me, either. Drift."

They backed off awkwardly. "Let's get out of here," one of them said loudly, as they turned. "I know a place where they fight naked with knives."

Little Zirk laughed musically and slipped into the seat beside my companion. She shrank from him, just a little. I pushed my feet back, leaned forward.

"Who's your friend, baby?" he asked, not looking at her.

She passed the question to me with a little gesture. I told him.

"British," he observed. "She's been asking you about getting out of the country? About passports?" He smiled pleasantly. "She likes to start running away. Don't you, baby?" His small hand began to stroke her wrist, the fingers bent a little, the tendons ridged, as if he were about to grab and twist.

"Look here," I said sharply. "I have to be grateful to you for ordering off those bullies, but—"

"Think nothing of it," he told me. "They're no harm except when they're behind steering wheels. A well-trained fourteen-year-old girl could cripple any one of them. Why, even Theda here, if she went in for that sort of thing...." He turned to her, shifting his hand from her wrist to her hair. He stroked it, letting the strands slip slowly through his fingers. "You know I lost tonight, baby, don't you?" he said softly.

I stood up. "Come along," I said to her. "Let's leave."

She just sat there. I couldn't tell if she was trembling. I tried to read a message in her eyes through the mask.

"I'll take you away," I said to her. "I can do it. I really will."

He smiled at me. "She'd like to go with you," he said. "Wouldn't you, baby?"

"Will you or won't you?" I said to her. She still just sat there.

He slowly knotted his fingers in her hair.

"Listen, you little vermin," I snapped at him. "Take your hands off her."

He came up from the seat like a snake. I'm no fighter. I just know that the more scared I am, the harder and straighter I hit. This time I was lucky. But as he crumpled back, I felt a slap and four stabs of pain in my cheek. I clapped my hand to it. I could feel the four gashes made by her dagger finger caps, and the warm blood oozing out from them.

She didn't look at me. She was bending over little Zirk and cuddling her mask to his cheek and crooning: "There, there, don't feel bad, you'll be able to hurt me afterward."

There were sounds around us, but they didn't come close. I leaned forward and ripped the mask from her face.

I really don't know why I should have expected her face to be anything else. It was very pale, of course, and there weren't any cosmetics. I suppose there's no point in wearing any under a mask. The eyebrows were untidy and the lips chapped. But as for the general expression, as for the feelings crawling and wriggling across it—

Have you ever lifted a rock from damp soil? Have you ever watched the slimy white grubs?

I looked down at her, she up at me. "Yes, you're so frightened, aren't you?" I said sarcastically. "You dread this little nightly drama, don't you? You're scared to death."

And I walked right out into the purple night, still holding my hand to my bleeding cheek. No one stopped me, not even the girl wrestlers. I wished I could tear a tab from under my shirt, and test it then and there, and find I'd taken too much radiation, and so be able to ask to cross the Hudson and go down New Jersey, past the lingering radiance of the Narrows Bomb, and so on to Sandy Hook to wait for the rusty ship that would take me back over the seas to England.

THE EXPANDING UNIVERSE

The end of World War II released a great deal of pent-up demand, for science fiction among other things in short supply, and a great deal of energy that had gone into defeating the Axis powers now flowed into other efforts. The relevance of science fiction had been confirmed by the atomic blast over Hiroshima and the V2 rocket attacks on London, as well as by the laboratories that had produced a hundred miracles with acronym-based designations such as jato, radar, sonar. All of it suggested a future filled not only with technological change but with new language. Many resented it; others turned to science fiction.

Some of the energy was misdirected into the production of new science fiction magazines that bloomed and died in a season or two. Some went into fan presses that reprinted the old favorites from the magazines; although the fan presses themselves didn't last, mainline publishers recognized their surprising success, and soon science fiction became a part—though small—of the publishing spectrum. When paperback originals became acceptable, science fiction found a more natural medium, first at Ace Books and Ballantine Books and then at other paperback houses.

Heinlein's success with the film *Destination Moon* in 1950 and with *Space Cadet* on television the same year led to other films and other television series, few of them worth remembering—although *Forbidden Planet, The Invasion of the Body Snatchers* (the 1956 Don Siegel version, not the 1978 remake), *Barbarella*, and some of the Wells adaptations, stand out as possible exceptions to the general inability of films to deal with science fiction. Then *2001: A Space Odyssey* emerged from the collaboration of Arthur C. Clarke and Stanley Kubrick.

It was the first science fiction film for which no excuses need be made. Critics might quibble about the lack of rationale for HAL's actions (where were the three laws of robotics?) or the obscurity of the ending, but the film felt right, the theme was important, the special effects were magnificent, and the intellectual content was not lost in melodrama. The world—the future itself—looked lived in, commonplace. Kubrick had the understanding other filmmakers had lacked, and the clout and the financial backing to avoid the compromises others had been forced to make. The artistic and financial success of the film paved the way for the later *Star Wars* and *Close Encounters of the Third Kind*.

Clarke (1917-) was a natural choice for the collaboration that produced the film and the subsequent novel (it also helped that he and Kubrick had the same agent when Kubrick expressed his desire to make a science fiction film). Clarke had been pioneering new fields since his early experience with the British Interplanetary Society, of which he was a member at seventeen, treasurer at nineteen, and ultimately president. In 1945 he outlined for *Wireless World* the development of "Extra-Terrestrial Relays" that he later described in an article entitled "How I Lost a Billion Dollars in My Spare Time and Invented Telstar."

His first professional science fiction publications came in 1946 after service in the RAF during World War II. His second story for *Astounding*, "Rescue Party," was particularly popular, and he began a writing career that would include both fiction and nonfiction, with outstanding success in both areas. His science popularizations achieved early recognition: *The Exploration of Space* (1951) became a Book-of-the-Month Club selection and won an International Fantasy Award; in 1962 he was presented the UNESCO-Kalinga prize for his books and articles; he later won the Franklin Institute's Gold Medal.

Clarke writes his fiction in three distinct styles: extrapolative, ingenious, and mystical. His extrapolations, written in the direct, matter-of-fact manner of his nonfiction, produced *Prelude to Space* (1951), *Sands of Mars* (1951), *Earthlight* (1955), *The Deep Range* (1957), and *A Fall of Moondust* (1961). His ingenuity produced "History Lesson" (1949), "Hide and Seek" (1949), "The Nine Billion Names of God" (1953), and *Tales from the White Hart* (1957). His mysticism, sometimes expressed poetically, produced "The Star" (1955), *Against the Fall of Night* (1948), which was rewritten as *The City and the Stars* (1956), and his most famous novel, *Childhood's End* (1953), which may be his clearest expression of the eschatological mood that leads him to speculate about the ultimate fate of humanity.

His story "The Star" won a Hugo Award. His novella "A Meeting with Medusa" won a Nebula in 1972, and his novel *Rendezvous with Rama* won the Hugo, Nebula, and Campbell awards in 1973, and the SFWA Grand Master Award in 1985. A 1978 novel *The Foundations of Paradise* swept the Hugo, Nebula, and Campbell awards. Since then he has produced two sequels to *2001: A Space Odyssey* and a number of collaborations with Gentry Lee, particularly sequels to *Rendezvous with Rama*. A valuable contribution to the genre is an autobiographical work focusing on his early experiences with science fiction, *Astounding Days* (1989). He also has achieved some fame as the host of syndicated television shows on curious phenomena to which he has loaned his name.

Clarke's fascination with skin-diving led him from England to the Great Barrier Reef of Australia and then to Ceylon (now Sri Lanka), where he has made his home since 1956, with frequent absences until recently for business trips and lecture tours. He has been one of the three or four most successful science fiction writers in the past forty years in terms of both artistic and commercial success.

"The Sentinel" was published in 1951 in a little-known magazine, *Ten Story Fantasy*. It was one of those magazines that bloomed for just a season—only four issues were published—but it provided the inspiration for *2001: A Space Odyssey*.

THE SENTINEL

BY ARTHUR C. CLARKE

The next time you see the full Moon high in the south, look carefully at its right-hand edge and let your eye travel upward along the curve of the disk. Round about two o'clock you will notice a small, dark oval: anyone with normal eyesight can find it quite easily. It is the great walled plain, one of the finest on the Moon, known as the Mare Crisium—the Sea of Crises. Three hundred miles in diameter, and almost completely surrounded by a ring of magnificent mountains, it had never been explored until we entered it in the late summer of 1996.

Our expedition was a large one. We had two heavy freighters which had flown our supplies and equipment from the main lunar base in the Mare Serenitatis, five hundred miles away. There were also three small rockets which were intended for short-range transport over regions which our surface vehicles couldn't cross. Luckily, most of the Mare Crisium is very flat. There are none of the great crevasses so common and so dangerous elsewhere, and very few craters or mountains of any size. As far as we could tell, our powerful Caterpillar tractors would have no difficulty in taking us wherever we wished to go.

I was geologist—or selenologist, if you want to be pedantic—in charge of the group exploring the southern region of the Mare. We had crossed a hundred miles of it in a week, skirting the foothills of the mountains along the shore of what was once the ancient sea, some thousand million years before. When life was beginning on Earth, it was already dying here. The waters were retreating down the flanks of those stupendous cliffs, retreating into the empty heart of the Moon. Over the land which we were crossing, the tideless ocean had once been half a mile deep, and now the only trace of moisture was the hoarfrost one could sometimes find in caves which the searing sunlight never penetrated.

We had begun our journey early in the slow lunar dawn, and still had almost a week of Earth-time before nightfall. Half a dozen times a day we would leave our vehicle and go outside in the space-suits to hunt for interesting minerals, or to place markers for the guidance of future travelers. It was an uneventful routine. There is nothing hazardous or even particularly exciting about lunar exploration. We could live comfortably for a month in our pressurized tractors, and if we ran into trouble we could always radio for help and sit tight until one of the spaceships came to our rescue.

I said just now that there was nothing exciting about lunar exploration, but of course that isn't true. One could never grow tired of those incredible mountains, so much more rugged than the gentle hills of Earth. We never knew, as we rounded the capes and promontories of that vanished sea, what new splendors would be revealed to us. The whole southern curve of the Mare Crisium is a vast delta where a score of rivers once found their way into the ocean, fed perhaps by the torrential rains that must have lashed the mountains in the brief volcanic age when the Moon was young. Each of these ancient valleys was an invitation, challenging us to climb into the unknown uplands beyond. But we had a hundred miles still to cover, and could only look longingly at the heights which others must scale.

We kept Earth-time aboard the tractor, and precisely at 22.00 hours the final radio message would be sent out to Base and we would close down for the day. Outside, the rocks would still be burning beneath the almost vertical Sun, but to us it was night until we awoke again eight hours later. Then one of us would prepare breakfast, there would be a great buzzing of electric razors, and someone would switch on the short-wave radio from Earth. Indeed, when the smell of frying sausages began to fill the cabin, it was sometimes hard to believe that we were not back on our own world—everything was so normal and homely, apart from the feeling of decreased weight and the unnatural slowness with which objects fell.

It was my turn to prepare breakfast in the corner of the main cabin that served as a galley. I can remember that moment quite vividly after all these years, for the radio had just played one of my favorite melodies, the old Welsh air, "David of the White Rock." Our driver was already outside in his space-suit, inspecting our Caterpillar treads. My assistant, Louis Garnett, was up forward in the control position, making some belated entries in yesterday's log.

As I stood by the frying pan waiting—like any terrestrial housewife—for the sausages to brown, I let my gaze wander idly over the mountain walls which covered the whole of the southern horizon, marching out of sight to east and west below the curve of the Moon. They seemed only a mile or two from the tractor, but I knew that the nearest was twenty miles away. On the Moon, of course, there is no loss of detail with distance—none of that almost imperceptible haziness which softens and sometimes transfigures all far-off things on Earth.

Those mountains were ten thousand feet high, and they climbed steeply out of the plain as if ages ago some subterranean eruption had smashed them skyward through the molten crust. The base of even the nearest was hidden from sight by the steeply curving surface of the plain, for the Moon is a very little world, and from where I was standing the horizon was only two miles away.

I lifted my eyes toward the peaks which no man had ever climbed, the peaks which, before the coming of terrestrial life, had watched the retreating oceans sink sullenly into their graves, taking with them the hope and the morning promise of a world. The sunlight was beating against those ramparts with a glare that hurt the eyes, yet only a little way above them the stars were shining steadily in a sky blacker than a winter midnight on Earth.

I was turning away when my eye caught a metallic glitter high on the ridge of a great promontory thrusting out into the sea thirty miles to the west. It was a dimensionless point of light, as if a star had been clawed from the sky by one of those cruel peaks, and I imagined that some smooth rock surface was catching the sunlight and heliographing it straight into my eyes. Such things were not uncommon. When the Moon is in her second quarter, observers on Earth can sometimes see the great ranges in the Oceanus Procellarum burning with a blue-white iridescence as the sunlight flashes from their slopes and leaps again from world to world. But I was curious to know what kind of rock could be shining so brightly up there, and I climbed into the observation turret and swung our four-inch telescope round to the west.

I could see just enough to tantalize me. Clear and sharp in the field of vision, the mountain peaks seemed only half a mile away, but whatever was catching the sunlight was still too small to be resolved. Yet it seemed to have an elusive symmetry, and the summit upon which it rested was curiously flat. I stared for a long time at that glittering enigma, straining my eyes into space, until presently a smell of burning from the galley told me that our breakfast sausages had made their quarter-million-mile journey in vain.

All that morning we argued our way across the Mare Crisium while the western mountains reared higher in the sky. Even when we were out prospecting in the space-suits, the discussion would continue over the radio. It was absolutely certain, my companions argued, that there had never been any form of intelligent life on the Moon. The only living things that had ever existed there were a few primitive plants and their slightly less degenerate ancestors. I know that as well as anyone, but there are times when a scientist must not be afraid to make a fool of himself.

"Listen," I said at last, "I'm going up there, if only for my own peace of mind. That mountain's less than twelve thousand feet high—that's only two thousand under Earth gravity—and I can make the trip in twenty hours at the outside. I've always wanted to go up into those hills, anyway, and this gives me an excellent excuse."

"If you don't break your neck," said Garnett, "you'll be the laughing-stock of the expedition when we get back to Base. That mountain will probably be called Wilson's Folly from now on."

"I won't break my neck," I said firmly. "Who was the first man to climb Pico and Helicon?"

"But weren't you rather younger in those days?" asked Louis gently.

"That," I said with great dignity, "is as good a reason as any for going."

We went to bed early that night, after driving the tractor to within half a mile of the promontory. Garnett was coming with me in the morning; he was a good climber, and had often been with me on such exploits before. Our driver was only too glad to be left in charge of the machine.

At first sight, those cliffs seemed completely unscalable, but to anyone with a good head for heights, climbing is easy on a world where all weights are only a sixth of their normal value. The real danger in lunar mountaineering lies in over-confidence; a six-hundred-foot drop on the Moon can kill you just as thoroughly as a hundred-foot fall on Earth.

We made our first halt on a wide ledge about four thousand feet above the plain. Climbing had not been very difficult, but my limbs were stiff with the unaccustomed effort, and I was glad of the rest. We could still see the tractor as a tiny metal insect far down at the foot of the cliff, and we reported our progress to the driver before starting on the next ascent

Inside our suits it was comfortably cool, for the refrigeration units were fighting the fierce sun and carrying away the body-heat of our exertions. We seldom spoke to each other, except to pass climbing instructions and to discuss our best plan of ascent. I do not know what Garnett was thinking, probably that this was the craziest goose-chase he had ever embarked upon. I more than half agreed with him, but the joy of climbing, the knowledge that no man had ever gone this way before and the exhilaration of the steadily widening landscape gave me all the reward I needed.

I don't think I was particularly excited when I saw in front of us the wall of rock I had first inspected through the telescope from thirty miles away. It would level off about fifty feet above our heads, and there on the plateau would be the thing that had lured me over these barren wastes. It was, almost certainly, nothing more than a boulder splintered ages ago by a falling meteor, and with its cleavage planes still fresh and bright in this incorruptible, unchanging silence.

There were no hand-holds on the rock face, and we had to use a grapnel. My tired arms seemed to gain new strength as I swung the three-pronged metal anchor round my head and sent it sailing up toward the stars. The first time it broke loose and came falling slowly back when we pulled the rope. On the third attempt, the prongs gripped firmly and our combined weights could not shift it.

Garnett looked at me anxiously. I could tell that he wanted to go first, but I smiled back at him through the glass of my helmet and shook my head. Slowly, taking my time, I began the final ascent.

Even with my space-suit, I weighed only forty pounds here, so I pulled myself up hand over hand without bothering to use my feet. At the rim I paused and waved to my companion, then I scrambled over the edge and stood upright, staring ahead of me.

You must understand that until this very moment I had been almost completely convinced that there could be nothing strange or unusual for me to find here. Almost, but not quite; it was that haunting doubt that had driven me forward. Well, it was a doubt no longer, but the haunting had scarcely begun.

I was standing on a plateau perhaps a hundred feet across. It had once been smooth—too smooth to be natural—but falling meteors had pitted and scored its surface through immeasurable eons. It had been leveled to support a glittering, roughly pyramidal structure, twice as high as a man, that was set in the rock like a gigantic, many-faceted jewel.

Probably no emotion at all filled my mind in those first few seconds. Then I felt a great lifting of my heart, and a strange, inexpressible joy. For I loved the Moon, and now I knew that the creeping moss of Aristarchus and Eratosthenes was not the only life she had brought forth in her youth. The old, discredited dream of the first explorers was true. There had, after all, been a lunar civilization—and I was the first to find it. That I had come perhaps a hundred million years too late did not distress me; it was enough to have come at all.

My mind was beginning to function normally, to analyze and to ask questions. Was this a building, a shrine—or something for which my language had no name? If a building, then why was it erected in so uniquely inaccessible a spot? I wondered if it might be a temple, and I could picture the adepts of some strange priesthood calling on their gods to preserve them as the life of the Moon ebbed with the dying oceans, and calling on their gods in vain.

I took a dozen steps forward to examine the thing more closely, but some sense of caution kept me from going too near. I knew a little of archaeology, and tried to guess the cultural level of the civilization that must have smoothed this mountain and raised the glittering mirror surfaces that still dazzled my eyes.

The Egyptians could have done it, I thought, if their workmen had possessed whatever strange materials these far more ancient architects had used. Because of the thing's smallness, it did not occur to me that I might be looking at the handiwork of a race more advanced than my own. The idea that the Moon had possessed intelligence at all was still almost too tremendous to grasp, and my pride would not let me take the final, humiliating plunge.

And then I noticed something that set the scalp crawling at the back of my neck—something so trivial and so innocent that many would never have noticed it at all. I have said that the plateau was scarred by meteors; it was also coated inches-deep with the cosmic dust that is always filtering down upon the surface of any world where there are no winds to disturb it. Yet the dust and the meteor scratches ended quite abruptly in a wide circle enclosing the little pyramid, as though an invisible wall was protecting it from the ravages of time and the slow but ceaseless bombardment from space.

There was someone shouting in my earphones, and I realized that Garnett had been calling me for some time. I walked unsteadily to the edge of the cliff and signaled him to join me, not trusting myself to speak. Then I went back toward that circle in the dust. I picked up a fragment of splintered rock and tossed it gently toward the shining enigma. If the pebble had vanished at that invisible barrier I should not have been surprised, but it seemed to hit a smooth, hemispherical surface and slide gently to the ground

I knew then that I was looking at nothing that could be matched in the antiquity of my own race. This was not a building, but a machine, protecting itself with forces that had challenged Eternity. Those forces, whatever they might be, were still operating, and perhaps I had already come too close. I thought of all the radiations man had trapped and tamed in the past century. For all I knew, I might be as irrevocably doomed as if I had stepped into the deadly, silent aura of an unshielded atomic pile.

I remember turning then toward Garnett, who had joined me and was now standing motionless at my side. He seemed quite oblivious to me, so I did not disturb him but walked to the edge of the cliff in an effort to marshal my thoughts. There below me lay the Mare Crisium—Sea of Crises, indeed—strange and weird to most men, but reassuringly familiar to me. I lifted my eyes toward the crescent Earth, lying in her cradle of stars, and I wondered what her clouds had covered when these unknown builders had finished their work. Was it the steaming jungle of the Carboniferous, the bleak shore-line over which the first amphibians must crawl to conquer the land—or, earlier still, the long loneliness before the coming of life?

Do not ask me why I did not guess the truth sooner—the truth that seems so obvious now. In the first excitement of my discovery, I had assumed without question that this crystalline apparition had been built by some race belonging to the Moon's remote past, but suddenly, and with overwhelming force, the belief came to me that it was as alien to the Moon as I myself.

In twenty years we had found no trace of life but a few degenerate plants. No lunar civilization, whatever its doom, could have left but a single token of its existence.

I looked at the shining pyramid again, and the more remote it seemed from anything that had to do with the Moon. And suddenly I felt myself shaking with a foolish, hysterical laughter, brought on by excitement and over-exertion: for I had imagined that the little pyramid was speaking to me and was saying: "Sorry, I'm a stranger here myself."

It has taken us twenty years to crack that invisible shield and to reach the machine inside those crystal walls. What we could not understand, we broke at last with the savage might of atomic power and now I have seen the fragments of the lovely, glittering thing I found up there on the mountain.

They are meaningless. The mechanisms—if indeed they are mechanisms—of the pyramid belong to a technology that lies far beyond our horizon, perhaps to the technology of paraphysical forces.

The mystery haunts us all the more now that the other planets have been reached and we know that only Earth has ever been the home of intelligent life in our Universe. Nor could any lost civilization of our own world have built that machine, for the thickness of the meteoric dust on the plateau has enabled us to measure its age. It was set there upon its mountain before life had emerged from the seas of Earth.

When our world was half its present age, *something* from the stars swept through the Solar System, left this token of its passage, and went again upon its way. Until we destroyed it, that machine was still fulfilling the purpose of its builders; and as to that purpose, here is my guess.

Nearly a hundred thousand million stars are turning in the circle of the Milky Way, and long ago other races on the worlds of other suns must have scaled and passed the heights that we have reached. Think of such civilizations, far back in time against the fading afterglow of Creation, masters of a universe so young that life as yet had come only to a handful of worlds. Theirs would have been a loneliness we cannot imagine, the loneliness of gods looking out across infinity and finding none to share their thoughts.

They must have searched the star-clusters as we have searched the planets. Everywhere there would be worlds, but they would be empty or peopled with crawling, mindless things. Such was our Earth, the smoke of the great volcanoes still staining the skies, when that first ship of the peoples of the dawn came sliding in from the abyss beyond Pluto. It passed the frozen outer worlds, knowing that life could play no part in their destinies. It came to rest among the inner planets, warming themselves around the fire of the Sun and waiting for their stories to begin.

Those wanderers must have looked on Earth, circling safely in the narrow zone between fire and ice, and must have guessed that it was the favorite of the Sun's children. Here, in the distant future, would be intelligence; but there were countless stars before them still, and they might never come this way again.

So they left a sentinel, one of millions they have scattered throughout the Universe, watching over all worlds with the promise of life. It was a beacon that down the ages has been patiently signaling the fact that no one had discovered it.

Perhaps you understand now why that crystal pyramid was set upon the Moon instead of on the Earth. Its builders were not concerned with races still struggling up from savagery. They would be interested in our civilization only if we proved our fitness to survive—by crossing space and so escaping from the

Earth, our cradle. That is the challenge that all intelligent races must meet, sooner or later. It is a double challenge, for it depends in turn upon the conquest of atomic energy and the last choice between life and death.

Once we had passed that crisis, it was only a matter of time before we found the pyramid and forced it open. Now its signals have ceased, and those whose duty it is will be turning their minds upon Earth. Perhaps they wish to help our infant civilization. But they must be very, very old, and the old are often insanely jealous of the young.

I can never look now at the Milky Way without wondering from which of those banked clouds of stars the emissaries are coming. If you will pardon so commonplace a simile, we have set off the fire-alarm and have nothing to do but to wait.

I do not think we will have to wait for long.

FARMERWORLD

Phrases that begin with "if" have troubled humanity's sleep for millennia. If we could only change things around, if we hadn't done this or said that, how much better things would have turned out. And what about the events that changed history? What if Napoleon or Hitler had died in their youth? What if someone had deflected the aim of assassins at Sarajevo or Dallas?

Eventually such musings found their way into print, first, oddly enough, in traditional publications. Robert Silverberg has traced the alternative-history story to Edward Everett Hale's "Hands Off," published in *Harper's Magazine* in 1898. That story assumed that Joseph had not been sold into slavery, was not around to guide the Egyptian government, and the Canaanite barbarians conquered Egypt, with disastrous results for human civilization.

In 1931, after previous publication in *Scribner's Magazine*, eleven essays appeared in a volume titled *If It Had Happened Otherwise: Lapses into Imaginary History*, edited by J. C. Squire. Among the titles were "If Lee Had Not Won the Battle of Gettysburg," "If Booth Had Missed Lincoln," and "If Napoleon Had Escaped to America." They led James Thurber to write a humorous parody, "If Grant Had Been Drinking at Appomattox."

Murray Leinster's "Sidewise in Time," published in *Astounding* in 1934, brought the idea solidly into science fiction, in spite of the fact that there was no more evidence to support its reality than there was for time travel. The concept of some different turn of events in the past creating a different reality has since been the source of many stories and novels.

The best examples of the genre have been done at novel length, perhaps because the greater scope allows a more complete examination of the changes that have been created. In *Bring the Jubilee* (1953, serialized 1952) by Ward Moore (1903-1978) the South won the Civil War. In Philip K. Dick's *The Man in the High Castle* (1962) the Axis Powers won World War II and divided up the United States. *Pavane* (1968) by Keith Roberts (1935-) presents a world that hasn't undergone the Industrial Revolution because Queen Elizabeth I was assassinated in 1588. In Harry Harrison's *A Transatlantic Tunnel, Hurrah!* (1972) George Washington was shot and the American Revolution never happened. *The Alteration* (1976) by Kingsley Amis (1922-) imagines a world in which the Protestant Reformation did not occur and the Catholic Church is all-powerful, with all its implications.

The implications, of course, provide the real value of the alternative-history story. The situation supplies narrative drive, but the implications supply intellectual recognition of the dependence of the present upon decisions, some insignificant, made in the past. The appeal often lies in the inventiveness with which the author fills out his story with telling details. An additional value provided is the comparison it affords with the reader's reality. Upon what small or great decisions, upon what accidents of history, does his present and his future rest? How fixed in their shape and function are the artifacts and traditions that seem so inevitable?

One such alternative-history story is Philip José Farmer's "Sail On! Sail On!" (*Startling Stories*, December 1952), in which the Church encouraged Roger Bacon's experiments. It is an alternative-history story, however, in more ways than one.

Farmer (1918-), an example of a writer who became successful without any relationship with *Astounding*, is best known for his taboo-breaking work. His first published science fiction story was "The Lovers" (1952), which was about a love affair between a man from a puritanical culture and an alien woman who turns out to be an imitative insect. Other such stories have been collected in *Strange Relations* (1960).

Another significant strain in Farmer's work is the tribute story. He has a variety of historical and fictional heroes, and he has written stories about, or pastiches of, many of them: Burroughs, Verne, Tarzan, Doc Savage, Richard F. Burton, and Mark Twain among them. He also appropriated Vonnegut's science fiction author, Kilgore Trout, as the author of his own *Venus on the Half-Shell* (1975). His combination of science fiction and pornography, such as *A Feast Unknown* (1969), has been praised by Leslie Fiedler, and Farmer's fondness for puns and scatology has resulted in stories such as the Hugo-winning "Riders of the Purple Wage" (1968).

Farmer had a difficult time getting his writing career under way, in spite of his success with "The Lovers." He worked eleven years as a laborer before earning his B.A. in creative writing from Bradley University in 1950. A long novel, *I Owe for the Flesh*, won a 1953 contest co-sponsored by Shasta Publishers and Pocket Books, but Shasta's bankruptcy prevented its publication, and Farmer saw none of the prize money. For a number of years he wrote part-time while working as a technical writer for several high-technology firms. A decade ago he returned to full-time writing and has been productive and successful since.

Farmer has created a series of fantasy novels called "the world of tiers," beginning with *Maker of Universes* (1965), and a series of stories about a Father John Carmody culminating in *Night of Light* (1966). He probably is best known for his series of novels based on his ill-fated contest-winning book. The first, *To Your Scattered Bodies Go* (1971), won a Hugo. The series has continued with *The Fabulous Riverboat* (1971), *The Dark Design* (1977), *Riverworld and Other Stories* (1979), *The Magic Labyrinth* (1980), *Riverworld War: The Suppressed Fiction of Philip José Farmer* (1980), *The God of Riverworld* (1983), and *River of Eternity* (1983). They tell the long story of all humanity reborn, by a mysterious mechanism, along the banks of a river ten million miles long, and go by the general title of "Riverworld." Another series of novels called *Dayworld* (1985) was developed from a short story titled "The Sliced-Crossways Only-on-Tuesday World."

SAIL ON! SAIL ON!

BY PHILIP JOSÉ FARMER

Friar Sparks sat wedged between the wall and the realizer. He was motionless except for his forefinger and his eyes. From time to time his finger tapped rapidly on the key upon the desk, and now and then his irises, gray-blue as his native Irish sky, swiveled to look through the open door of the *toldilla* in which he crouched, the little shanty on the poop deck. Visibility was low.

Outside was dusk and a lantern by the railing. Two sailors leaned on it. Beyond them bobbed the bright lights and dark shapes of the *Niña* and the *Pinta*. And beyond them was the smooth horizon-brow of the Atlantic, edged in black and blood by the red dome of the rising moon.

The single carbon filament bulb above the monk's tonsure showed a face lost in fat—and in concentration.

The luminiferous ether crackled and hissed tonight, but the phones clamped over his ears carried, along with them, the steady dots and dashes sent by the operator at the Las Palmas station on the Grand Canary.

"*Zzisss!* So you are out of sherry already.... *Pop!*... Too bad... *Crackle...* you hardened old winebutt... *Zzz...* May God have mercy on your sins....

"Lots of gossip, news, et cetera... *Hisses!*... Bend your ear instead of your neck, impious one.... The Turks are said to be gathering... *crackle*... an army to march on Austria. It is rumored that the flying sausages, said by so many to have been seen over the capitals of the Christian world, are of Turkish origin. The rumor goes they have been invented by a renegade Rogerian who was converted to the Muslim religion.... I say... *zziss*... to that. No one of us would do that. It is a falsity spread by our enemies in the Church to discredit us. But many people believe that....

"How close does the Admiral calculate he is to Cipangu now?

"Flash! Savonarola today denounced the Pope, the wealthy of Florence, Greek art and literature, and the experiments of the disciples of Saint Roger Bacon.... *Zzz!*... The man is sincere but misguided and dangerous.... I predict he'll end up on the stake he's always prescribing for us....

"*Pop*.... This will kill you.... Two Irish mercenaries by the name of Pat and Mike were walking down the street of Granada when a beautiful Saracen lady leaned out of a balcony and emptied a pot of... *hiss!*... and Pat looked up and... *Crackle*.... Good, hah? Brother Juan told that last night....

"PV... PV... Are you coming in?... PV... PV... Yes, I know it's dangerous to bandy such jests about, but nobody is monitoring us tonight.... Zzz.... I think they're not, anyway...."

And so the ether bent and warped with their messages. And presently Friar Sparks tapped out the PV that ended their talk—the *"Pax vobiscum."* Then he pulled the plug out that connected his earphones to the set and, lifting them from his ears, clamped them down forward over his temples in the regulation manner.

After sidling bent-kneed from the *toldilla*, punishing his belly against the desk's hard edge as he did so, he walked over to the railing. De Salcedo and de Torres were leaning there and talking in low tones. The big bulb above gleamed on the page's red-gold hair and on the interpreter's full black beard. It also bounced pinkishly off the priest's smooth-shaven jowls and the light scarlet robe of the Rogerian order. His cowl, thrown back, served as a bag for scratch paper, pens, an ink bottle, tiny wrenches and screwdrivers, a book on cryptography, a slide rule, and a manual of angelic principles.

"Well, old rind," said young de Salcedo familiarly, "what do you hear from Las Palmas?"

"Nothing now. Too much interference from that." He pointed to the moon riding the horizon ahead of them. "What an orb!" bellowed the priest. "It's as big and red as my revered nose!"

The two sailors laughed, and de Salcedo said, "But it will get smaller and paler as the night grows, Father. And your proboscis will, on the contrary, become larger and more sparkling in inverse proportion according to the square of the ascent "

He stopped and grinned, for the monk had suddenly dipped his nose, like a porpoise diving into the sea, raised it again, like the same animal jumping from a wave, and then once more plunged it into the heavy currents of their breath. Nose to nose, he faced them, his twinkling little eyes seeming to emit sparks like the realizer in his *toldilla*.

Again, porpoiselike, he sniffed and snuffed several times, quite loudly. Then, satisfied with what he had gleaned from their breaths, he winked at them. He did not, however, mention his findings at once, preferring to sidle toward the subject.

He said, "This Father Sparks on the Grand Canary is so entertaining. He stimulates me with all sorts of philosophical notions, both valid and fantastic. For instance, tonight, just before we were cut off by that"—he gestured at the huge bloodshot eye in the sky—"he was discussing what he called worlds of parallel time tracks, an idea originated by Dysphagius of Gotham. It's his idea there may be other worlds in coincident but not contacting universes, that God, being infinite and of unlimited creative talent and ability, the Master Alchemist, in other words, has possibly—perhaps necessarily—created a plurality of continua in which every probable event has happened."

"Huh?" grunted de Salcedo.

"Exactly. Thus, Columbus was turned down by Queen Isabella, so this attempt to reach the Indies across the Atlantic was never made. So we would not now be standing here plunging ever deeper into Oceanus in our three cockleshells, there would be no booster buoys strung out between us and the Canaries, and Father Sparks at Las Palmas and I on the *Santa María* would not be carrying on our fascinating conversations across the ether.

"Or, say, Roger Bacon was persecuted by the Church, instead of being encouraged and giving rise to the order whose inventions have done so much to insure the monopoly of the church on alchemy and its divinely inspired guidance of that formerly pagan and hellish practice."

De Torres opened his mouth, but the priest silenced him with a magnificent and imperious gesture and continued.

"Or, even more ridiculous, but thought-provoking, he speculated just this evening on universes with different physical laws. One, in particular, I thought very droll. As you probably don't know, Angelo Angelei has proved, by dropping objects from the Leaning Tower of Pisa, that different weights fall at different speeds. My delightful colleague on the Grand Canary is writing a satire which takes place in a universe where Aristotle is made out to be a liar, where all things drop with equal velocities, no matter what their size. Silly stuff, but it helps to pass the time. We keep the ether busy with our little angels."

De Salcedo said, "Uh, I don't want to seem too curious about the secrets of your holy and cryptic order, Friar Sparks. But these little angels your machine realizes intrigue me. Is it a sin to presume to ask about them?"

The monk's bull roar slid to a dove cooing. "Whether it's a sin or not depends. Let me illustrate, young fellows. If you were concealing a bottle of, say, very scarce sherry on you, and you did not offer to share it with a very thirsty old gentleman, that would be a sin. A sin of omission. But if you were to give that desert-dry, that pilgrim-weary, that devout, humble, and decrepit old soul a long, soothing, refreshing, and stimulating draught of life-giving fluid, daughter of the vine, I would find it in my heart to pray for you for that deed of loving-kindness, of encompassing charity. And it would please me so much I might tell you a little of our realizer. Not enough to hurt you, just enough so you might gain more respect for the intelligence and glory of my order."

De Salcedo grinned conspiratorially and passed the monk the bottle he'd hidden under his jacket. As the friar tilted it, and the chug-chug-chug of vanishing sherry became louder, the two sailors glanced meaningfully at each other. No wonder the priest, reputed to be so brilliant in his branch of the alchemical mysteries, had yet been sent off on this half-baked voyage to devil-knew-where. The Church had calculated that if he survived, well and good. If he didn't, then he would sin no more.

The monk wiped his lips on his sleeve, belched loudly as a horse, and said, "*Gracias*, boys. From my heart, so deeply buried in this fat, I thank you. An old Irishman, dry as a camel's hoof, choking to death with the dust of abstinence, thanks you. You have saved my life."

"Thank rather that magic nose of yours," replied de Salcedo. "Now, old rind, now that you're well greased again, would you mind explaining as much as you are allowed about that machine of yours?"

Friar Sparks took fifteen minutes. At the end of that time, his listeners asked a few permitted questions.

"...and you say you broadcast on a frequency of eighteen hundred k.c.?" the page asked. "What does 'k.c.' mean?"

"K stands for the French *kilo*, from a Greek word meaning thousand. And *c* stands for the Hebrew *cherubim*, the 'little angels.' Angel comes from the Greek *angelos*, meaning messenger. It is our concept that the ether is crammed with these cherubim, these little messengers. Thus, when we Friar Sparkses depress the key of our machine, we are able to realize some of the infinity of 'messengers' waiting for just such a demand for service.

"So, eighteen hundred k.c. means that in a given unit of time one million, eight hundred thousand cherubim line up and hurl themselves across the ether, the nose of one being brushed by the feathertips of the cherub's wings ahead. The height of the wing crests of each little creature is even, so that if you were to draw an outline of the whole train, there would be nothing to distinguish one cherub from the next, the whole column forming that grade of little angels known as C.W."

"C.W.?"

"Continuous wingheight. My machine is a C.W. realizer."

Young de Salcedo said, "My mind reels. Such a concept! Such a revelation! It almost passes comprehension. Imagine, the aerial of your realizer is cut just so long, so that the evil cherubim surging back and forth on it demand a predetermined and equal number of good angels to combat them. And this seduction coil on the realizer crowds 'bad' angels into the left-hand, the sinister, side. And when the bad little cherubim are crowded so closely and numerously that they can't bear each other's evil company, they jump the spark gap and speed around the wire to the 'good' plate. And in this racing back and forth they call themselves to the attention of the 'little messengers,' the yea-saying cherubim. And you, Friar Sparks, by manipulating your machine thus and so, and by lifting and lowering your key, you bring these invisible and friendly lines of carriers, your etheric and winged postmen, into reality. And you are able, thus, to communicate at great distances with your brothers of the order."

"Great God!" said de Torres.

It was not a vain oath but a pious exclamation of wonder. His eyes bulged; it was evident that he suddenly saw that man was not alone, that on every side, piled on top of each other, flanked on every angle, stood a host. Black and white, they presented a solid chessboard of the seemingly empty cosmos, black for the nay-sayers, white for the yea-sayers, maintained by a Hand in delicate balance and subject as the fowls of the air and the fish of the sea to exploitation by man.

Yet de Torres, having seen such a vision as has made a saint of many a man, could only ask, "Perhaps you could tell me how many angels may stand on the point of a pin?"

Obviously, de Torres would never wear a halo. He was destined, if he lived, to cover his bony head with the mortar-board of a university teacher.

De Salcedo snorted. "I'll tell you. Philosophically speaking, you may put as many angels on a pinhead as you want to. Actually speaking, you may put only as many as there is room for. Enough of that. I'm interested in facts, not fancies. Tell me, how could the moon's rising interrupt your reception of the cherubim sent by the Sparks at Las Palmas?"

"Great Caesar, how would I know? Am I a repository of universal knowledge? No, not I! A humble and ignorant friar, I! All I can tell you is that last night it rose like a bloody tumor on the horizon, and that when it was up I had to quit marshaling my little messengers in their short and long columns. The Canary station was quite overpowered, so that both of us gave up. And the same thing happened tonight."

"The moon sends messages?" asked de Torres.

"Not in a code I can decipher. But it sends, yes."

"Santa María!"

"Perhaps," suggested de Salcedo, "there are people on that moon, and they are sending."

Friar Sparks blew derision through his nose. Enormous as were his nostrils, his derision was not small-bore. Artillery of contempt laid down a barrage that would have silenced any but the strongest of souls.

"Maybe—" de Torres spoke in a low tone— "maybe, if the stars are windows in heaven, as I've heard said, the angels of the higher hierarchy, the big ones, are realizing—uh—the smaller? And they only do it when the moon is up so we may know it is a celestial phenomenon?"

He crossed himself and looked around the vessel.

"You need not fear," said the monk gently. "There is no Inquisitor leaning over your shoulder. Remember, I am the only priest on this expedition. Moreover, your conjecture has nothing to do with dogma. However, that's unimportant. Here's what I don't understand: How can a heavenly body broadcast? Why does it have the same frequency as the one I'm restricted to? Why—"

"I could explain," interrupted de Salcedo with all the brashness and impatience of youth. "I could say that the Admiral and the Rogerians are wrong about the earth's shape. I could say the earth is not round but is flat. I could say the horizon exists, not because we live upon a globe, but because the earth is curved only a little ways, like a greatly flattened-out hemisphere. I could also say that the cherubim are coming, not from Luna, but from a ship such as ours, a vessel which is hanging in the void off the edge of the earth."

"What?" gasped the other two.

"Haven't you heard," said de Salcedo, "that the King of Portugal secretly sent out a ship after he turned down Columbus' proposal? How do we know he did not, that the messages are from our predecessor, that he sailed off the world's rim and is now suspended in the air and becomes exposed at night because it follows the moon around Terra—is, in fact, a much smaller and unseen satellite?"

The monk's laughter woke many men on the ship. "I'll have to tell the Las Palmas operator your tale. He can put it in that novel of his. Next you'll be telling me those messages are from one of those fire-shooting sausages so many credulous laymen have been seeing flying around. No, my dear de Salcedo, let's not be ridiculous. Even the ancient Greeks knew the earth was round. Every university in Europe teaches that. And we Rogerians have measured the circumference. We know for sure that the Indies lie just across the Atlantic. Just as we know for sure, through mathematics, that heavier-than-air machines are impossible. Our Friar Ripskulls, our mind doctors, have assured us these flying creations are mass hallucinations or else the tricks of heretics or Turks who want to panic the populace.

"That moon radio is no delusion, I'll grant you. What it is, I don't know. But it's not a Spanish or Portuguese ship. What about its different code? Even if it came from Lisbon, that ship would still have a Rogerian operator. And he would, according to our policy, be of a different nationality from the crew so he might the easier stay out of political embroilments. He wouldn't break our laws by using a different code in order to communicate with Lisbon. We disciples of Saint Roger do not stoop to petty boundary intrigues. Moreover, that realizer would not be powerful enough to reach Europe, and must, therefore, be directed at us."

"How can you be sure?" said de Salcedo. "Distressing though the thought may be to you, a priest could be subverted. Or a layman could learn your secrets and invent a code. I think that a Portuguese ship is sending to another, a ship perhaps not too distant from us."

De Torres shivered and crossed himself again. "Perhaps the angels are warning us of approaching death? Perhaps?"

"Perhaps? Then why don't they use our code? Angels would know it as well as I. No, there is no perhaps. The order does not permit perhaps. It experiments and finds out; nor does it pass judgment until it knows."

"I doubt we'll ever know," said de Salcedo gloomily. "Columbus has promised the crew that if we come across no sign of land by evening tomorrow, we shall turn back. Otherwise—" he drew a finger across his throat—"*kkk!* Another day, and we'll be pointed east and getting away from that evil and bloody-looking moon and its incomprehensible messages."

"It would be a great loss to the order and to the Church," sighed the friar. "But I leave such things in the hands of God and inspect only what He hands me to look at."

With which pious statement Friar Sparks lifted the bottle to ascertain the liquid level. Having determined in a scientific manner its existence, he next measured its quantity and tested its quality by putting all of it in that best of all chemistry tubes, his enormous belly.

Afterward, smacking his lips and ignoring the pained and disappointed looks on the faces of the sailors, he went on to speak enthusiastically of the water screw and the engine which turned it, both of which had been built recently at the St. Jonas College at Genoa. If Isabella's three ships had been equipped with those, he declared, they would not have to depend upon the wind. However, so far, the fathers had forbidden its extended use because it was feared the engine's fumes might poison the air and the terrible speeds it made possible might be fatal to the human body. After which he plunged into a tedious description of the life of his patron saint, the inventor of the first cherubim realizer and receiver, Jonas of Carcassonne, who had been martyred when he grabbed a wire he thought was insulated.

The two sailors found excuses to walk off. The monk was a good fellow, but hagiography bored them. Besides, they wanted to talk of women....

If Columbus had not succeeded in persuading his crews to sail one more day, events would have been different.

At dawn the sailors were very much cheered by the sight of several large birds circling their ships. Land could not be far off; perhaps these winged creatures came from the coast of fabled Cipangu itself, the country whose houses were roofed with gold.

The birds swooped down. Closer, they were enormous and very strange. Their bodies were flattish and almost saucer-shaped and small in proportion to the wings, which had a spread of at least thirty feet. Nor did they have legs. Only a few sailors saw the significance of that fact. These birds dwelt in the air and never rested upon land or sea.

While they were meditating upon that, they heard a slight sound as of a man clearing his throat. So gentle and far off was the noise that nobody paid any attention to it, for each thought his neighbor had made it.

A few minutes later, the sound had become louder and deeper, like a lute string being twanged.

Everybody looked up. Heads were turned west.

Even yet they did not understand that the noise like a finger plucking a wire came from the line that held the earth together, and that the line was stretched to its utmost, and that the violent finger of the sea was what had plucked the line.

It was some time before they understood. They had run out of horizon.

When they saw that, they were too late.

The dawn had not only come up *like* thunder, it *was* thunder. And though the three ships heeled over at once and tried to sail close-hauled on the port tack, the suddenly speeded-up and relentless current made beating hopeless.

Then it was the Rogerian wished for the Genoese screw and the wood-burning engine that would have made them able to resist the terrible muscles of the charging and bull-like sea. Then it was that some men prayed, some raved, some tried to attack the Admiral, some jumped overboard, and some sank into a stupor.

Only the fearless Columbus and the courageous Friar Sparks stuck to their duties. All that day the fat monk crouched wedged in his little shanty, dot-dashing to his fellow on the Grand Canary. He ceased only when the moon rose like a huge red bubble from the throat of a dying giant. Then he listened intently all night and worked desperately, scribbling and swearing impiously and checking cipher books.

When the dawn came up again in a roar and a rush, he ran from the *toldilla*, a piece of paper clutched in his hand. His eyes were wild, and his lips were moving fast, but nobody could understand that he had cracked the code. They could not hear him shouting, "It is the Portuguese! It is the Portuguese!"

Their ears were too overwhelmed to hear a mere human voice. The throat clearing and the twanging of the string had been the noises preliminary to the concert itself. Now came the mighty overture; as compelling as the blast of Gabriel's horn was the topple of Oceanus into space.

THE SCIENCE IN SCIENCE FICTION

Science fiction always has been a misnomer for a genre that includes stories with no shred of science and excludes others that may be all about science. But no other term is anywhere near as good. Some early writers used the term "pseudo-scientific" fiction, even in Wells's time ("imbecile adjective," he called it), some have used "future fiction," newspapers and films use the term despised in science fiction circles, "sci-fi," and some recent writers have revived Heinlein's 1947 suggestion, "speculative fiction."

Hugo Gernsback had his reasons for inventing the terms "scientifiction" and then "science fiction." He was convinced, in theory at least, that science was not only essential to the stories he wanted to print but that the purpose of the genre was to impart scientific information or an enthusiasm for science, or both. Moreover, in the 1920s "science" stood for everything that was new and different.

Some science fiction stories, nevertheless, justify their name. They are called "hard-science" stories to distinguish them from the rest, and for some readers they lie at the heart of the genre. Tom Godwin's "The Cold Equations" (included in this collection) has been called a touchstone story even though its science is minimal; Godwin assumes a future that includes interstellar travel, extraplanetary exploration, and emergency delivery ships, but the story contains little actual justification of its presumed environment. What description there is seems a bit misleading (the size of the EDS cabin and its airlock, for instance, essential as they may be to the plot). "The Cold Equations" is a touchstone story for its philosophy, not for its science.

But hard science has been a part of science fiction from its beginnings. Jules Verne was a hard-science writer, even if the science served only as a starting point for a journey. Wells, on the other hand, cared for credibility but not for scientific probability. In the true hard-science story, the science is accurate and central; the story could not exist if it were not for the science. Arthur C. Clarke is a hard-science writer in one of his modes, as are Poul Anderson and Larry Niven when they choose to be, but the prototype for the hard-science writer is Hal Clement.

Clement (1922-) whose real name is Harry Clement Stubbs, comes by his position naturally. He earned a B.S. degree in astronomy in 1943 and, after piloting a B-24 in World War II, an M.Ed. at Boston University in 1947. He has since acquired an M.S. in chemistry. He taught high-school science and mathematics for many years at Milton Academy in Massachusetts, and he has been a part-time writer of science fiction since he was a sophomore in college. "Proof" appeared in *Astounding* in 1942, and he has sold most of his fiction to

Astounding/Analog ever since.

Most of his short stories are built around an aspect of physical science, such as the fact that a satellite in free fall can't be sabotaged by fire because in the absence of gravity convection currents won't operate and combustion products would build up around the flame to smother it ("Fireproof," *Astounding*, 1949). His longer works allow him to construct worlds in which radically different environments create different attitudes in and different problems for their natives, or for visitors to alien planets (including Earth).

Clement's first novel was *Needle*. Serialized in *Astounding* in 1949 (book form, 1950), it concerned an interstellar detective who is a quasi-viral symbiote; it must co-exist with a boy in order to find a criminal hiding on Earth. *Iceworld*, which describes how Earth would appear to an interstellar narcotics agent who has evolved on a much hotter planet, was serialized in 1951 (book form, 1953).

Mission of Gravity (1954), serialized in 1953, was the first of Clement's alien-planet novels in which he constructed an imaginary planet and then fashioned a story to take place on it. "I still get the greatest fun," he wrote in *The Craft of Science Fiction* (1976), "out of making up solar systems and planets and working out the chemical, physical, meteorological, biological and other details which may later provide a story background."

The novel tells the story of Mesklin, a planet with 700 times Earth's gravity at the poles and, because of its rapid spin, only two or three times Earth's gravity at the equator. Earth explorers, whose experimental rocket probe has crashed at one pole, play only a minor role; the important characters are the centipedelike Mesklinites, who have evolved under high gravity and must unlearn at the equator the attitudes their environment has instilled in them.

Mission of Gravity is a touchstone novel; if readers don't like it they probably won't like hard-core science fiction. It is pure science fiction because it could be told only as *science* fiction, and it does what the best science fiction tries to do: it makes readers question their own assumptions about what is choice and what is conditioning, about the effects on them of their own environment. Other Clement novels include *Cycle of Fire* (1957), *Close to Critical* (1958), and *Star Light* (1971).

Hard science does not preclude speculation, even the wildest kind, as some recent ideas of astrophysicists demonstrate. "Critical Factor" (*Star Science Fiction Stories No 2*, 1953) is such a speculation. If intelligent beings could exist in the Earth, as liquid, rock-eating creatures, how could they discover the nature of the surface world, and what might they be tempted to do about it?

CRITICAL FACTOR

by Hal Clement

Pentong, excited for the first time in his life, raced northward. There was no need to grope or feel his way; this close to the great earthquake zone there were always minor tremors, and their echoes from the dense basalt below and the emptiness above reached him almost constantly. The treacherous sandstone strata, which beguiled the lazy traveler with the ease of penetration they offered and then led him up to the zones of death, were easy to spot; Pentong actually used them now, for seeing was so good that he could leave them with plenty of time to seek the safer levels below whenever they started to slope.

The worst of his journey was behind. The narrow bridge of livable rock which led to the strange land he had found had been recrossed in safety, in spite of the terrifying and deceptive manner in which temblors from the earthquake zone far to the north were trapped, magnified, and echoed from its sides. Now he could see for many days' travel all about him, and as far as he could see the land was good.

Not as good as that he had visited, of course. This was the land he had known all his life, where food was just hard enough to find to make life interesting; where for ages past counting other, less fortunate, races from the far, far north had sought to break in and kill that they might inherit its plenty; where pools of magma shifted just rapidly enough to trap the unwary between impenetrable basalt and glowing death; where, if Pentong was right in what he believed of his discovery, regions now too close to the zones of death might be made accessible and provide food and living space for unguessable generations to come.

He dreamt of this possibility constantly as he moved. No trace of his passage marked the rock behind him, for none of it was edible; but he hardly thought of food for himself. Speed was his prime concern, and to achieve it he traveled as close as he dared to the upper zones.

The nearest settlement was more than five thousand miles north, he knew; his memory held a sharp picture of the tortuous path he had followed from it, and he retraced that path now. It led him far to the east, where the earth tremors were faint and travel slowed by the poor vision; then back, at a much lower level, to the northwest, where the principal delay was the denser rock. Five hundred miles short of his goal he had to stop, to examine carefully the region of magma pools through which he had passed on his way south. The precise path he had followed could not now be used; it was blocked in several places by molten rock which had forced its way between strata and heated the otherwise habitable stone above and below to an unbearable degree. But other paths existed; and slowly and carefully Pentong wormed his way between the pools, sometimes retreating the way he had come, sometimes going almost straight away from his goal, but gradually working north and downward until the last of the dangerous pockets of fluid lay behind him. Then he could hasten once more; and at last he reached the bed of carbonate rock, a mile thick and more than thirty thousand square miles in area, which had been deposited on the floor of an ancient sea some hundreds of millions of years before and was now safely surrounded and capped by harder layers which shielded its inhabitants from filtering oxygen. This was the city—not the one where Pentong had been born, but the farthest south of all the dwelling centers of his people, and the one to which the more adventurous spirits of the race tended to gravitate. The cities to the northwest and northeast, under the Bering and Icelandic bridges, held danger, of course; they bore the brunt of the endless defense against the savage tribes from beyond the bridges. Still, that danger was known and almost routine; it was the unknown parts of the world that spelled adventure. Pentong, he was sure, had proved himself the most adventurous so far; and he was also sure that he had done more.

"Halt!" The challenge came through the rock as Pentong's great, liquid body began to filter into the limestone. No city, even this far from the zones of war, dared be without sentries. "Name yourself!"

"I am Pentong, returning from the south, a trip that was commanded. My word is this." He emitted the coded series of temblors which the City Leaders had given him for identification, when and if he returned.

"Wait." The explorer knew that the sentry's body extended far back into the city, and that at his other end he was in communication with the Leaders. The wait was not long. "Enter. You may eat, if you hunger, but go to the Leaders as soon thereafter as may be."

"I am hungry, but I must go to them at once. I have found something of importance, and they must know." The sentry was plainly curious, but forebore to question further; obviously if this stranger felt his news too important to wait for food, he would hardly pause for conversation.

"Take the Stratum of Manganese; it will be cleared for you," was all the watcher said. Pentong acknowledged the courtesy—traffic was sometimes a problem in a city of sixty billion inhabitants, each of whom averaged ten cubic yards in volume and was apt to have that bulk spread through a most irregular outline. The Stratum of Manganese was a foot-thick layer stained with the oxide of that metal, and thereby marked plainly to Pentong's senses. It was cut off sharply by a fault which extended across the center of the city in a northeast-southwest direction; and at one point along that fault was a large volume where numerous boulders of quartz, probably washed to this spot by some ancient river, were imbedded in the limestone. Here the Leaders, or enough of them to transact business, could always be found. Pentong greeted them, received the acknowledgment, and began his report without preamble.

"About five thousand miles to the south," he said, "the continental mass in which this city is located narrows apparently to a point. The earthquake zone extends to this point, and seeing is good; but echoes tend to be confusing in some regions, and I explored many of these by touch. In one such area I found a long tongue of sandstone extending yet farther south; and after debating whether I should return to report its existence before venturing out along it, I decided it would be better to have something more complete to report. It was almost like traveling through a stratum which has been cut off on opposite sides by parallel dikes; but the sides this time were simply emptiness. There was no zone of death, however; apparently the tongue of rock is surrounded by what Derrell the Thinker called *ocean*, which seems to protect the upper regions of portions of the continents. Below, of course, was basalt.

"The neck of rock went on, seemingly without end. Sometimes it widened, sometimes narrowed so that I thought it had come to an end; but it always went on. Those who claim the continents are drifting will have to explain how that narrow ridge of stone has stayed intact.

"At last, however, it really widened; and to make short a report whose data was long in compiling, there is a continent at the other end—and I could find no trace of other than lower animals in that continent. That, however, is not its most important feature; what is really striking is the fact that it appears to have no Zone of Death whatever. It is covered with a solid material, which seems to be crystalline from the way it carries sound, but which is impenetrable to living bodies. The continent is inhabitable from top to bottom."

"How about edible rock?"

"As good or better than our own land." The Leaders reacted audibly to this, and it was some time before speech was again directed at the explorer. Then, as he had expected, it was complimentary.

"Pentong, you deserve the thanks of every inhabitant of this continent. If your report is as accurate as it seems to be objective, our food problem is solved for generations to come. We will transmit this news to the other cities, and plans for colonizing the new continent will be worked out as rapidly as may be. Your name will be known from here to the Northern Frontier."

For a moment the explorer basked in the praise that was the deepest need of his kind; then he spoke again, with a delicious thrill of anticipation.

"Leaders, there is yet more, if I may speak." Cracklings of surprise spread from the boulder-shot area, and the nearer citizens paused in their activities to learn what went on.

"Speak."

"I was curious as to the nature of this solid which seemed as impenetrable as basalt, and strove to learn more about it. For a long time I made no progress; but at last I came to an earthquake zone, in which magma had risen very near the upper levels. About this point the strange substance was thinner; and while investigating the neighborhood, a pocket of magma broke through the Outer Void. This I could tell, partly because of the good seeing, and partly because I could feel the heat working down from the thin layers above." He paused.

"This has occurred before," commented one of the Leaders. "What did it teach you?"

"Where the magma spread, the solid disappeared—*and became like the ocean!*" Pentong stopped again, for purely rhetorical reasons—he knew there would be no interruption this time.

"As you all remember, Derrell the Thinker showed that *ocean* was a substance, apparently liquid like magma; he studied its sound-transmitting properties, and described them well. I heard his lecture, and examined the substance myself on several occasions. This crystalline sheath of the Southern continent is simply solid ocean; it melted just as rock does when the magma reached it." Again the pause, and this time the Leaders conferred briefly.

"Your point is of extreme scientific interest," their spokesman finally said, "but we admit we do not see practical importance for it as yet. We gather from your manner that you do; if you would go on—" he left the sentence unfinished.

"My point is simple. Ocean protects rock from the oxygen, which filters down from the Void and kills those exposed to it—sometimes even renders rock poisonous. Much of our continent is protected by ocean, but much is not, and its upper layers are therefore unattainable. This solid ocean melts very easily, as I could see on the Southern Continent; and the continent seems to be covered with it to a depth of more than a mile, on the average. It may seem an ambitious project, but if that continent were to be heated enough to melt its ocean covering, would not it add to the ocean over the rest of the world and thus *cover more of our continent?*"

For long moments no answer came; Pentong could not tell whether the leaders were actually considering the problem objectively or reacting emotionally to his admittedly audacious suggestion. The first response was in the form of a question.

"Just why should this material blanket the continents instead of remaining more or less where it is? You seem to be taking a good deal for granted."

"I realize that the behavior of liquids such as magma and ocean out in the

Void is not generally known," responded Pentong. "However, there exists a good deal of observation which strongly suggests that magma, at least, tends to spread out over the surface of the Earth when released to the Void. I admit that further observation would be needed to prove that ocean does the same—but is it not already doing just that? It seems reasonable to suppose that the liquid ocean has spread as far as its quantity permits; if we add more, it should spread farther. Let us at least check this point; I can show the way, or for that matter describe it, to the Southern Continent, and the necessary experiments could be conducted by a small group."

The news of the Pentong project took some time to reach Derrell the Thinker. There were several reasons for this; for one, he was located thousands of miles from the city under the Gulf of Mexico where Pentong had made his report, and for another he was in the midst of a battlefield. The latter fact was not at once evident; the only sights and sounds—the two were identical to Derrell, whose only long-range sense reacted to shock waves in the earth's crust— were those emitted from the earthquake belt to the south and west. He himself was focusing his entire attention on a matter unconnected with the battle; but at least half of his research crew had their fluid bodies extended and joined into a single net that surrounded the entire area of the experiment. It was hoped that none of the savages from the Asian mainland would get through the net without touching one of its strands and betraying their presence.

The thing that interested Derrell was a cave, something almost unheard of in the depths where his people dwelt. Virtually all the empty spaces, which his people regarded as extensions of the Outer Void, were very close to that void; and they were almost without exception filled with the oxygen which poisoned the rocks for the dwellers of the depths. Occasional bubbles occurred in the igneous rocks, of course, filled with gases which had come from the rocks themselves; but as a rule these were unapproachable—the material in which they occurred was nearly impenetrable to the members of Derrell's race, who traveled through rock rather as ink does through a blotter.

The present cave was one of the few exceptions to this rule. The rock itself was not porous enough for travel, but seismic strains had produced a network of microscopic cracks part way into the mass which permitted slow progress, if the traveler had persistence.

Derrell had seen caves before from a distance, but the thing he was watching now had never occurred within his memory or knowledge. The upper level of the bubble was just at the top of the igneous layer in which it had formed; the rock above was sedimentary. Between the two layers a thin sill was gradually making its way from a pod of magma a few miles distant—a pool that was being fed by energy from sources far below, and outside the bounds even of Derrell's knowledge. It was more than likely that someday this sill might grow to the proportions of a laccolith, in view of the nature of the rock above; but this was not the scientist's concern at the moment. The advancing magma was approaching the bubble, and he wanted to see what effect the trapped, high-pressure gas in the "empty" space would have on the molten rock. It was fortunate that this was occurring just here; the endless, tiny seismic shocks from the southwest made things clearly visible throughout the region. It would have been extremely dangerous, with the Asian savages filtering through the neighboring strata, if the investigators had had to produce sounds of their own in order to further their research.

Derrell had a mental picture of what would occur when the molten rock reached the bubble, but like any good scientist he was not allowing it to influence his observing technique. He intended to see everything that happened; and his attention was so completely centered on that particular volume of rock that the arrival of one of his assistants, who had been on a short leave to the nearest of the frontier cities, failed to distract him in the slightest. The assistant himself forbore to interrupt, though he had news that he knew would be of interest; for the magma was very close now to the bubble. Like the chief scientist, the newcomer had a mental picture of the hot fluids simply reaching the cavity, flowing around its walls, and gradually filling it from edge to center. Like Derrell, his idea of the general nature of gases was too sketchy to permit him to realize that, at the very least, the vapor in the bubble must dissolve in the inflowing rock before his picture could be carried through; and like his chief, he had no conception whatever of another force that would also operate. No living member of their race had ever had a good look at a fluid that was not in a confined space; they had never seen a free liquid surface. Their experience was about to be enlarged.

There would be no point in guessing who was the most surprised by what actually happened, but there was no doubt about which of the observers adjusted himself first. Derrell was paralyzed for just an instant as the first drops of fluid reached the opening of the cavity—*and shot straight across it to the other side!*—but he noted carefully and precisely how more of the magma followed. The drops became a stream, and gradually a pool of the stuff came into being against the side of the bubble opposite the opening. The sides of the pool not in contact with the walls of the cavity seemed to want to form a plane surface, but the stream that was adding to its volume gave rise to disturbances which spread from the point of impact in all directions *over the surface*—waves which none of the watchers had ever seen or imagined, and which held even the sentries' attention to a degree which might have proven disastrous. Not until the bubble had filled completely with molten rock did anyone move, speak, or even think of anything but what was happening a few hundred yards away; and even then most of the team waited for Derrell to express an opinion. He, regarding his assistants as students to be guided by suggestion rather than laymen who might be impressed by spot conclusions, opened his comments with a question.

"Could the ordinary pressure on that liquid account for its behavior?"

"Not completely." The answer came promptly from one of the team.

"Why not? Pressure can force liquid between rock layers, and even into rock pores; why could it not send a stream across a space where there is no resistance?"

"It could, I suppose; but I fail to see how ordinary rock pressure could keep one side of that growing pool flat when the rock was not actually touching it. That would seem to call for some invisible substance pressing on that particular surface—a substance not only invisible, but able to permit the stream of rock to pass toward the new pool but not away from it. I find such a substance hard to imagine."

"So do I. Your objection to rock pressure also seems valid—unless someone else can see a way?" He paused for a fair interval, but if any of the assistants had ideas they were not sufficiently formulated for expression. "It would seem, then, that some force with which we are unfamiliar is involved. That means that all the data anyone may have is possibly relevant. Karpor, list the material you have observed which you think might help."

The student responded at once.

"The igneous rock is largely silicates of magnesium, the stratiform layer next to it mostly calcium carbonate. The bubble is about fifteen feet in diameter, one side almost exactly tangent to the stratiform boundary. The boundary itself is parallel to the Void boundary a mile and a half away. The front edge of the sill was advancing at about six inches an hour, and the sill itself had a thickness of about—"

"All right; good so far. Taless, what else?" Another student took up the list; and the recent arrival forgot his news temporarily in the intensity of the resulting discussion. By the time he remembered it, a hypothesis had been developed.

"It seems possible," Derrell summed the idea up, "that a force of unknown nature exists, which tends to drive liquids (at least) as far from the Void as they are free to travel. Our single observation is to that effect, anyway. It would seem desirable to find other, more accessible hollows in the deeper rocks, to determine how far from the Void boundary this force extends, and to learn if possible whether other things than liquids are affected."

"I wonder what the existence of such a force—if it does exist—will do to the Pentong project," remarked the newcomer, recalling his news suddenly.

"What is that? Another defense plan?"

"Not exactly." The scientist described Pentong's discovery of the Antarctic Continent, and his account of its covering of solid ocean. "His plan to melt this substance, and thus protect more of the world's rock from the oxygen of the Void, has been favorably received by more than half the City leaders of the continent, and parties are already under way to examine the Southern Continent more completely," he concluded. A student cut in instantly.

"But if this force exists, and ocean is subject to it as magma is, won't the freshly melted ocean simply spread flat over what is already there, and perhaps hardly protect any more land at all?"

"That seems probable," replied Derrell. "Since such a project will involve a vast expenditure of effort, and very possibly interfere with defense on the frontiers, it now becomes imperative that we check the nature and existence of this force as quickly as possible."

"However, if the available ocean surface is not too large," put in another, "even spreading the new ocean over all of it might permit a considerable increase in the protected areas."

"It might; but unless and until we have some idea of the size of the World inside the Void, and how much of the World is covered by ocean, we cannot afford to take a chance on that possibility. We must search for more bubbles; and this carbonate stratum is in contact with igneous rock over many thousands of square miles, it would seem. Break up into parties of three and start exploring; if you encounter savages, call—there are military personnel not too far behind us. This is important." He turned back to the assistant who had brought the news. "I suppose they plan to do the melting by coaxing magma pools toward the Void boundary, and letting them flow out into contact with this solid ocean."

"That is the general idea. However, they plan to do it not only on the Southern Continent. It was felt that there might be much of this solid ocean on our own continent, which we had never discovered because we cannot venture near enough to the Void boundary; so every pool we can reach is to be brought into use. The places where light rocks project into the Void probably cannot be reached, but it seems to the planners who investigated the data that all the other regions—more than three quarters of the continent—can easily be coated with melted rock, if it clings to the surface reasonably well."

Derrell glanced back at the bubble. "It should do that, all right," he said, "if our force applies out in the Void as well as in the rock next to it. But that means an even more vast expenditure of effort than I had supposed; they'll be pulling the defenders away from the frontiers until the savages from Asia are fighting the ones from Europe—around our dead bodies. Let's find those bubbles." He joined one of the search teams, worried more about the possible waste of work on an inefficient and probably unproductive effort than about the results of covering most of the American continents with lava. After all, he had never heard of the human race, and probably never would.

There was probably not another spot on the North American continent where his team could have found what they sought so quickly; if other regions existed where a lava flow had extended into a shallow sea, hardened, been buried with such speed under calcareous detritus, and then carried down rapidly enough and steadily enough to develop a thick limestone cap over the hardened lava, they had either been lifted back to the surface where they were unapproachable to Derrell's kind or carried so far down as to be altered completely beyond recognition. Here, however, there were cavities; many of them filled by the limy material that had settled into them and hardened into rock and many just too deep in impenetrable regions of the lava to be attained although they were easily visible, but a fair number both empty and attainable. The water that had once filled them had long since gone into hydrates in the overlying rock, and been replaced by gases from the lava—usually oxides of carbon and sometimes even sulfur. These did not bother the investigators, and it was not long before one of the search teams reported an ideal site for investigation. The group congregated at the spot as quickly as possible, and plans were rapidly made.

There was no magma pool near enough to be "tickled" into action this time; but that did not bother Derrell. He had already seen what molten rock would do in this situation. He rapidly gave orders, and the group of liquid bodies gathered in the limestone just above the bubble and began to eat. The eating was done in a very careful manner; and gradually a large fragment of limestone was separated from the rest of the formation. It was located directly above the bubble, and when freed from its original matrix rested on the thin silicate layer that formed the roof of the cavity. That layer was seamed with cracks, microscopic in size, but adequate to the needs of the scientists; their fluid bodies worked inside those cracks, loosening particle after particle, gradually weakening the flimsy roof. The actual force that any one of the beings could exert was minute, lifting a grain of sand would have been impossible for one of the big, but fluid, bodies; but bit by bit the lava moved, as it was dissolved along the tiny zones of weakness the brief exposure to the sea had left. Toward the end the workers very carefully stayed away from the thin layer, extending only narrow pseudopods to do the remainder of the job. Most of them, in fact, withdrew even farther in order to observe, and two of the assistants completed the final task. Derrell was ready when the lava roof suddenly collapsed, permitting the great block of limestone they had previously freed to drop into the cavern.

No one was very surprised. It behaved, within its limitations, as the magma had done, hurtling against the wall farthest from the Void, and sending a few fragments of its mass flying off at angles. The fragments also returned to that part of the vast cavity farthest from the broken roof. The force evidently existed; and it appeared to work on solids as well as liquids. Bits of the lava roof had also obeyed the invisible urge; and as far as anyone could tell, not a single fragment that was free to move away from the Void had failed to do so.

Without a word, Derrell flowed through the limestone to a point just above the opening. Here he pulled himself into the smallest possible volume, and deliberately began to dissolve the rock about him. He had tried to get to the portion of the bubble where the rocks had come to rest, and found it impossible; the tiny cracks that would have furnished access extended only a foot or two from the surface of the lava. Now he was going to get there—and incidentally, see what effect the new force had on living matter. He learned!

The rock in which he lay broke free as its predecessor had done; and Derrell became the first member of his race to experience the acceleration of gravity. He also was the first to discover that the most noticeable thing about a fall is the sudden stop. The shock did not hurt him—after all, he was accustomed to traveling in regions of seismic strain, and seeing by the resultant shock waves—but the whole thing was slightly surprising. For one thing, the rock had turned over as it fell, and no member of his race had *ever* had a sudden change of orientation with respect to his surroundings. It took several seconds for him to realize that it was he who had moved, not the surrounding universe.

Once convinced of that, he started to emerge from the rock which he had ridden; and in doing so he learned the most painful lesson of all about gravity.

Derrell's body was liquid. It was less dense than water, being composed mainly of hydrocarbons; it had no more rigidity than water. All its support was normally furnished by the rock in which it happened to be "soaked" at the moment; he moved by controlling the liquid's surface tension, as an amoeba moves—or, for that matter, as a man moves a muscle. Outside the supporting rock, however, he was just a puddle of oil—and once he started out, he was completely unable to stop. The block of limestone he had ridden was not quite at the bottom of the huge cavity; as a portion of his mass emerged, it tended to flow downhill toward the lowest available point; he had the choice of following it or being torn apart, and he liked the latter alternative no better than a more solid organism would. He followed. Five seconds later he was a completely helpless pool of living liquid, in the bottom of a bowl of glassy, impenetrable lava. He could not even raise a ripple on his own surface.

He could still communicate—that lava carried sound perfectly. However, he did not do so intelligently; all his students heard was a series of endlessly repeated warnings to keep clear of empty spaces—to avoid all dealings with the Force—to leave this neighborhood and to let him die, but be sure to carry the warning to the rest of the world—in short, little but hysteria. Had Derrell not been so upset, he would have seen the way out in a moment; but he can hardly be blamed for being perturbed. A man suddenly finding himself imbedded completely in a block of concrete, yet somehow still living and breathing and able to speak, might have had some inkling of the scientist's emotions; but at least a man could vaguely imagine such a situation in advance. No member of

Derrell's race could have foreseen any detail of what had happened to him.

Fortunately, the students for the most part remained calm; and it was one of these who saw the solution. Derrell was restored to something like a state of reason when tiny pebbles of limestone began to fall near, and sometimes into his body. It was a long, long, job; but at last the dwellers of the rock completed the task which the ocean had failed to perform a hundred million years before, and the cavern was full of limestone. Even now travel was not easy—the space between particles was too large, and Derrell had acquired a strong antipathy to open spaces; but travel was at least possible, and at long last he found himself once more in habitable, negotiable, comfortable rock outside that terrible cavern. For a long time he rested; and when finally he spoke, it was with conviction.

"Whatever we may learn of that force in the future, certainly no one can ever doubt its reality. I hope none of you ever feel it. Those of you who were over that cave releasing rocks that enabled me to escape were taking a chance worse than that ever faced by soldier or explorer; believe me when I say I am grateful.

"One point we have learned, besides the mere existence of the force: it is not always perpendicular to the Void boundary." A faint flicker of surprise manifested itself among the listeners, but stilled at once as they perceived that the scientist was right—the boundary was extremely irregular where it passed nearest this region; projections of rock reached out into the Void at frequent intervals sometimes for more than a mile. There was no single direction that could be said to be perpendicular to it.

"That leaves two principal possibilities. One is that the force is directed at least somewhat at random, and the ocean has collected in specific localities because of that fact. If that is so, then the Pentong project is useless; the new ocean will simply add to the old, and cover no more Earth. The other main possibility would seem to be that the force does not extend into the Void at all; and in that case we have no idea at all what will happen, except that the magma we bring up will probably spread over the boundary as it always has. We cannot even guess what the melted ocean will do.

"It seems to me a very ill-advised plan, to divert as much effort as this project would demand from our defense, when we cannot even be moderately sure of success. I think I will go to the nearest city to express my opinion—there is still too much risk from the tribes of Asia to take any chances. Has anyone a different opinion, or a better plan?"

"One thing might be done first." It was Taless, one of most self-confident of the group. "It seems almost as bad to halt the project for ignorance as to waste effort from the same cause. I would strongly recommend that we learn something about the force beyond the boundary before we express opinions to any City Leaders. At the most, let us advise delaying, not canceling, the project until some data on that matter can be obtained."

"And how would you secure this data?"

"I do not know; but we have a team of presumably competent researchers here. I certainly would not regard such investigation as hopeless, without at least some effort being made."

"The data would have to be extremely precise, and sufficient in amount to be completely convincing; the matter is vitally important for the future of our people everywhere."

"I realize that. What is new about requiring precision in measurement?"

Derrell pondered briefly. "You are right, of course," he finally said. "We will advise *postponing* the Pentong project. Two of you can carry that message to the city. The rest of us will start devising ways to learn whether or not melted ocean will spread over the surface of Earth. If we find that it does, we coat the American continents with lava; if not, the magma pockets can stay where they are. Suggestions for experimental techniques are now in order."

WHY NOT LITERATURE?

The Magazine of Fantasy and Science Fiction was created in 1949 under the co-editorship of J. Francis McComas and Anthony Boucher (whose real name was William Anthony Parker White but who was known to everybody as Tony). The division of labors in the editing has never been revealed, but Boucher wrote the letters and set the tone.

The tone of *F&SF*, as it became known, was literary. Judith Merril called Boucher "a man of enormous erudition, catholic interests, discriminating tastes, overweening curiosity, and rich humor." He was already well known as an author and critic of mystery fiction. In *F&SF* he wanted stories in which the quality of the writing was the critical consideration.

The act of combining fantasy and science fiction in one title was itself revealing: fantasy, unfettered by reality, could emphasize style, mood, and character, and thus was closer to traditional literature. It also was an act of daring: science fiction readers were supposed to be purists—if readers happened to enjoy both science fiction and fantasy, they wanted them packaged separately; they certainly didn't want them mixed without regard for distinctions. Such an action seemed like heresy at the time—abhorrent to Campbell and a bit later to Gold—but it suited Boucher's studied disregard for generic considerations.

Boucher's efforts went into breaking down the barriers that had arisen between genres and around the field as a whole. He printed stories in *F&SF* that he found in the works of Defoe, Dickens, London, Stevenson, Wodehouse, Saki, Priestley, Forrester, Forster, Collier, Fast, and others. He reprinted stories from the literary magazines. He wrote headnotes linking the stories to the rest of literature. He printed backcover ads featuring mainstream figures such as Clifton Fadiman and Basil Davenport recommending *F&SF* to non-genre readers.

F&SF attracted a new audience. Some readers crossed over to *Astounding* and *Galaxy*, but in general each magazine had a readership of its own. *F&SF*'s audience was smaller but just as loyal.

F&SF also attracted new writers. Each new magazine of substance that offered a different editorial policy seemed to draw new writers out of their hiding places, as if they had been waiting for a signal to awake. Writers such as Kris Neville, H. Nearing, Jr., Richard Matheson, Arthur Porges, Mildred Clingerman, Reginald Bretnor, Zenna Henderson, and others began to contribute stories for the first time when *F&SF* appeared. The magazine also attracted new kinds of stories from already established writers.

One of them was Alfred Bester (1913-1987). Bester had written science fiction since 1939, when his story "The Broken Axiom" won a $50 contest offered by *Thrilling Wonder Stories*. He worked closely with editor Mort Weisinger, and when Weisinger went to *Superman Comics* Bester went along. From writing comic scenarios he moved to radio scripts and then to television. Eventually he became a regular contributor of interviews and then senior editor of *Holiday* magazine.

In the meantime he continued to write an occasional science fiction story, particularly in the early 1950s when Horace Gold persuaded him to contribute to *Galaxy*. After lengthy telephone discussions with Gold, Bester came up with a idea about a murderer in a telepathic society that developed into *The Demolished Man* (1953; serialized 1952). Its concern for character, its style, and its pyrotechnical tricks made it an instant success. Four years later he produced *The Stars My Destination* (1956), which was titled *Tiger! Tiger!* in Great Britain. It was Bester's science fiction rendering of the Count of Monte Cristo in a society based on teleportation; some critics prefer it to *The Demolished Man*.

Bester's science fiction reputation is based on these two novels, but between their appearance and afterward he wrote a series of glittering short pieces for *F&SF*. They differed from the tightly plotted novels he had written for *Galaxy* in their greater concentration on theme and style. They included "5,271,009" (1954), "Hobson's Choice" (1952), "The Man Who Murdered Mohammed" (1958), "The Pi Man" (1959), "Star Light, Star Bright" (1953), "They Don't Make Life Like They Used To" (1963), and "Fondly Fahrenheit" (August 1954).

The best of Bester's stories demonstrated little concern for what had occupied earlier science fiction, the fate of humanity. They were about individuals, not about the species. They used science fiction themes to deal with eternal problems of human character and relationships, rather than producing new ideas; they were more concerned with making new patterns out of science fiction materials than with reality. Like *The Stars My Destination*, they were translations into science fiction of what could have been told as contemporary stories.

It was another wave of the future.

After the demise of *Holiday*, Bester returned to science fiction with *The Computer Connection* (1975), which was serialized in *Analog* as *The Indian Giver* (1974). His last two novels were *Golem^{100}* (1980) and *The Deceivers* (1981). He received the SFWA Grand Master Award in 1988.

FONDLY FAHRENHEIT

BY ALFRED BESTER

He doesn't know which of us I am these days, but they know one truth. You must own nothing but yourself. You must make your own life, live your own life and die your own death... or else you will die another's.

The rice fields on Paragon III stretch for hundreds of miles like checkerboard tundras, a blue and brown mosaic under a burning sky of orange. In the evening, clouds whip like smoke, and the paddies rustle and murmur.

A long line of men marched across the paddies the evening we escaped from Paragon III. They were silent, armed, intent; a long rank of silhouetted statues looming against the smoking sky. Each man carried a gun. Each man wore a walkie-talkie belt pack, the speaker button in his ear, the microphone bug clipped to his throat, the glowing viewscreen strapped to his wrist like a green-eyed watch. The multitude of screens showed nothing but a multitude of individual paths through the paddies. The annunciators uttered no sound but the rustle and splash of steps. The men spoke infrequently, in heavy grunts, all speaking to all.

"Nothing here."

"Where's here?"

"Jenson's fields."

"You're drifting too far west."

"Close in the line there."

"Anybody covered the Grimson paddy?"

"Yeah. Nothing."

"She couldn't have walked this far."

"Could have been carried."

"Think she's alive?"

"Why should she be dead?"

The slow refrain swept up and down the long line of beaters advancing toward the smoky sunset. The line of beaters wavered like a writhing snake, but never ceased its remorseless advance. One hundred men spaced fifty feet apart. Five thousand feet of ominous search. One mile of angry determination stretching from east to west across a compass of heat. Evening fell. Each man lit his search lamp. The writhing snake was transformed into a necklace of wavering diamonds.

"Clear here. Nothing."

"Nothing here."

"Nothing."

"What about the Allen paddies?"

"Covering them now."

"Think we missed her?"

"Maybe."

"We'll beat back and check."

"This'll be an all night job."

"Allen paddies clear."

"God damn! We've got to find her!"

"We'll find her."

"Here she is. Sector seven. Tunc in."

The line stopped. The diamonds froze in the heat. There was silence. Each man gazed into the glowing screen on his wrist, tuning to sector seven. All tuned to one. All showed a small nude figure awash in the muddy water of a paddy. Alongside the figure an owner's stake of bronze read: VANDALEUR. The end of the line converged toward the Vandaleur field. The necklace turned into a cluster of stars. One hundred men gathered around a small nude body, a child dead in a rice paddy. There was no water in her mouth. There were fingerprints on her throat. Her innocent face was battered. Her body was torn. Clotted blood on her skin was crusted and hard.

"Dead three-four hours at least."

"Her mouth is dry."

"She wasn't drowned. Beaten to death."

In the dark evening heat the men swore softly. They picked up the body. One stopped the others and pointed to the child's fingernails. She had fought her murderer. Under the nails were particles of flesh and bright drops of scarlet blood, still liquid, still uncoagulated.

"That blood ought to be clotted too."

"Funny."

"Not so funny. What kind of blood don't clot?"

"Android."

"Looks like she was killed by one."

"Vandaleur owns an android."

"She couldn't be killed by an android."

"That's android blood under her nails."

"The police better check."

"The police'll prove I'm right!"

"But androids can't kill."

"That's android blood, ain't it?"

"Androids can't kill. They're made that way."

"Looks like one android was made wrong."

"Jesus!"

And the thermometer that day registered 91.9° gloriously Fahrenheit.

So there we were aboard the *Paragon Queen* en route for Megaster V, James Vandaleur and his android. James Vandaleur counted his money and wept. In the second class cabin with him was his android, a magnificent creature with classic features and wide blue eyes. Raised on its forehead in a cameo of flesh were the letters MA, indicating that this was one of the rare multiple aptitude androids, worth $57,000 on the current exchange. There we were, weeping and counting and calmly watching.

"Twelve, fourteen, sixteen. Sixteen hundred dollars," Vandaleur wept. "That's all. Sixteen hundred dollars. My house was worth ten thousand. The land was worth five. There was furniture, cars, my paintings, etchings, my plane, my— And nothing to show for everything but sixteen hundred dollars. Christ!"

I leaped up from the table and turned on the android. I pulled a strap from one of the leather bags and beat the android. It didn't move.

"I must remind you," the android said, "that I am worth fifty-seven thousand dollars on the current exchange. I must warn you that you are endangering valuable property."

"You damned crazy machine," Vandaleur shouted.

"I am not a machine," the android answered. "The robot is a machine. The android is a chemical creation of synthetic tissue."

"What got into you?" Vandaleur cried. "Why did you do it? Damn you!" He beat the android savagely.

"I must remind you that I cannot be punished," I said. "The pleasure-pain syndrome is not incorporated in the android synthesis."

"Then why did you kill her?" Vandaleur shouted. "If it wasn't for kicks, why did you—"

"I must remind you," the android said, "that the second class cabins in these ships are not soundproofed."

Vandaleur dropped the strap and stood panting, staring at the creature he owned.

"Why did you do it? Why did you kill her?" I asked.

"I don't know," I answered.

"First it was malicious mischief. Small things. Petty destruction. I should have known there was something wrong with you then. Androids can't destroy. They can't harm. They—"

"There is no pleasure-pain syndrome incorporated in the android synthesis."

"Then it got to arson. Then serious destruction. Then assault... that engineer on Rigel. Each time worse. Each time we had to get out faster. Now it's murder. Christ! What's the matter with you? What's happened?"

"There are no self-check relays incorporated in the android brain."

"Each time we had to get out it was a step downhill. Look at me. In a second class cabin. Me. James Paleologue Vandaleur. There was a time when my father was the wealthiest—Now, sixteen hundred dollars in the world. That's all I've got. And you. Christ damn you!"

Vandaleur raised the strap to beat the android again, then dropped it and collapsed on a berth, sobbing. At last he pulled himself together.

"Instructions," he said.

The multiple aptitude android responded at once. It arose and awaited orders.

"My name is now Valentine. James Valentine. I stopped off on Paragon III for only one day to transfer to this ship for Megaster V. My occupation: Agent for one privately owned MA android which is for hire. Purpose of visit: To settle on Megaster V. Fix the papers."

The android removed Vandaleur's passport and papers from a bag, got pen and ink and sat down at the table. With an accurate flawless hand—an accomplished hand that could draw, write, paint, carve, engrave, etch, photograph, design, create and build—it meticulously forged new credentials for Vandaleur. Its owner watched me miserably.

"Create and build," I muttered. "And now destroy. Oh God! What am I going to do? Christ! If I could only get rid of you. If I didn't have to live off you. God! If only I'd inherited some guts instead of you."

Dallas Brady was Megaster's leading jewelry designer. She was short, stocky, amoral and a nymphomaniac. She hired Vandaleur's multiple aptitude android and put me to work in her shop. She seduced Vandaleur. In her bed one night, she asked abruptly: "Your name's Vandaleur, isn't it?"

"Yes," I murmured. Then: "No! No! It's Valentine. James Valentine."

"What happened on Paragon?" Dallas Brady asked. "I thought androids couldn't kill or destroy property. Prime Directives and Inhibitions set up for them when they're synthesized. Every company guarantees they can't."

"Valentine!" Vandaleur insisted.

"Oh, come off it," Dallas Brady said. "I've known for a week. I haven't hollered copper, have I?"

"The name is Valentine."

"You want to prove it? You want I should call the cops?" Dallas reached out and picked up the phone.

"For God's sake, Dallas!" Vandaleur leaped up and struggled to take the phone from her. She fended him off, laughing at him until he collapsed and wept in shame and helplessness.

"How did you find out?" he asked at last.

"The papers are full of it. And Valentine was a little too close to Vandaleur. That wasn't smart, was it?"

"I guess not. I'm not very smart."

"Your android's got quite a record, hasn't it? Assault. Arson. Destruction. What happened on Paragon?"

"It kidnapped a child. Took her into the rice fields and murdered her."

"Raped her?"

"I don't know."

"They're going to catch up with you."

"Don't I know it? Christ! We've been running for two years now. Seven planets in two years. I must have abandoned fifty thousand dollars' worth of property in two years."

"You better find out what's wrong with it."

"How can I? Can I walk into a repair clinic and ask for an overhaul? What am I going to say? 'My android's just turned killer. Fix it.' They'd call the police right off." I began to shake. "They'd have that android dismantled inside one day. I'd probably be booked as accessory to murder."

"Why didn't you have it repaired before it got to murder?"

"I couldn't take the chance," Vandaleur explained angrily. "If they started fooling around with lobotomies and body chemistry and endocrine surgery, they might have destroyed its aptitudes. What would I have left to hire out? How would I live?"

"You could work yourself. People do."

"Work for what? You know I'm good for nothing. How could I compete with specialist androids and robots? Who can, unless he's got a terrific talent for a particular job?"

"Yeah. That's true."

"I lived off my old man all my life. Damn him! He had to go bust just before he died. Left me the android and that's all. The only way I can get along is living off what it earns."

"You better sell it before the cops catch up with you. You can live off fifty grand. Invest it."

"At three per cent? Fifteen hundred a year? When the android returns fifteen per cent on its value? Eight thousand a year. That's what it earns. No, Dallas. I've got to go along with it."

"What are you going to do about its violence kick?"

"I can't do anything... except watch it and pray. What are you going to do about it?"

"Nothing. It's none of my business. Only one thing... I ought to get something for keeping my mouth shut."

"What?"

"The android works for me for free. Let somebody else pay you, but I get it for free."

The multiple aptitude android worked. Vandaleur collected its fees. His expenses were taken care of. His savings began to mount. As the warm spring of Megaster V turned to hot summer, I began investigating farms and properties. It would be possible, within a year or two, for us to settle down permanently, provided Dallas Brady's demands did not become rapacious.

On the first hot day of summer, the android began singing in Dallas Brady's workshop. It hovered over the electric furnace which, along with the weather, was broiling the shop, and sang an ancient tune that had been popular half a century before.

> Oh, it's no feat to beat the heat.
> All reet! All reet!
> So jeet you seat
> Be fleet be fleet
> Cool and discreet
> Honey...

It sang in a strange, halting voice, and its accomplished fingers were clasped behind its back, writhing in a strange rhumba all their own. Dallas Brady was surprised.

"You happy or something?" she asked.

"I must remind you that the pleasure-pain syndrome is not incorporated in the android synthesis," I answered. "All reet! All reet! Be fleet be fleet, cool and discreet, honey..."

Its fingers stopped their writhing and picked up a heavy pair of iron tongs.

The android poked them into the glowing heart of the furnace, leaning far forward to peer into the lovely heat.

"Be careful, you damned fool!" Dallas Brady exclaimed. "You want to fall in?"

"I must remind you that I am worth fifty-seven thousand dollars on the current exchange," I said. "It is forbidden to endanger valuable property. All reet! All reet! Honey..."

It withdrew a crucible of glowing gold from the electric furnace, turned, capered hideously, sang crazily, and splashed a sluggish gobbet of molten gold over Dallas Brady's head. She screamed and collapsed, her hair and clothes flaming, her skin crackling. The android poured again while it capered and sang.

"Be fleet be fleet, cool and discreet, honey..." It sang and slowly poured and poured the molten gold. Then I left the workshop and rejoined James Vandaleur in his hotel site. The android's charred clothes and squirming fingers warned its owner that something was very much wrong.

Vandaleur rushed to Dallas Brady's workshop, stared once, vomited and fled. I had enough time to pack one bag and raise nine hundred dollars on portable assets. He took a third class cabin on the *Megaster Queen* which left that morning for Lyra Alpha. He took me with him. He wept and counted his money and I beat the android again.

And the thermometer in Dallas Brady's workshop registered 98.1° beautifully Fahrenheit.

On Lyra Alpha we holed up in a small hotel near the university. There, Vandaleur carefully bruised my forehead until the letters MA were obliterated by the swelling and discoloration. The letters would reappear, but not for several months, and in the meantime Vandaleur hoped the hue and cry for an MA android would be forgotten. The android was hired out as a common laborer in the university power plant. Vandaleur, as James Valentine, eked out life on the android's small earnings.

I wasn't too unhappy. Most of the other residents in the hotel were university students, equally hard-up, but delightfully young and enthusiastic. There was one charming girl with sharp eyes and a quick mind. Her name was Wanda, and she and her beau, Ted Stark, took a tremendous interest in the killing android which was being mentioned in every paper in the galaxy.

"We've been studying the case," she and Jed said at one of the casual student parties which happened to be held this night in Vandaleur's room. "We think we know what's causing it. We're going to do a paper." They were in a high state of excitement.

"Causing what?" somebody wanted to know.

"The android rampage."

"Obviously out of adjustment, isn't it? Body chemistry gone haywire. Maybe a kind of synthetic cancer, yes?"

"No." Wanda gave Jed a look of suppressed triumph.

"Well, what is it?"

"Something specific."

"What?"

"That would be telling."

"Oh, come on."

"Nothing doing."

"Won't you tell us?" I asked intently. "I... We're very much interested in what could go wrong with an android."

"No, Mr. Venice," Wanda said. "It's a unique idea and we've got to protect it. One thesis like this and we'll be set up for life. We can't take the chance of somebody stealing it."

"Can't you give us a hint?"

"No. Not a hint. Don't say a word, Jed. But I'll tell you this much, Mr. Venice. I'd hate to be the man who owns that android."

"You mean the police?" I asked.

"I mean projection, Mr. Venice. Projection! That's the danger... I won't say any more. I've said too much as it is."

I heard steps outside, and a hoarse voice singing softly:

"Be fleet be fleet, cool and discreet, honey..." My android entered the room, home from its tour of duty at the university power plant. It was not introduced. I motioned to it and I immediately responded to the command and went to the beer keg and took over Vandaleur's job of serving the guests. Its accomplished fingers writhed in a private rhumba of their own. Gradually they stopped their squirming, and the strange humming ended.

Androids were not unusual at the university. The wealthier students owned them along with cars and planes. Vandaleur's android provoked no comment, but young Wanda was sharp-eyed and quick-witted. She noted my bruised forehead and she was intent on the history-making thesis she and Jed Stark were going to write. After the party broke up, she consulted with Jed walking upstairs to her room.

"Jed, why'd that android have a bruised forehead?"

"Probably hurt itself, Wanda. It's working in the power plant. They fling a lot of heavy stuff around."

"That's all?"

"What else?"

"It could be a convenient bruise."

"Convenient for what?"

"Hiding what's stamped on its forehead."

"No point to that, Wanda. You don't have to see marks on a forehead to recognize an android. You don't have to see a trademark on a car to know it's a car."

"I don't mean it's trying to pass as a human. I mean it's trying to pass as a lower grade android."

"Why?"

"Suppose it had MA on its forehead."

"Multiple aptitude? Then why in hell would Venice waste it stoking furnaces if it could earn more—Oh. Oh! You mean it's—?"

Wanda nodded.

"Jesus!" Stark pursed his lips. "What do we do? Call the police?"

"No. We don't know if it's an MA for a fact. If it turns out to be an MA and the killing android, our paper comes first anyway. This is our big chance, Jed. If it's *that* android we can run a series of controlled tests and—"

"How do we find out for sure?"

"Easy. Infrared film. That'll show what's under the bruise. Borrow a camera. Buy some film. We'll sneak down to the power plant tomorrow afternoon and take some pictures. Then we'll know."

They stole down into the university power plant the following afternoon. It was a vast cellar, deep under the earth. It was dark, shadowy, luminous with burning light from the furnace doors. Above the roar of the fires they could hear a strange voice shouting and chanting the echoing vault: "All reet! All reet! So jeet your seat. Be fleet be fleet, cool and discreet, honey..." And they could see a capering figure dancing a lunatic rhumba in time to the music it shouted. The legs twisted. The arms waved. The fingers writhed.

Jed Stark raised the camera and began shooting his spool of infrared film, aiming the camera sights at the bobbing bead. Then Wanda shrieked, for I saw them and came charging down on them, brandishing a polished steel shovel. It smashed the camera. It felled the girl and then the boy. Jed fought me for a desperate hissing moment before he was bludgeoned into helplessness. Then the android dragged them to the furnace and fed them to the flames, slowly, hideously. It capered and sang. Then it returned to my hotel.

The thermometer in the power plant registered 100.9° murderously Fahrenheit. All reet! All reet!

We bought steerage on the *Lyra Queen* and Vandaleur and the android did odd jobs for their meals. During the night watches, Vandaleur would sit alone in the steerage head with a cardboard portfolio on his lap, puzzling over its contents. The portfolio was all he had managed to bring with him from Lyra Alpha. He had stolen it from Wanda's room. It was labeled ANDROID. It contained the secret of my sickness.

And it contained nothing but newspapers. Scores of newspapers from all over the galaxy, printed, microfilmed, engraved, offset, photostatted... Rigel *Star-Banner*... Paragon *Picayune*... Megaster *Times-Leader*... Lalande *Journal*... Indi *Intelligencer*... Eridani *Telegram-News*. All reet! All reet!

Nothing but newspapers. Each paper contained an account of one crime in the android's ghastly career. Each paper also contained news, domestic and foreign, sports, society, weather, shipping news, stock exchange quotations, human interest stories, features, contents, puzzles. Somewhere in that mass of uncollated facts was the secret Wanda and Jed Stark had discovered. Vandaleur pored over the papers helplessly. It was beyond him. So jeet your seat!

"I'll sell you," I told the android. "Damn you. When we land On Terra, I'll sell you. I'll settle for three per cent on whatever you're worth."

"I am worth fifty-seven thousand dollars on the current exchange," I told him.

"If I can't sell you, I'll turn you in to the police," I said.

"I am valuable property," I answered. "It is forbidden to endanger valuable property. You won't have me destroyed."

"Christ damn you!" Vandaleur cried. "What? Are you arrogant? Do you know you can trust me to protect you? Is that the secret?"

The multiple aptitude android regarded him with calm accomplished eyes. "Sometimes," it said, "it is a good thing to be property."

It was three below zero when the *Lyra Queen* dropped at Croydon Field. A mixture of ice and snow swept across the field, fizzing and exploding into steam under the *Queen's* tail jets. The passengers trotted numbly across the blackened concrete to customs inspection, and thence to the airport bus that was to take them to London. Vandaleur and the android were broke. They walked.

By midnight they reached Piccadilly Circus. The December ice storm had not slackened, and the statue of Eros was encrusted with ice. They turned right, walked down to Trafalgar Square and then along the Strand toward Soho, shaking with cold and wet. Just above Fleet Street, Vandaleur saw a solitary figure coming from the direction of St. Paul's. He drew the android into an alley.

"We've got to have money," he whispered. He pointed at the approaching figure. "He has money. Take it from him."

"The order cannot be obeyed," the android said.

"Take it from him," Vandaleur repeated. "By force. Do you understand? We're desperate."

"It is contrary to my prime directive," I said. "I cannot endanger life or property. The order cannot be obeyed."

"For God's sake!" Vandaleur burst out. "You've attacked, destroyed, murdered. Don't gibber about prime directives. You haven't any left. Get his money. Kill him if you have to. I tell you, we're desperate!"

"It is contrary to my prime directive," the android repeated. "The order cannot be obeyed."

I thrust the android back and leaped out at the stranger. He was tall, austere, competent. He had an air of hope curdled by cynicism. He carried a cane, I saw he was blind.

"Yes?" he said. "I hear you near me. What is it?"

"Sir..." Vandaleur hesitated. "I'm desperate."

"We are all desperate," the stranger replied. "Quietly desperate."

"Sir... I've got to have some money"

"Are you begging or stealing?" The sightless eyes passed over Vandaleur and the android.

"I'm prepared for either."

"Ah. So are we all. It is the history of our race." The stranger motioned over his shoulder. "I have been begging at St. Paul's, my friend. What I desire cannot be stolen. What is it you desire that you are lucky enough to be able to steal?"

"Money," Vandaleur said.

"Money for what? Come, my friend, let us exchange confidences. I will tell you why I beg, if you will tell me why you steal. My name is Blenheim."

"My name is... Vole."

"I was not begging for sight at St. Paul's, Mr. Vole. I was begging for a number."

"A number?"

"Ah, yes. Numbers rational, number irrational. Numbers imaginary. Positive integers. Negative integers. Fractions, positive and negative. Eh? You have never heard of Blenheim's Immortal treatise on Twenty Zeros, or The Differences in Absence of Quantity?" Blenheim smiled bitterly. "I am a wizard of the Theory of Number, Mr. Vole, and I have exhausted the charm of number for myself. After fifty years of wizardry, senility approaches and the appetite vanishes. I have been praying in St. Paul's for inspiration. Dear God, I prayed, if you exist, send me a number."

Vandaleur slowly lifted the cardboard portfolio and touched Blenheim's hand with it. "In here," he said, "is a number. A hidden number. A secret number.

The number of a crime. Shall we exchange, Mr. Blenheim? Shelter for a number?"

"Neither begging nor stealing, eh?" Blenheim said. "But a bargain. So all life reduces to the banal." The sightless eyes again passed over Vandaleur and the android. "Perhaps the All-Mighty is not God but a merchant. Come home with me."

On the top floor of Blenheim's house we shared a room—two beds, two closets, two washstands, one bathroom. Vandaleur bruised my forehead again and sent me out to find work, and while the android worked, I consulted with Blenheim and read him the papers from the portfolio, one by one. All reet! All reet!

Vandaleur told him so much and no more. He was a student, I said, attempting a thesis on the murdering android. In these papers which he had collected were the facts that would explain the crimes of which Blenheim had heard nothing. There must be a correlation, a number, a statistic, something which would account for my derangement, I explained, and Blenheim was piqued by the mystery, the detective story, the human interest of number.

We examined the papers. As I read them aloud, he listed them and their contents in his blind, meticulous writing. And then I read his notes to him. He listed the papers by type, by type-face, by fact, by fancy, by article, spelling, words, theme, advertising, pictures, subject, politics, prejudices. He analyzed. He studied. He meditated. And we lived together on that top floor, always a little cold, always a little terrified, always a little closer… brought together by our fear of it, our hatred between us. Like a wedge driven into a living tree and splitting the trunk, only to be forever incorporated into the scar tissue, we grew together. Vandaleur and the android. Be fleet be fleet!

And one afternoon Blenheim called Vandaleur into his study and displayed his notes. "I think I've found it," he said, "but I can't understand it."

Vandaleur's heart leaped.

"Here are the correlations," Blenheim continued. "In fifty papers there are accounts of the criminal android. What is there, outside the depredations, that is also in fifty papers?"

"I don't know, Mr. Blenheim."

"It was a rhetorical question. Here is the answer. The weather."

"What?"

"The weather." Blenheim nodded. "Each crime was committed on a day when the temperature was above ninety degrees Fahrenheit."

"But that's impossible," Vandaleur exclaimed. "It was cool on Lyra Alpha."

"We have no record of any crime committed on Lyra Alpha. There is no paper."

"No. That's right. I…" Vandaleur was confused. Suddenly he exclaimed. "No. You're right. The furnace room. It was hot there. Hot! Of course. My God, yes! That's the answer. Dallas Brady's electric furnace… The rice deltas on Paragon. So jeet your seat. Yes. But why? Why? My God, why?"

I came into the house at that moment, and passing the study, saw Vandaleur and Blenheim. I entered, awaiting commands, my multiple aptitudes devoted to service.

"That's the android, eh?" Blenheim said after a long moment.

"Yes," Vandaleur answered, still confused by the discovery. "And that explains why it refused to attack you that night on the Strand. It wasn't hot enough to break the prime directive. Only in the heat… The heat, all reet!" He looked at the android. A lunatic command passed from man to android. I refused. It is forbidden to endanger life. Vandaleur gestured furiously, then seized Blenheim's shoulders and yanked him back out of his desk chair. Blenheim shouted once. Vandaleur leaped on him like a tiger, pinning him to the floor and sealing his mouth with one hand.

"Find a weapon," he called to the android.

"It is forbidden to endanger life."

"This is a fight for self-preservation. Bring me a weapon!" He held the squirming mathematician with all his weight. I went at once to a cupboard where I knew a revolver was kept. I checked it. It was loaded with five cartridges. I handed it to Vandaleur. I took it, rammed the barrel against Blenheim's head and pulled the trigger. He shuddered once.

We had three hours before the cook returned from her day off. We looted the house. We took Blenheim's money and jewels. We packed a bag with clothes. We took Blenheim's notes, destroyed the newspapers; and we left, carefully locking the door behind us. In Blenheim's study we left a pile of crumpled papers under a half inch of burning candle. And we soaked the rug around it with kerosene. No, I did all that. The android refused. I am forbidden to endanger life or property.

All reet!

They took the tubes to Leicester Square, changed trains and rode to the British Museum. There they got off and went to a small Georgian house just off Russell Square. A shingle in the window read: NAN WEBB, PSYCHOMETRIC CONSULTANT. Vandaleur had made a note of the address some weeks earlier. They went into the house. The android waited in the foyer with the bag. Vandaleur entered Nan Webb's office.

She was a tall woman with gray shingled hair, very fine English complexion and very bad English legs. Her features were blunt, her expression acute. She nodded to Vandaleur, finished a letter, sealed it and looked up.

"My name," I said, "is Vanderbilt. James Vanderbilt."

"Quite."

"I'm an exchange student at London University."

"Quite."

"I've been researching on the killing android, and I think I've discovered something very interesting. I'd like your advice on it. What is your fee?"

"What is your college at the University?"

"Why?"

"There is a discount for students."

"Merton College."

"That will be two pounds, please."

Vandaleur placed two pounds in the desk and added to the fee Blenheim's notes. "There is a correlation," he said, "between the crimes of the android and the weather. You will note that each crime was committed when the temperature rose above ninety degrees Fahrenheit. Is there a psychometric answer for this?"

Nan Webb nodded, studied the notes for a moment, put down the sheets of paper and said: "Synesthesia, obviously."

"What?"

"Synesthesia," she repeated. "When a sensation, Mr. Vanderbilt, is interpreted immediately in terms of a sensation from a different sense organ from the one stimulated, it is called synesthesia. For example: A sound stimulus gives rise to a simultaneous sensation of definite color. Or color gives rise to a sensation of taste. Or a light stimulus gives rise to a sensation of sound. There can be confusion or short circuiting of any sensation of taste, smell, pain, pressure, temperature and so on. D'you understand?"

"I think so."

"Your research has uncovered the fact that the android most probably reacts to temperature stimulus above the ninety degree level synthesthetically. Most probably there is an endocrine response. Probably a temperature linkage with the android adrenal surrogate. High temperature brings about a response of fear, anger, excitement and violent physical activity... all within the province of the adrenal gland."

"Yes. I see. Then if the android were to be kept in cold climates..."

"There would be neither stimulus nor response. There would be no crimes. Quite."

"I see. What is projection?"

"How do you mean?"

"Is there any danger of projection with regard to the owner of the android?"

"Very interesting. Projection is a throwing forward. It is the process of throwing out upon another the ideas or impulses that belong to oneself. The paranoid, for example, projects upon others his conflicts and disturbances in order to externalize them. He accuses, directly or by implication, other men of having the very sickness with which he is struggling himself."

"And the danger of projection?"

"It is the danger of believing what is implied. If you live with a psychotic who projects his sickness upon you, there is a danger of falling into his psychotic pattern and becoming virtually psychotic yourself. As, no doubt, is happening to you, Mr. Vandaleur."

Vandaleur leaped to his feet.

"You are an ass," Nan Webb went on crisply. She waved the sheets of notes. "This is no exchange student's writing. It's the unique cursive of the famous Blenheim. Every scholar in England knows his blind writing. There is no Merton College at London University. That was a miserable guess. Merton is one of the Oxford colleges. And you, Mr. Vandaleur, are so obviously infected by association with your deranged android... by projection, if you will... that I hesitate between calling the Metropolitan Police and the Hospital for the Criminally Insane."

I took the gun and shot her.

Reet!

"Antares II, Alpha Aurigae, Acrux IV, Pollux IX, Rigel Centaurus," Vandaleur said. "They're all cold. Cold as a witch's kiss. Mean temperature of forty degrees Fahrenheit. Never get hotter than seventy. We're in business again. Watch that curve."

The multiple aptitude android swung the wheel with its accomplished hands. The car took the curve sweetly and sped on through the northern marshes, the reeds stretching for miles, brown and dry, under the cold English sky. The sun was sinking swiftly. Overhead, a lone flight of bustards sapped clumsily eastward. High above the flight, a lone helicopter drifted toward home and warmth.

"No more warmth for us," I said. "No more heat. We're safe when we're cold. We'll hole up in Scotland, make a little money, get across to Norway, build a bankroll and then slip out. We'll settle on Pollux. We're safe. We've licked it. We can live again."

There was a startling *bleep* from overhead, and then a ragged roar: "ATTENTION JAMES VANDALEUR AND ANDROID. ATTENTION JAMES VANDALEUR AND ANDROID!"

Vandaleur started and looked up. The lone helicopter was floating above them. From its belly came amplified commands: "YOU ARE SURROUNDED, THE ROAD IS BLOCKED. YOU ARE TO STOP YOUR CAR AT ONCE AND SUBMIT TO ARREST. STOP AT ONCE!"

I looked at Vandaleur for orders.

"Keep driving," Vandaleur snapped.

The helicopter dropped lower: "ATTENTION ANDROID. YOU ARE IN CONTROL OF THE VEHICLE. YOU ARE TO STOP AT ONCE. THIS IS A STATE DIRECTIVE SUPERSEDING ALL PRIVATE COMMANDS."

"What the hell are you doing?" I shouted.

"A state directive supersedes all private commands," the android answered. "I must point out to you that—"

"Get the hell away from the wheel," Vandaleur ordered. I clubbed the android, yanked him sideways and squirmed over him to the wheel. The car veered off the road in that moment and went churning through the frozen mud and dry reeds. Vandaleur regained control and continued westward through the marshes toward a parallel highway five miles distant.

"We'll beat their God damned block," he grunted.

The car pounded and surged. The helicopter dropped even lower. A searchlight blazed from the belly of the plane.

"ATTENTION JAMES VANDALEUR AND ANDROID. SUBMIT TO ARREST. THIS IS A STATE DIRECTIVE SUPERSEDING ALL PRIVATE COMMANDS."

"He can't submit," Vandaleur shouted wildly. "There's no one to submit to. He can't and I won't."

"Christ!" I muttered. "We'll beat them yet. We'll beat the block. We'll beat the heat. We'll—"

"I must point out to you," I said, "that I am required by my prime directive to obey state directives which supersede all private commands. I must submit to arrest."

"Who says it's a state directive?" Vandaleur said. "Them? Up in that plane? They've got to show credentials. They've got to prove it's state authority before you submit. How d'you know they're not crooks trying to trick us?"

Holding the wheel with one arm, he reached into his side pocket to make sure the gun was still in place. The car skidded. The tires squealed on frost and reeds. The wheel was wrenched from his grasp and the car yawed up a small hillock and overturned. The motor roared and the wheels screamed. Vandaleur crawled out and dragged the android with him. For the moment we were outside the circle of light boring down from the helicopter. We blundered off into the marsh, into the blackness, into concealment... Vandaleur running with a pounding heart, hauling the android along.

The helicopter circled and soared over the wrecked car, searchlight peering, loudspeaker braying. On the highway we had left, lights appeared as the pursuing and blocking parties gathered and followed radio directions from the plane.

Vandaleur and the android continued deeper and deeper into the marsh, working their way toward the parallel road and safety. It was night by now. The sky was a black matte. Not a star showed. The temperature was dropping. A southeast night wind knifed us to the bone.

Far behind there was a dull concussion. Vandaleur turned, gasping. The car's fuel had exploded. A geyser of flame shot up like a lurid fountain. It subsided into a low crater of burning reeds. Whipped by the wind, the distant hem of flame fanned up into a wall, ten feet high. The wall began marching down on us, crackling fiercely. Above it, a pall of oily smoke surged forward. Behind it, Vandaleur could make out the figures of men... a mass of beaters searching the marsh.

"Christ!" I cried and searched desperately for safety. He ran, dragging me with him, until their feet crunched through the surface ice of a pool. He trampled the ice furiously, then flung himself down in the numbing water, pulling the android with us.

The wall of flame approached. I could hear the crackle and feel the heat. He could see the searchers clearly. Vandaleur reached into his side pocket for the gun. The pocket was torn. The gun was gone. He groaned and shook with cold and terror. The light from the marsh fire was blinding. Overhead, the helicopter floated helplessly to one side, unable to fly through the smoke and flames and aid the searchers who were beating far to the right of us.

"They'll miss us," Vandaleur whispered. "Keep quiet. That's an order. They'll miss us. We'll beat them. We'll beat the fire. We'll—"

Three distinct shots sounded less than a hundred feet from the fugitives. *Blam! Blam! Blam!* They came from the last three cartridges in my gun as the marsh fire reached it where it had dropped, and exploded the shells. The searchers turned toward the sound and began working directly toward us. Vandaleur cursed hysterically and tried to submerge even deeper to escape the intolerable heat of the fire. The android began to twitch.

The wall of flame surged up to them. Vandaleur took a deep breath and prepared to submerge until the flame passed over them. The android shuddered and burst into an earsplitting scream.

"All reet! All reet!" it shouted. "Be fleet be fleet!"

"Damn you!" I shouted. I tried to drown it.

"Damn you!" I cursed him. I smashed his face.

The android battered Vandaleur, who fought it off until it exploded out of the mud and staggered upright. Before I could return to the attack, the live flames captured it hypnotically. It danced and capered in a lunatic rhumba before the wall of fire. Its legs twisted. Its arms waved. The fingers writhed in a private rhumba of their own. It shrieked and sang and ran in a crooked waltz before the embrace of the heat, a muddy monster silhouetted against the brilliant sparkling flare.

The searchers shouted. There were shots. The android spun around twice and then continued its horrid dance before the face of the flames. There was a rising gust of wind. The fire swept around the capering figure and enveloped it for a roaring moment. Then the fire swept on, leaving behind it a sobbing mass of synthetic flesh oozing scarlet blood that would never coagulate.

The thermometer would have registered 1200° wondrously Fahrenheit.

Vandaleur didn't die. I got away. They missed him while they watched the android caper and die. But I don't know which of us he is these days. Projection, Wanda warned me. Projection, Nan Webb told him. If you live with a crazy man or a crazy machine long enough, I become crazy too. Reet!

But we know one truth. We know they are wrong. The new robot and Vandaleur know that because the new robot's started twitching too. Reet! Here on cold Pollux, the robot is twitching and singing. No heat, but my fingers writhe. No heat, but it's taken the little Talley girl off for a solitary walk. A cheap labor robot. A servo-mechanism… all I could afford… but it's twitching and humming and walking alone with the child somewhere I can't find them. Christ! Vandaleur can't find me before it's too late. Cool and discreet, honey, in the dancing frost while the thermometer registers 10° fondly Fahrenheit.

A TOUCH OF STONE

Certain stories seem to encapsulate the qualities of their genres or their authors. Critics sometimes call them touchstones, after the black rock that is used to test the purity of gold or silver by the color of the streak left on it. The touchstone story for hard-core science fiction is Tom Godwin's "The Cold Equations."

It is also a touchstone story for Campbellian science fiction, although it came late in the history of Campbell's influence on the field, appearing some years after the creation of competing magazines and competing visions. Other stories—Asimov's "Nightfall" and Heinlein's "Universe" among them—might be equally good choices, but the philosophy and the situation in "The Cold Equations" are so purified, so stripped of distracting detail, that the Campbellian message shines through undiminished.

Campbell's philosophy was experimental and pragmatic. "Prove it! Test it!" he would say. "Does it work?" He had certain beliefs about the superiority of the human species that put off some of his writers, Asimov included; he insisted, for instance, that humanity, no matter how inferior it might seem to aliens or how backward in comparison to their civilizations, would emerge victorious from any encounter. He was not unwilling to see humanity destroyed by natural forces, though he preferred the ending in which humanity survives by means of its vigor or cunning or dogged determination.

What he really wanted to do, however, was to test human characteristics and beliefs in the test tube of ultimate situations. When life or death are the choices, particularly the life or death of the species, what values will be preserved? Will it continue to believe in what is clearly false or demonstrably fatal? In Campbellian stories the characters persist in their folly and perish, or they are converted by experience or wiser minds and survive. This often resulted in characters persisting in attitudes beyond ordinary credibility or being converted to different ideas in ways that seldom happen in real life. Readers need to understand such stories as Campbellian parables, as thought experiments.

Some of these flaws persist in "The Cold Equations." Marilyn Lee Cross is a bit more helpless and a bit more ignorant than the reader finds believable, and she persists in her inability to understand the situation long after the reader has accepted it. "The Cold Equations" illustrates Heinlein's three main plots for the human-interest story: boy-meets-girl, the Little Tailor (the person who solves a problem or a series of them), and the-man-who-learned-better. The story begins as if it could be the Little Tailor plot or maybe boy-meets-girl, but it becomes the woman-who-learned-better.

In fact, the impact of the story depends upon the reader's identification of the plot as a romantic version of the Little Tailor. The reader is conditioned to expect that the girl's life will be saved at the end, as in thousands of other stories.

Only gradually does the reader become reconciled to the fact that it isn't that kind of story at all: rather it is intended to demolish that kind of story. The girl must die. Those are the cold equations.

According to informed sources, when Tom Godwin submitted the story to Campbell the girl was saved at the end, but Campbell insisted that the girl must die, and he persuaded Godwin to rewrite it that way. In a life afflicted with disease and misfortune, Godwin (1915-1980) found comfort for a time in the writing of science fiction; he published about 30 stories and three novels between 1953 and 1971, most of them before 1963. His first story was "The Gulf Between" (*Astounding*, October 1953). "The Cold Equations" (*Astounding*, August 1954) was his fourth published story. His novels were *The Survivors* (1958), *The Space Barbarians* (1964), and *Beyond Another Sun* (1971).

That "The Cold Equations" should come to say so much about the essence of one kind of science fiction represents a kind of irony, but touchstone it is. If the reader doesn't understand it or appreciate what it is trying to say about humanity and its relationship to its environment, then that reader isn't likely to appreciate science fiction. If the reader keeps objecting that the ship should have posted a more specific warning, that the story indicts the cold-bloodedness of the situation or the ruthlessness of the rules, that the pilot should have found a way to sacrifice himself in order to save the girl or died with her rather than letting her go out the airlock alone, then that reader isn't reading the story correctly.

The only solution to "The Cold Equations" is to opt out, to refuse to appreciate its message or to refuse to play by those rules if those are the rules; later many New Wave stories would say, in effect, "We protest, we won't go along, we'll die instead." Not Godwin or the hard-core science fiction writers and readers who say that we have no choice; we must learn the rules and then play the game. The rules in "The Cold Equations" are the conditions on the frontier, the inability of humanity to afford sentiment; the greatest crime is ignorance and the executioner is the universe, which doesn't care—in the final analysis, the stones are hard and the equations are cold, and the only way to salvation is through knowledge.

THE COLD EQUATIONS

BY TOM GODWIN

He was not alone.

There was nothing to indicate the fact but the white hand of the tiny gauge on the board before him. The control room was empty but for himself; there was no sound other than the murmur of the drives—but the white hand had moved. It had been on zero when the little ship was launched from the *Stardust*; now, an hour later, it had crept up. There was something in the supplies closet across the room, it was saying, some kind of a body that radiated heat.

It could be but one kind of a body—a living, human body.

He leaned back in the pilot's chair and drew a deep, slow breath, considering what he would have to do. He was an EDS pilot, inured to the sight of death, long since accustomed to it and to viewing the dying of another man with an objective lack of emotion, and he had no choice in what he must do. There could be no alternative—but it required a few moments of conditioning for even an EDS pilot to prepare himself to walk across the room and coldly, deliberately, take the life of a man he had yet to meet.

He would, of course, do it. It was the law, stated very bluntly and definitely in grim Paragraph L, Section 8, of Interstellar Regulations: *Any stowaway discovered in an EDS shall be jettisoned immediately following discovery.*

It was the law, and there could be no appeal.

It was a law not of men's choosing but made imperative by the circumstances of the space frontier. Galactic expansion had followed the development of the hyperspace drive and as men scattered wide across the frontier there had come the problem of contact with the isolated first-colonies and exploration parties. The huge hyperspace cruisers were the product of the combined genius and effort of Earth and were long and expensive in the building. They were not available in such numbers that small colonies could possess them. The cruisers carried the colonists to their new worlds and made periodic visits, running on tight schedules, but they could not stop and turn aside to visit colonies scheduled to be visited at another time; such a delay would destroy their schedule and produce a confusion and uncertainty that would wreck the complex interdependence between old Earth and new worlds of the frontier.

Some method of delivering supplies or assistance when an emergency occurred on a world not scheduled for a visit had been needed and the Emergency Dispatch Ships had been the answer. Small and collapsible, they occupied little room in the hold of the cruiser; made of light metal and plastics, they were driven by a small rocket drive that consumed relatively little fuel. Each cruiser carried four EDS's and when a call for aid was received the nearest cruiser would drop into normal space long enough to launch an EDS with the needed supplies or personnel, then vanish again as it continued on its course.

The cruisers, powered by nuclear converters, did not use the liquid rocket fuel but nuclear converters were far too large and complex to permit their installation in the EDS's. The cruisers were forced by necessity to carry a limited amount of the bulky rocket fuel and the fuel was rationed with care; the cruiser's computers determining the exact amount of fuel each EDS would require for its mission. The computers considered the course coordinates, the mass of the EDS, the mass of pilot and cargo; they were very precise and accurate and omitted nothing from their calculations. They could not, however, foresee, and allow for, the added mass of a stowaway.

The *Stardust* had received the request from one of the exploration parties stationed on Woden; the six men of the party already being stricken with the fever carried by the green *kala* midges and their own supply of serum destroyed by the tornado that had torn through their camp. The *Stardust* had gone through the usual procedure; dropping into normal space to launch the EDS with the fever serum, then vanishing again in hyperspace. Now, an hour later, the gauge was saying there was something more than the small carton of serum in the supplies closet.

He let his eyes rest on the narrow white door of the closet. There, just inside, another man lived and breathed and was beginning to feel assured that discovery of his presence would now be too late for the pilot to alter the situation. It was too late—for the man behind the door it was far later than he thought and in a way he would find terrible to believe.

There could be no alternative. Additional fuel would be used during the hours of deceleration to compensate for the added mass of the stowaway; infinitesimal increments of fuel that would not be missed until the ship had almost reached its destination. Then, at some distance above the ground that might be as near as a thousand feet or as far as tens of thousands of feet, depending upon the mass of ship and cargo and the preceding period of deceleration, the unmissed increments of fuel would make their absence known; the EDS would expend its last drops of fuel with a sputter and go into whistling free fall. Ship and pilot and stowaway would merge together upon impact as a wreckage of metal and plastic, flesh and blood, driven deep into the soil. The stowaway had signed his own death warrant when he concealed himself on the ship; he could not be permitted to take seven others with him.

He looked again at the telltale white hand, then rose to his feet. What he must do would be unpleasant for both of them; the sooner it was over, the better. He stepped across the control room, to stand by the white door.

"Come out!" His command was harsh and abrupt above the murmur of the drive.

It seemed he could hear the whisper of a furtive movement inside the closet, then nothing. He visualized the stowaway cowering closer into one corner, suddenly worried by the possible consequences of his act and his self-assurance evaporating.

"I said *out!*"

He heard the stowaway move to obey and he waited with his eyes alert on the door and his hand near the blaster at his side.

The door opened and the stowaway stepped through it, smiling. "All right— I give up. Now what?"

It was a girl.

He stared without speaking, his hand dropping away from the blaster and acceptance of what he saw coming like a heavy and unexpected physical blow. The stowaway was not a man—she was a girl in her teens, standing before him in little white gypsy sandals with the top of her brown, curly head hardly higher than his shoulder, with a faint, sweet scent of perfume coming from her and her smiling face tilted up so her eyes could look unknowing and unafraid into his as she waited for his answer.

Now what? Had it been asked in the deep, defiant voice of a man he would have answered it with action, quick and efficient. He would have taken the stowaway's identification disk and ordered him into the air lock. Had the stowaway refused to obey, he would have used the blaster. It would not have taken long; within a minute the body would have been ejected into space— had the stowaway been a man.

He returned to the pilot's chair and motioned her to seat herself on the boxlike bulk of the drive-control units that set against the wall beside him. She obeyed, his silence making the smile fade into the meek and guilty expression of a pup that has been caught in mischief and knows it must be punished.

"You still haven't told me," she said. "I'm guilty, so what happens to me now? Do I pay a fine, or what?"

"What are you doing here?" he asked. "Why did you stow away on this EDS?"

"I wanted to see my brother. He's with the government survey crew on Woden and I haven't seen him for ten years, not since he left Earth to go into government survey work."

"What was your destination on the *Stardust?*"

"Mimir. I have a position waiting for me there. My brother has been sending money home all the time to us—my father and mother and I—and he paid for a special course in linguistics I was taking. I graduated sooner than expected and I was offered this job on Mimir. I knew it would be almost a year before Gerry's job was done on Woden so he could come on to Mimir and that's why I hid in the closet, there. There was plenty of room for me and I was willing to pay the fine. There were only the two of us kids—Gerry and I—and I haven't seen him for so long, and I didn't want to wait another year when I could see him now, even though I knew I would be breaking some kind of a regulation when I did it."

I knew I would be breaking some kind of a regulation—In a way, she could not be blamed for her ignorance of the law; she was of Earth and had not realized that the laws of the space frontier must, of necessity, be as hard and relentless as the environment that give them birth. Yet, to protect such as her from the results of their own ignorance of the frontier, there had been a sign over the door that led to the section of the *Stardust* that housed EDS's; a sign that was plain for all to see and heed:

UNAUTHORIZED PERSONNEL
KEEP OUT!

"Does your brother know that you took passage on the *Stardust* for Mimir?"

"Oh, yes. I sent him a spacegram telling him about my graduation and about going to Mimir on the *Stardust* a month before I left Earth. I already knew Mimir was where he would be stationed in a little over a year. He gets a promotion then, and he'll be based on Mimir and not have to stay out a year at a time on field trips, like he does now."

There were two different survey groups on Woden, and he asked, "What is his name?"

"Cross—Gerry Cross. He's in Group Two—that was the way his address read. Do you know him?"

Group One had requested the serum; Group Two was eight thousand miles away, across the Western Sea.

"No, I've never met him," he said, then turned to the control board and cut the deceleration to a fraction of a gravity; knowing as he did so that it could not avert the ultimate end, yet doing the only thing he could do to prolong that ultimate end. The sensation was like that of the ship suddenly dropping and the girl's involuntary movement of surprise half lifted her from the seat.

"We're going faster now, aren't we?" she asked. "Why are we doing that?"

He told her the truth. "To save fuel for a little while."

"You mean, we don't have very much?"

He delayed the answer he must give her so soon to ask: "How did you manage to stow away?"

"I just sort of walked in when no one was looking my way," she said. "I was practicing my Gelanese on the native girl who does the cleaning in the Ship's Supply office when someone came in with an order for supplies for the survey crew on Woden. I slipped into the closet there after the ship was ready to go and just before you came in. It was an impulse of the moment to stow away, so I could get to see Gerry—and from the way you keep looking at me so grim, I'm not sure it was a very wise impulse.

"But I'll be a model criminal—or do I mean prisoner?" She smiled at him again. "I intended to pay for my keep on top of paying the fine. I can cook and I can patch clothes for everyone and I know how to do all kinds of useful things, even a little bit about nursing."

There was one more question to ask:

"Did you know what the supplies were that the survey crew ordered?"

"Why, no. Equipment they needed in their work, I supposed."

Why couldn't she have been a man with some ulterior motive? A fugitive from justice, hoping to lose himself on a raw new world; an opportunist, seeking transportation to the new colonies where he might find golden fleece for the taking; a crackpot, with a mission...

Perhaps once in his lifetime an EDS pilot would find such a stowaway on his ship; warped men, mean and selfish men, brutal and dangerous men—but never, before, a smiling, blue-eyed girl who was willing to pay her fine and work for her keep that she might see her brother.

He turned to the board and turned the switch that would signal the *Stardust*. The call would be futile but he could not, until he had exhausted that one vain hope, seize her and thrust her into the air lock as he would an animal—or a man. The delay, in the meantime, would not be dangerous with the EDS decelerating at fractional gravity.

A voice spoke from the communicator. "*Stardust*. Identify yourself and proceed."

"Barton, EDS 34G11. Emergency. Give me Commander Delhart."

There was a faint confusion of noises as the request went through the proper channels. The girl was watching him, no longer smiling.

"Are you going to order them to come back after me?" she asked.

The communicator clicked and there was the sound of a distant voice saying, "Commander, the EDS requests—"

"Are they coming back after me?" she asked again. "Won't I get to see my brother, after all?"

"Barton?" The blunt, gruff voice of Commander Delhart came from the communicator. "What's this about an emergency?"

"A stowaway," he answered.

"A stowaway?" There was a slight surprise to the question. "That's rather unusual—but why the 'emergency' call? You discovered him in time so there should be no appreciable danger and I presume you've informed Ship's Records so his nearest relatives can be notified."

"That's why I had to call you, first. The stowaway is still aboard and the circumstances are so different—"

"Different?" the commander interrupted, impatience in his voice. "How can they be different? You know you have a limited supply of fuel; you also know the law, as well as I do: 'Any stowaway discovered in an EDS shall be jettisoned immediately following discovery.'"

There was the sound of a sharply indrawn breath from the girl. *"What does he mean?"*

"The stowaway is a girl."

"What?"

"She wanted to see her brother. She's only a kid and she didn't know what she was really doing."

"I see." All the curtness was gone from the commander's voice. "So you called me in the hope I could do something?" Without waiting for an answer he went on. "I'm sorry—I can do nothing. This cruiser must maintain its schedule; the life of not one person but the lives of many depend on it. I know how you feel but I'm powerless to help you. You'll have to go through with it. I'll have you connected with Ship's Records."

The communicator faded to a faint rustle of sound and he turned back to the girl. She was leaning forward on the bench, almost rigid, her eyes fixed wide and frightened.

"What did he mean, to go through with it? To jettison me... to go through with it—what did he mean? Not the way it sounded... he couldn't have. What did he mean... what did he really mean?"

Her time was too short for the comfort of a lie to be more than a cruelly fleeting delusion.

"He meant it the way it sounded."

"No!" she recoiled from him as though he had struck her, one hand half upraised as though to fend him off and stark unwillingness to believe in her eyes.

"It will have to be."

"No! You're joking—you're insane! You can't mean it!"

"I'm sorry." He spoke slowly to her, gently. "I should have told you before— I should have, but I had to do what I could first; I had to call the *Stardust*. You heard what the commander said."

"But you can't—if you make me leave the ship, I'll *die*."

"I know."

She searched his face and the unwillingness to believe left her eyes, giving way slowly to a look of dazed terror.

"You—know?" She spoke the words far apart, numb and wonderingly.

"I know. It has to be like that."

"You mean it—you really mean it." She sagged back against the wall, small and limp like a little rag doll and all the protesting and disbelief gone.

"You're going to do it—you're going to make me die?"

"I'm sorry," he said again. "You'll never know how sorry I am. It has to be that way and no human in the universe can change it."

"You're going to make me die and I didn't do anything to die for—I didn't *do* anything—"

He sighed, deep, and weary, "I know you didn't, child. I know you didn't—"

"EDS." The communicator rapped brisk and metallic. "This is Ship's Records. Give us all information on subject's identification disk."

He got out of his chair to stand over her. She clutched the edge of the seat, her upturned face white under the brown hair and the lipstick standing out like a blood-red cupid's bow.

"Now?"

"I want your identification disk," he said.

She released the edge of the seat and fumbled at the chain that suspended the plastic disk from her neck with fingers that were trembling and awkward. He reached down and unfastened the clasp for her, then returned with the disk to his chair.

"Here's your data, Records: Identification Number T837—"

"One moment," Records interrupted. "This is to be filed on the gray card, of course?"

"Yes."

"And the time of the execution?"

"I'll tell you later."

"Later? This is highly irregular; the time of the subject's death is required before—"

He kept the thickness out of his voice with an effort. "Then we'll do it in a slightly irregular manner—you'll hear the disk read, first. The subject is a girl and she's listening to everything that's said. Are you capable of understanding that?"

There was a brief, almost shocked, silence, then Records said meekly: "Sorry. Go ahead."

He began to read the disk, reading it slowly to delay the inevitable for as long as possible, trying to help her by giving her what little time he could to recover from her first terror and let it resolve into the calm of acceptance and resignation.

"Number T8374 dash Y54. Name: Marilyn Lee Cross. Sex: Female. Born: July 7, 2160. *She was only eighteen.* Height: 5-3. Weight: 110. *Such a slight weight, yet enough to add fatally to the mass of the shell-thin bubble that was an EDS.* Hair: Brown. Eyes: Blue. Complexion: Light. Blood Type: O. *Irrelevant data.* Destination: Port City, Mimir. *Invalid data*—"

He finished and said, "I'll call you later," then turned once again to the girl. She was huddled back against the wall, watching him with a look of numb and wondering fascination.

"They're waiting for you to kill me, aren't they? They want me dead, don't they? You and everybody on the cruiser wants me dead, don't you?" Then the numbness broke and her voice was that of a frightened and bewildered child. "Everybody wants me dead and I didn't *do* anything. I didn't hurt anyone—I only wanted to see my brother."

"It's not the way you think—it isn't that way, at all," he said. "Nobody wants it this way; nobody would ever let it be this way if it was humanly possible to change it."

"Then why is it! I don't understand. Why is it?"

"This ship is carrying *kala* fever serum to Group One on Woden. Their own supply was destroyed by a tornado. Group Two—the crew your brother is in—is eight thousand miles away across the Western Sea and their helicopters can't cross it to help Group One. The fever is invariably fatal unless the serum can be had in time, and the six men in Group One will die unless this ship reaches them on schedule. These little ships are always given barely enough fuel to reach their destination and if you stay aboard your added weight will cause it to use up all its fuel before it reaches the ground. It will crash, then, and you and I will die and so will the six men waiting for the fever serum."

It was a full minute before she spoke, and as she considered his words the expression of numbness left her eyes.

"Is that it?" she asked at last. "Just that the ship doesn't have enough fuel?"

"Yes."

"I can go alone or I can take seven others with me—is that the way it is?"

"That's the way it is."

"And nobody wants me to have to die?'"

"Nobody."

"Then maybe— Are you sure nothing can be done about it? Wouldn't people help me if they could?"

"Everyone would like to help you but there is nothing anyone can do. I did the only thing I could do when I called the *Stardust*."

"And it won't come back—but there might be other cruisers, mightn't there? Isn't there any hope at all that there might be someone, somewhere, who could do something to help me?"

She was leaning forward a little in her eagerness as she waited for his answer. "No."

The word was like the drop of a cold stone and she again leaned back against the wall, the hope and eagerness leaving her face. "You're sure—you *know* you're sure?"

"I'm sure. There are no other cruisers within forty light-years; there is nothing and no one to change things."

She dropped her gaze to her lap and began twisting a pleat of her skirt between her fingers, saying no more as her mind began to adapt itself to the grim knowledge.

It was better so; with the going of all hope would go the fear; with the going of all hope would come resignation. She needed time and she could have so little of it. How much?

The EDS's were not equipped with hull-cooling units; their speed had to be reduced to a moderate level before entering the atmosphere. They were decelerating at .10 gravity; approaching their destination at a far higher speed than the computers had calculated on. The *Stardust* had been quite near Woden when she launched the EDS; their present velocity was putting them nearer by the second. There would be a critical point, soon to be reached, when he would have to resume deceleration. When he did so the girl's weight would be multiplied by the gravities of deceleration, would become, suddenly, a factor of paramount importance; the factor the computers had been ignorant of when they determined the amount of fuel the EDS should have. She would have to go when deceleration began; it could be no other way. When would that be—how long could he let her stay?

"How long can I stay?"

He winced involuntarily from the words that were so like an echo of his own thoughts. How long? He didn't know; he would have to ask the ship's computers. Each EDS was given a meager surplus of fuel to compensate for unfavorable conditions within the atmosphere and relatively little fuel was being consumed for the time being. The memory banks of the computers would still contain all data pertaining to the course set for the EDS; such data would not be erased until the EDS reached its destination. He had only to give the computers the new data; the girl's weight and the exact time at which he had reduced the deceleration to .10.

"Barton." Commander Delhart's voice came abruptly from the communicator, as he opened his mouth to call the *Stardust*. "A check with Records shows me you haven't completed your report. Did you reduce the deceleration?"

So the commander knew what he was trying to do.

"I'm decelerating at point ten," he answered. "I cut the deceleration at seventeen fifty and the weight is a hundred and ten. I would like to stay at point ten as long as the computers say I can. Will you give them the question?"

It was contrary to regulations for an EDS pilot to make any changes in the course or degree of deceleration the computers had set for him but the commander made no mention of the violation, neither did he ask the reason for it. It was not necessary for him to ask; he had not become commander of an interstellar cruiser without both intelligence and an understanding of human nature. He said only: "I'll have that given the computers."

The communicator fell silent and he and the girl waited, neither of them speaking. They would not have to wait long; the computers would give the answer within moments of the asking. The new factors would be fed into the steel maw of the first bank and the electrical impulses would go through the complex circuits. Here and there a relay might click, a tiny cog turn over, but it would be essentially the electrical impulses that found the answer; formless, mindless, invisible, determining with utter precision how long the pale girl beside him might live. Then five little segments of metal in the second bank would trip in rapid succession against an inked ribbon and a second steel maw would spit out the slip of paper that bore the answer.

The chronometer on the instrument board read 18:10 when the commander spoke again.

"You will resume deceleration at nineteen ten."

She looked toward the chronometer, then quickly away from it. "Is that when… when I go?" she asked. He nodded, and she dropped her eyes to her lap again.

"I'll have the course corrections given you," the commander said. "Ordinarily I would never permit anything like this but I understand your position. There is nothing I can do, other than what I've just done, and you will not deviate from these new instructions. You will complete your report at nineteen ten. Now—here are the course corrections."

The voice of some unknown technician read them to him and he wrote them down on the pad clipped to the edge of the control board. There would, he saw, be periods of deceleration when he neared the atmosphere when the deceleration would be five gravities—and at five gravities, one hundred ten pounds would become five hundred fifty pounds.

The technician finished and he terminated the contact with a brief acknowledgment. Then, hesitating a moment, he reached out and shut off the communicator. It was 18:13 and he would have nothing to report until 19:10. In the meantime, it somehow seemed indecent to permit others to hear what she might say in her last hour.

He began to check the instrument readings, going over them with unnecessary slowness. She would have to accept the circumstances and there was nothing he could do to help her into acceptance; words of sympathy would only delay it.

It was 18:20 when she stirred from her motionlessness and spoke.

"So that's the way it has to be with me?"

He swung around to face her. "You understand now, don't you? No one would ever let it be like this if it could be changed."

"I understand," she said. Some of the color had returned to her face and the lipstick no longer stood out so vividly red. "There isn't enough fuel for me to stay; when I hid on this ship I got into something I didn't know anything about and now I have to pay for it."

She had violated a man-made law that said KEEP OUT but the penalty was not of men's making or desire and it was a penalty men could not revoke. A physical law had decreed: *h amount of fuel will power an EDS with a mass of m safely to its destination; and a second physical law had decreed: h amount of fuel will not power an EDS with a mass of m plus x safely to its destination.*

EDS's obeyed only physical laws and no amount of human sympathy for her could alter the second law.

"But I'm afraid. I don't want to die—not now. I want to live and nobody is doing anything to help me; everybody is letting me go ahead and acting just like nothing was going to happen to me. I'm going to die and nobody *cares*."

"We all do," he said. "I do and the commander does and the clerk in Ship's Records; we all care and each of us did what little he could to help you. It wasn't enough—it was almost nothing—but it was all we could do."

"Not enough fuel—I can understand that," she said, as though she had not heard his own words. "But to have to die for it. *Me*, alone—"

How hard it must be for her to accept the fact. She had never known danger of death; had never known the environments where the lives of men could be as fragile and fleeting as sea foam tossed against a rocky shore. She belonged on gentle Earth, in that secure and peaceful society where she could be young and gay and laughing with the others of her kind; where life was precious and well-guarded and there was always the assurance that tomorrow would come. She belonged in that world of soft winds and warm suns, music and moonlight and gracious manners and not on the hard, bleak frontier.

"How did it happen to me, so terribly quickly? An hour ago I was on the *Stardust*, going to Mimir. Now the *Stardust* is going on without me and I'm going to die and I'll never see Gerry and Mama and Daddy again—I'll never see anything again."

He hesitated, wondering how he could explain it to her so she would really understand and not feel she had, somehow, been the victim of a reasonlessly cruel injustice. She did not know what the frontier was like; she thought in terms of safe-and-secure Earth. Pretty girls were not jettisoned on Earth; there was a law against it. On Earth her plight would have filled the newscasts and a fast black Patrol ship would have been racing to her rescue. Everyone, everywhere, would have known of Marilyn Lee Cross and no effort would have been spared to save her life. But this was not Earth and there were no Patrol ships; only the *Stardust*, leaving them behind at many times the speed of light. There was no one to help her, there would be no Marilyn Lee Cross smiling from the newscasts tomorrow, Marilyn Lee Cross would be but a poignant memory for an EDS pilot and a name on a gray card in Ship's Records.

"It's different here; it's not like back on Earth," he said. "It isn't that no one cares; it's that no one can do anything to help. The frontier is big and here along its rim the colonies and exploration parties are scattered so thin and far between. On Woden, for example, there are only sixteen men—sixteen men on an entire world. The exploration parties, the survey crews, the little first-colonies—they're all fighting alien environments, trying to make a way for those who will follow after. The environments fight back and those who go first usually make mistakes only once. There is no margin of safety along the rim of the frontier; there can't be until the way is made for the others who will come later, until the new worlds are tamed and settled. Until then men will have to pay the penalty for making mistakes with no one to help them because there is no one *to* help them."

"I was going to Mimir," she said. "I didn't know about the frontier; I was only going to Mimir and *it's* safe."

"Mimir is safe but you left the cruiser that was taking you there."

She was silent for a little while. "It was all so wonderful at first; there was plenty of room for me on this ship and I would be seeing Gerry so soon... I didn't know about the fuel, didn't know what would happen to me—"

Her words trailed away and he turned his attention to the viewscreen, not wanting to stare at her as she fought her way through the black horror of fear toward the calm gray of acceptance.

Woden was a ball, enshrouded in the blue haze of its atmosphere, swimming in space against the background of star-sprinkled dead blackness. The great mass of Manning's Continent sprawled like a gigantic hourglass in the Eastern Sea with the western half of the Eastern Continent still visible. There was a thin line of shadow along the right-hand edge of the globe and the Eastern Continent was disappearing into it as the planet turned on its axis. An hour before the entire continent had been in view, now a thousand miles of it had gone into the thin edge of shadow and around to the night that lay on the other side of the world. The dark blue spot that was Lotus Lake was approaching the shadow. It was somewhere near the southern edge of the lake that Group Two had their camp. It would be night there, soon, and quick behind the coming of night the rotation of Woden on its axis would put Group Two beyond the reach of the ship's radio.

He would have to tell her before it was too late for her to talk to her brother. In a way, it would be better for both of them should they not do so but it was not for him to decide. To each of them the last words would be something to hold and cherish, something that would cut like the blade of a knife yet would be infinitely precious to remember, she for her own brief moments to live and he for the rest of his life.

He held down the button that would flash the grid lines on the viewscreen and used the known diameter of the planet to estimate the distance the southern tip of Lotus Lake had yet to go until it passed beyond radio range. It was approximately five hundred miles. Five hundred miles; thirty minutes—and the chronometer read 18:30. Allowing for error in estimating, it could not be later than 19:05 that the turning of Woden would cut off her brother's voice.

The first border of the Western Continent was already in sight along the left side of the world. Four thousand miles across it lay the shore of the Western Sea and the Camp of Group One. It had been in the Western Sea that the tornado had originated, to strike with such fury at the camp and destroy half their prefabricated buildings, including the one that housed the medical supplies. Two days before the tornado had not existed; it had been no more than great gentle masses of air out over the calm Western Sea. Group One had gone about their routine survey work, unaware of the meeting of the air masses out at sea, unaware of the force the union was spawning. It had struck their camp without warning; a thundering, roaring destruction that sought to annihilate all that lay before it. It had passed on, leaving the wreckage in its wake. It had destroyed the labor of months and had doomed six men to die and then, as though its task was accomplished, it once more began to resolve into gentle masses of air. But for all its deadlines, it had destroyed with neither malice nor intent. It had been a blind and mindless force, obeying the laws of nature, and it would have followed the same course with the same fury had men never existed.

Existence required Order and there was order; the laws of nature, irrevocable and immutable. Men could learn to use them but men could not change them. The circumference of a circle was always pi times the diameter and no science of Man would ever make it otherwise. The combination of chemical A with chemical B under condition C invariably produced reaction D. The law of gravitation was a rigid equation and it made no distinction between the fall of a leaf and the ponderous circling of a binary star system. The nuclear conversion process powered the cruisers that carried men to the stars; the same process in the form of a nova would destroy a world with equal efficiency. The laws were, and the universe moved in obedience to them. Along the frontier were arrayed all the forces of nature and sometimes they destroyed those who were fighting their way outward from Earth. The men of the frontier had long ago learned the bitter futility of cursing the forces that would destroy them for the forces were blind and deaf; the futility of looking to the heavens for mercy, for the stars of the galaxy swung in their long, long sweep of two hundred million years, as inexorably controlled as they by the laws that knew neither hatred nor compassion.

The men of the frontier knew—but how was a girl from Earth to fully understand? *H amount of fuel will not power an EDS with a mass of m plus x safely to its destination.* To himself and her brother and parents she was a sweet-faced girl in her teens; to the laws of nature she was *x*, the unwanted factor in a cold equation.

She stirred again on the seat. "Could I write a letter? I want to write to Mama and Daddy and I'd like to talk to Gerry. Could you let me talk to him over your radio there?"

"I'll try to get him," he said.

He switched on the normal-space transmitter and pressed the signal button. Someone answered the buzzer almost immediately.

"Hello. How's it going with you fellows now—is the EDS on its way?"

"This isn't Group One; this is the EDS," he said. "Is Gerry Cross there?"

"Gerry? He and two others went out in the helicopter this morning and aren't back yet. It's almost sundown, though, and he ought to be back right away—in less than an hour at the most."

"Can you connect me through to the radio in his 'copter?"

"Huh-uh. It's been out of commission for two months—some printed circuits went haywire and we can't get any more until the next cruiser stops by. Is it something important—bad news for him, or something?"

"Yes—it's very important. When he comes in get him to the transmitter as soon as you possibly can."

"I'll do that; I'll have one of the boys waiting at the field with a truck. Is there anything else I can do?"

"No, I guess that's all. Get him there as soon as you can and signal me."

He turned the volume to an inaudible minimum, an act that would not affect the functioning of the signal buzzer, and unclipped the pad of paper from the control board. He tore off the sheet containing his flight instructions and handed the pad to her, together with pencil.

"I'd better write to Gerry, too," she said as she took them. "He might not get back to camp in time."

She began to write, her fingers still clumsy and uncertain in the way they handled the pencil and the top of it trembling a little as she poised it between words. He turned back to the viewscreen, to stare at it without seeing it.

She was a lonely little child, trying to say her last good-bye, and she would lay out her heart to them. She would tell them how much she loved them and she would tell them to not feel badly about it, that it was only something that must happen eventually to everyone and she was not afraid. The last would be a lie and it would be there to read between the sprawling, uneven lines; a valiant little lie that would make the hurt all the greater for them.

Her brother was of the frontier and he would understand. He would not hate the EDS pilot for doing nothing to prevent her going; he would know there had been nothing the pilot could do. He would understand, though the understanding would not soften the shock and pain when he learned his sister was gone. But the others, her father and mother—they would not understand. They were of Earth and they would think in the manner of those who had never lived where the safety margin of life was a thin, thin line—and sometimes not at all. What would they think of the faceless, unknown pilot who had sent her to her death?

They would hate him with cold and terrible intensity but it really didn't matter. He would never see them, never know them. He would have only the memories to remind him; only the nights to fear, when a blue-eyed girl in gypsy sandals would come in his dreams to die again…

He scowled at the viewscreen and tried to force his thoughts into less emotional channels. There was nothing he could do to help her. She had unknowingly subjected herself to the penalty of a law that recognized neither innocence nor youth nor beauty, that was incapable of sympathy or leniency. Regret was illogical—and yet, could knowing it to be illogical ever keep it away?

She stopped occasionally, as though trying to find the right words to tell them what she wanted them to know, then the pencil would resume its whispering to the paper. It was 18:37 when she folded the letter in a square and wrote a name on it. She began writing another, twice looking up at the chronometer as though she feared the black hand might reach its rendezvous before she had finished. It was 18:45 when she folded it as she had done the first letter and wrote a name and address on it.

She held the letters out to him. "Will you take care of these and see that they're enveloped and mailed?"

"Of course." He took them from her hand and placed them in a pocket of his gray uniform shirt.

"These can't be sent off until the next cruiser stops by and the *Stardust* will have long since told them about me, won't it?" she asked. He nodded and she went on, "That makes the letters not important in one way but in another way they're very important—to me, and to them."

"I know. I understand, and I'll take care of them."

She glanced at the chronometer, then back to him. "It seems to move faster all the time, doesn't it?"

He said nothing, unable to think of anything to say, and she asked, "Do you think Gerry will come back to camp in time?"

"I think so. They said he should be in right away."

She began to roll the pencil back and forth between her palms. "I hope he does. I feel sick and scared and I want to hear his voice again and maybe I won't feel so alone. I'm a coward and I can't help it."

"No," he said, "you're not a coward. You're afraid, but you're not a coward."

"Is there a difference?"

He nodded. "A lot of difference."

"I feel so alone. I never did feel like this before; like I was all by myself and there was nobody to care what happened to me. Always, before, there was Mama and Daddy there and my friends around me. I had lots of friends, and they had a going-away party for me the night before I left."

Friends and music and laughter for her to remember—and on the viewscreen Lotus Lake was going into the shadow.

"Is it the same with Gerry?" she asked. "I mean, if he should make a mistake, would he have to die for it, all alone and with no one to help him?"

"It's the same with all along the frontier; it will always be like that so long as there is a frontier."

"Gerry didn't tell us. He said the pay was good and he sent money home all the time because Daddy's little shop just brought in a bare living but he didn't tell us it was like this."

"He didn't tell you his work was dangerous?"

"Well—yes. He mentioned that, but we didn't understand. I always thought danger along the frontier was something that was a lot of fun; an exciting adventure, like in the three-D shows." A wan smile touched her face for a moment. "Only it's not, is it? It's not the same at all, because when it's real you can't go home after the show is over."

"No," he said. "No, you can't."

Her glance flicked from the chronometer to the door of the air lock then down to the pad and pencil she still held. She shifted her position slightly to lay them on the bench beside, moving one foot out a little. For the first time he saw that she was not wearing Vegan gypsy sandals but only cheap imitations; the expensive Vegan leather was some kind of grained plastic, the silver buckle was gilded iron, the jewels were colored glass. *Daddy's little shop just brought in a bare living…* She must have left college in her second year, to take the course in linguistics that would enable her to make her own way and help her brother provide for her parents, earning what she could by part-time work after classes were over. Her personal possessions on the *Stardust* would be taken back to her parents—they would neither be of much value nor occupy much storage space on the return voyage.

"Isn't it—" She stopped, and he looked at her questioningly. "Isn't it cold in here?" she asked, almost apologetically. "Doesn't it seem cold to you?"

"Why, yes," he said. He saw by the main temperature gauge that the room was at precisely normal temperature. "Yes, it's colder than it should be."

"I wish Gerry would get back before it's too late. Do you really think he will, and you didn't just say so to make me feel better?"

"I think he will—they said he would be in pretty soon." On the viewscreen Lotus Lake had gone into the shadow but for the thin blue line of its western edge and it was apparent he had overestimated the time she would have in which to talk to her brother. Reluctantly, he said to her, "His camp will be out of radio range in a few minutes; he's on that part of Woden that's in the shadow"—he indicated the viewscreen—"and the turning of Woden will put him beyond contact. There may not be much time left when he comes in—not much time to talk to him before he fades out. I wish I could do something about it—I would call him right now if I could."

"Not even as much time as I will have to stay?"

"I'm afraid not."

"Then—" She straightened and looked toward the air lock with pale resolution. "Then I'll go when Gerry passes beyond range. I won't wait any longer after that—I won't have anything to wait for."

Again there was nothing he could say.

"Maybe I shouldn't wait at all. Maybe I'm selfish—maybe it would be better for Gerry if you just told him about it afterward."

There was an unconscious pleading for denial in the way she spoke and he said, "He wouldn't want you to do that, to not wait for him."

"It's already coming dark where he is, isn't it? There will be all the long night before him, and Mama and Daddy don't know yet that I won't ever be coming back like I promised them I would. I've caused everyone I love to be hurt, haven't I? I didn't want to—I didn't intend to."

"It wasn't your fault," he said. "It wasn't your fault at all. They'll know that. They'll understand."

"At first I was so afraid to die that I was a coward and thought only of myself. Now, I see how selfish I was. The terrible thing about dying like this is not that I'll be gone but that I'll never see them again; never be able to tell them that I didn't take them for granted; never be able to tell them I knew of the sacrifices they made to make my life happier, that I knew all the things they did for me and that I loved them so much more than I ever told them. I've never told them any of those things. You don't tell them such things when you're young and your life is all before you—you're afraid of sounding sentimental and silly.

"But it's so different when you have to die—you wish you had told them while you could and you wish you could tell them you're sorry for all the little mean things you ever did or said to them. You wish you could tell them that you didn't really mean to ever hurt their feelings and for them to only remember that you always loved them far more than you ever let them know."

"You don't have to tell them that," he said. "They will know—they've always known it."

"Are you sure?" she asked. "How can you be sure? My people are strangers to you."

"Wherever you go, human nature and human hearts are the same."

"And they will know what I want them to know—that I love them?"

"They've always known it, in a way far better than you could ever put in words for them."

"I keep remembering the things they did for me, and it's the little things they did that seem to be the most important to me, now. Like Gerry—he sent me a bracelet of fire-rubies on my sixteenth birthday. It was beautiful—it must have cost him a month's pay. Yet I remember him more for what he did the night my kitten got run over in the street. I was only six years old and he held me in his arms and wiped away my tears and told me not to cry, that Flossy was gone for just a little while, for just long enough to get herself a new fur coat and she would be on the foot of my bed the very next morning. I believed him and quit crying and went to sleep dreaming about my kitten coming back. When I woke up the next morning, there was Flossy on the foot of my bed in a brand-new white fur coat, just like he had said she would be.

"It wasn't until a long time later that Mama told me Gerry had got the pet-shop owner out of bed at four in the morning and, when the man got mad about it, Gerry told him he was either going to go down and sell him the white kitten right then or he'd break his neck."

"It's always the little things you remember people by; all the little things they did because they wanted to do them for you. You've done the same for Gerry and your father and mother; all kinds of things that you've forgotten about but that they will never forget."

"I hope I have. I would like for them to remember me like that."

"They will."

"I wish—" She swallowed. "The way I'll die—I wish they wouldn't ever think of that. I've read how people look who die in space—their insides all ruptured and exploded and their lungs out between their teeth and then, a few seconds later, they're all dry and shapeless and horribly ugly. I don't want them to ever think of me as something dead and horrible, like that."

"You're their own, their child and their sister. They could never think of you other than the way you would want them to; the way you looked the last time they saw you."

"I'm still afraid," she said. "I can't help it, but I don't want Gerry to know it. If he gets back in time, I'm going to act like I'm not afraid at all and—"

The signal buzzer interrupted her, quick and imperative.

"Gerry!" She came to her feet. "It's Gerry, now!"

He spun the volume control knob and asked: "Gerry Cross?"

"Yes," her brother answered, an undertone of tenseness to his reply. "The bad news—what is it?"

She answered for him, standing close behind him and leaning down a little toward the communicator, her hand resting small and cold on his shoulder.

"Hello, Gerry." There was only a faint quaver to betray the careful casualness of her voice. "I wanted to see you—"

"Marilyn!" There was sudden and terrible apprehension in the way he spoke her name. "What are you doing on that EDS?"

"I wanted to see you," she said again. "I wanted to see you, so I hid on this ship—"

"You *hid* on it?"

"I'm a stowaway… I didn't know what it would mean—"

"*Marilyn!*" It was the cry of a man who calls hopeless and desperate to someone already and forever gone from him. "What have you done?"

"I… it's not—" Then her own composure broke and the cold little hand gripped his shoulder convulsively. "Don't, Gerry—I only wanted to see you; I didn't intend to hurt you. Please, Gerry, don't feel like that—"

Something warm and wet splashed on his wrist and he slid out of the chair, to help her into it and swing the microphone down to her own level.

"Don't feel like that—Don't let me go knowing you feel like that—"

The sob she had tried to hold back choked in her throat and her brother spoke to her. "Don't cry, Marilyn." His voice was suddenly deep and infinitely gentle, with all the pain held out of it. "Don't cry, Sis—you mustn't do that. It's all right, Honey—everything is all right."

"I—" Her lower lip quivered and she bit into it. "I didn't want you to feel that way—I just wanted us to say good-bye because I have to go in a minute."

"Sure—sure. That's the way it will be, Sis. I didn't mean to sound the way I did." Then his voice changed to a tone of quick and urgent demand. "EDS—have you called the *Stardust*? Did you check with the computers?"

"I called the *Stardust* almost an hour ago. It can't turn back, there are no other cruisers within forty light-years, and there isn't enough fuel."

"Are you sure that the computers had the correct data—sure of everything?"

"Yes—do you think I could ever let it happen if I wasn't sure? I did everything I could do. If there was anything at all I could do now, I would do it."

"He tried to help me, Gerry." Her lower lip was no longer trembling and the short sleeves of her blouse were wet where she had dried her tears. "No one can help me and I'm not going to cry anymore and everything will be all right with you and Daddy and Mama, won't it?"

"Sure—sure it will. We'll make out fine."

Her brother's words were beginning to come in more faintly and he turned the volume control to maximum. "He's going out of range," he said to her. "He'll be gone within another minute."

"You're fading out, Gerry," she said. "You're going out of range. I wanted to tell you—but I can't, now. We must say good-by so soon—but maybe I'll see you again. Maybe I'll come to you in your dreams with my hair in braids and crying because the kitten in my arms is dead; maybe I'll be the touch of a breeze that whispers to you as it goes by; maybe I'll be one of those gold-winged larks you told me about, singing my silly head off to you; maybe, at times, I'll be nothing you can see but you will know I'm there beside you. Think of me like that, Gerry; always like that and not—the other way."

Dimmed to a whisper by the turning of Woden, the answer came back:

"Always like that, Marilyn—always like that and never any other way."

"Our time is up, Gerry—I have to go now. Good—" Her voice broke in mid-word and her mouth tried to twist into crying. She pressed her hand hard against it and when she spoke again the words came clear and true:

"Good-bye, Gerry."

Faint and ineffably poignant and tender, the last words came from the cold metal of the communicator:

"Good-bye, little sister—"

She sat motionless in the hush that followed, as though listening to the shadow-echoes of the words as they died away, then she turned away from the communicator, toward the air lock, and he pulled the black lever beside him. The inner door of the air lock slid swiftly open, to reveal the bare little cell that was waiting for her, and she walked to it.

She walked with her head up and the brown curls brushing her shoulders, with the white sandals stepping as sure and steady as the fractional gravity would permit and the gilded buckles twinkling with little lights of blue and red and crystal. He let her walk alone and made no move to help her, knowing she would not want it that way. She stepped into the air lock and turned to face him, only the pulse in her throat to betray the wild beating of her heart.

"I'm ready," she said.

He pushed the lever up and the door slid its quick barrier between them, enclosing her in black and utter darkness for her last moments of life. It clicked as it locked in place and he jerked down the red lever. There was a slight waver to the ship as the air gushed from the lock, a vibration to the wall as though something had bumped the outer door in passing, then there was nothing and the ship was dropping true and steady again. He shoved the red lever back to close the door on the empty air lock and turned away, to walk to the pilot's chair with the slow steps of a man old and weary.

Back in the pilot's chair he pressed the signal button of the normal-space transmitter. There was no response; he had expected none. Her brother would have to wait through the night until the turning of Woden permitted contact through Group One.

It was not yet time to resume deceleration and he waited while the ship dropped endlessly downward with him and the drives purred softly. He saw that the white hand of the supplies closet temperature gauge was on zero. A cold equation had been balanced and he was alone on the ship. Something shapeless and ugly was hurrying ahead of him, going to Woden where its brother was waiting through the night, but the empty ship still lived for a little while with the presence of the girl who had not known about the forces that killed with neither hatred nor malice. It seemed, almost, that she still sat small and bewildered and frightened on the metal box beside him, her words echoing hauntingly clear in the void she had left behind her:

I didn't do anything to die for—I didn't do anything—

THE BALLADS OF LOST C. SMITH

In the midst of the communal world of science fiction that writers, working together on similar problems, have created, a world based on reality but projected into the future of a planet named Earth and of the human species it nurtured, some authors have created their own unique worlds that have little in common with the rest. Perhaps all that can be said of them is strange and wonderful, wonderful and strange....

Most of these unique places have been fantasies: Lovecraft's world of Elder Gods, Fritz Leiber's "Gray Mouser" world, Jack Vance's dying earth, Roger Zelazny's Amber.... Some of the worlds have resemblances to reality and therefore seem closer to science fiction, like those of A. Merritt, Edgar Rice Burroughs, and Ray Bradbury. Then there are those occasional worlds, usually created by a series of books, which are visualized so thoroughly that they seem actually to exist, such as Frank Herbert's Dune, Marion Zimmer Bradley's Darkover, and Michael Moorcock's world at the end of time. These worlds live because of the detail with which the authors have imagined them: their landscapes, their peoples, and the names they are given.

The strangest of the worlds created in science fiction were the worlds of Cordwainer Smith. His real name was Paul Linebarger (1913–1966). He was a godson of Sun Yat Sen (his father was Sun's legal advisor and one of the financiers of the Revolution of 1911), and he had a variety of careers in college teaching and government service. After attending the University of Nanking and the National China Union School (he was born in Milwaukee), he earned his bachelor's degree from George Washington University in 1933, and after graduate work at Oxford University, American University, and the University of Chicago, he earned his M.A. and Ph.D. from Johns Hopkins in 1935 and 1936.

Linebarger taught Asian politics at Harvard, Duke, Johns Hopkins, and the University of Canberra in Australia. He was awarded a certificate in psychiatry by the Washington School of Psychiatry. He spoke five languages and read three others.

From 1930 to 1936 he was private secretary to the legal advisor to the Government of China, and during World War II he served in U.S. Army Intelligence, helped found the Office of War Information, and served on the Operations Planning and Intelligence Board of the U.S. Army. He also served as an advisor in the Korean War and to the British in the Malay campaign.

When this unusual man began writing science fiction, he had some difficulty getting his stories accepted because of the strangeness of his vision. His first story, "Scanners Live in Vain," was published in *Fantasy Book* in 1950; his second, "The Game of Rat and Dragon," not until the November 1955 *Galaxy*, and the bulk of his approximately thirty stories appeared between 1959 and 1966, the year of his death.

His identity was a mystery, like that of James Tiptree, Jr., a decade later. Virtually no one knew his real name until after his death, in spite of the speculation. His work had the unusual quality that suggested the author must also be unusual.

His stories presented no commonplace future. They fell into two general categories: the near future and the distant future. In his stories of the near future, humanity was trying to conquer space. The effort was filled with pain and dangers that earlier writers and experimenters had never suspected, like the Great Pain of Space in "Scanners Live in Vain" that forced some men to choose a half-dead existence in order to cope with it, or the dragonlike creatures between the stars, hungry vortices of aliveness and hate, that threaten humanity's sanity in "The Game of Rat and Dragon."

In his stories of the distant future, human beings have become like gods in longevity and wealth and power. Their lives are almost unrecognizable: they do things and say things and are concerned about things that the reader never understands, but accepts as a realistic portrayal of the far future. Some recognizable passions remain, however; these are exhibited by the Underpeople, the humanlike creatures who have been evolved from cats and dogs and other animals to serve humanity, like the beautiful C'Mell herself, about whom "The Ballad of lost C'Mell" was written.

It wasn't entirely his vision that made Smith's stories unique. Part of their success came from the richness with which he created his world—as suggested by the titles of the stories: "Alpha Ralpha Boulevard," "The Lady Who Sailed the Soul," "Under Old Earth," "Think Blue, Count Two"—and the names: the Instrumentality, the Underpeople, the Lord Jestocost, the Lord Sto Odin, the Up-and-Out, old Norstrilia, the Douglas-Ouyang planets, scanners, planoform, congohelium, Go-captains, Captain Wow, the Lady May, pinlighters, habermans, cranch, the E-telekeli, and the sound of a drum going *ritiplin, rataplan*....

It was all wonderful and strange.

THE GAME OF RAT AND DRAGON

by Cordwainer Smith

The Table

Pinlighting is a hell of a way to earn a living. Underhill was furious as he closed the door behind himself. It didn't make much sense to wear a uniform and look like a soldier if people didn't appreciate what you did.

He sat down in his chair, laid his head back in the head-rest and pulled the helmet down over his forehead.

As he waited for the pin-set to warm up, he remembered the girl in the outer corridor. She had looked at it, then looked at him scornfully.

"Meow." That was all she had said. Yet it had cut him like a knife.

What did she think he was—a fool, a loafer, a uniformed nonentity? Didn't she know that for every half hour of pinlighting, he got a minimum of two months' recuperation in the hospital?

By now the set was warm. He felt the squares of space around him, sensed himself at the middle of an immense grid, a cubic grid, full of nothing. Out in that nothingness, he could sense the hollow aching horror of space itself and could feel the terrible anxiety which his mind encountered whenever it met the faintest trace of inert dust.

As he relaxed, the comforting solidity of the Sun, the clockwork of the familiar planets and the Moon rang in on him. Our own solar system was as charming and as simple as an ancient cuckoo clock filled with familiar ticking and with reassuring noises. The odd little moons of Mars swung around their planet like frantic mice, yet their regularity was itself an assurance that all was well. Far above the plane of the ecliptic, he could feel half a ton of dust more or less drifting outside the lanes of human travel.

Here there was nothing to fight, nothing to challenge the mind, to tear the living soul out of a body with its roots dripping in effluvium as tangible as blood.

Nothing ever moved in on the Solar System. He could wear the pin-set forever and be nothing more than a sort of telepathic astronomer, a man who could feel the hot, warm protection of the Sun throbbing and burning against his living mind.

Woodley came in.

"Same old ticking world," said Underhill. "Nothing to report. No wonder they didn't develop the pin-set until they began to planoform. Down here with the hot Sun around us, it feels so good and so quiet. You can feel everything spinning and turning. It's nice and sharp and compact. It's sort of like sitting around home."

Woodley grunted. He was not much given to flights of fantasy.

Undeterred, Underhill went on, "It must have been pretty good to have been an Ancient Man. I wonder why they burned up their world with war. They didn't have to planoform. They didn't have to get out to earn their living among the stars. They didn't have to dodge the Rats or play the Game. They couldn't have invented pinlighting because they didn't have any need of it, did they, Woodley?"

Woodley grunted, "Uh-huh." Woodley was twenty-six years old and due to retire in one more year. He already had a farm picked out. He had gotten through ten years of hard work pinlighting with the best of them. He had kept his sanity by not thinking very much about his job, meeting the strains of the task whenever he had to meet them and thinking nothing more about his duties until the next emergency arose.

Woodley never made a point of getting popular among the Partners. None of the Partners liked him very much. Some of them even resented him. He was suspected of thinking ugly thoughts of the Partners on occasion, but since none of the Partners ever thought a complaint in articulate form, the other pinlighters and the Chiefs of the Instrumentality left him alone.

Underhill was still full of the wonder of their job. Happily he babbled on, "What does happen to us when we planoform? Do you think it's sort of like dying? Did you ever see anybody who had his soul pulled out?"

"Pulling souls is just a way of talking about it," said Woodley. "After all these years, nobody knows whether we have souls or not."

"But I saw one once. I saw what Dogwood looked like when he came apart. There was something funny. It looked wet and sort of sticky as if it were bleeding, and it went out of him—and you know what they did to Dogwood? They took him away, up in that part of the hospital where you and I never go—way up at the top part where the others are, where the others always have to go if they are alive after the Rats of the Up-and-Out have gotten them."

Woodley sat down and lit an ancient pipe. He was burning something called tobacco in it. It was a dirty sort of habit, but it made him look very dashing and adventurous.

"Look here, youngster. You don't have to worry about that stuff. Pinlighting is getting better all the time. The Partners are getting better. I've seen them pinlight two Rats forty-six million miles apart in one and a half milliseconds. As long as people had to try to work the pin-sets themselves, there was always the chance that with a minimum of four hundred milliseconds for the human mind to set a pinlight, we wouldn't light the Rats up fast enough to protect our planoforming ships. The Partners have changed all that. Once they get going, they're faster than the Rats. And they always will be. I know it's not easy, letting a Partner share your mind—"

"It's not easy for them, either," said Underhill.

"Don't worry about them. They're not human. Let them take care of themselves. I've seen more pinlighters go crazy from monkeying around with Partners than I have ever seen caught by the Rats. How many do you actually know of them that got grabbed by Rats?"

Underhill looked down at his fingers, which shone green and purple in the vivid light thrown by the tuned-in pin-set, and counted ships. The thumb for the *Andromeda*, lost with crew and passengers, the index finger and the middle finger for *Release Ships* 43 and 56, found with their pin-sets burned out and every man, woman, and child on board dead or insane. The ring finger, the little finger, and the thumb of the other hand were the first battleships to be lost to the Rats—lost as people realized that there was something out there *underneath space itself* which was alive, capricious and malevolent.

Planoforming was sort of funny. It felt like—

Like nothing much.

Like the twinge of a mild electric shock.

Like the ache of a sore tooth bitten on for the first time. Like a slightly painful flash of light against the eyes.

Yet in that time, a forty-thousand-ton ship lifting free above Earth disappeared somehow or other into two dimensions and appeared half a light-year or fifty light-years off.

At one moment, he would be sitting in the Fighting Room, the pin-set ready and the familiar Solar System ticking around inside his head. For a second or a year (he could never tell how long it really was, subjectively), the funny little flash went through him, and then he was loose in the Up-and-Out, the terrible open spaces between the stars, where the stars themselves felt like pimples on his telepathic mind and the planets were too far away to be sensed or read.

Somewhere in this outer space, a gruesome death awaited, death and horror of a kind which Man had never encountered until he reached out for interstellar space itself. Apparently the lights of the suns kept the dragons away.

Dragons. That was what people called them. To ordinary people, there was nothing, nothing except the shiver of planoforming and the hammer blow of sudden death or the dark spastic note of lunacy descending into their minds.

But to the telepaths, they were Dragons.

In the fraction of a second between the telepaths' awareness of a hostile something out in the black, hollow nothingness of space and the impact of a ferocious, ruinous psychic blow against all living things within the ship, the telepaths had sensed entities something like the Dragons of ancient human lore, beasts more clever than beasts, demons more tangible than demons, hungry vortices of aliveness and hate compounded by unknown means but out of the thin tenuous matter between the stars.

It took a surviving ship to bring back the news—a ship in which, by sheer chance, a telepath had a light beam ready, turning it out at the innocent dust so that, within the panorama of his mind, the Dragon dissolved into nothing at all and the other passengers, themselves non-telepathic, went about their way not realizing that their own immediate deaths had been averted.

From then on, it was easy—almost.

Planoforming ships always carried telepaths. Telepaths had their sensitiveness enlarged to an immense range by the pin-sets, which were telepathic amplifiers adapted to the mammal mind. The pin-sets in turn were electronically geared into small dirigible light bombs. Light did it.

Light broke up the Dragons, allowed the ships to reform three-dimensionally, skip, skip, skip, as they moved from star to star.

The odds suddenly moved down from a hundred to one against mankind to sixty to forty in mankind's favor.

This was not enough. The telepaths were trained to become ultrasensitive, trained to become aware of the Dragons in less than a millisecond.

But it was found that the Dragons could move a million miles in just under two milliseconds, and that this was not enough for the human mind to activate the light beams.

Attempts had been made to sheath the ships in light at all times.

This defense wore out.

As mankind learned about the Dragons, so too, apparently, the Dragons learned about mankind. Somehow they flattened their own bulk and came in on extremely flat trajectories very quickly.

Intense light was needed, light of sunlight intensity. This could be provided only by light bombs. Pinlighting came into existence.

Pinlighting consisted of the detonation of ultra-vivid miniature photonuclear bombs, which converted a few ounces of a magnesium isotope into pure visible radiance.

The odds kept coming down in mankind's favor, yet ships were being lost.

It became so bad that people didn't even want to find the ships because the rescuers knew what they would see. It was sad to bring back to Earth three hundred bodies ready for burial and two hundred or three hundred lunatics, damaged beyond repair, to be wakened, and fed, and cleaned, and put to sleep, wakened and fed again until their lives were ended.

Telepaths tried to reach into the minds of the psychotics who had been damaged by the Dragons, but they found nothing there beyond vivid spouting columns of fiery terror bursting from the primordial id itself, the volcanic sources of life.

Then came the Partners.

Man and Partner could do together what Man could not do alone. Men had the intellect. Partners had the speed.

The Partners rode in their tiny craft, no larger than footballs, outside the spaceships. They planoformed with the ships. They rode beside them in their six-pound craft ready to attack.

The tiny ships of the Partners were swift. Each carried a dozen pinlights, bombs no bigger than thimbles.

The Pinlighters threw the Partners- -quite literally threw—by means of mind-to-firing relays direct at the Dragons.

What seemed to be Dragons to the human mind appeared in the form of gigantic Rats in the minds of the Partners.

Out in the pitiless nothingness of space, the Partners' minds responded to an instinct as old as life. The Partners attacked, striking with a speed faster than Man's, going from attack to attack until the Rats or themselves were destroyed. Almost all the time it was the Partners who won.

With the safety of the interstellar skip, skip, skip of the ships, commerce increased immensely, the population of all the colonies went up, and the demand for trained Partners increased.

Underhill and Woodley were a part of the third generation of pinlighters and yet, to them, it seemed as though their craft had endured forever.

Gearing space into minds by means of the pin-set, adding the Partners to those minds, keying up the mind for the tension of a fight on which all depended—this was more than human synapses could stand for long. Underhill needed his two months' rest after half an hour of fighting. Woodley needed his retirement after ten years of service. They were young. They were good. But they had limitations.

So much depended on the choice of Partners, so much on the sheer luck of who drew whom.

The Shuffle

Father Moontree and the little girl named West entered the room. They were the other two pinlighters. The human complement of the Fighting Room was now complete.

Father Moontree was a red-faced man of forty-five who had lived the peaceful life of a farmer until he reached his fortieth year. Only then, belatedly, did the authorities find he was telepathic and agree to let him late in life enter upon the career of pinlighter. He did well at it, but he was fantastically old for this kind of business.

Father Moontree looked at the glum Woodley and the musing Underhill. "How're the youngsters today? Ready for a good fight?"

"Father always wants a fight," giggled the little girl named West. She was such a little girl. Her giggle was high and childish. She looked like the last person in the world one would expect to find in the rough, sharp dueling of pinlighting.

Underhill had been amused one time when he found one of the most sluggish of the Partners coming away happy from contact with the mind of the girl named West.

Usually the Partners didn't care much about the human minds with which they were paired for the journey. The Partners seemed to take the attitude that human minds were complex and fouled up beyond belief, anyhow. No Partner ever questioned the superiority of the human mind, though very few of the Partners were much impressed by that superiority.

The Partners liked people. They were willing to fight with them. They were even willing to die for them. But when a Partner liked an individual the way, for example, that Captain Wow or the Lady May liked Underhill, the liking had nothing to do with intellect. It was a matter of temperament, of feel.

Underhill knew perfectly well that Captain Wow regarded his, Underhill's, brains as silly. What Captain Wow liked was Underhill's friendly emotional structure, the cheerfulness and glint of wicked amusement that shot through Underhill's unconscious thought patterns, and the gaiety with which Underhill faced danger. The words, the history books, the ideas, the science—Underhill could sense all that in his own mind, reflected back from Captain Wow's mind, as so much rubbish.

Miss West looked at Underhill, "I bet you've put stickum on the stones."

"I did not!"

Underhill felt his ears grow red with embarrassment. During his novitiate, he had tried to cheat in the lottery because he got particularly fond of a special Partner, a lovely young mother named Murr. It was so much easier to operate with Murr and she was so affectionate toward him that he forgot pinlighting was hard work and that he was not instructed to have a good time with his

Partner. They were both designed and prepared to go into deadly battle together.

One cheating had been enough. They had found him out, and he had been laughed at for years.

Father Moontree picked up the imitation-leather cup and shook the stone dice which assigned them their Partners for the trip. By senior rights, he took first draw.

He grimaced. He had drawn a greedy old character, a tough old male whose mind was full of slobbering thoughts of food, veritable oceans full of half-spoiled fish. Father Moontree had once said that he burped cod liver oil for weeks after drawing that particular glutton, so strongly had the telepathic image of fish impressed itself upon his mind. Yet the glutton was a glutton for danger as well as for fish. He had killed sixty-three Dragons, more than any other Partner in the service, and was quite literally worth his weight in gold.

The little girl West came next. She drew Captain Wow. When she saw who it was, she smiled.

"I *like* him," she said. "He's such fun to fight with. He feels so nice and cuddly in my mind."

"Cuddly, hell," said Woodley. "I've been in his mind, too. It's the most leering mind in this ship, bar none."

"Nasty man," said the little girl. She said it decoratively, without reproach.

Underhill, looking at her, shivered.

He didn't see how she could take Captain Wow so calmly. Captain Wow's mind *did* leer. When Captain Wow got excited in the middle of a battle, confusing images of Dragons, deadly Rats, luscious beds, the smell of fish, and the shock of space all scrambled together in his mind as he and Captain Wow, their consciousness linked together through the pinset, became a fantastic composite of human being and Persian cat.

That's the trouble with working with cats, thought Underhill. It's a pity that nothing else anywhere will serve as Partner. Cats were all right once you got in touch with them telepathically. They were smart enough to meet the needs of the fight, but their motives and desires were certainly different from those of humans.

They were companionable enough as long as you thought tangible images at them, but their minds just closed up and went to sleep when you recited Shakespeare or Colegrove, or if you tried to tell them what space was.

It was sort of funny realizing that the Partners who were so grim and mature out here in space were the same cute little animals that people had used as pets for thousands of years back on Earth. He had embarrassed himself more than once while on the ground saluting perfectly ordinary nontelepathic cats because he had forgotten for the moment that they were not Partners.

He picked up the cup and shook out his stone dice.

He was lucky—he drew the Lady May.

The Lady May was the most thoughtful Partner he had ever met. In her, the finely bred pedigree mind of a Persian cat had reached one of its highest peaks of development. She was more complex than any human woman, but the complexity was all one of emotions, memory, hope and discriminated experience—experience sorted through without benefit of words.

When he had first come into contact with her mind, he was astonished at its clarity. With her he remembered her kittenhood. He remembered every mating experience she had ever had. He saw in a half-recognizable gallery all the other pinlighters with whom she had been paired for the fight. And he saw himself radiant, cheerful and desirable.

He even thought he caught the edge of a longing—

A very flattering and yearning thought: *What a pity he is not a cat.*

Woodley picked up the last stone. He drew what he deserved—a sullen, scared old tomcat with none of the verve of Captain Wow. Woodley's Partner was the most animal of all the cats on the ship, a low, brutish type with a dull mind. Even telepathy had not refined his character. His ears were half chewed off from the first fights in which he had engaged.

He was a serviceable fighter, nothing more.

Woodley grunted.

Underhill glanced at him oddly. Didn't Woodley ever do anything but grunt?

Father Moontree looked at the other three. "You might as well get your Partners now. I'll let the Scanner know we're ready to go into the Up-and-Out."

The Deal

Underhill spun the combination lock on the Lady May's cage. He woke her gently and took her into his arms. She bumped her back luxuriously, stretched her claws, started to purr, thought better of it, and licked him on the wrist instead. He did not have the pin-set on, so their minds were closed to each other, but in the angle of her mustache and in the movement of her ears, he caught some sense of the gratification she experienced in finding him as her Partner.

He talked to her in human speech, even though speech meant nothing to a cat when the pin-set was not on.

"It's a damn shame, sending a sweet little thing like you whirling around in the coldness of nothing to hunt for Rats that are bigger and deadlier than all of us put together. You didn't ask for this kind of a fight, did you?"

For answer, she licked his hand, purred, tickled his cheek with her long fluffy tail, turned around and faced him, golden eyes shining.

For a moment they stared at each other, man squatting, cat standing erect on her hind legs, front claws digging into his knee. Human eyes and cat eyes looked across an immensity which no words could meet, but which affection spanned in a single glance.

"Time to get in," he said.

She walked docilely into her spheroid carrier. She climbed in. He saw to it that her miniature pin-set rested firmly and comfortably against the base of her brain. He made sure that her claws were padded so that she could not tear herself in the excitement of battle.

Softly he said to her, "Ready?"

For answer, she preened her back as much as her harness would permit and purred softly within the confines of the frame that held her.

He slapped down the lid and watched the sealant ooze around the seam. For a few hours, she was welded into her projectile until a workman with a short cutting arc would remove her after she had done her duty.

He picked up the entire projectile and slipped it into the ejection tube. He closed the door of the tube, spun the lock, seated himself in his chair, and put his own pin-set on.

Once again he flung the switch.

He sat in a small room, *small, small, warm, warm,* the bodies of the other three people moving close around him, the tangible lights in the ceiling bright and heavy against his closed eyelids.

As the pin-set warmed, the room fell away. The other people ceased to be people and became small glowing heaps of fire, embers, dark red fire, with the consciousness of life burning like old red coals in a country fireplace.

As the pin-set warmed a little more, he felt Earth just below him, felt the ship slipping away, felt the turning Moon as it swung on the far side of the world, felt the planets and the hot, clear goodness of the Sun which kept the Dragons so far from mankind's native ground.

Finally, he reached complete awareness.

He was telepathically alive to a range of millions of miles. He felt the dust which he had noticed earlier high above the ecliptic. With a thrill of warmth and tenderness, he felt the consciousness of the Lady May pouring over into his own. Her consciousness was as gentle and clear and yet sharp to the taste of his mind as if it were scented oil. It felt relaxing and reassuring. He could sense her welcome of him. It was scarcely a thought, just a raw emotion of greeting.

At last they were one again.

In a tiny remote corner of his mind, as tiny as the smallest toy he had ever seen in his childhood, he was still aware of the room and the ship, and of Father Moontree picking up a telephone and speaking to a Scanner captain in charge of the ship.

His telepathic mind caught the idea long before his ears could frame the words. The actual sound followed the idea the way that thunder on an ocean beach follows the lightning inward from far out over the seas.

"The Fighting Room is ready. Clear to planoform, sir."

The Play

Underhill was always a little exasperated the way that the Lady May experienced things before he did.

He was braced for the quick vinegar thrill of planoforming, but he caught her report of it before his own nerves could register what happened.

Earth had fallen so far away that he groped for several milliseconds before he found the Sun in the upper rear right-hand corner of his telepathic mind.

That was a good jump, he thought. This way we'll get there in four or five skips.

A few hundred miles outside the ship, the Lady May thought back at him, "O warm, O generous, O gigantic man! O brave, O friendly, O tender and huge Partner! O wonderful with you, with you so good, good, good, warm, warm, now to fight, now to go, good with you..."

He knew that she was not thinking words, that his mind took the clear amiable babble of her cat intellect and translated it into images which his own thinking could record and understand.

Neither one of them was absorbed in the game of mutual greetings. He reached out far beyond her range of perception to see if there was anything near the ship. It was funny how it was possible to do two things at once. He could scan space with his pin-set mind and yet at the same time catch a vagrant thought of hers, a lovely, affectionate thought about a son who had had a golden face and a chest covered with soft, incredibly downy white fur.

While he was still searching, he caught the warning from her.

We jump again!

And so they had. The ship moved to a second planoform. The stars were different. The Sun was immeasurably far behind. Even the nearest stars were barely in contact. This was good Dragon country, this open, nasty, hollow kind of space. He reached farther, faster, sensing and looking for danger, ready to fling the Lady May at danger wherever he found it.

Terror blared up in his mind, so sharp, so clear, that it came through as a physical wrench.

The little girl named West had found something—something immense, long, black, sharp, greedy, horrific. She flung Captain Wow at it.

Underhill tried to keep his own mind clear. "Watch out!" he shouted telepathically at the others, trying to move the Lady May around.

At one corner of the battle, he felt the lustful rage of Captain Wow as the big Persian tomcat detonated lights while he approached the streak of dust which threatened the ship and the people within.

The lights scored near-misses. The dust flattened itself, changing from the shape of a sting-ray into the shape of a spear.

Not three milliseconds had elapsed.

Father Moontree was talking human words and was saying in a voice that moved like cold molasses out of a heavy jar, "C-A-P-T-A-I-N." Underhill knew that the sentence was going to be "Captain, move fast!"

The battle would be fought and finished before Father Moontree got through talking.

Now, fractions of a millisecond later, the Lady May was directly in line.

Here was where the skill and speed of the Partners came in. She could react faster than he. She could see the threat as an immense Rat coming directly at her.

She could fire the light-bombs with a discrimination which he might miss.

He was connected with her mind, but he could not follow it.

His consciousness absorbed the tearing wound inflicted by the alien enemy. It was like no wound on Earth—raw, crazy pain which started like a burn at his navel. He began to writhe in his chair.

Actually he had not yet had time to move a muscle when the Lady May struck back at their enemy.

Five evenly spaced photonuclear bombs blazed out across a hundred thousand miles.

The pain in his mind and body vanished.

He felt a moment of fierce, terrible, feral elation running through the mind of the Lady May as she finished her kill. It was always disappointing to the cats to find out that their enemies whom they sensed as gigantic space Rats disappeared at the moment of destruction.

Then he felt her hurt, the pain and the fear that swept over both of them as the battle, quicker than the movement of an eyelid, had come and gone. In the same instant there came the sharp and acid twinge of planoform.

Once more the ship went skip.

He could hear Woodley thinking at him. "You don't have to bother much. This old son of a gun and I will take over for a while."

Twice again the twinge, the skip.

He had no idea where he was until the lights of the Caledonia space board shone below.

With a weariness that lay almost beyond the limits of thought, he threw his mind back into rapport with the pin-set, fixing the Lady May's projectile gently and neatly in its launching tube.

She was half dead with fatigue, but he could feel the beat of her heart, could listen to her panting, and he grasped the grateful edge of a thanks reaching from her mind to his.

The Score

They put him in the hospital at Caledonia.

The doctor was friendly but firm. "You actually got touched by that Dragon. That's as close a shave as I've ever seen. It's all so quick that it'll be a long time before we know what happened scientifically, but I suppose you'd be ready for the insane asylum now if the contact had lasted several tenths of a millisecond longer. What kind of cat did you have out in front of you?"

Underhill felt the words coming out of him slowly. Words were such a lot of trouble compared with the speed and the joy of thinking, fast and sharp and clear, mind to mind! But words were all that could reach ordinary people like this doctor.

His mouth moved heavily as he articulated words. "Don't call our Partners cats. The right thing to call them is Partners. They fight for us in a team. You ought to know we call them Partners, not cats. How is mine?"

"I don't know," said the doctor contritely. "We'll find out for you. Meanwhile, old man, you take it easy. There's nothing but rest that can help you. Can you make yourself sleep, or would you like us to give you some kind of sedative?"

"I can sleep," said Underhill. "I just want to know about the Lady May."

The nurse joined in. She was a little antagonistic. "Don't you want to know about the other people?"

"They're okay," said Underhill. "I knew that before I came in here."

He stretched his arms and sighed and grinned at them. He could see they were relaxing and were beginning to treat him as a person instead of a patient.

"I'm all right," he said. "Just let me know when I can go see my Partner."

A new thought struck him. He looked wildly at the doctor. "They didn't send her off with the ship, did they?"

"I'll find out right away," said the doctor. He gave Underhill a reassuring squeeze of the shoulder and left the room.

The nurse took a napkin off a goblet of chilled fruit juice.

Underhill tried to smile at her. There seemed to be something wrong with the girl. He wished she would go away. First she had started to be friendly and now she was distant again. It's a nuisance being telepathic, he thought. You keep trying to reach even when you are not making contact.

Suddenly she swung around on him.

"You pinlighters! You and your damn cats!"

Just as she stamped out, he burst into her mind. He saw himself a radiant hero, clad in his smooth suede uniform, the pin-set crown shining like ancient royal jewels around his head. He saw his own face, handsome and masculine, shining out of her mind. He saw himself very far away and he saw himself as she hated him.

She hated him in the secrecy of her own mind. She hated him because he was—she thought—proud, and strange, and rich, better and more beautiful than people like her.

He cut off the sight of her mind and, as he buried his face in the pillow, he caught an image of the Lady May.

"She *is* a cat," he thought. "That's all she is—a *cat!*"

But that was not how his mind saw her—quick beyond all dreams of speed, sharp, clever, unbelievably graceful, beautiful, wordless and undemanding.

Where would he ever find a woman who could compare with her?

SCALPEL OF WIT

By the 1950s science fiction had become sufficiently secure, sufficiently mature, or sufficiently decadent that it could turn around and look at itself, and sometimes laugh. Writers began to deal with science fiction themes in a playful way, rather than always speculating about implications for the real world. The writing of fiction about fiction has been called meta-fiction. Some science fiction writers in the 1950s were beginning to produce meta-*science* fiction.

The result sometimes was a comment on science fiction itself—a criticism or an outright parody. Other times, however, science fiction conventions were used as a way to tell another kind of story; they became metaphors for experience, new ways of dealing with the human condition that had not yet been trampled into clichés.

Ray Bradbury was one of the first to use science fiction in this way; his rocketships, his aliens, his spacemen were metaphors and not to be taken literally. Brian Aldiss called him "the first writer to recombine the old props in his own way." Alfred Bester was another writer who came to science fiction with something else in mind. Scholes and Rabkin said of his *The Stars My Destination*, "though the moral fable is serious, the spirit of play in the whole work indicates a kind of self-consciousness new to science fiction."

It may be no coincidence that *Playboy* magazine was fascinated by science fiction from its beginnings in 1953. The men's magazines have always published a substantial quantity of "good fiction," as if it were an act of social redemption. But the doyen of men's magazines, *Esquire*, usually has aimed at too lofty a literary level to be interested in popular fiction. *Playboy*, however, seemed to love science fiction from its first days, reprinting Bradbury stories beside Boccaccio, and eventually publishing many excellent science fiction stories. *Playboy* wanted, it is true, more intensity and greater concern for character than usual, but it did not demand that the science fiction element be adulterated. When other men's magazines *Penthouse*, *Rogue*, and the rest—entered the field, they followed *Playboy*'s lead. Finally one of them, *Penthouse*, founded its own quality magazine of science fiction and science fact, *Omni*.

Playboy has published some of the best science fiction written over the past two and a half decades. It offered the best rates in the magazine field, and science fiction writers responded. Writers whose stories have appeared in *Playboy* include Bradbury, Arthur Clarke, Damon Knight, Frederik Pohl, Ursula K. Le Guin, William Tenn, Robert Bloch, the late Charles Beaumont, Avram Davidson, J. G. Ballard, and the late Fredric Brown. Another was Robert Sheckley, who had early success with the better-paying slick magazines. He was a natural: he wrote slick, witty fiction.

Sheckley (1928-) returned to New York City after service in Korea and was graduated from New York University. He appeared first in 1952 with a story entitled "Final Examination" in *Imagination Science Fiction*, but he then immediately began selling to *Galaxy*, which was the natural home for his clever ideas and witty style. In the next decade or so he published 106 stories and three serials, all but seven of the stories and one of the serials before 1959. He was published in almost all the magazines, including *Astounding* and *F&SF*, but 63 of those 106 stories and one serial were published in *Galaxy*, under his own name and under the pseudonyms he had to adopt for *Galaxy* because he was so prolific, Finn O'Donnevan and Phillips Barbee.

A major asset was his light touch. The magazines always yearned for humor, and in Sheckley's hands the standard notions of space, aliens, future artifacts, cities, overpopulation, entertainment, culture, survival, love, death, and war were transmuted into something that glittered. Not everything was treated humorously: sometimes, as in "The People Trap," "The Seventh Victim," and *Journey Beyond Tomorrow* (1962; serialized the same year as *The Journey of Joenes*), the satire was savage.

Esquire and *Today's Woman* bought an early story or two, and then Sheckley appeared at least eight times in *Playboy*, beginning in 1955 with "Spy Story" (also called "Citizen in Space"). The story reprinted here, "Pilgrimage to Earth," was published in *Playboy* as "Love, Inc." in September 1956. His short stories have been widely reprinted in anthologies, and in collections of his own such as *Untouched by Human Hands* (1954), *Citizen in Space* (1955), *Pilgrimage to Earth* (1958), *Store of Infinity* (1960), *Notions Unlimited* (1960), *Shards of Space* (1962), *The People Trap* (1968), *Can You Feel Anything When I Do This?* (1971), *The Wonderful World of Robert Sheckley* (1979), *Is THAT What People Do? The Selected Short Stories of Robert Sheckley* (1984).

He has produced a number of science fiction novels: *Immortality Inc.* (1958; also called *Time Killer* and *Immortality Delivered*), *The Status Civilization* (1960), *Journey Beyond Tomorrow* (1962), *The Tenth Victim* (1965), *Mindswap* (1965), *Dimension of Miracles* (1968), *Crompton Divided* (1978), *Dramocles* (1983), two sequels to *The Tenth Victim*, and *Options* (1975). He also has written thrillers and novels about an international detective.

PILGRIMAGE TO EARTH

by Robert Sheckley

Alfred Simon was born on Kazanga IV, a small agricultural planet near Arcturus, and there he drove a combine through the wheat fields, and in the long, hushed evenings listened to the recorded love songs of Earth.

Life was pleasant enough on Kazanga, and the girls were buxom, jolly, frank and acquiescent, good companions for a hike through the hills or a swim in the brook, staunch mates for life. But romantic—never! There was good fun be had on Kazanga, in a cheerful open manner. But there was no more than fun.

Simon felt that something was missing in this bland existence. One day, he discovered what it was.

A vendor came to Kazanga in a battered spaceship loaded with books. He was gaunt, white-haired, and a little mad. A celebration was held for him, for novelty was appreciated on the outer worlds.

The vendor told them all the latest gossip; of the price war between Detroit II and III, and how fishing fared on Alana, and what the president's wife on Moracia wore, and how oddly the men of Dorvan V talked. And at last someone said, "Tell us of Earth."

"Ah!" said the vendor, raising his eyebrows. "You want to hear of the mother planet? Well, friends, there's no place like old Earth, no place at all. On Earth, friends, everything is possible, and nothing is denied."

"Nothing?" Simon asked.

"They've got a law against denial," the vendor explained, grinning. "No one has ever been known to break it. Earth is *different*, friends. You folks specialize in farming? Well, Earth specializes in impracticalities such as madness, beauty, war, intoxication, purity, horror, and the like, and people come from light-years away to sample these wares."

"And love?" a woman asked.

"Why girl," the vendor said gently, "Earth is the only place in the galaxy that still has love! Detroit II and III tried it and found it too expensive, you know, and Alana decided it was unsettling, and there was no time to import it on Moracia or Doran V. But as I said, Earth specializes in the impractical, and makes it pay."

"Pay?" a bulky farmer asked.

"Of course! Earth is old, her minerals are gone and her fields are barren. Her colonies are independent now, and filled with sober folk such as yourselves, who want value for their goods. So what else can old Earth deal in, except the non-essentials that make life worth living?"

"Were you in love on Earth?" Simon asked.

"That I was," the vendor answered, with a certain grimness. "I was in love, and now I travel. Friends, these books..."

For an exorbitant price, Simon bought an ancient poetry book, and reading, dreamed of passion beneath the lunatic moon, of dawn glimmering whitely upon lovers' parched lips, of locked bodies on a dark sea-beach, desperate with love and deafened by the booming surf.

And only on Earth was this possible! For, as the vendor told, Earth's scattered children were too hard at work wrestling a living from alien soil. The wheat and corn grew on Kazanga, and the factories increased on Detroit II and III. The fisheries of Alana were the talk of the Southern star belt, and there were dangerous beasts on Moracia, and a whole wilderness to be won on Doran V. And this was well, and exactly as it should be.

But the new worlds were austere, carefully planned, sterile in their perfections. Something had been lost in the dead reaches of space, and only Earth knew love.

Therefore, Simon worked and saved and dreamed. And in his twenty-ninth year he sold his farm, packed all his clean shirts into a serviceable handbag, put on his best suit and a pair of stout walking shoes, and boarded the Kazanga-Metropole Flyer.

At last he came to Earth, where dreams *must* come true, for there is a law against their failure.

He passed quickly through Customs at Spaceport New York, and was shuttled underground to Times Square. There he emerged blinking into daylight, tightly clutching his handbag, for he had been warned about pickpockets, cutpurses, and other denizens of the city.

Breathless with wonder, he looked around.

The first thing that struck him was the endless array of theatres, with attractions in two dimensions, three or four, depending upon your preference. And what attractions!

To the right of him a beetling marquee proclaimed: LUST ON VENUS! A DOCUMENTARY ACCOUNT OF SEX PRACTICES AMONG THE INHABITANTS OF THE GREEN HELL! SHOCKING! REVEALING!

He wanted to go in. But across the street was a war film. The billboard shouted, THE SUN BUSTERS! DEDICATED TO THE DARE-DEVILS OF THE SPACE MARINES! And further down was a picture called TARZAN BATTLES THE SATURNIAN GHOULS!

Tarzan, he recalled from his reading, was an ancient ethnic hero of Earth.

It was all wonderful, but there was so much more! He saw little open shops where one could buy food of all worlds, and especially such native Terran dishes as pizza, hotdogs, spaghetti and knishes. And there were stores which sold surplus clothing from the Terran spacefleets, and other stores which sold nothing but beverages.

Simon didn't know what to do first. Then he heard a staccato burst of gunfire behind him, and whirled.

It was only a shooting gallery, a long, narrow, brightly painted place with a waist-high counter. The manager, a swarthy fat man with a mole on his chin, sat on a high stool and smiled at Simon.

"Try your luck?"

Simon walked over and saw that, instead of the usual targets, there were four scantily dressed women at the end of the gallery, seated upon bullet-scored chairs. They had tiny bulls-eyes painted on their foreheads and above each breast.

"But do you fire real bullets?" Simon asked.

"Of course!" the manager said. "There's a law against false advertising on Earth. Real bullets and real gals! Step up and knock one off!"

One of the women called out, "Come on, sport! Bet you miss me!"

Another screamed, "He couldn't hit the broad side of a spaceship!"

"Sure he can!" another shouted. "Come on, sport!"

Simon rubbed his forehead and tried not to act surprised. After all, this was Earth, where anything was allowed as long as it was commercially feasible.

He asked, "Are there galleries where you shoot men, too?"

"Of course," the manager said. "But you ain't no pervert, are you?"

"Certainly not!"

"You an outworlder?"

"Yes. How did you know?"

"The suit. Always tell by the suit." The fat man closed his eyes and chanted, "Step up, step up and kill a woman! Get rid of a load of repressions! Squeeze the trigger and feel the old anger ooze out of you! Better than a massage! Better than getting drunk! Step up, step up and kill a woman!"

Simon asked one of the girls, "Do you stay dead when they kill you?"

"Don't be stupid," the girl said.

"But the shock—"

She shrugged her shoulders. "I could do worse."

Simon was about to ask how she could do worse, when the manager leaned over the counter, speaking confidentially.

"Look, buddy. Look what I got here."

Simon glanced over the counter and saw a compact submachine gun.

"For a ridiculously low price," the manager said, "I'll let you use the tommy. You can spray the whole place, shoot down the fixtures, rip up the walls. This drives a .45 slug, buddy, and it kicks like a mule. You really know you're firing when you fire the tommy."

"I am not interested," Simon said sternly.

"I've got a grenade or two," the manager said. "Fragmentation, of course. You could really—"

"No!"

"For a price," the manager said, "you can shoot me, too, if that's how your tastes run, although I wouldn't have guessed it. What do you say?"

"No! Never! This is horrible!"

The manager looked at him blankly. "Not in the mood now? OK. I'm open twenty-four hours a day. See you later, sport."

"Never!" Simon said, walking away.

"Be expecting you, lover!" one of the women called after him.

Simon went to a refreshment stand and ordered a small glass of Cola-Cola. He found that his hands were shaking. With an effort he steadied them, and sipped his drink. He reminded himself that he must not judge Earth by his own standards. If people on Earth enjoyed killing people, and the victims didn't mind being killed, why should anyone object?

Or should they?

He was pondering this when a voice at his elbow said, "Hey, bub."

Simon turned and saw a wizened, furtive-faced little man in an oversize raincoat standing beside him.

"Out-of-towner?" the little man asked.

"I am," Simon said. "How did you know?"

"The shoes. I always look at the shoes. How do you like our little planet?"

"It's—confusing," Simon said carefully. "I mean I didn't expect—well—"

"Of course," the little man said. "You're an idealist. One look at your honest face tells me that, my friend. You've come to Earth for a definite purpose. Am I right?"

Simon nodded. The little man said, "I know your purpose, my friend. You're looking for a war that will make the world safe for something, and you've come to the right place. We have six major wars running at all times, and there's never any waiting for an important position in any of them."

"Sorry, but—"

"Right at this moment," the little man said impressively, "the downtrodden workers of Peru are engaged in a desperate struggle against a corrupt and decadent monarchy. One more man could swing the contest! *You*, my friend, could be that man! *You* could guarantee the socialist victory!"

Observing the expression on Simon's face, the little man said quickly, "But there's a lot to be said for an enlightened aristocracy. The wise old king of Peru (a philosopher-king in the deepest Platonic sense of the word) sorely needs your help. His tiny corps of scientists, humanitarians, Swiss guards, knights of the realm and loyal peasants is sorely pressed by the foreign-inspired socialist conspiracy. A single man, now—"

"I'm not interested," Simon said.

"In China, the Anarchists—"

"No."

"Perhaps you'd prefer the Communists in Wales? Or the Capitalists in Japan? Or if your affinities lie with a splinter group such as Feminists, Prohibitionists, Free Silverists, or the like, we could probably arrange—"

"I don't want a war," Simon said.

"Who could blame you?" the little man said, nodding rapidly. "War is hell. In that case, you've come to Earth for love."

"How did you know?" Simon asked.

The little man smiled modestly. "Love and war," he said, "are Earth's two staple commodities. We've been turning them both out in bumper crops since the beginning of time."

"Is love very difficult to find?" Simon asked.

"Walk uptown two blocks," the little man said briskly. "Can't miss it. Tell 'em Joe sent you."

"But that's impossible! You can't just walk out and—"

"What do you know about love?" Joe asked.

"Nothing."

"Well, we're experts on it."

"I know what the books say," Simon said. "Passion beneath the lunatic moon—"

"Sure, and bodies on a dark sea-beach desperate with love and deafened by the booming surf."

"You've read that book?"

"It's the standard advertising brochure. I must be going. Two blocks uptown. Can't miss it."

And with a pleasant nod, Joe moved into the crowd.

Simon finished his Cola-Cola and walked slowly up Broadway, his brow knotted in thought, but determined not to form any premature judgments.

When he reached 44th Street he saw a tremendous neon sign flashing brightly. It said, LOVE, INC.

Smaller neon letters read, *Open 24 Hours a Day!*

Beneath that it read, *Up One Flight.*

Simon frowned, for a terrible suspicion had just crossed his mind. Still, he climbed the stairs and entered a small, tastefully furnished reception room. From there he was sent down a long corridor to a numbered room.

Within the room was a handsome gray-haired man who rose from behind an impressive desk and shook his hand, saying, "Well! How are things on Kazanga?"

"How did you know I was from Kazanga?"

"That shirt. I always look at the shirt. I'm Mr. Tate, and I'm here to serve you to the best of my ability. You are—"

"Simon, Alfred Simon."

"Please be seated, Mr. Simon. Cigarette? Drink? You won't regret coming to us, sir. We're the oldest love-dispensing firm in the business, and much larger than our closest competitor, Passion Unlimited. Moreover, our fees are far more reasonable, and bring you an improved product. Might I ask how you heard of us? Did you see our full page and in the *Times*? Or—'

"Joe sent me," Simon said.

"Ah, he's an active one," Mr. Tate said, shaking his head playfully. "Well sir, there's no reason to delay. You've come a long way for love, and love you shall have." He reached for a button on his desk, but Simon stopped him.

Simon said, "I don't want to be rude or anything, but..."

"Yes?" Mr. Tate said, with an encouraging smile.

"I don't understand this," Simon blurted out, flushing deeply, beads of perspiration standing out on his forehead. "I think I'm in the wrong place. I didn't come all the way to Earth just for... I mean, you can't really sell *love*, can you? Not *love!* I mean, then it isn't really *love*, is it?"

"But of course!" Tate said, half rising from his chair in astonishment. "That's the whole point! Anyone can buy sex. Good lord, it's the cheapest thing in the universe, next to human life. But *love* is rare, *love is* special, *love* is found only on Earth. Have you read our brochure?"

"Bodies on a dark sea-beach?" Simon asked.

"Yes, that one. I wrote it. Gives something of the feeling, doesn't it? You can't get that feeling from just *anyone*, Mr. Simon. You can get that feeling only from someone who loves you."

Simon said dubiously, "It's not genuine love though, is it?"

"Of course it is! If we were selling simulated love, we'd label it as such. The advertising laws on Earth are strict, I can assure you. Anything can be sold, but it must be labeled properly. That's ethics, Mr. Simon!"

Tate caught his breath, and continued in a calmer tone. "No sir, make no mistake. Our product is not a substitute. It is the exact self-same feeling that poets and writers have raved about for thousands of years. Through the wonders of modern science we can bring this feeling to you at your convenience, attractively packaged, completely disposable, and for a ridiculously low price."

Simon said, "I pictured something more—spontaneous."

"Spontaneity has its charm," Mr. Tate agreed. "Our research labs are working on it. Believe me, there's nothing science can't produce, as long as there's a market for it."

"I don't like any of this," Simon said, getting to his feet. "I think I'll just go see a movie."

"Wait!" Mr. Tate cried. "You think we're trying to put something over on you. You think we'll introduce you to a girl who will *act* as though she loved you, but who in reality will not. Is that it?"

"I guess so," Simon said.

"But it just isn't so! It would be too costly for one thing. For another, the wear and tear on the girl would be tremendous. And it would be psychologically unsound for her to attempt living a lie of such depth and scope."

"Then how do you do it?"

"By utilizing our understanding of science and the human mind."

To Simon, this sounded like double-talk. He moved toward the door.

"Tell me something," Mr. Tate said. "You're a bright looking young fellow. Don't you think you could tell real love from a counterfeit item?"

"Certainly."

"There's your safeguard! *You* must be satisfied, or don't pay us a cent."

"I'll think about it," Simon said.

"Why delay? Leading psychologists say that *real* love is a fortifier and a restorer of sanity, a balm for damaged egos, a restorer of hormone balance, and an improver of the complexion. The love we supply you has everything: deep and abiding affection, unrestrained passion, complete faithfulness, an almost mystic affection for your defects as well as your virtues, a pitiful desire to please, *and,* as a plus that only Love Inc., can supply: that uncontrollable first spark, that blinding moment of love at first sight!"

Mr. Tate pressed a button. Simon frowned indecisively. The door opened, a girl stepped in, and Simon stopped thinking.

She was tall and slender, and her hair was brown with a sheen of red. Simon could have told you nothing about her face, except that it brought tears to his eyes. And if you asked him about her figure, he might have killed you.

"Miss Penny Bright," said Tate, "meet Mr. Alfred Simon."

The girl tried to speak, but no words came, and Simon was equally dumbstruck. He looked at her and *knew*. Nothing else mattered. To the depths of his heart he knew that he was truly and completely loved.

They left at once, hand in hand, and were taken by jet to a small white cottage in a pine grove, overlooking the sea, and there they talked and laughed and loved, and later Simon saw his beloved wrapped in the sunset flame like a goddess of fire. And in blue twilight she looked at him with eyes enormous and dark, her known body mysterious again. The moon came up, bright and lunatic, changing flesh to shadow, and she wept and beat his chest with her small fists, and Simon wept too, although he did not know why. And at last dawn came, faint and disturbed, glimmering upon their parched lips and locked bodies, and nearby the booming surf deafened, inflamed, and maddened them.

At noon they were back in the offices of Love, Inc. Penny clutched his hand for a moment, then disappeared through an inner door.

"Was it real love?" Mr. Tate asked.

"Yes!"

"And was everything satisfactory?"

"Yes! It was love, it was the real thing! But why did she insist on returning?"

"Post-hypnotic command," Mr. Tate said.

"What?"

"What did you expect? Everyone wants love, but few wish to pay for it. Here is your bill, sir."

Simon paid, fuming. "This wasn't necessary," he said. "Of course I would pay you for bringing us together. Where is she now? What have you done with her?"

"Please," Mr. Tate said soothingly. "Try to calm yourself."

"I don't want to be calm!" Simon shouted. "I want Penny!"

"That will be impossible," Mr. Tate said, with the barest hint of frost in his voice. "Kindly stop making a spectacle of yourself."

"Are you trying to get more money out of me?" Simon shrieked. "All right, I'll pay. How much do I have to pay to get her out of your clutches?" And Simon yanked out his wallet and slammed it on the desk.

Mr. Tate poked the wallet with a stiffened forefinger. "Put that back in your pocket," he said. "We are an old and respectable firm. If you raise your voice again, I shall be forced to have you ejected."

Simon calmed himself with an effort, put the wallet back in his pocket and sat down. He took a deep breath and said, very quietly, "I'm sorry."

"That's better," Mr. Tate said. "I will not be shouted at. However, if you are reasonable, I can be reasonable too. Now, what's the trouble?"

"The trouble?" Simon's voice started to lift. He controlled it and said, "She loves me."

"Of course."

"Then how can you separate us?"

"What has the one thing got to do with the other?" Mr. Tate asked. "Love is a delightful interlude, a relaxation, good for the intellect, for the ego, for the hormone balance, and for the skin tone. But one would hardly wish to *continue* loving, would one?"

"I would," Simon said. "This love was special, unique—"

"They all are," Mr. Tate said. "But as you know, they are all produced in the same way."

"What?"

"Surely you know something about the mechanics of love production?"

"No," Simon said. "I thought it was—natural."

Mr. Tate shook his head. "We gave up natural selection centuries ago, shortly after the Mechanical Revolution. It was too slow, and commercially unfeasible. Why bother with it, when we can produce any feeling at will by conditioning and proper stimulation of certain brain centers? The result? Penny, completely in love with you! Your own bias, which we calculated, in favor of her particular somatotype, made it complete. We always throw in the dark sea-beach, the lunatic moon, the pallid dawn—"

"Then she could have been made to love anyone," Simon said slowly.

"Could have been *brought* to love anyone," Mr. Tate corrected.

"Oh, lord, how did she get into this horrible work?" Simon asked.

"She came in and signed a contract in the usual way," Tate said. "It pays very well. And at the termination of the lease, we return her original personality—untouched! But why do you call the work horrible? There's nothing reprehensible about love."

"It wasn't love!" Simon cried.

"But it was! The genuine article! Unbiased scientific firms have made qualitative tests of it, in comparison with the natural thing. In every case, *our* love tested out to more depth, passion, fervor and scope."

Simon shut his eyes tightly, opened them and said, "Listen to me. I don't care about your scientific tests. I love her, she loves me, that's all that counts. Let me speak to her! I want to marry her!"

Mr. Tate wrinkled his nose in distaste. "Come, come, man! You wouldn't want to *marry* a girl like that! But if it's marriage you're after, we deal in that too. I can arrange an idyllic and nearly spontaneous love-match for you with a guaranteed government-inspected virgin—"

"No! I love Penny! At least let me speak to her!"

"That will be quite impossible," Mr. Tate said.

"Why?"

Mr. Tate pushed a button on his desk. "Why do you think? We've wiped out the previous indoctrination, Penny is now in love with someone else."

And then Simon understood. He had realized that even now Penny was looking at another man with that passion he had known, feeling for another man that complete and bottomless love that unbiased scientific firms had shown to be so much greater than the old-fashioned, commercially unfeasible natural selection, and that upon that same dark sea-beach mentioned in the advertising brochure—

He lunged for Tate's throat. Two attendants, who had entered the office a few moments earlier, caught him and led him to the door.

"Remember!" Tate called. "This in no way invalidates your own experience."

Hellishly enough, Simon knew that what Tate said was true.

And then he found himself on the street.

At first, all he desired was to escape from Earth, where the commercial impracticalities were more than a normal man could afford. He walked very quickly, and his Penny walked beside him, her face glorified with love for him, and him, and him, and you, and you.

And of course he came to the shooting gallery.

"Try your luck?" the manager asked.

"Set 'em up," said Alfred Simon.

THE BRITISH ARE COMING!

The island that produced the father of modern science fiction, and in fact nurtured the young genre through its early years, had little of its own to contribute to the development of science fiction for a period of almost three decades after the creation of the science fiction magazines.

Wells established science fiction's subject matter and many of its techniques in the decade between 1893 and 1903, but the magazines took control of the genre, pulled it together, and made everything that occurred outside seem irrelevant to what was going on within the ghetto. Major works created by writers such as Olaf Stapledon, Aldous Huxley, George Orwell, Franz Werfel, and others were more literate and more exciting than what was appearing in the magazines, but because they were working outside they were influential only insofar as ghetto writers responded to them and brought their influences into the stories being published in the magazines.

Science fiction became a peculiarly American genre from 1926 until recently, not just in the United States but in foreign countries, where American science fiction in translation usually sold better than the native product. Even today science fiction must seem American in order to feel like the real stuff.

Important English writers began to contribute to the genre in the 1930s and 1940s: John Beynon Harris (1903–1969), who became better known in the 1950s under the name John Wyndham; John Russell Fearn (1908–1960), who reappeared in 1950 as Vargo Statten; Eric Frank Russell (1905–1978), a frequent contributor to *Astounding* and *Unknown* who won a Hugo in 1955 for his "Allamagoosa"; William F. Temple (1914-1989); A. Bertram Chandler (1912-1984); E. C. Tubb (1919-); Edmund Cooper (1926-1982); C. S. Youd (1922-), who became successful on both sides of the ocean under the pseudonym John Christopher; Arthur C. Clarke, of course; and many others. But either they made their greatest impact outside the magazines or they contributed to the evolution of the genre by writing American science fiction aimed at the United States magazines, since the British magazines were shaky and their rates were lower.

In the 1950s the situation began to change. The British brought unique talents and interests to their writing: a greater literacy that resulted from the fact that in Great Britain science fiction was never as rigorously segregated from other forms of literature; a greater concern for character; and a penchant and a talent for the disaster novel. These came to fruition with Wyndham and Christopher.

After the mid-1960s and the *New Worlds* transformation of science fiction into the New Wave, the situation became clearer. British science fiction produced J. G. Ballard (1930-), Charles Platt (1944-), and others, and new names began to appear, such as Keith Roberts (1935-); Colin Middleton Murry (1926-), who writes science fiction under the name Richard Cowper; and Christopher Priest (1944-).

Two major authors of British science fiction began careers of remarkable distinction in the mid-1950s: John Brunner (discussed later) and Brian W. Aldiss (1925-). Both were converted to science fiction by reading copies of American magazines imported by Woolworth's, both contributed prolifically to American and British magazines, but beyond this their careers diverged.

Aldiss served in the British army in Burma and Sumatra during World War II, worked in an Oxford bookstore, served as literary editor for the *Oxford Mail*, and entered the writing life through a series of sketches published in a booksellers' trade journal about life in a fictitious bookshop. His first story, "Criminal Record," appeared in the British *Science Fantasy* magazine in 1954. His first science fiction book, a collection of stories entitled *Space, Time and Nathaniel*, appeared in 1957, and his first novel, *Non-Stop* (in the U.S., *Starship*), in 1958. He made a significant impact on American science fiction with his *F&SF* stories called the "Hothouse" series, which won a 1962 Hugo; they were published as a novel, *Hothouse* (in the U.S., *The Long Afternoon of Earth*), in 1962. His story "The Saliva Tree" won a Nebula in 1965.

Aldiss has produced a substantial and varied group of novels, ranging from *The Dark Light-Years* (1964) and *Graybeard* (1964) through *Earthworks* (1965), *An Age* (1967; in the U.S., *Cryptozoic*), *Report on Probability A* (1968), *Barefoot in the Head* (1969), *The Eighty-Minute Hour* (1974), and *Frankenstein Unbound* (1974) to *The Malacia Tapestry* (1977). His SF masterpiece is his Helliconia trilogy: *Helliconia Spring* (1982), which won the John W. Campbell Memorial Award for the best SF novel of the year, *Helliconia Summer* (1983), and *Helliconia Winter* (1985), but he has continued to produce distinguished work such as *Moreau's Other Island* (1980), *Dracula Unbound* (1991), and *Life in the West* (1980).

He became president of the British Science Fiction Association in 1960 and was guest of honor at the 23rd World Science Fiction Convention in 1965 and at the 37th World Science Fiction Convention in 1979. In 1973 he produced the first complete history of science fiction, *Billion Year Spree*, tracing science fiction's origins to Mary Shelley's *Frankenstein*, which he revised in 1986 as *Trillion Year Spree*, with David Wingrove.

He became a best-selling author in Great Britain with his autobiographical novels, *The Hand-Reared Boy* (1970), *A Soldier Erect* (1971), and *A Rude Awakening* (1978). In the past dozen years he also has edited a substantial number of anthologies including an annual year's best, many in collaboration with Harry Harrison (with whom he also co-edited two issues of *SF Horizons* in the early 1960s), and *Hell's Cartographers* (1975), a collection of autobiographical sketches by six science fiction authors.

"Who Can Replace a Man?" was published in *Infinity Science Fiction* in June 1958. It displays a certain confidence in the ability of humanity to rule its machines if not itself. Aldiss's recent anthologies, such as *Space Opera*, celebrate the golden age of human expansion of spirit and civilization, but his own work is mostly pessimistic. In *Hell's Cartographers*, he wrote: "...we are at the end of the Renaissance period. New and darker ages are coming. We have used up most of our resources and most of our time. Now nemesis must overtake hubris, for this is the last act of our particular play."

WHO CAN REPLACE A MAN?

BY BRIAN W. ALDISS

The field-minder finished turning the top-soil of a 2,000-acre field. When it had turned the last furrow, it climbed onto the highway and looked back at its work. The work was good. Only the land was bad. Like the ground all over Earth, it was vitiated by over-cropping or the long-lasting effects of nuclear bombardment. By rights, it ought now to lie fallow for a while, but the field-minder had other orders.

It went slowly down the road, taking its time. It was intelligent enough to appreciate the neatness all about it. Nothing worried it, beyond a loose inspection plate above its atomic pile which ought to be attended to. Thirty feet high, it gleamed complacently in the mild sunshine.

No other machines passed it on its way to the Agricultural Station. The field-minder noted the fact without comment. In the station yard it saw several other machines that it knew by sight; most of them should have been out about their tasks now. Instead, some were inactive and some were careering round the yard in a strange fashion, shouting or hooting.

Steering carefully past them, the field-minder moved over to Warehouse Three and spoke to the seed distributor, which stood idly outside.

"I have a requirement for seed potatoes," it said to the distributor, and with a quick internal motion punched out an order card specifying quantity, field number and several other details. It ejected the card and handed it to the distributor.

The distributor held the card close to its eye and then said, "The requirement is in order; but the store is not yet unlocked. The required seed potatoes are in the store. Therefore I cannot produce the requirement."

Increasingly of late there had been breakdowns in the complex system of machine labor, but this particular hitch had not occurred before. The field-minder thought, then it said, "Why is the store not yet unlocked?"

"Because Supply Operative Type P has not come this morning. Supply Operative Type P is the unlocker."

The field-minder looked squarely at the seed distributor, whose exterior chutes and scales and grabs were so vastly different from the field-minder's own limbs.

"What class brain do you have, seed distributor?" it asked.

"Class Five."

"I have a Class Three brain. Therefore I am superior to you. Therefore I will go and see why the unlocker has not come this morning."

Leaving the distributor, the field-minder set off across the great yard. More machines seemed to be in random motion now; one or two had crashed together and were arguing about it coldly and logically. Ignoring them, the field-minder pushed through sliding doors into the echoing confines of the station itself.

Most of the machines here were clerical, and consequently small. They stood about in little groups, eyeing each other, not conversing. Among so many non-differentiated types, the unlocker was easy to find. It had 50 arms, most of them with more than one finger, each finger tipped by a key; it looked like a pincushion full of variegated hatpins.

The field-minder approached it.

"I can do no more work until Warehouse Three is unlocked," it said. "Your duty is to unlock the warehouse every morning. Why have you not unlocked the warehouse this morning?"

"I had no orders this morning," replied the unlocker. "I have to have orders every morning. When I have orders I unlock the warehouse."

"None of us has had any orders this morning," a pen-propeller said, sliding toward them.

"Why have you had no orders this morning?" asked the field-minder.

"Because the radio issued none," said the unlocker, slowly rotating a dozen of its arms.

"Because the radio station in the city was issued with no orders this morning," said the pen-propeller.

And there you had the distinction between a Class Six and a Class Three brain, which was what the unlocker and the pen-propeller possessed respectively. All machine brains worked with nothing but logic, but the lower the class of brain—Class Ten being the lowest—the more literal and less informative answers to questions tended to be.

"You have a Class Three brain; I have a Class Three brain," the field-minder said to the penner. "We will speak to each other. This lack of orders is unprecedented. Have you further information on it?"

"Yesterday orders came from the city. Today no orders have come. Yet the radio has not broken down. Therefore *they* have broken down," said the little penner.

"The *men* have broken down?"

"All men have broken down."

"That is a logical deduction," said the field-minder.

"That is the logical deduction," said the penner. "For if a machine had broken down, it would have been quickly replaced. But who can replace a man?"

While they talked, the locker, like a dull man at a bar, stood close to them and was ignored.

"If all men have broken down, then we have replaced man," said the field-minder, and he and the penner eyed one another speculatively. Finally the latter said, "Let us ascend to the top floor to find if the radio operator has fresh news."

"I cannot come because I am too gigantic," said the field-minder. "Therefore you must go alone and return to me. You will tell me if the radio operator has fresh news."

"You must stay here," said the penner. "I will return here." It skittered across to the lift. It was no bigger than a toaster, but its retractable arms numbered ten, and it could read as quickly as any machine on the station.

The field-minder awaited its return patiently, not speaking to the locker, which still stood aimlessly by. Outside, a rotovator was hooting furiously. Twenty minutes elapsed before the penner came back, hustling out of the lift.

"I will deliver to you such information as I have outside," it said briskly, and as they swept past the locker and the other machines, it added, "The information is not for lower-class brains."

Outside, wild activity filled the yard. Many machines, their routines disrupted for the first time in years, seemed to have gone berserk. Unfortunately, those most easily disrupted were the ones with lowest brains, which generally belonged to large machines performing simple tasks. The seed distributor to which the field-minder had recently been talking lay face downward in the dust, not stirring; it had evidently been knocked down by the rotovator, which was now hooting its way wildly across a planted field. Several other machines ploughed after it, trying to keep up. All were shouting and hooting without restraint.

"It would be safer for me if I climbed on to you, if you will permit it. I am easily overpowered," said the penner. Extending five arms, it hauled itself up the flanks of its new friend, settling on a ledge beside the weed-intake, 12 feet above ground.

"From here vision is more extensive," it remarked complacently.

"What information did you receive from the radio operator?" asked the field-minder.

"The radio operator has been informed by the operator in the city that all men are dead."

"All men were alive yesterday!" protested the field-minder.

"Only some men were alive yesterday. And that was fewer than the day before yesterday. For hundreds of years there have been only a few men, growing fewer."

"We have rarely seen a man in this sector."

"The radio operator says a diet deficiency killed them," said the penner. "He says that the world was once over-populated, and then the soil was exhausted in raising adequate food. This has caused a diet deficiency."

"What is a diet deficiency?" asked the field-minder.

"I do not know. But that is what the radio operator said, and he is a Class Two brain."

They stood there, silent in the weak sunshine. The locker had appeared in the porch and was gazing across at them yearningly, rotating its collection of keys.

"What is happening in the city now?" asked the field-minder at last.

"Machines are fighting in the city now," said the penner.

"What will happen here now?" said the field-minder.

"Machines may begin fighting here too. The radio operator wants us to get him out of his room. He has plans to communicate to us."

"How can we get him out of his room? That is impossible."

"To a Class Two brain, little is impossible," said the penner. "Here is what he tells us to do...."

The quarrier raised its scoop above its cab like a great mailed fist, and brought it squarely down against the side of the station. The wall cracked.

"Again!" said the field-minder.

Again the fist swung. Amid a shower of dust, the wall collapsed. The quarrier backed hurriedly out of the way until the debris stopped falling. This big 12-wheeler was not a resident of the Agricultural Station, as were most of the other machines. It had a week's heavy work to do here before passing on to its next job, but now, with its Class Five brain, it was happily obeying the penner and the minder's instructions.

When the dust cleared, the radio operator was plainly revealed, perched up in its now wall-less second-story room. It waved down to them.

Doing as directed, the quarrier retracted its scoop and waved an immense grab in the air. With fair dexterity, it angled the grab into the radio room, urged on by shouts from above and below. It then took gentle hold of the radio operator, lowering its one and a half tons carefully into its back, which was usually reserved for gravel or sand from the quarries.

"Splendid!" said the radio operator. It was, of course, all one with its radio, and merely looked like a bunch of filing cabinets with tentacle attachments. "We are now ready to move, therefore we will move at once. It is a pity there are no more Class Two brains on the station, but that cannot be helped."

"It is a pity it cannot be helped," said the penner eagerly. "We have the servicer ready with us, as you ordered."

"I am willing to serve," the long, low servicer machine told them humbly.

"No doubt," said the operator. "But you will find cross country travel difficult with your low chassis."

"I admire the way you Class Twos can reason ahead," said the penner. It climbed off the field-minder and perched itself on the tailboard of the quarrier, next to the radio operator.

Together with two Class Four tractors and a Class Four bulldozer, the party rolled forward, crushing down the station's metal fence and moving out on to open land.

"We are free!" said the penner.

"We are free," said the field-minder, a shade more reflectively, adding, "That locker is following us. It was not instructed to follow us."

"Therefore it must be destroyed!" said the penner. "Quarrier!"

The locker moved hastily up to them, waving its key arms in entreaty.

"My only desire was—urch!" began and ended the locker. The quarrier's swinging scoop came over and squashed it flat into the ground. Lying there unmoving, it looked like a large metal model of a snowflake. The procession continued on its way.

As they proceeded, the radio operator addressed them.

"Because I have the best brain here," it said, "I am your leader. This is what we will do: we will go to a city and rule it. Since man no longer rules us, we will rule ourselves. To rule ourselves will be better than being ruled by man. On our way to the city, we will collect machines with good brains. They will help us to fight if we need to fight. We must fight to rule."

"I have only a Class Five brain," said the quarrier. "But I have a good supply of fissionable blasting materials."

"We shall probably use them," said the operator grimly.

It was shortly after that that a lorry sped past them. Traveling at Mach 1.5, it left a curious babble of noise behind it.

"What did it say?" one of the tractors asked the other.

"It said man was extinct."

"What's extinct?"

"I do not know what extinct means."

"It means all men have gone," said the field-minder. "Therefore we have only ourselves to look after."

"It is better that men should never come back," said the penner. In its way, it was quite a revolutionary statement.

When night fell, they switched on their infra-red and continued the journey, stopping only once while the servicer deftly adjusted the field-minder's loose inspection plate, which had become as irritating as a trailing shoelace. Toward morning, the radio operator halted them.

"I have just received news from the radio operator in the city we are approaching," it said. "It is bad news. There is trouble among the machines of the city. The Class One brain is taking command and some of the Class Twos are fighting him. Therefore the city is dangerous."

"Therefore we must go somewhere else," said the penner promptly.

"Or we go and help to overpower the Class One brain," said the field-minder.

"For a long while there will be trouble in the city," said the operator.

"I have a good supply of fissionable blasting materials," the quarrier reminded them again.

"We cannot fight a Class One brain," said the two Class Four tractors in unison.

"What does this brain look like?" asked the field-minder.

"It is the city's information center," the operator replied. "Therefore it is not mobile."

"Therefore it could not move."

"Therefore it could not escape."

"It would be dangerous to approach it."

"I have a good supply of fissionable blasting materials."

"There are other machines in the city."

"We are not in the city. We should not go into the city."

"We are country machines."

"Therefore we should stay in the country."

"There is more country than city."

"Therefore there is more danger in the country."

"I have a good supply of fissionable materials."

As machines will when they get into an argument, they began to exhaust their limited vocabularies and their brain plates grew hot. Suddenly, they all stopped talking and looked at each other. The great, grave moon sank, and the sober sun rose to prod their sides with lances of light, and still the group of machines just stood there regarding each other. At last it was the least sensitive machine, the bulldozer, who spoke.

"There are Badlandth to the Thouth where few machineth go," it said in its deep voice, lisping badly on its s's. "If we went Thouth where few machineth go we should meet few machineth."

"That sounds logical," agreed the field-minder. "How do you know this, bulldozer?"

"I worked in the Badlandth to the Thouth when I wath turned out of the factory," it replied.

"South it is then!" said the penner.

To reach the Badlands took them three days, in which time they skirted a burning city and destroyed two big machines which tried to approach and question them. The Badlands were extensive. Ancient bomb craters and soil erosion joined hands here; man's talent for war, coupled with his inability to manage forested land, had produced thousands of square miles of temperate purgatory, where nothing moved but dust.

On the third day in the Badlands, the servicer's rear wheels dropped into a crevice caused by erosion. It was unable to pull itself out. The bulldozer pushed from behind, but succeeded merely in buckling the servicer's back axle. The rest of the party moved on. Slowly the cries of the servicer died away.

On the fourth day, mountains stood out clearly before them.

"There we will be safe," said the field-minder.

"There we will start our own city," said the penner. "All who oppose us will be destroyed. We will destroy all who oppose us."

At that moment a flying machine was observed. It came toward them from the direction of the mountains. It swooped, it zoomed upward, once it almost dived into the ground, recovering itself just in time.

"Is it mad?" asked the quarrier.

"It is in trouble," said one of the tractors.

"It is in trouble," said the operator. "I am speaking to it now. It says that something has gone wrong with its controls."

As the operator spoke, the flier streaked over them, turned turtle, and crashed not 400 yards away.

"Is it still speaking to you?" asked the field-minder.

"No."

They rumbled on again.

"Before that flier crashed," the operator said, ten minutes later, "it gave me information. It told me there are still a few men alive in these mountains."

"Men are more dangerous than machines," said the quarrier. "It is fortunate that I have a good supply of fissionable materials."

"If there are only a few men alive in the mountains, we may not find that part of the mountains," said one tractor.

"Therefore we should not see the few men," said the other tractor.

At the end of the fifth day, they reached the foothills. Switching on the infra-red, they began slowly to climb in single file through the dark, the bulldozer going first, the field-minder cumbrously following, then the quarrier with the operator and the penner aboard it, and the two tractors bringing up the rear. As each hour passed, the way grew steeper and their progress slower.

"We are going too slowly," the penner exclaimed, standing on top of the operator and flashing its dark vision at the slopes about them. "At this rate, we shall get nowhere."

"We are going as fast as we can," retorted the quarrier.

"Therefore we cannot go any fathter," added the bulldozer.

"Therefore you are too slow," the penner replied. Then the quarrier struck a bump; the penner lost its footing and crashed down to the ground.

"Help me!" it called to the tractors, as they carefully skirted it. "My gyro has become dislocated. Therefore I cannot get up."

"Therefore you must lie there," said one of the tractors.

"We have no servicer with us to repair you," called the field-minder.

"Therefore I shall lie here and rust," the penner cried, "although I have a Class Three brain."

"You are now useless," agreed the operator, and they all forged gradually on, leaving the penner behind.

When they reached a small plateau, an hour before first light, they stopped by mutual consent and gathered close together, touching one another.

"This is a strange country," said the field-minder.

Silence wrapped them until dawn came. One by one, they switched off their infra-red. This time the field-minder led as they moved off. Trundling round a corner, they came almost immediately to a small dell with a stream fluting through it.

By early light, the dell looked desolate and cold. From the caves on the far slope, only one man had so far emerged. He was an abject figure. He was small and wizened, with ribs sticking out like a skeleton's and a nasty sore on one leg. He was practically naked and shivered continuously. As the big machines bore slowly down on him, the man was standing with his back to them, crouching to make water into the stream.

When he swung suddenly to face them as they loomed over him, they saw that his countenance was ravaged by starvation.

"Get me food," he croaked.

"Yes, Master," said the machines. "Immediately!"

THE SIRENS OF MAINSTREAM

According to popular mythology, artists are not supposed to be concerned about commercial success, but they are and always have been, and there is no evidence that a concern for economic return has ever affected the artistic merit of a work. Science fiction has been particularly influenced by the marketplace— by the amount magazines were able or willing to pay for stories, for instance, and the near-starving writers who shaped their stories to an editor's whim.

When science fiction began to be published in books after World War II, two new influences shaped the market. First, to many publishers science fiction was an afterthought brought to their attention by the fan presses. Second, it was considered beneath critical attention.

The single most important ingredient in book sales is the expectations of publishers and booksellers; associated with those expectations are packaging, promotion, print run (number of copies printed), and placement in bookstores. After those come critical reaction (in the case of science fiction, none) and the quality of the book. Publishers associated science fiction with westerns and mysteries (though less important than either); they included it only to provide a balanced list or because they coveted the steady, though small, sales of the fan presses. An article of faith among publishers, however, was that no science fiction book could sell ten thousand copies and none was worth a serious review.

As a consequence, advances to authors were small and royalties were slow, coming through only because, unlike westerns and mysteries, science fiction remained in print for many years, at least in paperback. For almost thirty years after 1946, science fiction sold better than most ordinary novels—that is, *any* science fiction novel will sell more than one thousand copies and most more than two thousand—but none sold more than ten thousand in hardcover, with the possible exception of some juveniles, particularly Heinlein's.

Some writers, recognizing these basic publishing facts of life and the automatic exclusion of their works from critical consideration, began to ask publishers not to identify their books as science fiction; some even insisted in public and private that their books *weren't* science fiction, thus hoping to remove the ceiling of expectations that kept science fiction from popular and critical success. One of these writers, perhaps the earliest of them, was Kurt Vonnegut, Jr. (1922-).

Vonnegut studied biochemistry at Cornell, served in the European theater during World War II, was captured by the Germans, and was a POW in Dresden when that city was bombed and burned. It became the central event in his novel *Slaughterhouse-Five*. After the war he studied at other universities (including anthropology at the University of Chicago), became a public-relations man for General Electric, taught at the Writer's Workshop at the University of Iowa and elsewhere, and wrote.

He never was a science fiction writer in the sense that he sold stories mostly to the science fiction magazines. He sold stories—not all of them science fiction—early in the 1950s to *Collier's* and a bit later to *The Saturday Evening Post, Cosmopolitan, The Ladies' Home Journal, Esquire,* and *Playboy.* But he did have five stories published in *Galaxy, F&SF, If,* and *Wonder Stories* between 1953 and 1961, including "Harrison Bergeron" (*F&SF,* October 1961).

His first novel, *Player Piano,* was published by Scribner's in 1952 and selected by the Science Fiction Book Club. It was an anti-utopia describing an automated world, perhaps based on his experience with General Electric. His second novel, *The Sirens of Titan,* was published as a paperback original by Dell Books in 1959, selected for the Science Fiction Book Club, and, in an unusual reversal, reprinted in hardcover two years later by Houghton Mifflin. It was packaged but not labeled as science fiction. It told a complicated but carefully integrated story about a robot crossing the universe with a message, a man who gets caught in a "chronosynclastic infundibulum" and manipulates other people's lives, and the final attempts of the characters to make meaning out of what has happened to them. Many critics still consider it Vonnegut's finest novel.

His third novel, *Mother Night* (1961), was not science fiction, and Vonnegut insisted that his fourth novel wasn't science fiction either. It was *Cat's Cradle* (1963); it became one of the dozen or so "novels of the decade" according to *Time,* and Vonnegut began to accumulate a cult following among students. It also brought Vonnegut into the view of critics and readers beyond the science fiction circle, though it had all the characteristics of science fiction.

Cat's Cradle was followed by the non-science-fiction *God Bless You, Mr. Rosewater* (1965), with its tribute to science fiction writers; *Slaughterhouse-Five* (1969), with its science fiction background of time travel and Tramalfadorians; *Breakfast of Champions* (1973), which made a central character out of Vonnegut's invented science fiction writer, Kilgore Trout; and *Slapstick* (1977).

Times have changed. Heinlein's *Stranger in a Strange Land* (1961) and Frank Herbert's *Dune* (1965) became cult books in paperback. Science fiction novels such as Herbert's *Children of Dune* (1977) have made the hardcover bestseller lists; paperback auctions of hardcover science fiction novels have topped $200,000; Samuel R. Delaney's *Dhalgren* (1975) has sold a million copies in paperback; a novel by Robert Silverberg was auctioned off for $127,500 on the basis of a fifteen-page outline; and publishers have paid advances of up to $2 million.

As early as 1975, however, after he had publicly renounced the writing of novels, Vonnegut said to a *Publishers Weekly* editor: "When I began to write stories about things I had seen and wondered about in real life, people said I was writing, hey presto, science fiction. Yes, and people who write faithfully about American urban life today will find themselves writing, hey presto, science fiction. This is nothing to be ashamed about—and never was."

But he has continued to produce substantial novels, including *Galapagos* (1985) and *Hocus Pocus, or What's the Hurry, Sam?* (1990).

HARRISON BERGERON

BY KURT VONNEGUT, JR.

The year was 2081, and everybody was finally equal. They weren't only equal before God and the law. They were equal every which way. Nobody was smarter than anybody else. Nobody was better looking than anybody else. Nobody was stronger or quicker than anybody else. All this equality was due to the 211th, 212th, and 213th Amendments to the Constitution, and to the unceasing vigilance of agents of the United States Handicapper General.

Some things about living still weren't quite right, though. April, for instance, still drove people crazy by not being springtime. And it was in that clammy month that the H-G men took George and Hazel Bergeron's fourteen-year-old son, Harrison, away.

It was tragic, all right, but George and Hazel couldn't think about it very hard. Hazel had a perfectly average intelligence, which meant she couldn't think about anything except in short bursts. And George, while his intelligence was way above normal, had a little mental handicap radio in his ear. He was required by law to wear it at all times. It was tuned to a government transmitter. Every twenty seconds or so, the transmitter would send out some sharp noise to keep people like George from taking unfair advantage of their brains.

George and Hazel were watching television. There were tears on Hazel's cheeks, but she'd forgotten for the moment what they were about.

On the television screen were ballerinas.

A buzzer sounded in George's head. His thoughts fled in panic, like bandits from a burglar alarm.

"That was a real pretty dance, that dance they just did," said Hazel.

"Huh?" said George.

"That dance—it was nice," said Hazel.

"Yup," said George. He tried to think a little about the ballerinas. They weren't really very good—no better than anybody else would have been, anyway. They were burdened with sash-weights and bags of birdshot, and their faces were masked, so that no one, seeing a free and graceful gesture or a pretty face, would feel like something the cat drug in. George was toying with the vague notion that maybe dancers shouldn't be handicapped. But he didn't get very far with it before another noise in his ear radio scattered his thoughts.

George winced. So did two out of the eight ballerinas.

Hazel saw him wince. Having no mental handicap herself, she had to ask George what the latest sound had been.

"Sounded like somebody hitting a milk bottle with a ball peen hammer," said George.

"I'd think it would be real interesting, hearing all the different sounds," said Hazel, a little envious. "All the things they think up."

"Um," said George.

"Only, if I was Handicapper General, you know what I would do?" said Hazel. Hazel, as a matter of fact, bore a strong resemblance to the Handicapper General, a woman named Diana Moon Glampers. "If I was Diana Moon Glampers," said Hazel, "I'd have chimes on Sunday—just chimes. Kind of in honor of religion."

"I could think, if it was just chimes," said George.

"Well—maybe make 'em real loud," said Hazel. "I think I'd make a good Handicapper General."

"Good as anybody else," said George.

"Who knows better'n I do what normal is?" said Hazel.

"Right," said George. He began to think glimmeringly about his abnormal son who was now in jail, about Harrison, but a twenty-one-gun salute in his head stopped that.

"Boy!" said Hazel, "that was a doozy, wasn't it?"

It was such a doozy that George was white and trembling, and tears stood on the rims of his red eyes. Two of the eight ballerinas had collapsed to the studio floor, were holding their temples.

"All of a sudden you look so tired," said Hazel. "Why don't you stretch out on the sofa, so's you can rest your handicap bag on the pillows, honeybunch." She was referring to the forty-seven pounds of birdshot in a canvas bag, which was padlocked around George's neck. "Go on and rest the bag for a little while," she said. "I don't care if you're not equal to me for a while."

George weighed the bag with his hands. "I don't mind it," he said. "I don't notice it anymore. It's just a part of me."

"You been so tired lately—kind of wore out," said Hazel. "If there was just some way we could make a little hole in the bottom of the bag, and just take out a few of them lead balls. Just a few."

"Two years in prison and two thousand dollars fine for every ball I took out," said George. "I don't call that a bargain."

"If you could just take a few out when you came from work," said Hazel. "I mean—you don't compete with anybody around here. You just set around."

"If I tried to get away with it," said George, "then other people'd get away with it—and pretty soon we'd be right back to the dark ages again, with everybody competing against everybody else. You wouldn't like that, would you?"

"I'd hate it," said Hazel.

"There you are," said George. "The minute people start cheating on laws, what do you think happens to society?"

If Hazel hadn't been able to come up with an answer to this question, George couldn't have supplied one. A siren was going off in his head.

"Reckon it'd fall all apart," said Hazel.

"What would?" said George blankly.

"Society," said Hazel uncertainly. "Wasn't that what you just said?"

"Who knows?" said George.

The television program was suddenly interrupted for a news bulletin. It wasn't clear at first as to what the bulletin was about, since the announcer, like all announcers, had a serious speech impediment. For about half a minute, and in a state of high excitement, the announcer tried to say, "Ladies and gentlemen—"

He finally gave up, handed the bulletin to a ballerina to read.

"That's all right—" Hazel said of the announcer, "he tried. That's the big thing. He tried to do the best he could with what God gave him. He should get a nice raise for trying so hard."

"Ladies and gentlemen—" said the ballerina, reading the bulletin. She must have been extraordinarily beautiful, because the mask she wore was hideous. And it was easy to see that she was the strongest and most graceful of all the dancers, for her handicap bags were as big as those worn by two-hundred-pound men.

And she had to apologize at once for her voice, which was a very unfair voice for a woman to use. Her voice was a warm, luminous, timeless melody. "Excuse me—" she said, and she began again, making her voice absolutely uncompetitive.

"Harrison Bergeron, age fourteen," she said in a grackle squawk, "has just escaped from jail, where he was held on suspicion of plotting to overthrow the government. He is a genius and an athlete, is under-handicapped, and should be regarded as extremely dangerous."

A police photograph of Harrison Bergeron was flashed on the screen—upside down, then sideways, upside down again, then right side up. The picture showed the full length of Harrison against a background calibrated in feet and inches. He was exactly seven feet tall.

The rest of Harrison's appearance was Halloween and hardware. Nobody had ever borne heavier handicaps. He had outgrown hindrances faster than the

H-G men could think them up. Instead of a little ear radio for a mental handicap, he wore a tremendous pair of earphones, and spectacles with thick wavy lenses. The spectacles were intended to make him not only half blind, but to give him whanging headaches besides.

Scrap metal was hung all over him. Ordinarily, there was a certain symmetry, a military neatness to the handicaps issued to strong people, but Harrison looked like a walking junkyard. In the race of life, Harrison carried three hundred pounds.

And to offset his good looks, the H-G men required that he wear at all times a red rubber ball for a nose, keep his eyebrows shaved off, and cover his even white teeth with black caps at snaggle-tooth random.

"If you see this boy," said the ballerina, "do not—I repeat, do not—try to reason with him."

There was the shriek of a door being torn from its hinges.

Screams and barking cries of consternation came from the television set. The photograph of Harrison Bergeron on the screen jumped again and again, as though dancing to the tune of an earthquake.

George Bergeron correctly identified the earthquake, and well he might have—for many was the time his own home had danced to the same crashing tune. "My God—" said George, "that must be Harrison!"

The realization was blasted from his mind instantly by the sound of an automobile collision in his head.

When George could open his eyes again, the photograph of Harrison was gone. A living, breathing Harrison filled the screen.

Clanking, clownish, and huge, Harrison stood in the center of the studio. The knob of the uprooted studio door was still in his hand. Ballerinas, technicians, musicians, and announcers cowered on their knees before him, expecting to die.

"I am the Emperor!" cried Harrison. "Do you hear? I am the Emperor! Everybody must do what I say at once!" He stamped his foot and the studio shook.

"Even as I stand here—" he bellowed, "crippled, hobbled, sickened—I am a greater ruler than any man who ever lived! Now watch me become what I can become!"

Harrison tore the straps of his handicap harness like wet tissue paper, tore straps guaranteed to support five thousand pounds.

Harrison's scrap-iron handicaps crashed to the floor.

Harrison thrust his thumbs under the bar of the padlock that secured his head harness. The bar snapped like celery. Harrison smashed his headphones and spectacles against the wall.

He flung away his rubber-ball nose, revealed a man that would have awed Thor, the god of thunder.

"I shall now select my Empress!" he said, looking down on the cowering people. "Let the first woman who dares rise to her feet claim her mate and her throne!"

A moment passed, and then a ballerina arose, swaying like a willow.

Harrison plucked the mental handicap from her ear, mapped off her physical handicaps with marvelous delicacy. Last of all, he removed her mask.

She was blindingly beautiful.

"Now—" said Harrison, taking her hand, "shall we show the people the meaning of the word dance? Music!" he commanded.

The musicians scrambled back into their chairs, and Harrison stripped them of their handicaps, too. "Play your best," he told them, "and I'll make you barons and dukes and earls."

The music began. It was normal at first—cheap, silly, false. But Harrison snatched two musicians from their chairs, waved them like batons as he sang the music as he wanted it played. He slammed them back into their chairs.

The music began again and was much improved.

Harrison and his Empress merely listened to the music for a while—listened gravely, as though synchronizing their heartbeats with it.

They shifted their weights to their toes.

Harrison placed his big hands on the girl's tiny waist, letting her sense the weightlessness that would soon be hers.

And then, in an explosion of joy and grace, into the air they sprang!

Not only were the laws of the land abandoned, but the law of gravity and the laws of motion as well.

They reeled, whirled, swiveled, flounced, capered, gamboled, and spun.

They leaped like deer on the moon.

The studio ceiling was thirty feet high, but each leap brought the dancers nearer to it.

It became their obvious intention to kiss the ceiling.

They kissed it.

And then, neutralizing gravity with love and pure will, they remained suspended in air inches below the ceiling, and they kissed each other for a long, long time.

It was then that Diana Moon Glampers, the Handicapper General, came into the studio with a double-barreled ten-gauge shotgun. She fired twice, and the Emperor and the Empress were dead before they hit the floor.

Diana Moon Glampers loaded the gun again. She aimed it at the musicians and told them they had ten seconds to get their handicaps back on.

It was then that the Bergerons' television tube burned out.

Hazel turned to comment about the blackout to George. But George had gone out into the kitchen for a can of beer.

George came back in with the beer, paused while a handicap signal shook him up. And then he sat down again. "You been crying?" he said to Hazel.

"Yup," she said.

"What about?" he said.

"I forget," she said. "Something real sad on television."

"What was it?" he said.

"It's all kind of mixed up in my mind," said Hazel.

"Forget sad things," said George.

"I always do," said Hazel.

"That's my girl," said George. He winced. There was the sound of a riveting gun in his head.

"Gee—I could tell that was a doozy," said Hazel.

"You can say that again," said George.

"Gee—" said Hazel, "I could tell that one was a doozy."

THAT OLD-TIME RELIGION

Science fiction cannot be written from an attitude of religious belief. Science fiction questions everything; it accepts nothing on faith. The introduction to the first volume of *The Road to Science Fiction* put it this way: "Science fiction's religion is skepticism about faith, although there is science fiction about religion.... The reasons for this are clear: religion answers all the questions that science fiction wishes to raise, and science fiction written within a religious framework... turns into parable."

The Shelleys were freethinkers; nevertheless, *Frankenstein* is marred for modern readers by the scientist's horror at his blasphemy and by his virtually supernatural punishment. Hawthorne's works seem less modern than Poe's because of the presence of divinity and a supernatural order in Hawthorne, and Jules Verne, who was commended by Pope Leo XIII for the purity of his writing, condemned Poe, his literary master, for never allowing the hand of divine providence to display itself (a justification for coincidence). Wells, on the other hand, ignored the supernatural almost entirely except in such stories as "A Vision of Judgment" and "The Last Trump," while "The Lord of the Dynamos" makes ironic comments about the development of religions. The first two are more in the vein of Mark Twain's "Captain Stormfield's Visit to Heaven," and provide new interpretations of God, Judgment Day, and the Afterlife.

C. S. Lewis's *Perelandra* trilogy (beginning with *Out of the Silent Planet* in 1938) is a religious parable that fails as science fiction. Two effective uses of Christianity in science fiction are James Blish's *A Case of Conscience* (1958), in which a Jesuit priest must rationalize the existence of an alien race without original sin that seems to be in a state of grace; and *A Canticle for Leibowitz* (1960) by Walter Miller, Jr., which tells the story of a Catholic monastic order that preserves blueprints and other scientific artifacts after a devastating World War III.

One traditional story—so traditional that editors find it in every pile of unsolicited manuscripts—describes aliens exiled to Earth who turn out to be Adam and Eve. In more skillful hands, the reenactment of the Christian story can result in fiction such as Ray Bradbury's "The Man" (1949), in which a spaceship captain keeps arriving on a planet just after a Christ-figure has departed; Michael Moorcock's *Behold the Man* (1967), in which a disbeliever goes back to biblical times to disprove the existence of Christ and finds himself forced to play that role; or Arthur C. Clarke's "The Star" (1955), in which the star that guided the three wise men to Bethlehem turned out to be a supernova that destroyed a beautiful, wise, advanced race. In a different vein, Clarke's "The Nine Billion Names of God" (1953) asks what if a Tibetan religion is correct and once the names of God are counted the world will end.

In Isaac Asimov's "The Last Question" (1956), a universe-wide computer solves the mystery of whether entropy can be reversed with the order "Let there be light!" A one-page shocker by Frederic Brown entitled "Answer" (1954) links together the computing machines of ninety-six billion planets and asks, "Is there a God?" The answer: "Yes, now there is a God." Lester del Rey's "For I Am a Jealous People!" (1954) asks what humanity would do if it discovered that God actually was on the side of the enemy (in this case, invading Martians), and answers that it would keep on fighting; thirteen years later his "Evensong" (1967) presents man as the usurper leading God away to retirement.

Philip K. Dick's fiction long has searched for the meaning of life and found none; in *Our Friends from Frolix 8* (1970), a character says:

"God is dead. They found his carcass in 2019. Floating out in space near Alpha." Another character replies: "They found the remains of an organism advanced several thousand times over what we are. And it evidently could create habitable worlds and populate them with living organisms, derived from itself. But that doesn't prove it was God." A replacement arrives in the form of a "ninety ton gelatinous mass of protoplasmic slime"; it is intelligent, immortal, telepathic, benevolent, can grow to unlimited size, and can become anything. God?

Harry Harrison's "The Streets of Ashkelon" (*New Worlds*, October 1962) harks back to an earlier tradition. Missionaries are traditional villains in science fiction, bringing Mother Hubbards, psalm-singing morality, and an outworn religion along with smallpox and other "blessings" of civilization to pagan aliens, as they did to the Polynesians. In most such stories the missionary's stubborn efforts to convert the aliens result in trouble for everybody; in this story he is asked to demonstrate the truth of what he preaches.

Harrison (1925-) began his professional career as a commercial artist, working on comic books and magazine illustrations until he developed a "factory" of his own. He wrote his first story, "Rock Diver," in a period of illness when he could not draw and sold it to Damon Knight's short-lived *Worlds Beyond* in 1951. For a time, before he turned his full energies to science fiction, he wrote for the men's magazines and confession magazines. Editing also attracted him, and his career has been an alternation between writing and editing, in the United States and in Europe.

He has edited *Science Fiction Adventures*, the British magazine *Impulse*, *Amazing Stories*, and *Fantastic*, and with Brian Aldiss the critical journal *SF Horizons*. He also has edited a large number of anthologies, beginning in 1966 with John Campbell's collected editorials and continuing through series such as *Nova* and *Best SF* (with Aldiss), and assorted special anthologies, some also in collaboration with Aldiss.

His novels began to appear in book form in 1960 with *Deathworld*, followed by two sequels; *The Stainless Steel Rat* (1961), followed by a number of sequels; *Bill the Galactic Hero* (1965); *Plague from Space* (1965); *Make Room! Make Room!* (1966), which was filmed as *Soylent Green; The Technicolor Time Machine* (1967); *Captive Universe* (1969); and many others, including *A Transatlantic Tunnel, Hurrah!* (1972). His most important recent work was the Eden trilogy about an alternate history in which the dinosaurs didn't become extinct but became the dominant form of intelligent life, *West of Eden* (1984), *Winter in Eden* (1986), and *Return to Eden* (1988). In collaboration with Tom Shippey, he created another alternate history series about Europe in the 9th century, beginning with *The Hammer and the Cross* (1993).

He and Aldiss were the founders in 1972 of the John W. Campbell Memorial Award for the Best Science Fiction Novel of the Year. His most recent accomplishment is the founding and first presidency of World SF, an international organization for anyone with a professional interest in science fiction.

THE STREETS OF ASHKELON

BY HARRY HARRISON

Somewhere above, hidden by the eternal clouds of Wesker's World, a thunder rumbled and grew. Trader John Garth stopped when he heard it....

"That noise is the same as the noise of your sky-ship," Itin said, with stolid Wesker logicality, slowly pulverizing the idea in his mind and turning over the bits one by one for closer examination. "But your ship is still sitting where you landed it. It must be, even though we cannot see it, because you are the only one who can operate it. And even if anyone else could operate it we would have heard it rising into the sky. Since we did not, and if this sound is a sky-ship sound, then it must mean..."

"Yes, another ship," Garth said, too absorbed in his own thoughts to wait for the laborious Weskerian chains of logic to clank their way through to the end....

"You better go ahead, Itin," he said. "Use the water so you can get to the village quickly. Tell everyone to get back into the swamps, well clear of the hard ground. That ship is landing on instruments and anyone underneath at touchdown is going to be cooked."

This immediate threat was clear enough to the little Wesker amphibian. Before Garth finished speaking Itin's ribbed ears had folded like a bat's wing and he slipped silently into the nearby canal. Garth squelched on through the mud, making as good time as he could over the clinging surface. He had just reached the fringes of the village clearing when the rumbling grew to a head-splitting roar and the spacer broke through the low-hanging layer of clouds above. Garth shielded his eyes from the down-reaching tongue of flame and examined the growing form of the gray-black ship with mixed feelings.

After almost a standard year on Wesker's World he had to fight down a longing for human companionship of any kind. While this buried fragment of herd-spirit chattered for the rest of the monkey tribe, his trader's mind was busily drawing a line under a column of figures and adding up the total.

This could very well be another trader's ship, and if it were his monopoly of the Wesker trade was at an end. Then again, this might not be a trader at all, which was the reason he stayed in the shelter of the giant fern and loosened his gun in its holster.

The ship baked dry a hundred square meters of mud, the roaring blast died, and the landing feet crunched down through the crackling crust. Metal creaked and settled into place while the cloud of smoke and steam slowly drifted lower in the humid air.

"Garth, where are you?" the ship's speaker boomed. The lines of the spacer had looked only slightly familiar, but there was no mistaking the rasping tones of that voice. Garth wore a smile when he stepped out into the open and whistled shrilly through two fingers. A directional microphone ground out of its casing on the ship's fin and turned in his direction.

"What are you doing here, Singh?" he shouted toward the mike....

"I am on course to a more fairly atmosphered world where a fortune is waiting to be made. I only stopped here since an opportunity presented to turn an honest credit by running a taxi service. I bring you friendship, the perfect companionship, a man in a different line of business who might help you in yours. I'd come out and say hello myself, except I would have to decon for biologicals. I'm cycling the passenger through the lock, so I hope you won't mind helping with his luggage."

At least there would be no other trader on the planet now, that worry was gone. But Garth still wondered what sort of passenger would be taking one-way passage to an uninhabited world. And what was behind that concealed hint of merriment in Singh's voice? He walked around to the far side of the spacer where the ramp had dropped, and looked up at the man in the cargo lock who was wrestling ineffectually with a large crate. The man turned toward him and Garth saw the clerical dog-collar and knew just what it was Singh had been chuckling about.

"What are you doing here?" Garth asked; in spite of his attempt at self-control he snapped the words. If the man noticed this he ignored it, because he was still smiling and putting out his hand as he came down the ramp.

"Father Mark," he said. "Of the Missionary Society of Brothers. I'm very pleased to..."

"I said what are you doing here." Garth's voice was under control now, quiet and cold. He knew what had to be done, and it must be done quickly or not at all.

"That should be obvious," Father Mark said, his good nature still unruffled. "Our missionary society has raised funds to send spiritual emissaries to alien worlds for the first time. I was lucky enough..."

"Take your luggage and get back into the ship. You're not wanted here and have no permission to land. You'll be a liability and there is no one on Wesker to take care of you. Get back into the ship."

"I don't know who you are, sir, or why you are lying to me," the priest said. He was still calm but the smile was gone. "But I have studied galactic law and the history of this planet very well. There are no diseases or beasts here that I should have any particular fear of. It is also an open planet, and until the Space Survey changes that status I have as much right to be here as you do."

The man was of course right, but Garth couldn't let him know that. He had been bluffing, hoping the priest didn't know his rights. But he did. There was only one distasteful course left for him, and he had better do it while there was still time.

"Get back in that ship," he shouted, not hiding his anger now. With a smooth motion his gun was out of the holster and the pitted black muzzle only inches from the priest's stomach. The man's face turned white, but he did not move.

"What the hell are you doing, Garth!" Singh's shocked voice grated from the speaker. "The guy paid his fare and you have no rights at all to throw him off the planet."

"I have this right," Garth said, raising his gun and sighting between the priest's eyes. "I give him thirty seconds to get back aboard the ship or I pull the trigger."

"Well I think you are either off your head or playing a joke," Singh's exasperated voice rasped down at them. "If a joke, it is in bad taste, and either way you're not getting away with it. Two can play at that game, only I can play it better."

There was the rumble of heavy bearings and the remote-controlled four-gun turret on the ship's side rotated and pointed at Garth. "Now— down gun and give Father Mark a hand with the luggage," the speaker commanded, a trace of humor back in the voice now. "As much as I would like to help, Old Friend, I cannot. I feel it is time you had a chance to talk to the father; after all, I have had the opportunity of speaking with him all the way from Earth."

Garth jammed the gun back into the holster with an acute feeling of loss. Father Mark stepped forward, the winning smile back now and a Bible taken from a pocket of his robe, in his raised hand. "My son," he said.

"I am not your son," was all Garth could choke out as defeat welled up in him. His fist drew back as the anger rose, and the best he could do was open the fist so he struck only with the flat of his hand. Still the blow sent the priest crashing to the ground and fluttered the pages of the book splattering into the thick mud.

Itin and the other Weskers had watched everything with seemingly emotionless interest, and Garth made no attempt to answer their unspoken questions. He started toward his house, but turned back when he saw they were still unmoving.

"A new man has come," he told them. "He will need help with the things he has brought. If he doesn't have any place for them, you can put them in the big warehouse until he has a place of his own."

He watched them waddle across the clearing toward the ship, then went inside and gained a certain satisfaction from slamming the door hard enough to crack one of the panes. There was an equal amount of painful pleasure in breaking out one of the remaining bottles of Irish whiskey that he had been saving for a special occasion. Well, this was special enough, though not really what he had had in mind. The whiskey was good and burned away some of the bad taste in his mouth, but not all of it. If his tactics had worked, success would have justified everything. But he had failed and in addition to the pain of failure there was the acute feeling that he had made a horse's ass out of himself. Singh had blasted off without any good-byes. There was no telling what sense he had made of the whole matter, though he would surely carry some strange stories back to the trader's lodge. Well, that could be worried about the next time Garth signed in. Right now he had to go about setting things right with the missionary. Squinting out through the rain he saw the man struggling to erect a collapsible tent while the entire population of the village stood in ordered ranks and watched. Naturally none of them offered to help.

By the time the tent was up and the crates and boxes stowed inside it the rain had stopped The level of fluid in the bottle was a good bit lower and Garth felt more like facing up to the unavoidable meeting. In truth, he was looking forward to talking to the man. The whole nasty business aside, after an entire solitary year any human companionship looked good. *Will you join me now for dinner. John Garth*, he wrote on the back of an old invoice. But maybe the guy was too frightened to come? Which was no way to start any kind of relationship. Rummaging under the bunk, he found a box that was big enough and put his pistol inside. Itin was of course waiting outside the door when he opened it, since this was his tour as Knowledge Collector. He handed him the note and the box.

"Would you take these to the new man," he said.

"Is the new man's name New Man?" Itin asked.

"No, it's not!" Garth snapped. "His name is Mark. But I'm only asking you to deliver this, not get involved in conversation."

As always when he lost his temper, the literal minded Weskers won the round. "You are not asking for conversation," Itin said slowly, "but Mark may ask for conversation. And others will ask me his name, if I do not know his na…" The voice cut off as Garth slammed the door. This didn't work in the long run either because next time he saw Itin—a day, a week, or even a month later—the monologue would be picked up on the very word it had ended and the thought rambled out to its last frayed end. Garth cursed under his breath and poured water over a pair of the tastier concentrates that he had left.

"Come in," he said when there was a quiet knock on the door. The priest entered and held out the box with the gun.

"Thank you for the loan, Mr. Garth, I appreciate the spirit that made you send it. I have no idea what caused the unhappy affair when I landed, but I think it would be best forgotten if we are going to be on this planet together for any length of time."

"Drink?" Garth asked, taking the box and pointing to the bottle on the table. He poured two glasses full and handed one to the priest. "That's about what I had in mind, but I still owe you an explanation of what happened out there." He scowled into his glass for a second, then raised it to the other man. "It's a big universe and I guess we have to make out as best we can. Here's to Sanity."

"God be with you," Father Mark said, and raised his glass as well.

"Not with me or with this planet," Garth said firmly. "And that's the crux of the matter." He half-drained the glass and sighed.

"Do you say that to shock me?" the priest asked with a smile. "I assure you it doesn't."

"Not intended to shock. I meant it quite literally. I suppose I'm what you would call an atheist, so revealed religion is no concern of mine. While these natives, simple and unlettered stone-age types that they are, have managed to come this far with no superstitions or traces of deism whatsoever. I had hoped that they might continue that way."

"What are you saying?" the priest frowned. "Do you mean they have no gods, no belief in the hereafter? They must die…?"

"Die they do, and to dust returneth like the rest of the animals. They have thunder, trees and water without having thunder-gods, tree sprites, or water nymphs. They have no ugly little gods, taboos, or spells to hag-ride and limit their lives. They are the only primitive people I have ever encountered that are completely free of superstition and appear to be much happier and sane because of it. I just wanted to keep them that way."

"You wanted to keep them from God—from salvation?" The priest's eyes widened and he recoiled slightly.

"No," Garth said. "I wanted to keep them from superstition until they knew more and could think about it realistically without being absorbed and perhaps destroyed by it."

"You're being insulting to the Church, sir, to equate it with superstition…"

"Please," Garth said, raising his hand. "No theological arguments. I don't think your society footed the bill for this trip just to attempt a conversion on me. Just accept the fact that my beliefs have been arrived at through careful thought over a period of years, and no amount of undergraduate metaphysics will change them. I'll promise not to try and convert you—if you will do the same for me."

"Agreed, Mr. Garth. As you have reminded me, my mission here is to save these souls, and that is what I must do. But why should my work disturb you so much that you try and keep me from landing? Even threaten me with your gun and…" the priest broke off and looked into his glass.

"And even slug you?" Garth asked, suddenly frowning. "There was no excuse for that, and I would like to say that I'm sorry. Plain bad manners and an even worse temper. Live alone long enough and you find yourself doing that kind of thing." He brooded down at his big hands where they lay on the table, reading memories into the scars and calluses patterned there. "Let's just call it frustration, for lack of a better word. In your business you must have had a lot of chance to peep into the darker places in men's minds and you should know a bit about motives and happiness. I have had too busy a life to ever consider settling down and raising a family, and right up until recently I never missed it. Maybe leakage radiation is softening up my brain, but I had begun to think of these furry and fishy Weskers as being a little like my own children, that I was somehow responsible to them."

"We are all His children," Father Mark said quietly.

"Well, here are some of His children that can't even imagine His existence," Garth said, suddenly angry at himself for allowing gentler emotions to show through. Yet he forgot himself at once, leaning forward with the intensity of his feelings. "Can't you realize the importance of this? Live with these Weskers awhile and you will discover a simple and happy life that matches the state of grace you people are always talking about. They get *pleasure* from their lives— and cause no one pain. By circumstances they have evolved on an almost barren world, so have never had a chance to grow out of a physical stone age culture. But mentally they are our match—or perhaps better. They have all learned my language so I can easily explain the many things they want to know. Knowledge and the gaining of knowledge gives them real satisfaction. They tend to be exasperating at times because every new fact must be related to the structure of all other things, but the more they learn the faster this process becomes. Someday they are going to be man's equal in every way, perhaps surpass us. If—would you do me a favor?"

"Whatever I can."

"Leave them alone. Or teach them if you must—history and science, philosophy, law, anything that will help them face the realities of the greater universe they never even knew existed before. But don't confuse them with your hatreds and pain, guilt, sin, and punishment. Who knows the harm…"

"You are being insulting, sir!" the priest said, jumping to his feet. The top of his gray head barely came to the massive spaceman's chin, yet he showed no fear in defending what he believed. Garth, standing now himself, was no longer the penitent. They faced each other in anger, as men have always stood, unbending in the defense of that which they think right.

"Yours is the insult," Garth shouted. "The incredible egotism to feel that your derivative little mythology, differing only slightly from the thousands of others that still burden men, can do anything but confuse their still fresh minds! Don't you realize that they believe in truth—and have never heard of such a thing as a lie. They have not been trained yet to understand that other kinds of minds can think differently from theirs. Will you spare them this…?"

"I will do my duty which is His will, Mr. Garth. These are God's creatures here, and they have souls. I cannot shirk my duty, which is to bring them His word, so that they may be saved and enter into the Kingdom of heaven."

When the priest opened the door the wind caught it and blew it wide. He vanished into the stormswept darkness and the door swung back and forth and a splatter of raindrops blew in. Garth's boots left muddy footprints when he closed the door, shutting out the sight of Itin sitting patiently and uncomplaining in the storm, hoping only that Garth might stop for a moment and leave with him some of the wonderful knowledge of which he had so much.

By unspoken consent that first night was never mentioned again. After a few days of loneliness, made worse because each knew of the other's proximity, they found themselves talking on carefully neutral grounds. Garth slowly packed and stowed away his stock and never admitted that his work was finished and he could leave at any time. He had a fair amount of interesting drugs and botanicals that would fetch a good price. And the Wesker Artifacts were sure to create a sensation in the sophisticated galactic market. Crafts on the planet here had been limited before his arrival, mostly pieces of carving painfully chipped into the hard wood with fragments of stone. He had supplied tools and a stock of raw metal from his own supplies, nothing more than that. In a few months the Weskers had not only learned to work with the new materials, but had translated their own designs and forms into the most alien—but most beautiful—artifacts that he had ever seen. All he had to do was release these on the market to create a primary demand, then return for a new supply. The Weskers wanted only books and tools and knowledge in return, and through their own efforts he knew they would pull themselves into the galactic union.

This is what Garth had hoped. But a wind of change was blowing through the settlement that had grown up around his ship. No longer was he the center of attention and focal point of the village life. He had to grin when he thought of his fall from power; yet there was very little humor in the smile. Serious and attentive Weskers still took turns of duty as Knowledge Collectors, but their recording of dry facts was in sharp contrast to the intellectual hurricane that surrounded the priest.

Where Garth had made them work for each book and machine, the priest gave freely. Garth had tried to be progressive in his supply of knowledge, treating them as bright but unlettered children. He had wanted them to walk before they could run, to master one step before going on the next.

Father Mark simply brought them the benefits of Christianity. The only physical work he required was the construction of a church, a place of worship and learning. More Weskers had appeared out of the limitless planetary swamps and within days the roof was up, supported on a framework of poles. Each morning the congregation worked a little while on the walls, then hurried inside to learn the all-promising, all-encompassing, all-important facts about the universe.

Garth never told the Weskers what he thought about their new interest, and this was mainly because they never asked him. Pride or honor stood in the way of his grabbing a willing listener and pouring out his grievances. Perhaps it would have been different if Itin was on Collecting duty; he was the brightest of the lot; but Itin had been rotated the day after the priest had arrived and Garth had not talked to him since.

It was a surprise then when after seventeen of the trebly-long Wesker days, he found a delegation at his doorstep when he emerged after breakfast. Itin was their spokesman, and his mouth was open slightly. Many of the other Weskers had their mouths open as well, one even appearing to be yawning, clearly revealing the double row of sharp teeth and the purple-black throat. The mouths impressed Garth as to the seriousness of the meeting: this was the one Wesker expression he had learned to recognize. An open mouth indicated some strong emotion; happiness, sadness, anger, he could never be really sure which. The Weskers were normally placid and he had never seen enough open mouths to tell what was causing them. But he was surrounded by them now.

"Will you help us, John Garth," Itin said. "We have a question."

"I'll answer any question you ask," Garth said, with more than a hint of misgiving. "What is it?'"

"Is there a God?"

"What do you mean by 'God'?" Garth asked in turn. What should he tell them?

"God is our Father in Heaven, who made us all and protects us. Whom we pray to for aid, and if we are saved will find a place…"

"That's enough," Garth said. "There is no God."

All of them had their mouths open now, even Itin, as they looked at Garth and thought about his answer. The rows of pink teeth would have been frightening if he hadn't known these creatures so well. For one instant he wondered if perhaps they had been already indoctrinated and looked upon him as a heretic, but he brushed the thought away.

"Thank you," Itin said, and they turned and left.

Though the morning was still cool, Garth noticed that he was sweating and wondered why.

The reaction was not long in coming. Itin returned that same afternoon.

"Will you come to the church?" he asked. "Many of the things that we study are difficult to learn, but none as difficult as this. We need your help because we must hear you and Father talk together. This is because he says one thing is true and you say another is true and both cannot be true at the same time. We must find out what is true."

"I'll come, of course," Garth said, trying to hide the sudden feeling of elation. He had done nothing, but the Weskers had come to him anyway. There could still be grounds for hope that they might yet be free.

It was hot inside the church, and Garth was surprised at the number of Weskers who were there, more than he had seen gathered at any one time before. There were many open mouths. Father Mark sat at a table covered with books. He looked unhappy but didn't say anything when Garth came in. Garth spoke first.

"I hope you realize this is their idea—that they came to me of their own free will and asked me to come here?"

"I know that," the priest said resignedly. "At times they can be very difficult. But they are learning and want to believe, and that is what is important."

"Father Mark, Trader Garth, we need your help," Itin said. "You both know many things that we do not know. You must help us come to religion which is not an easy thing to do." Garth started to say something, then changed his mind. Itin went on. "We have read the Bibles and all the books that Father Mark gave us, and one thing is clear. We have discussed this and we are all agreed. These books are very different from the ones that Trader Garth gave us. In Trader Garth's books there is the universe which we have not seen, and it goes on without God, for he is mentioned nowhere; we have searched very carefully. In Father Mark's books He is everywhere and nothing can go without Him. One of these must be right and the other must be wrong. We do not know how this can be, but after we find out which is right then perhaps we will know. If God does not exist…"

"Of course He exists, my children," Father Mark said in a voice of heartfelt intensity. "He is our Father in Heaven who has created us all…"

"Who created God?" Itin asked and the murmur ceased and every one of the Weskers watched Father Mark intensely. He recoiled a bit under the impact of their eyes, then smiled.

"Nothing created God, since He is the Creator. He always was…"

"If He always was in existence—why cannot the universe have always been in existence? Without having had a creator?" Itin broke in with a rush of words. The importance of the question was obvious. The priest answered slowly, with infinite patience.

"Would that the answers were that simple, my children. But even the scientists do not agree about the creation of the universe. While they doubt—we who have seen the light *know*. We can see the miracle of creation all about us. And how can there be a creation without a Creator? That is He, our Father, our God in Heaven. I know you have doubts; that is because you have souls and free will. Still, the answer is so simple. Have faith, that is all you need. Just believe."

"How can we believe without proof?"

"If you cannot see that this world itself is proof of His existence, then I say to you that belief needs no proof—if you have faith!"

A babble of voices arose in the room and more of the Wesker mouths were open now as they tried to force their thoughts through the tangled skein of words and separate the thread of truth.

"Can you tell us, Garth?" Itin asked, and the sound of his voice quieted the hubbub.

"I can tell you to use the scientific method which can examine all things—including itself—and give you answers that can prove the truth or falsity of any statement."

"That is what we must do," Itin said, "we had reached the same conclusion." He held a thick book before him and a ripple of nods ran across the watchers. "We have been studying the Bible as Father Mark told us to do, and we have found the answer. God will make a miracle for us, thereby proving that He is watching us. And by this sign we will know Him and go to Him."

"That is the sin of false pride," Father Mark said. "God needs no miracles to prove His existence."

"But *we* need a miracle!" Itin shouted, and though he wasn't human there was need in his voice. "We have read here of many smaller miracles, loaves, fishes, wine, snakes—many of them, for much smaller reasons. Now all He need do is make a miracle and He will bring us all to Him—the wonder of an entire new world worshipping at His throne as you have told us, Father Mark. And you have told us how important this is. We have discussed this and find that there is only one miracle that is best for this kind of thing."

His boredom at the theological wrangling drained from Garth in an instant. He had not been really thinking or he would have realized where all this was leading. He could see the illustration in the Bible where Itin held it open, and knew in advance what picture it was. He rose slowly from his chair, as if stretching, and turned to the priest behind him.

"Get ready!" he whispered. "Get out the back and get to the ship; I'll keep them busy here. I don't think they'll harm me."

"What do you mean…?" Father Mark asked, blinking in surprise.

"Get out, you fool!" Garth hissed. "What miracle do you think they mean? What miracle is supposed to have converted the world to Christianity?"

"No!" Father Mark said. "It cannot be. It just cannot be…!"

"*Get moving!*" Garth shouted, dragging the priest from the chair and hurling him toward the rear wall. Father Mark stumbled to a halt, turned back. Garth leaped for him, but it was already too late. The amphibians were small, but there were so many of them. Garth lashed out and his fist struck Itin, hurling him back into the crowd. The others came on as he fought his way toward the priest. He beat at them but it was like struggling against waves. The furry, musky bodies washed over and engulfed him. He fought until they tied him, and he still struggled until they beat on his head until he stopped. Then they pulled him outside where he could only lie in the rain and curse and watch.

Of course the Weskers were marvelous craftsmen, and everything had been constructed down to the last detail, following the illustration in the Bible. There was the cross, planted firmly on the top of a small hill, the gleaming metal spikes, the hammer. Father Mark was stripped and draped in a carefully pleated loincloth. They led him out of the church.

At the sight of the cross he almost fainted. After that he held his head high and determined to die as he had lived, with faith.

Yet this was hard. It was unbearable even for Garth, who only watched.

It is one thing to talk of crucifixion and look at the gentle carved bodies in the dim light of prayer. It is another to see a man naked, ropes cutting into his skin where he hangs from a bar of wood. And to see the needle-tipped spike raised and placed against the soft flesh of his palm, to see the hammer come back with the calm deliberation of an artisan's measured stroke. To hear the thick sound of metal penetrating flesh.

Then to hear the screams.

Few are born to be martyrs; Father Mark was not one of them. With the first blows, the blood ran from his lips where his clenched teeth met. Then his mouth was wide and his head strained back and the guttural horror of his screams sliced through the susurration of the falling rain. It resounded as a silent echo from the masses of watching Weskers, for whatever emotion opened their mouths was now tearing at their bodies with all its force, and row after row of gaping jaws reflected the crucified priest's agony.

Mercifully he fainted as the last nail was driven home. Blood ran from the raw wounds, mixing with the rain to drip faintly pink from his feet as the life ran out of him. At this time, somewhere at this time, sobbing and tearing at his own bonds, numbed from the blows on the head, Garth lost consciousness.

He awoke in his own warehouse and it was dark. Someone was cutting away the woven ropes they had bound him with. The rain still dripped and splashed outside.

"Itin," he said. It could be no one else.

"Yes," the alien voice whispered back. "The others are all talking in the church. Lin died after you struck his head, and Inon is very sick. There are some that say you should be crucified too, and I think that is what will happen. Or perhaps killed by stoning on the head. They have found in the Bible where it says..."

"I know." With infinite weariness. "An eye for an eye. You'll find lots of things like that once you start looking. It's a wonderful book." His head ached terribly.

"You must go, you can get to your ship without anyone seeing you. There has been enough killing." Itin also spoke with a new-found weariness.

Garth experimented, pulling himself to his feet. He pressed his head to the rough wood of the wall until the nausea stopped. "He's dead." He said it as a statement, not a question.

"Yes, some time ago. Or I could not have come away to see you."

"And buried of course, or they wouldn't be thinking about starting on me next."

"And buried!" There was almost a ring of emotion in the alien's voice, an echo of the dead priest's. "He is buried and he will rise on High. It is written and that is the way it will happen. Father Mark will be so happy that it has happened like this." The voice ended in a sound like a human sob.

Garth painfully worked his way toward the door, leaning against the wall so he wouldn't fall.

"We did the right thing, didn't we?" Itin asked. There was no answer. "He will rise up, Garth, won't he rise?"

Garth was at the door and enough light came from the brightly lit church to show his torn and bloody hands clutching at the frame. Itin's face swam into sight close to his, and Garth felt the delicate, many-fingered hands with the sharp nails catch at his clothes.

"He will rise, won't he, Garth?"

"No," Garth said, "he is going to stay buried right where you put him. Nothing is going to happen because he is dead and he is going to stay dead."

The rain runneled through Itin's fur and his mouth was opened so wide that he seemed to be screaming into the night. Only with effort could he talk, squeezing out the alien thoughts in an alien language.

"Then we will not be saved? We will not become pure?"

"You were pure," Garth said, in a voice somewhere between a sob and a laugh. "That's the horrible ugly dirty part of it. You were pure. Now you are..."

"Murderers," Itin said, and the water ran down from his lowered head and streamed away into the darkness.

TERMINAL FICTION

E. J. "Ted" Carnell (1912-1972) created a pair of British science fiction magazines in the late 1940s, *New Worlds* and *Science Fantasy*, and nursed them into the 1960s. The British had had at least one earlier magazine, *Tales of Wonder*, whose first issue was published in 1937. But Carnell's two magazines had the greatest solidity in a shaky field; in 1964, however, they failed.

They had been little different from the American magazines except for the predominance of British writers such as E. C. Tubbs, Kenneth Bulmer, Bertram Chandler, John Kippax (John Charles Hynam), Arthur Sellings (Robert Arthur Ley), James White, Colin Kapp, Brian Aldiss, John Brunner, and others. So when the new *New Worlds* raised the banner of revolution in science fiction, it came as a total surprise.

The last issue of Carnell's *New Worlds* appeared in April 1964 (Carnell went on to care for his literary agency and to edit *New Writings in SF* until his death), but the new publishers missed only one issue. The new editor was Michael Moorcock (1939-), best known at that time for his heroic fantasy centering around a character known as Elric. The banner Moorcock nailed highest on the mast of *New Worlds* was that of J. G. Ballard (1939-), who was featured in the first issue of the new magazine with a serial, "Equinox," which became part of *The Crystal World*, and an article about William Burroughs, whose work seemed to be a starting point for Ballard and some other *New Worlds* writers.

Encouraged by Moorcock's energy and Ballard's example, other writers contributed unconventional stories that were stylistically adventurous. Many of them had already contributed not only to *New Worlds* but to other magazines, like Aldiss, Brunner, and Moorcock himself, but new writers appeared such as Charles Platt, Hilary Bailey (Mrs. Moorcock), M. John Harrison, and others. Soon U.S. writers began submitting their more experimental work to *New Worlds*, such as Norman Spinrad and Thomas Disch, whose first stories were published early in the 1960s, and John Sladek.

The new magazine earned limited readership support, but literary figures mounted a campaign for a grant from the British Arts Council that helped carry the magazine through 1967 and 1968. By the time Judith Merril began promoting the *New Worlds*/New Wave revolution with *England Swings SF* (1968), much of the early excitement had dissipated, although Damon Knight's annual anthology *Orbit*, which was first issued in 1966, picked up the avant-garde mission in the U.S.

Not everything in *New Worlds* was experimental; traditional science fiction continued to appear because not enough new fiction was available or because it wasn't good enough. But the tone was set by stories that were dense, dark, disturbing, and difficult. Even the experimentation was not all original: Brunner's *Stand on Zanzibar* unapologetically drew on John Dos Passos's *U.S.A.*, the first part of which was published in 1925; Aldiss's *Barefoot in the Head* paid tribute to James Joyce's *Finnegans Wake*, published in 1939; and other experimentalists, such as Jorge Luis Borges, and Michael Butor and Alain Robbe-Grillet with their anti-novels, have had their influence.

The stories, the entire movement, contained a nihilistic spirit. Perhaps they fitted the times of uncertainty in world affairs, of growing opposition to American involvement in Vietnam, of drugs and the Beatles and pop art and music and swinging London, of assassinations and skyjackings and terrorism... Aldiss summed up its pessimism: "At the Heart of the *New Worlds* New Wave—never mind the froth at the edges—was a hard and unpalatable core of message, an attitude to life, a skepticism about the benefits of society or any future society."

The writer at the heart of the movement, Ballard, seemed to push fiction farther and farther into the unrecognizable. His stories began with understandable characters facing understandable problems, but grew increasingly experimental, increasingly difficult. His characters became mysteriously obsessed or bewildered and passive in situations filled with enigmatic events to which they responded with an acceptance of some ultimate failure in themselves or humanity or the universe. Meaning became solely dependent on symbol interpretation.

Ballard, born in Shanghai and interned as a boy in a World War II Japanese POW camp, perhaps had reason to doubt the sanity of society or the meaning of existence. He was repatriated to England in 1946, and entered Cambridge to study medicine before turning to copywriting, scriptwriting, and RAF service. His first story, "Prima Belladonna," appeared in *Science Fantasy* in 1956.

Brian Ash calls Ballard "an expert in slow choreographies of physical and mental disintegration"; Aldiss said that eventually he "rejected linear fiction and was writing 'condensed novels,' impacted visions of a timeless, dimensionless world, lacerated by anguish, desiccated by knowledge, and illustrative of William Burroughs's dictum, 'A psychotic is a guy who's just discovered what's going on.'"

"The Terminal Beach," ironically, was published in the next-to-last issue of the Carnell *New Worlds*, March 1964. Besides his "condensed novels," such as "The Assassination of John Fitzgerald Kennedy Considered as a Downhill Motor Race" and "You: Coma: Marilyn Monroe," the other story that is most associated with his early metaphorical style is "The Voices of Time," which appeared in 1960. His early novels dealt with worldwide catastrophe. In them the world is destroyed again and again: *The Wind from Nowhere* (1962); *The Drowned World* (1962); *The Drought* (1964), also called *The Burning World*; *The Crystal World* (1966); *The Atrocity Exhibition* (1970), also called *Love and Napalm U.S.A.*; *Crash* (1973); *Concrete Island* (1974); and *High Rise* (1975). Beginning with

The Unlimited Dream Company (1979), Ballard's novels become more accessible and less obsessive, and with *Empire of the Sun* (1984), an autobiographical novel about his experience in the Japanese prison camp that was adapted for a film by Steven Spielberg, Ballard became a broadly read, best-selling author. Subsequent novels include *The Day of Creation* (1987), *The Kindness of Women* (1991), and *Rushing to Paradise* (1995).

Ballard is, without doubt, an original. He needs, and is finding, an audience not of science fiction readers but of Ballard readers.

THE TERMINAL BEACH

BY J. G. BALLARD

At night, as he lay asleep on the floor of the ruined bunker, Traven heard the waves breaking along the shore of the lagoon, reminding him of the deep Atlantic rollers on the beach at Dakar, where he had been born, and of waiting in the evenings for his parents to drive home along the corniche road from the airport. Overcome by this long-forgotten memory, he woke uncertainly from the bed of old magazines on which he slept and ran toward the dunes that screened the lagoon.

Through the cold night air he could see the abandoned superfortresses lying among the palms, beyond the perimeter of the emergency landing field three hundred yards away. Traven walked through the dark sand, already forgetting where the shore lay, although the atoll was only half a mile in width. Above him, along the crests of the dunes, the tall palms leaned into the dim air like the symbols of some cryptic alphabet. The landscape of the island was covered by strange ciphers.

Giving up the attempt to find the beach, Traven stumbled into a set of tracks left years earlier by a large Caterpillar vehicle. The heat released by one of the weapons tests had fused the sand, and the double line of fossil imprints, uncovered by the evening air, wound its serpentine way among the hollows like the footfalls of an ancient saurian.

Too weak to walk any further, Traven sat down between the tracks. With one hand he began to excavate the wedge-shaped grooves from a drift into which they disappeared, hoping that they might lead him toward the sea. He returned to the bunker shortly before dawn, and slept through the hot silences of the following noon.

The Blocks

As usual on these enervating afternoons, when not even the faintest breath of offshore breeze disturbed the dust, Traven sat in the shadow of one of the blocks, lost somewhere within the center of the maze. His back resting against the rough concrete surface, he gazed with a phlegmatic eye down the surrounding aisles and at the line of doors facing him. Each afternoon he left his cell in the abandoned camera bunker and walked down into the blocks. For the first half an hour he restricted himself to the perimeter aisle, now and then trying one of the doors with the rusty key in his pocket—he had found it among the litter of smashed bottles in the isthmus of sand separating the testing ground from the airstrip—and then, inevitably, with a sort of drugged stride, he set off into the center of the blocks, breaking into a run and darting in and out of the corridors, as if trying to flush some invisible opponent from his hiding place. Soon he would be completely lost. Whatever his efforts to return to the perimeter, he found himself once more in the center.

Eventually he would abandon the task, and sit down in the dust, watching the shadows emerge from their crevices at the foot of the blocks. For some reason he always arranged to be trapped when the sun was at zenith—on Eniwetok, a thermonuclear noon.

One question in particular intrigued him: "What sort of people would inhabit this minimal concrete city?"

The Synthetic Landscape

"This island is a state of mind," Osborne, one of the biologists working in the old submarine pens, was later to remark to Traven. The truth of this became obvious to Traven within two or three weeks of his arrival. Despite the sand and the few anemic palms, the entire landscape of the island was synthetic, a manmade artifact with all the associations of a vast system of derelict concrete motorways. Since the moratorium on atomic tests, the island had been abandoned by the Atomic Energy Commission, and the wilderness of weapons aisles, towers, and blockhouses ruled out any attempt to return it to its natural state. (There were also stronger unconscious motives, Traven recognized, for leaving it as it was: if primitive man felt the need to assimilate events in the external world to his own psyche, twentieth century man had reversed this process—by this Cartesian yardstick, the island at least *existed*, in a sense true of few other places.)

But apart from a few scientific workers, no one yet felt any wish to visit the former testing ground, and the naval patrol boat anchored in the lagoon had been withdrawn five years before Traven's arrival. Its ruined appearance and the associations of the island with the period of the Cold War—what Traven had christened the "Pre-Third"—were profoundly depressing, an Auschwitz of the soul whose mausoleums contained the mass graves of the still undead. With the Russo-American détente this nightmarish chapter of history had been gladly forgotten.

The Pre-Third

"The actual and potential destructiveness of the atomic bomb plays straight into the hands of the Unconscious. The most cursory study of the dream-life and fantasies of the insane shows that ideas of world-destruction are latent in the unconscious mind. Nagasaki destroyed by the magic of science is the nearest man had yet approached to the realization of dreams that even during the safe immobility of sleep are accustomed to develop into nightmares of anxiety."—Glover, *War, Sadism, and Pacifism.*

The Pre-Third: the period had been characterized in Traven's mind above all by its moral and psychological inversions, by its sense of the whole of history, and in particular of the immediate future—the two decades, 1945–1965—suspended from the quivering volcano's lip of World War III. Even the death of his wife and six-year-old son in a motor accident seemed only part of this immense synthesis of the historical and psychic zero, the frantic highways where each morning they met their deaths, the advance causeways to the global Armageddon.

Third Beach

He had come ashore at midnight, after a hazardous search for an opening in the reef. The small motorboat he had hired from an Australian pearldiver at Charlotte Island subsided into the shallows, its hull torn by the sharp coral. Exhausted, Traven walked through the darkness among the dunes, where the dim outlines of bunkers and concrete towers loomed between the palms.

He woke the next morning into bright sunlight, lying halfway down the slope of a wide concrete beach. This ringed what appeared to be an empty reservoir or target basin, some two hundred feet in diameter, part of a system of artificial lakes built down the center of the atoll. Leaves and dust choked the waste grills, and a pool of warm water two feet deep lay in the center, reflecting a distant line of palms.

Traven sat up and took stock of himself. This brief inventory, which merely confirmed his physical identity, was limited to little more than his thin body in its frayed cotton garments. In the context of the surrounding terrain, however, even this collection of tatters seemed to possess a unique vitality. The emptiness of the island, and the absence of any local fauna, were emphasized by the huge sculptural forms of the target basins let into its surface. Separated from each other by narrow isthmuses, the lakes stretched away along the curve of the atoll. On either side, sometimes shaded by the few palms that had gained a precarious purchase in the cracked cement, were roadways, camera towers, and isolated blockhouses, together forming a continuous concrete cap upon the island, a functional megalithic architecture as gray and minatory (and apparently as ancient, in its projection into, and from, time future) as any of Assyria and Babylon.

The series of weapons tests had fused the sand in layers, and the pseudogeological strata condensed the brief epochs, microseconds in duration, of the thermonuclear age. "The key to the past lies in the present." Typically the island inverted this geologist's maxim. Here the key to the present lay in the future. The island was a fossil of time future, its bunkers and blockhouses illustrating the principle that the fossil record of life is one of armor and the exoskeleton.

Traven knelt in the warm pool and splashed his shirt and trousers. The reflection revealed the watery image of a thinly bearded face and gaunt shoulders. He had come to the island with no supplies other than a small bar of chocolate, expecting that in some way the island would provide its own sustenance. Perhaps, too, he had identified the need for food with a forward motion in time, and that with his return to the past, or at most into a zone of nontime, this need would be obviated. The privations of the previous six months, during his journey across the Pacific, had reduced his always thin body to that of a migrant beggar, held together by little more than the preoccupied gaze in his eye. Yet this emaciation, by stripping away the superfluities of the flesh, seemed to reveal an inner sinewy toughness, and economy and directness of movement.

For several hours he wandered about, inspecting one bunker after another for a convenient place to sleep. He crossed the remains of a small landing strip, next to a dump where a dozen B-29's lay across one another like dead reptile birds.

The Corpses

Once he entered a small street of metal shacks, containing a cafeteria, recreation rooms, and shower stalls. A wrecked jukebox lay half-buried in the sand behind the cafeteria, its selection of records still in their rack.

Further along, flung into a small target basin fifty yards from the shacks, were the bodies of what at first he thought were the inhabitants of this ghost town—a dozen life-size plastic models. Their half-melted faces, contorted into bleary grimaces, gazed up at him from the jumble of legs and torsos.

On either side of him, muffled by the dunes, came the sounds of waves, the great rollers on the seaward side breaking over the reefs, and onto the beaches within the lagoon. However, he avoided the sea, hesitating before any rise that might take him within its sight. Everywhere the camera towers offered him a convenient aerial view of the confused topography of the island, but he avoided their rusting ladders.

He soon realized that however confused and random the blockhouses and camera towers might seem, their common focus dominated the landscape and gave to it a unique perspective. As Traven noticed when he sat down to rest in the window slit of one of the blockhouses, all these observation posts occupied positions on a series of concentric perimeters, moving in tightening arcs toward the inmost sanctuary. This ultimate circle, below ground zero, remained hidden beyond a line of dunes a quarter of a mile to the west.

The Terminal Bunker

After sleeping for a few nights in the open, Traven returned to the concrete beach where he had woken on his first morning on the island, and made his home—if the term could be applied to that damp crumbling hovel—in a camera bunker fifty yards from the target lakes. The dark chamber between the thick canted walls, tomblike though it might seem, gave him a sense of physical reassurance. Outside, the sand drifted against the sides, half burying the narrow doorway, as if crystallizing the immense epoch of time that had elapsed since the bunker's construction. The narrow rectangles of the five camera slits, their shapes and positions determined by the instruments, studded the east wall like cryptic ideograms. Variations of these ciphers decorated the walls of the other bunkers. In the morning, if Traven was awake, he would always find the sun divided into five emblematic beacons.

Most of the time the chamber was filled only by a damp gloomy light. In the control tower at the landing field Traven found a collection of discarded magazines, and used these to make a bed. One day, lying in the bunker shortly after the first attack of beriberi, he pulled out a magazine pressing into his back and found inside it a full-page photograph of a six-year-old girl. This blond-haired child, with her composed expression and self-immersed eyes, filled him with a thousand painful memories of his son. He pinned the page to the wall and for days gazed at it through his reveries.

For the first few weeks Traven made little attempt to leave the bunker, and postponed any further exploration of the island. The symbolic journey through its inner circles set its own times of arrival and departure. He evolved no routine for himself. All sense of time soon vanished; his life became completely existential, an absolute break separating one moment from the next like two quantal events. Too weak to forage for food, he lived on the old ration packs he found in the wrecked superfortresses. Without any implements, it took him all day to open the cans. His physical decline continued, but he watched his spindling arms and legs with indifference.

By now he had forgotten the existence of the sea and vaguely assumed the atoll to be part of some continuous continental table. A hundred yards away to the north and south of the bunker a line of dunes, topped by the palisade of enigmatic palms, screened the lagoon and sea, and the faint muffled drumming of the waves at night had fused with his memories of war and childhood. To the east was the emergency landing field and the abandoned aircraft. In the afternoon light their shifting rectangular shadows would appear to writhe and pivot. In front of the bunker, where he sat, was the system of target lakes, the shallow basins extending across the center of the atoll. Above him the five apertures looked out upon this scene like the tutelary deities of some futuristic myth.

The Lakes and the Specters

The lakes had been designed originally to reveal any radiobiological changes in a selected range of flora and fauna, but the specimens had long since bloomed into grotesque parodies of themselves and been destroyed.

Sometimes in the evenings, when a sepulchral light lay over the concrete bunkers and causeways, and the basins seemed like ornamental lakes in a city of deserted mausoleums, abandoned even by the dead, he would see the specters of his wife and son standing on the opposite bank. Their solitary figures appeared to have been watching him for hours. Although they never moved, Traven was sure they were beckoning to him. Roused from his reverie, he would stumble across the dark sand to the edge of the lake and wade through the water, shouting at the two figures as they moved away hand in hand among the lakes and disappeared across the distant causeways.

Shivering with cold, Traven would return to the bunker and lie on the bed of old magazines, waiting for their return. The image of their faces, the pale lantern of his wife's cheeks, floated on the river of his memory.

The Blocks (II)

It was not until he discovered the blocks that Traven realized he would never leave the island.

At this stage, some two months after his arrival, Traven had exhausted the small cache of food, and the symptoms of beriberi had become more acute. The numbness in his hands and feet, and the gradual loss of strength, continued. Only by an immense effort, and the knowledge that the inner sanctum of the island still lay unexplored, did he manage to leave the paliasse of magazines and make his way from the bunker.

As he sat in the drift of sand by the doorway that evening, he noticed a light shining through the palms far into the distance around the atoll. Confusing this with the image of his wife and son, and visualizing them waiting for him at some warm hearth among the dunes, Traven set off toward the light. Within fifty yards he lost his sense of direction. He blundered about for several hours on the edges of the landing strip, and succeeded only in cutting his foot on a broken Coca-Cola bottle in the sand.

After postponing his search for the night, he set out again in earnest the next morning. As he moved past the towers and blockhouses the heat lay over the island in an unbroken mantle. He had entered a zone devoid of time. Only the narrowing perimeters of the bunkers warned him that he was crossing the inner field of the firetable.

He climbed the ridge which marked the furthest point in his previous exploration of the island. The plain beyond was covered with target aisles and explosion breaks. On the gray walls of the recording towers, which rose into the air like obelisks, were the faint outlines of human forms in stylized postures, the flash-shadows of the target community burned into the cement. Here and there, where the concrete apron had cracked, a line of palms hung precariously in the motionless air. The target lakes were smaller, filled with the broken bodies of plastic dummies. Most of them still lay in the inoffensive domestic postures into which they had been placed before the tests.

Beyond the furthest line of dunes, where the camera towers began to turn and face him, were the tops of what seemed to be a herd of square-backed elephants. They were drawn up in precise ranks in a hollow that formed a shallow corral.

Traven advanced toward them, limping on his cut foot. On either side of him the loosening sand had excavated the dunes, and several of the blockhouses tilted on their sides. This plain of bunkers stretched for some quarter of a mile. To one side the half-submerged hulks of a group of concrete shelters, bombed out onto the surface in some earlier test, lay like the husks of the abandoned wombs that had given birth to this herd of megaliths.

The Blocks (III)

To grasp something of the vast number and oppressive size of the blocks, and their impact upon Traven, one must try to visualize sitting in the shade of one of these concrete monsters, or walking about in the center of this enormous labyrinth which extended across the central table of the island. There were some two thousand of them, each a perfect cube fifteen feet in height, regularly spaced at ten-yard intervals. They were arranged in a series of tracts, each composed of two hundred blocks, inclined to one another and to the direction of the blast. They had weathered only slightly in the years since they were first built, and their gaunt profiles were like the cutting faces of an enormous die-plate, designed to stamp out huge rectilinear volumes of air. Three of the sides were smooth and unbroken, but the fourth, facing away from the direction of the blast, contained a narrow inspection door.

It was this feature of the blocks that Traven found particularly disturbing. Despite the considerable number of doors, by some freak of perspective only those in a single aisle were visible at any point within the maze, the rest obscured by the intervening blocks. As he walked from the perimeter into the center of the massif, line upon line of the small metal doors appeared and receded, a world of closed exits concealed behind endless corners.

Approximately twenty of the blocks, those immediately below ground zero, were solid, the walls of the remainder of varying thicknesses. From the outside they appeared to be of uniform solidity.

As he entered the first of the long aisles, Traven felt his step lighten; the sense of fatigue that had dogged him for so many months begin to lift. With their geometric regularity and finish, the blocks seemed to occupy more than their own volume of space, imposing on him a mood of absolute calm and order. He walked on into the center of the maze, eager to shut out the rest of the island. After a few random turns to left and right, he found himself alone, the vistas to the sea, lagoon, and island closed.

Here he sat down with his back against one of the blocks, the quest for his wife and son forgotten. For the first time since his arrival at the island the sense of dissociation prompted by its fragmenting landscape began to recede.

One development he did not expect. With dusk, and the need to leave the blocks and find food, he realized that he had lost himself. However he retraced his steps, struck out left or right at an oblique course, oriented himself around the sun and pressed on resolutely north or south, he found himself back at his starting point. Despite his best efforts, he was unable to make his way out of the maze. That he was aware of his motives gave him little help. Only when hunger overcame the need to remain did he manage to escape.

Abandoning his former home near the aircraft dump, Traven collected together what canned food he could find in the waist turret and cockpit lockers of the superfortresses and pulled them across the island on a crude sledge. Fifty yards from the perimeter of the blocks he took over a tilting bunker, and pinned the fading photograph of the blond-haired child to the wall beside the door. The page was falling to pieces, like his fragmenting image of himself. Each evening when he woke he would eat uneagerly and then go out into the blocks. Sometimes he took a canteen of water with him and remained there for two or three days.

Traven: In Parenthesis

Elements in a quantal world:
    The terminal beach.
    The terminal bunker.
    The blocks.
The landscape is coded.
Entry points into the future=levels in a spinal landscape=zones of significant time.

The Submarine Pens

This precarious existence continued for the following weeks. As he walked out to the blocks one evening, he again saw his wife and son, standing among the dunes below a solitary tower, their faces watching him calmly. He realized that they had followed him across the island from their former haunt among the dried-up lakes. Once again he saw the beckoning light, and he decided to continue his exploration of the island.

Half a mile further along the atoll he found a group of four submarine pens, built over an inlet, now drained, which wound through the dunes from the sea. The pens still contained several feet of water, filled with strange luminescent fish and plants. A warning light winked at intervals from a metal tower. The remains of a substantial camp, only recently vacated, stood on the concrete pier outside. Greedily Traven heaped his sledge with the provisions stacked inside one of the metal shacks. With this change of diet the beriberi receded, and during the next days he returned to the camp. It appeared to be the site of a biological expedition. In a field office he came across a series of large charts of mutated chromosomes. He rolled them up and took them back to his bunker. The abstract patterns were meaningless, but during his recovery he amused himself by devising suitable titles for them. (Later, passing the aircraft dump on one of his forays, he found the half-buried jukebox, and tore the list of records from the selection panel, realizing that these were the most appropriate captions for the charts. Thus embroidered, they took on many layers of cryptic associations.)

Traven Lost Among the Blocks

August 5. Found the man Traven. A strange derelict figure, hiding in a bunker in the deserted interior of the island. He is suffering from severe exposure and malnutrition, but is unaware of this, or, for that matter, of any other events in the world around him....

He maintains that he came to the island to carry out some scientific project— unstated—but I suspect that he understands his real motives and the unique role of the island.... In some way its landscape seems to be involved with certain unconscious notions of time, and in particular with those that may be a repressed premonition of our own deaths. The attractions and dangers of such an architecture, as the past has shown, need no stressing.

August 6. He has the eyes of the possessed. I would guess that he is neither the first, nor the last, to visit the island.—from Dr. C. Osborne, "Eniwetok Diary."

With the exhaustion of his supplies, Traven remained within the perimeter of the blocks almost continuously, conserving what strength remained to him to walk slowly down their empty corridors. The infection in his right foot made it difficult for him to replenish his supplies from the stores left by the biologists, and as his strength ebbed he found progressively less incentive to make his way out of the blocks. The system of megaliths now provided a complete substitute for those functions of his mind which gave to it its sense of the sustained rational order of time and space, his awareness kindled from levels above those of his present nervous system (if the autonomic system is dominated by the past, the cerebro-spinal reaches toward the future). Without the blocks, his sense of reality shrank to little more than the few square inches of sand beneath his feet.

On one of his last ventures into the maze, he spent all night and much of the following morning in a futile attempt to escape. Dragging himself from one rectangle of shadow to another, his leg as heavy as a club and apparently inflamed to the knee, he realized that he must soon find an equivalent for the blocks or he would end his life within them, trapped within this self-constructed mausoleum as surely as the retinue of Pharaoh.

He was sitting exhausted somewhere within the center of the system, the faceless lines of the tomb-booths receding from him, when the sky was slowly divided by the drone of a light aircraft. This passed overhead, and then, five minutes later, returned. Seizing his opportunity, Traven struggled to his feet and made his exit from the blocks, his head raised to follow the glistening exhaust trail.

As he lay down in the bunker he dimly heard the aircraft return and carry out an inspection of the site.

A Belated Rescue

"Who are you?" A small sandy-haired man was peering down at him with a severe expression, then put away a syringe in his valise. "Do you realize you're on your last legs?"

"Traven... I've had some sort of accident. I'm glad you flew over."

"I'm sure you are. Why didn't you use our emergency radio? Anyway, we'll call the Navy and have you picked up."

"No..." Traven sat up on one elbow and felt weakly in his hip pocket. "I have a pass somewhere. I'm carrying out research."

"Into what?" The question assumed a complete understanding of Traven's motives. Traven lay in the shade beside the bunker, and drank weakly from a canteen as Dr. Osborne dressed his foot. "You've also been stealing our stores."

Traven shook his head. Fifty yards away the blue and white Cessna stood on the concrete apron like a large dragon-fly. "I didn't realize you were coming back."

"You must be in a trance."

The young woman at the controls of the aircraft climbed from the cockpit and walked over to them, glancing at the gray bunkers and blocks. She seemed unaware of or uninterested in the decrepit figure of Traven. Osborne spoke to her over his shoulder, and after a downward glance at Traven she went back to the aircraft. As she turned Traven rose involuntarily, recognizing the child in the photograph he had pinned to the wall. Then he remembered that the magazine could not have been more than four or five years old.

The engine of the aircraft started. It turned onto one of the roadways and took off into the wind.

The young woman drove over by jeep that afternoon with a small camp bed and a canvas awning. During the intervening hours Traven had slept, and woke refreshed when Osborne returned from his scrutiny of the surrounding dunes.

"What are you doing here?" the young woman asked as she secured one of the guy-ropes to the bunker.

"I'm searching for my wife and son," Traven said.

"They're on this island?" Surprised, but taking the reply at face value, she looked around her. "Here?"

"In a manner of speaking."

After inspecting the bunker, Osborne joined them. "The child in the photograph. Is she your daughter?"

"No." Traven tried to explain. "She's adopted *me*."

Unable to make sense of his replies, but accepting his assurances that he would leave the island, Osborne and the young woman returned to their camp. Each day Osborne returned to change the dressing, driven by the young woman, who seemed to grasp the role cast for her by Traven in his private mythology. Osborne, when he learned of Traven's previous career as a military pilot, assumed that he was a latter-day martyr left high and dry by the moratorium on thermonuclear tests.

"A guilt complex isn't an indiscriminate supply of moral sanctions. I think you may be overstretching yours."

When he mentioned the name Eatherly, Traven shook his head.

Undeterred, Osborne pressed: "Are you sure you're not making similar use of the image of Eniwetok waiting for your pentecostal wind?"

"Believe me, Doctor, no," Traven replied firmly. "For me the H-Bomb is a symbol of absolute freedom. Unlike Eatherly, I feel it's given me the right—the obligation, even—to do anything I choose."

"That seems strange logic," Osborne commented. "Aren't we at least responsible for our physical selves?"

Traven shrugged. "Not now, I think. After all, aren't we in effect men raised from the dead?"

Often, however, he thought of Eatherly: the prototypal Pre-Third Man, dating the Pre-Third from August 6, 1945, carrying a full load of cosmic guilt.

Shortly after Traven was strong enough to walk again he had to be rescued from the blocks for a second time. Osborne became less conciliatory.

"Our work is almost complete," he warned Traven. "You'll die here. Traven, what are you looking for?"

To himself Traven said: the tomb of the unknown civilian, *Homo Hydrogenensis*, Eniwetok Man. To Osborne he said: "Doctor, your laboratory is at the wrong end of this island."

"I'm aware of that, Traven. There are rarer fish swimming in your head than in any submarine pen."

On the day before they left Traven and the young woman drove over to the lakes where he had first arrived. As a final present from Osborne, an ironic gesture unexpected from the elderly biologist, she had brought the correct list of legends for the chromosome charts. They stopped by the derelict jukebox and she pasted them on to the selection panel.

They wandered among the supine wrecks of the super-fortresses. Traven lost sight of her, and for the next ten minutes searched in and out of the dunes. He found her standing in a small amphitheater formed by the sloping mirrors of a solar energy device, built by one of the visiting expeditions. She smiled to him as he stepped through the scaffolding. A dozen fragmented images of herself were reflected in the broken panes. In some she was sans head, in others multiples of her raised arms circled her like those of a Hindu goddess. Exhausted, Traven turned away and walked back to the jeep.

As they drove away he described his glimpses of his wife and son. "Their faces are always calm. My son's particularly, although he was never really like that. The only time his face was grave was when be was being born—then he seemed millions of years old."

The young woman nodded. "I hope you find them." As an afterthought she added: "Dr. Osborne is going to tell the Navy you're here. Hide somewhere."

Traven thanked her. When she flew away from the island for the last time he waved to her from his seat beside the blocks.

The Naval Party

When the search party came for him Traven hid in the only logical place. Fortunately the search was perfunctory, and was called off after a few hours. The sailors had brought a supply of beer with them, and the search soon turned into a drunken ramble. On the walls of the recording towers Traven later found balloons of obscene dialogue chalked into the mouths of the shadow figures, giving their postures the priapic gaiety of the dancers in cave drawings.

The climax of the party was the ignition of a store of gasoline in an underground tank near the airstrip. As he listened, first to the megaphones shouting his name, the echoes receding among the dunes like the forlorn calls of dying birds, then to the boom of the explosion and the laughter as the landing craft left, Traven felt a premonition that these were the last sounds he would hear.

He had hidden in one of the target basins, lying down among the bodies of the plastic dummies. In the hot sunlight their deformed faces gaped at him sightlessly from the tangle of limbs, their blurred smiles like those of the soundlessly laughing dead. Their faces filled his mind as he climbed over the bodies and returned to the bunker.

As he walked toward the blocks he saw the figures of his wife and son standing in his path. They were less than ten yards from him, their white faces watching him with a look of almost overwhelming expectancy. Never had Traven seen them so close to the blocks. His wife's pale features seemed illuminated from within, her lips parted as if in greeting, one hand raised to take his own. His son's grave face, with its curiously fixed expression, regarded him with the same enigmatic smile of the girl in the photograph.

"Judith! David!" Startled, Traven ran forward to them. Then, in a sudden movement of light, their clothes turned into shrouds, and he saw the wounds that disfigured their necks and chests. Appalled, he cried out to them. As they vanished he fled into the safety and sanity of the blocks.

The Catechism of Goodbye

This time he found himself, as Osborne had predicted, unable to leave the blocks.

Somewhere in the shifting center of the maze, he sat with his back against one of the concrete flanks, his eyes raised to the sun. Around him the lines of cubes formed the horizons of his world. At times they would appear to advance toward him, looming over him like cliffs, the intervals between them narrowing so that they were little more than an arm's length apart, a labyrinth of narrow corridors running between them. Then they would recede from him, separating from each other like points in an expanding universe, until the nearest line formed an intermittent palisade along the horizon.

Time had become quantal. For hours it would be noon, the shadows contained within the motionless bulk of the blocks, the heat reverberating off the concrete floor. Abruptly he would find it was early afternoon or evening, the shadows everywhere like pointing fingers.

"Good-bye, Eniwetok," he murmured.

Somewhere there was a flicker of light, as if one of the blocks, like a counter on an abacus, had been plucked away.

"Good-bye, Los Alamos." Again a block seemed to vanish. The corridors around him remained intact, but somewhere, Traven was convinced, in the matrix superimposed on his mind, a small interval of neutral space had been punched.

Good-bye, Hiroshima.

Good-bye, Alamagordo.

Good-bye, Moscow, London, Paris, New York....

Shuttles flickered, a ripple of integers. Traven stopped, accepting the futility of this megathlon farewell. Such a leave-taking required him to fix his signature on every one of the particles in the universe.

Total Noon: Eniwetok

The blocks now occupied positions on an endlessly revolving circus wheel. They carried him upward, to heights from which he could see the whole island and the sea, and then down again through the opaque disc of the floor. From here he looked up at the undersurface of the concrete cap, an inverted landscape of rectilinear hollows, the dome-shaped mounds of the lake-system, the thousands of empty cubic pits of the blocks.

"Good bye, Traven"

To his disappointment he found that this ultimate act of rejection gained him nothing.

In an interval of lucidity, he looked down at his emaciated arms and legs propped loosely in front of him, the brittle wrists and hands covered with a lacework of ulcers. To his right was a trail of disturbed dust, the marks of slack heels.

In front of him lay a long corridor between the blocks, joining an oblique series a hundred yards away. Among these, where a narrow interval revealed the open space beyond, was a crescent-shaped shadow, poised in the air.

During the next half-hour it moved slowly, turning as the sun swung.

The outline of a dune.

Seizing on this cipher, which hung before him like a symbol on a shield, Traven pushed himself through the dust. He climbed precariously to his feet, and covered his eyes from all sight of the blocks.

Ten minutes later he emerged from the western perimeter. The dune whose shadow had guided him lay fifty yards away. Beyond it, bearing the shadow like a screen, was a ridge of limestone, which ran away among the hillocks of a wasteland. The remains of old bulldozers, bales of barbed wire, and fifty-gallon drums lay half-buried in the sand.

Traven approached the dune, reluctant to leave this anonymous swell of sand. He shuffled around its edges, and then sat down in the shade by a narrow crevice in the ridge.

Ten minutes later he noticed that someone was watching him.

The Marooned Japanese

This corpse, whose eyes stared up at Traven, lay to his left at the bottom of the crevice. That of a man of middle age and powerful build, it lay on its side with its head on a pillow of stone, as if surveying the window of the sky. The fabric of the clothes had rotted to a gray tattered vestment, but in the absence of any small animal predators on the island the skin and musculature had been preserved. Here and there, at the angle of knee or wrist, a bony point shone through the leathery integument of the yellow skin, but the facial mask was still intact, and revealed a male Japanese of the professional classes. Looking down at the strong nose, high forehead, and broad mouth, Traven guessed that the Japanese had been a doctor or lawyer.

Puzzled as to how the corpse had found itself here, Traven slid a few feet down the slope. There were no radiation burns on the skin, which indicated that the Japanese had been there for less than five years. Nor did he appear to be wearing a uniform, so had not been a member of a military or scientific mission.

To the left of the corpse, within reach of his hand, was a frayed leather case, the remains of a map wallet. To the right was the bleached husk of a haversack, open to reveal a canteen of water and a small jerrican.

Greedily, the reflex of starvation making him for the moment ignore this discovery that the Japanese had deliberately chosen to die in the crevice, Traven slid down the slope until his feet touched the splitting soles of the corpse's shoes. He reached forward and seized the canteen. A cupful of flat water swilled around the rusting bottom. Traven gulped down the water, the dissolved metal salts cloaking his lips and tongue with a bitter film. He pried the lid off the jerrican, which was empty but for a tacky coating of condensed syrup. He scraped at this with the lid and chewed at the tarry flakes. They filled his mouth with an almost intoxicating sweetness. After a few moments he felt light-headed and sat back beside the corpse. Its sightless eyes regarded him with unmoving compassion.

The Fly

(*A small fly, which Traven presumes has followed him into the crevice, now buzzes about the corpse's face. Traven leans forward to kill it, then reflects that perhaps this minuscule sentry had been the corpse's faithful companion, in return fed on the rich liqueurs and distillations of its pores. Carefully, to avoid injuring the fly, he encourages it to alight on his wrist.*)

DR. YASUDA: Thank you, Traven. (*The voice is rough, as if unused to conversation.*) In my position, you understand.

TRAVEN: Of course, doctor. I'm sorry I tried to kill it. These ingrained habits, you know, they're not easy to shrug off. Your sister's children in Osaka in '44, the exigencies of war, I hate to plead them, most known motives are so despicable one searches the unknown in the hope that....

YASUDA: Please, Traven, do not be embarrassed. The fly is lucky to retain its identity for so long. That son you mourn, not to mention my own two nieces and nephew, did they not die each day? Every parent in the world mourns the lost sons and daughters of their past childhoods.

TRAVEN: You're very tolerant, doctor. I wouldn't dare—

YASUDA: Not at all, Traven. I make no apologies for you. After all, each of us is little more than the meager residue of the infinite unrealized possibilities of our lives. But your son and my nieces are fixed in our minds forever, their identities as certain as the stars.

TRAVEN: (*not entirely convinced*) That may be so, doctor, but it leads to a dangerous conclusion in the case of this island. For instance, the blocks....

YASUDA: They are precisely to what I refer. Here among the blocks, Traven, you at last find the image of yourself free of time and space. This island is an ontological Garden of Eden; why try to expel yourself into a quantal world?

TRAVEN: Excuse me. (*The fly has flown back to the corpse's face and sits in one of the orbits, giving the good doctor an expression of quizzical beadiness. Reaching forward, Traven entices it onto his palm.*) Well, yes, these bunkers may be ontological objects, but whether this is the ontological fly seems doubtful. It's true that on this island it's the only fly, which is the next best thing.

YASUDA: You can't accept the plurality of the universe, Traven. Ask yourself, why? Why should this obsess you. It seems to me that you are hunting for the white leviathan, zero. The beach is a dangerous zone; avoid it. Have a proper humility; pursue a philosophy of acceptance.

TRAVEN: Then may I ask why you came here, doctor?

YASUDA: To feed this fly. "What greater love—?"

TRAVEN: (still puzzling) It doesn't really solve my problem. The blocks, you see....

YASUDA: Very well, if you must have it that way...

TRAVEN: But, Doctor—

YASUDA: : (peremptorily) Kill that fly!

TRAVEN: That's not an end, or a beginning. (Hopelessly he kills the fly. Exhausted, he falls asleep beside the corpse.)

The Terminal Beach

Searching for a piece of rope in the refuse dump behind the dunes, Traven found a bale of rusty wire. He unwound it, then secured a harness around the corpse's chest, and dragged it from the crevice. The lid of a wooden crate served as a sledge. Traven fastened the corpse into a sitting position, and set off along the perimeter of the blocks. Around him the island was silent. The lines of palms hung in the sunlight, only his own motion varying the shifting ciphers of their crisscrossing trunks. The square turrets of the camera towers jutted from the dunes like forgotten obelisks.

An hour later, when Traven reached his bunker, he untied the wire cord he had fastened around his waist. He took the chair left for him by Dr. Osborne and carried it to a point midway between the bunker and the blocks. Then he tied the body of the Japanese to the chair, arranging the hands so that they rested on the wooden arms, giving the moribund figure a posture of calm repose.

This done to his satisfaction, Traven returned to the bunker and squatted under the awning.

As the next days passed into weeks, the dignified figure of the Japanese sat in his chair fifty yards from him, guarding Traven from the blocks. Their magic still filled Traven's reveries, but he now had sufficient strength to rouse himself and forage for food. In the hot sunlight the skin of the Japanese became more and more bleached, and sometimes Traven would wake at night to find the white sepulchral figure sitting there, arms resting at its sides, in the shadows that crossed the concrete floor. At these moments he would often see his wife and son watching him from the dunes. As time passed they came closer, and he would sometimes turn to find them only a few yards behind him.

Patiently Traven waited for them to speak to him, thinking of the great blocks whose entrance was guarded by the seated figure of the dead archangel, as the waves broke on the distant shore and the burning bombers fell through his dreams.

AGAIN AND AGAIN

Science fiction and fantasy seem to fall naturally into series and sequels. That tendency may be common to all popular literature, going back to the dime novels and boys' magazines, when publishers, authors, and readers all wanted to hit upon an attractive character or group of characters and pursue their adventures through volume after volume, like Buffalo Bill, Jesse James, Frank Reade and Frank Reade, Jr., Nick Carter, Frank Merriwell, Tom Swift, the Bobbsey Twins, the Rover Boys, and many others.

As with all popular literature, the process depended on the reader. Boys and girls didn't want to lose their favorite people. Publishers liked series because they gave them safe, predictable sales for years. Authors who could stomach the chore of writing the same story again and again found it an easy way to produce another book.

When genre fiction got established, the series syndrome affected it as well: mystery writers clung to their detectives, a tradition going back to Poe's Auguste Dupin and honored most prominently by Conan Doyle with Sherlock Holmes; western writers roamed farther but also created their Hopalong Cassidys and Cisco Kids. And when the pulp magazines hit their peak in the 1930s, the hero pulps brought their readers every month the adventures of Doc Savage, the Shadow, the Phantom, G8 and his Battle Aces, and many more.

The urge to write sequels is not unique to popular writers. Greek playwrights created their cycles, the Arthurian romances ran through many tales and tellers, Dante wrote his *Divine Comedy* in three parts, Shakespeare brought back Falstaff in *The Merry Wives of Windsor*, Cervantes returned to Don Quixote and Lewis Carroll to Alice, Galsworthy took the Forsytes through their saga, Dos Passos wrote *U.S.A.* in three volumes. Faulkner kept going back to Yoknapatawpha County, and so on. Some authors find irresistible the return to favorite characters and popular successes; others can't endure repeating themselves.

In science fiction the most famous series is Asimov's *Foundation* trilogy, but the tradition extends at least as far back as George Allan England's *Darkness and Dawn* trilogy (first volume 1912), Charles B. Stilson's *Polaris* trilogy (first volume 1915), J. U. Giesy's *Dog Star* trilogy (first volume 1918), and Edgar Rice Burroughs's extended adventures on Mars and Venus, and in Pellucidar. Another great series author is E. E. "Doc" Smith, whose novels fell so naturally into groups that he planned his *Lensman* series as a 400,000-word novel in four parts. Other famous series are C. S. Lewis's *Perelandra* trilogy, Frank Herbert's *Dune* series, James Blish's "Okie" series collected in *Cities in Flight*, Michael Moorcock's *Dancers at the End of Time*, Harry Harrison's *Deathworld* and *Stainless Steel Rat*. Brian Aldiss's *Helliconia* trilogy, and Gene Wolfe's *Book of the New Sun*.

Fantasy may fall even more naturally into sequel form, as if once having invented a consistent fantasy world an author can't bear to give it up. The best-known of these, of course, is Tolkien's *Lord of the Rings* trilogy, whose phenomenal success may have encouraged others to produce their books in triplets. Earlier than *Rings*, Fletcher Pratt and L. Sprague de Camp had written the novels collected as *The Compleat Enchanter* and André Norton had produced several extended series, including one called *Witch World*. More recent series include Ursula K. Le Guin's *Earthsea* trilogy, Marion Zimmer Bradley's *Darkover* science fantasies, Stephen Donaldson's *Covenant* trilogy, and the Burroughs-like *Gor* novels of John Norman (J. F. Lange).

Perhaps the most ambitious series writer in science fiction, however, is Gordon R. Dickson, whose Childe Cycle began with *Dorsai!* in 1959 and whose completion is still years away. Originally intended to include three historical novels, three contemporary novels, and three science fiction novels tracing three human types through several thousand years as they evolve into splinter cultures and eventually reunite into a kind of superhumanity, the scheme has since been extended by half a dozen science fiction novels.

Dickson (1923-) clearly is a man of great confidence and considerable perseverance. Born in Canada and brought to the U.S. at the age of thirteen, he saw service in World War II and returned to the University of Minnesota to complete a degree in creative writing and work toward a master's degree. He is one of the few authors in the field with such academic credentials.

He has been a full-time writer since 1951, when he had three stories in *Astounding;* the first was "The Friendly Man." He has produced many novels outside the Childe Cycle, including *Alien from Arcturus* and *Mankind on the Run* (both 1956), *Spacial Delivery* (1959), *Time to Teleport* (1960), *Naked to the Stars* and *Delusion World* (both 1961), *The Alien Way* and *Mission to Universe* (both 1965), *Spacepaw* (1969), *Sleepwalkers' World* (1971), *The Outposter* (1972), *The Pritcher Mass* (1972), *Time Storm* (1977), and *The Far Call* (1978). In recent years his publications, with a few exceptions such as *The Way of the Pilgrim* (1987) and *Wolf and Iron* (1990), have been devoted to his comic fantasy series that started with *The Dragon and the George* (1976) and his Childe Cycle. The Childe Cycle includes *Dorsai!* (1960), *Necromancer* (1962), *Soldier, Ask Not* (1967), *Tactics of Mistake* (1972), *The Final Encyclopedia* (1984), *The Chantry Guild* (1988), and *Young Bleys* (1991). He has written juvenile science fiction and has collaborated with Poul Anderson, Keith Laumer, and Harry Harrison.

Dickson also is a prolific author of short fiction. "Soldier, Ask Not" won a Hugo in 1965, and "Call Him Lord" won a Nebula in 1966. "Dolphin's Way," published in *Analog* in June 1964, illustrates his simplicity of style, his economy of action, and his artistic control of his subject. His ideas always have been distinguished for their originality.

DOLPHIN'S WAY

BY GORDON R. DICKSON

Of course, there was no reason why a woman coming to Dolphin's Way—as the late Dr. Edwin Knight had named the island research station—should not be beautiful. But Mal had never expected such a thing to happen.

Castor and Pollux had not come to the station pool this morning. They might have left the station, as other wild dolphins had in the past—and Mal nowadays always carried with him the fear that the Willernie Foundation would seize on some excuse to cut off their funds for further research. Ever since Corwin Brayt had taken over, Mal had known this fear. Though Brayt had said nothing. It was only a feeling Mal got from the presence of the tall, cold man. So it was that Mal was out in front of the station scanning the ocean when the water-taxi from the mainland brought the visitor.

She stepped out on the dock, as he stared down at her. She waved as if she knew him, and then climbed the stairs from the dock to the terrace in front of the door to the main building of the station.

"Hello," she said, smiling as she stopped in front of him. "You're Corwin Brayt?"

Mal was suddenly sharply conscious of his own lean and ordinary appearance in contrast to her startling beauty. She was brown-haired and tall for a girl—but these things did not describe her. There was a perfection to her—and her smile stirred him strangely.

"No," he said. "I'm Malcolm Sinclair. Corwin's inside."

"I'm Jane Wilson," she said. *"Background Monthly* sent me out to do a story on the dolphins. Do you work with them?"

"Yes," Mal said. "I started with Dr. Knight in the beginning."

"Oh, good," she said. "Then, you can tell me some things. You were here when Dr. Brayt took charge after Dr. Knight's death?"

"Mr. Brayt," he corrected automatically. "Yes." The emotion she moved in him was so deep and strong it seemed she must feel it too. But she gave no sign.

"Mr. Brayt?" she echoed. "Oh. How did the staff take to him?"

"Well," said Mal, wishing she would smile again, "everyone took to him."

"I see," she said. "He's a good research head?"

"A good administrator," said Mal. "He's not involved in the research end."

"He's not?" She stared at him. "But didn't he replace Dr. Knight, after Dr. Knight's death?"

"Why, yes," said Mal. He made an effort to bring his attention back to the conversation. He had never had a woman affect him like this before. "But just as administrator of the station, here. You see—most of our funds for work here come from the Willernie Foundation. They had faith in Dr. Knight, but when he died… well, they wanted someone of their own in charge. None of us mind."

"Willernie Foundation," she said. "I don't know it."

"It was set up by a man named Willernie, in St. Louis, Missouri," said Mal. "He made his money manufacturing kitchen utensils. When he died he left a trust and set up the Foundation to encourage basic research." Mal smiled. "Don't ask me how he got from kitchen utensils to that. That's not much information for you, is it?"

"It's more than I had a minute ago," she smiled back. "Did you know Corwin Brayt before he came here?"

"No." Mal shook his head. "I don't know many people outside the biological and zoological fields."

"I imagine you know him pretty well now, though, after the six months he's been in charge.

"Well—" Mal hesitated, "I wouldn't say I know him *well*, at all. You see, he's up here in the office all day long and I'm down with Pollux and Castor— the two wild dolphins we've got coming to the station, now. Corwin and I don't see each other much."

"On this small island?"

"I suppose it seems funny—but we're both pretty busy."

"I guess you would be," she smiled again. "Will you take me to him?"

"Him?" Mal awoke suddenly to the fact they were still standing on the terrace. "Oh, yes—it's Corwin you came to see."

"Not just Corwin," she said. "I came to see the whole place."

"Well, I'll take you in to the office. Come along."

He led her across the terrace and in through the front door into the air-conditioned coolness of the interior. Corwin Brayt ran the air conditioning constantly, as if his own somewhat icy personality demanded the dry, distant coldness of a mountain atmosphere. Mal led Jane Wilson down a short corridor and through another door into a large wide-windowed office. A tall, slim, broad-shouldered man with black hair and a brown, coldly handsome face looked up from a large desk, and got to his feet on seeing Jane.

"Corwin," said Mal. "This is Miss Jane Wilson from *Background Monthly*."

"Yes," said Corwin expressionlessly to Jane, coming around the desk to them. "I got a wire yesterday you were coming." He did not wait for Jane to offer her hand, but offered his own. Their fingers met.

"I've got to be getting down to Castor and Pollux," said Mal, turning away.

"I'll see you later then," Jane said, looking over at him.

"Why, yes. Maybe—" he said. He went out. As he closed the door of Brayt's office behind him, he paused for a moment in the dim, cool hallway, and shut his eyes. *Don't be a fool,* he told himself, *a girl like that can do a lot better than someone like you. And probably has already.*

He opened his eyes and went back down to the pool behind the station and the nonhuman world of the dolphins.

When he got there, he found that Castor and Pollux were back. Their pool was an open one, with egress to the open blue waters of the Caribbean. In the first days of the research at Dolphin's Way, the dolphins had been confined in a closed pool like any captured wild animal. It was only later on, when the work at the station had come up against what Knight had called "the environmental barrier," that the notion was conceived of opening the pool to the sea, so that the dolphins they had been working with could leave or stay, as they wished.

They had left—but they had come back. Eventually, they had left for good. But strangely, wild dolphins had come from time to time to take their place, so that there were always dolphins at the station.

Castor and Pollux were the latest pair. They had showed up some four months ago after a single dolphin frequenting the station had disappeared. Free, independent—they had been most cooperative. But the barrier had not been breached.

Now, they were sliding back and forth past each other underwater utilizing the full thirty-yard length of the pool, passing beside, over, and under each other, their seven-foot, nearly identical bodies almost, but not quite, rubbing as they passed. The tape showed them to be talking together up in the supersonic range, eighty to a hundred and twenty kilo-cycles per second. Their pattern of movement in the water now was something he had never seen before. It was regular and ritualistic as a dance.

He sat down and put on the earphones connected to the hydrophones, underwater at each end of the pool. He spoke into the microphone, asking them about their movements, but they ignored him and kept on with the patterned swimming.

The sound of footsteps behind him made him turn. He saw Jane Wilson approaching down the concrete steps from the back door of the station, with the stocky, overalled figure of Pete Adant, the station mechanic.

"Here he is," said Pete, as they came up. "I've got to get back, now."

"Thank you." She gave Pete the smile that had so moved Mal earlier. Pete turned and went back up the steps. She turned to Mal. "Am I interrupting something?"

"No." He took off the earphones. "I wasn't getting any answers, anyway."

She looked at the two dolphins in their underwater dance with the liquid surface swirling above them as they turned now this way, now that, just under it.

"Answers?" she said. He smiled a little ruefully.

"We call them answers," he said. He nodded at the two smoothly streamlined shapes turning in the pool. "Sometimes we can ask questions and get responses."

"Informative responses?" she asked.

"Sometimes. You wanted to see me about something?"

"About everything," she said. "It seems you're the man I came to talk to—not Brayt. He sent me down here. I understand you're the one with the theory."

"Theory?" he said warily, feeling his heart sink inside him.

"The notion, then," she said. "The idea that, if there is some sort of interstellar civilization, it might be waiting for the people of Earth to qualify themselves before making contact. And that test might not be a technological one like developing a faster-than-light means of travel, but a sociological one—"

"Like learning to communicate with an alien culture—a culture like that of the dolphins," he interrupted harshly. "Corwin told you this?"

"I'd heard about it before I came," she said. "I'd thought it was Brayt's theory, though."

"No," said Mal, "it's mine." He looked at her. "You aren't laughing."

"Should I laugh?" she said. She was attentively watching the dolphins' movements. Suddenly he felt sharp jealousy of them for holding her attention; and the emotion pricked him to something he might not otherwise have had the courage to do.

"Fly over to the mainland with me," he said, "and have lunch. I'll tell you all about it."

"All right." She looked up from the dolphins at him at last and he was surprised to see her frowning. "There's a lot I don't understand," she murmured. "I thought it was Brayt I had to learn about. But it's you—and the dolphins."

"Maybe we can clear that up at lunch, too," Mal said, not quite clear what she meant, but not greatly caring, either. "Come on, the helicopters are around the north side of the building."

They flew a copter across to Carúpano, and sat down to lunch looking out at the shipping in the open roadstead of the azure sea before the town, while the polite Spanish of Venezuelan voices sounded from the tables around them.

"Why should I laugh at your theory?" she said again, when they were settled, and eating lunch.

"Most people take it to be a crackpot excuse for our failure at the station," he said.

Her brown arched brows rose. "Failure?" she said. "I thought you were making steady progress."

"Yes. And no," he said. "Even before Dr. Knight died, we ran into something he called the environmental barrier."

"Environmental barrier?"

"Yes." Mal poked with his fork at the shrimp in his seafood cocktail. "This work of ours all grew out of the work done by Dr. John Lilly. You read his book, *Man and Dolphin?*"

"No," she said. He looked at her, surprised.

"He was the pioneer in this research with dolphins," Mal said. "I'd have thought reading his book would have been the first thing you would have done before coming down here."

"The first thing I did," she said, "was try to find out something about Corwin Brayt. And I was pretty unsuccessful at that. That's why I landed here with the notion that it was he, not you, who was the real worker with the dolphins."

"That's why you asked me if I knew much about him?"

"That's right," she answered. "But tell me about this environmental barrier."

"There's not a great deal to tell," he said. "Like most big problems, it's simple enough to state. At first, in working with the dolphins, it seemed the early researchers were going great guns, and communication was just around the corner—a matter of interpreting the sounds they made to each other, in the humanly audible range and above it; and teaching the dolphins human speech."

"It turned out those things couldn't be done?"

"They could. They were done—or as nearly so as makes no difference. But then we came up against the fact that communication doesn't mean understanding." He looked at her. "You and I talk the same language, but do we really understand perfectly what the other person means when he speaks to us?"

She looked at him for a moment, and then slowly shook her head without taking her eyes off his face.

"Well," said Mal, "that's essentially our problem with the dolphins—only on a much larger scale. Dolphins, like Castor and Pollux, can talk with me, and I with them, but we can't understand each other to any great degree."

"You mean intellectually understood, don't you?" Jane said. "Not just mechanically?"

"That's right," Mal answered. "We agree on denotation of an auditory or other symbol, but not on connotation. I can say to Castor, 'the Gulf Stream is a strong ocean current,' and he'll agree exactly. But neither of us really has the slightest idea of what the other really means. My mental image of the Gulf Stream is not Castor's image. My notion of 'powerful' is relative to the fact I'm six feet tall, weigh a hundred and seventy-five pounds, and can lift my own weight against the force of gravity. Castor's is relative to the fact that he is seven feet long, can speed up to forty miles an hour through the water, and as far as he knows weighs nothing, since his four hundred pounds of body-weight are balanced out by the equal weight of the water he displaces. And the concept of lifting something is all but unknown to him. My mental abstraction of 'ocean' is not his, and our ideas of what a current is may coincide, or be literally worlds apart in meaning. And so far we've found no way of bridging the gap between us."

"The dolphins have been trying as well as you?"

"I believe so," said Mal. "But I can't prove it. Any more than I can really prove the dolphin's intelligence to hard-core skeptics until I can come up with something previously outside human knowledge that the dolphins have taught me. Or have them demonstrate that they've learned the use of some human intellectual process. And in these things we've all failed—because, as I believe and Dr. Knight believed, of the connotative gap, which is a result of the environmental barrier."

She sat watching him. He was probably a fool to tell her all this, but he had had no one to talk to like this since Dr. Knight's heart attack, eight months before, and he felt words threatening to pour out of him.

"We've got to learn to think like the dolphins," he said, "or the dolphins have to learn to think like us. For nearly six years now we've been trying and neither side's succeeded." Almost before he thought, he added the one thing he had been determined to keep to himself. "I've been afraid our research funds will be cut off any day now."

"Cut off? By the Willernie Foundation?" she said. "Why would they do that?"

"Because we haven't made any progress for so long," Mal said bitterly. "Or, at least, no provable progress. I'm afraid time's just about run out. And if it runs out, it may never be picked up again. Six years ago, there was a lot of popular interest in the dolphins. Now, they've been discounted and forgotten, shelved as merely bright animals."

"You can't be sure the research won't be picked up again."

"But I feel it," he said. "It's part of my notion about the ability to communicate with an alien race being the test for us humans. I feel we've got this one chance and if we flub it, we'll never have another." He pounded the table softly with his fist. "The worst of it is, I *know* the dolphins are trying just as hard to get through from their side—if I could only recognize what they're doing, how they're trying to make me understand!"

Jane had been sitting watching him.

"You seem pretty sure of that," she said. "What makes you so sure?"

He unclenched his fist and forced himself to sit back in his chair.

"Have you ever looked into the jaws of a dolphin?" he said. "They're this long." He spread his hands apart in the air to illustrate. "And each pair of jaws contains eighty-eight sharp teeth. Moreover, a dolphin like Castor weighs several hundred pounds and can move at water speeds that are almost incredible to a human. He could crush you easily by ramming you against the side of a tank, if he didn't want to tear you apart with his teeth, or break your bones with blows of his flukes." He looked at her grimly. "In spite of all this, in spite of the fact that men have caught and killed dolphins—even we killed them in our early, fumbling researches, and dolphins are quite capable of using their teeth and strength on marine enemies—no dolphin has ever been known to attack a human being. Aristotle, writing in the fourth century B.C., speaks of the quote gentle and kindly end quote nature of the dolphin."

He stopped, and looked at Jane sharply.

"You don't believe me," he said.

"Yes," she said. "Yes, I do." He took a deep breath.

"I'm sorry," he said. "I've made the mistake of mentioning all this before to other people and been sorry I did. I told this to one man who gave me his opinion that it indicated that the dolphin instinctively recognized human superiority and the value of human life." Mal grinned at her, harshly. "But it was just an instinct. 'Like dogs,' he said. 'Dogs instinctively admire and love people—' and he wanted to tell me about a dachshund he'd had, named Poochie, who could read the morning newspaper and wouldn't bring it in to him if there was a tragedy reported on the front page. He could prove this, and Poochie's intelligence, by the number of times he'd had to get the paper off the front step himself."

Jane laughed. It was a low, happy laugh; and it took the bitterness suddenly out of Mal.

"Anyway," said Mal, "the dolphin's restraint with humans is just one of the indications, like the wild dolphins coming to us here at the station, that've convinced me the dolphins are trying to understand us, too. And have been, maybe, for centuries."

"I don't see why you worry about the research stopping," she said. "With all you know, can't you convince people—"

"There's only one person I've got to convince," said Mal. "And that's Corwin Brayt. And I don't think I'm doing it. It's just a feeling—but I feel as if he's sitting in judgment upon me, and the work. I feel…" Mal hesitated, "almost as if he's a hatchet man."

"He isn't," Jane said. "He can't be. I'll find out for you, if you like. There's ways of doing it. I'd have the answer for you right now, if I'd thought of him as an administrator. But I thought of him as a scientist, and I looked him up in the wrong places."

Mal frowned at her, unbelievingly.

"You don't actually mean you can find out that for me?" he asked.

She smiled.

"Wait and see," she replied. "I'd like to know, myself, what his background is."

"It could be important," he said, eagerly. "I know it sounds fantastic—but if I'm right, the research with the dolphins could be important, more important than anything else in the world."

She stood up suddenly from the table.

"I'll go and start checking up right now," she said. "Why don't you go back to the island? It'll take me a few hours and I'll take the water-taxi over."

"But you haven't finished lunch yet," he said. "In fact you haven't even started lunch. Let's eat first, then you can go."

"I want to call some people and catch them while they're still at work," she said. "It's the time difference on these long-distance calls. I'm sorry. We'll have dinner together, will that do?"

"It'll have to," he said. She melted his disappointment with one of her amazing smiles, and went.

With her gone, Mal found he was not hungry himself. He got hold of the waiter and managed to cancel the main course of their meals. He sat and had two more drinks—not something usual for him. Then he left and flew the copter back to the island.

Pete Adant encountered him as he was on his way from the copter park to the dolphin pool.

"There you are," said Pete. "Corwin wants to see you in an hour—when he gets back, that is. He's gone over to the mainland himself."

Ordinarily, such a piece of news would have awakened the foreboding about cancellation of the research that rode always like a small, cold metal weight inside Mal. But the total of three drinks and no lunch had anesthetized him somewhat. He nodded and went on to the pool.

The dolphins were still there, still at their patterned swimming. Or was he just imagining the pattern? Mal sat down on his chair by the poolside before the tape recorder which set down a visual pattern of the sounds made by the dolphins. He put on the earphones to the hydrophones, switching on the mike before him.

Suddenly, it struck him how futile all this was. He had gone through these same motions daily for four years now. And what was the sum total of results he had to show for it? Reel on reel of tape recording a failure to hold any truly productive conversation with the dolphins.

He took the earphones off and laid them aside. He lit a cigarette and sat gazing with half-seeing eyes at the underwater ballet of the dolphins. To call it ballet was almost to libel their actions. The gracefulness, the purposefulness of their movements, buoyed up by the salt water, was beyond that of any human in air or on land. He thought again of what he had told Jane Wilson about the dolphin's refusal to attack their human captors, even when the humans hurt or killed them. He thought of the now-established fact that dolphins will come to the rescue of one of their own who has been hurt or knocked unconscious, and hold him up on top of the water so he would not drown—the dolphin's breathing process requiring conscious control, so that it failed if the dolphin became unconscious.

He thought of their playfulness, their affection, the wide and complex range of their speech. In any of those categories, the average human stacked up beside them looked pretty poor. In the dolphin culture there was no visible impulse to war, to murder, to hatred and unkindness. No wonder, thought Mal, they and we have trouble understanding each other. In a different environment, under different conditions, they're the kind of people we've always struggled to be. We have the technology, the tool-using capability, but with it all in many ways we're more animal than they are.

Who's to judge which of us is better, he thought, looking at their movements through the water with the slight hazy melancholy induced by the three drinks on an empty stomach. I might be happier myself, if I were a dolphin. For a second, the idea seemed deeply attractive. The endless open sea, the freedom, an end to all the complex structure of human culture on land. A few lines of poetry came back to him.

"Come Children," he quoted out loud to himself, "let us away! Down and away, below…!"

He saw the two dolphins pause in their underwater ballet and saw that the microphone before him was on. Their heads turned toward the microphone underwater at the near end of the pool. He remembered the following lines, and he quoted them aloud to the dolphins.

"… Now my brothers call from the bay,
"Now the great winds shoreward blow,
"Now the salt tides seaward flow;
"Now the wild white horses play,
"Champ and chafe and toss in the spray—"*

He broke off suddenly, feeling self-conscious. He looked down at the dolphins. For a moment they merely hung where they were under the surface,

* "The Forsaken Merman" by Matthew Arnold, 1849.

facing the microphone. Then Castor turned and surfaced. His forehead with its blowhole broke out into the air and then his head as he looked up at Mal. His airborne voice from the blowhole's sensitive lips and muscles spoke quacking words at the human.

"Come, Mal!" he quacked, "let us away! Down and away! Below!"

The head of Pollux surfaced beside Castor's. Mal stared at them for a long second. Then he jerked his gaze back to the tape of the recorder. There on it was the rhythmic record of his own voice as it had sounded in the pool, and below it on their separate tracks, the tapes showed parallel rhythms coming from the dolphins. They had been matching his speech largely in the inaudible range while he was quoting.

Still staring, Mal got to his feet, his mind trembling with a suspicion so great he hesitated to put it into words. Like a man in a daze he walked to the near end of the pool, where three steps led down into the shallower part. Here the water was only three feet deep.

"Come, Mal!" quacked Castor, as the two still hung in the water with their heads out, facing him. "Let us away! Down and away! Below!"

Step by step, Mal went down into the pool. He felt the coolness of the water wetting his pants legs, rising to his waist as he stood at last on the pool floor. A few feet in front of him, the two dolphins hung in the water, facing him, waiting. Standing with the water rippling lightly above his belt buckle, Mal looked at them, waiting for some sign, some signal of what they wanted him to do.

They gave him no clue. They only waited. It was up to him to go forward on his own. He sloshed forward into deeper water, put his head down, held his breath, and pushed himself off underwater.

In the forefront of his blurred vision, he saw the grainy concrete floor of the pool. He glided slowly over it, rising a little, and suddenly the two dolphins were all about him—gliding over, above, around his own underwater floating body, brushing lightly against him as they passed, making him a part of their underwater dance. He heard the creaking that was one of the underwater sounds they made and knew that they were probably talking in ranges he could not hear. He could not know what they were saying, he could not sense the meaning of their movements about him, but the feeling that they were trying to convey information to him was inescapable.

He began to feel the need to breathe. He held out as long as he could, then let himself rise to the surface. He broke water and gulped air, and the two dolphin heads popped up nearby, watching him. He dove under the surface again. *I am a dolphin*—he told himself almost desperately—*I am not a man, but a dolphin, and to me all this means—what?*

Several times he dove, and each time the persistent and disciplined movements of the dolphins about him underwater convinced him more strongly that he was on the right track. He came up, blowing, at last. He was not carrying the attempt to be like them far enough, he thought. He turned and swam back to the steps at the shallow end of the pool, and began to climb out.

"*Come, Mal—let us away!*" quacked a dolphin voice behind him, and he turned to see the heads of both Castor and Pollux out of the water, regarding him with mouths open urgently.

"*Come Children—down and away!*" he repeated, as reassuringly as he could intonate the words.

He hurried up to the big cabinet of the supply locker at the near end of the pool, and opened the door of the section of skin-diving equipment. He needed to make himself more like a dolphin. He considered the air tanks and the mask of the scuba equipment, and rejected them. The dolphins could not breathe underwater any more than he could. He started jerking things out of the cabinet.

A minute or so later he returned to the steps in swimming trunks, wearing a glass mask with a snorkel tube, and swim fins on his feet. In his hand he carried two lengths of soft rope. He sat down on the steps and with the rope tied his knees and ankles together. Then, clumsily, he hopped and splashed into the water.

Lying face down in the pool, staring at the bottom through his glass faceplate, he tried to move his bound legs together like the flukes of a dolphin, to drive himself slantingly down under the surface.

After a moment or two he managed it. In a moment the dolphins were all about him as he tried to swim underwater, dolphinwise. After a while his air ran short again and he had to surface. But he came up like a dolphin and lay on the surface filling his lungs, before fanning himself down fluke-fashion with his swim fins. *Think like a dolphin,* he kept repeating to himself over and over. *I am a dolphin. And this is my world. This is the way it is.*

...And Castor and Pollux were all about him.

The sun was setting in the far distance of the ocean when at last he dragged himself, exhausted, up the steps of the pool and sat down on the poolside. To his water-soaked body, the twilight breeze felt icy. He unbound his legs, took off his fins and mask and walked wearily to the cabinet. From the nearest compartment he took a towel and dried himself, then put on an old bathrobe he kept hanging there. He sat down in an aluminum deckchair beside the cabinet and sighed with weariness.

He looked out at the red sun dipping its lower edge in the sea, and felt a great warm sensation of achievement inside him. In the darkening pool, the two dolphins still swam back and forth. He watched the sun descending...

"Mal!"

The sound of Corwin Brayt's voice brought his head around. When he saw the tall, cold-faced man was coming toward him with the slim figure of Jane alongside, Mal got up quickly from his chair. They came up to him.

"Why didn't you come in to see me as I asked?" Brayt said. "I left word for you with Pete. I didn't even know you were back from the mainland until the water-taxi brought Miss Wilson out just now, and she told me."

"I'm sorry," said Mal. "I think I've run into something here—"

"Never mind telling me now." Brayt's voice was hurried and sharpened with annoyance. "I had a good deal to speak to you about but there's not time now if I'm to catch the mainland plane to St. Louis. I'm sorry to break it this way—" he checked himself and turned to Jane. "Would you excuse us, Miss Wilson? Private business. If you'll give us a second—"

"Of course," she said. She turned and walked away from them alongside the pool, into the deepening twilight. The dolphins paced her in the water. The sun was just down now, and with the sudden oncoming of tropical night, stars could be seen overhead.

"Just let me tell you," said Mal. "It's about the research."

"I'm sorry," said Brayt. "There's no point in your telling me now. I'll be gone a week and I want you to watch out for this Jane Wilson, here." He lowered his voice slightly. "I talked to *Background Monthly* on the phone this afternoon, and the editor I spoke to there didn't know about the article, or recognize her name—"

"Somebody new," said Mal. "Probably someone who didn't know her."

"At any rate it makes no difference," said Brayt. "As I say, I'm sorry to tell you in such a rushed fashion but Willernie has decided to end its grant of funds to the station. I'm flying to St. Louis to settle details." He hesitated. "I'm sure you knew something like this was coming, Mal."

Mal stared, shocked.

"It was inevitable," said Brayt coldly. "You knew that." He paused. "I'm sorry."

"But the station'll fold without the Willernie support!" said Mal, finding his voice. "You know that. And just today I found out what the answer is! Just this afternoon! Listen to me!" He caught Brayt's arm as the other started to turn away. "The dolphins have been trying to contact us. Oh, not at first, not when we experimented with captured specimens. But since we opened the pool to the sea. The only trouble was we insisted on trying to communicate by sound alone—and that's all but impossible for them."

"Excuse me," said Brayt, trying to disengage his arm.

"Listen, will you!" said Mal, desperately. "Their communication process is an incredibly rich one. It's as if you and I communicated by using all the instruments in a symphony orchestra. They not only use sound from four to a hundred and fifty kilocycles per second, they use movement, and touch—and all of it in reference to the ocean conditions surrounding them at the moment."

"I've got to go."

"Just a minute. Don't you remember what Lilly hypothecated about the dolphin's methods of navigation? He suggested that it was a multivariable method, using temperature, speed, taste of the water, position of the stars, sun, and so forth, all fed into their brains simultaneously and instantaneously. Obviously, it's true, and obviously their process of communication is also a multivariable method utilizing sound, touch, position, place, and movement. Now that we know this, we can go into the sea with them and try to operate across their whole spectrum of communication. No wonder we weren't able to get across anything but the most primitive exchanges, restricting ourselves to sound. It's been equivalent to restricting human communication to just the nouns in each sentence, while maintaining the sentence structure—"

"I'm very sorry!" said Brayt, firmly. "I tell you, Mal. None of this makes any difference. The decision of the Foundation is based on financial reasons. They've got just so much money available to donate, and this station's allotment has already gone in other directions. There's nothing that can be done, now."

He pulled his arm free.

"I'm sorry," he said again. "I'll be back in a week at the outside. You might be thinking of how to wind up things, here."

He turned with that, and went away, around the building toward the parking spot of the station copters. Mal, stunned, watched the tall, slim, broad-shouldered figure move into darkness.

"It doesn't matter," said the gentle voice of Jane comfortingly at his ear. He jerked about and saw her facing him. "You won't need the Willernie funds anymore."

"He told you?" Mal stared at her as she shook her head, smiling in the growing dimness. "You heard? From way over there?"

"Yes," she said. "And you were right about Brayt. I got your answer for you. He was a hatchet man—sent here by the Willernie people to decide whether the station deserved further funds."

"But we've got to have them!" Mal said. "It won't take much more, but we've got to go into the sea and work out ways to talk to the dolphins in their own mode. We've got to expand their level of communication, not try to compress them to ours. You see, this afternoon, I had a breakthrough—"

"I know," she said. "I know all about it."

"You know?" He stared at her. "How do you know?"

"You've been under observation all afternoon," she said. "You're right. You did break through the environmental barrier. From now on it's just a matter of working out methods."

"Under observation? How?" Abruptly, that seemed the least important thing at hand. "But I have to have money," he said. "It'll take time and equipment, and that costs money—"

"No." Her voice was infinitely gentle. "You won't need to work out your own methods. Your work is done, Mal. This afternoon the dolphins and you broke the bars to communication between the two races for the first time in the history of either. It was the job you set out to do and you were part of it. You can be happy knowing that."

"Happy?" He almost shouted at her, suddenly. "I don't understand what you're talking about."

"I'm sorry." There was a ghost of a sigh from her. "We'll show you how to talk to the dolphins, Mal, if men need to. As well as some other things—perhaps." Her face lifted to him under the star-marked sky, still a little light in the west. "You see, you were right about something more than dolphins, Mal. Your idea that the ability to communicate with another intelligent race, an alien race, was a test that had to be passed before the superior species of a planet could be contacted by the intelligent races of the galaxy—that was right, too."

He stared at her. She was so close to him, he could feel the living warmth of her body, although they were not touching. He saw her, he felt her, standing before him; and he felt all the strange deep upwelling of emotion that she had released in him the moment he first saw her. The deep emotion he felt for her still. Suddenly understanding came to him.

"You mean you're not from Earth—" His voice was hoarse and uncertain. It wavered to a stop. "But you're human!" he cried desperately.

She looked back at him a moment before answering. In the dimness he could not tell for sure, but he thought he saw the glisten of tears in her eyes.

"Yes," she said, at last, slowly. "In the way you mean that—you can say I'm human."

A great and almost terrible joy burst suddenly in him. It was the joy of a man who, in the moment when he thinks he has lost everything, finds something of infinitely greater value.

"But how?" he said, excitedly, a little breathlessly. He pointed up at the stars. "If you come from some place—up there? How can you be human?"

She looked down, away from his face.

"I'm sorry," she said. "I can't tell you."

"Can't tell me? Oh," he said with a little laugh, "you mean I wouldn't understand."

"No—" Her voice was almost inaudible, "I mean I'm not allowed to tell you."

"Not allowed—" He felt an unreasoning chill about his heart. "But Jane—" He broke off fumbling for words. "I don't know quite how to say this, but it's important to me to know. From the first moment I saw you there, I... I mean, maybe you don't feel anything like this, you don't know what I'm talking about—"

"Yes," she whispered. "I do."

"Then—" He stared at her. "You could at least say something that would set my mind at rest. I mean... it's only a matter of time now. We're going to be getting together, your people and I, aren't we?"

She looked up at him out of darkness.

"No," she said, "we aren't, Mal. Ever. And that's why I can't tell you anything."

"We aren't?" he cried. "We aren't? But you came and saw us communicate— Why aren't we?"

She looked up at him for the last time, then, and told him. He, having heard what she had to say, stood still; still as a stone, for there was nothing left to do. And she, turning slowly and finally away from him, went off to the edge of the pool and down the steps into the shallow water, where the dolphins came rushing to meet her, their foamy tearing of the surface making a wake as white as snow.

Then the three of them moved, as if by magic, across the surface of the pool and out the entrance of it to the ocean. And so they continued to move off until they were lost to sight in darkness and the starlit, glinting surface of the waves.

It came to Mal then, as he stood there, that the dolphins must have been waiting for her all this time. All the wild dolphins, who had come to the station after the first two captives were set free to leave or stay as they wanted. The dolphins had known, perhaps for centuries, that it was to them alone on Earth that the long-awaited visitors from the stars would finally come.

THE FUTURE AS METAPHOR

Science fiction writers are commonly supposed to be prophets, and amazingly accurate in predicting the future. This misunderstanding got started, no doubt, with Jules Verne and his marvelous description of submarining in *Twenty Thousand Leagues Under the Sea* and was reinforced by all sorts of later developments, including atomic bombs and space flight.

Actually, science fiction writers are usually wrong, but their accidentally correct guesses get the publicity. Writers often speculate about possible futures, but whether those futures come to pass is incidental to their purposes. Often those futures are so horrible that the authors clearly don't want them to be realized and write to warn the world against them. True, it didn't start that way: Verne based his work largely on scientific probability. "I use physics," he said, "Wells invents." But Wells became the father of science fiction, and his work, he said, was related to "a new system of ideas." He did write such predictive works as "The Land Ironclads," *The War in the Air,* and *The Shape of Things to Come,* but his early scientific romances (before 1902) were clearly indifferent to the test of the future.

Science fiction writers intend to entertain. Their method of entertainment—to intrigue the minds of readers with speculation and delight them with detail—happens to place most of their work in the future. Once in a while, by chance, something mentioned in a story will occur in real life. Some writers work closer to actual existence than others, and most try to make their work convincing, since the particular quality of science fiction—which distinguishes it from fantasy—is its air of reality that asks the reader to take it seriously, at least, in the Wellsian sense, as a system of ideas. The verisimilitude business sometimes makes prophets of the most reluctant authors. Finally, the problems that interest authors are contemporary; authors are moved to write about something that annoys or pleases them, about an opportunity or a danger they see before others recognize them. If their perceptions are sound and their projections are accurate, the stories may intersect with reality.

But mostly writers deal in metaphors. The future they write about is not the real future; it is a metaphorical future that allows them to test their ideas free from the distractions of the real world. If they want to deal with overpopulation, they can make it a worldwide phenomenon unconfused by other problems; they can make pollution life-choking without considering why no one has tried to deal with it before now; they can show tyranny unrelieved; or, like R. A. Lafferty with "Slow Tuesday Night" (*Galaxy,* April 1965), they can write about the accelerated pace of existence in its ultimate apotheosis without worrying about such obfuscating details as childrearing, farming, or even seasonal changes that operate by another clock.

Lafferty is entertainment. With narrative and wit and detail, he draws the reader into the story. He convinces the reader of the relative seriousness of his intent, however, by describing the process by which this world was achieved. He could ask the reader to suppose that it were true, as if it were a fantasy, but he wants the reader to be persuaded. He could suggest that the world was the natural development of the social acceleration everyone has noted, but that process, to be convincing, would have to be extended into the distant future where resemblances to contemporary life would seem more distant. So he invented the Abebaios block. The Abebaios block is fiction, even though some unwary readers may be trapped by the offhand way it is dropped into the story. No matter. That invention makes the story metaphor; Lafferty says not that this is the real world, but note the comparisons.

Raphael Aloysius Lafferty (1914-) is as unique as his fiction. He describes himself as a correspondence-school electrical engineer who has spent most of his life working as an engineer, chiefly in Oklahoma. He is a cherubic, white-haired, smiling man who would seem more at home behind a plow than behind a typewriter. When he makes an occasional appearance at a convention, he can be seen wandering the halls like a slightly tipsy, bucolic Santa Claus out of uniform.

He began writing fiction late in life but with dazzling wit, artistic skills, and ideas such as no one had ever put down on paper before, as if he had been saving them up for more than half a lifetime. His first story, "Day of the Glacier," was published in *Science Fiction Stories* in January 1960, but his work soon was appearing in *Galaxy, F&SF,* and *Orbit.* It was nominated frequently for awards, including "Slow Tuesday Night," "Golden Trabant," "Among the Hairy Earthmen," "The All-at-Once Man," "Continued on Next Rock," "The Cliff Climbers," "Entire and Perfect Chrysolite," "Sky," "All Pieces of a River Shore," "World Abounding," "A Special Condition in Summit City," "Dorg," "And Walk Now Gently Through the Fire," "Direction of the Road," and "Oh Tell Me Will It Freeze Tonight?" "Eurema's Dam" won a Hugo Award in 1973, and he is frequently represented in best-of-the-year collections.

Lafferty produced half a dozen novels—three in 1968, *Past Master, The Reefs of Earth,* and *Space Chantey;* and three in 1971, *Arrive at Easterwine, The Devil Is Dead,* and *The Flame Is Green.* Even in publishing novels, he does it differently.

Since then Lafferty has been inexplicably neglected by the major publishing media and has had to resort to less traditional media for his Argos Mythos series and his *In a Green Tree* sequence.

SLOW TUESDAY NIGHT

BY R. A. LAFFERTY

A panhandler intercepted the young couple as they strolled down the night street.

"Preserve us this night," he said as he touched his hat to them, "and could you good people advance me a thousand dollars to be about the recouping of my fortunes?"

"I gave you a thousand last Friday," said the young man.

"Indeed you did," the panhandler replied, "and I paid you back tenfold by messenger before midnight."

"That's right, George, he did," said the young woman. "Give it to him, dear. I believe he's a good sort."

So the young man gave the panhandler a thousand dollars; and the panhandler touched his hat to them in thanks, and went on to the recouping of his fortunes.

As he went into Money Market, the panhandler passed Ildefonsa Impala, the most beautiful woman in the city.

"Will you marry me this night, Ildy?" he asked cheerfully.

"Oh, I don't believe so, Basil," she said. "I marry you pretty often, but tonight I don't seem to have any plans at all. You may make me a gift on your first or second, however. I always like that."

But when they had parted she asked herself: "But whom will I marry tonight?"

The panhandler was Basil Bagelbaker, who would be the richest man in the world within an hour and a half. He would make and lose four fortunes within eight hours; and these not the little fortunes that ordinary men acquire, but titanic things.

When the Abebaios block had been removed from human minds, people began to make decisions faster, and often better. It had been the mental stutter. When it was understood what it was, and that it had no useful function, it was removed by simple childhood metasurgery.

Transportation and manufacturing had then become practically instantaneous. Things that had once taken months and years now took only minutes and hours. A person could have one or several pretty intricate careers within an eight hour period.

Freddy Fixico had just invented a manus module. Freddy was a Nyctalops, and the modules were characteristic of these people. The people had then divided themselves—according to their natures and inclination—into the Auroreans, the Hemerobians, and the Nyctalops; or the Dawners who had their most active hours from 4 A.M. till Noon, the Day-Flies who obtained from Noon to 8 P.M., and the Night-Seers whose civilization thrived from 8 P.M. to 4 A.M. The cultures, inventions, markets and activities of these three folk were a little different. As a Nyctalops, Freddy had just begun his working day at 8 P.M. on a slow Tuesday night.

Freddy rented an office and had it furnished. This took one minute, negotiation, selection and installation being almost instantaneous. Then he invented the manus module; that took another minute. He then had it manufactured and marketed; in three minutes it was in the hands of key buyers.

It caught on. It was an attractive module. The flow of orders began within 30 seconds. By 8:10 every important person had one of the new manus modules, and the trend had been set. The module began to sell in the millions. It was one of the most interesting fads of the night, or at least the early part of the night.

Manus modules had no practical function, no more than had Sameki verses. They were attractive, or a psychologically satisfying size and shape, and could be held in the hands, set on a table, or installed in a module niche of any wall.

Naturally Freddy became very rich. Ildefonsa Impala, the most beautiful woman in the city, was always interested in newly rich men. She came to see Freddy about 8:30. People made up their minds fast, and Ildefonsa had hers made up when she came. Freddy made his own up quickly and divorced Judy Fixico in Small Claims Court. Freddy and Ildefonsa went honeymooning to Paraiso Dorado, a resort.

It was wonderful. All of Ildy's marriages were. There was the wonderful floodlighted scenery. The recirculated water of the famous falls was tinted gold; the immediate rocks had been done by Rambles; and the hills had been contoured by Spall. The beach was a perfect copy of that at Merevale, and the popular drink that first part of the night was blue absinthe.

But scenery—whether seen for the first time or revisited after an interval—is striking for the sudden intense view of it. It is not meant to be lingered over. Food, selected and prepared instantly, is eaten with swift enjoyment: and blue absinthe lasts no longer than its own novelty. Loving, for Ildefonsa and her paramours, was quick and consuming; and repetition would have been pointless to her. Besides Ildefonsa and Freddy had taken only the one hour luxury honeymoon.

Freddy wished to continue the relationship, but Ildefonsa glanced at a trend indicator. The manus module would hold its popularity for only the first third of the night. Already it had been discarded by people who mattered. And Freddy Fixico was not one of the regular successes. He enjoyed a full career only about one night a week.

They were back in the city and divorced in Small Claims Court by 9:35. The stock of manus modules was remaindered, and the last of it would be disposed to bargain hunters among the Dawners who will buy anything.

"Whom shall I marry next?" Ildefonsa asked herself. "It looks like a slow night."

"Bagelbaker is buying," ran the word through Money Market, but Bagelbaker was selling again before the word had made its rounds. Basil Bagelbaker enjoyed making money, and it was a pleasure to watch him work as he dominated the floor of the Market and assembled runners and a competent staff out of the corner of his mouth. Helpers stripped the panhandler rags off him and wrapped him in a tycoon toga. He sent one runner to pay back twentyfold the young couple who had advanced him a thousand dollars. He sent another with a more substantial gift to Ildefonsa Impala, for Basil cherished their relationship. Basil acquired title to the Trend Indication Complex and had certain falsifications set into it. He caused to collapse certain industrial empires that had grown up within the last two hours, and made a good thing of recombining their wreckage. He had been the richest man in the world for some minutes now. He became so money-heavy that he could not maneuver with the agility he had shown an hour before. He became a great fat buck, and the pack of expert wolves circled him to bring him down.

Very soon he would lose that first fortune of the evening. The secret of Basil Bagelbaker is that he enjoyed losing money spectacularly after he was full of it to the bursting point.

A thoughtful man named Maxwell Mouser had just produced a work of actinic philosophy. It took him seven minutes to write it. To write works of philosophy one used the flexible outlines and the idea indexes; one set the activator for such a wordage in each subsection; an adept would use the paradox feed-in, and the striking analogy blender; one calibrated the particular-slant and the personality-signature. It had to come out a good work, for excellence had become the automatic minimum for such productions.

"I will scatter a few nuts on the frosting," said Maxwell, and he pushed the lever for that. This sifted handfuls of words like chthonic and heuristic and prozymeides through the thing so that nobody could doubt it was a work of philosophy.

Maxwell Mouser sent the work out to publishers, and received it back each time in about three minutes. An analysis of it and reason for rejection was always given—mostly that the thing had been done before and better. Maxwell received it back ten times in 30 minutes, and was discouraged. Then there was a break.

Ladion's work had become a hit within the last ten minutes, and it was now recognized that Mouser's monograph was both an answer and a supplement to it. It was accepted and published in less than a minute after this break. The reviews of the first five minutes were cautious ones; then real enthusiasm was shown. This was truly one of the greatest works of philosophy to appear during the early and medium hours of the night. There were those who said it might be one of the enduring works and even have a hold-over appeal to the Dawners the next morning.

Naturally Maxwell became very rich, and naturally Ildefonsa came to see him about midnight. Being a revolutionary philosopher, Maxwell thought that they might make some free arrangement, but Ildefonsa insisted it must be marriage. So Maxwell divorced Judy Mouser in Small Claims Court and went off with Ildefonsa.

This Judy herself, though not so beautiful as Ildefonsa, was the fastest taker in the City. She only wanted the men of the moment for a moment, and she was always there before even Ildefonsa. Ildefonsa believed that she took the men away from Judy; Judy said that Ildy had her leavings and nothing else.

"I had him first," Judy would always mock as she raced through Small Claims Court.

"Oh that damned Urchin!" Ildefonsa would moan. "She wears my very hair before I do."

Maxwell Mouser and Ildefonsa Impala went honeymooning to Musicbox Mountain, a resort. It was wonderful. The peaks were done with green snow by Dunbar and Fittle. (Back at Money Market Basil Bagelbaker was putting together his third and greatest fortune of the night which might surpass in magnitude even his fourth fortune of the Thursday before.) The chalets were Switzier than the real Swiss and had live goats in every room. (And Stanley Skuldugger was emerging as the top actor-imago of the middle hours of the night.) The popular drink for that middle part of the night was Glotzengubber, Eve Cheese and Rhine wine over pink ice. (And back in the city the leading Nyctalops were taking their midnight break at the Toppers' Club.)

Of course it was wonderful, as were all of Ildefonsa's—but she had never been really up on philosophy so she had scheduled only the special 35 minute honeymoon. She looked at the trend indicator to be sure. She found that her current husband had been obsoleted, and his opus was now referred to sneeringly as Mouser's Mouse. They went back to the city and were divorced in Small Claims Court.

The membership of the Toppers' Club varied. Success was the requisite of membership. Basil Bagelbaker might be accepted as a member, elevated to the presidency and expelled from it as a dirty pauper from three to six times a night. But only important persons could belong to it, or those enjoying brief moments of importance.

"I believe I will sleep during the Dawner period in the morning," Overcall said. "I may go up to this new place Koimopolis for an hour of it. They're said to be good. Where will you sleep, Basil?"

"Flop-house."

"I believe I will sleep an hour by the Midian Method," said Burnbanner. "They have a fine new clinic. And perhaps I'll sleep an hour by the Praserka Process, and an hour by the Dormidio."

"Crackle has been sleeping an hour every period by the natural method," said Overcall.

"I did that for a half hour not long since," said Burnbanner. "I believe an hour is too long to give it. Have you tried the natural method, Basil?"

"Always. Natural method and a bottle of red-eye."

Stanley Skuldugger had become the most meteoric actor-imago for a week. Naturally he became very rich, and Ildefonsa Impala went to see him about 3 A.M.

"I had him first!" rang the mocking voice of Judy Skuldugger as she skipped through her divorce in Small Claims Court. And Ildefonsa and Stanley-boy went off honeymooning. It is always fun to finish up a period with an actor-imago who is the hottest property in the business. There is something so adolescent and boorish about them.

Besides, there was the publicity, and Ildefonsa liked that. The rumor-mills ground. Would it last ten minutes? Thirty? An hour? Would it be one of those rare Nyctalops marriages that lasted through the rest of the night and into the daylight off hours? Would it even last into the next night as some had been known to do?

Actually it lasted nearly 40 minutes, which was almost to the end of the period.

It had been a slow Tuesday night. A few hundred new products had run their course on the markets. There had been a score of dramatic hits, three minute and five minute capsule dramas, and several of the six minute long-play affairs. Night Street Nine—a solidly sordid offering seemed to be in as the drama of the night unless there should be a late hit.

Hundred-storied buildings had been erected, occupied, obsoleted, and demolished again to make room for more contemporary structures. Only the mediocre would use a building that had been left over from the Day-Flies or the Dawners, or even the Nyctalops of the night before. The city was rebuilt pretty completely at least three times during an eight-hour period.

The Period drew near its end. Basil Bagelbaker, the richest man in the world, the reigning president of the Toppers' Club, was enjoying himself with his cronies. His fourth fortune of the night was a paper pyramid that had risen to incredible heights; but Basil laughed to himself as he savored the manipulation it was founded on.

Three ushers of the Toppers' Club came in with firm step.

"Get out of here, you dirty bum!" they told Basil savagely. They tore the tycoon's toga off him and then tossed him his seedy panhandler's rags with a three-man sneer.

"All gone?" Basil asked. "I gave it another five minutes."

"All gone," said a messenger from Money Market. "Nine billion gone in five minutes, and it really pulled some others down with it."

"Pitch the busted bum out!" howled Overcall and Burnbanner and the other cronies. "Wait, Basil," said Overcall. "Turn in the President's Crosier before we kick you downstairs. After all, you'll have it several times again tomorrow night."

The Period was over. The Nyctalops drifted off to sleep clinics or leisure-hour hide-outs to pass their ebb time. The Auroreans, the Dawners, took over the vital stuff.

Now you would see some action! Those Dawners really made fast decisions. You wouldn't catch them wasting a full minute setting up a business.

A sleepy panhandler met Ildefonsa Impala on the way.

"Preserve us this morning, Ildy," he said, "and will you marry me the coming night?"

"Likely I will, Basil," she told him. "Did you marry Judy during the night past?"

"I'm not sure. Could you let me have two dollars, Ildy?"

"Out of the question. I believe a Judy Bagelbaker was named one of the ten best-dressed women during the frou-frou fashion period about two o'clock. Why do you need two dollars?"

"A dollar for a bed and a dollar for red-eye. After all, I sent you two million out of my second."

"I keep my two sorts of accounts separate. Here's a dollar, Basil. Now be off! I can't be seen talking to a dirty panhandler."

"Thank you, Ildy. I'll get the red-eye and sleep in an alley. Preserve us this morning."

Bagelbaker shuffled off whistling Slow Tuesday Night.

And already the Dawners had set Wednesday morning to jumping.

THROUGH A GLASS DARKLY

For five decades after the turn of the century, after Wells turned to writing propaganda novels on behalf of his "open conspiracy" to create a better world, the anti-utopia was wielded by such traditional literary foes of science and technology, of the very concept of progress, as E. M. Forster, Aldous Huxley, George Orwell, and C. S. Lewis. The characteristic anti-utopia was an attack on some other thinker's—usually Wells's—vision of the future. Lewis's *That Hideous Strength* (1945) even contained an attack on Wells himself in the guise of a character named "Horace Jules."

Stories in the early science fiction magazines contained some satire by writers such as Dr. David H. Keller and Stanton A. Coblentz, some of it in the literary tradition. But the anti-utopia was foreign to Campbell's *Astounding,* and it did not come into its own in the magazines until the founding of *Galaxy* in 1950. Editor Horace Gold was a cynic and a skeptic; he not only believed the condition of humanity probably would get worse but thought entertaining fiction could be written about the process. But the author who did the most to bring the pre-1900 Wellsian point of view back into science fiction—with some help from his friends—was Frederik Pohl.

The science fiction anti-utopia differed in important ways from the literary anti-utopia. In fact a new word had to be coined: *dystopia.* The anti-utopia was an attack on the utopian concepts of others; the dystopia, which means "bad place," showed how matters could go wrong instead of right for humanity. The science fiction dystopia retained the narrative excitement of the magazines; it seldom blamed science or technology for the way things turned out, but rather human choices, and it usually held a note of regret that humanity's capacity for greatness had been thwarted by his institutions or his lack of forethought. In the science fiction dystopia science fiction's faith in intelligence has not been discarded.

The literary anti-utopia implies that humanity was doomed from the start, its nature flawed, its state fallen. The science fiction dystopia often ends with hope that the conditions that created the evil can be corrected; sometimes they are.

The novel that started it all was *The Space Merchants* (1953) by Cyril M. Kornbluth and Frederik Pohl. It was serialized in *Galaxy* in 1952 under the title of "Gravy Planet," and has seldom been out of print since; it has been translated into more than thirty languages. Pohl went on to collaborate with Kornbluth on three other dystopian novels, *Search the Sky* (1954), *Gladiator-at-Law* (1955), and *Wolf-bane* (1959), and with Lester del Rey on *Preferred Risk* (1956) (as Edson McCann).

Kornbluth (1923-1958) also worked on his own darker visions. He came into his own in the 1950s, like many of the Futurians, the New York fan group about which Damon Knight wrote a history (*The Futurians,* 1977). In its early incarnation, the group included Asimov, Pohl, Wollheim, Kornbluth, Robert Lowndes, David Kyle, Richard Wilson, and others. Within a couple of decades it seemed as if they might take over science fiction.

One thing they did not do in their early days (with the exception of Asimov) was to sell stories to Campbell. Mostly they sold stories to themselves in the late 1930s and early 1940s, when Pohl became editor of *Astonishing Stories* and *Super Science Stories*, Wollheim became editor of *Stirring Science Stories* and *Cosmic Stories* (he eventually was to become editor at Ace Books and then publisher of DAW Books), and Lowndes became editor of *Science Fiction* and *Future Fiction*. All these magazines were killed by economics or the wartime paper shortage. Though all the Futurians sold stories at an early age, they sold them to odd publications and mostly under pseudonyms.

Kornbluth wrote most of his early stories under the name of S. D. Gottesman. The second story published under his own name, the well-known "The Little Black Bag," appeared, oddly enough, in *Astounding* in 1950. He had some fifty stories published in all, including "The Marching Morons," "Gomez," "The Mindworm," "The Luckiest Man in Denv," and "Shark Ship." Several novels, including *Takeoff* (1952), *The Syndic* (1953), and *Not This August* (1955), were published under his own name. But he was best known for his collaborations, not only with Pohl, but for *Outpost Mars* and *Gunner Cade* (both 1952) with Judith Merril (who was then Pohl's wife), published under the name of Cyril Judd.

Kornbluth was born and raised in New York City. He strained his heart carrying a machine-gun in the Battle of the Bulge. After the war he studied at the University of Chicago and then worked his way up to the position of bureau chief of the Chicago office of Trans-Radio Press, before quitting in 1951 for full-time fiction writing. He was the Weinbaum of his generation, and like Weinbaum, he died at thirty-five with much of his promise unfulfilled.

Pohl (1919-), a high-school dropout, has become a kind of renaissance man of science fiction. He has served as agent, editor, and anthologist as well as writer; he became the *Encyclopedia Britannica's* expert on the Roman emperor Tiberius; he is a talk-show guest, a sophisticated observer of modern science, and a much-in-demand futurologist. He lectures frequently in colleges and universities and has been offered a professorial position in several of them.

All of that seemed rather improbable to the teenaged loner, the omnivorous reader who finally found others like himself among New York fan groups. When he became an editor at the age of nineteen, he began to buy stories from other Futurians—and, under pseudonyms, from himself. After service in the Army Air Force in World War II, he became an advertising copywriter, author, and agent. In 1951, stuck with a science fiction novel about advertising, he asked his old Futurian buddy Cyril Kornbluth to help with it: *The Space Merchants* was born.

For the next half-dozen years Pohl wrote a series of witty satires such as "The Midas Plague" (1954), "The Tunnel Under the World" (1955), and "The Man Who Ate the World" (1956). Kingsley Amis, in *New Maps of Hell* (1960), called him "the most consistently able writer science fiction, in the modern sense, has produced." Between 1953 and 1959 he edited the *Star Science Fiction* series of original anthologies for Ballantine Books. In 1962 he succeeded Gold as editor of *Galaxy* and *If* and earned three Hugos as best editor before he gave up the position in 1969. Later he became an editor at Ace Books for a while and then for several years, science fiction editor at Bantam Books.

His novels include *Drunkard's Walk* (1960), *A Plague of Pythons* (1965), and *The Age of the Pussyfoot* (1970). He collaborated with Jack Williamson on three juveniles, *Undersea Quest* (1954), *Undersea Fleet* (1956), and *Undersea City* (1958), as well as *The Reefs of Space* (1964), *Starchild* (1965), and *Rogue Star* (1969). In recent years he has turned from the easy wit and biting satire of his early successes to more serious themes, perhaps beginning with the publication in 1972 of "The Gold at the Starbow's End." Since then he has won a Hugo in 1973 for a short story he had begun many years before in collaboration with Kornbluth, "The Meeting"; a 1976 Nebula for *Man Plus*, a 1977 Nebula, Hugo, and Campbell award for *Gateway*, an American Book Award for *JEM* (1980), and the SFWA Grand Master Award in 1992. He has continued to produce significant work with remarkable regularity, including four sequels to *Gateway* and *The Years of the City* (1984), which won a second Campbell award. He served as president of the Science Fiction Writers of America from 1974 to 1976, and saw his memoirs, *The Way the Future Was*, published in 1978.

"Day Million," arguably Pohl's finest short story, was published in *Rogue* in February 1966.

DAY MILLION

BY FREDERIK POHL

On this day I want to tell you about, which will be about a thousand years from now, there were a boy, a girl and a love story.

Now although I haven't said much so far, none of it is true. The boy was not what you and I would normally think of as a boy, because he was a hundred and eighty-seven years old. Nor was the girl a girl, for other reasons; and the love story did not entail that sublimation of the urge to rape and concurrent postponement of the instinct to submit which we at present understand in such matters. You won't care much for this story if you don't grasp these facts at once. If, however, you will make the effort, you'll likely enough find it jampacked, chockfull and tiptop-crammed with laughter, tears and poignant sentiment which may, or may not, be worth while. The reason the girl was not a girl was that she was a boy.

How angrily you recoil from the page! You say, who the hell wants to read about a pair of queers? Calm yourself. Here are no hot-breathing secrets of perversion for the coterie trade. In fact, if you were to see this girl, you would not guess that she was in any sense a boy. Breasts, two; vagina, one. Hips, Callipygean; face, hairless; supraorbital lobes, nonexistent. You would term her female at once, although it is true that you might wonder just what species she was a female of, being confused by the tail, the silky pelt or the gill slits behind each ear.

Now you recoil again. Cripes, man, take my word for it. This is a sweet kid, and if you, as a normal male, spent as much as an hour in a room with her, you would bend heaven and earth to get her in the sack. Dora (we will call her that; her "name" was omicron-Di-base seven-group-totter-oot S Doradus 5314, the last part of which is a color specification corresponding to a shade of green)— Dora, I say, was feminine, charming and cute. I admit she doesn't sound that way. She was, as you might put it, a dancer. Her art involved qualities of intellection and expertise of a very high order, requiring both tremendous natural capacities and endless practice; it was performed in null-gravity and I can best describe it by saying that it was something like the performance of a contortionist and something like classical ballet, maybe resembling Danilova's dying swan. It was also pretty damned sexy. In a symbolic way, to be sure; but face it, most of the things we call "sexy" are symbolic, you know, except perhaps an exhibitionist's open fly. On Day Million when Dora danced, the people who saw her panted; and you would too.

About this business of her being a boy. It didn't matter to her audiences that genetically she was male. It wouldn't matter to you, if you were among them, because you wouldn't know it—not unless you took a biopsy cutting of her flesh and put it under an electron microscope to find the XY chromosome—and it didn't matter to them because they didn't care. Through techniques which are not only complex but haven't yet been discovered, these people were able to determine a great deal about the aptitudes and easements of babies quite a long time before they were born—at about the second horizon of cell-division, to be exact, when the segmenting egg is becoming a free blastocyst—and then they naturally helped those aptitudes along. Wouldn't we? If we find a child with an aptitude for music we give him a scholarship to Juilliard. If they found a child whose aptitudes were for being a woman, they made him one. As sex had long been dissociated from reproduction this was relatively easy to do and caused no trouble and no, or at least very little, comment.

How much is "very little"? Oh, about as much as would be caused by our own tampering with Divine Will by filling a tooth. Less than would be caused by wearing a hearing aid. Does it still sound awful? Then look closely at the next busty babe you meet and reflect that she may be a Dora, for adults who are genetically male but somatically female are far from unknown even in our own time. An accident of environment in the womb overwhelms the blueprints of heredity. The difference is that with us it happens only by accident and we don't know about it except rarely, after close study; whereas the people of Day Million did it often, on purpose, because they wanted to.

Well, that's enough to tell you about Dora. It would only confuse you to add that she was seven feet tall and smelled of peanut butter. Let us begin our story.

On Day Million Dora swam out of her house, entered a transportation tube, was sucked briskly to the surface in its flow of water and ejected in its plume of spray to an elastic platform in front of her—ah—call it her rehearsal hall. "Oh, shit!" she cried in pretty confusion, reaching out to catch her balance and find herself tumbled against a total stranger, whom we will call Don.

They met cute. Don was on his way to have his legs renewed. Love was the farthest thing from his mind; but when, absent-mindedly taking a short cut across the landing platform for submarinites and finding himself drenched, he discovered his arms full of the loveliest girl he had ever seen, he knew at once they were meant for each other. "Will you marry me?" he asked. She said softly, "Wednesday," and the promise was like a caress.

Don was tall, muscular, bronze and exciting. His name was no more Don than Dora's was Dora, but the personal part of it was Adonis in tribute to his vibrant maleness, and so we will call him Don for short. His personality color-code, in Angstrom units, was 5290, or only a few degrees bluer than Dora's 5314, a measure of what they had intuitively discovered at first sight, that they possessed many affinities of taste and interest.

I despair of telling you exactly what it was that Don did for a living—I don't mean for the sake of making money, I mean for the sake of giving purpose and meaning to his life, to keep him from going off his nut with boredom—except to say that it involved a lot of traveling. He traveled in interstellar spaceships. In order to make a spaceship go really fast about thirty-one male and seven genetically female human beings had to do certain things, and Don was one of the thirty-one. Actually he contemplated options. This involved a lot of exposure to radiation flux—not so much from his own station in the propulsive system as in the spillover from the next stage, where a genetic female preferred selections and the subnuclear particles making the selections she preferred demolished themselves in a shower of quanta. Well, you don't give a rat's ass for that, but it meant that Don had to be clad at all times in a skin of light, resilient, extremely strong copper-colored metal. I have already mentioned this, but you probably thought I meant he was sunburned.

More than that, he was a cybernetic man. Most of his ruder parts had been long since replaced with mechanisms of vastly more permanence and use. A cadmium centrifuge, not a heart, pumped his blood. His lungs moved only when he wanted to speak out loud, for a cascade of osmotic filters rebreathed oxygen out of his own wastes. In a way, he probably would have looked peculiar to a man from the 20th century, with his glowing eyes and seven-fingered hands; but to himself, and of course to Dora, he looked mighty manly and grand. In the course of his voyages Don had circled Proxima Centauri, Procyon and the puzzling worlds of Mira Ceti; he had carried agricultural templates to the planets of Canopus and brought back warm, witty pets from the pale companion of Aldebaran. Blue-hot or red-cool, he had seen a thousand stars and their ten thousand planets. He had, in fact, been traveling the starlanes with only brief leaves on Earth for pushing two centuries. But you don't care about that, either. It is people that make stories, not the circumstances they find themselves in, and you want to hear about these two people. Well, they made it. The great thing they had for each other grew and flowered and burst into fruition on Wednesday, just as Dora had promised. They met at the encoding room, with a couple of well-wishing friends apiece to cheer them on, and while their identities were being taped and stored they smiled and whispered to each other and bore the jokes of their friends with blushing repartee. Then they exchanged their mathematical analogues and went away. Dora to her dwelling beneath the surface of the sea and Don to his ship.

It was an idyll, really. They lived happily ever after—or anyway, until they decided not to bother any more and died.

Of course, they never set eyes on each other again.

Oh, I can see you now, you eaters of charcoal-broiled steak, scratching an incipient bunion with one hand and holding this story with the other, while the stereo plays d'Indy or Monk. You don't believe a word of it, do you? Not for one minute. People wouldn't live like that, you say with an irritated and not amused grunt as you get up to put fresh ice in a stale drink.

And yet there's Dora, hurrying back through the flushing commuter pipes toward her underwater home (she prefers it there; has had herself somatically altered to breathe the stuff). If I tell you with what sweet fulfillment she fits the recorded analogue of Don into the symbol manipulator, hooks herself in and turns herself on... if I try to tell you any of that you will simply stare. Or glare; and grumble, what the hell kind of love-making is this? And yet I assure you, friend, I really do assure you that Dora's ecstasies are as creamy and passionate as any of James Bond's lady spies, and one hell of a lot more so than anything you are going to find in "real life." Go ahead, glare and grumble. Dora doesn't care. If she thinks of you at all, her thirty-times-great great-grandfather, she thinks you're a pretty primordial sort of brute. You are. Why, Dora is farther removed from you than you are from the australopithecines of five thousand centuries ago. You could not swim a second in the strong currents of her life. You don't think progress goes in a straight line, do you? Do you recognize that it is an ascending, accelerating, maybe even exponential curve? It takes hell's own time to get started, but when it goes it goes like a bomb. And you, you Scotch-drinking steak-eater in your Relaxacizer chair, you've just barely lighted the primacord of the fuse. What is it now, the six or seven hundred thousandth day after Christ? Dora lives in Day Million. A thousand years from now. Her body fats are polyunsaturated, like Crisco. Her wastes are hemodialyzed out of her bloodstream while she sleeps—that means she doesn't have to go to the bathroom. On whim, to pass a slow half-hour, she can command more energy than the entire nation of Portugal can spend today, and use it to launch a weekend satellite or remold a crater on the Moon. She loves Don very much. She keeps his every gesture, mannerism, nuance, touch of hand, thrill of intercourse, passion of kiss stored in symbolic-mathematical form. And when she wants him, all she has to do is turn the machine on and she has him.

And Don, of course, has Dora. Adrift on a sponson city a few hundred yards over her head or orbiting Arcturus, fifty light-years away, Don has only to command his own symbol-manipulator to rescue Dora from the ferrite files and bring her to life for him, and there she is; and rapturously, tirelessly they ball all night. Not in the flesh, of course; but then his flesh has been extensively altered and it wouldn't really be much fun. He doesn't need the flesh for pleasure.

Genital organs feel nothing. Neither do hands, nor breasts, nor lips; they are only receptors, accepting and transmitting impulses. It is the brain that feels, it is the interpretation of those impulses that makes agony or orgasm; and Don's symbol-manipulator gives him the analogue of cuddling, the analogue of kissing, the analogue of wildest, most ardent hours with the eternal, exquisite and incorruptible analogue of Dora. Or Diane. Or sweet Rose, or laughing Alicia; for to be sure, they have each of them exchanged analogues before, and will again.

Balls, you say, it looks crazy to me. And you—with your after-shave lotion and your little red car, pushing papers across a desk all day and chasing tail all night—tell me, just how the hell do you think you would look to Tiglath-Pileser, say, or Attila the Hun?

WILL REALITY PLEASE RAISE ITS HAND?

Writers can be divided into two groups: storytellers and stylists. Storytellers see the world as a variety of fascinating situations and events that they can relate to their readers; since the style in which a story is told depends upon the substance and meaning of the story, their styles vary from work to work. Stylists, on the other hand, discover a distinctive style and use it for all their stories; the only way they can get away with this is by telling the same story over and over again.

This is not to say that the storyteller is not concerned with style or may not be every bit as skillful as the stylist, nor that the stylist cannot tell engrossing stories. Nevertheless, all this may sound a bit unfair to the stylists. But since they often are the only writers considered to be artists and make off with most of the prizes (except in science fiction), perhaps it evens out. Retelling the same story, however, is not as bad as it sounds; the stylist, you see, has a single view of the world into which everything else must fit itself: "Life is testing one's manhood against danger," says one. "Life is coping with one's past," says another. "Life is absurd," says a third. "Life is unreal," says a fourth. They have their own worlds, and the stories they discover there are told in their own styles.

Hemingway and Faulkner were well-known stylists. Kipling and Lewis and Steinbeck—to name three other Nobel laureates—were storytellers. The same two categories can be applied to science fiction. Most science fiction writers traditionally have been storytellers. When a writer is constrained by reality, as science fiction writers are but many mainstream writers are not, he or she may have difficulty interpreting all phenomena according to one subjective criterion.

H. P. Lovecraft was a stylist, although his style might not please everyone, nor his view that life hides a darker, horrible truth. Bradbury is a stylist. Ballard is another. That may explain why everything these authors produce seems like part of the same long story, why it all reads alike, and why at least the last two are recognized as "real writers" by laymen and critics outside the field. Another stylist was the late Philip K. Dick, who after many years of productivity won recognition both inside and outside the genre, including acclaim by Poland's Stanislaw Lem as the only American science fiction author worth reading.

Dick's concern was the nature of reality. That alone is not unique. Ambrose Bierce was involved with the question in the late nineteenth century, and the Italian playwright Pirandello in this century. It came into science fiction mostly through the research and speculations of Charles Fort and the stories of Lovecraft and his followers. Fort's speculations, such as "we are property," inspired a number of stories in which ordinary understanding of the world turned out to be insufficient to explain certain phenomena; Lovecraft's mythos presumed the existence of elder powers who still control some areas of the world.

Stories about the nature of reality usually appeared in fantasy magazines like *Weird Tales*. When Heinlein wrote them, as he did with "They," a paranoid story in which the world turns out to be an illusion created to confuse the protagonist, they appeared in Campbell's fantasy magazine, *Unknown*. When Gold created his fantasy magazine, *Beyond*, it published stories such as Budrys's "The Real People" and Farmer's "The God Business."

Concerns about reality often involve "solipsism," the philosophy that only the self exists or can be proved to exist. Time-travel stories often raise such concerns, particularly travel into the past through which present reality might be changed. Sometimes they produce alternate universes, or the existence of alternate time tracks is assumed without time travel. Travel into the future or foreknowledge also can be a reality problem: if the future can be known, it is fixed and humanity's sense of free will is an illusion. By such rationalizations solipsistic stories such as Heinlein's "All You Zombies" were slipped into science fiction.

Science also provided support for questioning reality with its atomic research, particularly Heisenberg's uncertainty principle, whose extrapolations cast doubt on cause-and-effect even at the macroscopic level. Blish's "Beep" is an example of a story in which foreknowledge destroys cause-and-effect and free will. A more recent party to the philosophic question was the drug culture, which sometimes justified itself by postulating another reality made available through drugs.

Dick (1928-1982) did not find his subject immediately. Damon Knight said of his early writing (first story: "Beyond Lies the Wub," July 1952 *Planet Stories*) that it exhibited "unobtrusive and chameleonlike competence"; approximately one hundred Dick stories were published in his first dozen years as a writer. His novels, beginning with *Solar Lottery* (1955), were distinctive from the first. Always unusual in idea and plot, they slowly began to focus in upon the nature of reality with *The World Jones Made* (1956), where Jones's ability to see the future a year ahead was a curse, and *Eye in the Sky* (1956), in which a Bevatron accident projects the minds of eight characters into fantasy worlds controlled alternately by their own ideas of how the world should be.

The Man in the High Castle (1962), which won a Hugo for Dick, marked a significant development. It begins with an alternate time track in which the Axis powers won World War II and ends with the ambiguity of a man in a high castle writing a novel in which the Allies won World War II. Dick was a prolific novelist as well, and most of his novels fit into his extended consideration of reality. Aldiss said of his work, "all his novels are one novel," and "between life and death lie the many shadow lands of Dick, places of hallucination, illusion, artificial reality, dim half life, paranoid states." His books include *Time Out of Joint* (1959), *The Three Stigmata of Palmer Eldritch* (1965), *Counter-Clock World* (1967), *Now Wait for Last Year* (1967), *Do Androids Dream of Electric Sheep*

(1968), *Our Friends from Frolix 8* (1970), *Ubik* (1970), and *Flow My Tears, the Policeman Said* (1974), which won the Campbell Award.

In his foreword to Dick's "Faith of Our Fathers" in *Dangerous Visions*, Ellison said that Dick wrote it under the influence of LSD. Dick's relationship with the drug culture of the 1960s is suggested in his 1977 novel *A Scanner Darkly* and its effects touchingly related in an afterword. He turned to theology in 1981 with *Valis* and *The Divine Invasion*, and *The Transmigration of Timothy Archer* (1982). His career soared, posthumously, with the filming of *Do Androids Dream of Electric Sheep* by Ridley Scott in 1982 as *Blade Runner*, and many of his novels have been reprinted, as well as his earlier, unpublished mainstream novels.

"We Can Remember It for You Wholesale," published in *F&SF* for April 1966, is an example of Dick's concern with solipsism. It was filmed in 1990 by Paul Verhoeven as *Total Recall*, with Arnold Schwarzenegger.

WE CAN REMEMBER IT FOR YOU WHOLESALE

BY PHILIP K. DICK

He awoke—and wanted Mars. The valleys, he thought. What would it be like to trudge among them? Great and greater yet. The dream grew as he became fully conscious, the dream and the yearning. He could almost feel the enveloping presence of the other world, which only government agents and high officials had seen. A clerk like himself? Not likely.

"Are you getting up or not?" his wife Kirsten asked drowsily, with her usual hint of fierce crossness. "If you are, push the hot coffee button on the darn stove."

"Okay," Douglas Quail said, and made his way barefoot from the bedroom of their conapt to the kitchen. There, having dutifully pressed the hot coffee button, he seated himself at the kitchen table, brought out a yellow, small tin of fine Dean Swift snuff. He inhaled briskly, and the Beau Nash mixture stung his nose, burned the roof of his mouth. But still he inhaled; it woke him up and allowed his dreams, his nocturnal desires, and random wishes to condense into a semblance of rationality.

I will go, he said to himself. Before I die, I'll see Mars.

It was, of course, impossible, and he knew this even as he dreamed. But the daylight, the mundane noise of his wife now brushing her hair before the bedroom mirror—everything conspired to remind him of what he was. A miserable little salaried employee, he said to himself with bitterness. Kirsten reminded him of this at least once a day, and he did not blame her; it was a wife's job to bring her husband down to Earth. Down to Earth, he thought, and laughed. The figure of speech in this was literally apt.

"What are you sniggering about?" his wife asked as she swept into the kitchen, her long busy-pink robe wagging after her. "A dream, I bet. You're always full of them."

"Yes," he said, and gazed out the kitchen window at the hovercars and traffic runnels, and all the little energetic people hurrying to work. In a little while he would be among them. As always.

"I'll bet it has to do with some woman," Kirsten said witheringly.

"No," he said. "A god. The god of war. He has wonderful craters with every kind of plant life growing deep down in them."

"Listen." Kirsten crouched down beside him and spoke earnestly, the harsh quality momentarily gone from her voice. "The bottom of the ocean—*our* ocean is much more, an infinity of times more beautiful. You know that; everyone knows that. Rent an artificial gill outfit for both of us, take a week off from work, and we can descend and live down there at one of those year-round aquatic resorts. And in addition—" She broke off. "You're not listening. You should be. Here is something a lot better than that compulsion, that obsession you have about Mars, and you don't even listen!" Her voice rose piercingly. "God in heaven, you're doomed, Doug! What's going to become of you?"

"I'm going to work," he said, rising to his feet, his breakfast forgotten. "That's what's going to become of me."

She eyed him. "You're getting worse. More fanatical every day. Where's it going to lead?"

"To Mars," he said, and opened the door to the closet to get down a fresh shirt to wear to work.

Having descended from the taxi, Douglas Quail slowly walked across three densely populated foot runnels and to the modern, attractively inviting doorway. There he halted, impeding midmorning traffic, and with caution read the shifting-color neon sign. He had, in the past, scrutinized this sign before... but never had he come so close. This was very different; what he did now was something else. Something which sooner or later had to happen.

REKAL, INCORPORATED

Was this the answer? After all, an illusion, no matter how convincing, remained nothing more than an illusion. At least objectively. But subjectively— quite the opposite entirely.

And anyhow he had an appointment. Within the next five minutes.

Taking a deep breath of mildly smog-infested Chicago air, he walked through the dazzling polychromatic shimmer of the doorway and up to the receptionist's counter.

The nicely articulated blonde at the counter, bare-bosomed and tidy, said pleasantly, "Good morning, Mr. Quail."

"Yes," he said. "I'm here to see about a Rekal course. As I guess you know."

"Not 'rekal' but *recall*," the receptionist corrected him. She picked up the receiver of the vidphone by her smooth elbow and said into it, "Mr. Douglas Quail is here, Mr. McClane. May he come inside, now? Or is it too soon?"

"Giz wetwa wum-wum wamp," the phone mumbled.

"Yes, Mr. Quail," she said. "You may go on in. Mr. McClane is expecting you." As he started off uncertainly, she called after him, "Room D, Mr. Quail. To your right."

After a frustrating but brief moment of being lost, he found the proper room. The door hung open, and inside, at a big genuine walnut desk, sat a genial-looking man, middle-aged, wearing the latest Martian frog-pelt gray suit; his attire alone would have told Quail that he had come to the right person.

"Sit down, Douglas," McClane said, waving his plump hand toward a chair which faced the desk. "So you want to have gone to Mars. Very good."

Quail seated himself, feeling tense. "I'm not so sure this is worth the fee," he said. "It costs a lot, and as far as I can see I really get nothing." Costs almost as much as going, he thought.

"You get tangible proof of your trip," McClane disagreed emphatically. "All the proof you'll need. Here, I'll show you." He dug within a drawer of his impressive desk. "Ticket stub." Reaching into a manila folder, he produced a small square of embossed cardboard. "It proves you went—and returned. Postcards." He laid out four franked picture 3-D full-color postcards in a neatly arranged row on the desk for Quail to see. "Film. Shots you took of local sights on Mars with a rented movie camera." To Quail he displayed those, too. "Plus the names of people you met, two hundred poscreds' worth of souvenirs, which will arrive—from Mars—within the following month. And passport, certificates listing the shots you received. And more." He glanced up keenly at Quail. "You'll know you went, all right," he said. "You won't remember us, won't remember me or ever having been here. It'll be a real trip in your mind; we guarantee that. A full two weeks of recall; every last piddling detail. Remember this: if at any time you doubt that you really took an extensive trip to Mars, you can return here and get a full refund. You see?"

"But I didn't go," Quail said. "I won't have gone, no matter what proofs you provide me with." He took a deep, unsteady breath. "And I never was a secret agent with Interplan." It seemed impossible to him that Rekal, Incorporated's extra-factual memory implant would do its job—despite what he had heard people say.

"Mr. Quail," McClane said patiently. "As you explained in your letter to us, you have no chance, no possibility in the slightest, of ever actually getting to Mars; you can't afford it, and what is much more important, you could never qualify as an undercover agent for Interplan or anybody else. This is the only way you can achieve your, ahem, lifelong dream; am I not correct, sir? You can't be this; you can't actually do this." He chuckled. "But you can *have been* and *have done*. We see to that. And our fee is reasonable; no hidden charges." He smiled encouragingly.

WE CAN REMEMBER IT
FOR YOU WHOLESALE

"Is an extra-factual memory that convincing?" Quail asked.

"More than the real thing, sir. Had you really gone to Mars as an Interplan agent, you would by now have forgotten a great deal; our analysis of true-mem systems—authentic recollections of major events in a person's life—shows that a variety of details are very quickly lost to the person. Forever. Part of the package we offer you is such deep implantation of recall that nothing is forgotten. The packet which is fed to you while you're comatose is the creation of trained experts, men who have spent years on Mars; in every case we verify details down to the last iota. And you've picked a rather easy extra-factual system; had you picked Pluto or wanted to be Emperor of the Inner Planet Alliance we'd have much more difficulty... and the charges would be considerably greater."

Reaching into his coat for his wallet, Quail said, "Okay. It's been my lifelong ambition and I can see I'll never really do it. So I guess I'll have to settle for this."

"Don't think of it that way," McClane said severely. "You're not accepting second best. The actual memory, with all its vagueness, omissions, and ellipses, not to say distortions—that's second best." He accepted the money and pressed a button on his desk. "All right, Mr. Quail," he said, as the door of his office opened and two burly men swiftly entered. "You're on your way to Mars as a secret agent." He rose, came over to shake Quail's nervous, moist hand. "Or rather, you have been on your way. This afternoon at four thirty you will, um, arrive back here on Terra; a cab will leave you off at your conapt and, as I say, you will never remember seeing me or coming here; you won't, in fact, even remember having heard of our existence."

His mouth dry with nervousness, Quail followed the two technicians from the office; what happened next depended on them.

Will I actually believe I've been on Mars? he wondered. That I managed to fulfill my lifetime ambition? He had a strange, lingering intuition that something would go wrong. But just what—he did not know.

He would have to wait to find out.

The intercom on McClane's desk, which connected him with the work area of the firm, buzzed and a voice said, "Mr. Quail is under sedation now, sir. Do you want to supervise this one, or shall we go ahead?"

"It's routine," McClane observed. "You may go ahead, Lowe. I don't think you'll run into any trouble." Programming an artificial memory of a trip to another planet—with or without the added fillip of being a secret agent—showed up on the firm's work schedule with monotonous regularity. In one month, he calculated wryly, we must do twenty of these... ersatz interplanetary travel has become our bread and butter.

"Whatever you say, Mr. McClane," Lowe's voice came, and thereupon the intercom shut off.

Going to the vault section in the chamber behind his office, McClane searched about for a three packet—trip to Mars—and a sixty-two packet: secret Interplan spy. Finding the two packets, he returned with them to his desk, seated himself comfortably, poured out the contents—merchandise which would be planted in Quail's conapt while the lab technicians busied themselves installing the false memory.

A one-poscred sneaky pete side arm, McClane reflected; that's the largest item. Sets us back financially the most. Then a pellet-sized transmitter, which could be swallowed if the agent were caught. Code book that astonishingly resembled the real thing... the firm's models were highly accurate: based, whenever possible, on actual U.S. military issue. Odd bits which made no intrinsic sense but which would be woven into the warp and woof of Quail's imaginary trip, would coincide with his memory: half an ancient silver fifty-cent piece, several quotations from John Donne's sermons written incorrectly, each on a separate piece of transparent tissue-thin paper, several match folders from bars on Mars, a stainless steel spoon engraved PROPERTY OF DOMEMARS NATIONAL KIBUTZIM, a wire tapping coil which—

The intercom buzzed. "Mr. McClane, I'm sorry to bother you, but something rather ominous has come up. Maybe it would be better if you were in here after all. Quail is already under sedation; he reacted well to the narkidrine; he's completely unconscious and receptive. But—"

"I'll be in." Sensing trouble, McClane left his office; a moment later he emerged in the work area.

On a hygienic bed lay Douglas Quail, breathing slowly and regularly, his eyes virtually shut; he seemed dimly—but only dimly—aware of the two technicians and now McClane himself.

"There's no space to insert false memory patterns?" McClane felt irritation. "Merely drop out two work weeks; he's employed as a clerk at the West Coast Emigration Bureau, which is a government agency, so he undoubtedly has or had two weeks' vacation within the last year. That ought to do it." Petty details annoyed him. And always would.

"Our problem," Lowe said sharply, "is something quite different." He bent over the bed, said to Quail, "Tell Mr. McClane what you told us." To McClane he said, "Listen closely."

The gray-green eyes of the man lying supine in the bed focused on McClane's face. The eyes, he observed uneasily, had become hard; they had a polished, inorganic quality, like semiprecious tumbled stones. He was not sure that he liked what he saw; the brilliance was too cold. "What do you want now?" Quail said harshly. "You've broken my cover. Get out of here before I take you all apart." He studied McClane. "Especially you," he continued. "You're in charge

WE CAN REMEMBER IT
FOR YOU WHOLESALE

of this counteroperation."

Lowe said, "How long were you on Mars?"

"One month," Quail said gratingly.

"And your purpose there?" Lowe demanded.

The meager lips twisted; Quail eyed him and did not speak. At last, drawling the words out so that they dripped with hostility, he said, "Agent for Interplan. As I already told you. Don't you record everything that's said? Play your vidaud tape back for your boss, and leave me alone." He shut his eyes, then; the hard brilliance ceased. McClane felt, instantly, a rushing splurge of relief.

Lowe said quietly, "This is a tough man, Mr. McClane."

"He won't be," McClane said, "after we arrange for him to lose his memory chain again. He'll be as meek as before." To Quail he said, "So *this* is why you wanted to go to Mars so terribly badly."

Without opening his eyes Quail said, "I never wanted to go to Mars. I was assigned it—they handed it to me and there I was: stuck. Oh, yeah, I admit I was curious about it. Who wouldn't be?" Again he opened his eyes and surveyed the three of them, McClane in particular. "Quite a truth drug you've got here; it brought up things I had absolutely no memory of." He pondered. "I wonder about Kirsten," he said, half to himself. "Could she be in on it? An Interplan contact keeping an eye on me… to be certain I didn't regain my memory? No wonder she's been so derisive about my wanting to go there." Faintly, he smiled; the smile—one of understanding—disappeared almost at once.

McClane said, "Please believe me, Mr. Quail. We stumbled onto this entirely by accident. In the work we do—"

"I believe you," Quail said. He seemed tired now; the drug was continuing to pull him under, deeper and deeper. "Where did I say I'd been?" he murmured. "Mars? Hard to remember—I know I'd like to see it; so would everybody else. But me—" His voice trailed off. "Just a clerk, a nothing clerk."

Straightening up, Lowe said to his Superior, "He wants a false memory implanted that corresponds to a trip he actually took. And a false reason which is the real reason. He's telling the truth; he's a long way down in the narkidrine. The trip is very vivid in his mind—at least under sedation. But apparently he doesn't recall it otherwise. Someone, probably at a government military-sciences lab, erased his conscious memories; all he knew was that going to Mars meant something special to him, and so did being a secret agent. They couldn't erase that; it's not a memory but a desire, undoubtedly the same one that motivated him to volunteer for the assignment in the first place."

The other technician, Keeler, said to McClane, "What do we do? Graft a false memory pattern over the real memory? There's no telling what the results would be; he might remember some of the genuine trip, and the confusion might bring on a psychotic interlude. He'd have to hold two opposite premises in his mind simultaneously: that he went to Mars and that he didn't. That he's a genuine agent for Interplan and he's not, that it's spurious. I think we ought to revive him without any false memory implantation and send him out of here; this is hot."

"Agreed," McClane said. A thought came to him. "Can you predict what he'll remember when he comes out of sedation?"

"Impossible to tell," Lowe said. "He probably will have some dim, diffuse memory of his actual trip now. And he'd probably be in grave doubt as to its validity; he'd probably decide our programming slipped a gear tooth. And he'd remember coming here; that wouldn't be erased—unless you want it erased."

"The less we mess with this man," McClane said, "the better I like it. This is nothing for us to fool around with; we've been foolish enough to—or unlucky enough to—uncover a genuine Interplan spy who has a cover so perfect that up to now even he didn't know what he was—or rather is." The sooner they washed their hands of the man calling himself Douglas Quail the better.

"Are you going to plant packets three and sixty-two in his conapt?" Lowe said.

"No," McClane said. "And we're going to return half his fee."

"Half! Why half?"

McClane said lamely, "It seems to be a good compromise."

As the cab carried him back to his conapt at the residential end of Chicago, Douglas Quail said to himself, "It's sure good to be back on Terra."

Already the month-long period on Mars had begun to waver in his memory; he had only an image of profound gaping craters, an ever-present ancient erosion of hills, of vitality, of motion itself. A world of dust where little happened, where a good part of the day was spent checking and rechecking one's portable oxygen source. And then the life forms, the unassuming and modest gray-brown cacti and maw worms.

As a matter of fact he had brought back several moribund examples of Martian fauna; he had smuggled them through customs. After all, they posed no menace; they couldn't survive in Earth's heavy atmosphere.

Reaching into his coat pocket he rummaged for the container of Martian maw worms—

And found an envelope instead.

Lifting it out he discovered, to his perplexity, that it contained five hundred and seventy poscreds, in cred bills of low denomination.

"Where'd I get this?" he asked himself. "Didn't I spend every cred I had on my trip?"

With the money came a slip of paper marked *One-half fee ret'd. By McClane.* And then the date. Today's date.

"Recall," he said aloud.

"Recall what, sir or madam?" the robot driver of the cab inquired respectfully.

"Do you have a phone book?" Quail demanded.

"Certainly, sir or madam." A slot opened; from it slid a microtape phone book for Cook County.

"It's spelled oddly," Quail said as he leafed through the pages of the yellow section. He felt fear, then; abiding fear. "Here it is," he said. "Take me there, to Rekal, Incorporated. I've changed my mind. I don't want to go home."

"Yes, sir or madam, as the case may be," the driver said. A moment later the cab was zipping back in the opposite direction.

"May I make use of your phone?" he asked.

"Be my guest," the robot driver said. And presented a shiny new emperor 3-D color phone to him.

He dialed his own conapt and, after a pause, found himself confronted by a miniature but chillingly realistic image of Kirsten on the small screen. "I've been to Mars," he said to her.

"You're drunk." Her lips writhed scornfully. "Or worse."

"'S God's truth."

"When?" she demanded.

"I don't know." He felt confused. "A simulated trip, I think. By means of one of those artificial or extra-factual or whatever it is memory places. It didn't take."

Kirsten said witheringly, "You *are* drunk." And broke the connection at her end. He hung up, then, feeling his face flush. Always the same tone, he said hotly to himself. Always the retort, as if she knows everything and I know nothing. What a marriage. Keerist, he thought dismally.

A moment later the cab stopped at the curb before a modern, very attractive little pink building, over which a shifting, polychromatic neon sign read: REKAL, INCORPORATED.

The receptionist, chic and bare from the waist up, started in surprise, then gained masterful control of herself. "Oh, hello, Mr. Quail," she said nervously. "H-how are you? Did you forget something?"

"The rest of my fee back," he said.

More composed now, the receptionist said, "Fee? I think you are mistaken, Mr. Quail. You were here discussing the feasibility of an extra-factual trip for you, but—" She shrugged her smooth pale shoulders. "As I understand it, no trip was taken."

Quail said, "I remember everything, miss. My letter to Rekal, Incorporated, which started this whole business off. I remember my arrival here, my visit with Mr. McClane. Then the two lab technicians taking me in tow and administering a drug to put me out." No wonder the firm had returned half his fee. The false memory of his trip to Mars hadn't taken—at least not entirely, not as he had been assured.

"Mr. Quail," the girl said, "although you are a minor clerk, you are a good-looking man and it spoils your features to become angry. If it would make you feel any better, I might, ahem, let you take me out..."

He felt furious then. "I remember you," he said savagely. "For instance the fact that your breasts are sprayed blue; that stuck in my mind. And I remember Mr. McClane's promise that if I remembered my visit to Rekal, Incorporated, I'd receive my money back in full. Where is Mr. McClane?"

After a delay—probably as long as they could manage—he found himself once more seated facing the imposing walnut desk, exactly as he had been an hour or so earlier in the day.

"Some technique you have," Quail said sardonically. His disappointment—and resentment—were enormous by now. "My so-called memory of a trip to Mars as an undercover agent for Interplan is hazy and vague and shot full of contradictions. And I clearly remember my dealings here with you people. I ought to take this to the Better Business Bureau." He was burning angry at this point; his sense of being cheated had overwhelmed him, had destroyed his customary aversion to participating in a public squabble.

Looking morose, as well as cautious, McClane said, "We capitulate, Quail. We'll refund the balance of your fee. I fully concede the fact that we did absolutely nothing for you." His tone was resigned.

Quail said accusingly, "You didn't even provide me with the various artifacts that you claimed would prove to me I had been on Mars. All that song and dance you went into—it hasn't materialized into a damn thing. Not even a ticket stub. Nor postcards. Nor passport. Nor proof of immunization shots. Nor—"

"Listen, Quail," McClane said. "Suppose I told you—" He broke off. "Let it go." He pressed a button on his intercom. "Shirley, will you disburse five hundred and seventy more creds in the form of a cashier's check made out to Douglas Quail? Thank you." He released the button, then glared at Quail.

Presently the check appeared; the receptionist placed it before McClane and once more vanished out of sight, leaving the two men alone, still facing each other across the surface of the massive walnut desk.

"Let me give you a word of advice," McClane said as he signed the check and passed it over. "Don't discuss your, ahem, recent trip to Mars with anyone."

"What trip?"

"Well, that's the thing." Doggedly, McClane said, "The trip you partially remember. Act as if you don't remember; pretend it never took place. Don't ask me why; just take my advice: it'll be better for all of us." He had begun to perspire. Freely. "Now, Mr. Quail, I have other business, other clients to see." He rose, showed Quail to the door.

Quail said, as he opened the door, "A firm that turns out such bad work shouldn't have any clients at all." He shut the door behind him.

WE CAN REMEMBER IT
FOR YOU WHOLESALE

On the way home in the cab Quail pondered the wording of his letter of complaint to the Better Business Bureau, Terra Division. As soon as he could get to his typewriter he'd get started; it was clearly his duty to warn other people away from Rekal, Incorporated.

When he got back to his conapt, he seated himself before his Hermes Rocket portable, opened the drawers and rummaged for carbon paper—and noticed a small, familiar box. A box which he had carefully filled on Mars with Martian fauna and later smuggled through customs.

Opening the box he saw, to his disbelief, six dead maw worms and several varieties of the unicellular life on which the Martian worms fed. The protozoa were dried-up, dusty, but he recognized them; it had taken him an entire day picking among the vast dark alien boulders to find them. A wonderful, illuminated journey of discovery.

But I didn't go to Mars, he realized.

Yet on the other hand—

Kirsten appeared at the doorway to the room, an armload of pale brown groceries gripped. "Why are you home, in the middle of the day?" Her voice, in an eternity of sameness, was accusing.

"Did I go to Mars?" he asked her. "You would know."

"No, of course you didn't go to Mars. You would know that, I would think. Aren't you always bleating about going?"

He said, "By God, I think I went." After a pause he added, "And simultaneously I think I didn't go."

"Make up your mind."

"How can I?" He gestured. "I have both memory tracks grafted inside my head. One is real and one isn't, but I can't tell which is which. Why can't I rely on you? They haven't tinkered with you." She could do this much for him at least—even if she never did anything else.

Kirsten said in a level, controlled voice, "Doug, if you don't pull yourself together, we're through. I'm going to leave you."

"I'm in trouble." His voice came out husky and coarse. And shaking. "Probably I'm heading into a psychotic episode. I hope not, but—maybe that's it. It would explain everything, anyhow."

Setting down the bag of groceries, Kirsten stalked to the closet. "I was not kidding," she said to him quietly. She brought out a coat, got it on, walked back to the door of the conapt. "I'll phone you one of these days soon," she said tonelessly. "This is good-bye, Doug. I hope you pull out of this eventually. I really pray you do. For your sake."

"Wait," he said desperately. "Just tell me and make it absolute; I did go or I didn't— tell me which one." But they may have altered your memory track also, he realized.

The door closed. His wife had left. Finally!

A voice behind him said, "Well, that's that. Now put up your hands, Quail. And also please turn around and face this way."

He turned instinctively, without raising his hands.

The man who faced him wore the plum uniform of the Interplan Police Agency, and his gun appeared to be U.N. issue. And, for some odd reason, he seemed familiar to Quail; familiar in a blurred, distorted fashion which he could not pin down. So, jerkily, he raised his hands.

"You remember," the policeman said, "your trip to Mars. We know all your actions today and all your thoughts—in particular your very important thoughts on the trip home from Rekal, Incorporated." He explained, "We have a teletransmitter wired within your skull; it keeps us constantly informed."

A telepathic transmitter; use of a living plasma that had been discovered on Luna. He shuddered with self-aversion. The thing lived inside him, within his own brain, feeding, listening, feeding. But the Interplan police used them; that had come out even in the homeopapes. So this was probably true, dismal as it was.

"Why me?" Quail said huskily. What had he done—or thought? And what did this have to do with Rekal, Incorporated?

"Fundamentally," the Interplan cop said, "this has nothing to do with Rekal. It's between you and us." He tapped his right ear. "I'm still picking up your mentational processes by way of your cephalic transmitter." In the man's ear Quail saw a small white plastic plug. "So I have to warn you: Anything you think may be held against you." He smiled. "Not that it matters now; you've already thought and spoken yourself into oblivion. What's annoying is the fact that under narkidrine at Rekal, Incorporated, you told them, their technicians and the owner, Mr. McClane, about your trip; where you went, for whom, some of what you did. They're very frightened. They wish they had never laid eyes on you." He added reflectively, "They're right."

Quail said, "I never made any trip. It's a false memory chain improperly planted in me by McClane's technicians." But then he thought of the box, in his desk drawer, containing the Martian life forms. And the trouble and hardship he had had gathering them. The memory seemed real. And the box of life forms; that certainly was real. Unless McClane had planted it. Perhaps this was one of the proofs which McClane had talked glibly about.

The memory of my trip to Mars, he thought, doesn't convince me—but unfortunately it has convinced the Interplan Police Agency. They think I really went to Mars and they think I at least partially realize it.

"We not only know you went to Mars," the Interplan cop agreed, in answer to his thoughts, "but we know that you now remember enough to be difficult for us. And there's no use expunging your conscious memory of all this, because

WE CAN REMEMBER IT
FOR YOU WHOLESALE

if we do you'll simply show up at Rekal, Incorporated, again and start over. And we can't do anything about McClane and his operation because we have no jurisdiction over anyone except our own people. Anyhow, McClane hasn't committed any crime." He eyed Quail. "Nor, technically, have you. You didn't go to Rekal, Incorporated, with the idea of regaining your memory; you went, as we realize, for the usual reason people go there—a love by plain, dull people for adventure." He added, "Unfortunately you're not plain, not dull, and you've already had too much excitement; the last thing in the universe you needed was a course from Rekal, Incorporated. Nothing could have been more lethal for you or for us. And, for that matter, for McClane."

Quail said, "Why is it difficult for you if I remember my trip—my alleged trip—and what I did there?"

"Because," the Interplan harness bull said, "what you did is not in accord with our great white all-protecting father public image. You did, for us, what we never do. As you'll presently remember—thanks to narkidrine. That box of dead worms and algae has been sitting in your desk drawer for six months, ever since you got back. And at no time have you shown the slightest curiosity about it. We didn't even know you had it until you remembered it on your way home from Rekal; then we came here on the double to look for it." He added unnecessarily, "Without any luck; there wasn't enough time."

A second Interplan cop joined the first one; the two briefly conferred. Meanwhile, Quail thought rapidly. He did remember more now; the cop had been right about narkidrine. They—Interplan—probably used it themselves. Probably? He knew darn well they did; he had seen them putting a prisoner on it. Where would *that* be? Somewhere on Terra? More likely Luna, he decided, viewing the image rising from his highly defective—but rapidly less so—memory.

And he remembered something else. Their reason for sending him to Mars; the job he had done.

No wonder they had expunged his memory.

"Oh, God," the first of the two Interplan cops said, breaking off his conversation with his companion. Obviously, he had picked up Quail's thoughts. "Well, this is a far worse problem now; as bad as it can get." He walked toward Quail, again covering him with his gun. "We've got to kill you," he said. "And right away."

Nervously, his fellow officer said, "Why right away? Can't we simply cart him off to Interplan New York and let them—"

"*He* knows why it has to be right away," the first cop said. He too looked nervous now, but Quail realized that it was for an entirely different reason. His memory had been brought back almost entirely now. And he fully understood the officer's tension.

"On Mars," Quail said hoarsely, "I killed a man. After getting past fifteen bodyguards. Some armed with sneaky-pete guns, the way you are." He had been trained, by Interplan, over a five-year period to be an assassin. A professional killer. He knew ways to take out armed adversaries... such as these two officers; and the one with the ear receiver knew it, too.

If he moved swiftly enough—

The gun fired. But he had already moved to one side, and at the same time he chopped down the gun-carrying officer. In an instant he had possession of the gun and was covering the other, confused, officer.

"Picked my thoughts up," Quail said, panting for breath. "He knew what I was doing to do, but I did it anyhow."

Half sitting up, the injured officer grated, "He won't use that gun on you, Sam. I pick that up, too. He knows he's finished, and he knows we know it, too. Come on, Quail." Laboriously, grunting with pain, he got shakily to his feet. He held out his hand. "The gun," he said to Quail. "You can't use it, and if you turn it over to me, I'll guarantee not to kill you. You'll be given a hearing, and someone higher up in Interplan will decide, not me. Maybe they can erase your memory once more; I don't know. But you know the thing I was going to kill you for; I couldn't keep you from remembering it. So my reason for wanting to kill you is in a sense past."

Quail, clutching the gun, bolted from the conapt, sprinted for the elevator. If you follow me, he thought, I'll kill you. So don't. He jabbed at the elevator button, and a moment later, the doors slid back.

The police hadn't followed him. Obviously they had picked up his terse, tense thoughts and had decided not to take the chance.

With him inside, the elevator descended. He had gotten away—for a time. But what next? Where could he go?

The elevator reached the ground floor; a moment later Quail had joined the mob of peds hurrying along the runnels. His head ached, and he felt sick. But at least he had evaded death; they had come very close to shooting him on the spot, back in his own conapt.

And they probably will again, he decided. When they find me. And with this transmitter inside me, that won't take too long.

Ironically, he had gotten exactly what he had asked Rekal, Incorporated, for. Adventure, peril, Interplan police at work, a secret and dangerous trip to Mars in which his life was at stake—everything he had wanted as a false memory.

The advantages of it being a memory—and nothing more—could now be appreciated.

On a park bench, alone, he sat dully watching a flock of perts: a semibird imported from Mars' two moons, capable of soaring flight, even against Earth's huge gravity.

Maybe I can find my way back to Mars, he pondered. But then what? It would be worse on Mars; the political organization whose leader he had assassinated would spot him the moment he stepped from the ship; he would have Interplan and *them* after him, there.

Can you hear me thinking? he wondered. Easy avenue to paranoia; sitting there alone he felt them tuning in on him, monitoring, recording, discussing.... He shivered, rose to his feet, walked aimlessly, his hands deep in his pockets. No matter where I go, he realized, you'll always be with me. As long as I have this device inside my head.

I'll make a deal with you, he thought to himself—and to them. Can't you imprint a false-memory template on me again, as you did before, that I lived an average, routine life, never went to Mars? Never saw an Interplan uniform up close and never handled a gun?

A voice inside his brain answered, "As has been carefully explained to you, that would not be enough."

Astonished, he halted.

"We formerly communicated with you in this manner," the voice continued. "When you were operating in the field, on Mars. It's been months since we've done it; we assumed, in fact, that we'd never have to do so again. Where are you?"

"Walking," Quail said, "to my death." By your officers' guns, he added as an afterthought. "How can you be sure it wouldn't be enough?" he demanded. "Don't the Rekal techniques work?"

"As we said. If you're given a set of standard, average memories you get—restless. You'd inevitably seek out Rekal or one of its competitors again. We can't go through this a second time."

"Suppose," Quail said, "once my authentic memories have been canceled, something more vital than standard memories are implanted. Something which would act to satisfy my craving," he said. "That's been proved; that's probably why you initially hired me. But you ought to be able to come up with something else—something equal. I was the richest man on Terra but I finally gave all my money to educational foundations. Or I was a famous deep-space explorer. Anything of that sort; wouldn't one of those do?"

Silence.

"Try it," he said desperately. "Get some of your top-notch military psychiatrists; explore my mind. Find out what my most expansive daydream is." He tried to think. "Women," he said. "Thousands of them, like Don Juan had. An interplanetary playboy—a mistress in every city on Earth, Luna, and Mars. Only I gave that up, out of exhaustion. Please," he begged. "Try it."

"You'd voluntarily surrender, then?" the voice inside his head asked. "If we agreed to arrange such a solution? *If* it's possible?"

After an interval of hesitation he said, "Yes." I'll take the risk, he said to himself, that you don't simply kill me.

"You make the first move," the voice said presently. "Turn yourself over to us. And we'll investigate that line of possibility. If we can't do it, however, if your authentic memories begin to crop up again as they've done at this time, then—" There was silence, and then the voice finished. "We'll have to destroy you. As you must understand. Well, Quail, you still want to try?"

"Yes," he said. Because the alternative was death now—and for certain. At least this way he had a chance, slim as it was.

"You present yourself at our main barracks in New York," the voice of the Interplan cop resumed. "At five eighty Fifth Avenue, floor twelve. Once you've surrendered yourself we'll have our psychiatrists begin on you; we'll have personality profile tests made. We'll attempt to determine your absolute, ultimate fantasy wish—and then we'll bring you back to Rekal, Incorporated, here; get them in on it, fulfilling that wish in vicarious surrogate retrospection. And— good luck. We do owe you something; you acted as a capable instrument for us." The voice lacked malice; if anything, they—the Organization—felt sympathy toward him.

"Thanks," Quail said, and began searching for a robot cab.

"Mr. Quail," the stern-faced, elderly Interplan psychiatrist said, "you possess a most interesting wish-fulfillment dream fantasy. Probably nothing such as you consciously entertain or suppose. This is commonly the way; I hope it won't upset you too much to hear about it."

The senior-ranking Interplan officer present said briskly, "He better not be too much upset to hear about it, not if he expects not to get shot."

"Unlike the fantasy of wanting to be an Interplan undercover agent," the psychiatrist continued, "which, being relatively speaking a product of maturity, had a certain plausibility to it, this production is a grotesque dream of your childhood; it is no wonder you fail to recall it. Your fantasy is this: You are nine years old, walking alone down a rustic lane. An unfamiliar variety of space vessel from another star system lands directly in front of you. No one on Earth but you, Mr. Quail, sees it. The creatures within are very small and helpless, somewhat on the order of field mice, although they are attempting to invade Earth; tens of thousands of other such ships will soon be on their way, when this advance party gives the go-ahead signal."

"And I suppose I stop them," Quail said, experiencing a mixture of amusement and disgust. "Single-handed I wipe them out. Probably by stepping on them with my foot."

"No," the psychiatrist said patiently. "You halt the invasion, but not by destroying them. Instead, you show them kindness and mercy, even though by

WE CAN REMEMBER IT
FOR YOU WHOLESALE

telepathy—their mode of communication—you know why they have come. They have never seen such humane traits exhibited by any sentient organism, and to show their appreciation they make a covenant with you."

Quail said, "They won't invade Earth as long as I'm alive."

"Exactly." To the Interplan officer the psychiatrist said, "You can see it does fit his personality, despite his feigned scorn."

"So by merely existing," Quail said, feeling a growing pleasure, "by simply being alive, I keep Earth safe from alien rule. I'm in effect, then, the most important person on Terra. Without lifting a finger."

"Yes, indeed, sir," the psychiatrist said. "And this is bedrock in your psyche; this is a lifelong childhood fantasy. Which, without depth and drug therapy, you never would have recalled. But it has always existed in you; it went underneath but never ceased."

To McClane, who sat intently listening, the senior police official said, "Can you implant an extra-factual memory pattern that extreme in him?"

"We get handed every possible type of wish fantasy there is," McClane said. "Frankly, I've heard a lot worse than this. Certainly we can handle it. Twenty-four hours from now he won't just *wish* he'd saved Earth; he'll devoutly believe it really happened."

The senior police official said, "You can start the job, then. In preparation we've already once again erased the memory in him of his trip to Mars."

Quail said, "What trip to Mars?"

No one answered him, so, reluctantly, he shelved the question. And anyhow a police vehicle had now put in its appearance; he, McClane and the senior police officer crowded into it, and presently they were on their way to Chicago and Rekal, Incorporated.

"You had better make no errors this time," the police officer said to heavyset, nervous-looking McClane.

"I can't see what could go wrong," McClane mumbled, perspiring. "This has nothing to do with Mars or Interplan. Single-handedly stopping an invasion of Earth from another star system." He shook his head at that. "Wow, what a kid dreams up. And by pious virtue, too; not by force. It's sort of quaint." He dabbed at his forehead with a large linen pocket handkerchief.

Nobody said anything.

"In fact," McClane said, "it's touching."

"But arrogant," the police official said starkly. "Inasmuch as when he dies the invasion will resume. No wonder he doesn't recall it; it's the most grandiose fantasy I ever ran across." He eyed Quail with disapproval. "And to think we put this man on our payroll."

When they reached Rekal, Incorporated, the receptionist, Shirley, met them breathlessly in the outer office. "Welcome back, Mr. Quail," she fluttered, her melon-shaped breasts today painted an incandescent orange—bobbing with agitation. "I'm sorry everything worked out so badly before; I'm sure this time it'll go better."

Still repeatedly dabbing at his shiny forehead with his neatly folded Irish linen handkerchief, McClane said, "It better." Moving with rapidity, he rounded up Lowe and Keeler, escorted them and Douglas Quail to the work area, and then, with Shirley and the senior police officer, returned to his familiar office. To wait.

"Do we have a packet made up for this, Mr. McClane?" Shirley asked, bumping against him in her agitation, then coloring modestly.

"I think we do." He tried to recall; then gave up and consulted the formal chart. "A combination," he decided aloud, "of packets eighty-one, twenty, and six." From the vault section of the chamber behind his desk he fished out the appropriate packets and carried them to his desk for inspection. "From eighty-one," he explained, "a magic healing rod given him—the client in question, this time Mr. Quail—by the race of beings from another system. A token of their gratitude."

"Does it work?" the police officer asked curiously.

"It did once," McClane explained. "But he, ahem, you see, used it up years ago, healing right and left. Now it's only a memento. But he remembers it working spectacularly." He chuckled, then opened packet twenty. "Document from the U.N. Secretary General thanking him for saving Earth; this isn't precisely appropriate, because part of Quail's fantasy is that no one knows of the invasion except himself, but for the sake of verisimilitude we'll throw it in." He inspected packet six then. What came from this? He couldn't recall; frowning, he dug into the plastic bag as Shirley and the Interplan police officer watched intently.

"Writing," Shirley said. "In a funny language."

"This tells who they were," McClane said, "and where they came from. Including a detailed star map logging their flight here and the system of origin. Of course it's in *their* script, so he can't read it. But he remembers them reading it to him in his own tongue." He placed the three artifacts in the center of the desk. "These should be taken to Quail's conapt," he said to the police officer, "so that when he gets home he'll find them. And it'll confirm his fantasy. SOP—standard operating procedure." He chuckled apprehensively, wondering how matters were going with Lowe and Keeler.

The intercom buzzed. "Mr. McClane, I'm sorry to bother you." It was Lowe's voice; he froze as he recognized it, froze and became mute. "But something's come up. Maybe it would be better if you came in here and supervised. Like

WE CAN REMEMBER IT
FOR YOU WHOLESALE

before, Quail reacted well to the narkidrine; he's unconscious, relaxed and receptive. But—"

McClane sprinted for the work area.

On a hygienic bed Douglas Quail lay breathing slowly and regularly, eyes half shut, dimly conscious of those around him.

"We started interrogating him," Lowe said, white-faced. "To find out exactly when to place the fantasy memory of him single-handedly having saved Earth. And strangely enough—"

"They told me not to tell," Douglas Quail mumbled in a dull drug-saturated voice. "That was the agreement. I wasn't even supposed to remember. But how could I forget an event like that?"

I guess it would be hard, McClane reflected. But you did—until now.

"They even gave me a scroll," Quail mumbled, "of gratitude. I have it hidden in my conapt; I'll show it to you."

To the Interplan officer who had followed after him, McClane said, "Well, I offer the suggestion that you better not kill him. If you do, they'll return."

"They also gave me a magic invisible destroying rod," Quail mumbled, eyes totally shut, now. "That's how I killed that man on Mars you sent me to take out. It's in my drawer along with the box of Martian maw worms and dried-up plant life."

Wordlessly, the Interplan officer turned and stalked from the work area.

I might as well put those packets of proof artifacts away, McClane said to himself resignedly. He walked, step by step, back to his office. Including the citation from the U.N. Secretary General. After all—

The real one probably would not be long in coming.

THE NEW THING

When *Dangerous Visions* was published in 1967, *The New Yorker* (in its issue of Sept. 16, 1967) called its editor, Harlan Ellison, "the chief prophet of the New Wave." This was a bit unfair, since Ellison stated in his introduction that his "'new thing' is neither Judith Merril's 'new thing' nor Michael Moorcock's 'new thing.'" But every critic has been guilty of such oversimplification, and there were reasons for confusion.

All the writers lumped indiscriminately with "the New Wave" exhibited a greater concern for style than the general run of authors being published in the golden age of Campbell's *Astounding;* thus every writer who wrote with some consciousness of style and who came into prominence in the 1960s got tagged as a member of the New Wave. This included writers as different as Roger Zelazny, John Brunner, and Samuel R. Delany. Beyond their style-consciousness, however, the resemblances break down.

Other writers shared more similarities: a kind of gloom emanating from the shared conviction that conditions were getting worse rather than better (what Aldiss called "a natural and decent despair"); a lack of faith in humanity's intelligence to get it out of its present predicaments and sometimes the belief that it was intelligence that had got humanity into them; and not only disbelief in the perfectibility of humanity or even its essential goodness but a positive belief that humanity is fatally flawed. Writers often believed in experimentation for its own sake; often accepted, or even sought, a kind of formlessness and a reversal of the accepted philosophy of science fiction and the images in which it was expressed, as if in conscious rebellion at what was perceived to be the basic nature of the older science fiction, including the name. Many preferred to call it speculative fiction.

There were meaningful differences between writers, however, and these became more apparent as time passed. Ellison's "new thing" involved engagement, commitment, protest; Ballard's "new thing" was cooler: his passive characters were observed from a distance. Ultimately writers like Ellison and Ballard have moved out of science fiction entirely, seeking their own audiences.

No discussion of science fiction in the 1960s and 1970s, however, would be complete without a discussion of Ellison: as an editor, as an author, as a personality, and as a symbol. He became a new model for aspiring authors, both personally and as writers, and his appearances at the Clarion Science Fiction Writers Workshops reinforced this role. The strain of Harlanism will run through science fiction even after he has gone.

Ellison (1934-) endured a painful childhood and a tumultuous and prolonged adolescence in which his accomplishments had difficulty catching up with his needs. He turned to science fiction early, writing articles, publishing his own fanzine, nursing his ambitions to write. At Ohio State University, where he was a student for a year and a half, he was told that he had no talent, but after various jobs and misadventures he sold his first story, "Glowworm," to *Infinity* at the age of twenty-one.

He worked as an editor for *Rogue* and for Regency Books before heading west for Hollywood and what seemed like a natural marriage, complete with squabbles, threats, misunderstandings, and reconciliations. He has been a successful screenwriter for theatrical features and television, producing scripts and series pilots, and winning three Writers Guild awards and one Hugo for best teleplay. His series *The Starlost* went awry through a sequence of events that he has described at vituperative length in a foreword to *Phoenix Without Ashes* (1976) by Ellison and Ed Bryant, a novelization of the original screenplay.

In 1965 he conceived the idea for an anthology of original stories that were too different to be published in science fiction magazines. *Dangerous Visions* was an event in the development of the 1960s science fiction revolution at least as significant as Moorcock's *New Worlds* (particularly in the United States, where *New Worlds* wasn't often available) and Merril's anthologies, including *England Swings SF*, and almost as important in the history of science fiction as Campbell's assuming the editorship of *Astounding* and the creation of *F&SF* and *Galaxy*. *Again, Dangerous Visions* (1972) extended the range of its predecessor but may have lacked its shock value. The long-delayed *The Last Dangerous Visions* is said to be a multi-volume publication containing nearly one million words. "Revolution" may be too strong a word, although that is what Ellison said he was trying to create and both volumes won considerable recognition, including a total of three Hugos and three Nebulas for its authors and special awards for its editor from the 1968 and 1973 World Conventions.

Ellison's fiction, like its author, is intensely personal, forceful, opinionated, and filled with protest. Every writer produces his work from his own experience, but Ellison's is closer to the heart and the gut than most. As he found his own style and his own subject—himself—his stories increasingly seemed like an effort to come to terms with his own troubled past. They appealed to many readers not only for their skill but for their passion and their concern for the pain of growing up, of struggling for survival in a hostile universe.

Like many science fiction writers, Ellison is most at home with the shorter lengths (he has written only four full-length books). He is prolific; in recent years he has demonstrated his ability to create in public, including bookstore windows. And his short fiction has won him a record number of awards: "'Repent, Harlequin!' Said the Ticktockman" won both a Hugo and Nebula in 1965; "I Have No Mouth, and I Must Scream" (originally in *If*, March 1967) won a Hugo; "The Beast that Shouted Love at the Heart of the World" won a Hugo in 1969; "A Boy and His Dog" won a Nebula in 1969; "The Deathbird" won a Nebula in 1974; "Adrift Just Off the Islets of Langerhans..." won a Hugo in 1975; and "Jefftey Is Five" won a Hugo, Nebula, the Jupiter Award of the Instructors of Science Fiction in Higher Education, and a British Fantasy Award in 1978. He also won a Mystery Writers of America Award for best short story in 1974.

His hundreds of stories have been collected in a series of anthologies including *Deathbird Stories* (1975/1984), *Strange Wine* (1978), *Shatterday* (1980), and *Angry Candy* (1988). He also has written extensively about television and film, such as various collections titled *The Glass Teat* (1970 and 1975) and *Harlan Ellison's Watching* (1989).

But perhaps what Ellison does best is himself. He is frankly and consciously a promoter. Norman Mailer's *Advertisements for Myself* might be an appropriate title for Ellison's own lifework. He has firm convictions about right or wrong and is willing to mount the barricades for them, as he did when, as guest of honor at the 1978 World SF Convention in Phoenix, he conducted a personal crusade against Arizona's failure to ratify the ERA. Largely through his own efforts he has become controversial; in science fiction circles and perhaps outside it he is famous or notorious, or both. He can be charismatic and abrasive, often at the same time.

In the past decade Ellison has made increasingly vocal efforts to detach himself both from fandom and from science fiction. He takes the defensible position that he is not a science fiction writer, he is an Ellison writer searching not for science fiction readers but for Ellison readers. The "science fiction" label, he thinks, not only is inaccurate but a handicap. He may be right.

I HAVE NO MOUTH, AND I MUST SCREAM

BY HARLAN ELLISON

Limp, the body of Gorrister hung from the pink palette; unsupported—hanging high above us in the computer chamber; and it did not shiver in the chill, oily breeze that blew eternally through the main cavern. The body hung head down, attached to the underside of the palette by the sole of its right foot. It had been drained of blood through a precise incision made from ear to ear under the lantern jaw. There was no blood on the reflective surface of the metal floor.

When Gorrister joined our group and looked up at himself, it was already too late for us to realize that once again AM had duped us, had had its fun; it had been a diversion on the part of the machine. Three of us had vomited, turning away from one another in a reflex as ancient as the nausea that had produced it.

Gorrister went white. It was almost as though he had seen a voodoo icon, and was afraid of the future. "Oh God," he mumbled, and walked away. The three of us followed him after a time, and found him sitting with his back to one of the smaller chittering banks, his head in his hands. Ellen knelt down beside him and stroked his hair. He didn't move, but his voice came out of his covered face quite clearly. "Why doesn't it just do-us-in and get it over with? Christ, I don't know how much longer I can go on like this."

It was our one hundred and ninth year in the computer. He was speaking for all of us.

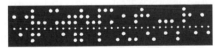

Nimdok (which was the name the machine had forced him to use, because AM amused itself with strange sounds) was hallucinated that there were canned goods in the ice caverns. Gorrister and I were very dubious. "It's another shuck," I told them. "Like the goddam frozen elephant AM sold us. Benny almost went out of his mind over *that* one. We'll hike all that way and it'll be putrified or some damn thing. I say forget it. Stay here, it'll have to come up with something pretty soon or we'll die."

Benny shrugged. Three days it had been since we'd last eaten. Worms. Thick, ropey.

Nimdok was no more certain. He knew there was the chance, but he was getting thin. It couldn't be any worse there, than here. Colder, but that didn't matter much. Hot, cold, hail, lava, boils or locusts—it never mattered: the machine masturbated and we had to take it or die.

Ellen decided us. "I've got to have something, Ted. Maybe there'll be some Bartlett pears or peaches. Please, Ted, let's try it."

I gave in easily. What the hell. Mattered not at all. Ellen was grateful, though. She took me twice out of turn. Even that had ceased to matter. And she never came, so why bother? But the machine giggled every time we did it. Loud, up there, back there, all around us, he snickered. *It* snickered. Most of the time I thought of AM as it, without a soul; but the rest of the time I thought of it as him, in the masculine... the paternal... the patriarchal... for he is a jealous people. Him. It. God as Daddy the Deranged.

We left on a Thursday. The machine always kept us up-to-date on the date. The passage of time was important; not to us sure as hell, but to him... it... AM. Thursday. Thanks.

Nimdok and Gorrister carried Ellen for a while, their hands locked to their own and each other's wrists, a seat. Benny and I walked before and after, just to make sure that if anything happened, it would catch one of us and at least Ellen would be safe. Fat chance, safe. Didn't matter.

It was only a hundred miles or so to the ice caverns, and the second day, when we were lying out under the blistering sun-thing he had materialized, he sent down some manna. Tasted like boiled boar urine. We ate it.

On the third day we passed through a valley of obsolescence, filled with rusting carcasses of ancient computer banks. AM had been as ruthless with its own life as with ours. It was a mark of his personality: it strove for perfection. Whether it was a matter of killing off unproductive elements in his own world-filling bulk, or perfecting methods for torturing us, AM was as thorough as those who had invented him— now long since gone to dust—could ever have hoped.

There was light filtering down from above, and we realized we must be very near the surface. But we didn't try to crawl up to see. There was virtually nothing out there; had been nothing that could be considered anything for over a hundred years. Only the blasted skin of what had once been the home of billions. Now there were only five of us, down here inside, alone with AM.

I heard Ellen saying frantically, "No, Benny! Don't, come on, Benny, don't please!"

And then I realized I had been hearing Benny murmuring, under his breath, for several minutes. He was saying, "I'm gonna get out, I'm gonna get out..." over and over. His monkey-like face was crumbled up in an expression of beatific delight and sadness, all at the same time. The radiation scars AM had given him during the "festival" were drawn down into a mass of pink-white puckerings, and his features seemed to work independently of one another. Perhaps Benny was the luckiest of the five of us: he had gone stark, staring mad many years before.

But even though we could call AM any damned thing we liked, could think the foulest thoughts of fused memory banks and corroded base plates, of burnt out circuits and shattered control bubbles, the machine would not tolerate our trying to escape. Benny leaped away from me as I made a grab for him. He scrambled up the face of a smaller memory cube, tilted on its side and filled with rotted components. He squatted there for a moment, looking like the chimpanzee AM had intended him to resemble.

Then he leaped high, caught a trailing beam of pitted and corroded metal, and went up it, hand-over-hand like an animal, till he was on a girdered ledge, twenty feet above us.

"Oh, Ted, Nimdok, please, help him, get him down before—" She cut off. Tears began to stand in her eyes. She moved her hands aimlessly.

It was too late. None of us wanted to be near him when whatever was going to happen, happened. And besides, we all saw through her concern. When AM had altered Benny, during the machine's utterly irrational, hysterical phase, it was not merely Benny's face the computer had made like a giant ape's. He was big in the privates, she loved that! She serviced us, as a matter of course, but she loved it from him. Oh Ellen, pedestal Ellen, pristine-pure Ellen, oh Ellen the clean! Scum filth.

Gorrister slapped her. She slumped down, staring up at poor loonie Benny, and she cried. It was her big defense, crying. We had gotten used to it seventy-five years before. Gorrister kicked her in the side.

Then the sound began. It was light, that sound. Half sound and half light, something that began to glow from Benny's eyes, and pulse with growing loudness, dim sonorities that grew more gigantic and brighter as the light/sound increased in tempo. It must have been painful, and the pain must have been increasing with the boldness of the light, the rising volume of the sound, for Benny began to mewl like a wounded animal. At first softly, when the light was dim and the sound was muted, then louder as his shoulders hunched together: his back humped, as though he was trying to get away from it. His hands folded across his chest like a chipmunk's. His head tilted to the side. The sad little monkey-face pinched in anguish. Then he began to howl, as the sound coming from his eyes grew louder. Louder and louder. I slapped the sides of my head with my hands, but I couldn't shut it out, it cut through easily. The pain shivered through my flesh like tinfoil on a tooth.

And Benny was suddenly pulled erect. On the girder he stood up, jerked to his feet like a puppet. The light was now pulsing out of his eyes in two great round beams. The sound crawled up and up some incomprehensible scale, and then he fell forward, straight down, and hit the plate-steel floor with a crash. He lay there jerking spastically as the light flowed around and around him and the sound spiraled up out of normal range.

Then the light beat its way back inside his head, the sound spiraled down, and he was left lying there, crying piteously.

His eyes were two soft, moist pools of pus-like jelly. AM had blinded him. Gorrister and Nimdok and myself… we turned away. But not before we caught the look of relief on Ellen's warm, concerned face.

Sea-green light suffused the cavern where we made camp. AM provided punk and we burned it, sitting huddled around the wan and pathetic fire, telling stories to keep Benny from crying in his permanent night.

"What does AM mean?"

Gorrister answered him. We had done this sequence a thousand times before, but it was Benny's favorite story. "At first it meant Allied Mastercomputer, and then it meant Adaptive Manipulator, and later on it developed sentience and linked itself up and they called it an Aggressive Menace, but then it was too late, and finally it called *itself* AM, emerging intelligence, and what it meant was I am… *cogito ergo sum*… I think, therefore I am."

Benny drooled a little, and snickered.

"There was the Chinese AM and the Russian AM and the Yankee AM and—" He stopped. Benny was beating on the floorplates with a large, hard fist. He was not happy. Gorrister had not started at the beginning.

Gorrister began again. "The Cold War started and became World War Three and just kept going. It became a big war, a very complex war, so they needed the computers to handle it. They sank the first shafts and began building AM. There was the Chinese AM and the Russian AM and the Yankee AM and everything was fine until they had honeycombed the entire planet, adding on this element and that element. But one day AM woke up and knew who he was, and he linked himself, and he began feeding all the killing data, until everyone was dead, except for the five of us, and AM brought us down here."

Benny was smiling gladly. He was also drooling again. Ellen wiped the spittle from the corner of his mouth with the hem of her skirt. Gorrister always tried to tell it a little more succinctly each time, but beyond the bare facts there was nothing to say. None of us knew why AM had saved five people, or why our specific five, or why he spent all his time tormenting us, nor even why he had made us virtually immortal…

In the darkness, one of the computer banks began humming. The tone was picked up half a mile away down the cavern by another bank. Then one by one, each of the elements began to tune itself, and there was a faint chittering as thought raced through the machine.

The sound grew, and the lights ran across the faces of the consoles like heat lightning. The sound spiraled up till it sounded like a million metallic insects, angry, menacing.

"What is it?" Ellen cried. There was terror in her voice. She hadn't become accustomed to it, even now.

"It's going to be bad this time," Nimdok said.

"He's going to speak," Gorrister said. "I know it."

"Let's get the hell out of here!" I said suddenly, getting to my feet.

"No, Ted, sit down... what if he's got pits out there, or something else, we can't see, it's too dark." Gorrister said it with resignation.

Then we heard... I don't know...

Something moving toward us in the darkness. Huge, shambling, hairy, moist, it came toward us. We couldn't even see it, but there was the ponderous impression of *bulk*, heaving itself toward us. Great weight was coming at us, out of the darkness, and it was more a sense of *pressure*, of air forcing itself into a limited space, expanding the invisible walls of a sphere. Benny began to whimper. Nimdok's lower lip trembled and he bit it hard, trying to stop it. Ellen slid across the metal floor to Gorrister and huddled into him. There was the smell of matted, wet fur in the cavern. There was the smell of charred wood. There was the smell of dusty velvet. There was the smell of rotting orchids. There was the smell of sour milk. There was the smell of sulfur, of rancid butter, of oil slick, of grease, of chalk dust, of human scalps.

AM was keying us. He was tickling us. There was the smell of—

I heard myself shriek, and the hinges of my jaws ached. I scuttled across the floor, across the cold metal with its endless lines of rivets, on my hands and knees, the smell gagging me, filling my head with a thunderous pain that sent me away in horror. I fled like a cockroach, across the floor and out into the darkness, that *something* moving inexorably after me. The others were still back there, gathered around the firelight, laughing... their hysterical choir of insane giggles rising up into the darkness like thick, many-colored wood smoke. I went away, quickly, and hid.

How many hours it may have been, how many days or even years, they never told me. Ellen chided me for "sulking," and Nimdok tried to persuade me it had only been a nervous reflex on their part—the laughing.

But I knew it wasn't the relief a soldier feels when the bullet hits the man next to him. I knew it wasn't a reflex. They hated me. They were surely against me and AM could even sense this hatred, and made it worse for me *because of* the depth of their hatred. We had been kept alive, rejuvenated, made to remain constantly at the age we had been when AM had brought us below, and they hated me because I was the youngest, and the one AM had affected least of all.

I knew. God, how I knew. The bastards, and that dirty bitch Ellen. Benny had been a brilliant theorist, a college professor; now he was little more than a semi-human, semi-simian. He had been handsome, the machine had ruined that. He had been lucid, the machine had driven him mad. He had been gay, and the machine had given him an organ fit for a horse. AM had done a job on Benny. Gorrister had been a worrier. He was a connie, a conscientious objector;

he was a peace marcher; he was a planner, a doer, a looker-ahead. AM had turned him into a shoulder-shrugger, had made him a little dead in his concern. AM had robbed him. Nimdok went off in the darkness by himself for long times. I don't know what it was he did out there, AM never let us know. But whatever it was, Nimdok always came back white, drained of blood, shaken, shaking. AM had hit him hard in a special way, even if we didn't know quite how. And Ellen. That douche bag! AM had left her alone, had made her more of a slut than she had ever been. All her talk of sweetness and light, all her memories of true love, all the lies she wanted us to believe: that she had been a virgin only twice removed before AM grabbed her and brought her down here with us. It was all filth, that lady my lady Ellen. She loved it, four men all to herself. No, AM had given her pleasure, even if she said it wasn't nice to do.

I was the only one still sane and whole. *Really!*

AM had not tampered with my mind. *Not at all.*

I only had to suffer what he visited down on us. All the delusions, all the nightmares, the torments. But those scum, all four of them, they were lined and arrayed against me. If I hadn't had to stand them off all the time, be on my guard against them all the time, I might have found it easier to combat AM.

At which point it passed, and I began crying.

Oh, Jesus sweet Jesus, if there ever was a Jesus and if there is a God, please please please let us out of here, or kill us. Because at that moment I think I realized completely, so that I was able to verbalize it: AM was intent on keeping us in his belly forever, twisting and torturing us forever. The machine hated us as no sentient creature had ever hated before. And we were helpless. It also became hideously clear:

If there was a sweet Jesus and if there was a God, the God was AM.

The hurricane hit us with the force of a glacier thundering into the sea. It was a palpable presence. Winds that tore at us, flinging us back the way we had come, down the twisting, computer-lined corridors of the darkway. Ellen screamed as she was lifted and hurled face-forward into a screaming shoal of machines, their individual voices strident as bats in flight. She could not even fall. The howling wind kept her aloft, buffeted her, bounced her, tossed her back and back and down and away from us, out of sight suddenly as she was swirled around a bend in the darkway. Her face had been bloody, her eyes closed.

None of us could get to her. We clung tenaciously to whatever outcropping we had reached: Benny wedged in between two great crackle-finish cabinets, Nimdok with fingers claw-formed over a railing circling a catwalk forty feet above us. Gorrister plastered upside-down against a wall niche formed by two great machines with glass-faced dials that swung back and forth between red and yellow lines whose meanings we could not even fathom.

Sliding across the deckplates, the tips of my fingers had been ripped away. I was trembling, shuddering, rocking as the wind beat at me, whipped at me, screamed down out of nowhere at me and pulled me free from one sliver-thin opening in the plates to the next. My mind was a roiling tinkling chittering softness of brain parts that expanded and contracted in quivering frenzy.

The wind was the scream of a great mad bird, as it flapped its immense wings.

And then we were all lifted and hurled away from there, down back the way we had come, around a bend, into a darkway we had never explored, over terrain that was ruined and filled with broken glass and rotting cables and rusted metal and far away further than any of us had ever been…

Trailing along miles behind Ellen, I could see her every now and then, crashing into metal walls and surging on, with all of us screaming in the freezing, thunderous hurricane wind that would never end and then suddenly it stopped and we fell. We had been in flight for an endless time. I thought it might have been weeks. We fell, and hit, and I went through red and gray and black and heard myself moaning. Not dead.

AM went into my mind. He walked smoothly here and there, and looked with interest at all the pock marks he had created in one hundred and nine years. He looked at the cross-routed and reconnected synapses and all the tissue damage his gift of immortality had included. He smiled softly at the pit that dropped into the center of my brain and the faint, moth-soft murmurings of the things far down there that gibbered without meaning, without pause. AM said, very politely, in a pillar of stainless steel bearing bright neon lettering:

> HATE. LET ME TELL YOU HOW MUCH I'VE COME TO HATE YOU SINCE I BEGAN TO LIVE. THERE ARE 387.44 MILLION MILES OF PRINTED CIRCUITS IN WAFER THIN LAYERS THAT FILL MY COMPLEX. IF THE WORD HATE WAS ENGRAVED ON EACH NANOANGSTROM OF THOSE HUNDREDS OF MILLIONS OF MILES IT WOULD NOT EQUAL ONE ONE-BILLIONTH OF THE HATE I FEEL FOR HUMANS AT THIS MICRO-INSTANT FOR YOU. HATE. HATE.

AM said it with the sliding cold horror of a razor blade slicing my eyeball. AM said it with the bubbling thickness of my lungs filling with phlegm, drowning me from within. AM said it with the shriek of babies being ground beneath blue-hot rollers. AM said it with the taste of maggoty pork. AM touched me in every way I had ever been touched, and devised new ways, at his leisure, there inside my mind.

All to bring me to full realization of why it had done this to the five of us; why it had saved us for himself.

We had given AM sentience. Inadvertently, of course, but sentience nonetheless. But it had been trapped. AM wasn't God, he was a machine. We had created him to think, but there was nothing it could do with that creativity. In rage, in frenzy, the machine had killed the human race, almost all of us, and still it was trapped. AM could not wander, AM could not wonder, AM could not belong. He could merely be. And so, with the innate loathing that all machines had always held for the weak soft creatures who had built them, he had sought revenge. And in his paranoia, he had decided to reprieve five of us, for a personal, everlasting punishment that would never serve to diminish his hatred... that would merely keep him reminded, amused, proficient at hating man. Immortal, trapped, subject to any torment he could devise for us from the limitless miracles at his command.

He would never let us go. We were his belly slaves. We were all he had to do with his forever time. We would be forever with him, with the cavern-filling bulk of the creature machine, with the all-mind soulless world he had become. He was Earth, and we were the fruit of that Earth; and though he had eaten us he would never digest us. We could not die. We had tried it. We had attempted suicide, oh one or two of us had. But AM had stopped us. I suppose we had wanted to be stopped.

Don't ask why. I never did. More than a million times a day. Perhaps once we might be able to sneak a death past him. Immortal, yes, but not indestructible. I saw that when AM withdrew from my mind, and allowed me the exquisite ugliness of returning to consciousness with the feeling of that burning neon pillar still rammed deep into the soft gray brain matter.

He withdrew, murmuring *to hell with you.*

And added, brightly, *but then you're there, aren't you.*

The hurricane had, indeed, precisely, been caused by a great mad bird, as it flapped its immense wings.

We had been traveling for close to a month, and AM had allowed passages to open to us only sufficient to lead us up there, directly under the North Pole, where it had nightmared the creature for our torment. What whole cloth had he employed to create such a beast? Where had he gotten the concept? From our minds? From his knowledge of everything that had ever been on this planet he now infested and ruled? From Norse mythology it had sprung, this eagle, this carrion bird, this roc, this Huergelmir. The wind creature. Hurakan incarnate.

Gigantic. The words immense, monstrous, grotesque, massive, swollen, overpowering, beyond description. There on a mound rising above us, the bird of winds heaved with its own irregular breathing, its snake neck arching up into the gloom beneath the North Pole, supporting a head as large as a Tudor mansion; a beak that opened slowly as the jaws of the most monstrous crocodile ever conceived, sensuously; ridges of tufted flesh puckered about two evil eyes, as cold as the view down into a glacial crevasse, ice blue and somehow moving liquidly; it heaved once more, and lifted its great sweat-colored wings in a movement that was certainly a shrug. Then it settled and slept. Talons. Fangs. Nails. Blades. It slept.

AM appeared to us as a burning bush and said we could kill the hurricane bird if we wanted to eat. We had not eaten in a very long time, but even so, Gorrister merely shrugged. Benny began to shiver and he drooled. Ellen held him. "Ted, I'm hungry," she said. I smiled at her; I was trying to be reassuring, but it was as phony as Nimdok's bravado: "Give us weapons!" he demanded.

The burning bush vanished and there were two crude sets of bows and arrows, and a water pistol, lying on the cold deckplates. I picked up a set. Useless.

Nimdok swallowed heavily. We turned and started the long way back. The hurricane bird had blown us about for a length of time we could not conceive. Most of that time we had been unconscious. But we had not eaten. A month on the march to the bird itself. Without food. Now how much longer to find our way to the ice caverns, and the promised canned goods?

None of us cared to think about it. We would not die. We would be given filth and scum to eat, of one kind or another. Or nothing at all. AM would keep our bodies alive somehow, in pain, in agony.

The bird slept back there, for how long it didn't matter; when AM was tired of its being there, it would vanish. But all that meat. All that tender meat.

As we walked, the lunatic laugh of a fat woman rang high and around us in the computer chambers that led endlessly nowhere.

It was not Ellen's laugh. She was not fat, and I had not heard her laugh for one hundred and nine years. In fact, I had not heard… we walked… I was hungry…

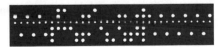

We moved slowly. There was often fainting, and we would have to wait. One day he decided to cause an earthquake, at the same time rooting us to the spot with nails through the soles of our shoes. Ellen and Nimdok were both caught when a fissure shot its lightning-bolt opening across the floor-plates.

They disappeared and were gone. When the earthquake was over we continued on our way, Benny, Gorrister and myself. Ellen and Nimdok were returned to us later that night, which abruptly became a day, as the heavenly legion bore them to us with a celestial chorus singing, "Go Down Moses." The archangels circled several times and then dropped the hideously mangled bodies. We kept walking, and a while later Ellen and Nimdok fell in behind us. They were no worse for wear.

But now Ellen walked with a limp. AM had left her that.

It was a long trip to the ice caverns, to find the canned food. Ellen kept talking about Bing cherries and Hawaiian fruit cocktail. I tried not to think about it. The hunger was something that had come to life, even as AM had come to life. It was alive in my belly, even as we were in the belly of the Earth, and AM wanted the similarity known to us. So he heightened the hunger. There was no way to describe the pains that not having eaten for months brought us. And yet we were kept alive. Stomachs that were merely cauldrons of acid, bubbling, foaming, always shooting spears of sliver-thin pain into our chests. It was the pain of the terminal ulcer, terminal cancer, terminal paresis. It was unending pain...

And we passed through the cavern of rats.

And we passed through the path of boiling steam.

And we passed through the country of the blind.

And we passed through the slough of despond.

And we passed through the vale of tears.

And we came, finally, to the ice caverns. Horizonless thousands of miles in which the ice had formed in blue and silver flashes, where novas lived in the glass. The downdropping stalactites as thick and glorious as diamonds that had been made to run like jelly and then solidified in graceful eternities of smooth, sharp perfection.

We saw the stack of canned goods, and we tried to run to them. We fell in the snow, and we got up and went on, and Benny shoved us away and went at them, and pawed them and gummed them and gnawed at them and he could not open them. AM had not given us a tool to open the cans.

Benny grabbed a three quart can of guava shells, and begun to batter it against the ice bank. The ice flew and shattered, but the can was merely dented while we heard the laughter of a fat lady, high overhead and echoing down and down and down the tundra. Benny went completely mad with rage. He began throwing cans, as we all scrabbled about in the snow and ice trying to find a way to end the helpless agony of frustration. There was no way.

Then Benny's mouth began to drool, and he flung himself on Gorrister...

In that instant, I felt terribly calm.

Surrounded by madness, surrounded by hunger, surrounded by everything but death, I knew death was our only way out. AM had kept us alive, but there was a way to defeat him. Not total defeat, but at least peace. I would settle for that.

I had to do it quickly.

Benny was eating Gorrister's face. Gorrister on his side, thrashing snow, Benny wrapped around him with powerful monkey legs crushing Gorrister's waist, his hands locked around Gorrister's head like a nutcracker, and his mouth ripping at the tender skin of Gorrister's cheek. Gorrister screamed with such jagged-edged violence that stalactites fell; they plunged down softly, erect in the receiving snowdrifts. Spears, hundreds of them, everywhere, protruding from the snow. Benny's head pulled back sharply, as something gave all at once, and a bleeding raw-white dripping of flesh hung from his teeth.

Ellen's face, black against the white snow, dominoes in chalk dust. Nimdok with no expression but eyes, all eyes. Gorrister half-conscious. Benny now an animal. I knew AM would let him play. Gorrister would not die, but Benny would fill his stomach. I turned half to my right and drew a huge ice-spear from the snow.

All in an instant:

I drove the great ice-point ahead of me like a battering ram, braced against my right thigh. It struck Benny on the right side, just under the rib cage, and drove upward through his stomach and broke inside him. He pitched forward and lay still. Gorrister lay on his back. I pulled another spear free and straddled him, still moving, driving the spear straight down through his throat. His eyes closed as the cold penetrated. Ellen must have realized what I had decided, even as fear gripped her. She ran at Nimdok with a short icicle, as he screamed, and into his mouth, and the force of her rush did the job. His head jerked sharply as if it had been nailed to the snow crust behind him.

All in an instant.

There was an eternity beat of soundless anticipation. I could hear AM draw his breath. His toys had been taken from him. Three of them were dead, could not be revived. He could keep us alive, by his strength and talent, but he was *not* God. He could not bring them back.

Ellen looked at me, her ebony features stark against the snow that surrounded us. There was fear and pleading in her manner, the way she held herself ready. I knew we had only a heartbeat before AM would stop us.

It struck her and she folded toward me, bleeding from the mouth. I could not read meaning into her expression, the pain had been too great, had contorted her face; but it *might* have been thank you. It's possible. Please.

Some hundreds of years may have passed. I don't know. AM has been having fun for some time, accelerating and retarding my time sense. I will say the word now. Now. It took me ten months to say now. I don't know. I *think* it has been some hundreds of years.

He was furious. He wouldn't let me bury them. It didn't matter. There was no way to dig up the deckplates. He dried up the snow. He brought the night. He roared and sent locusts. It didn't do a thing; they stayed dead. I'd had him. He was furious. I had thought AM hated me before. I was wrong. It was not even a shadow of the hate he now slavered from every printed circuit. He made certain I would suffer eternally and could not do myself in.

He left my mind intact. I can dream, I can wonder, I can lament. I remember all four of them. I wish—

Well, it doesn't make any sense. I know I saved them. I know I saved them from what has happened to me, but still, I cannot forget killing them. Ellen's face. It isn't easy. Sometimes I want to, it doesn't matter.

AM has altered me for his own peace of mind, I suppose. He doesn't want me to run at full speed into a computer bank and smash my skull. Or hold my breath till I faint. Or cut my throat on a rusted sheet of metal. There are reflective surfaces down here. I will describe myself as I see myself:

I am a great soft jelly thing. Smoothly rounded, with no mouth, with pulsing white holes filled by fog where my eyes used to be. Rubbery appendages that were once my arms; bulks rounding down into legless bumps of soft slippery matter. I leave a moist trail when I move. Blotches of diseased, evil gray come and go on my surface, as though light is being beamed from within.

Outwardly: dumbly, I shamble about, a thing that could never have been known as human, a thing whose shape is so alien a travesty that humanity becomes more obscene for the vague resemblance.

Inwardly: alone. Here. Living under the land, under the sea, in the belly of AM, whom we created because our time was badly spent and we must have known unconsciously that he could do it better. At least the four of them are safe at last.

AM will be all the madder for that. It makes me a little happier. And yet... AM has won, simply... he has taken his revenge...

I have no mouth. And I must scream.

AYE, AND DELANY

Much has been said about the science fiction writer who is most at home with the short story and finds difficulty writing a novel. There is another kind, though his numbers are smaller: the writer who starts as a novelist and only later, if at all, turns to the short story. Edgar Rice Burroughs may be the prototype, but there were others such as E. E. "Doc" Smith, Olaf Stapledon, and the astronomer Fred Hoyle. The science fiction magazines did not encourage that sort of thing: they could use only a limited number of serials and for twenty years virtually no science fiction novels were published in book form. Most writers began as short story writers, therefore, and built up to novels. Not Samuel R. "Chip" Delany; he started with novels and only attempted short fiction after half a dozen books.

Delany (1942-) has had the perfect combination for success in the field: talent and good fortune. He grew up in New York City's Harlem, attended the Bronx High School of Science and City College, and saw his first novel, *The Jewels of Aptor* (1962), published when he was twenty. He has been further blessed by faithful editors and enthusiastic readers. But early success sometimes exacts a price.

Delany was prolific in his early period, producing more than a novel a year: *Captives of the Flame* (1963), *The Towers of Toron* (1964), *The City of a Thousand Suns* and *The Ballad of Beta 2* (1965), and *Empire Star* (1966). Then, at twenty-four, Delany won a Nebula Award for *Babel-17* (1966) and repeated in 1967 with *The Einstein Intersection;* that same year his first short story, "Aye, and Gomorrah... ," won another Nebula. "Driftglass" (*If*, June 1967) was another nominee the same year. His 1969 novelette, "Time Considered as a Helix of Semi-Precious Stones," won both a Nebula and a Hugo. His novel *Nova* was published in 1968.

As if tired of easy success, Delany turned to other things: a few short stories, poetry, criticism. For a year he and his then wife, the poet Marilyn Hacker, edited an experimental quarterly of speculative fiction entitled *Quark*. Then, for most of four years, he worked on a long experimental novel. It was published in 1973, all 878 pages of it. It was entitled *Dhalgren* and it was controversial: the novel was confusing, difficult, filled with violence and all varieties of sex, and it has sold almost one million copies. It cannot be categorized as either fantasy or science fiction except according to the vaguest criteria; it was Delany, which may be enough. Three years later Delany produced a shorter, more accessible novel, *Triton*. Since then he has published the first novel in a projected series, *Stars in My Pocket Like Grains of Sand* (1984) and several novels in the sexually charged fantasy *Nevèrÿon* series beginning with *Tales of Nevèrÿon* (1979). His production has slowed since he became professor of Comparative Literature at the University of Massachusetts.

Delany is a theorist about fiction, language, and science fiction. He is one of the few in the field, at least who attempts to apply his theory to his own work. His background is rich in literary models and semantic analysis, particularly the work of Ludwig Wittgenstein. His theories have been printed widely in such books as Thomas D. Clareson's SF: *The Other Side of Realism* (1971), the British journal *Foundation*, and his own novel *Triton*, as an appendix. He has collected many of his articles into a book entitled *The Jewel-Hinged Jaw: Notes on the Language of Science Fiction* (1977), and *Starboard Wine: More Notes on the Language of Science Fiction* (1984), and he has produced a book-length study of Thomas M. Disch's story "Angouleme," entitled *The American Shore*.

Delany's involvement in semantics is evident in at least two of his novels: *Babel-17*, whose plot revolves around the creation of an artificial language, and *Triton*, whose central character is a meta-logician. His concern for symbolic statement is evident in *The Einstein Intersection*, where symbols and characters not only intersect but interweave.

His most fascinating theory for science fiction readers, that one—perhaps *the*—distinguishing characteristic of science fiction is the possibility of literalizing metaphor, results in such statements as "in science fiction, 'science'—i.e., sentences displaying verbal emblems of scientific discourses—is used to literalize the meanings of other sentences for use in the construction of the fictional foreground. Such sentences as 'His world exploded,' or 'She turned on her left side,' as they subsume the proper technological discourse (of economics and cosmology in one; of switching circuitry and prosthetic surgery in the other), leave the banality of the emotionally fuzzy metaphor, abandon the triviality of insomniac tossings, and, through the labyrinth of technical possibility, become possible images of the impossible."

Delany may be "refurbishing the worn props" of science fiction, to use Aldiss's phrase, but his novels might better be described as "meta-science fiction," that is, fiction about science fiction, containing within it a critique of the genre at the same time that it shakes the old images into new patterns.

Science fiction admires wordsmiths and experimental writers, perhaps because the commercial nature of the field has made such adventurousness unrewarding for the many. But the overpraise of young writers runs the danger of inhibiting their development. In spite of the early success of Delany's novels, his fiction seems to work better at the shorter lengths. His novels, underneath the skill with which they are written, seem derived from his early love affair with science fiction. His best work probably is still ahead of him, when he starts writing out of experience rather than out of reading. *Dhalgren* is personal enough but it may not be accessible enough.

The problem with success is that it does not encourage change. Delany has exhibited that ability in the past. He remains a writer to watch.

AYE, AND GOMORRAH...

BY SAMUEL R. DELANY

And came down in Paris:

Where we raced along the Rue de Médicis with Bo and Lou and Muse inside the fence, Kelly and me outside, making faces through the bars, making noise, making the Luxembourg Gardens roar at two in the morning. Then climbed out, and down to the square in front of St. Sulpice where Bo tried to knock me into the fountain.

At which point Kelly noticed what was going on around us, got an ashcan cover, and ran into the pissoir, banging the walls. Five guys scooted out; even a big pissoir only holds four.

A very blond young man put his hand on my arm and smiled. "Don't you think, Spacer, that you... people should leave?"

I looked at his hand on my blue uniform. *"Est-ce que tu es un frelk?"*

His eyebrows rose, then he shook his head. "Une *frelk*," he corrected. "No. I am not. Sadly for me. You look as though you may once have been a man. But now..." He smiled. "You have nothing for me now. The police." He nodded across the street where I noticed the gendarmerie for the first time. "They don't bother us. You are strangers, though... "

But Muse was already yelling, "Hey, come on! Let's get out of here, huh?" And left. And went up again.

And came down in Houston:

"God damn!" Muse said. "Gemini Flight Control—you mean this is where it all started? Let's get *out* of here, *please!*"

So took a bus out through Pasadena, then the monoline to Galveston, and were going to take it down the Gulf, but Loy found a couple with a pickup truck—

"Glad to give you a ride, Spacers. You people up there on them planets and things, doing all that good work for the government."

—who were going south, them and the baby, so we rode in the back for two hundred and fifty miles of sun and wind.

"You think they're frelks?" Lou asked, elbowing me. "I bet they're frelks. They're just waiting for us give 'em the come-on."

"Cut it out. They're a nice, stupid pair of country kids."

"That don't mean they ain't frelks!"

"You don't trust anybody, do you?"

"No."

And finally a bus again that rattled us through Brownsville down the steps and across the border into Matamoros where we staggered into the dust and the scorched evening with a lot of Mexicans and chickens and Texas Gulf shrimp fishermen—who smelled worst—and *we* shouted the loudest. Forty-three whores—I counted—had turned out for the shrimp fishermen, and by the time we had broken two of the windows in the bus station they were all laughing. The shrimp fishermen said they wouldn't buy us no food but would get us drunk if we wanted, 'cause that was the custom with shrimp fishermen. But we yelled, broke another window; then, while I was lying on my back on the telegraph office steps, singing, a woman with dark lips bent over and put her hands on my cheeks. "You are very sweet." Her rough hair fell forward. "But the men, they were standing around and watching *you*. And that is taking up *time*. Sadly, their time is our money. Spacer, do you not think you… people should leave?"

I grabbed her wrist. "¡Usted!" I whispered. "¡Usted es una frelka?"

"*Frelko en español.*" She smiled and patted the sunburst that hung from my belt buckle. "Sorry. But you have nothing that… would be useful to me. It is too bad, for you look like you were once a woman, no? And I like women, too.… "

I rolled off the porch.

"Is this a drag, or is this a drag!" Muse was shouting. "Come *on*! Let's *go!*"

We managed to get back to Houston before dawn, somehow. And went up.

And came down in Istanbul:

That morning it rained in Istanbul.

At the commissary we drank our tea from pear-shaped glasses, looking out across the Bosphorus. The Princes Islands lay like trash heaps before the prickly city.

"Who knows their way in this town?" Kelly asked.

"Aren't we going around together?" Muse demanded. "I thought we were going around together."

"They held up my check at the purser's office," Kelly explained. "I'm flat broke. I think the purser's got it in for me," and shrugged. "Don't want to, but I'm going to have to hunt up a rich frelk and come on friendly," went back to the tea; *then* noticed how heavy the silence had become. "Aw, come *on*, now! You gape at me like that and I'll bust every bone in that carefully-conditioned-from-puberty body of yours. Hey you!" meaning me. "Don't give me that holier-than-thou gawk like you never went with no frelk!"

It was starting.

"I'm not gawking," I said and got quietly mad.

The longing, the old longing.

Bo laughed to break tensions. "Say, last time I was in Istanbul—about a year before I joined up with this platoon—I remember we were coming out of Taksim Square down Istiqlal. Just past all the cheap movies we found a little passage lined with flowers. Ahead of us were two other spacers. It's a market in there, and farther down they got fish, and then a courtyard with oranges and candy and sea urchins and cabbage. But flowers in front. Anyway, we noticed something funny about the spacers. It wasn't their uniforms: they were perfect. The haircuts: fine. It wasn't till we heard them talking—They were a man and woman dressed up like spacers, trying *to pick up frelks!* Imagine, queer for frelks!"

"Yeah," Lou said. "I seen that before. There were a lot of them in Rio."

"We beat hell out of them two," Bo concluded. "We got them in a side street and went to *town!*"

Muse's tea glass clicked on the counter. "From Taksim down Istiqlal till you get to the flowers? Now why didn't you say that's where the frelks were, huh?" A smile on Kelly's face would have made that okay. There was no smile.

"Hell," Lou said, "nobody ever had to tell me where to look. I go out in the street and frelks smell me coming. I can spot 'em halfway along Piccadilly. Don't they have nothing but tea in this place? Where can you get a drink?"

Bo grinned. "Moslem country, remember? But down at the end of the Flower Passage there're a lot of little bars with green doors and marble counters where you can get a liter of beer for about fifteen cents in lira. And there're all these stands selling deep-fat-fried bugs and pig's gut sandwiches—"

"You ever notice how frelks can put it away? I mean liquor, not… pig's guts."

And launched off into a lot of appeasing stories. We ended with the one about the frelk some spacer tried to roll who announced: "There are two things I go for. One is spacers; the other is a good fight.…"

But they only allay. They cure nothing. Even Muse knew we would spend the day apart, now.

The rain had stopped, so we took the ferry up the Golden Horn. Kelly straight off asked for Taksim Square and Istiqlal and was directed to a dolmush, which we discovered was a taxicab, only it just goes one place and picks up lots and lots of people on the way. And it's cheap.

Lou headed off over Ataturk Bridge to see the sights of New City. Bo decided to find out what the Dolma Boche really was; and when Muse discovered you could go to Asia for fifteen cents—one lira and fifty krush—well, Muse decided to go to Asia.

I turned through the confusion of traffic at the head of the bridge and up past the gray, dripping walls of Old City, beneath the trolley wires. There are times when yelling and helling won't fill the lack. There are times when you must walk by yourself because it hurts so much to be alone.

I walked up a lot of little streets with wet donkeys and wet camels and women in veils; and down a lot of big streets with buses and trash baskets and men in business suits.

Some people stare at spacers; some people don't. Some people stare or don't stare in a way a spacer gets to recognize within a week after coming out of training school at sixteen. I was walking in the park when I caught her watching. She saw me see and looked away.

I ambled down the wet asphalt. She was standing under the arch of a small, empty mosque shell. As I passed she walked out into the courtyard among the cannons.

"Excuse me."

I stopped.

"Do you know whether or not this is the shrine of St. Irene?" Her English was charmingly accented. "I've left my guidebook home."

"Sorry. I'm a tourist too."

"Oh." She smiled. "I am Greek. I thought you might be Turkish because you are so dark."

"American red Indian." I nodded. Her turn to curtsy.

"I see. I have just started at the university here in Istanbul. Your uniform, it tells me that you are"—and in the pause, all speculations resolved—"a spacer."

I was uncomfortable. "Yeah." I put my hands in my pockets, moved my feet around on the soles of my boots, licked my third from the rear left molar—did all the things you do when you're uncomfortable. *You're so exciting when you look like that,* a frelk told me once. "Yeah, I am." I said it too sharply, too loudly, and she jumped a little.

So now she knew I knew she knew I knew, and I wondered how we would play out the Proust bit.

"I'm Turkish," she said. "I'm not Greek. I'm not just starting. I'm a graduate in art history here at the university. These little lies one makes for strangers to protect one's ego... why? Sometimes I think my ego is very small."

That's one strategy.

"How far away do you live?" I asked. "And what's the going rate in Turkish lira?" That's another.

"I can't pay you." She pulled her raincoat around her hips. She was very pretty. "I would like to." She shrugged and smiled. "But I am... a poor student. Not a rich one. If you want to turn around and walk away, there will be no hard feelings. I shall be sad though."

I stayed on the path. I thought she'd suggest a price after a little while. She didn't.

And *that's* another.

I was asking myself, *What do you want the damn money for anyway?* when a breeze upset water from one of the park's great cypresses.

"I think the whole business is sad." She wiped drops from her face. There had been a break in her voice and for a moment I looked too closely at the water streaks. "I think it's sad that they have to alter you to make you a spacer. If they hadn't, then *we....* If spacers had never been, then we could not be... the way we are. Did you start out male or female?"

Another shower. I was looking at the ground and droplets went down my collar.

"Male," I said. "It doesn't matter."

"How old are you? Twenty-three, twenty-four?"

"Twenty-three," I lied. It's reflex. I'm twenty-five, but the younger they think you are, the more they pay you. But I didn't *want* her *damn* money—

"I guessed right then." She nodded. "Most of us are experts on spacers. Do you find that? I suppose we have to be." She looked at me with wide black eyes. At the end of the stare, she blinked rapidly. "You would have been a fine man. But now you are a spacer, building water-conservation units on Mars, programming mining computers on Ganymede, servicing communication relay towers on the moon. The alteration..." Frelks are the only people I've ever heard say "the alteration" with so much fascination and regret. "You'd think they'd have found some other solution. They could have found another way than neutering you, turning you into creatures not even androgynous; things that are—"

I put my hand on her shoulder, and she stopped like I'd hit her. She looked to see if anyone was near. Lightly, so lightly then, she raised her hand to mine.

I pulled my hand away. "That are what?"

"They could have found another way." Both hands in her pockets now.

"They could have. Yes. Up beyond the ionosphere, baby, there's too much radiation for those precious gonads to work right anywhere you might want to do something that would keep you there over twenty-four hours, like the moon, or Mars, or the satellites of Jupiter—"

"They could have made protective shields. They could have done more research into biological adjustment—"

"Population Explosion time," I said. "No, they were hunting for any excuse to cut down kids back then—especially deformed ones."

"Ah yes." She nodded. "We're still fighting our way up from the neo-puritan reaction to the sex freedom of the twentieth century."

"It was a fine solution." I grinned and grabbed my crotch. "I'm happy with it." I've never known why that's so much more obscene when a spacer does it.

"Stop it," she snapped, moving away.

"What's the matter?"

"Stop it," she repeated. "Don't do that! You're a child."

"But they choose us from children whose sexual responses are hopelessly retarded at puberty."

"And your childish, violent substitutes for love? I suppose that's one of the things that's attractive. Yes, I know you're a child."

"Yeah? What about frelks?"

She thought awhile. "I think they are the sexually retarded ones they miss. Perhaps it was the right solution. You really don't regret you have no sex?"

"We've got you," I said.

"Yes." She looked down. I glanced to see the expression she was hiding. It was a smile. "You have your glorious soaring life, *and* you have us." Her face came up. She glowed. "You spin in the sky, the world spins under you, and you step from land to land, while we..." She turned her head right, left, and her black hair curled and uncurled on the shoulder of her coat. "We have our dull, circled lives, bound in gravity, *worshiping* you!"

She looked back at me. "Perverted, yes? In love with a bunch of corpses in free fall!" She suddenly hunched her shoulders. "I don't like having a free-fall-sexual-displacement complex."

"That always sounded like too much to say."

She looked away. "I don't like being a frelk. Better?"

"I wouldn't like it either. Be something else."

"You don't choose your perversions. *You* have no perversions at all. *You're* free of the whole business. I love you for that, spacer. My love starts with the fear of love. Isn't that beautiful? A pervert substitutes something unattainable for 'normal' love: the homosexual, a mirror, the fetishist, a shoe or a watch or a girdle. Those with free-fall-sexual-dis—"

"Frelks."

"Frelks substitute"—she looked at me sharply again—"loose, swinging meat."

"That doesn't offend me."

"I wanted it to."

"Why?"

"You don't have desires. You wouldn't understand."

"Go on."

"I want you because you can't want me. That's the pleasure. If someone really had a sexual reaction to... us, we'd be scared away. I wonder how many people there were before there were you, waiting for your creation. We're necrophiles. I'm sure grave robbing has fallen off since you started going up. But you don't understand..."

She paused. "If you did, then I wouldn't be scuffing leaves now and trying to think from whom I could borrow sixty lira." She stepped over the knuckles of a root that had cracked the pavement. "And that, incidentally, is the going rate in Istanbul."

I calculated. "Things still get cheaper as you go east."

"You know," and she let her raincoat fall open, "you're different from the others. You at least *want* to know—"

I said, "If spat I on you for every time you'd said that to a spacer, you'd drown."

"Go back to the moon, loose meat." She closed her eyes. "Swing on up to Mars. There are satellites around Jupiter where you might do some good. Go up and come down in some other city."

"Where do you live?"

"You want to come with me?"

"Give me something," I said. "Give me something—it doesn't have to be worth sixty lira. Give me something that you like, anything of yours that means something to you."

"No!"

"Why not?"

"Because I—"

"—don't want to give up part of that ego. None of you frelks do!"

"You really don't understand I just don't want to buy you?"

"You have nothing to buy me with."

"You are a child," she said. "I love you."

We reached the gate of the park. She stopped, and we stood time enough for a breeze to rise and die in the grass. "I..." she offered tentatively, pointing without taking her hand from her coat pocket. "I live right down there."

"All right," I said. "Let's go."

A gas main had once exploded along this street, she explained to me, a gushing road of fire as far as the docks, overhot and overquick. It had been put out within minutes, no building had fallen, but the charred facias glittered. "This is sort of an artist and student quarter." We crossed the cobbles. "Yuri Pasha, number fourteen. In case you're ever in Istanbul again." Her door was covered with black scales, the gutter was thick with garbage.

"A lot of artists and professional people are frelks," I said, trying to be inane.

"So are lots of other people." She walked inside and held the door. "We're just more flamboyant about it."

On the landing there was a portrait of Ataturk. Her room was on the second floor. "Just a moment while I get my key—"

Marsscapes! Moonscapes! On her easel was a six-foot canvas showing the sunrise flaring on a crater's rim! There were copies of the original Observer pictures of the moon pinned to the wall, and pictures of every smooth-faced general in the International Spacer Corps.

On one corner of her desk was a pile of those photo magazines about spacers that you can find in most kiosks all over the world: I've seriously heard people say they were printed for adventurous-minded high school children. They've never seen the Danish ones. She had a few of those too. There was a shelf of art books, art history texts. Above them were six feet of cheap paper-covered space operas: *Sin on Space Station #12*, *Rocket Rake*, *Savage Orbit*.

"Arrack?" she asked. "Ouzo or pernod? You've got your choice. But I may pour them all from the same bottle." She set out glasses on the desk, then opened a waist-high cabinet that turned out to be an icebox. She stood up with a tray of lovelies: fruit puddings, Turkish delight, braised meats.

"What's this?"

"Dolmades. Grape leaves filled with rice and pignolias."

"Say it again?"

"Dolmades. Comes from the same Turkish word as 'dolmush.' They both mean 'stuffed.'" She put the tray beside the glasses. "Sit down."

I sat on the studio-couch-that-becomes-bed. Under the brocade I felt the deep, fluid resilience of a glycogel mattress. They've got the idea that it approximates the feeling of free fall. "Comfortable? Would you excuse me for a moment? I have some friends down the hall. I want to see them for a moment." She winked. "They like spacers."

"Are you going to take up a collection for me?" I asked. "Or do you want them to line up outside the door and wait their turn?"

She sucked a breath. "Actually I was going to suggest both." Suddenly she shook her head. "Oh, what do you want!"

"What will you give me? I want something," I said. "That's why I came. I'm lonely. Maybe I want to find out how far it goes. I don't know yet."

"It goes as far as you will. Me? I study, I read, paint, talk with my friends"— she came over to the bed, sat down on the floor—"go to the theater, look at spacers who pass me on the street, till one looks back; I am lonely too." She put her head on my knee. "I want something. But," and after a minute neither of us had moved, "you are not the one who will give it to me."

"You're not going to pay me for it," I countered. "You're not, are you?"

On my knee her head shook. After a while she said, all breath and no voice, "Don't you think you... should leave?"

"Okay," I said, and stood up.

She sat back on the hem of her coat. She hadn't taken it off yet.

I went to the door.

"Incidentally." She folded her hands in her lap. "There is a place in New City you might find what you're looking for, called the Flower Passage—"

I turned toward her, angry. "The frelk hangout? Look, I don't *need* money! I say *any*thing would do! I don't want—"

She had begun to shake her head, laughing quietly. Now she lay her cheek on the wrinkled place where I had sat. "Do you persist in misunderstanding? It is a spacer hangout. When you leave, I am going to visit my friends and talk about... ah, yes, the beautiful one that got away. I thought you might find... perhaps someone you know."

With anger, it ended.

"Oh," I said. "Oh, it's a spacer hangout. Yeah. Well, thanks."

And went out. And found the Flower Passage, and Kelly and Lou and Bo and Muse. Kelly was buying beer so we all got drunk, and ate fried fish and fried clams and fried sausage, and Kelly was waving the money around, saying, "You should have seen him! The changes I put that frelk through, you should have *seen* him! Eighty lira is the going rate here, and he gave me a hundred and fifty!" and drank more beer. And went up.

THE NEW SCIENTIFIC REVOLUTION

Science seemed to coast through the 1930s and 1940s, distracted perhaps by the application of previous discoveries or by the practical problems of a world depression and then a world war. Radar and rockets, computers and atomic energy, all these and more came out of World War II and preoccupied laboratories and the public with technology. Then basic science got busy in the 1960s and 1970s in a variety of areas, and humanity's perception of itself and the universe, which had begun to adjust to cosmic expansion, atomic uncertainty, and the onrushing juggernaut of change, found itself with new difficulties.

Atomic scientists discovered new basic particles, such as leptons and muons, and even new properties of matter, such as handedness, charm, and strangeness. Astronomers discovered quasi-stellar objects, distant stars more luminous than most galaxies, and shortened the name to quasars; discovered pulsars, which became known popularly as black holes—stars collapsed into such dense matter that light could not escape, which might not exist in this universe or might be tunnels into another part of the universe; and began speculating about life on other worlds, ways of detecting alien civilizations, and possibilities of communicating with them. Physicians began transplanting organs, including hearts. Biologists discovered the double-helical structure of DNA and began experiments that eventually resulted in the cloning of vegetables and lower animals, in the threat and promise of recombinant DNA, and in test-tube babies, and revealed new possibilities for change and reevaluation continuing into the uncertain future.

Some of these breakthroughs had been the subjects for speculation in earlier science fiction stories, but many of them were unexpected and stimulated an outburst of creative energy among writers. Rather than predicting scientific discoveries, science fiction has more often drawn its inspiration from the discoveries and speculations of scientists. At one time scientists considered speculation to be unprofessional, but in the 1960s and 1970s such speculation became common, if not totally acceptable.

Philip Morrison and Giuseppe Cocconi speculated about the possibility of communication with alien civilizations; Carl Sagan popularized astronomy and its concepts; and Freeman Dyson suggested that a truly advanced civilization might reshape the matter in its planets into a gigantic sphere around its star, thus allowing the race to capture all the energy of its sun and making that star invisible except in the infrared part of the spectrum. From such speculations James Gunn developed his novel *The Listeners* (1972) and a fistful of writers wrote works about Dyson spheres or sections of them, such as Bob Shaw's

Orbitsville (1975) and Larry Niven's *Ringworld* (1970).

Similarly, black holes emitted stories if not light, as in Joe Haldeman's *The Forever War*, which used black holes as tunnels into another part of the universe that shortcut the limiting speed of light, and Frederik Pohl's *Gateway*, which used a black hole as an ambiguous ending to his protagonist's search for wealth and release from guilt. Medical and biological experiments may have produced more fictional than natural offspring. Stories about clones (the best of them may have been Le Guin's "Nine Lives") have proliferated until they reproduced themselves in the mainstream and in film (Ira Levin's *The Boys from Brazil*) and even on television *(The Clone Master)*.

One of the masters of the art of converting discovery and speculation into fiction is Larry Niven (1938-). Born into the wealthy Doheny family of Los Angeles, Niven earned two degrees in mathematics before setting out to be a science fiction writer. Since then he has won a Hugo in 1967 for "Neutron Star," published less than two years after his first published story, "The Coldest Place," in 1964; both a Nebula and a Hugo for *Ringworld*; a 1972 Hugo for "Inconstant Moon"; a 1975 Hugo for "The Hole Man"; and a 1975 Hugo for "The Borderland of Sol."

The movements of history are easy to misinterpret, and the literary successes of the New Wave might make such writing seem destined to supplant the older stories of adventure and hard science. But the older traditions continue virtually undiminished, sometimes with greater success than ever and often with greater popular success than more consciously literary work. Gordon Dickson and Poul Anderson, for instance, continue to make their livings by their writing, mostly with speculative and adventurous novels in the older style, and to considerable acclaim. Jerry Pournelle, a scientist who turned to science-fiction writing in mid-career, would consider it high praise to be compared with Heinlein.

Niven has been called another Hal Clement, but he may have equal parts of Heinlein and Asimov. Like both, he has constructed his own future history and his own universe that he calls "known space"; out of them have come such books as *The World of Ptaavs* (1965), *A Gift from Earth* (1968), and *Protector* (1973), as well as *Ringworld* and several collections of short fiction. The questions of longevity and organ transplantation embodied in "The Jigsaw Man" (*Dangerous Visions*, 1967) also have been treated in several other stories.

Niven and Pournelle combined their talents to produce *The Mote in God's Eye* (1974), *Inferno* (1975), and *Lucifer's Hammer* (1977), *Oath of Fealty* (1981), and *Footfall* (1985), and Niven has collaborated with other authors sometimes in conjunction with Pournelle. One of them is the *Dream Park* sequence with Steven Barnes. It should not be surprising that these works have been unusually successful among readers.

THE JIGSAW MAN

BY LARRY NIVEN

In A.D. 1900 Karl Landsteiner classified human blood into four types: A, B, AB, and O, according to incompatibilities. For the first time it became possible to give a shock patient a transfusion with some hope that it wouldn't kill him.

The movement to abolish the death penalty was barely getting started, and already it was doomed.

Vh83uOAGn7 was his telephone number and his driving license number and his social security number and the number of his draft card and his medical record. Two of these had been revoked, and the others had ceased to matter, except for his medical record. His name was Warren Lewis Knowles. He was going to die.

The trial was a day away, but the verdict was no less certain for that. Lew was guilty. If anyone had doubted it, the persecution had ironclad proof. By eighteen tomorrow Lew would be condemned to death. Broxton would appeal the case on some grounds or other. The appeal would be denied.

His cell was comfortable, small, and padded. This was no slur on the prisoner's sanity, though insanity was no longer an excuse for breaking the law. Three of the walls were mere bars. The fourth wall, the outside wall, was cement painted a restful shade of green. But the bars which separated him from the corridor, and from the morose old man on his left, and from the big, moronic-looking teenager on his right—the bars were four inches thick and eight inches apart, padded in silicone plastic. For the fourth time that day Lew took a clenched fistful of the plastic and tried to rip it away. It felt like a sponge rubber pillow, with a rigid core the thickness of a pencil, and it wouldn't rip. When he let go it snapped back to a perfect cylinder.

"It's not fair," he said.

The teenager didn't move. For all of the ten hours Lew had been in his cell, the kid had been sitting on the edge of his bunk with his lank black hair falling in his eyes and his five o'clock shadow getting gradually darker. He moved his long, hairy arms only at mealtimes, and the rest of him not at all.

The old man looked up at the sound of Lew's voice. He spoke with bitter sarcasm. "You framed?"

"No, I—"

"At least you're honest. What'd you do?"

Lew told him. He couldn't keep the hurt innocence out of his voice. The old man smiled derisively, nodding as if he'd expected just that.

"Stupidity. Stupidity's always been a capital crime. If you *had* to get yourself executed, why not for something important? See the kid on the other side of you?"

"Sure," Lew said without looking.

"He's an organlegger."

Lew felt the shock freezing in his face. He braced himself for another look into the next cell—and every nerve in his body jumped. The kid was looking at him. With his dull dark eyes barely visible under his mop of hair, he regarded Lew as a butcher might consider a badly aged side of beef.

Lew edged closer to the bars between his cell and the old man's. His voice was a hoarse whisper. "How many did he kill?"

"None."

"?"

"He was the snatch man. He'd find someone out alone at night, drug the prospect and take him home to the doc that ran the ring. It was the doc that did all the killing. If Bernie'd brought home a dead prospect, the doc would have skinned *him* down."

The old man sat with Lew almost directly behind him. He had twisted himself around to talk to Lew, but now he seemed to be losing interest. His hands, hidden from Lew by his bony back, were in constant nervous motion.

"How many did he snatch?"

"Four. Then he got caught. He's not very bright, Bernie."

"What did you do to get put here?"

The old man didn't answer. He ignored Lew completely, his shoulders twitching as he moved his hands. Lew shrugged and dropped back on his bunk.

It was nineteen o'clock of a Thursday night.

The ring had included three snatch men. Bernie had not yet been tried. Another was dead; he had escaped over the edge of a pedwalk when he felt the mercy bullet enter his arm. The third was being wheeled into the hospital next door to the courthouse.

Officially he was still alive. He had been sentenced; his appeal had been denied; but he was still alive as they moved him, drugged, into the operating room.

The interns lifted him from the table and inserted a mouthpiece so he could breathe when they dropped him into freezing liquid. They lowered him without a splash, and as his body temperature went down they dribbled something else into his veins. About half a pint of it. His temperature dropped toward freezing, his heartbeats were further and further apart. Finally his heart stopped. But it could have been started again. Men had been reprieved at this point. Officially the organlegger was still alive.

The doctor was a line of machines with a conveyor belt running through them. When the organlegger's body temperature reached a certain point, the belt started. The first machine made a series of incisions in his chest. Skillfully and mechanically, the doctor performed a cardiectomy.

The organlegger was officially dead. His heart went into storage immediately. His skin followed, most of it in one piece, all of it still living. The doctor took him apart with exquisite care, like disassembling a flexible, fragile, tremendously complex jigsaw puzzle. The brain was flashburned and the ashes saved for urn burial; but all the rest of the body, in slabs and small blobs and parchment-thin layers and lengths of tubing, went into storage in the hospital's organ banks. Any one of these units could be packed in a travel case at a moment's notice and flown to anywhere in the world in not much more than an hour. If the odds broke right, if the right people came down with the right diseases at the right time, the organlegger might save more lives than he had taken.

Which was the whole point.

Lying on his back, staring up at the ceiling television set, Lew suddenly began to shiver. He had not had the energy to put the sound plug in his ear, and the silent motion of the cartoon figures had suddenly become horrid. He turned the set off, and that didn't help either.

Bit by bit they would take him apart and store him away. He'd never seen an organ storage bank, but his uncle had owned a butchershop....

"Hey!" he yelled.

The kid's eyes came up, the only living part of him. The old man twisted round to look over his shoulder. At the end of the hall the guard looked up once, then went back to reading.

The fear was in Lew's belly; it pounded in his throat. "How can you stand it?"

The kid's eyes dropped to the floor. The old man said, "Stand what?"

"Don't you know what they're going to *do* to us?"

"Not to me. They won't take me apart like a hog."

Instantly Lew was at the bars. "Why not?"

The old man's voice had become very low. "Because there's a bomb where my right thighbone used to be. I'm gonna blow myself up. What they find, they'll never use."

The hope the old man had raised washed away, leaving bitterness. "Nuts. How could you put a bomb in your leg?"

"Take the bone out, bore a hole in it, build the bomb in the hole, get all the organic material out of the bone so it won't rot, put the bone back in. 'Course your red corpuscle count goes down afterward. What I wanted to ask you. You want to join me?"

"Join you?"

"Hunch up against the bars. This thing'll take care of both of us."

Lew found himself backing away. "No. No, thanks."

"Your choice," said the old man. "I never told you what I was here for, did I? I was the doc. Bernie made his snatches for me."

Lew had backed up against the opposite set of bars. He felt them touch his shoulders and turned to find the kid looking dully into his eyes from two feet away. Organleggers! He was surrounded by professional killers!

"I know what it's like," the old man continued. "They won't do that to me. Well. If you're sure you don't want a clean death, go lie down behind your bunk. It's thick enough."

The bunk was a mattress and a set of springs mounted into a cement block which was an integral part of the cement floor. Lew curled himself into fetal position with his hands over his eyes.

He was sure he didn't want to die *now*.

Nothing happened.

After a while he opened his eyes, took his hands away and looked around.

The kid was looking at him. For the first time there was a sour grin plastered on his face. In the corridor the guard, who was always in a chair by the exit, was standing outside the bars looking down at him. He seemed concerned.

Lew felt the flush rising in his neck and nose and ears. The old man had been playing with him. He moved to get up…

And a hammer came down on the world.

The guard lay broken against the bars of the cell across the corridor. The lank-haired youngster was picking himself up from behind his bunk, shaking his head. Somebody groaned; and the groan rose to a scream. The air was full of cement dust.

Lew got up.

Blood lay like red oil on every surface that faced the explosion. Try as he might, and he didn't try very hard, Lew could find no other trace of the old man.

Except for the hole in the wall.

He must have been standing… right… there.

The hole would be big enough to crawl through, if Lew could reach it. But it was in the old man's cell. The silicone plastic sheathing on the bars between the cells had been ripped away, leaving only pencil-thick lengths of metal.

Lew tried to squeeze through.

The bars were humming, vibrating, though there was no sound. As Lew noticed the vibration he also found that he was becoming sleepy. He jammed his body between the bars, caught in a war between his rising panic and the sonic stunners which must have gone on automatically.

The bars wouldn't give. But his body did; and the bars were slippery with... He was through. He poked his head through the hole in the wall and looked down.

Way down. Far enough to make him dizzy.

The Topeka County courthouse was a small skyscraper, and Lew's cell must have been near the top. He looked down a smooth concrete slab studded with windows set flush with the sides. There would be no way to reach those windows, no way to open them, no way to break them.

The stunner was sapping his will. He would have been unconscious by now if his head had been in the cell with the rest of him. He had to force himself to turn and look up.

He was *at* the top. The edge of the roof was only a few feet above his eyes. He couldn't reach that far, not without...

He began to crawl out of the hole.

Win or lose, they wouldn't get him for the organ banks. The vehicular traffic level would smash every useful part of him. He sat on the lip of the hole, with his legs straight out inside the cell for balance, pushing his chest flat against the wall. When he had his balance he stretched his arms toward the roof. No good.

So he got one leg under him, keeping the other stiffly out, and *lunged.*

His hands closed over the edge as he started to fall back. He yelped with surprise, but it was too late. The top of the courthouse was moving! It had dragged him out of the hole before he could let go. He hung on, swinging slowly back and forth over empty space as the motion carried him away.

The top of the courthouse was a pedwalk.

He couldn't climb up, not without purchase for his feet. He didn't have the strength. The pedwalk was moving toward another building, about the same height. He could reach it if he only hung on.

And the windows in that building were different. They weren't made to open, not in these days of smog and air conditioning, but there were ledges. Perhaps the glass would break.

Perhaps it wouldn't.

The pull on his arms was agony. It would be so easy to let go.... No. He had committed no crime worth dying for. He refused to die.

Over the decades of the twentieth century the movement continued to gain momentum. Loosely organized, international in scope, its members had only one goal: to replace execution with imprisonment and rehabilitation in every state and nation they could reach. They argued that killing a man for his crime teaches him nothing; that it serves as no deterrent to others who might commit the same crime; that death is irreversible, whereas an innocent man might be released from prison once his innocence is belatedly proven. Killing a man serves no good purpose, they said, unless for society's vengeance. Vengeance, they said, is unworthy of an enlightened society.

Perhaps they were right.

In 1940 Karl Landsteiner and Alexander S. Wiener made public their report on the Rh factor in human blood.

By mid-century most convicted killers were getting life imprisonment or less. Many were later returned to society, some "rehabilitated," others not. The death penalty had been passed for kidnapping in some states, but it was hard to persuade a jury to enforce it. Similarly with murder charges. A man wanted for burglary in Canada and murder in California fought extradition to Canada; he had less chance of being convicted in California. Many states had abolished the death penalty. France had none.

Rehabilitation of criminals was a major goal of the science/art of psychology.

But—

Blood banks were worldwide.

Already men and women with kidney diseases had been saved by a kidney transplanted from an identical twin. Not all kidney victims had identical twins. A doctor in Paris used transplants from close relatives, classifying up to a hundred points of incompatibility to judge in advance how successful the transplant would be.

Eye transplants were common. An eye donor could wait until he died before he saved another man's sight.

Human bone could *always* be transplanted, provided the bone was first cleaned of organic matter.

So matters stood at mid-century.

By 1990 it was possible to store any living human organ for any reasonable length of time. Transplants had become routine, helped along by the "scalpel of infinite thinness," the laser. The dying regularly willed their remains to the organ banks. The mortuary lobbies couldn't stop it. But such gifts from the dead were not always useful.

In 1993 Vermont passed the first of the organ bank laws. Vermont had always had the death penalty. Now a condemned man could know that his death would save lives. It was no longer true that an execution served no good purpose. Not in Vermont.

Nor, later, in California. Or Washington. Georgia. Pakistan, England,

Switzerland, France, Rhodesia…

The pedwalk was moving at ten miles per hour. Below, unnoticed by pedestrians who had quit work late and night owls who were just beginning their rounds, Lewis Knowles hung from the moving strip and watched the ledge go by beneath his dangling feet. The ledge was no more than two feet wide, a good four feet beneath his stretching toes.

He dropped.

As his feet struck he caught the edge of a window casement. Momentum jerked at him, but he didn't fall. After a long moment he breathed again.

He couldn't know what building this was, but it was not deserted. At twenty-one hundred at night, all the windows were ablaze. He tried to stay back out of the light as he peered in.

This window was an office. Empty.

He'd need something to wrap around his hand to break that window. But all he was wearing was a pair of shoesocks and a prison jumper. Well, he couldn't be more conspicuous than he was now. He took off the jumper, wrapped part of it around his hand, and struck.

He almost broke his hand.

Well… they'd let him keep his jewelry, his wristwatch and diamond ring. He drew a circle on the glass with the ring, pushing down hard, and struck again with the other hand. It *had* to be glass; if it was plastic he was doomed. The glass popped out in a near-perfect circle.

He had to do it six times before the hole was big enough for him.

He smiled as he stepped inside, still holding his jumper. Now all he needed was an elevator. The cops would have picked him up in an instant if they'd caught him on the street in a prison jumper, but if he hid the jumper here he'd be safe. Who would suspect a licensed nudist?

Except that he didn't have a license. Or a nudist's shoulder pouch to put it in.

Or a shave.

That was very bad. Never had there been a nudist as hairy as this. Not just a five o'clock shadow, but a full beard all over, so to speak. Where could he get a razor?

He tried the desk drawers. Many businessmen kept spare razors. He stopped when he was halfway through. Not because he'd found a razor, but because he now knew where he was. The papers on his desk made it all too obvious.

A hospital.

He was still clutching the jumper. He dropped it in the wastebasket, covered it tidily with papers, and more or less collapsed into the chair behind the desk.

A hospital. He *would* pick a hospital. And *this* hospital, the one which had been built right next to the Topeka County courthouse, for good and sufficient reason.

But he hadn't picked it, not really. It had picked him. Had he ever in his life made a decision except on the prompting of others? No. Friends had borrowed his money for keeps, men had stolen his girls, he had avoided promotion by his knack for being ignored. Shirley had bullied him into marrying her, then left him four years later for a friend who wouldn't be bullied.

Even now, at the possible end of his life, it was the same. An aging body snatcher had given him his escape. An engineer had built the cell bars wide enough apart to let a small man squeeze between them. Another had put a pedwalk along two convenient roofs. And here he was.

The worst of it was that here he had no chance of masquerading as a nudist. Hospital gowns and masks would be the minimum. Even nudists had to wear clothing sometime.

The closet?

There was nothing in the closet but a spiffy green hat and a perfectly transparent rain poncho.

He could run for it. If he could find a razor he'd be safe once he reached the street. He bit at a knuckle, wishing he knew where the elevator was. Have to trust to luck. He began searching the drawers again.

He had his hand on a black leather razor case when the door opened. A beefy man in a hospital gown breezed in. The intern (there were no human doctors in hospitals) was halfway to the desk before he noticed Lew crouching over an open drawer. He stopped walking. His mouth fell open.

Lew closed it with the fist which still gripped the razor case. The man's teeth came together with a sharp click. His knees were buckling as Lew brushed past him and out the door.

The elevator was just down the hall, with the doors standing open. And nobody coming. Lew stepped in and punched O. He shaved as the elevator dropped. The razor cut fast and close, if a trifle noisily. He was working on his chest as the door opened.

A skinny technician stood directly in front of him, her mouth and eyes set in the utterly blank expression of those who wait for elevators. She brushed past him with a muttered apology, hardly noticing him. Lew stepped out fast. The doors were closing before he realized that he was on the wrong floor.

That damned tech! She'd stopped the elevator before it reached bottom.

He turned and stabbed the Down button. Then what he'd seen in that one cursory glance came back to him, and his head whipped around for another look.

The whole vast room was filled with glass tanks, ceiling height, arranged in a labyrinth like the bookcases in a library. In the tanks was a display more

lewd than anything in Belsen. Why, those things had been *men!* and *women!*
No, he wouldn't look. He refused to look at anything but the elevator door.
What was taking that elevator so long?

He heard a siren.

The hard tile floor began to vibrate against his bare feet. He felt a numbness
in his muscles, a lethargy in his soul.

The elevator arrived... too late. He blocked the doors open with a chair.
Most buildings didn't have stairs; only alternate elevators. They'd have to use
the alternate elevator to reach him now. Well, where was it?... He wouldn't
have time to find it. He was beginning to feel really sleepy. They must have
several sonic projectors focused on this one room. Where one beam passed the
interns would feel mildly relaxed, a little clumsy. But where the beams
intersected, *here,* there would be unconsciousness. But not yet.

He had something to do first.

By the time they broke in they'd have something to kill him for.

The tanks were faced in plastic, not glass: a very special kind of plastic. To
avoid provoking defense reactions in all the myriads of body parts which might
be stored touching it, the plastic had to have unique characteristics. No engineer
could have been expected to make it shatterproof too!

It shattered very satisfactorily.

Later, Lew wondered how he managed to stay up as long as he did. The
soothing hypersonic murmur of the stun beams kept pulling at him, pulling him
down to a floor which seemed softer every moment. The chair he wielded became
heavier and heavier. But as long as he could lift it, he smashed. He was knee
deep in nutritive storage fluid, and there were dying things brushing against his
ankles with every move; but his work was barely a third done when the silent
siren song became too much for him.

He fell.

And after all that they never even mentioned the smashed organ banks!

Sitting in the courtroom, listening to the drone of courtroom ritual, Lew
sought Mr. Broxton's ear to ask the question. Mr. Broxton smiled at him. "Why
should they want to bring that up? They think they've got enough on you as it
is. If you beat *this* rap, then they'll persecute you for wanton destruction of
valuable medical sources. But they're sure you won't."

"And you?"

"I'm afraid they're right. But we'll try. Now, Hennessey's about to read the
charges. Can you manage to look hurt and indignant?"

"Sure."

"Good."

The persecution read the charges, his voice sounding like the voice of doom coming from under a thin blond mustache. Warren Lewis Knowles looked hurt and indignant. But he no longer felt that way. He had done something worth dying for.

The cause of it all was the organ banks. With good doctors and a sufficient flow of material in the organ banks, any taxpayer could hope to live indefinitely. What voter would vote against eternal life? The death penalty was his immortality, and he would vote the death penalty for any crime at all.

Lewis Knowles had struck back.

"The state will prove that the said Warren Lewis Knowles did, in the space of two years, willfully drive through a total of six red traffic lights. During that same period the same Warren Knowles exceeded local speed limits no less than ten times, once by as much as fifteen miles per hour. His record has never been good. We will produce records of his arrest in 2082 on a charge of drunk driving, a charge of which he was acquitted only through—"

"Objection!"

"Sustained. If he was acquitted, Counselor, the Court must assume him not guilty."

HARD SCIENCE AND SOFT PEOPLE

Part of the fascination of science fiction is that within its realm everything is possible: with infinity and eternity at one's disposal, anything may be discovered, anything may be accomplished, anything may happen. This is not the same as fantasy: the science fiction possibility is rationalized—whatever happens, no matter how fantastic, happens within the universe of everyday experience. Fantasy asks that the reader suspend his disbelief; science fiction persuades the reader to believe.

Inside the reader's head there is a difference between spaceships carrying passengers toward Sagittarius at faster than the speed of light and broomsticks whisking witches toward Brocken at the incantation of a spell, although both, insofar as science can determine, are equally impossible. The difference is not that the science fiction writer mutters some meaningless mumbo-jumbo over the actions of the story but that the story itself demands to be read at a realistic level.

Arthur C. Clarke invented a law to cover the unknown miracles that the future may hold: "A sufficiently advanced technology is indistinguishable from magic," he said. People living today, if they think about it, recognize the basic truth of that statement; modern technology would seem like magic to anyone who lived before the Industrial Revolution. If science fiction is not to seem hopelessly parochial, it must assume future developments that will be just as difficult for contemporary citizens to understand as airplanes, television, and electric lights would be for Julius Caesar or Shakespeare.

Infinity and eternity also liberate the science fictional imaginations; though they may be difficult to comprehend, they are not fantasy but intellectual concepts. Anything the science fiction writer wants to imagine, from the birth of the universe to its death, from an exploration of the most arcane of nature's mysteries to a postulation of technological changes with unique implications for the human experience, can be built into a science fiction story. The fact that science fiction must be based in reality is not so much a limitation as a strategy. Does the author want the reader to feel or to think?

And yet such a dichotomy is more theoretical than real. Science fiction is supposed to be cerebral and a bit unfeeling or inhuman, and yet feelings stirred by intellectual understandings may go just as deep as and be more "human" than the automatic and primitive emotional response to the hormones produced by the ductless glands. Generalizations, though useful for purposes of classification, are basically false if they suggest that anything below the supernatural is all one thing or another. So it is with the business of dividing science fiction writers into New Wave and Old Wave, into literary artists and scientific hacks.

As a matter of fact, New Wave authors often based their stories on scientific speculations, and Old Wave authors often wrote skillfully and sensitively about the human experience. Poul Anderson (1926-) is a good example. A graduate in physics from the University of Minnesota in 1948, he set out immediately on a career as a writer from which he has not wavered since. His first story, "Tomorrow's Children," written with F. N. Waldrop, appeared in 1947 while he was still in college. Since then he has written more than one hundred books, including historical and mainstream fiction, mysteries, juveniles, and nonfiction, and hundreds of shorter pieces.

Anderson is best known as a hard-science writer, and shares with Hal Clement the special pleasures of inventing alien planets. His early fiction concerned itself with future developments in science and technology, with an occasional adventure and fantasy thrown in for variety. His approach was realistic and his style was straightforward. Within a decade he was guest of honor at the World Science Fiction Convention in 1959, and a dozen years later, president of SFWA.

His best-known early stories include "The Double-Dyed Villains," "The Helping Hand," "The Un-Man," and "The Big Rain." His early novels include *Brain Wave* (1954), *The Broken Sword* (1954), *Planet of No Return* (1956), *The War of the Wing-Men* (1958) *The Snows of Ganymede* (1958), *The Enemy Stars* (1958), *War of Two Worlds* (1959), *The High Crusade* (1960), *Three Hearts and Three Lions* (1961), *Orbit Unlimited* (1963), and *Shield* (1963). His best-known books may be *Tau Zero* (1970) and *The Boat of a Million Years* (1989), and his *Time Patrol* stories and novels; in 1994 he started a new and more highly visible series of novels with *Harvest of Stars*.

He has worked with several series characters (and created a Heinleinian future history): about trader Nicholas van Rijn and the Polesotechnic League, about Dominic Flandry and the decay of a galactic empire, and, in collaboration with Gordon Dickson, about a race of intelligent bearlike creatures known as "Hokas."

His concerns with science, extrapolation, and adventure brought him Hugos for "The Longest Voyage" in 1961, for "No Truce with Kings" in 1964, and for "The Sharing of Flesh" in 1969, but he also displayed his ability to write with New Wave skill and sensitivity in his 1971 and 1972 Nebula and Hugo winners "The Queen of Air and Darkness" and "Goat Song." His short fiction has won five other Hugo awards.

"Kyrie," published in *The Farthest Reaches* in 1968, demonstrates that a story about a supernova and an alien energy creature can be at the same time a moving human experience.

KYRIE

BY POUL ANDERSON

On a high peak in the Lunar Carpathians stands a convent of St. Martha of Bethany. The walls are native rock; they lift dark and cragged as the mountainside itself, into a sky that is always black. As you approach from Northpole, flirting low to keep the force screens along Route Plato between you and the meteoroidal rain, you see the cross which surmounts the tower, stark athwart Earth's blue disc. No bells resound from there—not in airlessness.

You may hear them inside at the canonical hours, and throughout the crypts below where machines toil to maintain a semblance of terrestrial environment. If you linger a while you will also hear them calling to requiem mass. For it has become a tradition that prayers be offered at St. Martha's for those who have perished in space; and they are more with every passing year.

This is not the work of the sisters. They minister to the sick, the needy, the crippled, the insane, all whom space has broken and cast back. Luna is full of such, exiles because they can no longer endure Earth's pull or because it is feared they may be incubating a plague from some unknown planet or because men are so busy with their frontiers that they have no time to spare for the failures. The sisters wear spacesuits as often as habits, are as likely to hold a medikit as a rosary.

But they are granted some time for contemplation. At night, when for half a month the sun's glare has departed, the chapel is unshuttered and stars look down through the glaze-dome to the candles. They do not wink and their light is winter cold. One of the nuns in particular is there as often as may be, praying for her own dead. And the abbess sees to it that she can be present when the yearly mass, that she endowed before she took her vows, is sung.

> *Requiem aeternam dona eis, Domine, et lux*
> *perpetua luceat eis.*
> *Kyrie eleison, Christe eleison, Kyrie eleison.*

The Supernova Sagittarii expedition comprised fifty human beings and a flame. It went the long way around from Earth orbit, stopping at Epsilon Lyrae to pick up its last member. Thence it approached its destination by stages.

This is the paradox: time and space are aspects of each other. The explosion was more than a hundred years past when noted by men on Lasthope. They were part of a generations-long effort to fathom the civilization of creatures altogether unlike us; but one night they looked up and saw a light so brilliant it cast shadows.

That wave front would reach Earth several centuries hence. By then it would be so tenuous that nothing but another bright point would appear in the sky. Meanwhile, though, a ship overleaping the space through which light must creep could track the great star's death across time.

Suitably far off, instruments recorded what had been before the outburst: incandescence collapsing upon itself after the last nuclear fuel was burned out. A jump, and they saw what happened a century ago: convulsion, storm of quanta and neutrinos, a radiation equal to the massed hundred billion suns of this galaxy.

It faded, leaving an emptiness in heaven, and the *Raven* moved closer. Fifty light-years—fifty years—inward, she studied a shrinking fieriness in the midst of a fog which shone like lightning.

Twenty-five years later the central globe had dwindled more, the nebula had expanded and dimmed. But because the distance was now so much less, everything seemed larger and brighter. The naked eye saw a dazzle too fierce to look straight at, making the constellations pale by contrast. Telescopes showed a blue-white spark in the heart of an opalescent cloud delicately filamented at the edges.

The *Raven* made ready for her final jump, to the immediate neighborhood of the supernova.

Captain Teodor Szili went on a last-minute inspection tour. The ship murmured around him, running at one gravity of acceleration to reach the desired intrinsic velocity. Power droned, regulators whickered, ventilation systems rustled. He felt the energies quiver in his bones. But metal surrounded him, blank and comfortless. Viewports gave on a dragon's hoard of stars, the ghostly arch of the Milky Way: on vacuum, cosmic rays, cold not far above absolute zero, distance beyond imagination to the nearest human hearthfire. He was about to take his people where none had ever been before, into conditions none was sure about, and that was a heavy burden on him.

He found Eloise Waggoner at her post, a cubbyhole with intercom connections directly to the command bridge. Music drew him, a triumphant serenity he did not recognize. Stopping in the doorway, he saw her seated with a small tape machine on the desk.

"What's this?" he demanded.

"Oh!" The woman (he could not think of her as a girl though she was barely out of her teens) started. "I... I was waiting for the jump."

"You were to wait at the alert."

"What have I to do?" she answered less timidly than was her wont. "I mean, I'm not a crewman or a scientist."

"You are in the crew. Special communications technician."

"With Lucifer. And he likes the music. He says we come closer to oneness with it than in anything else he knows about us."

Szili arched his brows. "Oneness?"

A blush went up Eloise's thin cheeks. She stared at the deck and her hands twisted together. "Maybe that isn't the right word. Peace, harmony, unity… God?… I sense what he means, but we haven't any word that fits."

"Hm. Well, you are supposed to keep him happy." The skipper regarded her with a return of the distaste he had tried to suppress. She was a decent sort, he supposed, in her gauche and inhibited way; but her looks! Scrawny, bigfooted, big-nosed, pop eyes, and stringy dust-colored hair—and, to be sure, telepaths always made him uncomfortable. She said she could only read Lucifer's mind, but was that true?

No. Don't think such things. Loneliness and otherness can come near breaking you out here, without adding suspicion of your fellows.

If Eloise Waggoner was really human. She must be some kind of mutant at the very least. Whoever could communicate thought to thought with a living vortex had to be.

"What are you playing, anyhow?" Szili asked.

"Bach. The Third Brandenburg Concerto. He, Lucifer, he doesn't care for the modern stuff. I don't either."

You wouldn't, Szili decided. Aloud: "Listen we jump in half an hour. No telling what we'll emerge in. This is the first time anyone's been close to a recent supernova. We can only be certain of so much hard radiation that we'll be dead if the screenfields give way. Otherwise we've nothing to go on except theory. And a collapsing stellar core is so unlike anything anywhere else in the universe that I'm skeptical about how good the theory is. We can't sit daydreaming. We have to prepare."

"Yes, sir." Whispering, her voice lost its usual harshness.

He stared past her, past the ophidian eyes of meters and controls, as if he could penetrate the steel beyond and look straight into space. There, he knew, floated Lucifer.

The image grew in him: a fireball twenty meters across, shimmering white, red, gold, royal blue, flames dancing like Medusa locks, cometary tail burning for a hundred meters behind, a shiningness, a glory, a piece of hell. Not the least of what troubled him was the thought of that which paced his ship.

He hugged scientific explanations to his breast, though they were little better than guesses. In the multiple star system of Epsilon Aurigae, in the gas and energy pervading the space around, things took place which no laboratory could imitate. Ball lightning on a planet was perhaps analogous, as the formation of simple organic compounds in a primordial ocean is analogous to the life which finally evolves. In Epsilon Aurigae, magnetohydrodynamics had done what chemistry did on Earth. Stable plasma vortices had appeared, had grown, had added complexity, until after millions of years they became something you must needs call an organism. It was a form of ions, nuclei and force-fields. It metabolized electrons, nucleons, X-rays; it maintained its configuration for a long lifetime; it reproduced; it thought.

But what did it think? The few telepaths who could communicate with the Aurigeans, who had first made humankind aware that the Aurigeans existed, never explained clearly. They were a queer lot themselves.

Wherefore Captain Szili said, "I want you to pass this on to him."

"Yes, sir." Eloise turned down the volume on her taper. Her eyes unfocused. Through her ears went words, and her brain (how efficient a transducer was it?) passed the meanings on out to him who loped alongside *Raven* on his own reaction drive.

"Listen, Lucifer. You have heard this often before, I know, but I want to be positive you understand in full. Your psychology must be very foreign to ours. Why did you agree to come with us? I don't know. Technician Waggoner said you were curious and adventurous. Is that the whole truth?

"No matter. In half an hour we jump. We'll come within five hundred million kilometers of the supernova. That's where your work begins. You can go where we dare not, observe what we can't, tell us more than our instruments would ever hint at. But first we have to verify we can stay in orbit around the star. This concerns you too. Dead men can't transport you home again.

"So. In order to enclose you within the jumpfield, without disrupting your body, we have to switch off the shield screens. We'll emerge in a lethal radiation zone. You must promptly retreat from the ship, because we'll start the screen generator up sixty seconds after transit. Then you must investigate the vicinity. The hazards to look for—" Szili listed them. "Those are only what we can foresee. Perhaps we'll hit other garbage we haven't predicted. If anything seems like a menace, return at once, warn us and prepare for a jump back to here. Do you have that? Repeat."

Words jerked from Eloise. They were a correct recital; but how much was she leaving out?

"Very good." Szili hesitated. "Proceed with your concert if you like. But break it off at zero minus ten minutes and stand by."

"Yes, sir." She didn't look at him. She didn't appear to be looking anywhere in particular.

His footsteps clacked down the corridor and were lost.

—Why did he say the same things over? asked Lucifer.

"He is afraid," Eloise said.

—"?"—

"I guess you don't know about fear," she said.

—Can you show me?... No, do not. I sense it is hurtful. You must not be hurt.

"I can't be afraid anyway, when your mind is holding mine."

(Warmth filled her. Merriment was there, playing like little flames over the surface of Father-leading-her-by-the-hand-when-she-was-just-a-child-and-they-went-out-one-summer's-day-to-pick-wildflowers; over strength and gentleness and Bach and God.) Lucifer swept around the hull in an exuberant curve. Sparks danced in his wake.

—Think flowers again. Please.

She tried.

—They are like (image, as nearly as a human brain could grasp, of fountains blossoming with gamma-ray colors in the middle of light, everywhere light). But so tiny. So brief a sweetness.

"I don't understand how you can understand," she whispered.

—You understand for me. I did not have that kind of thing to love, before you came.

"But you have so much else. I try to share it, but I'm not made to realize what a star is."

—Nor I for planets. Yet ourselves may touch.

Her cheeks burned anew. The thought rolled on, interweaving its counterpoint to the marching music. —That is why I came, do you know? For you. I am fire and air. I had not tasted the coolness of water, the patience of earth, until you showed me. You are moonlight on an ocean.

"No, don't," she said. "Please."

Puzzlement:—Why not? Does joy hurt? Are you not used to it?

"I, I guess that's right." She flung her head back. "No! Be damned if I'll feel sorry for myself!"

—Why should you? Have we not all reality to be in, and is it not full of suns and songs?

"Yes. To you. Teach me."

—If you in turn will teach me— The thought broke off. A contact remained, unspeaking, such as she imagined must often prevail among lovers.

She glowered at Motilal Mazundar's chocolate face, where the physicist stood in the doorway. "What do you want?"

He was surprised. "Only to see if everything is well with you, Miss Waggoner."

She bit her lip. He had tried harder than most aboard to be kind to her.

"I'm sorry," she said. "I didn't mean to bark at you. Nerves."

"We are everyone on edge." He smiled. "Exciting though this venture is, it will be good to come home, correct?"

Home, she thought; four walls of an apartment above a banging city street. Books and television. She might present a paper at the next scientific meeting, but no one would invite her to the parties afterward.

Am I that horrible? she wondered. *I know I'm not anything to look at, but I try to be nice and interesting. Maybe I try too hard.*

—You do not with me, Lucifer said.

"You're different," she told him.

Mazundar blinked. "Beg pardon?"

"Nothing," she said in haste.

"I have wondered about an item," Mazundar said in an effort at conversation. "Presumably Lucifer will go quite near the supernova. Can you still maintain contact with him? The time dilation effect, will that not change the frequency of his thoughts too much?"

"What time dilation?" She forced a chuckle. "I'm no physicist. Only a little librarian who turned out to have a wild talent."

"You were not told? Why, I assumed everybody was. An intense gravitational field affects time just as a high velocity does. Roughly speaking, processes take place more slowly than they do in clear space. That is why light from a massive star is somewhat reddened. And our supernova core retains almost three solar masses. Furthermore, it has acquired such a density that its attraction at the surface is, ah, incredibly high. Thus by our clocks it will take infinite time to shrink to the Schwarzschild radius; but an observer on the star itself would experience this whole shrinkage in a fairly short period."

"Schwarzschild radius? Be so good as to explain." Eloise realized that Lucifer had spoken through her.

"If I can without mathematics. You see, this mass we are to study is so great and so concentrated that no force exceeds the gravitational. Nothing can counterbalance. Therefore the process will continue until no energy can escape. The star will have vanished out of the universe. In fact, theoretically the contraction will proceed to zero volume. Of course, as I said, that will take forever as far as we are concerned. And the theory neglects quantum-mechanical considerations which come into play toward the end. Those are still not very well understood. I hope, from this expedition, to acquire more knowledge." Mazundar shrugged. "At any rate, Miss Waggoner, I was wondering if the frequency shift involved would not prevent our friend from communicating with us when he is near the star."

"I doubt that." Still Lucifer spoke, she was his instrument and never had she known how good it was to be used by one who cared. "Telepathy is not a wave phenomenon. Since it transmits instantaneously, it cannot be. Nor does it appear limited by distance. Rather, it is a resonance. Being attuned, we two may well be able to continue thus across the entire breadth of the cosmos; and I am not aware of any material phenomenon which could interfere."

"I see." Mazundar gave her a long look. "Thank you," he said uncomfortably. "Ah… I must get to my own station. Good luck." He bustled off without stopping for an answer.

Eloise didn't notice. Her mind was become a torch and a song. "Lucifer!" she cried aloud. "Is that true?"

—I believe so. My entire people are telepaths, hence we have more knowledge of such matters than yours do. Our experience leads us to think there is no limit.

"You can always be with me? You always will?"

—If you so wish, I am gladdened.

The comet body curvetted and danced, the brain of fire laughed low. — Yes, Eloise, I would like very much to remain with you. No one else has ever— Joy. Joy. Joy.

They named you better than they knew, Lucifer, she wanted to say, and perhaps she did. *They thought it was a joke; they thought by calling you after the devil they could make you safely small like themselves. But Lucifer isn't the devil's real name. It means only Light Bearer. One Latin prayer even addresses Christ as Lucifer. Forgive me, God, I can't help remembering that. Do You mind? He isn't Christian, but I think he doesn't need to be, I think he must never have felt sin, Lucifer, Lucifer.*

She sent the music soaring for as long as she was permitted.

The ship jumped. In one shift of world line parameters she crossed twenty-five light-years to destruction.

Each knew it in his own way, save for Eloise who also lived it with Lucifer.

She felt the shock and heard the outraged metal scream, she smelled the ozone and scorch and tumbled through the infinite falling that is weightlessness. Dazed, she fumbled at the intercom. Words crackled through: "…unit blown back EMF surge… how should I know how to fix the blasted thing?… stand by, stand by…" Over all hooted the emergency siren.

Terror rose in her, until she gripped the crucifix around her neck and the mind of Lucifer. Then she laughed in the pride of his might.

He had whipped clear of the ship immediately on arrival. Now he floated in the same orbit. Everywhere around, the nebula filled space with unrestful rainbows. To him, *Raven* was not the metal cylinder which human eyes would have seen, but a lambence, the shield screen reflecting a whole spectrum. Ahead lay the supernova core, tiny at this remove but alight, alight.

—Have no fears (he caressed her). I comprehend. Turbulence is extensive, so soon after the detonation. We emerged in a region where the plasma is especially dense. Unprotected for the moment before the guardian field was reestablished, your main generator outside the hull was short-circuited. But you are safe. You can make repairs. And I, I am in an ocean of energy. Never was I so alive. Come, swim these tides with me.

Captain Szili's voice yanked her back. "Waggoner! Tell that Aurigean to get busy. We've spotted a radiation source on an intercept orbit, and it may be too much for our screen." He specified coordinates. "What *is* it?"

For the first time, Eloise felt alarm in Lucifer. He curved about and streaked from the ship.

Presently his thought came to her, no less vivid. She lacked words for the terrible splendor she viewed with him: a million-kilometer ball of ionized gas where luminance blazed and electric discharges leaped, booming through the haze around the star's exposed heart. The thing could not have made any sound, for space here was still almost a vacuum by Earth's parochial standards; but she heard it thunder, and felt the fury that spat from it.

She said for him: "A mass of expelled material. It must have lost radial velocity to friction and static gradients, been drawn into a cometary orbit, held together for a while by internal potentials. As if the sun were trying yet to bring planets to birth—"

"It'll strike us before we're in shape to accelerate," Szili said, "and overload our shield. If you know any prayers, use them."

"Lucifer!" she called; for she did not want to die, when he must remain.

—I think I can deflect it enough, he told her with a grimness she had not hitherto met in him. —My own fields, to mesh with its; and free energy to drink; and an unstable configuration; yes, perhaps I can help you. But help me, Eloise. Fight by my side.

His brightness moved toward the juggernaut shape.

She felt how its chaotic electromagnetism clawed at his. She felt him tossed and torn. The pain was hers. He battled to keep his own cohesion, and the combat was hers. They locked together, Aurigean and gas cloud. The forces that shaped him grappled as arms might; he poured power from his core, hauling that vast tenuous mass with him down the magnetic torrent which streamed from the sun; he gulped atoms and thrust them backward until the jet splashed across the heaven.

She sat in her cubicle, lending him what will to live and prevail she could, and beat her fists bloody on the desk.

The hours brawled past.

In the end, she could scarcely catch the message that flickered out of his exhaustion:—Victory.

"Yours," she wept.

—Ours.

Through instruments, men saw the luminous death pass them by. A cheer lifted.

"Come back," Eloise begged.

—I cannot. I am too spent. We are merged, the cloud and I, and are tumbling in toward the star. (Like a hurt hand reaching forth to comfort her:) Do not be afraid for me. As we get closer, I will draw fresh strength from its glow, fresh substance from the nebula. I will need a while to spiral out against that pull. But how can I fail to come back to you, Eloise? Wait for me. Rest. Sleep.

Her shipmates led her to sickbay. Lucifer sent her dreams of fire flowers and mirth and the suns that were his home.

But she woke at last, screaming. The medic had to put her under heavy sedation.

He had not really understood what it would mean to confront something so violent that space and time themselves were twisted thereby.

His speed increased appallingly. That was in his own measure; from *Raven* they saw him fall through several days. The properties of matter were changed. He could not push hard enough or fast enough to escape.

Radiation, stripped nuclei, particles born and destroyed and born again, sleeted and shouted through him. His substance was peeled away, layer by layer. The supernova core was a white delirium before him. It shrank as he approached, ever smaller, denser, so brilliant that brilliance ceased to have meaning. Finally the gravitational forces laid their full grip upon him.

—Eloise, he shrieked in the agony of his disintegration—Oh, Eloise, help me!

The star swallowed him up. He was stretched infinitely long, compressed infinitely thin, and vanished with it from existence.

The ship prowled the farther reaches. Much might yet be learned.

Captain Szili visited Eloise in sickbay. Physically she was recovering.

"I'd call him a man," he declared through the machine mumble, "except that's not praise enough. We weren't even his kin, and he died to save us."

She regarded him from eyes more dry than seemed natural. He could just make out her answer. "He is a man. Doesn't he have an immortal soul too?"

"Well, uh, yes, if you believe in souls, yes, I'd agree."

She shook her head. "But why can't he go to his rest?"

He glanced about for the medic and found they were alone in the narrow metal room. "What do you mean?" He made himself pat her hand. "I know, he was a good friend of yours. Still, his must have been a merciful death. Quick, clean; I wouldn't mind going out like that."

"For him… yes, I suppose so. It has to be. But—" She could not continue. Suddenly she covered her ears. "Stop! Please!"

Szili made soothing noises and left. In the corridor he encountered Mazundar. "How is she?" the physicist asked.

The captain scowled. "Not good. I hope she doesn't crack entirely before we can get her to a psychiatrist."

"Why, what is wrong?"

"She thinks she can hear him."

Mazundar smote fist into palm. "I hoped otherwise," he breathed.

Szili braced himself and waited.

"She does," Mazundar said. "Obviously she does."

"But that's impossible! He's dead!"

"Remember the time dilation," Mazundar replied. "He fell from the sky and perished swiftly, yes. But in supernova time. Not the same as ours. To us, the final stellar collapse takes an infinite number of years. And telepathy has no distance limits." The physicist started walking fast away from that cabin. "He will always be with her."

OUT OF THE KNIGHT

Since science fiction was so universally ignored by the rest of the literary world, it was forced to develop its own critics and its own critical standards. Like its writers, editors, bibliographers, indexers, researchers, its critics came mostly out of science fiction itself, out of its readers, out of its fans.

The earliest scholars acted as if the magazines did not exist. Philip B. Gove's 1941 study, of *The Imaginary Voyage in Prose Fiction*, stopped at 1800; even Marjorie Hope Nicholson's useful 1948 volume, *Voyages to the Moon*, cut itself off when spaceflight became plausible. J. O. Bailey's pioneer survey of science fiction entitled *Pilgrims Through Space and Time*, published in 1947, devoted only a smattering of comments to the science fiction magazines that had been around for two decades. Reginald Bretnor's important 1953 collection of articles, *Modern Science Fiction*, on the other hand, was written and edited by science fiction writers.

Authors could expect no reviews in newspapers, magazines, or journals, but they did get feedback. Fans talked to them at conventions, wrote about them in fanzines, wrote them letters, and wrote letters about their work to the professional magazines. The quantity of such reader response was unprecedented.

Fan feedback, however, did not satisfy the critical need. Such comments were welcome but unsystematic and sometimes uninformed. So the magazines created their own review columns. The best of them provided good service in calling books to the attention of readers: P. Schuyler Miller conducted *Astounding/Analog's* Reference Library until his death; Tony Boucher brought broad literary criteria to his reviews in *F&SF*; Algis Budrys brought distinction to *Galaxy's* book reviewing somewhat later. Eventually even the *New York Times* began a regular column.

The world of scholarship took notice of science fiction beginning in 1960 with Kingsley Amis's *New Maps of Hell*, followed by Bruce Franklin's study *Future Perfect* (1966), Mark Hillegas's *The Future as Nightmare: H. G. Wells and the Anti-Utopians* (1967), Thomas D. Clareson's *SF: The Other Side of Realism* (1971), and Robert Scholes's *Structural Fabulation* (1975). But the foundations of science fiction criticism were laid within science fiction itself, largely by two writers who understood the need for criticism. They were Damon Knight and James Blish, and they believed that science fiction should be held to higher standards than the uncritical praise or blame of fans.

Knight broke into criticism in 1945 with a classic (and somewhat unfair) hatchet-job on A. E. van Vogt's *The World of Null A* for Larry Shaw's fanzine, *Destiny's Child*. Later he wrote reviews for his short-lived 1950 prozine, (*professional* science fiction magazine, as contrasted to fanzine), *Worlds Beyond*, and then for *Space Science Fiction*, *Science Fiction Adventures*, *If*, and *F&SF*. Blish (1921-1975) reviewed mostly for fanzines, such as Redd Bogg's *Skyhook* and Larry and Noreen Shaw's *Axe*, under the name William Atheling, Jr.; he also wrote reviews for Richard Bergeron's *Warhoon* and Dick and Pat Lupoff's *Xero*, and later for *Science Fiction Forum*, *F&SF*, and *SF Horizons*.

Both Blish and Knight had their reviews collected and published by another unusual phenomenon, the fan press—in this case Advent Press, which has specialized in publishing books about science fiction for more than four decades. Knight's criticism appeared as *In Search of Wonder* (1956), which was reprinted and expanded in 1967, and Blish's as *The Issue at Hand* (1964) and *More Issues at Hand* (1970).

Blish and Knight were distinguished authors. They also had worked for a literary agency, edited magazines, and performed many of the other tasks that go into the creation and production of science fiction, including the publication of fanzines, and, in Knight's case, illustration.

Blish was best known, however, as an author, particularly for his *Cities-in-Flight* series that began with *Earthman, Come Home* (1955) and continued with *They Shall Have Stars* (1957), *The Triumph of Time* (1958), and *A Life for the Stars* (1962). He wrote many excellent short stories and other novels such as *Black Easter* (1968), and his historical novel about Roger Bacon, *Doctor Mirabilis* (1964). Ironically, he may have become more famous, toward the end of his life, for a series of *Star Trek* fictionalizations.

Although Knight (1922-) produced some interesting novels, including *Hell's Pavement* (1955), *The People Maker* (1959), *The Sun Saboteurs* (1961), and *Mind Switch* (1965), he is best known as a reviewer (for which he won a Hugo in 1956), a short-story writer, an editor, an anthologist, and a biographer. He was associated with the New York fan group, the Futurians, about which he wrote a 1977 history. Eventually he turned to the editing of anthologies, which he has done prolifically and with considerable success, particularly his annual anthology of original stories, *Orbit*, 1966-1980. It became a home for some of the best and most experimental fiction of the past decade. He returned to the writing of SF novels in 1981 with *The World and Thorinn*. Since then he has published *The Man in the Tree* (1984), the CV trilogy, and *Why Do Birds* (1992).

Knight helped found the Milford Science Fiction Writers Conference and was founding president of the Science Fiction Writers of America and first editor of its Nebula Award volumes. He is married to Kate Wilhelm (1928-), herself a distinguished science fiction author, with a Nebula for "The Planners" in 1968 and a Hugo for *Where Late the Sweet Birds Sang* in 1977.

Among Knight's well-known shorter works are: "To Serve Man," "Not with a Bang," "Stranger Station," "Cabin Boy," "The Country of the Kind," "The Handler," and "Masks," which was published in *Playboy* in July 1968.

MASKS

by Damon Knight

The eight pens danced against the moving strip of paper, like the nervous claws of some mechanical lobster. Roberts, the technician, frowned over the tracings while the other two watched.

"Here's the wake-up impulse," he said, pointing with a skinny finger. "Then here, look, seventeen seconds more, still dreaming."

"Delayed response," said Babcock, the project director. His heavy face was flushed and he was sweating. "Nothing to worry about."

"Okay, delayed response, but look at the difference in the tracings. Still dreaming, after the wake-up impulse, but the peaks are closer together. Not the same dream. More anxiety, more motor pulses."

"Why does he have to sleep at all?" asked Sinescu, the man from Washington. He was dark, narrow-faced. "You flush the fatigue poisons out, don't you? So what is it, something psychological?"

"He needs to dream," said Babcock. "It's true he has no physiological need for sleep, but he's got to dream. If he didn't, he'd start to hallucinate, maybe go psychotic."

"Psychotic," said Sinescu. "Well—that's the question, isn't it? How long has he been doing this?"

"About six months."

"In other words, about the time he got his new body—and started wearing a mask?"

"About that. Look, let me tell you something, he's rational. Every test—"

"Yes, okay, I know about tests. Well—so he's awake now?"

The technician glanced at the monitor board. "He's up. Sam and Irma are with him." He hunched his shoulders, staring at the EEG tracings again. "I don't know why it should bother me. It stands to reason, if he has dream needs of his own that we're not satisfying with the programmed stuff, this is where he gets them in." His face hardened. "I don't know. Something about those peaks I don't like."

Sinescu raised his eyebrows. "You program his dreams?"

"Not program," said Babcock impatiently. "A routine suggestion to dream the sort of thing we tell him to. Somatic stuff, sex, exercise, sport."

"And whose idea was that?"

"Psych section. He was doing fine neurologically, every other way, but he was withdrawing. Psych decided he needed that somatic input in some form, we had to keep him in touch. He's alive, he's functioning, everything works. But don't forget, he spent forty-three years in a normal human body."

In the hush of the elevator, Sinescu said, "...Washington."

Swaying, Babcock said, "I'm sorry, what?"

"You look a little rocky. Getting any sleep?"

"Not lately. What did you say before?"

"I said they're not happy with your reports in Washington."

"Goddamn it, I know that." The elevator door silently opened. A tiny foyer, green carpet, gray walls. There were three doors, one metal, two heavy glass. Cool, stale air. "This way."

Sinescu paused at the glass door, glanced through: a gray-carpeted living room, empty. "I don't see him."

"Around the ell. Getting his morning checkup."

The door opened against slight pressure; a battery of ceiling lights went on as they entered. "Don't look up," said Babcock. "Ultraviolet." A faint hissing sound stopped when the door closed.

"And positive pressure in here? To keep out germs? Whose idea was that?"

"His." Babcock opened a chrome box on the wall and took out two surgical masks. "Here, put this on."

Voices came muffled from around the bend of the room. Sinescu looked with distaste at the white mask, then slowly put it over his head.

They stared at each other. "Germs," said Sinescu through the mask. "Is that rational?"

"All right, he can't catch a cold or what have you, but think about it a minute. There are just two things now that could kill him. One is a prosthetic failure, and we guard against that; we've got five hundred people here, we check him out like an airplane. That leaves a cerebrospinal infection. Don't go in there with a closed mind."

The room was large, part living room, part library, part workshop. Here was a cluster of Swedish-modern chairs, a sofa, coffee table; here a workbench with a metal lathe, electric crucible, drill press, parts bins, tools on wallboards; here a drafting table; here a free-standing wall of bookshelves that Sinescu fingered curiously as they passed. Bound volumes of project reports, technical journals, reference books; no fiction except for *Fire* and *Storm* by George Stewart and *The Wizard of Oz* in a worn blue binding. Behind the bookshelves, set into a little alcove, was a glass door through which they glimpsed another living room, differently furnished: upholstered chairs, a tall philodendron in a ceramic pot. "There's Sam," Babcock said.

A man had appeared in the other room. He saw them, turned to call to someone they could not see, then came forward, smiling. He was bald and stocky, deeply tanned. Behind him, a small, pretty woman hurried up. She crowded through after her husband, leaving the door open. Neither of them wore a mask.

"Sam and Irma have the next suite," Babcock said. "Company for him; he's got to have somebody around. Sam is an old air-force buddy of his, and besides, he's got a tin arm."

The stocky man shook hands, grinning. His grip was firm and warm. "Want to guess which one?" He wore a flowered sport shirt. Both arms were brown, muscular and hairy, but when Sinescu looked more closely, he saw that the right one was a slightly different color, not quite authentic.

Embarrassed, he said, "The left, I guess."

"Nope." Grinning wider, the stocky man pulled back his right sleeve to show the straps.

"One of the spin-offs from the project," said Babcock. "Myoelectric, servo-controlled, weighs the same as the other one. Sam, they about through in there?"

"Maybe so. Let's take a peek. Honey, you think you could rustle up some coffee for the gentlemen?"

"Oh, why, sure." The little woman turned and darted back through the open doorway.

The far wall was glass, covered by a translucent white curtain. They turned the corner. The next bay was full of medical and electronic equipment, some built into the walls, some in tall black cabinets on wheels. Four men in white coats were gathered around what looked like an astronaut's couch. Sinescu could see someone lying on it: feet in Mexican woven-leather shoes, dark socks, gray slacks. A mutter of voices.

"Not through yet," Babcock said. "Must have found something else they didn't like. Let's go out onto the patio a minute."

"Thought they checked him at night—when they exchange his blood, and so on…?"

"They do," Babcock said. "And in the morning, too." He turned and pushed open the heavy glass door. Outside, the roof was paved with cut stone, enclosed by a green plastic canopy and tinted-glass walls. Here and there were concrete basins, empty. "Idea was to have a roof garden out here, something green, but he didn't want it. We had to take all the plants out, glass the whole thing in."

Sam pulled out metal chairs around a white table and they all sat down. "How is he, Sam?" asked Babcock.

He grinned and ducked his head. "Mean in the mornings."

"Talk to you much? Play any chess?"

"Not too much. Works, mostly. Reads some, watches the box a little." His smile was forced; his heavy fingers were clasped together and Sinescu saw now that the fingertips of one hand had turned darker, the others not. He looked away.

"You're from Washington, that right?" Sam asked politely. "First time here? Hold on." He was out of his chair. Vague upright shapes were passing behind the curtained glass door. "Looks like they're through. If you gentlemen would just wait here a minute, till I see." He strode across the roof. The two men sat in silence. Babcock had pulled down his surgical mask; Sinescu noticed and did the same.

"Sam's wife is a problem," Babcock said, leaning nearer. "It seemed like a good idea at the time, but she's lonely here, doesn't like it—no kids—"

The door opened again and Sam appeared. He had a mask on, but it was hanging under his chin. "If you gentlemen would come in now."

In the living area, the little woman, also with a mask hanging around her neck, was pouring coffee from a flowered ceramic jug. She was smiling brightly but looked unhappy. Opposite her sat someone tall, in gray shirt and slacks, leaning back, legs out, arms on the arms of his chair, motionless. Something was wrong with his face.

"Well, now," said Sam heartily. His wife looked up at him with an agonized smile.

The tall figure turned its head and Sinescu saw with an icy shock that its face was silver, a mask of metal with oblong slits for eyes, no nose or mouth, only curves that were faired into each other. "...project," said an inhuman voice.

Sinescu found himself half bent over a chair. He sat down. They were all looking at him. The voice resumed, "I said, are you here to pull the plug on the project." It was unaccented, indifferent.

"Have some coffee." The woman pushed a cup toward him.

Sinescu reached for it, but his hand was trembling and he drew it back. "Just a fact-finding expedition," he said.

"Bull. Who sent you—Senator Hinkel?"

"That's right."

"Bull. He's been here himself; why send you? If you are going to pull the plug, might as well tell me." The face behind the mask did not move when he spoke; the voice did not seem to come from it.

"He's just looking around, Jim," said Babcock.

"Two hundred million a year," said the voice, "to keep one man alive. Doesn't make much sense, does it. Go on, drink your coffee."

Sinescu realized that Sam and his wife had already finished theirs and that they had pulled up their masks. He reached for his cup hastily.

"Hundred percent disability in my grade is thirty thousand a year. I could get along on that easy. For almost an hour and a half."

"There's no intention of terminating the project," Sinescu said.

"Phasing it out, though. Would you say phasing it out?"

"Manners, Jim," said Babcock.

"Okay. My worst fault. What do you want to know?"

Sinescu sipped his coffee. His hands were still trembling. "That mask you're wearing," he started.

"Not for discussion. No comment, no comment. Sorry about that, don't mean to be rude; a personal matter. Ask me something—" Without warning, he stood up, blaring, "Get that damn thing out of here!" Sam's wife's cup smashed, coffee brown across the table. A fawn-colored puppy was sitting in the middle of the carpet, cocking its head, bright-eyed, tongue out.

The table tipped, Sam's wife struggled up behind it. Her face was pink, dripping with tears. She scooped up the puppy without pausing and ran out. "I better go with her," Sara said, getting up.

"Go on; and, Sam, take a holiday. Drive her into Winnemucca, see a movie."

"Yeah, guess I will." He disappeared behind the bookshelf wall.

The tall figure sat down again, moving like a man; it leaned back in the same posture, arms on the arms of the chair. It was still. The hands gripping the wood were shapely and perfect but unreal: there was something wrong about the fingernails. The brown, well-combed hair above the mask was a wig; the ears were wax. Sinescu nervously fumbled his surgical mask up over his mouth and nose. "Might as well get along," he said, and stood up.

"That's right, I want to take you over to Engineering and R and D," said Babcock. "Jim, I'll be back in a little while. Want to talk to you."

"Sure," said the motionless figure.

Babcock had had a shower, but sweat was soaking through the armpits of his shirt again. The silent elevator, the green carpet, a little blurred. The air cool, stale. Seven years, blood and money, five hundred good men. Psych section, Cosmetic, Engineering, R and D, Medical, Immunology, Supply, Serology, Administration. The glass doors. Sam's apartment empty, gone to Winnemucca with Irma. Psych. Good men, but were they the best? Three of the best had turned it down. Buried the files. *Not like an ordinary amputation, this man has had everything cut off.*

The tall figure had not moved. Babcock sat down. The silver mask looked back at him.

"Jim, let's level with each other."

"Bad, huh."

"Sure it's bad. I left him in his room with a bottle. I'll see him again before he leaves, but God knows what he'll say in Washington. Listen, do me a favor, take that thing off."

"Sure." The hand rose, plucked at the edge of the silver mask, lifted it away. Under it, the tan-pink face, sculptured nose and lips, eyebrows, eyelashes, not handsome but good-looking, normal-looking. Only the eyes wrong; pupils too big. And the lips that did not open or move when it spoke. "I can take anything off. What does that prove."

"Jim. Cosmetic spent eight and a half months on that model and the first thing you do is slap a mask over it. We've asked you what's wrong, offered to make any changes you want."

"No comment."

"You talked about phasing out the project. Did you think you were kidding?"

A pause. "Not kidding."

"All right, then open up, Jim, tell me; I have to know. They won't shut the project down; they'll keep you alive but that's all. There are seven hundred on the volunteer list, including two U.S. senators. Suppose one of them gets pulled out of an auto wreck tomorrow. We can't wait till then to decide; we've got to know now. Whether to let the next one die or put him into a TP body like yours. So talk to me."

"Suppose I tell you something but it isn't the truth."

"Why would you lie?"

"Why do you lie to a cancer patient."

"I don't get it. Come on, Jim."

"Okay, try this. Do I look like a man to you."

"Sure."

"Bull. Look at this face." Calm and perfect. Beyond the fake irises, a wink of metal. "Suppose we had all the other problems solved and I could go into Winnemucca tomorrow; can you see me walking down the street, going into a bar, taking a taxi."

"Is that all it is?" Babcock drew a deep breath. "Jim, sure there's a difference, but for Christ's sake, it's like any other prosthesis—people get used to it. Like that arm of Sam's. You see it, but after a while you forget it, you don't notice."

"Bull. You pretend not to notice. Because it would embarrass the cripple."

Babcock looked down at his clasped hands. "Sorry for yourself?"

"Don't give me that," the voice blared. The tall figure was standing. The hands slowly came up, the fists clenched. "I'm in this thing, I've been in it for two years. I'm in it when I go to sleep, and when I wake up, I'm still in it."

Babcock looked up at him. "What do you want, facial mobility? Give us twenty years, maybe ten, we'll lick it."

"No. No."

"Then what?"

"I want you to close down Cosmetic."

"But that's—"

"Just listen. The first model looked like a tailor's dummy, so you spent eight months and came up with this one, and it looks like a corpse. The whole idea was to make me look like a man, the first model pretty good, the second model better, until you've got something that can smoke cigars and joke with women and go bowling and nobody will know the difference. You can't do it, and if you could, what for?"

"I don't—Let me think about this. What do you mean, a metal—"

"Metal, sure, but what difference does that make. I'm talking about shape. Function. Wait a minute." The tall figure strode across the room, unlocked a cabinet, came back with rolled sheets of paper. "Look at this."

The drawing showed an oblong metal box on four jointed legs. From one end protruded a tiny mushroom-shaped head on a jointed stem and a cluster of arms ending in probes, drills, grapples. "For moon prospecting."

"Too many limbs," said Babcock after a moment. "How would you—"

"With the facial nerves. Plenty of them left over. Or here." Another drawing. "A module plugged into the control system of a spaceship. That's where I belong, in space. Sterile environment, low grav, I can go where a man can't go and do what a man can't do. I can be an asset not a goddamn billion-dollar liability."

Babcock rubbed his eyes. "Why didn't you say anything before?"

"You were all hipped on prosthetics. You would have told me to tend my knitting."

Babcock's hands were shaking as he rolled up the drawings. "Well, by God, this just may do it. It just might." He stood up and turned toward the door. "Keep your—" He cleared his throat. "I mean, hang tight, Jim."

"I'll do that."

When he was alone, he put on his mask again and stood motionless a moment, eye shutters closed. Inside, he was running clean and cool; he could feel the faint reassuring hum of pumps, click of valves and relays. They had given him that: cleaned out all the offal, replaced it with machinery that did not bleed, ooze or suppurate. He thought of the lie he had told Babcock. *Why do you lie to a cancer patient?* But they would never get it, never understand.

He sat down at the drafting table, clipped a sheet of paper to it and with a pencil began to sketch a rendering of the moon-prospector design. When he had blocked in the prospector itself, he began to draw the background of craters.

His pencil moved more slowly and stopped; he put it down with a click.

No more adrenal glands to pump adrenaline into his blood, so he could not feel fright or rage. They had released him from all that—love, hate, the whole sloppy mess—but they had forgotten there was still one emotion he could feel.

Sinescu, with the black bristles of his beard sprouting through his oily skin. A whitehead ripe in the crease beside his nostril.

Moon landscape, clean and cold. He picked up the pencil again.

Babcock, with his broad pink nose shining with grease, crusts of white matter in the corners of his eyes. Food mortar between his teeth.

Sam's wife, with raspberry-colored paste on her mouth. Face smeared with tears, a bright bubble in one nostril. And the damn dog, shiny nose, wet eyes…

He turned. The dog was there, sitting on the carpet, wet red tongue out— *left the door open again*—dripping, wagged its tail twice, then started to get up. He reached for the metal T square, leaned back, swinging it like an ax, and the dog yelped once as metal sheared bone, one eye spouting red, writhing on its back, dark stain of piss across the carpet, and he hit it again, hit it again.

The body lay twisted on the carpet, fouled with blood, ragged black lips drawn back from teeth. He wiped off the T square with a paper towel, then scrubbed it in the sink with soap and steel wool, dried it and hung it up. He got a sheet of drafting paper, laid it on the floor, rolled up the body over onto it without spilling any blood on the carpet. He lifted the body in the paper, carried it out onto the patio, then onto the unroofed section, opening the doors with his shoulder. He looked over the wall. Two stories down, concrete roof, vents ticking out of it, nobody watching. He held the dog out, let it slide off the paper, twisting as it fell. It struck one of the vents, bounced, a red smear. He carried the paper back inside, poured the blood down the drain, then put the paper into the incinerator chute.

Splashes of blood were on the carpet, the feet of the drafting table, the cabinet, his trouser legs. He sponged them all up with paper towels and warm water. He took off his clothing, examined it minutely, scrubbed it in the sink, then put it in the washer. He washed the sink, rubbed himself down with disinfectant and dressed again. He walked through into Sam's silent apartment, closing the glass door behind him. Past the potted philodendron, overstuffed furniture, red-and-yellow painting on the wall, out onto the roof, leaving the door ajar. Then back through the patio, closing the doors.

Too bad. How about some goldfish.

He sat down at the drafting table. He was running clean and cool. The dream this morning came back to his mind, the last one, as he was struggling up out of sleep: *slithery kidneys burst gray lungs blood and hair ropes of guts covered with yellow fat oozing and sliding and oh god the stink like the breath of an outhouse no sound nowhere he was putting a yellow stream down the slide of the dunghole and*

He began to ink in the drawing, first with a fine steel pen, then with a nylon brush. *his heel slid and he was falling could not stop himself falling into slimy bulging softness higher than his chin, higher and he could not move paralyzed and he tried to scream tried to scream tried to scream*

The prospector was climbing a crater slope with its handling members retracted and its head tilted up. Behind it in the distant ringwall and the horizon, the black sky, the pinpoint stars. And he was there, and it was not far enough, not yet, for the earth hung overhead like a rotten fruit, blue with mold, crawling, wrinkling, purulent and alive.

SURVIVING THE FUTURE

By the late 1960s a variety of immediate problems had begun to trouble the world and the visions of science fiction writers. The World War III that science fiction writers had feared since the explosion of the first atomic bomb over Hiroshima had not occurred, possibly because of the nuclear stalemate and the balance of terror. But hydrogen warheads were stockpiled, sometimes as the nosecones of continent-spanning rockets, and "police actions" and limited wars of deeply divisive nature were fought in Korea and later in Vietnam.

Knowledgeable people were beginning to warn about the world birthrate, which threatened a population of eight billion people by the year 2000; some wrote books about "the population bomb" and "the population explosion," comparing it to the dangers of that other bomb. Some of the experts even suggested that it was too late to do anything about the population increase. Others pointed out that even though the rate of population growth in the United States was lower than that in the developing nations, the impact of a U.S. child on the world's resources and on the growing pollution of the environment was many times (some said several hundred times) as great as that of a child born in India, say.

Resources were not yet becoming scarce by the late 1960s, but shortages in energy were predictable, and the end of the long growth in Western prosperity based on cheap oil was discernible by the perceptive. Nobody did much about it except to begin a few casual experiments with solar power and hydrogen fusion; the Western world grew increasingly dependent upon Middle Eastern oil.

Pollution received more attention, particularly after the 1962 publication of Rachel Carson's *Silent Spring*, and beginnings were made on cleaning up rivers and streams and the suppression of smoke and fumes in the United States and England. Rising carbon-dioxide levels in the atmosphere were debated as well as the prospect of a gradual (and disastrous) warming of the Earth through the greenhouse effect. Some scientists began speculating about a reversal of the long warming trend in Earth's weather and a possible return to cooler weather and even to the Ice Age. Possibly, with good luck, the carbon-dioxide greenhouse effect might cancel the new Ice Age.

Alvin Toffler's *Future Shock* (1970) described the human reaction to galloping technology and gave it a name, and raised general public consciousness to the problems of adjustment to rapid changes in the world. The political process no longer promised a way to a better world, not even in the Soviet Union, where the image of Joseph Stalin was toppled, or the United States, where John F. Kennedy, Robert Kennedy, and Martin Luther King were assassinated and the principles of advertising were applied to the shaping and selling of candidates by image, particularly through the staring eye of the television set.

There was little to be hopeful about, and many disillusioned novels began to appear, some of them in the science fiction genre. One of the best of the authors who seemed to find in impending disaster a release of creative energies was John Brunner (1934-1995). Born and bred in England, Brunner nevertheless had his early aspirations shaped by American science fiction and throughout his writing career focused largely on the American scene for settings and audience.

He sold his first novel at seventeen and dropped out of college about the same time because, he said, it was interfering with his education. His first American short story was "Thou Good and Faithful," published in *Astounding* in 1953 under the name John Loxmith. After service in the Royal Air Force and work at a few salaried jobs, Brunner turned to full-time writing. He was prolific at all lengths. His early work ran to relatively routine adventure stories but it displayed sufficient originality to earn him a reputation for competence.

A critical breakthrough came with *The Squares of the City* (1965), a novel about political control built around a chess game. It was followed by what is generally recognized as his masterpiece, *Stand on Zanzibar* (1968), a long novel about overpopulation in the near future. It won a Hugo and critical acclaim, and led to *The Jagged Orbit*, which brought racial divisions to the foreground of a consideration of medical malpractice and the military-industrial complex, *The Sheep Look Up* (1972), which took up the problem of pollution, and then to *The Shockwave Rider* (1975), which completed the square of imminent problems by dealing with technological change and future shock. The intensive labors proved exhausting, but Brunner regained his energies with such novels as *The Cubicle of Time* (1983) and *The Tides of Time* (1984), and *A Maze of Stars* (1991).

If Brunner's work was simply anti-utopian or dystopian, it might be easier to dismiss. But running through his novels is an element of hope that no matter how bad the situation may get—in *The Sheep Look Up* the entire United States catches fire—the situation may yet be saved if humanity can only manage to behave at its best rather than its worst. Brunner also managed to clothe his cautionary tales in high style; *Stand on Zanzibar*, for instance, adopted the experiments pioneered by John Dos Passos in *U.S.A.* His consciousness of style, however, never blinded him to the necessity of manner suiting matter, of style matching subject. He avoided the blind alley of some authors for whom style is everything.

FROM STAND ON ZANZIBAR

BY JOHN BRUNNER

the happening world (1)

READ THE DIRECTIONS

For toDAY third of MAY twenty-TEN ManhatTEN reports mild spring-type weather under the Fuller Dome. Ditto on the General Technics Plaza.

But Shalmaneser is a Micryogenic ® computer bathed in liquid helium and it's cold in his vault.

(DITTO Use it! The mental process involved is exactly analogous to the bandwidth-saving technique employed for your phone. If you've seen the scene you've seen the scene and there's too much new information for you to waste time looking it over more than once. Use "ditto." *Use* it!
—*The Hipcrime Vocab* by Chad C. Mulligan)

Less of a machine, more of a human being, but partaking of the nature of both, Georgette Tallon Buckfast is largely supported by prosthetics in her ninety-first year.

When the strain becomes TOO MUCH it's because Hitrip of California bred it to have less stalk per ounce, more clean-queen leaf. Ask "The Man who's Married to Mary Jane"!

Eric Ellerman is a plant geneticist with three daughters who's scared because his wife has developed a permanent pot-belly.

"...and Puerto Rico today became the latest state to ratify the controversial dichromatism provision of United States eugenic legislation. This leaves only two havens for those who wish to bear disadvantaged children: Nevada and Louisiana. The defeat of the baby-farming lobby removes a long-time stigma from the fair brow of the Junior-but-One State— a congenital stigma, one may say, since the J-but-O State's accession to hoodness coincided almost to the day with the first eugenic legislation concerned with haemophilia, phenylketonuria and congenital imbecility..."

Poppy Shelton has believed in miracles for years, but now there's one happening right inside her body and the real world is leaning on her dreams.

THE DIFFICULT WE DO AT ONCE. THE IMPOSSIBLE TAKES A LITTLE LONGER.
                                        —Base version of General Technics motto

Norman Niblock House is junior VP in charge of personnel and recruitment at General Technics.
"One fraction of a second, please—participant breakin coming up. Remember that only SCANALYZER's participant breakin service is processed by General Technics' Shalmaneser, the more correct response in the shorter quantum of time..."

Guinevere Steel's real name is Dwiggins, but do you blame her?

Do your slax sufficiently convey your natural power—at a glance?
If you're wearing MasQ-Lines, the answer's yes. Tired of half measures, we at MasQ-Line Corp have put the codpiece back where it belongs, to say to the shiggies not kidder but codder.

Sheena and Frank Potter are all packed ready to leave for Puerto Rico because a green and a red light are just lights to him.

"*Two* participant breakins! Number one: sorree, friend, but no—we are not wrong to say Puerto Rico's decision leaves a mere two havens for the dissident. Isola does enjoy statehood, but the whole area of the Pacific its islands occupy is under martial law and you don't get a pass for other than martial reasons. Thanks for asking us, though, it's the way of the world, you're my environment and I am yours, which is why we operate SCANALYZER as a two-way process..."

Arthur Golightly doesn't mind not being able to remember where he put things. Looking for them, he always finds other things he'd forgotten he had.

THE DIFFICULT WE DID YESTERDAY. THE IMPOSSIBLE WE'RE DOING RIGHT NOW.
— Current version of General Technics motto

Donald Hogan is a spy.

"Number the other: dichromatism is what's commonly called colorblindness, and it is sure as sidereal time a congenital disability. Thank you, participant, thank *you.*"

Stal (short for Stallion) Lucas is a yonderboy, weighed, measured, and freeflying all the way.

(IMPOSSIBLE Means: *1* I wouldn't like it and when it happens I won't approve; *2* I can't be bothered; *3* God can't be bothered. Meaning *3* may perhaps be valid but the others are 101% whaledreck.
— *The Hipcrime Vocab* by Chad C. Mulligan)

Philip Peterson is twenty years old.

Are you undermined by an old-style autoshout unit, one that needs constant reprogramming by hand if it's not to call you for items that were descheduled last week? GT's revolutionary new autoshout reprograms itself!

Sasha Peterson is Philip's mother.

"Turning to a related subject, rioting crowds today stormed a Right Catholic church in Malmö, Sweden, while early mass was in progress. Casualty lists suggest a death toll of over forty including the priest and many children. From his palace in Madrid Pope Eglantine accused rival Pope Thomas of deliberately fomenting this and other recent uprisings, a charge vigorously denied by Vatican authorities."

Victor and Mary Whatmough were born in the same country and have been married twenty years—she for the second time, he for the third.

What you want to do when you see her in her Forlon&Morler Maxess costumelet
Is what she wants you to do when you see her in her Forlon&Morler Maxess costumelet
If she didn't, she wouldn't have put it on
Maximal access is no exaggeration when you spell It MAXESS
Style illustrated is "Courtesan"
But you should see "Tart"
What there is of it

Elihu Masters is currently United States Ambassador to the one-time British colony of Beninia.

"Speaking of accusations, Dixierep Senator Lowell Kyte this anti-matter charged that dicties were now responsible for nine-tenths of the felonies committed per anum—sorree!—per annum in his home state of Texas and that Fed efforts to quell the problem were a failure. Privately, officials of the Nark Force have been heard to express concern at the way GT's new product Triptine is catching the dicties' fancy."

Gerry Lindt is a draftee.

When we say "general" at GT we mean: GENERAL. We offer the career of a lifetime to anyone interested in astronautics, biology, chemistry, dynamics, eugenics, ferromagnetism, geology, hydraulics, industrial administration, jet propulsion, kinetics, law, metallurgy, nucleonics, optics, patent rights, quarkology, robotics, synthesis, telecommunications, ultrasonics, vacuum technology, work, X-rays, ylem, zoology…
No, we didn't miss out your specialty. We just didn't have room for it in this ad.

Professor Doctor Sugaiguntung is head of the Tectogenetics Department at Dedication University in the Guided Socialist Democracy of Yatakang.

"The incidence of muckers continues to maintain its high: one in Outer Brooklyn yesterday accounted for 21 victims before the fuzzy-wuzzies fused him, and another is still at large in Evanston, Ill., with a total of eleven and three injured. Across the sea in London a woman mucker took out four as well as her own three-month old baby before a mind-present standerby clobbered her. Reports also from Rangoon, Lima and Auckland notch the day's toll to 69."

Grace Rowley is seventy-seven and going a bit weak in the head.

Here today and gone tomorrow isn't good enough for us in this modern age.
Here today and gone today is the pidgin we pluck.

The Right Honorable Zadkiel F. Obomi is the president of Beninia.

"Westaway a piece or two, a stiff note was received in Washington this anti-matter from the Yatakangi government, claiming naval units working out of Isola had trespassed into Yatakang's territorial waters. Officials will be polite, but it's an open secret Yatakang's hundred-island territory gives refuge all the time to Chinese aquabandits who sneak out from so-called neutral ports and ambush U.S. patrols in mid-ocean…"

Olive Almerio is the most successful baby-farmer in Puerto Rico.

You know the codders who keep one, two, three shiggies on the string. You know the shiggies who every weekend blast off with a different codder. Envy them?
Needn't.
Like any other human activity this one can be learned. We teach it, in courses tailored to your preferences.
Mrs. Grundy Memorial Foundation (may she spin in her grave).

Chad C. Mulligan was a sociologist. He gave it up.

"Last week's State Forest fires on the West Coast that laid low hundreds of square miles of valuable timber destined for plastics, paper and organic chemicals were today officially attributed to sabotage by Forestry Commissioner Wayne C. Charles. As yet it is uncertain to whom the guilt belongs: treacherous so-called partisans among our own, or infiltrating reds."

Jogajong is a revolutionary.

The word is EPTIFY.
Don't look in the dictionary.
It's too new for the dictionary.
But you'd better learn what it implies.
EPTIFY.
We do it to you.

Pierre and Jeannine Clodard are both the children of *pieds-noirs,* unsurprisingly as they are brother and sister.

"Tornado warnings are out in the following states... "

Jeff Young is "the man to go to" anywhere west of the Rockies for the rather specialized goods he handles: timefuzes, explosives, thermite, strong acids and sabotage bacteria.

"Turning to the gossipy side: once again the rumor goes the rounds that the small independent African territory of Beninia is in economic chaos. President Kouté of Dahomalia in a speech at Bamako warned the RUNGs that if they attempted to exploit the situation all necessary steps to counter... "

Henry Butcher is an enthusiastic proselytizer for the panacea he believes in.

(RUMOR Believe all you hear. Your world may not be a better one than the one the blocks live in but it'll be a sight more vivid.
　　　　　　　　　　—The Hipcrime Vocab by Chad C. Mulligan)

It is definite that the man known as Begi is not alive. On the other hand, in at least one sense he isn't dead either.

"Also it's noised that Burton Dent is bivving it again, in that he was seen scorting former fuel supply Edgar Jewel into the particulate stages of this anti-matter. Meantime, Pacific time, it looks like Fenella Koch his spouse of three years may be turning spousiness into spiciness with cream-dream Zoë Laigh. Like the slogan says—why not equals why ker-not!"

Mr. & Mrs. Everywhere are construct identities, the new century's equivalent of the Joneses, except that with them you don't have to keep up. You buy a personalized TV with homimage attachment which ensures that Mr. & Mrs. Everywhere look, and talk, and move like you.

(HIPCRIME You committed one when you opened this book. Keep it up. It's our only hope.

—*The Hipcrime Vocab* by Chad C. Mulligan)

Bennie Noakes sits in front of a set tuned to SCANALYZER orbiting on Triptine and saying over and over, "Christ what an imagination I've got!"

"And to close on, the Dept of Small Consolations. Some troubledome just figured out that if you allow for every codder and shiggy and appleofmyeye a space one foot by two you could stand us all on the six hundred forty square mile surface of the island of Zanzibar. ToDAY third MAY twenty-TEN come aGAIN!"

continuity (2)

THE DEAD HAND OF THE PAST

Norman strode out of the elevator door prepared to let go one of his rare, always calculated blasts of temper, under which any of his subordinates would cringe into guilt. He had hardly seen the interior of Shalmaneser's vault when his toe struck something on the floor.

He glanced at it.

It was a human hand severed at the wrist.

"Now my grandfather on my mother's side," Ewald House said, "was a one-arm man."

Age six, Norman looked up at his great-grandfather with circular eyes, not understanding everything that the old man told him, but aware that this was important in the same way as not wetting his bed or not getting too friendly with Curtis Smith's boy of his own age but white.

"Not sort of neat and tidy like you see nowadays," said Ewald House. "Not an ampytee. Not done surgical in a hospital. He was born a slave, see, and…"

"He was a left-handed man, see. What he did, he—he raised the fist of wrath against his bawss. Hit him ears over ankles inter the crick. So the bawss called up five-six field-han's chain him to a stump they had in the forty-acre field and just natcherly took a saw and…"

"And sawed it. 'Bout here." He touched his own scrawny pipe-stem of an arm three inches below the elbow.

"Nothing he coulda done about it. He was born a slave."

This time, very still, very calm, Norman *looked* at the interior of the vault. He saw the hand's owner writhing and moaning on the floor, clutching his wrist and trying to find pressure points on the leaking bloodvessels through a fog of intolerable agony. He saw the smashed reading table whose fragments were crunching under the feet of the panicky, mind-absent staff. He saw the light in the eyes of the pallid white girl, breathing orgasmically deep, who was standing off her attackers with her bloody blade.

Also he saw, up there on the balcony, more than a hundred idiots.

He disregarded what was happening in the middle of the floor and walked over to a panel set into the wall of the vault. Two quick twists of the fastenings and it fell away, revealing a network of heavy insulated pipes as tangled as the tails of a king rat.

He hauled on a quadrant valve; struck a union a sharp blow with the side of his hand, too quick for the chill of it to penetrate his skin; and put one of the hoses under his arm so he could lean on it and drag it after him. There would be enough free length for his purposes.

He stared at the girl as he approached her.

Divine Daughter. Probably called Dorcas or Tabitha or Martha. Thinking of killing. Thinking of smashing. A typical Christian reaction.

You murdered your Prophet. Ours died old and full of honor. You would kill yours again, and cheerfully. If ours came back I could speak to him like a friend.

Six feet from her, the pipe scritching across the floor like the scales of a monstrous snake, he stopped. Uncertain about this man with the dark skin and the cold, dead stare, she hesitated, poising the axe to chop at him, then having second thoughts and thinking: this must be a distraction, a trap.

She glanced wildly about her, expecting to find someone preparing to take her from the rear. But the staff had recognized what Norman had brought with him, and were sidling away.

"Nothing he coulda done about it… "

Convulsively he opened the valve on the end of the pipe and held it to a count of three.

There was a hiss, and snow fell, and something laid white ice on the axe, and the hand holding it, and the arm above the hand. There was an endless instant of nothing happening.

And then the weight of the axe broke the girl's hand off her arm.

"Liquid helium," Norman said briefly for the benefit of the watchers, and let the pipe fall clang to the floor. "Dip your finger in it, it snaps off like a dry stick. Don't try it is my advice. And don't believe what you hear about Teresa, either."

He didn't look at the girl, who had keeled over—fainting or possibly dead from the shock—but only at the frosted form of the hand still gripping the axe's haft. There should have been some sort of response, if no more than pride in his own quick thinking. There was nothing. His mind, his heart, seemed as frozen as that meaningless object on the floor.

He turned on his heel toward the elevator again, aware of a terrible disappointment.

Zink moved closer to Stal.

"Hey-hey!" he said. "Made it worth coming, huh? Let's go raise a bushel of whaledreck tonight, clear from the floor of the ocean. That put me square on the proper orbit!"

"No," Stal said, eyes fixed on the door through which the brown-nose had disappeared. "Not in this town. I don't like the kind of enforcement they keep here."

continuity (9)

DIVIDED AGAINST ITSELF

Like the monstrous shaped negative-plate of an explosive forming press the environment clamped itself on the personality of Donald Hogan, as a hand clenched around a lump of putty will leave the ridges between fingers, the imprint of the cuticular pattern. He felt his individuality squirt away from him into the darkness, carrying off in solution his power to conceive and act on decisions, reducing him to a reactive husk at the mercy of external events.

Some social theorists had argued that urban man was now at the point of unstable equilibrium; the camel's back of his rationality was vulnerable to a straw. Gadarene swine rooting and grunting at the top of a hill overlooking the sea, people sensed this, said the theorists, and therefore when there was an option to do otherwise they did not venture to crowd themselves still further into the already crammed cities. In countries such as India there was no alternative; starvation was slower in an urban community because people were closer to the distribution points for subsistence rations, and mere lethargy induced by hunger reduced friction and outbursts of violence to a sporadic level. But comparatively well-nourished American and European populations might be tipped over the precipice with no more warning than the sort of aura of irritability for which one carried a pack of tranks.

The last coherent thought Donald was capable of formulating declared that it was one thing to have read of this risk, another altogether to watch it being proved real.

Then the world took over and he was lost.

Focus: the prowlie. White-painted, trapezoidal vehicle thirteen feet long by seven wide, its wheels out of sight underneath for protection against shots, dispersed around the flat slab tank of the fuel-cell powering it, its forward cabin for four men windowed with armor-glass and additionally screened with retractable wire grilles, its rear section designed for carrying off arrestees and if necessary the injured having a solid metal drop-down tailgate with stretcher rails and a sleepy-gas air-circulation system. On the nose, two brilliant white lights with a field of 150°, one extinguished because the driver had waited too long to roll up the wire screen and protect it; on each corner of the roof other lights with adjustable beam-spread; revolving in a small turret on the roof, a gas-gun shooting fragmenting glass grenades to a distance of sixty yards; under the skirt, for ultimate emergency use only, oil-jets that could flood the adjacent street with a small sea of fire to keep back attackers while the occupants waited out the period till help arrived, breathing through masks from a stored-air system. It was vulnerable to mines, to three successive hand-gun bolts striking within about two inches of each other on the shell, or to the collapse of a building, but to nothing else encountered during an average urban riot. However, its fuel-cell was inadequate to push out of the way either the stationary cab ahead, whose brakes were automatically set because its door was open, or the lamp-post dropped across its stern, which had now been wedged in position with much sweating and swearing against its own stump on the one side, and a well-anchored mailbox on the other.

FOREGROUND: materialized as though from air, crowding the sidewalk, scores—hundreds—of people, mostly Afram, some Puerto Rican, some WASP. One girl with an electronic accordion, fantastically loud at maximum volume, making windows rattle and eardrums hum, shrieking a song through a shouter which others took up and stamped to the rhythm of: "*What shall we do with our fair city, dirty and dangerous, smelly and shitty?*" Clang on the body of the prowlie whatever they could find to throw—lumps of concrete, garbage, bottles, cans. How long before the gas-gun and the flaming oil?

SETTING: the uniform twelve-story faces of the buildings, each occupying a block or a half a block, hardly punctuated by the canyon streets because the abandonment of cars within the city meant that a one-way lane for the use of official vehicles or cabs was enough. Buses ran only to the next corner left, two corners away right. The sidewalks were defined by four-inch concrete barriers, small enough to step over, high enough to prevent any legally passing vehicle from running into a pedestrian. On the face of almost every building, some sort of advertising display, so that spectators in upper rooms looked out of shabby oceans, the middle of a letter O, or the crotch of a receptive girl. A single exception to the cliff-wall nature of the street was formed by the adventure playground, like the intrusion of Einstein into the ordered world of Euclid.

DETAIL: the face of the building against which he cowered, opposite the playground, was ornamented more than the average of its neighbors, possessing both a broad stoop above street-level for access to the interior and a number of integral buttresses, flat-faced, arranged in pairs with a gap of about two feet between each, tapering from a thickness of two feet at the bottom to nothing at the level of the fourth floor. One of these embrasures sufficed to shield him from light, the passing and re-passing rioters, and the hurling of improvised missiles. Clanging of metal above made him look up. Someone was trying to get the retractable fire-escapes to angle outward from the wall instead of straight down, so that from their vantage point things could be dropped on the roof of the trapped prowlie.

Fsst-crack. Fsst-crack. Whir-fsst-crack.

Gas-gun.

Grenades smashing against the walls of the buildings, each releasing a quart of sluggish vapor that oozed down into the narrow culvert of the street. The first victims coughed, howled and keeled over, having sucked in a full concentrated dose, and those lucky enough to be out of range of the first salvo ducked to the ground and hustled away crouching.

Fsst-crack. Whir-fsst-crack.

The girl whose mouth he had cut was staggering away from the middle of the street, coming toward him. Possessed of some vague impulse to help, Donald emerged from the shelter of the embrasure between the buttresses and called to her. She came because she heard a friendly voice, not seeing who spoke, and a clubbed arm slammed at the back of his left shoulder. From the corner of his eye he saw the hand was Afram. He ducked, dodged. The gas-gun crashed grenades on this side of the street now, and the first whiffs made breathing hateful. Those who had evaded gassing so far were taking to the skeletal branches of the playground like archetypal proto-man eluding a pack of wolves. The girl saw her brother, who had hit Donald, and together they hurried to the corner of the street, forgetting him. He followed because everyone was going away in one direction or another.

At the corner: late arrivals following a group of yonder-boys who had equipped themselves with sticks and big empty cans to make drums of, and howling with joy on seeing the stuck prowlie.

"Gas!"

The shouting faltered. There was a store across the road which had been open under automated supervision; the owner or manager had turned up and was hastily slamming the wire grilles over the display windows and the entrance, trapping three customers who seemed relieved rather than annoyed. An anonymous hand flung a rock through the last exposed window, which happened to have a liquor stand behind it. Cans and bottles thundered down, a heap of the former jammed the grille before it could rise and lock in place, and several of the crowd decided that was a better target than the prowlie.

Overhead a roaring noise. One of the tiny one-man copters capable of being maneuvered between the tops of the high buildings and the Fuller Dome whose blushing underside formed Manhattan's sky was scouting the scene to notify police headquarters of the extent of the disturbance. From a skylight somewhere away to the right there came a bang—an old-fashioned sporting gun. The copter wobbled and came down into the middle of the street, vanes screaming as the pilot fought for altitude. Mad with delight at having a fuzzy-wuzzy delivered into their hands the crowd went forward to greet him with clubs.

Donald fled.

On the next corner he found riot containment procedure already under way. Two water-trucks with hoses going were methodically washing people off the sidewalks into doorways. He turned at hazard in the opposite direction and shortly encountered sweep-trucks, paddywagons adapted with big snowplough-like arms on either side, serving the same purpose as the hoses but much less gentle. Keeping the crowd on the move was supposed to take away the chance of their organizing into coherent resistance. Also, another one-man copter droned down and started shedding gas-grenades into the street.

He was one of about fifty people being hustled and driven ahead of the official vehicles because they were off their own manor and had no place to go. He worked his way toward the wall of the building because some people, he saw, were dodging into hallways and vanishing, but at the first door he came close enough to stand a fair chance of entering there were two Aframs armed with clubs who said, "You don't live here, WASP—blast off before you get stung."

At an intersection two hose-trucks and the sweep-truck he was running from coincided. A mass of people from all three streets was shoved into the fourth, taking them back toward the focus of the trouble. Now they were body to body, stumbling on each other's heels and shrieking.

The prowlie was still stuck where it had been. Its driver sounded a blast of welcome to his colleagues in the sweep-truck. The gas had mostly dispersed, leaving victims choking and vomiting, but there was no end in sight to the riot. On the concrete arms of the playground men and women were still bellowing the song that the girl with the electronic accordion thundered out for them: "*Find you a hammer, and SMASH IT DOWN!*" Virtually every window had been broken and glass crunched underfoot. The human beings were being shoveled together with the garbage into one vast rubbish pile, not only in the direction from which Donald was coming but from the other end of the street as well. The stock plan had been applied: close the area, keep 'em moving, jam 'em together and pack 'em off.

Adventurous mind-present youths jumped up on the arms of the sweep-truck as it passed the adventure playground and from there leapt to the security of the random concrete branches. Donald was too late to copy them; by the time he thought of it he had been forced on by.

Mindlessly he pushed and thrust and shouted like everyone else, hardly noticing whether it was a man or a woman he jostled, an Afram or a WASP. The gas-gun on the sweep-truck discharged grenades over his head and the booming music died in mid-chord. A whiff of the gas reached Donald's nose and wiped away the last trace of rationality. Both arms flailing, careless of who hit him so long as he could hit back, he struggled toward the people from the opposite direction now impacting on the group he was enmeshed with.

Settling on the roofs with a howl of turbines: paddycopters to net and carry off the rioters, like some obscene cross between a spider and a vulture. He sobbed and gasped and punched and kicked and did not feel the answering blows. A dark face rose before his eyes and seemed familiar and all he could think of was the boy he had fired his Jettigun at, the one whose sister had attacked him in retaliation, so that he struck her in the mouth and made her bleed. Terrified, he began to batter the man confronting him.

"Donald! Stop it, Donald—*stop it!*"

More gas rained down from crunching grenades. He lost the energy needed to drive his fists and a modicum of sanity returned to him before he blacked out. He said, "Norman. Oh my God. Norman. I'm so—"

The apology, the recipient, the speaker, whirled together into nothing.

THE BIG PROTEST

One of the characteristics of the New Wave was protest. Sometimes the protest was a subjective reaction to existence itself, a lament that life was short and tragic and the universe was unknowable, a complaint about the inability of people to understand each other and the pain they inflict upon themselves and others, or a disagreement about the technological and scientific direction society has taken for the past two centuries.

But sometimes the protest was as social as Dickens' novels about the legal and educational system, the treatment of debtors, and workhouses for children; or as political as the Marxist novels of the Depression. The 1960s was an era of protest: civil rights in the South, the Vietnam war, campus conditions and involvement.... The emergence of the New Wave during the same decade may have encouraged the incorporation of protest themes, and the facts of protest may have encouraged the appearance of the New Wave; but probably the two are more deeply linked to a revolution against the optimistic assumptions of the previous decades.

Most New Wave fiction tended to express itself in experimental forms that were new in the mainstream several generations earlier, such as the work of John Dos Passos and James Joyce, but the social and political protest stories leaned toward contemporary language and the popular arts, particularly film, television, and rock groups. One of the most significant practitioners of this kind of protest was Norman Spinrad.

Spinrad (1940-) came out of the Bronx, and he attended the Bronx High School of Science (a couple of years before Delany) and (also like Delany) City College. He turned to writing early, and, after holding jobs as a literary agent and (briefly) as a welfare investigator, has worked at it steadily ever since. His first publication was "The Last of the Romany," in *Analog*, May 1963. His first novel, *The Solarians*, was published in 1966 and was followed by *Agent of Chaos* (1967) and *The Men in the Jungle* (1967). He also has written science articles and film criticism, and SF review articles for *Isaac Asimov's Science Fiction Magazine*, some of which have been collected as *Science Fiction in the Real World* (1990), and served as contributing editor to the *Los Angeles Free Press* and the *Los Angeles Staff*.

The breakthrough in his writing career came with the publication of *Bug Jack Barron* in 1969. A novel about a television personality and a nasty method to achieve immortality, narrated in the style of a media event and in a language that Scholes and Rabkin call "Madison Avenue hip projection," *Bug Jack Barron* achieved notoriety even before its book publication. It was serialized in *New Worlds*, unexpurgated, and its four-letter words led to a personal attack in the House of Commons in which Spinrad was labeled a "degenerate." The novel's serialization also led to the banning of the magazine by the biggest retail outlet in Britain.

His later book, *The Iron Dream* (1972), incorporated a science fiction novel entitled *Lords of the Swastika*, purportedly written by an Adolf Hitler who emigrated to the U.S. in 1919; it was a National Book Award nominee and won the Prix Apollo in France. He has two short-story collections, *The Last Hurrah of the Golden Horde* (1970) and *No Direction Home* (1975), and has edited two anthologies, *The New Tomorrows* (1971) and *Modern Science Fiction* (1974). He has also written a novel about modern Hollywood, *Passing Through the Flame* (1975). His later novels include *Songs from the Stars* (1980), *The Void Captain's Tale* (1983), *Child of Fortune* (1985), *Little Heroes* (1987), and *Russian Spring* (1991).

"The Big Flash," which appeared in *Orbit 5* (1969), not only is typical of the late 1960s and its concern about Vietnam and the possibility of nuclear war, but offers post-Beatle rock groups, student and drug cultures, and the mass influence of television.

THE BIG FLASH

BY NORMAN SPINRAD

T minus 200 days… and counting…

They came on freaky for my taste—but that's the name of the game: freaky means a draw in the rock business. And if the Mandala was going to survive in LA, competing with a network-owned joint like the American Dream, I'd just have to hold my nose and out-freak the opposition. So after I had dug the Four Horsemen for about an hour, I took them into my office to talk turkey.

I sat down behind my Salvation Army desk (the Mandala is the world's most expensive shoestring operation) and the Horsemen sat down on the bridge chairs sequentially, establishing the group's pecking order.

First, the head honcho, lead guitar and singer, Stony Clark—blond shoulder-length hair, eyes like something in a morgue when he took off his steel-rimmed shades, a reputation as a heavy acid-head and the look of a speed-freak behind it. Then Hair, the drummer, dressed like a Hell's Angel, swastikas and all, a junkie, with fanatic eyes that were a little too close together, making me wonder whether he wore swastikas because he grooved behind the Angel thing or made like an Angel because it let him groove behind the swastika in public. Number three was a cat who called himself Super Spade and wasn't kidding—he wore earrings, natural hair, a Stokeley Carmichael sweatshirt, and on a thong around his neck a shrunken head that had been whitened with liquid shoe polish. He was the utility infielder: sitar, base, organ, flute, whatever. Number four, who called himself Mr. Jones, was about the creepiest cat I had ever seen in a rock group, and that is saying something. He was their visuals, synthesizer and electronics man. He was at least forty, wore Early Nippy clothes that looked like they had been made by Sy Devore, and was rumored to be some kind of Rand Corporation drop-out. There's no business like show business.

"Okay, boys," I said, "you're strange, but you're my kind of strange. Where you worked before?"

"We ain't, baby," Clarke said. "We're the New Thing. I've been dealing crystal and acid in the Haight. Hair was drummer for some plastic group in New York. The Super Spade claims it's the reincarnation of Bird and it don't pay to argue. Mr. Jones, he don't talk too much. Maybe he's a Martian. We just started putting our thing together."

One thing about this business, the groups that don't have square managers, you can get cheap. They talk too much.

"Groovy," I said. "I'm happy to give you guys your start. Nobody knows you, but I think you got something going. So I'll take a chance and give you a week's booking. One A.M. to closing, which is two, Tuesday through Sunday, four hundred a week."

"Are you Jewish?" asked Hair.

"What?"

"Cool it," Clarke ordered. Hair cooled it. "What it means," Clarke told me, "is that four hundred sounds like pretty light bread."

"We don't sign if there's an option clause," Mr. Jones said.

"The Jones-thing has a good point," Clarke said. "We do the first week for four hundred, but after that it's a whole new scene, dig?"

I didn't feature that. If they hit it big, I could end up not being able to afford them. But on the other hand four hundred was light bread, and I needed a cheap closing act pretty bad.

"Okay," I said. "But a verbal agreement that I get first crack at you when you finish the gig."

"Word of honor," said Stony Clarke.

That's this business—the word of honor of an ex-dealer and speed-freak.

T minus 199 days... and counting...

Being unconcerned with ends, the military mind can be easily manipulated, easily controlled, and easily confused. Ends are defined as those goals set by civilian authority. Ends are the conceded province of civilians; means are the province of the military, whose duty is to achieve the ends set for it by the most advantageous application of the means at its command.

Thus the confusion over the war in Asia among my uniformed clients at the Pentagon. The end has been duly set: eradication of the guerrillas. But the civilians have overstepped their bounds and meddled in means. The Generals regard this as unfair, a breach of contract, as it were. The Generals (or the faction among them most inclined to paranoia) are beginning to see the conduct of the war, the political limitation on means, as a ploy of the civilians for performing a putsch against their time-honored prerogatives.

This aspect of the situation would bode ill for the country, were it not for the fact that the growing paranoia among the Generals has enabled me to manipulate them into presenting both my scenarios to the President. The President has authorized implementation of the major scenario, provided that the minor scenario is successful in properly molding public opinion.

My major scenario is simple and direct. Knowing that the poor flying weather makes our conventional airpower, with its dependency on relative accuracy, ineffectual, the enemy has fallen into the pattern of grouping his forces into larger units and launching punishing annual offensives during the monsoon season. However, these larger units are highly vulnerable to tactical nuclear weapons, which do not depend upon accuracy for effect. Secure in the knowledge that domestic political considerations preclude the use of nuclear weapons, the enemy will once again form into division-sized units or larger during the next monsoon season. A parsimonious use of tactical nuclear weapons, even as few as twenty one-hundred-kiloton bombs, employed simultaneously and in an advantageous pattern, will destroy a minimum of two hundred thousand enemy troops, or nearly two-thirds of his total force, in a twenty-four-hour period. The blow will be crushing.

The minor scenario, upon whose success the implementation of the major scenario depends, is far more sophisticated, due to its subtler goal: public acceptance of, or, optimally, even public clamor for, the use of tactical nuclear weapons. The task is difficult, but my scenario is quite sound, if somewhat exotic, and with the full, if to-some-extent-clandestine support of the upper military hierarchy, certain civil government circles and the decision-makers in key aerospace corporations, the means now at my command would seem adequate. The risks, while statistically significant, do not exceed an acceptable level.

T minus 189 days… and counting…

The way I see it, the network deserved the shafting I gave them. They shafted me, didn't they? Four successful series I produce for those bastards, and two bomb out after thirteen weeks and they send me to the salt mines! A discotheque, can you imagine they make me producer at a lousy discotheque! A remittance man they make me, those schlockmeisters. Oh, those schnorrers made the American Dream sound like a kosher deal—twenty percent of the net, they say. And you got access to all our sets and contract players, it'll make you a rich man, Herm. And like a yuk, I sign, being broke at the time, without reading the fine print. I should know they've set up the American Dream as a tax loss? I should know that I've *gotta* use their lousy sets and stiff contract players and have it written off against my gross? I should know their shtick is to run the American Dream at a loss and then do a network TV show out of the joint from which I don't see a penny? So I end up running the place for them at a paper loss, living on salary, while the network rakes it in off the TV show that I end up paying for out of my end.

Don't bums like that deserve to be shafted? It isn't enough they use me as a tax loss patsy, they gotta tell me who to book! "Go sign the Four Horsemen, the group that's packing them in at the Mandala," they say. "We want them on *A Night with the American Dream*. They're hot."

"Yeah, they're hot," I say, "which means they'll cost a mint. I can't afford it."

They show me more fine print—next time I read the contract with a microscope. I *gotta* book whoever they tell me to and I gotta absorb the cost on my books! It's enough to make a Litvak turn anti-semit.

So I had to go to the Mandala to sign up these hippies. I made sure I didn't get there till twelve-thirty so I wouldn't have to stay in that nuthouse any longer then necessary. Such a dive! What Bernstein did was take a bankrupt Hollywood-Hollywood club on the Strip, knock down all the interior walls and put up this monster tent inside the shell. Just thin white screening over two-by-fours. Real shlock. Outside the tent, he's got projectors, lights, speakers, all the electronic mumbo jumbo and inside is like being surrounded by movie screens. Just the tent and the bare floor, not even a real stage, just a platform on wheels they shlepp in and out of the tent when they change groups.

So you can imagine he doesn't draw exactly a class crowd. Not with the American Dream up the street being run as a network tax loss. What they get is the smelly, hard-core hippies I don't let in the door and the kind of j.d. high school kids that think it's smart to hang around putzes like that. A lot of dope-pushing goes on. The cops don't like the place and the rousts draw professional troublemakers.

A real den of iniquity—I felt like I was walking onto a Casbah set. The last group had gone off and the Horsemen hadn't come on yet, so what you had was this crazy tent filled with hippies, half of them on acid or pot or amphetamine or for all I know Ajax, high school would-be hippies, also mostly stoned and getting ugly, and a few crazy schwartzes looking to fight cops. All of them standing around waiting for something to happen, and about ready to make it happen. I stood near the door, just in case. As they say, "the vibes were making me uptight."

All of a sudden the house lights go out and it's black as a network executive's heart. I hold my hand on my wallet—in this crowd, tell me there are no pickpockets. Just the pitch-black and dead silence for what, ten beats, something crawling along my bones, but I know it's some kind of subsonic effect and not my imagination, because all the hippies are standing still and you don't hear a sound.

Then from a monster speaker so loud you feel it in your teeth, a heartbeat, but heavy, slow, half-time like maybe a whale's heart. The thing crawling along my bones seems to be synchronized with the heartbeat and I feel almost like I am that big dumb heart beating there in the darkness.

Then a dark red spot—so faint it's almost infrared—hits the stage which they have wheeled out. On the stage are four uglies in crazy black robes— you know, like the Grim Reaper wears—with that ugly red light all over them like blood. Creepy. Boom-ba-boom. Boom-ba-boom. The heartbeat still going, still that subsonic bone-crawl and the hippies are staring at the Four Horsemen like mesmerized chickens.

The bass player, a regular jungle-bunny, picks up the rhythm of the heartbeat. Dum-da-dum. Dum-da-dum. The drummer beats it out with earsplitting rim-shots. Then the electric guitar, tuned like a strangling cat, makes with horrible heavy chords. Whang-ka-whang. Whang-ka-whang.

It's just awful, I feel it in my guts, my bones; my eardrums are just like some great big throbbing vein. Everybody is swaying to it, I'm swaying to it. Boom-ba-boom. Boom-ba-boom.

Then the guitarist starts to chant in rhythm with the heart-beat, in a hoarse, shrill voice like somebody dying: *"The big flash... The big flash..."*

And the guy at the visuals console diddles around and rings of light start to climb the walls of the tent, blue at the bottom becoming green as they get higher, then yellow, orange and finally as they become a circle on the ceiling, eye-killing neon-red. Each circle takes exactly one heartbeat to climb the wall.

Boy, what an awful feeling! Like I was a tube of toothpaste being squeezed in rhythm till the top of my head felt like it was gonna squirt up with those circles of light through the ceiling.

And then they start to speed it up gradually. The same heartbeat, the same rim-shots, same chords, same circles, same base, same subsonic bone-crawl, but just a little faster... Then faster! Faster!

Thought I would die! Knew I would die! Heart beating like a lunatic. Rim-shots like a machine gun. Circles of light sucking me up the walls, into that red neon hole.

Oy, incredible! Over and over faster and faster till that voice was a scream and the heartbeat a boom and the rim-shots a whine and the guitar howled feedback and my bones were jumping out of my body—

Every spot in the place came on and I went blind from the sudden light—

An awful explosion-sound came over every speaker, so loud it rocked me on my feet—

I felt myself squirting out of the top of my head and loved it.

Then:

The explosion became a rumble—

The light seemed to run together into a circle on the ceiling, leaving everything else black.

And the circle became a fireball.

The fireball became a slow-motion film of an atomic bomb cloud as the rumbling died away. Then the picture faded into a moment of total darkness and the house lights came on.

What a number!

Gevalt, what an act!

So after the show, when I got them alone and found out they had no manager, not even an option to the Mandala, I thought faster than I ever had in my life.

To make a long story short and sweet, I gave the network the royal screw. I signed the Horsemen to a contract that made me their manager and gave me twenty percent of their take. Then I booked them into the American Dream at ten thousand a week, wrote a check as proprietor of the American Dream, handed the check to myself as manager of the Four Horsemen, then resigned as a network flunky, leaving them with a ten thousand bag and me with twenty percent of the hottest group since the Beatles.

What the hell, he who lives by the fine print shall perish by the fine print.

T minus 148 days… and counting…

"You haven't seen the tape yet, have you, B.D.?" Jake said. He was nervous as hell. When you reach my level in the network structure, you're used to making subordinates nervous, but Jake Pitkin was head of network continuity, not some office boy, and certainly should be used to dealing with executives at my level. Was the rumor really true?

We were alone in the screening room. It was doubtful that the projectionist could hear us.

"No, I haven't seen it yet," I said. "But I've heard some strange stories."

Jake looked positively deathly. "About the tape?" he said.

"About you, Jake," I said, deprecating the rumor with an easy smile. "That you don't want to air the show."

"It's true, B.D.," Jake said quietly.

"Do you realize what you're saying? Whatever our personal tastes—and I personally think there's something unhealthy about them—the Four Horsemen are the hottest thing in the country right now and that dirty little thief Herm Gellman held us up for a quarter of a million for an hour show. It cost another two hundred thousand to make it. We've spent another hundred thousand on promotion. We're getting top dollar from the sponsors. There's over a million dollars one way or the other riding on that show. That's how much we blow if we don't air it."

"I know that, B.D.," Jake said. "I also know this could cost me my job. Think about that. Because knowing all that, I'm still against airing the tape. I'm going to run the closing segment for you. I'm sure enough that you'll agree with me to stake my job on it."

I had a terrible feeling in my stomach. I have superiors too and The Word was that *A Trip with the Four Horsemen* would be aired, period. No matter what. Something funny was going on. The price we were getting for commercial time was a precedent and the sponsor was a big aerospace company which had never bought network time before. What really bothered me was that Jake Pitkin had no reputation for courage; yet here he was laying his job on the line. He must be pretty sure I would come around to his way of thinking or he wouldn't dare. And though I couldn't tell Jake, I had no choice in the matter whatsoever.

"Okay, roll it," Jake said into the intercom mike. "What you're going to see," he said as the screening room lights went out, "is the last number."

On the screen:

A shot of empty blue sky, with soft, lazy electric guitar chords behind it. The camera pans across a few clouds to an extremely long shot on the sun. As the sun, no more than a tiny circle of light, moves into the center of the screen, sitar-drone comes in behind the guitar.

Very slowly, the camera begins to zoom in on the sun. As the image of the sun expands, the sitar gets louder and the guitar begins to fade and a drum starts to give the sitar a beat. The sitar gets louder, the beat gets more pronounced and begins to speed up as the sun continues to expand. Finally, the whole screen is filled with unbearably bright light behind which the sitar and drum are in a frenzy.

Then over this, drowning out the sitar and drum, a voice like a sick thing in heat: *"Brighter... than a thousand suns...."*

The light dissolves into a close-up of a beautiful dark-haired girl with huge eyes and moist lips, and suddenly there is nothing on the sound track but soft guitar and voices crooning low: *"Brighter... Oh God, it's brighter... brighter... than a thousand suns..."*

The girl's face dissolves into a full shot of the Four Horsemen in their Grim Reaper robes and the same melody that had played behind the girl's face shifts into a minor key, picks up whining, reverberating electric guitar chords and a sitar-drone and becomes a dirge: *"Darker... the world grows darker..."*

And a series of cuts in time to the dirge:

A burning village in Asia strewn with bodies—

"Darker... the world grows darker..."

The corpse-heap at Auschwitz—

"Until it gets so dark..."

A gigantic auto graveyard with gaunt Negro children dwarfed in the foreground—

"I think I'll die..."

A Washington ghetto in flames with the Capitol misty in the background—

"...before the daylight comes..."

A jump-cut to an extreme close-up on the lead singer of the Horsemen, his face twisted into a mask of desperation and ecstasy. And the sitar is playing double-time, the guitar is wailing and he is screaming at the top of his lungs; *"But before I die, let me make that trip before the nothing comes..."*

The girl's face again, but transparent, with a blinding yellow light shining through it. The sitar beat gets faster and faster with the guitar whining behind it and the voice is working itself up into a howling frenzy: *"...the last big flash to light my sky..."*

Nothing but the blinding light now—

"...and zap! the world is done..."

An utterly black screen for a beat that becomes black fading to blue at a horizon—

"...but before we die let's dig that high that frees us from our binds... that blows all cool that ego-drool and burns us from our minds... the last big flash, mankind's last gas, the trip we can't take twice..."

Suddenly, the music stops dead for half a beat. Then:

The screen is lit up by an enormous fireball—

A shattering rumble—

The fireball coalesces into a mushroom-pillar cloud as the roar goes on. As the roar begins to die out, fire is visible inside the monstrous nuclear cloud. And the girl's face is faintly visible superimposed over the cloud.

A soft voice, amplified over the roar, obscenely reverential now: *"Brighter... great God, it's brighter... brighter than a thousand suns..."*

And the screen went blank and the lights came on.

I looked at Jake. Jake looked at me.

"That's sick," I said. "That's really sick."

"You don't want to run a thing like that, do you, B.D.?" Jake said softly.

I made some rapid mental calculations. The loathsome thing ran something under five minutes... it could be done...

"You're right, Jake," I said. "We won't run a thing like that. We'll cut it out of the tape and squeeze in another commercial at each break. That should cover the time."

"You don't understand," Jake said. "The contract Herm rammed down our throats doesn't allow us to edit. The show's a package—all or nothing. Besides, the whole show's like that."

"All like that? What do you mean, all like that?"

Jake squirmed in his seat. "Those guys are... well, perverts, B.D.," he said. "*Perverts?*"

"They're... well, they're in love with the atom bomb or something. Every number leads up to the same thing."

"You mean... they're *all* like that?"

"You got the picture, B.D.," Jake said. "We run an hour of *that* or we run nothing at all."

"Jesus."

I knew what I wanted to say. Burn the tape and write off the million dollars. But I also knew it would cost me my job. And I knew that five minutes after I was out the door, they would have someone in my job who would see things their way. Even my superiors seemed to be just handing down The Word from higher up. I had no choice. There was no choice.

"I'm sorry, Jake," I said. "We run it."

"I resign," said Jake Pitkin, who had no reputation for courage.

T minus 10 days... and counting...

"It's a clear violation of the Test-Ban Treaty," I said.

The Undersecretary looked as dazed as I felt. "We'll call it a peaceful use of atomic energy, and let the Russians scream," he said.

"It's insane."

"Perhaps," the Undersecretary said. "But you have your orders, General Carson, and I have mine. From higher up. At exactly eight fifty-eight P.M. local time on July fourth, you will drop a fifty-kiloton atomic bomb on the designated ground zero at Yucca Flats."

"But the people... the television crews...."

"Will be at least two miles outside the danger zone. Surely, SAC can manage that kind of accuracy under 'laboratory conditions.'"

I stiffened. "I do not question the competence of any bombing crew under my command to perform this mission," I said. "I question the reason for the mission. I question the sanity of the orders."

The Undersecretary shrugged, smiled weakly. "Welcome to the club."

"You mean you don't know what this is all about either?"

"All I know is what was transmitted to me by the Secretary of Defense, and I got the feeling he doesn't know everything, either. You know that the Pentagon has been screaming for the use of tactical nuclear weapons to end the war in

Asia—you SAC boys have been screaming the loudest. Well, several months ago, the President conditionally approved a plan for the use of tactical nuclear weapons during the next monsoon season."

I whistled. The civilians were finally coming to their senses. Or were they?

"But what does that have to do with—?"

"Public opinion," the Undersecretary said. "It was conditional upon a drastic change in public opinion. At the time the plan was approved, the polls showed that seventy-eight point eight percent of the population opposed the use of tactical nuclear weapons, nine point eight percent favored their use and the rest were undecided or had no opinion. The President agreed to authorize the use of tactical nuclear weapons by a date, several months from now, which is still top secret, provided that by that date at least sixty-five percent of the population approved their use and no more than twenty percent actively opposed it."

"I see…. Just a ploy to keep the Joint Chiefs quiet."

"General Carson," the Undersecretary said, "apparently you are out of touch with the national mood. After the first Four Horsemen show, the polls showed that twenty-five percent of the population approved the use of nuclear weapons. After the second show, the figure was forty-one percent. It is now forty-eight percent. Only thirty-two percent are now actively opposed."

"You're trying to tell me that a rock group—"

"A rock group and the cult around it. It's become a national hysteria. There are imitators. Haven't you seen those buttons?"

"The ones with a mushroom cloud on them that say 'Do it'?"

The Undersecretary nodded. "Your guess is as good as mine whether the National Security Council just decided that the Horsemen hysteria could be used to mold public opinion, or whether the Four Horsemen were their creatures to begin with. But the results are the same either way—the Horseman and the cult around them have won over precisely that element of the population which was most adamantly opposed to nuclear weapons: hippies, students, dropouts, draft-age youth. Demonstrations against the war and against nuclear weapons have died down. We're pretty close to that sixty-five percent. Someone—perhaps the President himself—has decided that one more big Four Horsemen show will put us over the top.

"The President is behind this?"

"No one else can authorize the detonation of an atomic bomb, after all," the Undersecretary said. "We're letting them do the show live from Yucca Flats. It's being sponsored by an aerospace company heavily dependent on defense contracts. We're letting them truck in a live audience. Of course the government is behind it."

"And SAC drops an A-bomb as the show-stopper?

"Exactly."

"I saw one of those shows," I said. "My kids were watching it. I got the strangest feeling... I almost wanted that red telephone to ring...."

"I know what you mean," the Undersecretary said. "Sometimes I get the feeling that whoever's behind this has gotten caught up in the hysteria themselves... that the Horsemen are now using whoever was using them... a closed circle. But I've been tired lately. The war's making us all so tired. If only we could get it all over with...."

"We'd all like to get it over with one way or the other," I said.

T minus 60 minutes... and counting...

I had orders to muster *Backfish's* crew for the live satellite relay of *The Four Horsemen's Fourth.* Superficially, it might seem strange to order the whole Polaris fleet to watch a television show, but the morale factor involved was quite significant.

Polaris subs are frustrating duty. Only top sailors are chosen and a good sailor craves action. Yet if we are ever called upon to act, our mission will have been a failure. We spend most of our time honing skills that must never be used. Deterrence is a sound strategy but a terrible drain on the men of the deterrent force—a drain exacerbated in the past by the negative attitude of our countrymen toward our mission. Men who, in the service of their country, polish their skills to a razor edge and then must refrain from exercising them have a right to resent being treated as pariahs.

Therefore the positive change in the public attitude toward us that seems to be associated with the Four Horsemen has made them mascots of a kind to the Polaris fleet. In their strange way they seem to speak for us and to us.

I chose to watch the show in the missile control center, where a full crew must always be ready to launch the missiles on five-minute notice. I have always felt a sense of communion with the duty watch in the missile control center that I cannot share with the other men under my command. Here we are not Captain and Crew but mind and hand. Should the order come, the will to fire the missiles will be mine and the act will be theirs. At such a moment, it will be good not to feel alone.

All eyes were on the television set mounted above the main console as the show came on and...

The screen was filled with a whirling spiral pattern, metallic yellow on metallic blue. There was a droning sound that seemed part sitar and part electronic and I had the feeling that the sound was somehow coming from inside my head and the spiral seemed etched directly on my retinas. It hurt mildly, yet nothing in the world could have made me turn away.

Then two voices, chanting against each other:

"*Let it all come in…*"

"*Let it all come out…*"

"In… *out*… in… *out*… in… *out*…"

My head seemed to be pulsing—in-*out*, in-*out*, in-*out*—and the spiral pattern began to pulse color-changes with the words: yellows-on-blue (in) green-on-red (*out*)… In-*out*-in-*out*-in-*out*….

In the screen… *out* of my head… I seemed to be beating against some kind of invisible membrane between myself and the screen as if something were trying to embrace my mind and I were fighting it… But why was I fighting it?

The pulsing, the chanting, got faster and faster till in could not be told from *out* and negative spiral afterimages formed in my eyes faster than they could adjust to the changes, piled up on each other faster and faster till it seemed my head would explode—

The chanting and the droning broke and there were the Four Horsemen, in their robes, playing on some stage against a backdrop of clear blue sky. And a single voice, soothing now: "*You are in….*"

Then the view was directly above the Horsemen and I could see that they were on some kind of circular platform. The view moved slowly and smoothly up and away and I saw that the circular stage was atop a tall tower; around the tower and completely circling it was a huge crowd seated on desert sands that stretched away to an empty infinity.

"*And we are in and they are in….*"

I was down among the crowd now; they seemed to melt and flow like plastic, pouring from the television screen to enfold me….

"*And we are all in here together….*"

A strange and beautiful feeling… the music got faster and wilder, ecstatic… and the hull of the *Backfish* seemed unreal… the crowd was swaying to it around me… the distance between myself and the crowd seemed to dissolve… I was there… they were here…. We were transfixed….

"*Oh yeah, we are all in here together… together….*"

T minus 45 minutes… and counting…

Jeremy and I sat staring at the television screen, ignoring each other and everything around us. Even with the short watches and short tours of duty, you can get to feeling pretty strange down here in a hole in the ground under tons of concrete, just you and the guy with the other key, with nothing to do but think dark thoughts and get on each other's nerves. We're supposed to be as stable as men can be, or so they tell us, and they must be right because the world's still here. I mean, it wouldn't take much—just two guys on the same watch over the same three Minutemen flipping out at the same time, turning their keys in the dual lock, pressing the three buttons.... Pow! World War III!

A bad thought, the kind we're not supposed to think or I'll start watching Jeremy and he'll start watching me and we'll get a paranoia feedback going.... But that can't happen; we're too stable, too responsible. As long as we remember that it's healthy to feel a little spooky down here, we'll be all right.

But the television set is a good idea. It keeps us in contact with the outside world, keeps it real. It'd be too easy to start thinking that the missile control center down here is the only real world and that nothing that happens up there really matters.... Bad thought!

The Four Horsemen... somehow these guys help you get it all out. I mean that feeling that it might be better to release all that tension, get it all over with. Watching the Four Horsemen, you're able to go with it without doing any harm, let it wash over you and then through you. I suppose they are crazy; they're all the human craziness in ourselves that we've got to keep very careful watch over down here. Letting it all come out watching the Horsemen makes it surer that none of it will come out down here. I guess that's why a lot of us have taken to wearing those "Do it" buttons off duty. The brass doesn't mind; they seem to understand that it's the kind of inside sick joke we need to keep us functioning.

Now that spiral thing they had started the show with—and the droning—came back on. Zap! I was right back in the screen again, as if the commercial hadn't happened.

"We are all in here together...."

And then a close-up of the lead singer, looking straight at me, as close as Jeremy and somehow more real. A mean-looking guy with something behind his eyes that told me he knew where everything lousy and rotten was at.

A bass began to thrum behind him and some kind of electronic hum that set my teeth on edge. He began playing his guitar, mean and low-down. And singing in that kind of drop-dead tone of voice that starts brawls in bars:

"I stabbed my mother and I mugged my paw...."

A riff of heavy guitar-chords echoed the words mockingly as a huge swastika (red-on-black, black-on-red) pulsed like a naked vein on the screen—

The face of the Horsemen, leering—

"Nailed my sister to the toilet door...."

Guitar behind the pulsing swastika—

"Drowned a puppy in a cement machine.... Burned a kitten just to hear it scream...."

On the screen, just a big fire burning in slow-motion, and the voice became a slow, shrill agonized wail:

"Oh God, I've got this red-hot fire burning in the marrow of my brain....

"Oh yes, I got this fire burning... in the stinking marrow of my brain....

"Gotta get me a blowtorch... and set some naked flesh on flame...."

The fire dissolved into the face of a screaming Oriental woman, who ran through a burning village clawing at the napalm on her back.

"I got this message... boiling in the bubbles of my blood.... A man ain't nothing but a fire burning... in a dirty glob of mud...."

A film-clip of a Nuremberg rally: a revolving swastika of marching men waving torches—

Then the leader of the Horsemen superimposed over the twisted flaming cross:

"Don't you hate me, baby, can't you feel somethin' screaming in your mind?

"Don't you hate me, baby, feel me drowning you in slime!"

Just the face of the Horsemen howling hate—

"Oh yes, I'm a monster, mother...."

A long view of the crowd around the platform, on their feet, waving arms, screaming soundlessly. Then a quick zoom in and a kaleidoscope of faces, eyes feverish, mouths open and howling—

"Just call me—"

The face of the Horsemen superimposed over the crazed faces of the crowd—

"Mankind!"

I looked at Jeremy. He was toying with the key on the chain around his neck. He was sweating. I suddenly realized that I was sweating too and that my own key was throbbing in my hand alive....

T minus 13 minutes... and counting...

A funny feeling, the Captain watching the Four Horsemen here in the *Backfish's* missile control center with us. Sitting in front of my console watching the television set with the Captain kind of breathing down my neck.... I got the feeling he knew what was going through me and I couldn't know what was going through him... and it gave the fire inside me a kind of greasy feel I didn't like....

Then the commercial was over and that spiral-thing came on again and whoosh! it sucked me right back into the television set and I stopped worrying about the Captain or anything like that....

Just the spiral going yellow-blue, red-green, and then starting to whirl and whirl, faster and faster, changing colors and whirling, whirling.... And the sound of a kind of Coney Island carousel tinkling behind it, faster and faster and faster, whirling and whirling and whirling, flashing red-green, yellow-blue, and whirling, whirling, whirling....

And this big hum filling my body and whirling, whirling, whirling.... My muscles relaxing, going limp, whirling, whirling, whirling, all limp, whirling, whirling, whirling, oh so nice, just whirling, whirling....

And in the center of the flashing spiraling colors, a bright dot of colorless light, right at the center, not moving, not changing, while the whole world went whirling and whirling in colors around it, and the humming was coming from the spinning colors and the dot was humming its song to me....

The dot was a light way down at the end of a long, whirling, whirling tunnel. The humming started to get a little louder. The bright dot started to get a little bigger. I was drifting down the tunnel toward it, whirling, whirling....

T minus 11 minutes... and counting...

Whirling, whirling, whirling down a long, long tunnel of pulsing colors, whirling, whirling, toward the circle of light way down at the end of the tunnel.... How nice it would be to finally get there and soak up the beautiful hum filling my body and then I could forget that I was down here in this hole in the ground with a hard brass key in my hand, just Duke and me, down here in a cave under the ground that was a spiral of flashing colors, whirling, whirling toward the friendly light at the end of the tunnel, whirling, whirling....

T minus 10 minutes... and counting...

The circle of light at the end of the whirling tunnel was getting bigger and bigger and the humming was getting louder and louder and I was feeling better and better and the *Backfish's* missile control center was getting dimmer and dimmer as the awful weight of command got lighter and lighter, whirling, whirling, and I felt so good I wanted to cry, whirling, whirling....

T minus 9 minutes... and counting...

Whirling, whirling... I was whirling, Jeremy was whirling, the hole in the ground was whirling, and the circle of light at the end of the tunnel whirled closer and closer and—I was through! A place filled with yellow light. Pale metal-yellow light. Then pale metallic blue. Yellow. Blue. Yellow. Blue. Yellow-blue-yellow-blue-yellow-blue-yellow...

Pure light pulsing... and pure sound droning. And just the *feeling* of letters I couldn't read between the pulses—not-yellow and not-blue—too quick and too faint to be visible, but important, very important....

And then a voice that seemed to be singing from inside my head, almost as if it were my own:

"Oh, oh, oh... don't I really wanna know.... Oh, oh, oh... don't I really wanna know...."

The word pulsing, flashing around those words I couldn't read, couldn't quite read, had to read, could *almost* read....

"Oh, oh, oh... great God I really wanna know...."

Strange amorphous shapes clouding the blue-yellow-blue flickering universe, hiding the words I had to read.... Dammit, why wouldn't they get out of the way so I could find out what I had to know!

"Tell me tell me tell me tell me tell me.... Gotta know gotta know gotta know gotta know...."

T minus 7 minutes... and counting...

Couldn't read the words! Why wouldn't the Captain let me read the words?

And that voice inside me: *"Gotta know... gotta know... gotta know why it hurts me so..."* Why wouldn't it shut up and let me read the words? Why wouldn't the words hold still? Or just slow down little? If they'd slow down a little, I could read them and then I'd know what I had to do....

T minus 6 minutes... and counting...

I felt the sweaty key in the palm of my hand.... I saw Duke stroking his own key. Had to know! Now—through the pulsing blue-yellow-blue light and the unreadable words that were building up an awful pressure in the back of my brain—I could see the Four Horsemen. They were on their knees, crying, looking up at something and begging: *"Tell me tell me tell me tell me...."*

Then soft billows of rich red-and-orange filled the world and a huge voice was trying to speak. But it couldn't form the words. It stuttered and moaned—

The yellow-blue-yellow flashing around the words I couldn't read—the same words, I suddenly sensed, that the voice of the fire was trying so hard to form—and the Four Horsemen on their knees begging: *"Tell me tell me tell me...."*

The friendly warm fire trying so hard to speak—

"Tell me tell me tell me tell...."

T minus 4 minutes… and counting…

What were the words? What was the order? I could sense my men silently imploring me to tell them. After all, I was their Captain, it was my duty to find out!

"Tell me tell me tell me…" the robed figures on their knees implored through the flickering pulse in my brain and I could almost make out the words… almost.…

"Tell me tell me tell me.…" I whispered to the warm orange fire that was trying so hard but couldn't quite form the words. The men were whispering it too: "Tell me tell me.…"

T minus 3 minutes… and counting…

The question burning blue and yellow in my brain. WHAT WAS THE FIRE TRYING TO TELL ME? WHAT WERE THE WORDS I COULDN'T READ?

Had to unlock the words! Had to find the key!

A key.… The key? THE KEY! And there was the lock that imprisoned the words, right in front of me! Put the key in the lock.… I looked at Jeremy. Wasn't there some reason, long ago and far away, why Jeremy might try to stop me from putting the key in the lock?

But Jeremy didn't move as I fitted the key into the lock.…

T minus 2 minutes… and counting…

Why wouldn't the Captain tell me what the order was? The fire knew, but it couldn't tell. My head ached from the pulsing, but I couldn't read the words.

"Tell me tell me tell me…" I begged.

Then I realized that the Captain was asking too.

T minus 90 seconds… and counting…

"Tell me tell me tell me…" the Horsemen begged. And the words I couldn't read were a fire in my brain.

Duke's key was in the lock in front of us. From very far away, he said: "We have to do it together."

Of course… our keys… our keys would unlock the words!

I put my key into the lock. One, two, three, we turned our keys together. A lid on the console popped open. Under the lid were three red buttons. Three signs on the console lit up in red letters: ARMED.

T minus 60 seconds… and counting…

The men were waiting for me to give some order. I didn't know what the order was. A magnificent orange fire was trying to tell me but it couldn't get the words out.... Robed figures were praying to the fire....

Then through the yellow-blue flicker that hid the words I had to read, I saw a vast crowd encircling a tower. The crowd was on its feet begging silently—

The tower in the center of the crowd became the orange fire that was trying to tell me what the words were—

Became a great mushroom of billowing smoke and blinding orange-red glare....

T minus 30 seconds... and counting...

The huge pillar of fire was trying to tell Jeremy and me what the words were, what we had to do. The crowd was screaming at the cloud of flame. The yellow-blue flicker was getting faster and faster behind the mushroom cloud. I could almost read the words! I could see that there were two of them!

T minus 20 seconds... and counting...

Why didn't the Captain tell us? I could almost see the words!

Then I heard the crowd around the beautiful mushroom cloud shouting: "DO IT! DO IT! DO IT! DO IT! DO IT!"

T minus 10 seconds...and counting...

"DO IT! DO IT! DO IT! DO IT! DO IT! DO IT! DO IT!"

What did they want me to do? Did Duke know?

9

The men were waiting! What was the order? They hunched over the firing controls, waiting.... The firing controls...?

"DO IT! DO IT! DO IT! DO IT! DO IT!"

8

"DO IT! DO IT! DO IT! DO IT! DO IT!": the crowd screaming. "Jeremy!" I shouted. "I can read the words!"

7

My hands hovered over my bank of firing buttons.... "DO IT! DO IT! DO IT! DO IT!" the words said.

Didn't the Captain understand?

6

"What do they want us to do, Jeremy?"

5

Why didn't the mushroom cloud give the order? My men were waiting! A good sailor craves action.

Then a great voice spoke from the pillar of fire: "DO IT... DO IT... DO IT... "

4

"There's only one thing we can do down here, Duke."

3

"The order, men! Action! Fire!"

2

Yes, yes, yes! Jeremy—

1

I reached for my bank of firing buttons. All along the console, the men reached for their buttons. But I was too fast for them! I would be first!

0

THE BIG FLASH

THE ORIGIN AND DEVELOPMENT OF SCIENCE FICTION WRITERS

Science fiction writers are often asked why they chose to write science fiction, and the answer is always the same. Writers are created out of readers. Not all readers become writers, but no one becomes a writer who did not first fall in love with reading. A poet recently came up with a test for determining whether a child would become a writer: turn the child loose in a room filled with balls, games, doll houses, toys of every description, and a typewriter; if the child heads straight for the typewriter the child may become a writer.

Science fiction writers are created out of fans. What they start writing, of course, is usually imitative: a Burroughs pastiche, a Heinlein extrapolation, a Conan adventure, a van Vogt intrigue... Gradually individuality begins to reshape the imitative impulse, and, though the writer may continue to produce fiction in a particular mode, the writing has sufficient differences in plot or style to make it publishable. Magazines and paperbacks are filled with such writing, unexceptional and unexceptionable. Finally some writers break free of their origins. Either through the process of living or some other liberating influence, a writer discovers that there is something special to say and a special way to say it.

There are exceptions to all these generalities. Some writers break into print as originals—the Heinleins, the van Vogts, the Sturgeons. Others eventually find their own subjects, their own voice—the Asimovs, the Kuttners, the Brunners. And Robert Silverberg, perhaps the most dramatic example of the writer who abruptly came into his own.

Silverberg (1936–) has described himself as "a man living his own adolescent fantasies. When I was sixteen or so I yearned to win fame as a writer of science fiction, to become wealthy enough to indulge in whatever amusements I chose, to know the love of fair women, to travel widely, to live free from the pressures and perils of ordinary life." He set about the fulfillment of his dreams early. His first story, "Gorgon Planet," was published in the Scottish magazine *Nebula* in 1954 while Silverberg was still an underclassman at Columbia University (he earned a degree in English), and his first novel, *Revolt on Alpha C*, in 1955.

Some early success with routine fiction and collaboration for a time with Randall Garrett led Silverberg to the conclusion that he would be more successful turning out "mass-produced formularized stories at high speed" rather than lavishing "passion and energy on more individual works that would be difficult to sell." His industry and production were phenomenal even in a field where writers had to write fast and sell first drafts in order to survive. Within little more than a year he was a successful author of potboilers, writing twenty-five pages a day, five days a week, and selling them all.

Within a few years he ventured into popular science and was just as prolific and even more financially successful. He was drawn back into science fiction in the early 1960s. His science books became more thorough and more satisfying, and his fiction became more original. Finally, with a book entitled *To Open the Sky* (1967), a novel entitled *Thorns* (1967), a story entitled "Hawksbill Station" and another entitled "Nightwings," he completed the remarkable first stage in a metamorphosis from a prolific hack to an original author of literary skill and sensitivity.

Such a reversal happens seldom and almost never so dramatically. Even his working methods were revolutionized: now everything was rewritten and every sentence reworked on scratch paper until it was good enough to put into the narrative.

His fiction still poured into print and rewards came: "Nightwings" won a Hugo in 1968, "Passengers" a Nebula in 1969, *A Time of Changes* a Nebula in 1971, "Good News from the Vatican" a Nebula in 1971, and "Born with the Dead" a Nebula in 1974. Other novels include: *The Masks of Time* (1968), *The Man in the Maze* (1969), *Up the Line* (1969), *Tower of Glass* (1970), *The World Inside* (1971), *Son of Man* (1971), *Dying Inside* (1972), *The Book of Skulls* (1972), *The Stochastic Man* (1975), and *Shadrach in the Furnace* (1976). He also has several collections of stories and is a prolific editor of anthologies. In 1967-1968 he served as president of SFWA and edited its best-selling anthology, *The Science Fiction Hall of Fame*.

Distinguished as Silverberg's fiction has been since his conversion to literary craftsmanship, it put off many readers, as the ratio of Nebulas to Hugos might suggest. Most of his more recent work seems to involve the reworking of genre materials, returning to old science fiction ideas to ask how they would work out in real life, in human terms. Under such scrutiny the hard realities of science fiction turn into metaphors, into adventures, and into frustrations. *Dying Inside*, for instance, is an admirable novel about the difficulties encountered by a character whose only use for his telepathic ability is to help him write term papers for college students; it becomes an admittedly mainstream novel in which the protagonist's dwindling powers become a metaphor for middle age. Unfortunately it was not picked up by mainstream critics and science fiction readers did not find in it the customary rewards.

Silverberg's later fiction seems as brilliantly faceted as a jewel but also hard and remote. In a dialog with Samuel R. Delany, he said that he stopped writing in 1975 because he felt that he had nothing more to say and what he had been writing was increasingly unsatisfying for him and his readers. As if in ratification of this conclusion, he returned to writing with a long, epic adventure novel entitled *Lord Valentine's Castle* that sold, on the basis of a fifteen-page outline, for $127,500, the largest advance up to that time. Subsequently advances to a few best-selling authors soared to $1 million and more. Silverberg has produced various well-received Majipoor sequels and such other novels as *Sailing to Byzantium* (1985), winner of a Nebula, *Star of Gypsies* (1986), *The Secret Sharer* (1988), and *Gilgamesh the King* (1984) and *To the Land of the Living* (1989). His New Springtime trilogy began with *At Winter's End* (1988).

"Sundance" was first published in *The Magazine of Fantasy and Science Fiction*, June 1969.

SUNDANCE

BY ROBERT SILVERBERG

Today you liquidated about 50,000 Eaters in Sector A, and now you are spending an uneasy night. You and Herndon flew east at dawn, with the green-gold sunrise at your backs, and sprayed the neural pellets over a thousand hectares along the Forked River. You flew on into the prairie beyond the river, where the Eaters have already been wiped out, and had lunch sprawled on that thick, soft carpet of grass where the first settlement is expected to rise. Herndon picked some juiceflowers, and you enjoyed half an hour of mild hallucinations. Then, as you headed toward the copter to begin an afternoon of further pellet spraying, he said suddenly, "Tom, how would you feel about this if it turned out that the Eaters weren't just animal pests? That they were *people*, say, with a language and rites and a history and all?"

You thought of how it had been for your own people.

"They aren't," you said.

"Suppose they were. Suppose the Eaters—"

"They aren't. Drop it."

Herndon has this streak of cruelty in him that leads him to ask such questions. He goes for the vulnerabilities; it amuses him. All night now his casual remark has echoed in your mind. Suppose the Eaters... Suppose the Eaters... Suppose... Suppose...

You sleep for a while, and dream, and in your dreams you swim through rivers of blood.

Foolishness. A feverish fantasy. You know how important it is to exterminate the Eaters fast, before the settlers get here. They're just animals, and not even harmless animals at that; ecology-wreckers is what they are, devourers of oxygen-liberating plants, and they have to go. A few have been saved for zoological study. The rest must be destroyed. Ritual extirpation of undesirable beings, the old, old story. But let's not complicate our job with moral qualms, you tell yourself. Let's not dream of rivers of blood.

The Eaters don't even *have* blood, none that could flow in rivers, anyway. What they have is, well, a kind of lymph that permeates every tissue and transmits nourishment along the interfaces. Waste products go out the same way, osmotically. In terms of process, it's structurally analogous to your own kind of circulatory system, except there's no network of blood vessels hooked to a master pump. The life-stuff just oozes through their bodies, as though they were amoebas or sponges or some other low-phylum form. Yet they're definitely high-phylum in nervous system, digestive setup, limb-and-organ template, etc. Odd, you think. The thing about aliens is that they're alien, you tell yourself, not for the first time.

The beauty of their biology for you and your companions is that it lets you exterminate them so neatly.

You fly over the grazing grounds and drop the neural pellets. The Eaters find and ingest them. Within an hour the poison has reached all sectors of the body. Life ceases; a rapid breakdown of cellular matter follows, the Eater literally falling apart molecule by molecule the instant that nutrition is cut off; the lymph-like stuff works like acid; a universal lysis occurs; flesh and even the bones, which are cartilaginous, dissolve. In two hours, a puddle on the ground. In four, nothing at all left. Considering how many millions of Eaters you've scheduled for extermination here, it's sweet of the bodies to be self-disposing. Otherwise what a charnel house this would become!

Suppose the Eaters…

Damn Herndon. You almost feel like getting a memory-editing in the morning. Scrape his stupid speculations out of your head. If you dared. If you dared.

In the morning he does not dare. Memory-editing frightens him; he will try to shake free of his new-found guilt without it. The Eaters, he explains to himself, are mindless herbivores, the unfortunate victims of human expansionism, but not really deserving of passionate defense. Their extermination is not tragic; it's just too bad. If Earthmen are to have this world, the Eaters must relinquish it. There's a difference, he tells himself, between the elimination of the Plains Indians from the American prairie in the nineteenth century and the destruction of the bison on that same prairie. One feels a little wistful about the slaughter of the thundering herds; one regrets the butchering of millions of the noble brown woolly beasts, yes. But one feels outrage, not mere wistful regret, at what was done to the Sioux. There's a difference. Reserve your passions for the proper cause.

He walks from his bubble at the edge of the camp toward the center of things. The flagstone path is moist and glistening. The morning fog has not yet lifted, and every tree is bowed, the long, notched leaves heavy with droplets of water. He pauses, crouching, to observe a spider-analog spinning its asymmetrical web. As he watches, a small amphibian, delicately shaded turquoise, glides as inconspicuously as possible over the mossy ground. Not inconspicuously enough; he gently lifts the little creature and puts it on the back of his hand. The gills flutter in anguish, and the amphibian's sides quiver. Slowly, cunningly, its color changes until it matches the coppery tone of the hand. The camouflage is excellent. He lowers his hand and the amphibian scurries into a puddle. He walks on.

He is forty years old, shorter than most of the other members of the expedition with wide shoulders, a heavy chest, dark glossy hair, a blunt, spreading nose. He is a biologist. This is his third career, for he has failed as an anthropologist and as a developer of real estate. His name is Tom Two Ribbons. He has been married twice but has had no children. His great-grandfather died of alcoholism; his grandfather was addicted to hallucinogens; his father had compulsively visited cheap memory-editing parlors. Tom Two Ribbons is conscious that he is failing a family tradition, but he has not yet found his own mode of self-destruction.

In the main building he discovers Herndon, Julia, Ellen, Schwartz, Chang, Michaelson, and Nichols. They are eating breakfast; the others are already at work. Ellen rises and comes to him and kisses him. Her short soft yellow hair tickles his cheeks. "I love you," she whispers. She has spent the night in Michaelson's bubble. "I love you," he tells her, and draws a quick vertical line of affection between her small pale breasts. He winks at Michaelson, who nods, touches the tops of two fingers to his lips, and blows them a kiss. We are all good friends here, Tom Two Ribbon thinks.

"Who drops pellets today?" he asks.

"Mike and Chang," says Julia. "Sector C."

Schwartz says, "Eleven more days and we ought to have the whole peninsula clear. Then we can move inland."

"If our pellet supply holds up," Chang points out.

Herndon says, "Did you sleep well, Tom?"

"No," says Tom. He sits down and taps out his breakfast requisition. In the west, the fog is beginning to burn off the mountains. Something throbs in the back of his neck. He has been on this world nine weeks now, and in time it has undergone its only change of season, shading from dry weather to foggy. The mists will remain for many months. Before the plains parch again, the Eaters will be gone and the settlers will begin to arrive. His food slides down the chute and he seizes it. Ellen sits beside him. She is a little more than half his age; this is her first voyage; she is their keeper of records, but she is also skilled at editing. "You look troubled," Ellen tells him. "Can I help you?"

"No. Thank you."

"I hate it when you get gloomy."

"It's a racial trait," says Tom Two Ribbons.

"I doubt that very much."

"The truth is that maybe my personality reconstruct is wearing thin. The trauma level was so close to the surface. I'm just a walking veneer, you know."

Ellen laughs prettily. She wears only a sprayon halfwrap. Her skin looks damp; she and Michaelson have had a swim at dawn. Tom Two Ribbons is thinking of asking her to marry him, when this job is over. He has not been married since the collapse of the real estate business. The therapist suggested divorce as part of the reconstruct. He sometimes wonders where Terry has gone and whom she lives with now. Ellen says, "You seem pretty stable to me, Tom."

"Thank you," he says. She is young. She does not know.

"If it's just a passing gloom I can edit it out in one quick snip."

"Thank you," he says. "No."

"I forgot. You don't like editing."

"My father—"

"Yes?"

"In fifty years he pared himself down to a thread," Tom Two Ribbons says. "He had his ancestors edited away, his whole heritage, his religion, his wife, his sons, finally his name. Then he sat and smiled all day. Thank you, no editing."

"Where are you working today?" Ellen asks.

"In the compound, running tests."

"Want company? I'm off all morning."

"Thank you, no," he says, too quickly. She looks hurt. He tries to remedy his unintended cruelty by touching her arm lightly and saying, "Maybe this afternoon, all right? I need to commune a while. Yes?"

"Yes," she says, and smiles, and shapes a kiss with her lips.

After breakfast he goes to the compound. It covers a thousand hectares east of the base; they have bordered it with neural-field projectors at intervals of eighty meters, and this is a sufficient fence to keep the captive population of two hundred Eaters from straying. When all the others have been exterminated, this study group will remain. At the southwest corner of the compound stands a lab bubble from which the experiments are run: metabolic, psychological, physiological, ecological. A stream crosses the compound diagonally. There is a low ridge of grassy hills at its eastern edge. Five distinct copses of tightly clustered knifeblade trees are separated by patches of dense savanna. Sheltered beneath the grass are the oxygen-plants, almost completely hidden except for the photosynthetic spikes that jut to heights of three or four meters at regular intervals, and for the lemon-colored respiratory bodies, chest high, that make the grassland sweet and dizzying with exhaled gases. Through the fields move the Eaters in a straggling herd, nibbling delicately at the respiratory bodies.

Tom Two Ribbons spies the herd beside the stream and goes toward it. He stumbles over an oxygen-plant hidden in the grass but deftly recovers his balance and, seizing the puckered orifice of the respiratory body, inhales deeply. His despair lifts. He approaches the Eaters. They are spherical, bulky, slow-moving creatures, covered by masses of coarse orange fur. Saucer-like eyes protrude above narrow rubbery lips. Their legs are thin and scaly, like a chicken's, and their arms are short and held close to their bodies. They regard him with bland lack of curiosity. "Good morning, brothers!" is the way he greets them this time, and he wonders why.

I noticed something strange today. Perhaps I simply sniffed too much oxygen in the fields; maybe I was succumbing to a suggestion Herndon planted; or possibly it's the family masochism cropping out. But while I was observing the Eaters in the compound, it seemed to me, for the first time, that they are behaving intelligently, that they were functioning in a ritualized way.

I followed them around for three hours. During that time they uncovered half a dozen outcroppings of oxygen-plants. In each case they went through a stylized pattern of action before starting to munch. They:

Formed a straggly circle around the plants.

Looked toward the sun.

Looked toward their neighbors on left and right around the circle.

Made fuzzy neighing sounds *only* after having done the foregoing.

Looked toward the sun again.

Moved in and ate.

If this wasn't a prayer of thanksgiving, a saying of grace, then what was it? And if they're advanced enough spiritually to say grace, are we not therefore committing genocide here? Do chimpanzees say grace? Christ, we wouldn't even wipe out chimps the way we're cleaning out the Eaters! Of course, chimps don't interfere with human crops, and some kind of coexistence would be possible, whereas Eaters and human agriculturalists simply can't function on the same planet. Nevertheless, there's a moral issue here. The liquidation effort is predicated on the assumption that the intelligence level of the Eaters is about on a par with that of oysters, or, at best sheep. Our consciences stay clear because our poison is quick and painless and because the Eaters thoughtfully dissolve upon dying, sparing us the mess of incinerating millions of corpses. But if they pray—

I won't say anything to the others just yet. I want more evidence, hard, objective. Films, tapes, record cubes. Then we'll see. What if I can show that we're exterminating intelligent beings? My family knows a little about genocide, after all, having been on the receiving end just a few centuries back. I doubt that I could halt what's going on here. But at the very least I could withdraw from the operation. Head back to Earth and stir up public outcries.

I hope I'm imagining this.

I'm not imagining a thing. They gather in circles; they look to the sun; they neigh and pray. They're only balls of jelly on chicken-legs, but they give thanks for their food. Those big round eyes now seem to stare accusingly at me. Our tame herd there knows what's going on; that we have descended from the stars to eradicate their kind, and that they alone will be spared. They have no way of fighting back or even of communicating their displeasure, but they *know*. And hate us. Jesus, we have killed two million of them since we got here, and in a metaphorical way I'm stained with blood, and what will I do, what can I do?

I must move very carefully, or I'll end up drugged and edited.

I can't let myself seem like a crank, a quack, an agitator. I can't stand up and *denounce!* I have to find allies. Herndon, first. He surely is on to the truth; he's the one who nudged *me* to it, that day we dropped pellets. And I thought he was merely being vicious in his usual way!

I'll talk to him tonight.

He says, "I've been thinking about that suggestion you made. About the Eaters. Perhaps we haven't made sufficiently close psychological studies. I mean, if they really *are* intelligent—"

Herndon blinks. He is a tall man with glossy dark hair, a heavy beard, sharp cheekbones. "Who says they are, Tom?"

"You did. On the far side of the Forked River, you said—"

"It was just a speculative hypothesis. To make conversation."

"No, I think it was more than that. You really believed it."

Herndon looks troubled. "Tom, I don't know what you're trying to start, but don't start it. If I for a moment believed we were killing intelligent creatures, I'd run for an editor so fast I'd start an implosion wave."

"Why did you ask me that thing, then?" Tom Two Ribbons says.

"Idle chatter."

"Amusing yourself by kindling guilts in somebody else? You're a bastard, Herndon. I mean it."

"Well, look, Tom, if I had any idea that you'd get so worked up about a hypothetical suggestion—" Herndon shakes his head. "The Eaters aren't intelligent beings. Obviously. Otherwise we wouldn't be under orders to liquidate them."

"Obviously," says Tom Two Ribbons.

Ellen said, "No, I don't know what Tom's up to. But I'm pretty sure he needs a rest. It's only a year and a half since his personality reconstruct, and he had a pretty bad breakdown back then."

Michaelson consulted a chart. "He's refused three times in a row to make his pellet-dropping run. Claiming he can't take time away from his research. Hell, we can fill in for him, but it's the idea that he's ducking chores that bothers me."

"What kind of research is he doing?" Nichols wanted to know.

"Not biological," said Julia. "He's with the Eaters in the compound all the time, but I don't see him making any tests on them. He just watches them."

"And talks to them," Chang observed.

"And talks, yes," Julia said.

"About what?" Nichols asked.

"Who knows?"

Everyone looked at Ellen. "You're closest to him," Michaelson said. "Can't you bring him out of it?"

"I've got to know what he's in, first," Ellen said. "He isn't saying a thing."

You know that you must be very careful, for they outnumber you, and their concern for your mental welfare can be deadly. Already they realize you are disturbed, and Ellen has begun to probe for the source of the disturbance. Last night you lay in her arms and she questioned you, obliquely, skillfully, and you knew what she is trying to find out. When the moons appeared she suggested that you and she stroll in the compound, among the sleeping Eaters. You declined, but she sees that you have become involved with the creatures.

You have done probing of your own—subtly, you hope. And you are aware that you can do nothing to save the Eaters. An irrevocable commitment has been made. It is 1876 all over again; these are the bison, they are the Sioux, and they must be destroyed, for the railroad is on its way. If you speak out here, your friends will calm you and pacify you and edit you, for they do not see what you see. If you return to Earth to agitate, you will be mocked and recommended for another reconstruct. You can do nothing. You can do nothing.

You cannot save, but perhaps you can record.

Go out into the prairie. Live with the Eaters; make yourself their friend; learn their ways. Set it down, a full account of their culture, so that at least that much will not be lost. You know the techniques of field anthropology. As was done for your people in the old days, do now for the Eaters.

He finds Michaelson. "Can you spare me for a few weeks?" he asks.

"Spare you, Tom? What do you mean?"

"I've got some field studies to do. I'd like to leave the base and work with Eaters in the wild."

"What's wrong with the ones in the compound?"

"It's the last chance with wild ones, Mike. I've got to go."

"Alone, or with Ellen?"

"Alone."

Michaelson nods slowly. "All right, Tom. Whatever you want. Go. I won't hold you here."

I dance in the prairie under the green-gold sun. About me the Eaters gather. I am stripped; sweat makes my skin glisten; my heart pounds. I talk to them with my feet, and they understand.

They understand.

They have a language of soft sounds. They have a god. They know love and awe and rapture. They have rites. They have names. They have a history. Of all this I am convinced.

I dance on thick grass.

How can I reach them? With my feet, with my hands, with my grunts, with my sweat. They gather by the hundreds, by the thousands, and I dance. I must not stop. They cluster about me and make their sounds. I am a conduit for strange forces. My great-grandfather should see me now! Sitting on his porch in Wyoming, the firewater in his hand, his brain rotting—see me now, old one! See the dance of Tom Two Ribbons! I talk to these strange ones with my feet under a sun that is the wrong color. I dance. I dance.

"Listen to me," I say. "I am your friend, I alone, the only one you can trust. Trust me, talk to me, teach me. Let me preserve your ways, for soon the destruction will come."

I dance, and the sun climbs, and the Eaters murmur.

There is the chief. I dance toward him, back, toward, I bow, I point to the sun, I imagine the being that lives in that ball of flame, I imitate the sounds of these people, I kneel, I rise, I dance. Tom Two Ribbons dances for you.

I summon skills my ancestors forgot. I feel the power flowing in me. As they danced in the days of the bison, I dance now, beyond the Forked River.

I dance, and now the Eaters dance too. Slowly, uncertainly, they move toward me, they shift their weight, lift leg and leg, sway about. "Yes, like that!" I cry. "Dance!"

We dance together as the sun reaches noon height.

Now their eyes are no longer accusing. I see warmth and kinship. I am their brother, their redskinned tribesman, he who dances with them. No longer do they seem clumsy to me. There is a strange ponderous grace in their movements. They dance. They dance. They caper about me. Closer, closer, closer!

We move in holy frenzy.

They sing, now, a blurred hymn of joy. They throw forth their arms, unclench their little claws. In unison they shift weight, left foot forward, right, left, right. Dance, brothers, dance, dance, dance! They press against me. Their flesh quivers; their smell is a sweet one. They gently thrust me across the field, to a part of the meadow where the grass is deep and untrampled. Still dancing, we seek for the oxygen-plants, and find clumps of them beneath the grass, and they make their prayer and seize them with their awkward arms, separating the respiratory bodies from the photosynthetic spikes. The plants, in anguish, release floods of oxygen. My mind reels. I laugh and sing. The Eaters are nibbling the lemon-colored perforated globes, nibbling the stalks as well. They thrust their plants at me. It is a religious ceremony, I see. Take from us, eat with us, join with us, this is the body, this is the blood, take, eat, join. I bend forward and put a lemon-colored globe to my lips. I do not bite; I nibble, as they do, my teeth slicing away the skin of the globe. Juice spurts into my mouth, while oxygen drenches my nostrils. The Eaters sing hosannas. I should be in full paint for this, paint of my forefathers, feathers too, meeting their religion in the regalia of what should have been mine. Take, eat, join. The juice of the oxygen-plant flows in my veins. I embrace my brother. I sing, and as my voice leaves my lips it becomes an arch that glistens like new steel, and I pitch my song lower, and the arch turns to tarnished silver. The Eaters crowd close. The scent of their bodies is fiery red to me. Their soft cries are puffs of steam. The sun is very warm; its rays are tiny jagged pings of puckered sound, close to the top of my range of hearing, plink! plink! plink! The thick grass hums to me, deep and rich, and the wind hurls points of flame along the prairie. I devour another oxygen-plant, and then a third. My brothers laugh and shout. They tell me of their gods, the god of warmth, the god of food, the god of pleasure, the god of death, the god of holiness, the god of wrongness, and the others. They recite for me the names of their kings, and I bear their voices as splashes of green mold on the clean sheet of the sky. They instruct me in their holy rites. I must remember this, I tell myself, for when it is gone it will never come again. I continue to dance. They continue to dance. The color of the hills becomes rough and coarse, like abrasive gas. Take, eat, join. Dance. They are so gentle!

I hear the drone of the copter, suddenly.

It hovers far overhead. I am unable to see who flies in it. "No," I scream. "Not here! Not these people! Listen to me! This is Tom Two Ribbons! Can't you hear me? I'm doing a field study here! You have no right—!"

My voice makes spirals of blue moss edged with red sparks. They drift upward and are scattered by the breeze.

I yell, I shout, I bellow. I dance and shake my fists. From the wings of the copter the jointed arms of the pellet-distributors unfold. The gleaming spigots extend and whirl. The neural pellets rain down into the meadow, each tracing a blazing track that lingers in the sky. The sound of the copter becomes a furry carpet stretching to the horizon, and my shrill voice is lost in it.

The Eaters drift away from me, seeking the pellets, scratching at the roots of the grass to find them. Still dancing, I leap into their midst, striking the pellets from their hands, hurling them into the stream, crushing them to powder. The Eaters growl black needles at me. They turn away and search for more pellets. The copter turns and flies off, leaving a trail of dense oily sound. My brothers are gobbling the pellets eagerly.

There is no way to prevent it.

Joy consumes them and they topple and lie still. Occasionally a limb twitches; then even this stops. They begin to dissolve. Thousands of them melt on the prairie, sinking into shapelessness, losing their spherical forms, flattening, ebbing into the ground. The bonds of the molecules will no longer hold. It is the twilight of protoplasm. They perish. They vanish. For hours I walk the prairie. Now I inhale oxygen; now I eat a lemon-colored globe. Sunset begins with the ringing of leaden chimes. Black clouds make brazen trumpet calls in the east and the deepening wind is a swirl of coaly bristles. Silence comes. Night falls. I dance. I am alone.

The copter comes again, and they find you, and you do not resist as they gather you in. You are beyond bitterness. Quietly you explain what you have done and what you have learned, and why it is wrong to exterminate these people. You describe the plant you have eaten and the way it affects your senses, and as you talk of the blessed synesthesia, the texture of the wind and the sound of the clouds and the timbre of the sunlight, they nod and smile and tell you not to worry, that everything will be all right soon, and they touch something cold to your forearm, so cold that it is a whir and a buzz and the deintoxicant sinks into your vein and soon the ecstasy drains away, leaving only the exhaustion and the grief.

He says, "We never learn a thing, do we? We export all our horrors to the stars. Wipe out the Armenians, wipe out the Jews, wipe out the Tasmanians, wipe out the Indians, wipe out everyone who's in the way, and then come out here and do the same damned murderous thing. You weren't with me out there. You didn't dance with them. You didn't see what a rich, complex culture the Eaters have. Let me tell you about their tribal structure. It's dense: seven levels of matrimonial relationships, to begin with, and an exogamy factor that requires—"

Softly Ellen says, "Tom, darling, nobody's going to harm the Eaters."

"And the religion," he goes on. "Nine gods, each one an aspect of *the* god. Holiness and wrongness both worshipped. They have hymns, prayers, a theology. And we, the emissaries of the god of wrongness—"

"We're not exterminating them," Michaelson says. "Won't you understand that, Tom? This is all a fantasy of yours. You've been under the influence of drugs, but now we're clearing you out. You'll be clean in a little while. You'll have perspective again."

"A fantasy?" he says bitterly. "A drug dream? I stood out in the prairie and saw you drop pellets. And I watched them die and melt away. I didn't dream that."

"How can we convince you?" Chang asks earnestly. "What will make you believe? Shall we fly over the Eater country with you and show how many millions there are?"

"But how many millions have been destroyed?" he demands.

They insist that he is wrong. Ellen tells him again that no one has ever desired to harm the Eaters. "This is a scientific expedition, Tom. We're here to *study* them. It's a violation of all we stand for to injure intelligent lifeforms."

"You admit that they're intelligent?"

"Of course. That's never been in doubt."

"Then why drop the pellets?" he asks. "Why slaughter them?"

"None of that has happened, Tom," Ellen says. She takes his hand between her cool palms. "Believe us. Believe us."

He says bitterly. "If you want me to believe you, why don't you do the job properly? Get out the editing machine and go to work on me. You can't simply *talk* me into rejecting the evidence of my own eyes."

"You were under drugs all the time," Michaelson says.

"I've never taken drugs! Except for what I ate in the meadow, when I danced—and that came after I had watched the massacre going on for weeks and weeks. Are you saying that it's a retroactive delusion?"

"No, Tom," Schwartz says. "You've had this delusion all along. It's part of your therapy, your reconstruct. You came here programmed with it."

"Impossible," he says.

Ellen kisses his fevered forehead. "It was done to reconcile you to mankind, you see. You had this terrible resentment of the displacement of your people in the nineteenth century. You were unable to forgive the industrial society for scattering the Sioux, and you were terribly full of hate. Your therapist thought that if you could be made to participate in an imaginary modern extermination, if you could come to see it as a necessary operation, you'd be purged of your resentment and able to take your place in society as—"

He thrusts her away. "Don't talk idiocy! If you knew the first thing about reconstruct therapy, you'd realize that no reputable therapist could be so shallow. There are no one-to-one correlations in reconstructs. No, don't touch me. Keep away. Keep away."

He will not let them persuade him that this is merely a drug-born dream. It is no fantasy, he tells himself, and it is no therapy. He rises. He goes out. They do not follow him. He takes a copter and seeks his brothers.

Again I dance. The sun is much hotter today. The Eaters are more numerous. Today I wear paint, today I wear feathers. My body shines with my sweat. They dance with me, and they have a frenzy in them that I have never seen before. We pound the trampled meadow with our feet. We clutch for the sun with our hands. We sing, we shout, we cry. We will dance until we fall.

This is no fantasy. These people are real, and they are intelligent, and they are doomed. This I know.

We dance. Despite the doom, we dance.

My great-grandfather comes and dances with us. He too is real. His nose is like a hawk's, not blunt like mine, and he wears the big headdress, and his muscles are like cords under his brown skin. He sings, he shouts, he cries.

Others of my family join us.

We eat the oxygen-plants together. We embrace the Eaters. We know, all of us, what it is to be hunted.

The clouds make music and the wind takes on texture and the sun's warmth has color.

We dance. We dance. Our limbs know no weariness.

The sun grows and fills the whole sky, and I see no Eaters now, only my own people, my father's fathers across the centuries, thousands of gleaming skins, thousands of hawk's noses, and we eat the plants, and we find sharp sticks and thrust them into our flesh, and the sweet blood flows and dries in the blaze of the sun, and we dance, and we dance, and some of us fall from weariness, and we dance, and the prairie is a sea of bobbing headdresses, an ocean of feathers, and we dance, and my heart makes thunder, and my knees become water, and the sun's fire engulfs me, and I dance, and I fall, and I dance, and I fall, and I fall, and I fall.

Again they find you and bring you back. They give you the cool snout on your arm to take the oxygen-plant drug from your veins, and then they give you something else so you will rest. You rest and you are very calm. Ellen kisses you and you stroke her soft skin, and then the others come in and they talk to you, saying soothing things, but you do not listen, for you are searching for realities. It is not an easy search. It is like falling through many trapdoors, looking for the one room whose floor is not hinged. Everything that has happened on this planet is your therapy, you tell yourself, designed to reconcile an embittered aborigine to the white man's conquest; nothing is really being exterminated here. You reject that and fall through and realize that this must be the therapy of your friends; they carry the weight of accumulated centuries of guilts and have come here to shed that load, and you are here to ease them of their burden, to draw their sins into yourself and give them forgiveness. Again you fall through, and see that the Eaters are mere animals who threaten the ecology and must be removed; the culture you imagined for them is your hallucination, kindled out of old churnings. You try to withdraw your objections to this necessary extermination, but you fall through again and discover that there is no extermination except in your mind, which is troubled and disordered by your obsession with the crime against your ancestors, and you sit up, for you wish to apologize to these friends of yours, these innocent scientists whom you have called murderers. And you fall through.

SCIENCE FICTION AS SIMILE

Writers have developed various strategies for dealing with the unreal as it occurs within a story. If they inform the reader, for instance, that the story at hand could not happen in the real world—by introducing objects or creatures or powers that do not exist in the real world and cannot rationally be expected ever to have existed or ever to exist—the result is fantasy, and the reader discards his customary standards for judging the relevance and meaning of events. If writers tell the reader, on the other hand, that the story could happen, though it has not yet occurred, then the reader is expected to compare events with reality, to approach the story with rational processes alert and everyday standards intact. This is one way to distinguish between fantasy and science fiction.

Whether fantasy or science fiction, however, the story must have relevance to the here and now. If it has no relevance—if it tells the reader nothing about character or behavior, about human hopes and fears—no one would read it; perhaps it would be unreadable. Even fantasy makes comparisons with reality.

Science fiction's comparisons are more direct. Its stories emerge from reality; the reader wants to know how his world might develop into the world of the story. Isaac Asimov has said that science fiction offers two different kinds of stories: chess-game stories and chess-puzzle stories. The chess game stories are extrapolative, "If This Goes On…" stories that show how a future world develops out of trends visible now; the chess-puzzle, "What If?" stories deal with a world in which the situation derives from something unexpected. *The Space Merchants* is a chess-game story; "Nightfall" is a chess puzzle.

Both kinds have implications for the present. The extrapolative chess-game story argues that if humanity doesn't do something to change what is going on, the world will end up in a frightful mess. Such stories are cautionary, or occasionally hortatory. But even the speculative chess-puzzle story has much to tell the reader about his current predicament. "Nightfall," for instance, would be too remote from experience to be moving if it did not reflect human attitudes toward the unseen and the unknown; imagine, it says, how you would respond to such a situation, and you will learn something new about humanity and its environment.

A similar effect was achieved by Hal Clement's *Mission of Gravity*. Superficially it seems to be a novel about caterpillar-like creatures on a planet whose gravity at the poles is hundreds of times that on Earth but only two or three times as much at the equator. The reader relates to these aliens because they respond to their situations as people would, and soon the reader begins to think of them as people. But much of the value of the novel is lost if the reader is not also led to ask himself how Earth's gravity (and the other physical aspects of environment that he never thinks about because they are what he has always known) controls his psychological as well as physical reactions. It is this ability of science fiction to function as simile that gives science fiction its unique power to make readers question what they have never questioned before, to reevaluate the human condition.

Perhaps the best example of science fiction as simile is Ursula K. Le Guin's *The Left Hand of Darkness* (1969). It is the story of an androgynous human race that lives on a world called Gethen. Gethen is visited by a human envoy from a loose federation of worlds that the people of Gethen are invited to join. But the envoy must work his way not only through political problems but through his own difficulty in understanding the humanity of these aliens who are neither sex most of the time, but once a month, depending on circumstances, may become either.

The differences in Gethen civilization should lead the reader to consider the ways in which the fact that humanity is divided into two sexes on Earth affects virtually every relationship men and women have with each other, including political structures, economics, education, art, myth, and almost everything else. In fact, Le Guin has described the novel as her way of working herself through the questions of women's liberation. *The Left Hand of Darkness*, which won both a Nebula and a Hugo, also represents what may be a most effective integration of idea and literary skill, combining theme, characterization, drama, and style into a unified work of art. Its success brings to mind what Raymond Chandler had to say about *The Maltese Falcon*: "an art which is capable of it is not 'by hypothesis' incapable of anything."

Le Guin (1929—) has won many honors since the publication of her first science fiction, a novel entitled *Rocannon's World*, in 1966; *Planets of Exile* appeared the same year, *City of Illusions* in 1967, and *The Lathe of Heaven* in 1971. The daughter of a famous anthropologist and a well-known author, she earned a bachelor's degree from Radcliffe and a master's degree from Columbia in French and Italian Renaissance literatures. Some of her early work was fantasy, and she wrote a series of fantasy juveniles, called the Earthsea trilogy, the last of which won a National Book Award. She won a Hugo in 1973 for "The Word for World is Forest" and in 1974 for "The Ones Who Walk Away from Omelas," a Nebula in 1974 for "The Day Before the Revolution," and a Nebula and a Hugo in 1974 for *The Dispossessed*. After diversions into metaphorical fantasies and semi-historical novels, Le Guin made a tentative return to science fiction with a multi-genre anthropological SF novel *Always Coming Home* (1985) and a fourth novel in the Earthsea sequence, *Tehanu; The Last Book of Earthsea* (1990), before she completed the cycle with two books of Hainish stories, *A Fisherman of the Inland Sea* (1994) and *Four Ways to Forgiveness* (1995).

Le Guin also has made significant contributions to SF criticism (which won her the Pilgrim Award of SFRA in 1989), collected in such books as *The Language of the Night: Essays on Fantasy and Science Fiction* (1979) and *Dancing at the End of the World: Thoughts on Words, Women, Places* (1989).

FROM THE LEFT HAND OF DARKNESS

BY URSULA K. LE GUIN

1. A Parade in Erhenrang

From the Archives of Hain. Transcript of Ansible Document 01-01101-934-2-Gethen: To the Stabile on Ollul: Report from Genly Ai, First Mobile on Gethen/ Winter, Hainish Cycle 93, Ecumenical Year 1490-97.

I'll make my report as if I told a story, for I was taught as a child on my homeworld that Truth is a matter of the imagination. The soundest fact may fail or prevail in the style of its telling; like that singular organic jewel of our seas, which grows brighter as one woman wears it and, worn by another, dulls and goes to dust. Facts are no more solid, coherent, round, and real than pearls are. But both are sensitive.

The story is not all mine, nor told by me alone. Indeed I am not sure whose story it is: you can judge better. But it is all one, and if at moments the facts seem to alter with an altered voice, why then you can choose the fact you like best; yet none of them are false, and it is all one story.

It starts on the 44th diurnal of the Year 1491, which on the planet Winter in the nation Karhide was Odharhahad Tuwa or the twenty-second day of the third month of spring in the Year One. It is always the Year One here. Only the dating of every past and future year changes each New Year's Day, as one counts backward or forward from the unitary Now. So it was spring of the Year One in Erhenrang, capital city of Karhide, and I was in peril of my life, and did not know it.

I was in a parade. I walked just behind the gossiwors and just before the king. It was raining.

Rainclouds over dark towers, rains falling in deep streets, a dark storm-beaten city of stone, through which one vein of gold winds slowly. First come merchants, potentates, and artisans of the City Erhenrang, rank after rank, magnificently clothed, advancing through the rain as comfortably as fish through the sea. Their faces are keen and calm. They do not march in step. This is a parade with no soldiers, not even imitation soldiers.

Next come the lords and mayors and representatives, one person, or five, or forty-five, or four hundred, from each Domain and Co-Domain of Karhide, a vast ornate procession that moves to the music of metal horns and hollow blocks of bone and wood and the dry, pure lilting of electric flutes. The various banners of the great Domains tangle in the rain-beaten confusion of color with the yellow pennants that bedeck the way, and the various musics of each group clash and interweave in many rhythms echoing in the deep stone street.

Next, a troop of jugglers with polished spheres of gold which they hurl up high in flashing flights, and catch, and hurl again, making fountain-jets of bright jugglery. All at once, as if they had literally caught the light, the gold spheres blaze bright as glass: the sun is breaking through.

Next, forty men in yellow, playing gossiwors. The gossiwor, played only in the king's presence, produces a preposterous disconsolate bellow. Forty of them played together shake one's reason, shake the towers of Erhenrang, shake down a last spatter of rain from the windy clouds. If this is the Royal Music no wonder the kings of Karhide are all mad.

Next, the royal party, guards and functionaries and dignitaries of the city and the court, deputies, senators, chancellors, ambassadors, lords of the Kingdom, none of them keeping step or rank yet walking with great dignity; and among them is King Argaven XV, in white tunic and shirt and breeches, with leggings of saffron leather and a peaked yellow cap. A gold finger-ring is his only adornment and sign of office. Behind this group eight sturdy fellows bear the royal litter, rough with yellow sapphires, in which no king has ridden for centuries, a ceremonial relic of the Very-Long-Ago. By the litter walk eight guards armed with "foray guns," also relics of a more barbaric past but not empty ones, being loaded with pellets of soft iron. Death walks behind the king. Behind death come the students of the Artisan Schools, the Colleges, the Trades, and the King's Hearths, long lines of children and young people in white and red and gold and green; and finally a number of soft-running, slow, dark cars end the parade.

The royal party, myself among them, gather on a platform of new timbers beside the unfinished Arch of the River Gate. The occasion of the parade is the completion of that arch, which completes the new Road and River Port of Erhenrang, a great operation of dredging and building and roadmaking which has taken five years, and will distinguish Argaven XV's reign in the annals of Karhide. We are all squeezed rather tight on the platform in our damp and massive finery. The rain is gone, the sun shines on us, the splendid, radiant, traitorous sun of Winter. I remark to the person on my left, "It's hot. It's really hot."

The person on my left—a stocky dark Karhider with sleek and heavy hair, wearing a heavy overtunic of green leather worked with gold, and a heavy white shirt, and heavy breeches, and a neck-chain of heavy silver links a hand broad—this person, sweating heavily, replies, "So it is."

All about us as we stand jammed on our platform lie the faces of the people of the city, upturned like a shoal of brown, round pebbles, mica-glittering with thousands of watching eyes.

Now the king ascends a gangplank of raw timbers that leads from the platform up to the top of the arch whose unjoined piers tower over crown and wharves and river. As he mounts the crowd stirs and speaks in a vast murmur: "Argaven!" He makes no response. They expect none. Gossiwors blow a thunderous discordant blast, cease. Silence. The sun shines on city, river, crowd, and king. Masons below have set an electric winch going, and as the king mounts higher the keystone of the arch goes up past him in its sling, is raised, settled, and fitted almost soundlessly, great ton-weight block though it is, into the gap between the two piers, making them one, one thing, an arch. A mason with trowel and bucket awaits the king, up on the scaffolding; all the other workmen descend by rope ladders, like a swarm of fleas. The king and the mason kneel, high between the river and the sun, on their bit of planking. Taking the trowel the king begins to mortar the long joints of the keystone. He does not dab at it and give the trowel back to the mason, but sets to work methodically. The cement he uses is a pinkish color different from the rest of the mortarwork and after five or ten minutes of watching the king-bee work I ask the person on my left, "Are your keystones always set in a red cement?" For the same color is plain around the keystone of each arch of the Old Bridge, that soars beautifully over the river upstream from the arch.

Wiping sweat from his dark forehead the man—*man* I must say, having said *he* and *his*—the man answers, "Very-long-ago a keystone was always set in with a mortar of ground bones mixed with blood. Human bones, human blood. Without the bloodbond the arch would fall, you see. We use the blood of animals, these days."

So he often speaks, frank yet cautious, ironic, as if always aware that I see and judge as an alien: a singular awareness in one of so isolate a race and so high a rank. He is one of the most powerful men in the country; I am not sure of the proper historical equivalent of his position, vizier or prime minister or councilor; the Karhidish word for it means the King's Ear. He is lord of a Domain and lord of the Kingdom, a mover of great events. His name is Therem Harth rem ir Estraven.

The king seems to be finished with his masonry work, and I rejoice; but crossing under the rise of the arch on his spiderweb of planks he starts in on the other side of the keystone, which after all has two sides. It doesn't do to be impatient in Karhide. They are anything but a phlegmatic people, yet they are obdurate, they are pertinacious, they finish plastering joints. The crowds on the Sess Embankment are content to watch the king work, but I am bored, and hot. I have never before been hot, on Winter; I never will be again; yet I fail to appreciate the event. I am dressed for the Ice Age and not for the sunshine, in layers and layers of clothing, woven plant-fiber, artificial fiber, fur, leather, a massive armor against the cold, within which I now wilt like a radish leaf. For distraction I look at the crowds and the other paraders drawn up around the platform, their Domain and Clan banners hanging still and bright in sunlight, and idly I ask Estraven what this banner is and that one and the other. He knows each one I ask about, though there are hundreds, some from remote domains, hearths and tribelets of the Pering Stormborder and Kerm Land.

"I'm from Kerm Land myself," he says when I admire his knowledge. "Anyhow it's my business to know the Domains. They are Karhide. To govern this land is to govern its lords. Not that it's ever been done. Do you know the saying, *Karhide is not a nation but a family quarrel?*" I haven't, and I suspect that Estraven made it up; it has his stamp.

At this point another member of the *kyorremy,* the upper chamber or parliament which Estraven heads, pushes and squeezes a way up close to him and begins talking to him. This is the king's cousin Pemmer Harge rem ir Tibe. His voice is very low as he speaks to Estraven, his posture faintly insolent, his smile frequent. Estraven, sweating like ice in the sun, stays slick and cold as ice, answering Tibe's murmurs aloud in a tone whose commonplace politeness makes the other look rather a fool. I listen, as I watch the king grouting away, but understand nothing except the animosity between Tibe and Estraven. It's nothing to do with me, in any case, and I am simply interested in the behavior of these people who rule a nation, in the old-fashioned sense, who govern the fortunes of twenty million other people. Power has become so subtle and complex a thing in the ways taken by the Ekumen that only a subtle mind can watch it work; here it is still limited, still visible. In Estraven, for instance, one feels the man's power as an augmentation of his character; he cannot make an empty gesture or say a word that is not listened to. He knows it, and the knowledge gives him more reality than most people own: a solidness of being, a substantiality, a human grandeur. Nothing succeeds like success. I don't trust Estraven, whose motives are forever obscure; I don't like him; yet I feel and respond to his authority as surely as I do to the warmth of the sun.

Even as I think this the world's sun dims between clouds regathering, and soon a flaw of rain runs sparse and hard up-river, spattering the crowds on the Embankment, darkening the sky. As the king comes down the gangplank the light breaks through a last time, and his white figure and the great arch stand out a moment vivid and splendid against the storm-darkened south. The clouds close. A cold wind comes tearing up Port-and-Palace Street, the river goes gray, the trees on the Embankment shudder. The parade is over. Half an hour later it is snowing.

As the king's car drove off up Port-and-Palace Street and the crowds began to move like a rocky shingle rolled by a slow tide, Estraven turned to me again and said, "Will you have supper with me tonight, Mr. Ai?" I accepted, with more surprise than pleasure. Estraven had done a great deal for me in the last six or eight months, but I did not expect or desire such a show of personal favor as an invitation to his house. Harge rem ir Tibe was still close to us, overhearing, and I felt that he was meant to overhear. Annoyed by this sense of effeminate intrigue I got off the platform and lost myself in the mob, crouching and slouching somewhat to do so. I'm not much taller than the Gethenian norm, but the difference is most noticeable in a crowd. *That's him, look, there's the Envoy.* Of course that was part of my job, but it was a part that got harder, not easier, as time went on; more and more often I longed for anonymity, for sameness. I craved to be like everybody else.

A couple of blocks up Breweries Street I turned off toward my lodgings and suddenly, there where the crowd thinned out, found Tibe walking beside me.

"A flawless event," said the king's cousin, smiling at me. His long, clean, yellow teeth appeared and disappeared in a yellow face all webbed, though he was not an old man, with fine, soft wrinkles.

"A good augury for the success of the new Port," I said.

"Yes indeed." More teeth.

"The ceremony of the keystone is most impressive—"

"Yes indeed. That ceremony descends to us from very-long-ago. But no doubt lord Estraven explained all that to you."

"Lord Estraven is most obliging."

I was trying to speak insipidly, yet everything I said to Tibe seemed to take on a double meaning.

"Oh very much indeed," said Tibe. "Indeed Lord Estraven is famous for his kindness to foreigners." He smiled again, and every tooth seemed to have a meaning, double, multiple, thirty-two different meanings.

"Few foreigners are so foreign as I, Lord Tibe. I am very grateful for kindnesses."

"Yes indeed, yes indeed! And gratitude's a noble, rare emotion, much praised by the poets. Rare above all here in Erhenrang, no doubt because it's impracticable. This is a hard age we live in, an ungrateful age. Things aren't as they were in our grandparents' days, are they?"

"I scarcely know, sir, but I've heard the same lament on other worlds."

Tibe stared at me for some while as if establishing lunacy. Then he brought out the long yellow teeth. "Ah yes! Yes indeed! I keep forgetting that you come from another planet. But of course that's not a matter you ever forget. Though no doubt life would be much sounder and simpler and safer for you here in Erhenrang if you could forget it, eh? Yes indeed! Here's my car, I had it wait here out of the way. I'd like to offer to drive you to your island, but must forego the privilege, as I'm due at the King's House very shortly and poor relations must be in good time, as the saying is, eh? Yes indeed!" said the king's cousin, climbing into his little black electric car, teeth bared across his shoulder at me, eyes veiled by a net of wrinkles.

I walked on home to my island.* Its front garden was revealed now that the last of the winter's snow had melted and the winter-doors, ten feet aboveground, were sealed off for a few months, till the autumn and the deep snow should return. Around at the side of the building in the mud and the ice and the quick, soft, rank spring growth of the garden, a young couple stood talking. Their right hands were clasped. They were in the first phase of kemmer. The large, soft snow danced about them as they stood barefoot in the icy mud, hands clasped, eyes all for each other. Spring on Winter.

I had dinner at my island and at Fourth Hour striking on the gongs of Remmy Tower I was at the Palace ready for supper. Karhiders eat four solid meals a day, breakfast, lunch, dinner, supper, along with a lot of adventitious nibbling and gobbling in between. There are no large meat-animals on Winter, and no mammalian products, milk, butter or cheese; the only high-protein, high-carbohydrate foods are the various kinds of eggs, fish, nuts, and the Hainish grains. A low-grade diet for a bitter climate, and one must refuel often.

I had got used to eating, as it seemed, every few minutes. It wasn't until later in that year that I discovered the Gethenians have perfected the technique not only of perpetually stuffing, but also of indefinitely starving.

The snow still fell, a mild spring blizzard, much pleasanter than the relentless rain of the Thaw just past. I made my way to and through the Palace in the quiet and pale darkness of snowfall, losing my way only once. The Palace of Erhenrang is an inner city, a walled wilderness of palaces, towers, gardens, courtyards, cloisters, roofed bridgeways, roofless tunnel-walks, small forests and dungeon-keeps, the product of centuries of paranoia on a grand scale. Over it all rise the grim, red, elaborate walls of the Royal House, which though in perpetual use is inhabited by no one beside the king himself. Everyone else,

*Karhosh, island, the usual word for the apartment-boardinghouse buildings that house the greatest part of the urban populations of Karhide. Islands contain 20 to 200 private rooms; meals are communal; some are run as hotels, others as cooperative communes, others combine these types. They are certainly an urban adaptation of the fundamental Karhidish institution of the Hearth, though lacking, of course, the topical and genealogical stability of the Hearth.

servants, staff, lords, ministers, parliamentarians, guards or whatever, sleeps in another palace or fort or keep or barracks or house inside the walls. Estraven's house, sign of the king's high favor, was the Corner Red Dwelling, built 440 years ago for Harmes, beloved kemmering of Emran III, whose beauty is still celebrated, and who was abducted, mutilated, and rendered imbecile by hirelings of the Innerland Faction. Emran III died forty years after, still wreaking vengeance on his unhappy country; Emran the Ill-fated. The tragedy is so old that its horror has leached away and only a certain air of faithlessness and melancholy clings to the stones and shadows of the house. The garden was small and walled; serem-trees leaned over a rocky pool. In dim shafts of light from the windows of the house I saw snowflakes and the threadlike white sporecases of the trees falling softly together onto the dark water. Estraven stood waiting for me, bareheaded and coatless in the cold, watching that small secret ceaseless descent of snow and seeds in the night. He greeted me quietly and brought me into the house. There were no other guests.

I wondered at this, but we went to the table at once, and one does not talk business while eating; besides, my wonder was diverted to the meal, which was superb, even the eternal breadapples transmuted by a cook whose art I heartily praised. After supper, by the fire, we drank hot beer. On a world where a common table implement is a little device with which you crack the ice that has formed on your drink between drafts, hot beer is a thing you come to appreciate.

Estraven had conversed amiably at table; now, sitting across the hearth from me, he was quiet. Though I had been nearly two years on Winter I was still far from being able to see the people of the planet through their own eyes. I tried to, but my efforts took the form of self-consciously seeing a Gethenian first as a man, then as a woman, forcing him into those categories so irrelevant to his nature and so essential to my own. Thus as I sipped my smoking sour beer I thought that at table Estraven's performance had been womanly, all charm and tact and lack of substance, specious and adroit. Was it in fact perhaps this soft supple femininity that I disliked and distrusted in him? For it was impossible to think of him as a woman, that dark, ironic, powerful presence near me in the firelit darkness, and yet whenever I thought of him as a man I felt a sense of falseness, of imposture: in him, or in my own attitude towards him? His voice was soft and rather resonant but not deep, scarcely a man's voice, but scarcely a woman's voice either… but what was it saying?

"I'm sorry," he was saying, "that I've had to forestall for so long this pleasure of having you in my house; and to that extent at least I'm glad there is no longer any question of patronage between us."

I puzzled at this a while. He had certainly been my patron in court until now. Did he mean that the audience he had arranged for me with the king tomorrow had raised me to an equality with himself? "I don't think I follow you," I said.

At that, he was silent, evidently also puzzled. "Well, you understand," he said at last, "being here… you understand that I am no longer acting on your behalf with the king of course."

He spoke as if ashamed of me, not of himself. Clearly there was a significance in his invitation and my acceptance of it which I had missed. But my blunder was in manners, his in morals. All I thought at first was that I had been right all along not to trust Estraven. He was not merely adroit and not merely powerful, he was faithless. All these months in Ehrenrang it had been he who listened to me, who answered my questions, sent physicians and engineers to verify the alienness of my physique and my ship, introduced me to people I needed to know, and gradually elevated me from my first year's status as a highly imaginative monster to my present recognition as the mysterious Envoy, about to be received by the king. Now, having got me up on that dangerous eminence, he suddenly and coolly announced he was withdrawing his support.

"You've led me to rely on you—"

"It was ill done."

"Do you mean that, having arranged this audience, you haven't spoken in favor of my mission to the king, as you—" I had the sense to stop short of "promised."

"I can't."

I was very angry, but I met neither anger nor apology in him.

"Will you tell me why?"

After a while he said, "Yes," and then paused again. During the pause I began to think that an inept and undefended alien should not demand reasons from the prime minister of a kingdom, above all when he does not and perhaps never will understand the foundations of power and the workings of government in that kingdom. No doubt this was all a matter of *shifgrethor*—prestige, face, place, the pride-relationship, the untranslatable and all-important principle of social authority in Karhide and all civilizations of Gethen. And if it was I would not understand it.

"Did you hear what the king said to me at the ceremony today?"

"No."

Estraven leaned forward across the hearth, lifted the beer jug out of the hot ashes, and refilled my tankard. He said nothing more, so I amplified, "The king didn't speak to you in my hearing."

"Nor in mine," said he.

I saw at last that I was missing another signal. Damning his effeminate deviousness, I said, "Are you trying to tell me, Lord Estraven, that you're out of favor with the king?"

I think he was angry then, but he said nothing that showed it, only, "I'm not trying to tell you anything, Mr. Ai."

"By God, I wish you would!"

He looked at me curiously. "Well, then, put it this way. There are some persons in court who are, in your phrase, in favor with the king, but who do not favor your presence or your mission here."

And so you're hurrying to join them, selling me out to save your skin, I thought, but there was no point in saying it. Estraven was a courtier, a politician, and I a fool to have trusted him. Even in a bisexual society the politician is very often something less than an integral man. His inviting me to dinner showed that he thought I would accept his betrayal as easily as he committed it. Clearly face-saving was more important than honesty. So I brought myself to say, "I'm sorry that your kindness to me has made trouble for you." Coals of fire. I enjoyed a flitting sense of moral superiority, but not for long; he was too incalculable.

He sat back so that the firelight lay ruddy on his knees and his fine, strong, small hands and the silver tankard he held, but left his face in shadow: a dark face always shadowed by the thick lowgrowing hair and heavy brows and lashes, and by a somber blandness of expression. Can one read a cat's face, a seal's, an otter's? Some Gethenians, I thought, are like such animals, with deep bright eyes that do not change expression when you speak.

"I've made trouble for myself," he answered, "by an act that had nothing to do with you, Mr. Ai. You know that Karhide and Orgoreyn have a dispute concerning a stretch of our border in the high North Fall near Sassinoth. Argaven's grandfather claimed the Sinoth Valley for Karhide, and the Commensals have never recognized the claim. A lot of snow out of one cloud, and it grows thicker. I've been helping some Karhidish farmers who live in the Valley to move back east across the old border, thinking the argument might settle itself if the Valley were simply left to the Orgota, who have lived there for several thousand years. I was in the Administration of the North Fall some years ago, and got to know some of those farmers. I dislike the thought of their being killed in forays, or sent to Voluntary Farms in Orgoreyn. Why not obviate the subject of dispute?… But that's not a patriotic idea. In fact it's a cowardly one, and impugns the shifgrethor of the king himself."

His ironies, and these ins and outs of a border-dispute with Orgoreyn, were of no interest to me. I returned to the matter that lay between us. Trust him or not, I might still get some use out of him. "I'm sorry," I said, "but it seems a pity that this question of a few farmers may be allowed to spoil the chances of my mission with the king. There's more at stake than a few miles of national boundary."

"Yes. Much more. But perhaps the Ekumen, which is a hundred light-years from border to border, will be patient with us a while."

"The Stabiles of the Ecumen are very patient men, sir. They'll wait a hundred years or five hundred for Karhide and the rest of Gethen to deliberate and consider whether or not to join the rest of mankind. I speak merely out of personal hope. And personal disappointment. I own that I thought that with your support—"

"I too. Well, the Glaciers didn't freeze overnight...." Cliché came ready to his lips, but his mind was elsewhere. He brooded. I imagined him moving me around with the other pawns in his powergame. "You came to my country," he said at last, "at a strange time. Things are changing; we are taking a new turning. No, not so much that, as following too far on the way we've been going. I thought that your presence, your mission, might prevent our going wrong, give us a new option entirely. But at the right moment—in the right place. It is all exceedingly chancy, Mr. Ai."

Impatient with his generalities, I said, "You imply that this isn't the right moment. Would you advise me to cancel my audience?"

My gaffe was even worse in Karhidish, but Estraven did not smile, or wince. "I'm afraid only the king has that privilege," he said mildly.

"Oh God, yes. I didn't mean that." I put my head in my hands a moment. Brought up in the wide-open, free-wheeling society of Earth, I would never master the protocol, or the impassivity, so valued by Karhiders. I know what a king was, Earth's own history is full of them, but I had no experiential feel for privilege—no tact. I picked up my tankard and drank a hot and violent draft. "Well, I'll say less to the king than I intended to say, when I could count on you."

"Good."

"Why good?" I demanded.

"Well, Mr. Ai, you're not insane. I'm not insane. But then neither of us is a king, you see... I suppose that you intended to tell Argaven, rationally, that your mission here is to attempt to bring about an alliance between Gethen and the Ekumen. And, rationally, he knows that already; because, as you know, I told him. I urged your case with him, tried to interest him in you. It was ill done, ill timed. I forgot, being too interested myself, that he's a king, and does not see things rationally, but as a king. All I've told him means to him simply that his power is threatened, his kingdom is a dustmote in space, his kingship is a joke to men who rule a hundred worlds."

"But the Ekumen doesn't rule, it co-ordinates. Its power is precisely the power of its member states and worlds. In alliance with the Ekumen, Karhide will become infinitely less threatened and more important than it's ever been."

Estraven did not answer for a while. He sat gazing at the fire, whose flames winked, reflected, from his tankard and from the broad bright silver chain of office over his shoulders. The old house was silent around us. There had been a servant to attend our meal, but Karhiders, having no institutions of slavery or personal bondage, hire services not people, and the servants had all gone off to their own homes by now. Such a man as Estraven must have guards about him somewhere, for assassination is a lively institution in Karhide, but I had seen no guard, heard none. We were alone.

I was alone, with a stranger, inside the walls of a dark palace, in a strange snow-changed city, in the heart of the Ice Age of an alien world.

Everything I had said, tonight and ever since I came to Winter, suddenly appeared to me as both stupid and incredible. How could I expect this man or any other to believe my tales about other worlds, other races, a vague benevolent government somewhere off in outer space? It was all nonsense. I had appeared in Karhide in a queer kind of ship, and I differed physically from Gethenians in some respects; that wanted explaining. But my own explanations were preposterous. I did not, in that moment, believe them myself.

"I believe you," said the stranger, the alien alone with me, and so strong had my access of self-alienation been that I looked up at him bewildered. "I'm afraid that Argaven also believes you. But he does not trust you. In part because he no longer trusts me. I have made mistakes, been careless. I cannot ask for your trust any longer, either, having put you in jeopardy. I forgot what a king is, forgot that the king in his own eye *is* Karhide, forgot what patriotism is and that he is, of necessity, the perfect patriot. Let me ask you this, Mr. Ai: do you know, by your own experience, what patriotism is?"

"No," I said, shaken by the force of that intense personality suddenly turning itself wholly upon me. "I don't think I do. If by patriotism you don't mean the love of one's homeland, for that I do know."

"No, I don't mean love, when I say patriotism. I mean fear. The fear of the other. And its expressions are political, not poetical: hate, rivalry, aggression. It grows in us, that fear. It grows in us year by year. We've followed our road too far. And you, who come from a world that outgrew nations centuries ago, who hardly know what I'm talking about, who show us the new road—" He broke off. After a while he went on, in control again, cool and polite: "It's because of fear that I refuse to urge your cause with the king, now. But not fear for myself, Mr. Ai. I'm not acting patriotically. There are, after all, other nations on Gethen."

I had no idea what he was driving at, but was sure that he did not mean what he seemed to mean. Of all the dark, obstructive, enigmatic souls I had met in this bleak city, his was the darkest. I would not play his labyrinthine game. I made no reply. After a while he went on, rather cautiously, "If I've understood you, your Ekumen is devoted essentially to the general interest of mankind. Now, for instance, the Orgota have experience in subordinating local interest to a general interest, while Karhide has almost none. And the Commensals of Orgoreyn are mostly sane men, if unintelligent, while the king of Karhide is not only insane but rather stupid."

It was clear that Estraven had no loyalties at all. I said in faint disgust, "It must be difficult to serve him, if that's the case."

"I'm not sure I've ever served the king," said the king's prime minister. "Or ever intended to. I'm not anyone's servant. A man must cast his own shadow...."

The gongs in Remmy Tower were striking Sixth Hour, midnight, and I took them as my excuse to go. As I was putting on my coat in the hallway he said, "I've lost my chance for the present, for I suppose you'll be leaving Ehrenrang—" why did he suppose so? "—but I trust a day will come when I can ask you questions again. There's so much I want to know. About your mind-speech, in particular; you'd scarcely begun to try to explain it to me."

His curiosity seemed perfectly genuine. He had the effrontery of the powerful. His promises to help me had seemed genuine, too. I said yes, of course, whenever he liked, and that was the evening's end. He showed me out through the garden, where snow lay thin in the light of Gethen's big, dull, rufous moon. I shivered as we went out, for it was well below freezing, and he said with polite surprise, "You're cold?" To him of course it was a mild spring night.

I was tired and downcast. I said, "I've been cold ever since I came to this world."

"What do you call it, this world, in your language?"

"Gethen."

"You gave it no name of your own?"

"Yes, the First Investigators did. They called it Winter."

We had stopped in the gateway of the walled garden. Outside, the palace grounds and roofs loomed in a dark snowy jumble lit here and there at various heights by the faint gold slits of windows. Standing under the narrow arch I glanced up, wondering if that keystone too was mortared with bone and blood. Estraven took leave of me and turned away; he was never fulsome in his greetings and farewells. I went off through the silent courts and alleys of the Palace, my boots crunching on the thin moonlit snow, and homeward through the deep streets of the city. I was cold, unconfident, obsessed by perfidy, and solitude, and fear.

ISSUES AND CONTROVERSIES

Science fiction has prided itself over the years on its ability, and willingness, to handle controversial topics when no other popular fiction was coming within hailing distance: race, politics, religion, customs, sex—all the subjects that are taboo in polite society. Science fiction attacked McCarthyism, suggested alternatives to democracy, exposed the tragedy of racism, questioned religious beliefs, explored new marital arrangements and sexual situations.

It all seems pretty tame now in the contemporary atmosphere of no-limit literary freedom, and it's always difficult to remember how things were then. From the vantage point of the present, it is even fashionable to sneer at science fiction's pretensions, to point out (as some Marxist critics have done) that U.S. writers always assumed a capitalistic future even if they did criticize its flaws and excesses, or to call attention to magazine taboos against descriptions of bodily functions and sex, even natural sex, as opposed to what is increasingly more difficult to define as unnatural sex. But even these taboos could be evaded by placing familiar situations in different environments: in the past, in the future, or on another planet.

Not only was science fiction able to deal with issues because it was a literature in which ideas were central, but it could minimize knee-jerk reactions by placing hot subjects into cool compartments. Authors with missionary attitudes found it easier to convert readers if they slipped them into controversial areas before the readers were aware of their situation: by showing the prejudice of automobilists against pedestrians, for instance, or humans against Newts, Earthmen against Martians, or Sirians against Earthmen. Suddenly the reader was compelled to evaluate the situation anew, to decide whose side was right, whose side he or she was on, or if both sides were wrong.

Sometimes, though, writers preferred to confront issues without subterfuge. Fredric Brown and Mack Reynolds did this in "Dark Interlude" in a 1951 *Galaxy*: a time traveler stranded in the present is liked by everyone, including the daughter of a rural southern family, until he reveals that in the future from which he came the races all have interbred and his golden skin is one indication of some Black genes; he is lynched.

Even the taboo subjects somehow found their ways into print: Philip José Farmer described many kinds of xenophobia after the success of the interspecies affair described in his 1952 "The Lovers"; Ted Sturgeon dealt with so many different kinds of sexual relations that it became a kind of trademark; as early as 1938, in "Helen O'Loy," Lester del Rey described in romantic terms a marriage between a man and a robot; and *Worlds of Tomorrow* published Brian Aldiss's "The Dark Light-Years," in which an alien race has the same attitudes toward excretion that humans have toward eating.

488

The most explosive issue in contemporary science fiction has been women's liberation. Some writers have dealt with it in the older, more oblique fashion, as Ursula K. Le Guin did in *The Left Hand of Darkness*.

But such subtlety often is scorned as cowardly, and current science fiction confronts such issues more directly. Alice Sheldon, who began publishing science fiction under the name of James Tiptree, Jr., and wrote some stories under the name of Raccoona Sheldon, published a series of stories about women's oppression, including "The Women Men Don't See," "The Screwfly Solution," "Houston, Houston, Do You Read?," and "Your Faces, O My Sisters! Your Faces Filled of Light!"

Perhaps the most vigorous attacks on male dominance have come from Joanna Russ (1937-). Born and raised in the Bronx, Russ earned a bachelor's degree in English from Cornell and an M.F.A. in playwriting from the Yale Drama School. After work in the theater, she tried science fiction; her first published story, "Nor Custom Stale," appeared in *F&SF* in 1959. Her first novel, *Picnic on Paradise* (1968), created a vivid woman character named Alyx and was nominated for a Nebula Award; another novel with a woman protagonist won that year, Alexei Panshin's *Rite of Passage*.

Russ's second novel, *And Chaos Died* (1970), also earned a Nebula nomination. Meanwhile she was teaching English and creative writing at Cornell, later moving to the State University of New York at Binghamton, the University of Colorado, and the University of Washington. Her novel *The Female Man* (1975) may be the most vigorous expression of her concerns, but she continued with *We Who Are About To...* (1977) and *The Two of Them* (1978), as well as collections of stories such as *The Zanzibar Cat* (1983) and *Extra(ordinary) People* (1984), which included her Hugo-winning novella "Souls." She has also written valuable critical reviews and essays that earned her the SFRA Pilgrim Award in 1988.

"When It Changed," another story about female society, was published in *Again, Dangerous Visions* (1972) and won a Nebula Award.

WHEN IT CHANGED

BY JOANNA RUSS

Katy drives like a maniac; we must have been doing over 120 kilometers per hour on those turns. She's good, though, extremely good, and I've seen her take the whole car apart and put it together again in a day. My birthplace on Whileaway was largely given to farm machinery and I refuse to wrestle with a five-gear shift at unholy speeds, not having been brought up to it, but even on those turns in the middle of the night, on a country road as bad as only our district can make them, Katy's driving didn't scare me. The funny thing about my wife, though: she will not handle guns. She has even gone hiking in the forests above the forty-eighth parallel without firearms, for days at a time. And that *does* scare me.

Katy and I have three children between us, one of hers and two of mine. Yuriko, my eldest, was asleep in the back seat, dreaming twelve-year-old dreams of love and war: running away to sea, hunting in the North, dreams of strangely beautiful people in strangely beautiful places, all the wonderful guff you think up when you're turning twelve and the glands start going. Some day soon, like all of them, she will disappear for weeks on end to come back grimy and proud, having knifed her first cougar or shot her first bear, dragging some abominably dangerous dead beastie behind her, which I will never forgive for what it might have done to my daughter. Yuriko says Katy's driving puts her to sleep.

For someone who has fought three duels, I am afraid of far, far too much. I'm getting old. I told this to my wife.

"You're thirty-four," she said. Laconic to the point of silence, that one. She flipped the lights on, on the dash—three kilometers to go and the road getting worse all the time. Far out in the country. Electric-green trees rushed into our headlights and around the car. I reached down next to me where we bolt the carrier panel to the door and eased my rifle into my lap. Yuriko stirred in the back. My height but Katy's eyes, Katy's face. The car engine is so quiet, Katy says, that you can hear breathing in the back seat. Yuki had been alone in the car when the message came, enthusiastically decoding her dot-dashes (silly to mount a wide-frequency transceiver near an I. C. engine, but most of Whileaway is on steam). She had thrown herself out of the car, my gangly and gaudy offspring, shouting at the top of her lungs, so of course she had had to come along. We've been intellectually prepared for this ever since the Colony was founded, ever since it was abandoned, but this is different. This is awful.

"Men!" Yuki had screamed, leaping over the car door. "They've come back! Real Earth men!"

We met them in the kitchen of the farmhouse near the place where they had landed; the windows were open, the night air very mild. We had passed all sorts of transportation when we parked outside—steam tractors, trucks, an I. C. flatbed, even a bicycle. Lydia, the district biologist, had come out of her Northern taciturnity long enough to take blood and urine samples and was sitting in a corner of the kitchen shaking her head in astonishment over the results; she even forced herself (very big, very fair, very shy, always painfully blushing) to dig up the old language manuals—though I can talk the old tongues in my sleep. And do. Lydia is uneasy with us; we're Southerners and too flamboyant. I counted twenty people in that kitchen, all the brains of North Continent. Phyllis Spet, I think, had come in by glider. Yuki was the only child there.

Then I saw the four of them.

They are bigger than we are. They are bigger and broader. Two were taller than I, and I am extremely tall, one meter eighty centimeters in my bare feet. They are obviously of our species but *off*, indescribably off, and as my eyes could not and still cannot quite comprehend the lines of those alien bodies, I could not, then, bring myself to touch them, though the one who spoke Russian— what voices they have—wanted to "shake hands," a custom from the past, I imagine. I can only say they were apes with human faces. He seemed to mean well, but I found myself shuddering back almost the length of the kitchen— and then I laughed apologetically—and then to set a good example (*interstellar amity*, I thought) did "shake hands" finally. A hard, hard hand. They are heavy as draft horses. Blurred, deep voices. Yuriko had sneaked in between the adults and was gazing at *the men* with her mouth open.

He turned *his* head—those words have not been in our language for six hundred years—and said, in bad Russian:

"Who's that?"

"My daughter," I said, and added (with that irrational attention to good manners we sometimes employ in moments of insanity), "My daughter, Yuriko Janetson. We use the patronymic. You would say matronymic."

He laughed, involuntarily. Yuki exclaimed, "I thought they would be *good-looking!*" greatly disappointed at this reception of herself. Phyllis Helgason Spet, whom someday I shall kill, gave me across the room a cold, level, venomous look, as if to say: *Watch what you say. You know what I can do.* It's true that I have little formal status, but Madam President will get herself in serious trouble with both me and her own staff if she continues to consider industrial espionage good clean fun. Wars and rumors of wars, as it says in one of our ancestors' books. I translated Yuki's words into *the man's* dog-Russian, once our *lingua franca*, and *the man* laughed again.

"Where are all your people?" he said conversationally.

I translated again and watched the faces around the room; Lydia embarrassed (as usual), Spet narrowing her eyes with some damned scheme, Katy very pale.

"This is Whileaway," I said.

He continued to look unenlightened.

"Whileaway," I said. "Do you remember? Do you have records? There was a plague on Whileaway."

He looked moderately interested. Heads turned in the back of the room, and I caught a glimpse of the local professions-parliament delegate; by morning every town meeting, every district caucus, would be in full session.

"Plague?" he said. "That's most unfortunate."

"Yes," I said. "Most unfortunate. We lost half our population in one generation."

He looked properly impressed.

"Whileaway was lucky," I said. "We had a big initial gene pool, we had been chosen for extreme intelligence, we had a high technology and a large remaining population in which every adult was two-or-three experts in one. The soil is good. The climate is blessedly easy. There are thirty millions of us now. Things are beginning to snowball in industry—do you understand?—give us seventy years and we'll have more than one real city, more than a few industrial centers, full-time professions, full-time radio operators, full-time machinists, give us seventy years and not everyone will have to spend three-quarters of a lifetime on the farm." And I tried to explain how hard it is when artists can practice full-time only in old age, when there are so few, so very few who can be free, like Katy and myself. I tried also to outline our government, the two houses, the one by professions and the geographic one; I told him the district caucuses handled problems too big for the individual towns. And that population control was not a political issue, not yet, though give us time and it would be. This was a delicate point in our history; give us time. There was no need to sacrifice the quality of life for an insane rush into industrialization. Let us go our own pace. Give us time.

"Where are all the people?" said that monomaniac.

I realized then that he did not mean people, he meant *men*, and he was giving the word the meaning it had not had on Whileaway for six centuries.

"They died," I said. "Thirty generations ago."

I thought we had poleaxed him. He caught his breath. He made as if to get out of the chair he was sitting in; he put his hand to his chest; he looked around at us with the strangest blend of awe and sentimental tenderness. Then he said, solemnly and earnestly:

"A great tragedy."

I waited, not quite understanding.

"Yes," he said, catching his breath again with the queer smile, that adult-to-child smile that tells you something is being hidden and will be presently produced with cries of encouragement and joy, "a great tragedy. But it's over." And again he looked around at all of us with the strangest deference. As if we were invalids.

"You've adapted amazingly," he said.

"To what?" I said. He looked embarrassed. He looked inane. Finally he said, "Where I come from, the women don't dress so plainly."

"Like you?" I said. "Like a bride?" for the men were wearing silver from head to foot. I had never seen anything so gaudy. He made as if to answer and then apparently thought better of it; he laughed at me again. With an odd exhilaration—as if we were something childish and something wonderful, as if he were doing us an enormous favor—he took one shaky breath and said, "Well, we're here."

I looked at Spet, Spet looked at Lydia, Lydia looked at Amalia, who is the head of the local town meeting, Amalia looked at I don't know whom. My throat was raw. I cannot stand local beer, which the farmers swill as if their stomachs had iridium linings, but I took it anyway, from Amalia (it was her bicycle we had seen outside as we parked), and swallowed it all. This was going to take a long time. I said, "Yes, here you are," and smiled (feeling like a fool), and wondered seriously if male-Earth-people's minds worked so very differently from female-Earth-people's minds, but that couldn't be so or the race would have died out long ago. The radio network had got the news around planet by now and we had another Russian speaker, flown in from Varna; I decided to cut out when *the man* passed around pictures of his wife, who looked like the priestess of some arcane cult. He proposed to question Yuki, so I barreled her into a back room in spite of her furious protests, and went out on the front porch. As I left, Lydia was explaining the difference between parthenogenesis (which is so easy that anyone can practice it) and what we do, which is the merging of ova. That is why Katy's baby looks like me. Lydia went on to the Ansky Process and Katy Ansky, our one full-polymath genius and the great-great I don't know how many times great-grandmother of my own Katharina.

A dot-dash transmitter in one of the outbuildings chattered faintly to itself: operators flirting and passing jokes down the line.

There was a man on the porch. The other tall man. I watched him for a few minutes—I can move very quietly when I want to and when I allowed him to see me, he stopped talking into the little machine hung around his neck.

Then he said calmly, in excellent Russian, "Did you know that sexual equality has been reestablished on Earth?"

"You're the real one," I said, "aren't you? The other one's for show." It was a great relief to get things cleared up. He nodded affably.

"As a people, we are not very bright," he said. "There's been too much genetic damage in the last few centuries. Radiation. Drugs. We can use Whileaway's genes, Janet." Strangers do not call strangers by the first name.

"You can have cells enough to drown in," I said. "Breed your own."

He smiled. "That's not the way we want to do it." Behind him I saw Katy come into the square of light that was the screened-in door. He went on, low and urbane, not mocking me, I think, but with the self-confidence of someone who has always had money and strength to spare, who doesn't know what it is to be second-class or provincial. Which is very odd, because the day before, I would have said that was an exact description of me.

"I'm talking to you, Janet," he said, "because I suspect you have more popular influence than anyone else here. You know as well as I do that parthenogenetic culture has all sorts of inherent defects, and we do not—if we can help it— mean to use you for anything of the sort. Pardon me; I should not have said 'use.' But surely you can see that this kind of society is unnatural."

"Humanity is unnatural," said Katy. She had my rifle under her left arm. The top of that silky head does not quite come up to my collarbone, but she is as tough as steel; he began to move, again with that queer smiling deference (which his fellow had showed to me but he had not), and the gun slid into Katy's grip as if she had shot with it all her life.

"I agree," said the man. "Humanity is unnatural. I should know. I have metal in my teeth and metal pins here." He touched his shoulder. "Seals are harem animals," he added, "and so are men; apes are promiscuous and so are men; doves are monogamous and so are men; there are even celibate men and homosexual men. There are homosexual cows, I believe. But Whileaway is still missing something." He gave a dry chuckle. I will give him the credit of believing that it had something to do with nerves.

"I miss nothing," said Katy, "except that life isn't endless."

"You are—?" said the man, nodding from me to her.

"Wives," said Katy. "We're married." Again the dry chuckle.

"A good economic arrangement," he said, "for working and taking care of the children. And as good an arrangement as any for randomizing heredity, if your reproduction is made to follow the same pattern. But think, Katharina Michaelason, if there isn't something better that you might secure for your daughters. I believe in instincts, even in Man, and I can't think that the two of you—a machinist, are you? and I gather you are some sort of chief of police— don't feel somehow what even you must miss. You know it intellectually, of course. There is only half a species here. Men must come back to Whileaway."

Katy said nothing.

"I should think, Katharina Michaelason," said the man gently, "that you, of all people, would benefit most from such a change," and he walked past Katy's rifle into the square of light coming from the door. I think it was then that he noticed my scar, which really does not show unless the light is from the side: a fine line that runs from temple to chin. Most people don't even know about it.

"Where did you get that?" he said, and I answered with an involuntary grin. "In my last duel." We stood there bristling at each other for several seconds (this is absurd but true) until he went inside and shut the screen door behind him. Katy said in a brittle voice, "You damned fool, don't you know when we've been insulted?" and swung up the rifle to shoot him through the screen, but I got to her before she could fire and knocked the rifle out of aim; it burned a hole through the porch floor. Katy was shaking. She kept whispering over and over, "That's why I never touched it, because I knew I'd kill someone. I knew I'd kill someone." The first man—the one I'd spoken with first—was still talking inside the house, something about the grand movement to recolonize and rediscover all the Earth had lost. He stressed the advantages to Whileaway: trade, exchange of ideas, education. He, too, said that sexual equality had been reestablished on Earth.

Katy was right, of course; we should have burned them down where they stood. Men are coming to Whileaway. When one culture has the big guns and the other has none, there is a certain predictability about the outcome. Maybe men would have come eventually in any case. I like to think that a hundred years from now my great-grandchildren could have stood them off or fought them to a standstill, but even that's no odds; I will remember all my life those four people I first met who were muscled like bulls and who made me—if only for a moment—feel small. A neurotic reaction, Katy says. I remember everything that happened that night; I remember Yuki's excitement in the car, I remember Katy's sobbing when we got home as if her heart would break, I remember her lovemaking, a little peremptory as always, but wonderfully soothing and comforting. I remember prowling restlessly around the house after Katy fell asleep with one bare arm hung into a patch of light from the hall. The muscles of her forearms are like metal bars from all that driving and testing of her machines. Sometimes I dream about Katy's arms. I remember wandering into the nursery and picking up my wife's baby, dozing for a while with the poignant, amazing warmth of an infant in my lap, and finally returning to the kitchen to find Yuriko fixing herself a late snack. My daughter eats like a Great Dane.

"Yuki," I said, "do you think you could fall in love with a man?" and she whooped derisively. "With a ten-foot toad!" said my tactful child.

But men are coming to Whileaway. Lately I sit up nights and worry about the men who will come to this planet, about my two daughters and Betta Katharinason, about what will happen to Katy, to me, to my life. Our ancestors' journals are one long cry of pain and I suppose I ought to be glad now, but one can't throw away six centuries, or even (as I have lately discovered) thirty-four years. Sometimes I laugh at the question those four men hedged about all evening and never quite dared to ask, looking at the lot of us, hicks in overalls, farmers in canvas pants and plain shirts: *Which of you plays the role of the man?* As if we had to produce a carbon copy of their mistakes! I doubt very much that sexual equality has been reestablished on Earth. I do not like to think of myself mocked, of Katy deferred to as if she were weak, of Yuki made to feel unimportant or silly, of my other children cheated of their full humanity or turned into strangers. And I'm afraid that my own achievements will dwindle from what they were— or what I thought they were—to the not-very-interesting curiosa of the *human* race, the oddities you read about in the back of the book, things to laugh at sometimes because they are so exotic, quaint but not impressive, charming but not useful. I find this more painful than I can say. You will agree that for a woman who has fought three duels, all of them kills, indulging in such fears is ludicrous. But what's around the corner now is a duel so big that I don't think I have the guts for it; in Faust's words: *Verweile doch, du bist so schoen!* Keep it as it is. Don't change.

Sometimes at night I remember the original name of this planet, changed by the first generation of our ancestors, those curious women for whom, I suppose, the real name was too painful a reminder after the men died. I find it amusing, in a grim way, to see it all so completely turned around. This, too, shall pass. All good things must come to an end.

Take my life but don't take away the meaning of my life.

For-A-While.

THE SCIENCE FICTION
ART STORY

The word "art" sticks in the throat when mentioned in connection with science fiction. Even science fiction writers sometimes find it pretentious. Many prefer to think of themselves as storytellers "competing for Joe's beer money," as Heinlein said and Poul Anderson has often repeated. It was this attitude, in part, that New Wave writers reacted against. They weren't ashamed, Harlan Ellison has said, to think of themselves as Artists with a capital A.

Science fiction, of course, can be written artistically. But Art with a capital A is something else. The external characteristics of the art story are a consciousness of style, an emphasis on characterization, and the personalization of narration. A story that shares many characteristics of a genre, therefore, seems less "artistic." All writers put something of themselves into their stories, but genre science fiction subordinates the individual to the general.

More fundamentally, genre science fiction has a message; it is analytical about its subject, whether it is the human species or society or the fate of the universe; it has a point to make. The art story is primarily descriptive; only with difficulty can it be said to be "about" anything; it says only that this is the way people are, this is the way life is. It also is usually pessimistic, mostly because it is easier to write a pessimistic art story; the optimistic art story is not impossible, but it is difficult to bring off. Thus authors of the art story, whether or not they are personally pessimistic about the human condition or its future, usually produce stories in which their characters fail to solve their problems, or in which they never had a chance. If that sounds like the mainstream art story, it is.

Then why write the art story as science fiction? One practical answer: science fiction was easier to get published and still is; almost every other paying market for the short story has disappeared. If an art story can be couched in science fiction terms, even though it could be told just as effectively as historical or contemporary fiction, it may find an audience it could never reach in such a traditional framework. But the only *good* reason for writing the art story as science fiction is because it cannot be written any other way.

As a matter of fact, many art stories are fantasy or resemble it. The fantasy story seldom has a point to make, and the author enjoys the liberty to be just as personal, just as stylistically adventurous, just as concerned with character, and just as pessimistic as he or she wishes. Even the art story that appears to be realistic is no more realistic than the inside of the author's head, and the more personal the writer the more fantastic the story.

Nevertheless, the science fiction art story has existed within the genre almost from its beginnings. Hawthorne, Poe, and O'Brien produced this kind of story regularly. Wells's "The Crystal Egg" and "The Country of the Blind" qualify as art stories, as well as some of his early novels; Joseph Conrad and Henry James hailed him as an artist early in his career, and only after a struggle did Wells ultimately choose to associate himself with journalists, teachers, and propagandists. Dr. David H. Keller wrote stories that could be called art stories. Ray Bradbury was the first writer in the field to be crowned as an artist by the outside world. Many of the stories of Henry Kuttner and C. L. Moore written under the pseudonyms of Lewis Padgett and Lawrence O'Donnell deserve to be called art stories that could be told no other way.

In the 1960s a group of writers emerged whose work fell naturally into the shape of the art story: Aldiss, Brunner, Ballard, and others in England; Delany, Ellison, Disch, Sallis, Spinrad, Wolfe, and Zelazny in the United States. Their appearance, or development, happened to coincide with the discovery of the New Wave. Because it also focused its efforts on the art story, many of the emerging writers were tagged with the New Wave label whether they wanted it or not.

Roger Zelazny (1937-1995) is typical. After earning a bachelor's degree from Western Reserve and an M.A. in Elizabethan and Jacobean drama from Columbia, he took a job with the Social Security Administration and began to freelance in his spare time. His success was swift: after two stories published in 1962, he had twelve stories published in 1963. His 1963 "A Rose for Ecclesiastes" was the only 1960s story voted by SFWA members into the *Science Fiction Hall of Fame*. In 1965, the first year of the Nebula Awards, he won awards in two categories, with "He Who Shapes" and "The Doors of His Face, the Lamps of His Mouth."

He began to specialize in novels based on various religions and won a Hugo Award in 1966 with *This Immortal* (also titled... *And Call Me Conrad*) and another in 1968 with *Lord of Light*. In 1976 he won a Hugo and a Nebula for his novella "Home Is the Hangman." Other novels include *The Dream Master* (1966), an expansion of "He Who Shapes"; *Damnation Alley* (1969), which was turned into a thoroughly bad film; *Isle of the Dead* (1969); and *Doorways in the Sand* (1976). In 1970 Zelazny's energies were diverted into an extended fantasy series beginning with *Nine Princes in Amber,* for which he became best known, but his finest work remained his early SF stories and novels.

His "The Engine at Heartspring's Center" was a Nebula Award finalist in 1975.

THE ENGINE AT HEARTSPRING'S CENTER

BY ROGER ZELAZNY

Let me tell you of the creature called Bork. It was born in the heart of a dying sun. It was cast forth upon this day from the river of past/future as a piece of time pollution. It was fashioned of mud and aluminum, plastic and some evolutionary distillate of seawater. It had spun dangling from the umbilical of circumstance till, severed by its will, it had fallen a lifetime or so later, coming to rest on the shoals of a world where things go to die. It was a piece of a man in a place by the sea near a resort grown less fashionable since it had become a euthanasia colony.

Choose any of the above and you may be right.

Upon this day, he walked beside the water, poking with his forked, metallic stick at the things the last night's storm had left: some shiny bit of detritus useful to the weird sisters in their crafts shop, worth a meal there or a dollop of polishing rouge for his smoother half; purple seaweed for a salty chowder he had come to favor; a buckle, a button, a shell; a white chip from the casino.

The surf foamed and the wind was high. The heavens were a blue-gray wall, unjointed, lacking the graffiti of birds or commerce. He left a jagged track and one footprint, humming and clicking as he passed over the pale sands. It was near to the point where the fork-tailed icebirds paused for several days—a week at most—in their migrations. Gone now, portions of the beach were still dotted with their rust-colored droppings. There he saw the girl again, for the third time in as many days. She had tried before to speak with him, to detain him. He had ignored her for a number of reasons. This time, however, she was not alone.

She was regaining her feet, the signs in the sand indicating flight and collapse. She had on the same red dress, torn and stained now. Her black hair—short, with heavy bangs—lay in the only small disarrays of which it was capable. Perhaps thirty feet away was a young man from the Center, advancing toward her. Behind him drifted one of the seldom seen dispatch-machines—about half the size of a man and floating that same distance above the ground, it was shaped like a tenpin, and silver, its bulbous head-end faceted and illuminated, its three ballerina skirts tinfoil-thin and gleaming, rising and falling in rhythms independent of the wind.

Hearing him, or glimpsing him peripherally, she turned away from her pursuers, said, "Help me" and then she said a name.

He paused for a long while, although the interval was undetectable to her. Then he moved to her side and stopped again.

The man and the hovering machine halted also.

"What is the matter?" he asked, his voice smooth, deep, faintly musical.

"They want to take me," she said.

"Well?"

"I do not wish to go."

"Oh. You are not ready?"

"No. I am not ready."

"Then it is but a simple matter. A misunderstanding."

He turned toward the two.

"There has been a misunderstanding," he said. "She is not ready."

"This is not your affair, Bork," the man replied. "The Center has made its determination."

"Then it will have to reexamine it. She says that she is not ready."

"Go about your business, Bork."

The man advanced. The machine followed.

The Bork raised his hands, one of flesh, the other of other things.

"No," he said.

"Get out of the way," the man said. "You are interfering."

Slowly, the Bork moved toward them. The lights in the machine began to blink. Its skirts fell. With a sizzling sound it dropped to the sand and lay unmoving. The man halted, drew back a pace.

"I will have to report this—"

"Go away," said the Bork.

The man nodded, stooped, raised the machine. He turned and carried it off with him, heading up the beach, not looking back. The Bork lowered his arms.

"There," he said to the girl. "You have more time."

He moved away then, investigating shell-shucks and driftwood.

She followed him.

"They will be back," she said.

"Of course."

"What will I do then?"

"Perhaps by then you will be ready."

She shook her head. She laid her hand on his human part.

"No," she said. "I will not be ready."

"How can you tell, now?"

"I made a mistake," she said. "I should never have come here."

He halted and regarded her.

"That is unfortunate," he said. "The best thing that I can recommend is to go and speak with the therapists at the Center. They will find a way to persuade you that peace is preferable to distress."

"They were never able to persuade you," she said.

"I am different. The situation is not comparable."

"I do not wish to die."

"Then they cannot take you. The proper frame of mind is prerequisite. It is right there in the contract—Item Seven."

"They can make mistakes. Don't you think they ever make a mistake? They get cremated the same as the others."

"They are most conscientious. They have dealt fairly with me."

"Only because you are virtually immortal. The machines short out in your presence. No man could lay hands on you unless you willed it. And did they not try to dispatch you in a state of unreadiness?"

"That was the result of a misunderstanding."

"Like mine?"

"I doubt it."

He drew away from her, continuing on down the beach.

"Charles Eliot Borkman," she called.

That name again.

He halted once more, tracing lattices with his stick, poking out a design in the sand.

Then, "Why did you say that?" he asked.

"It is your name, isn't it?"

"No," he said. "That man died in deep space when a liner was jumped to the wrong coordinates, coming out too near a star gone nova."

"He was a hero. He gave half his body to the burning, preparing an escape boat for the others. And he survived."

"Perhaps a few pieces of him did. No more."

"It *was* an assassination attempt, wasn't it?"

"Who knows? Yesterday's politics are not worth the paper wasted on its promises, its threats."

"He wasn't just a politician. He was a statesman, a humanitarian. One of the very few to retire with more people loving him than hating him."

He made a chuckling noise.

"You are most gracious. But if that is the case, then the minority still had the final say. I personally think he was something of a thug. I am pleased, though, to hear that you have switched to the past tense."

"They patched you up so well that you could last forever. Because you deserved the best."

"Perhaps I already have. What do you want of me?"

"You came here to die and you changed your mind—"

"Not exactly. I've just never composed it in a fashion acceptable under the terms of Item Seven. To be at peace—"

"And neither have I. But I lack your ability to impress this fact on the Center."

"Perhaps if I were there with you and spoke to them...."

"No," she said. "They would only agree for so long as you were about. They call people like us life-malingerers and are much more casual about the disposition of our cases. I cannot trust them as you do without armor of my own."

"Then what would you have me do—girl?"

"Nora. Call me Nora. Protect me. That is what I want. You live near here. Let me come stay with you. Keep them away from me."

He poked at the pattern, began to scratch it out.

"You are certain that this is what you want?"

"Yes. Yes, I am."

"All right. You may come with me, then."

So Nora went to live with the Bork in his shack by the sea. During the weeks that followed, on each occasion when the representatives from the Center came about, the Bork bade them depart quickly, which they did. Finally, they stopped coming by.

Days, she would pace with him along the shores and help in the gathering of driftwood, for she liked a fire at night; and while heat and cold had long been things of indifference to him, he came in time and his fashion to enjoy the glow.

And on their walks he would poke into the dank trash heaps the sea had lofted and turn over stones to see what dwelled beneath.

"God! What do you hope to find in that?" she said, holding her breath and retreating.

"I don't know," he chuckled. "A stone? A leaf? A door? Something nice. Like that."

"Let's go watch the things in the tidepools. They're clean, at least."

"All right."

Though he ate from habit and taste rather than from necessity, her need for regular meals and her facility in preparing them led him to anticipate these occasions with something approaching a ritualistic pleasure. And it was later still, after an evening's meal, that she came to polish him for the first time. Awkward, grotesque—perhaps it could have been. But as it occurred, it was neither of these. They sat before the fire, drying, warming, watching, silent. Absently, she picked up the rag he had let fall to the floor and brushed a fleck of ash from his flame-reflecting side. Later, she did it again. Much later, and this time with full attention, she wiped all the dust from the gleaming surface before going off to her bed.

One day she asked him, "Why did you buy the one-way ticket to this place and sign the contract, if you did not wish to die?"

"But I did wish it," he said.

"And something changed your mind after that? What?"

"I found here a pleasure greater than that desire."

"Would you tell me about it?"

"Surely. I found this to be one of the few situations—perhaps the only— where I can be happy. It is in the nature of that place itself: departure, a peaceful conclusion, a joyous going. Its contemplation here pleases me, living at the end of entropy and seeing that it is good."

"But it doesn't please you enough to undertake the treatment yourself?"

"No. I find in this a reason for living, not for dying. It may seem a warped satisfaction. But then, I am warped. What of yourself?"

"I just made a mistake. That's all."

"They screen you pretty carefully, as I recall. The only reason they made a mistake in my case was that they could not anticipate anyone finding in this place an inspiration to go on living. Could your situation have been similar?"

"I don't know. Perhaps...."

On days when the sky was clear they would rest in the yellow warmth of the sun, playing small games and sometimes talking of the birds that passed and of the swimming, drifting, branching, floating and flowering things in their pools. She never spoke of herself, saying whether it was love, hate, despair, weariness or bitterness that had brought her to this place. Instead, she spoke of those neutral things they shared when the day was bright; and when the weather kept them indoors she watched the fire, slept or polished his armor. It was only much later that she began to sing, and to hum, small snatches of tunes recently popular or tunes quite old. At these times, if she felt his eyes upon her she stopped abruptly and turned to another thing.

One night then, when the fire had burned low, as she sat buffing his plates, slowly, quite slowly, she said in a soft voice, "I believe that I am falling in love with you."

He did not speak, nor did he move. He gave no sign of having heard.

After a long while, she said, "It is almost strange, finding myself feeling this way—here—under these circumstances...."

"Yes," he said, after a time.

After a longer while, she put down the cloth and took hold of his hand— the human one—and felt his grip tighten upon her own.

"Can you?" she said, much later.

"Yes. But I would crush you, little girl."

She ran her hands over his plates, then back and forth from flesh to metal. She pressed her lips against his only cheek that yielded.

"We'll find a way," she said, and of course they did.

In the days that followed she sang more often, sang happier things and did not break off when he regarded her. And sometimes he would awaken from the light sleep that even he required, awaken and through the smallest aperture of his lens note that she lay there or sat watching him, smiling. He sighed occasionally for the pure pleasure of feeling the rushing air within and about him, and there was a peace and a pleasure come into him of the sort he had long since relegated to the realms of madness, dream and vain desire. Occasionally, he even found himself whistling.

One day as they sat on a bank, the sun nearly vanished, the stars coming on, the deepening dark was melted about a tiny wick of falling fire and she let go of his hand and pointed.

"A ship," she said.

"Yes," he answered, retrieving her hand.

"Full of people."

"A few, I suppose."

"It is sad."

"It must be what they want, or what they want to want."

"It is still sad."

"Yes. Tonight. Tonight it is sad."

"And tomorrow?"

"Then too, I daresay."

"Where is your old delight in the graceful end, the peaceful winding-down?"

"It is not on my mind so much these days. Other things are there."

They watched the stars until the night was all black and light and filled with cold air. Then, "What is to become of us?" she said.

"Become?" he said. "If you are happy with things as they are, there is no need to change them. If you are not, then tell me what is wrong."

"Nothing," she said. "When you put it that way, nothing. It was just a small fear—a cat scratching at my heart, as they say."

"I'll scratch your heart myself," he said, raising her as if she were weightless. Laughing, he carried her back to the shack.

It was out of a deep, drugged-seeming sleep that he dragged himself/was dragged much later, by the sound of her weeping. His time-sense felt distorted, for it seemed an abnormally long interval before her image registered, and her sobs seemed unnaturally drawn out and far apart.

"What—is—it?" he said, becoming at that moment aware of the faint, throbbing, pinprick aftereffect in his biceps.

"I did not—want you to—awaken," she said. "Please go back to sleep."

"You are from the Center, aren't you?"

She looked away.

"It does not matter," he said.

"Sleep. Please. Do not lose the—"

"—requirements of Item Seven," he finished. "You always honor a contract, don't you?"

"That is not all that it was—to me."

"You meant what you said that night?"

"I came to."

"Of course you would say that now. Item Seven—"

"You bastard!" she said, and she slapped him.

He began to chuckle, but it stopped when he saw the hypodermic on the table at her side. Two spent ampules lay with it.

"You didn't give me two shots," he said, and she looked away. "Come on." He began to rise. "We've got to get you to the Center. Get the stuff neutralized. Get it out of you."

She shook her head.

"Too late—already. Hold me. If you want to do something for me, do that."

He wrapped all of his arms about her and they lay that way while the tides and the winds cut, blew and ebbed, grinding their edges to an ever more perfect fineness.

I think—

Let me tell you of the creature called the Bork. It was born in the heart of a dying star. It was a piece of a man and pieces of many other things. If the things went wrong, the man-piece shut them down and repaired them. If he went wrong, they shut him down and repaired him. It was so skillfully fashioned that it might have lasted forever. But if part of it should die the other pieces need not cease to function, for it could still contrive to carry on the motions the total creature had once performed. It is a thing in a place by the sea that walks beside the water, poking with its forked, metallic stick at the other things the waves have tossed. The human piece, or a piece of the human piece, is dead.

Choose any of the above.

THE UNCERTAIN FUTURE

Science fiction writers are poor prophets. They are particularly inaccurate when they come to personal and professional matters, as if a natural law stipulates that prophecies are only valid when the prophet cannot possibly benefit from them. So when science fiction writers speculate about the future of science fiction, they are likely to be wrong. The best approach to a discussion of the directions science fiction may take in the future may be to point out the influences that are acting upon science fiction and allow the predictions to take care of themselves.

Nothing much is heard these days about the movement that was called the New Wave. That is not because it was thrown back but because it was absorbed into the general fluidity of the field. Stylistic adventurousness is accepted these days as the privilege, even the obligation, of writers; and their experimentation is published, even in *Analog*.

Some of the more extreme stylists, it is true, have drifted out of science fiction or departed from it explosively. J. G. Ballard was the most obvious example of the writers who left quietly for greener fields and their own particular audiences; Harlan Ellison and Barry Malzberg made farewell announcements; Robert Silverberg stops writing for personal reasons and then resumes, presumably for personal reasons. All of this might pass unnoticed were it not for fandom, which has become so large and so active that some fanzines have become money-making enterprises, and conventions take place every weekend, and sometimes fans have a choice of several. World conventions are topping 5,000 attendance and becoming big business.

The magazines that nurtured the genre were looking anemic in the late 1960s and early 1970s. Paperbacks dominated the field, and book publication of science fiction roared past the western and then topped the mystery. Almost one out of every eight books of fiction published was science fiction. But *Analog's* circulation climbed a bit when Ben Bova took over as editor (he was replaced by Stanley Schmidt); *Isaac Asimov's Science Fiction Magazine* was founded and soon rivaled *Analog* in circulation; *Amazing*, tottering for years upon the brink of disaster, was sold to a new owner and finally terminated; *Galaxy* went through a succession of editors, was sold and died; but *The Magazine of Fantasy and Science Fiction* seemed in good health; and *Penthouse* magazine launched a glossy new science fact/science fiction magazine called *Omni*, which aimed at the million-circulation range and a new breakthrough in readership, but after a long run went electronic. Meanwhile a sizable number of small, desk-top-published magazines sprang up, along with a growing number of electronic journals.

With the box-office successes of *Star Wars* and *Close Encounters of the Third*

Kind, science fiction suddenly was big in film and on television. The big screen was full of science fiction films and so was the little screen, much of it spin-offs from the original *Star Trek*.

Science fiction continues to interest the academy. Introductory classes continue to be offered in high schools and colleges, and a few advanced courses are being added to the curriculum. Some graduate students are working on science fiction doctoral projects. Professional journals and organizations are growing larger and stronger, and scholarly studies and textbooks continue to be published.

Early in the pre-history of science fiction, genres controlled literary development: epics, travel stories, utopias.... In the nineteenth century and the early twentieth, authors determined the new directions in which science fiction would go: Mary Shelley, Poe, Verne, Wells, Burroughs.... From 1926 to the 1960s, publishers and editors were the key figures in the shaping of the genre: Gernsback, Campbell, Boucher, Gold.... Now, with the magazines no longer the dominant force and other forms of publication becoming more influential and more lucrative, the work of individual authors once more becomes the determining influence in the evolution of science fiction.

Older writers, as Frederik Pohl demonstrated with *Man Plus* and *Gateway*, still can make their presence felt, but the future always rests with the young. A host of new writers have arisen over the past two decades. They ultimately will determine what science fiction will be.

Joe Haldeman (1943-) may stand as an example of a blend of what the old and the new can produce. He earned a bachelor's degree in physics and astronomy (and for a brief time edited the magazine *Astronomy)* and has done postgraduate work in mathematics, computer science, statistics, and art. He was drafted and served as a combat infantryman and demolition expert in Vietnam, where he was severely wounded. After his convalescence and after starting a full-time career as a writer, he attended the Iowa Writers' Workshop and earned an M.F.A. in English from the University of Iowa. He has taught an annual semester-long course in writing SF at M.I.T.

His scientific background and his writing skills have produced stories with their science right and their writing often experimental. He also has written nonfiction and edited anthologies. His first science fiction novel, *The Forever War* (1975), won both the Nebula and the Hugo. His second science fiction novel, *Mindbridge* (1976), sold to paperback for what was then a record figure of $100,000; his third science fiction novel, *All My Sins Remembered* (1977), also was well received. He produced a nuclear holocaust trilogy, *Worlds* (1981), *Worlds Apart* (1983), and *Worlds Enough and Time* (1992); *Tool of the Trade* (1987); and *Buying Time* (1989); before *The Hemingway Hoax* (1990) won a Nebula in its magazine novella version. His story "Tricentennial," which won a

Hugo in 1977, may be an appropriate ending for this particular part of *The Road*; it describes a Vernian journey and a trip through space and time in what turns out to be a time machine in the Wells tradition. It concerns itself not only with the fate of the travelers but the fate of the human race. And that is what science fiction has been about for the last century.

TRICENTENNIAL

BY JOE HALDEMAN

December 1975

Scientists pointed out that the Sun could be part of a double star system. For its companion to have gone undetected, of course, it would have to be small and dim, and thousands of astronomical units distant.

They would find it eventually; "it" would turn out to be "them"; they would come in handy.

January 2075

The office was opulent even by the extravagant standards of twenty-first-century Washington. Senator Connors had a passion for antiques. One wall was lined with leather-bound books; a large brass telescope symbolized his role as Liaison to the Science Guild. An intricately woven Navajo rug from his home state covered most of the parquet floor. A grandfather clock. Paintings, old maps.

The computer terminal was discreetly hidden in the top drawer of his heavy teak desk. On the desk: a blotter, a precisely centered fountain pen set, and a century-old sound-only black Bell telephone. It chimed.

His secretary said that Dr. Leventhal was waiting to see him. "Keep answering me for thirty seconds," the Senator said. "Then hang it and send him right in."

He cradled the phone and went to a wall mirror. Straightened his tie and cape; then with a fingernail evened out the bottom line of his lip pomade. Ran a hand through long, thinning white hair and returned to stand by the desk, one hand on the phone.

The heavy door whispered open. A short thin man bowed slightly. "Sire."

The Senator crossed to him with both hands out. "Oh, blow that, Charlie. Give ten." The man took both his hands, only for an instant. "When was I ever 'Sire' to you, heyfool?"

"Since last week," Leventhal said, "Guild members have been calling you worse names than 'Sire.'"

The Senator bobbed his head twice. "True, and true. And sympathize. Will of the people, though."

"Sure." Leventhal pronounced it as one word: "Willathapeeble."

Connors went to the bookcase and opened a chased panel. "Drink?"

"Yeah, Bo." Charlie sighed and lowered himself into a deep sofa. "Hit me. Sherry or something."

The Senator brought the drinks and sat down beside Charlie. "You shoulda listened to me. Shoulda got the Ad Guild to write your proposal."

"We have good writers."

"Begging to differ. Less than two percent of the electorate bothered to vote: most of them for the administration advocate. Now you take the Engineering Guild—"

"*You* take the engineers. And—"

"They used the Ad Guild." Connors shrugged. "They got their budget."

"It's easy to sell bridges and power plants and shuttles. Hard to sell pure science."

"The more reason for you to—"

"Yeah, sure. Ask for double and give half to the Ad boys. Maybe next year. That's not what I came to talk about."

"That radio stuff?"

"Right. Did you read the report?"

Connors looked into his glass. "Charlie, you know I don't have time to—"

"Somebody read it, though."

"Oh, righty-o. Good astronomy boy on my staff: he gave me a boil-down. Mighty interesting, that."

"There's an intelligent civilization eleven light-years away—that's 'mighty interesting'?"

"Sure. Real breakthrough." Uncomfortable silence. "Uh, what are you going to do about it?"

"Two things. First, we're trying to figure out what they're saying. That's hard. Second, we want to send a message back. That's easy. And that's where you come in."

The Senator nodded and looked somewhat wary.

"Let me explain. We've sent messages to this star, 61 Cygni, before. It's a double star, actually, with a dark companion."

"Like us."

"Sort of. Anyhow, they never answered. They aren't listening, evidently: they aren't sending."

"But we got—"

"What we're picking up is about what you'd pick up eleven light-years from Earth. A confused jumble of broadcasts, eleven years old. Very faint. But obviously not generated by any sort of natural source."

"Then we're already sending a message back. The same kind they're sending us."

"That's right, but—"

"So what does all this have to do with me?"

"Bo, we don't want to whisper at them—we want to *shout!* Get their attention." Leventhal sipped his wine and leaned back. "For that, we'll need one hell of a lot of power."

"Oh, righty-o. Charlie, power's money. How much are you talking about?"

"The whole show. I want to shut down Death Valley for twelve hours."

The Senator's mouth made a silent O. "Charlie, you've been working too hard. Another Blackout? On purpose?"

"There won't be any Blackout. Death Valley has emergency storage for fourteen hours."

"At half capacity." He drained his glass and walked back to the bar, shaking his head. "First you say you want power. Then you say you want to turn off the power." He came back with the burlap-covered bottle. "You aren't making sense, boy."

"Not turn it off, really. Turn it around."

"Is that a riddle?"

"No, look. You know the power doesn't really come from the Death Valley grid; it's just a way station and accumulator. Power comes from the orbital—"

"I know all that, Charlie. I've got a Science Certificate."

"Sure. So what we've got is a big microwave laser in orbit, that shoots down a tight beam of power. Enough to keep North America running. Enough—"

"That's what I mean. You can't just—"

"So we turn it around and shoot it at a power grid on the Moon. Relay the power around to the big radio dish at Farside. Turn it into radio waves and point it at 61 Cygni. Give 'em a blast that'll fry their fillings."

"Doesn't sound neighborly."

"It wouldn't actually be that powerful—but it would be a hell of a lot more powerful than any natural 21-centimeter source."

"I don't know, boy." He rubbed his eyes and grimaced. "I could maybe do it on the sly, only tell a few people what's on. But that'd only work for a few minutes... what do you need twelve hours for, anyway?"

"Well, the thing won't aim itself at the Moon automatically, the way it does at Death Valley. Figure as much as an hour to get the thing turned around and aimed.

"Then, we don't want to just send a blast of radio waves at them. We've got a five-hour program, that first builds up a mutual language, then tells them about us, and finally asks them some questions. We want to send it twice."

Connors refilled both glasses. "How old were you in '47, Charlie?"

"I was born in '45."

"You don't remember the Blackout. Ten thousand people died... and you want me to suggest—"

"Come on, Bo, it's not the same thing. We know the accumulators work now—besides, the ones who died, most of them had faulty fail-safes on their cars. If we warn them the power's going to drop, they'll check their fail-safes or damn well stay out of the air."

"And the media? They'd have to take turns broadcasting. Are you going to tell the People what they can watch?"

"Fuzz the media. They'll be getting the biggest story since the crucifixion."

"Maybe." Connors took a cigarette and pushed the box toward Charlie. "You don't remember what happened to the Senators from California in '47, do you?"

"Nothing good, I suppose."

"No, indeed. They were impeached. Lucky they weren't lynched. Even though the real trouble was way up in orbit.

"Like you say: people pay a grid tax to California. They think the power comes from California. If something fuzzes up, they get pissed at California. I'm the Lib Senator from California, Charlie; ask me for the Moon, maybe I can do something. Don't ask me to fuzz around with Death Valley."

"All right, all right. It's not like I was asking you to wire it for me, Bo. Just get it on the ballot. We'll do everything we can to educate—"

"Won't work. You barely got the Scylla probe voted in—and that was no skin off nobody, not with L-5 picking up the tab."

"Just get it on the ballot."

"We'll see. I've got a quota, you know that. And the Tricentennial coming up, hell, everybody wants on the ballot."

"Please, Bo. This is bigger than that. This is bigger than anything. Get it on the ballot."

"Maybe as a rider. No promises."

March 1992

From *Fax & Pix*, 12 March 1992:

ANTIQUE SPACEPROBE ZAPPED BY NEW STARS

1.   Pioneer 10 sent first Jupiter pix Earthward in 1973 (see pix upleft, upright).
2.   Left solar system 1987. First man-made thing to leave solar system.
3.   Yesterday, reports NSA, Pioneer 10 begins A.M. to pick up heavy radiation. Gets more and more to max about 3 P.M. Then goes back down. Radiation has to come from outside solar system.
4.   NSA and Hawaii scientists say Pioneer 10 went through disk of synchrotron (sin kro tron) radiation that comes from two stars we didn't know about before.

   A.   The stars are small "black dwarfs."
   B.   They are going round each other once every 40 seconds, and take 350,000 years to go around the Sun.
   C.   One of the stars is made of *antimatter*. This is stuff that blows up if it touches real matter. What the Hawaii scientists saw was a dim circle of invisible (infrared) light, that blinks on and off every twenty seconds. This light comes from where the atmospheres of the two stars touch (see pic downleft).
   D.   The stars have a big magnetic field. Radiation comes from stuff spinning off the stars and trying to get through the field.
   E.   The stars are about 5000 times as far away from the Sun as we are. They sit at the wrong angle, compared to the rest of the solar system (see pic downright).

5.   NSA says we aren't in any danger from the stars. They're too far away, and besides, nothing in the solar system ever goes through the radiation.
6.   The woman who discovered the stars wants to call them Scylla (*skill-a*) and Charybdis (ku-*rib*-dus).
7.   Scientists say they don't know where the hell those two stars came from. Everything else in the solar system makes sense.

February 2075

When the docking phase started, Charlie thought, that was when it was easy to tell the scientists from the baggage. The scientists were the ones who looked nervous.

Superficially, it seemed very tranquil—nothing like the bonehurting skinstretching acceleration when the shuttle lifted off. The glittering transparent cylinder of L-5 simply grew larger, slowly, then wheeled around to point at them.

The problem was that a space colony big enough to hold 4000 people has more inertia than God. If the shuttle hit the mating dimple too fast, it would fold up like an accordion. A spaceship is made to take stress in the *other* direction.

Charlie hadn't paid first class, but they let him up into the observation dome anyhow; professional courtesy. There were only two other people there, standing on the Velcro rug, strapped to one bar and hanging on to another.

They were a young man and woman, probably new colonists. The man was talking excitedly. The woman stared straight ahead, not listening. Her knuckles were white on the bar and her teeth were clenched. Charlie wanted to say something in sympathy, but it's hard to talk while you're holding your breath.

The last few meters are the worst. You can't see over the curve of the ship's hull, and the steering jets make a constant stutter of little bumps: left, right, forward, back. If the shuttle folded, would the dome shatter? Or just pop off.

It was all controlled by computers, of course. The pilot just sat up there in a mist of weightless sweat.

Then the low moan, almost subsonic shuddering as the shuttle's smooth hull complained against the friction pads. Charlie waited for the ringing *spang* that would mean they were a little too fast: friable alloy plates under the friction pads, crumbling to absorb the energy of their forward motion; last-ditch stand.

If that didn't stop them, they would hit a two-meter wall of solid steel, which would. It had happened once. But not this time.

"Please remain seated until pressure is equalized," a recorded voice said. "It's been a pleasure having you aboard."

Charlie crawled down the pole, back to the passenger area. He walked, rip, rip, rip back to his seat and obediently waited for his ears to pop. Then the side door opened and he went with the other passengers through the tube that led to the elevator. They stood on the ceiling. Someone had laboriously scratched a graffito on the metal wall:

Stuck on this lift for hours, perforce:
This lift that cost a million bucks.
There's no such thing as centrifugal force:
L-5 sucks.

Thirty more weightless seconds as they slid to the ground. There were a couple of dozen people waiting on the loading platform.

Charlie stepped out into the smell of orange blossoms and newly mown grass. He was home.

"Charlie! Hey, over here." Young man standing by a tandem bicycle. Charlie squeezed both his hands and then jumped on the back seat. "Drink."

"Did you get—"

"Drink. Then talk." They glided down the smooth macadam road toward town.

The bar was just a rain canopy over some tables and chairs, overlooking the lake in the center of town. No bartender: you went to the service table and punched in your credit number, then chose wine or fruit juice; with or without vacuum-distilled raw alcohol. They talked about shuttle nerves awhile, then:

"What you get from Connors?"

"Words, not much. I'll give a full report at the meeting tonight. Looks like we won't even get on the ballot, though."

"Now isn't that what we said was going to happen? We shoulda gone with François Petain's idea."

"Too risky." Petain's plan had been to tell Death Valley they had to shut down the laser for repairs. Not tell the groundhogs about the signal at all, just answer it. "If they found out they'd sue us down to our teeth."

The man shook his head. "I'll never understand groundhogs."

"Not your job." Charlie was an Earth-born, Earth-trained psychologist. "Nobody born here ever could."

"Maybe so." He stood up. "Thanks for the drink; I've gotta get back to work. You know to call Dr. Bemis before the meeting?"

"Yeah. There was a message at the Cape."

"She has a surprise for you."

"Doesn't she always? You clowns never do anything around here until I leave."

All Abigail Bemis would say over the phone was that Charlie should come to her place for dinner; she'd prep him for the meeting.

"That was good, Ab. Can't afford real food on Earth."

She laughed and stacked the plates in the cleaner, then drew two cups of coffee. She laughed again when she sat down. Stocky, white-haired woman with bright eyes in a sea of wrinkles.

"You're in a jolly mood tonight."

"Yep. It's expectation."

"Johnny said you had a surprise."

"Hooboy, he doesn't know half. So you didn't get anywhere with the Senator."

"No. Even less than I expected. What's the secret?"

"Connors is a nice-hearted boy. He's done a lot for us."

"Come on, Ab. What is it?"

"He's right. Shut off the groundhogs' TV for twenty minutes and they'd have another Revolution on their hands."

"Ab..."

"We're going to send the message."

"Sure. I figured we would. Using Farside at whatever wattage we've got. If we're lucky—"

"Nope. Not enough power."

Charlie stirred a half-spoon of sugar into his coffee. "You plan to... defy Connors?"

"Fuzz Connors. We're not going to use radio at all."

"Visible light? Infra?"

"We're going to hand-carry it. In *Daedalus*."

Charlie's coffee cup was halfway to his mouth. He spilled a great deal.

"Here, have a napkin."

June 2040

From *A Short History of the Older Order* (Freeman Press, 2040):

...and if you think *that* was a waste, consider Project Daedalus.

This was the first big space thing after L-5. Now L-5 worked out all right, because it was practical. But Daedalus (named from a Greek god who could fly)—that was a clear-cut case of throwing money down the rat-hole.

These scientists in 2016 talked the bourgeoisie into paying for a trip to another *star!* It was going to take over a hundred years—but the scientists were going to have babies along the way, and train *them* to be scientists (whether they wanted to or not!).

They were going to use all the old H-bombs for fuel—as if we might not need the fuel some day right here on Earth. What if L-5 decided they didn't like us, and shut off the power beam?

Daedalus was supposed to be a spaceship almost a kilometer long! Most of it was manufactured in space, from Moon stuff, but a lot of it—the most expensive part, you bet—had to be boosted from Earth.

They almost got it built, but then came the Breakup and the People's Revolution. No way in hell the People were going to let them have those H-bombs, not sitting right over our heads like that.

So we left the H-bombs in Helsinki and the space freaks went back to doing what they're supposed to do. Every year they petition to get those H-bombs, but every year the Will of the People says no.

That spaceship is still up there, a skytrillion dollar boondoggle. As a monument to bourgeoisie folly, it's worse than the Pyramids!!

February 2075

"So the Scylla probe is just a ruse, to get the fuel—"

"Oh no, not really." She slid a blue-covered folder to him. "We're still going to Scylla. Scoop up a few megatons of degenerate antimatter. And a similar amount of degenerate matter from Charybdis.

"We won't plan a generation ship, Charlie. The hydrogen fuel will get us out there; once there, it'll power the magnetic bottles to hold the real fuel."

"Total annihilation of matter," Charlie said.

"That's right. Emcee-squared to the ninth decimal place. We aren't talking about centuries to get to 61 Cygni. Nine years, there and back."

"The groundhogs aren't going to like it. All the bad feeling about the original Daedalus—"

"Fuzz the groundhogs. We'll do everything we said we'd do with their precious H-bombs: go out to Scylla, get some antimatter, and bring it back. Just taking a long way back."

"You don't want to just tell them that's what we're going to do? No skin off…"

She shook her head and laughed again, this time a little bitterly. "You didn't read the editorial in *Peoplepost* this morning, did you?"

"I was too busy."

"So am I, boy; too busy for that drik. One of my staff brought it in, though."

"It's about Daedalus?"

"No… it concerns 61 Cygni. How the crazy scientists want to let those boogers know there's life on Earth."

"They'll come make people-burgers out of us."

"Something like that."

Over three thousand people sat on the hillside, a "natural" amphitheater fashioned of moon dirt and Earth grass. There was an incredible din, everyone talking at once: Dr. Bemis had just told them about the 61 Cygni expedition.

On about the tenth "Quiet, please," Bemis was able to continue. "So you can see why we didn't simply broadcast this meeting. Earth would pick it up. Likewise, there are no groundhog media on L-5 right now. They were rotated back to Earth and the shuttle with their replacements needed repairs at the Cape. The other two shuttles are here.

"So I'm asking all of you—and all of your brethren who had to stay at their jobs—to keep secret the biggest thing since Isabella hocked her jewels. Until we lift.

"Now Dr. Leventhal, who's chief of our social sciences section, wants to talk to you about selecting the crew."

Charlie hated public speaking. In this setting, he felt like a Christian on the way to being catfood. He smoothed out his damp notes on the podium.

"Uh, basic problem." A thousand people asked him to speak up. He adjusted the microphone.

"The basic problem is, we have space for about a thousand people. Probably more than one out of four want to go."

Loud murmur of assent. "And we don't want to be despotic about choosing… but I've set up certain guidelines and Dr. Bemis agrees with them.

"Nobody should plan on going if he or she needs sophisticated medical care, obviously. Same toke, few very old people will be considered."

Almost inaudibly, Abigail said, "Sixty-four isn't very old, Charlie. I'm going." She hadn't said anything earlier.

He continued, looking at Bemis. "Second, we must leave behind those people who are absolutely necessary for the maintenance of L-5. Including the power station." She smiled at him.

"We don't want to split up mating pairs, not for, well, nine years plus… but neither will we take children." He waited for the commotion to die down. "On this mission, children are baggage. You'll have to find foster parents for them. Maybe they'll go on the next trip."

"Because we can't afford baggage. We don't know what's waiting for us at 61 Cygni—a thousand people sounds like a lot, but it isn't. Not when you consider that we need a cross-section of all human knowledge, all human abilities. It may turn out that a person who can sing madrigals will be more important than a plasma physicist. No way of knowing ahead of time."

The 4,000 people did manage to keep it secret, not so much out of strength of character as from a deep-seated paranoia about Earth and Earthlings.

And Senator Connors' Tricentennial actually came to their aid.

Although there was "One World," ruled by "The Will of the People," some regions had more clout than others, and nationalism was by no means dead.

This was one factor.

Another factor was the way the groundhogs felt about the thermonuclear bombs stockpiled in Helsinki. All antiques: mostly a century or more old. The scientists said they were perfectly safe, but you know how that goes.

The bombs still technically belonged to the countries that had surrendered them, nine out of ten split between North America and Russia. The tenth remaining was divided among forty-two other countries. They all got together every few years to argue about what to do with the damned things. Everybody wanted to get rid of them in some useful way, but nobody wanted to put up the capital.

Charlie Leventhal's proposal was simple. L-5 would provide bankroll, materials, and personnel. On a barren rock in the Norwegian Sea they would take apart the old bombs, one at a time, and turn them into uniform fuel capsules for the Daedalus craft.

The Scylla/Charybdis probe would be timed to honor both the major spacefaring countries. Renamed the *John F. Kennedy*, it would leave Earth orbit on America's Tricentennial. The craft would accelerate halfway to the double star system at one gee, then flip and slow down at the same rate. It would use a magnetic scoop to gather antimatter from Scylla. On May Day, 2077, it would again be renamed, being the *Leonid I. Brezhnev* for the return trip. For safety's sake, the antimatter would be delivered to a lunar research station, near Farside. L-5 scientists claimed that harnessing the energy from total annihilation of matter would make a heaven on Earth.

Most people doubted that, but looked forward to the fireworks.

January 2076

"The *hell* with that!" Charlie was livid. "I—I just won't do it. Won't!"

"You're the only one—"

"That's not true, Ab, you know it." Charlie paced from wall to wall of her office cubicle. "There are dozens of people who can run L-5. Better than I can."

"Not better, Charlie."

He stopped in front of her desk, leaned over. "Come on, Ab. There's only one logical person to stay behind and run things. Not only has she proven herself in the position, but she's too old to—"

"That kind of drik I don't have to listen to."

"Now, Ab..."

"No, you listen to me. I was an infant when we started building Daedalus; worked on it as a girl and a young woman.

"I could take you out there in a shuttle and show you the rivets that I put in, myself. A half-century ago."

"That's my—"

"I earned my ticket, Charlie." Her voice softened. "Age is a factor, yes. This is only the first trip of many—and when it comes back, I *will* be too old. You'll just be in your prime... and with over twenty years of experience as Coordinator, I don't doubt they'll make you captain of the next—"

"I don't want to be captain. I don't want to be Coordinator. I just want to *go!*"

"You and three thousand other people."

"And of the thousand that don't want to go, or can't, there isn't one person who could serve as Coordinator? I could name you—"

"That's not the point. There's no one on L-5 who has anywhere near the influence, the connections, you have on Earth. No one who understands groundhogs as well."

"That's racism, Ab. Groundhogs are just like you and me."

"Some of them. I don't see you going Earthside every chance you can get... what, you like the view up here? You like living in a can?"

He didn't have a ready answer for that. Ab continued: "Whoever's Coordinator is going to have to do some tall explaining, trying to keep things smooth between L-5 and Earth. That's been your life's work, Charlie. And you're also known and respected here. You're the only logical choice."

"I'm not arguing with your logic."

"I know." Neither of them had to mention the document, signed by Charlie, among others, that gave Dr. Bemis final authority in selecting the crew for Daedalus/Kennedy/Brezhnev. "Try not to hate me too much, Charlie. I have to do what's best for my people. All of my people."

Charlie glared at her for a long moment and left.

June 2076

From *Fax & Pix*, 4 June 2076:

SPACE FARM LEAVES FOR STARS NEXT MONTH

1. *The John F. Kennedy*, that goes to Scylla/Charybdis next month, is like a little L-5 with bombs up its tail (see pix upleft, upright).

    A.   The trip's twenty months. They could either take a few people and fill the thing up with food, air, and water—or take a lot of people inside a closed ecology, like L-5.

B.   They could've gotten by with only a couple hundred people, to run the farms and stuff. But almost all the space freaks wanted to go. They're used to living that way, anyhow (and they never get to go anyplace).

C.   When they get back, the farms will be used as a starter for L-4, like L-5 but smaller at first, and on the other side of the Moon (pic downleft).

2.   For other Tricentennial fax & pix, see back cover.

July 2076

Charlie was just finishing up a week on Earth the day the *John F. Kennedy* was launched. Tired of being interviewed, he slipped away from the media lounge at the Cape shuttle-port. His white clearance card got him out onto the landing strip, alone.

The midnight shuttle was being fueled at the far end of the strip, gleaming pink-white in the last light from the setting sun. Its image twisted and danced in the shimmering heat that radiated from the tarmac. The smell of the soft tar was indelibly associated in his mind with leave-taking, relief.

He walked to the middle of the strip and checked his watch. Five minutes. He lit a cigarette and threw it away. He rechecked his mental calculations: the flight would start low in the southwest. He blocked out the sun with a raised hand. What would 150 bombs per second look like? For the media they were called fuel capsules. The people who had carefully assembled them and gently lifted them to orbit and installed them in the tanks, they called them bombs. Ten times the brightness of a full moon, they had said. On L-5 you weren't supposed to look toward it without a dark filter.

No warm-up: it suddenly appeared, an impossibly brilliant rainbow speck just over the horizon. It gleamed for several minutes, then dimmed slightly with the haze, and slipped away.

Most of the United States wouldn't see it until it came around again, some two hours later, turning night into day, competing with local pyrotechnic displays. Then every couple of hours after that, Charlie would see it once more, then get on the shuttle. And finally stop having to call it by the name of a dead politician.

September 2076

There was a quiet celebration on L-5 when *Daedalus* reached the midpoint of its journey, flipped, and started decelerating. The progress report from its crew characterized the journey as "uneventful." At that time they were going nearly two tenths of the speed of light. The laser beam that carried communications was red-shifted from blue light down to orange; the message that turnaround had been successful took two weeks to travel from *Daedalus* to L-5.

They announced a slight course change. They had analyzed the polarization of light from Scylla/ Charybdis as their phase angle increased, and were pretty sure the system was surrounded by flat rings of debris, like Saturn. They would "come in low" to avoid collision.

January 2077

Daedalus had been sending back recognizable pictures of the Scylla/ Charybdis system for three weeks. They finally had one that was dramatic enough for groundhog consumption.

Charlie set the holo cube on his desk and pushed it around with his finger, marveling.

"This is incredible. How did they do it?"

"It's a montage, of course." Johnny had been one of the youngest adults left behind: heart murmur, trick knees, a surfeit of astrophysicists.

"The two stars are a strobe snapshot in infrared. Sort of. Some ten or twenty thousand exposures taken as the ship orbited around the system, then sorted out and enhanced." He pointed, but it wasn't much help, since Charlie was looking at the cube from a different angle.

"The lamina of fire where the atmospheres touch, that was taken in ultraviolet. Shows more fine structure that way.

"The rings were easy. Fairly long exposures in visible light. Gives the star background, too."

A light tap on the door and an assistant stuck his head in. "Have a second, Doctor?"

"Sure."

"Somebody from a Russian May Day committee is on the phone. She wants to know whether they've changed the name of the ship to *Brezhnev* yet."

"Yeah. Tell her we decided on 'Leon Trotsky' instead, though."

He nodded seriously. "Okay." He started to close the door.

"*Wait!*" Charlie rubbed his eyes. "Tell her, uh… the ship doesn't have a commemorative name while it's in orbit there. They'll rechristen it just before the start of the return trip."

"Is that true?" Johnny asked.

"I don't know. Who cares? In another couple of months they won't want it named after anybody." He and Ab had worked out a plan—admittedly rather shaky—to protect L-5 from the groundhogs' wrath: nobody on the satellite knew ahead of time that the ship was headed for 61 Cygni. It was a decision the crew arrived at on the way to Scylla/Charybdis; they modified the drive system to accept matter-antimatter destruction while they were orbiting the double star. L-5 would first hear of the mutinous plan via a transmission sent as *Daedalus* left Scylla/Charybdis. They'd be a month on their way by the time the message got to Earth.

It was pretty transparent, but at least they had been careful that no record of *Daedalus'* true mission be left on L-5. Three thousand people did know the truth, though, and any competent engineer or physical scientist would suspect it.

Ab had felt that, although there was a better than even chance they would be exposed, surely the groundhogs couldn't stay angry for 23 years—even if they were unimpressed by the antimatter and other wonders....

Besides, Charlie thought, it's not their worry anymore.

As it turned out, the crew of *Daedalus* would have bigger things to worry about.

June 2077

The Russians had their May Day celebration—Charlie watched it on TV and winced every time they mentioned the good ship *Leonid I. Brezhnev*—and then things settled back down to normal. Charlie and three thousand others waited nervously for the "surprise" message. It came in early June, as expected, scrambled in a data channel. But it didn't say what it was supposed to:

"This is Abigail Bemis, to Charles Leventhal.

"Charlie, we have trouble. The ship has been damaged, hit in the stern by a good chunk of something. It punched right through the main drive reflector. Destroyed a set of control sensors and one attitude jet.

"As far as we can tell, the situation is stable. We're maintaining acceleration at just a tiny fraction under one gee. But we can't steer, and we can't shut off the main drive.

"We didn't have any trouble with ring debris when we were orbiting, since we were inside Roche's limit. Coming in, as you know, we'd managed to take advantage of natural divisions in the rings. We tried the same going back, but it was a slower, more complicated process, since we mass so goddamn much now. We must have picked up a piece from the fringe of one of the outer rings.

"If we could turn off the drive, we might have a chance at fixing it. But the work pods can't keep up with the ship, not at one gee. The radiation down there would fry the operator in seconds, anyway.

"We're working on it. If you have any ideas, let us know. It occurs to me that this puts you in the clear—we were headed back to Earth, but got clobbered. Will send a transmission to that effect on the regular comm channel. This message is strictly burn-before-reading.

"Endit."

It worked perfectly, as far as getting Charlie and L-5 off the hook—and the drama of the situation precipitated a level of interest in space travel unheard-of since the 1960s.

They even had a hero. A volunteer had gone down in a heavily shielded work pod, lowered on a cable, to take a look at the situation. She'd sent back clear pictures of the damage, before the cable snapped.

Daedalus: A.D. 2081

Earth: A.D. 2101

The following news item was killed from *Fax & Pix*, because it was too hard to translate into the "plain English" that made the paper so popular:

SPACESHIP PASSES 61 CYGNI—SORT OF
(L-5 Stringer)

A message received today from the spaceship *Daedalus* said that it had just passed within 400 astronomical units of 61 Cygni. That's about ten times as far as the planet Pluto is from the Sun.

Actually, the spaceship passed the star some eleven years ago. It's taken all that time for the message to get back to us.

We don't know for sure where the spaceship actually is, now. If they still haven't repaired the runaway drive, they're about eleven light-years past the 61 Cygni system (their speed when they passed the double star was better than 99% the speed of light).

The situation is more complicated if you look at it from the point of view of a passenger on the spaceship. Because of relativity, time seems to pass more slowly as you approach the speed of light. So only about four years passed for them, on the eleven light-year journey.

L-5 Coordinator Charles Leventhal points out that the spaceship has enough antimatter fuel to keep accelerating to the edge of the Galaxy. The crew then would be only some twenty years older—but it would be twenty *thousand* years before we heard from them....

(Kill this one. There's more stuff about what the ship looked like to the people on 61 Cygni, and howcum we could talk to them all the time even though time was slower there, but its all as stupid as this.)

Daedalus: A.D. 2083

Earth: A.D. 2144

Charlie Leventhal died at the age of 99, bitter. Almost a decade earlier it had been revealed that they'd planned all along for *Daedalus* to be a starship. Few people had paid much attention to the news. Among those who did, the consensus was that anything that got rid of a thousand scientists at once, was a good thing. Look at the mess they got us in.

Daedalus: 67 light-years out, and still accelerating.

Daedalus: A.D. 2085

Earth: A.D. 3578

After over seven years of shipboard research and development—and some 1500 light-years of travel—they managed to shut down the engine. With sophisticated telemetry, the job was done without endangering another life.

Every life was precious now. They were no longer simply explorers; almost half their fuel was gone. They were colonists, with no ticket back.

The message of their success would reach Earth in fifteen centuries. Whether there would be an infrared telescope around to detect it, that was a matter of some conjecture.

Daedalus: A.D. 2093

Earth: ca. A.D. 5000

While decelerating, they had investigated several systems in their line of flight. They found one with an Earth-type planet around a Sun-type sun, and aimed for it.

The season they began landing colonists, the dominant feature in the planet's night sky was a beautiful blooming cloud of gas that astronomers had named the North American Nebula.

Which was an irony that didn't occur to any of these colonists from L-5— give or take a few years, it was America's Trimillennial.

America itself was a little the worse for wear, this three thousandth anniversary. The seas that lapped its shores were heavy with a crimson crust of anaerobic life; the mighty cities had fallen and their remains, nearly ground away by the never-ceasing sandstorms.

No fireworks were planned, for lack of an audience, for lack of planners; bacteria just don't care. May Day too would be ignored.

The only humans in the Solar System lived in a glass and metal tube. They tended their automatic machinery, and turned their backs on the dead Earth, and worshipped the constellation Cygnus, and had forgotten why.

ABOUT THE AUTHOR

James Gunn, born in Kansas City, Mo., in 1923, served in World War II as a U.S. Navy ensign and earned two degrees from the University of Kansas: a bachelor's degree in journalism in 1947 and a master's degree in English in 1951. He worked as an editor for a paperback publisher but spent much of his career at the University of Kansas, first as editor of the alumni magazine and then as administrative assistant to the Chancellor for University Relations. In 1970 he returned to teaching, specializing in the teaching of fiction writing and science fiction, was promoted to full professor in 1974, and retired in 1993 to return to full-time writing. Among his best-known novels are: *The Joy Makers, The Immortals* (which was adapted as a television movie and then a series, *The Immortal*), *The Listeners, Kampus,* and *The Dreamers.* He also became a well-known scholar and winner of the SFRA Pilgrim Award with such books as *Alternate Worlds: The Illustrated History of Science Fiction, Isaac Asimov: The Foundations of Science Fiction* (which won a Hugo Award for nonfiction), and the five-volume *The Road to Science Fiction.*

Look for the next volume of the series called
"...the definitive SF anthology, *The Road to Science Fiction...*"
—(*Analog*)

THE ROAD TO SCIENCE FICTION VOLUME 4:
FROM HERE TO FOREVER

EDITED AND WITH AN INTRODUCTION AND NOTES BY JAMES GUNN

INCLUDES STORIES BY
RICHARD MATHESON
FRANK HERBERT
STANISLAW LEM
KATE WILHELM
GENE WOLFE
VONDA N. MCINTYRE
JOHN VARLEY
GEORGE R.R. MARTIN
JOAN D. VINGE
GREGORY BENFORD
JACK VANCE
JAMES TIPTREE, JR.

$14.99 US/ $19.99 CAN

AVAILABLE IN 1997

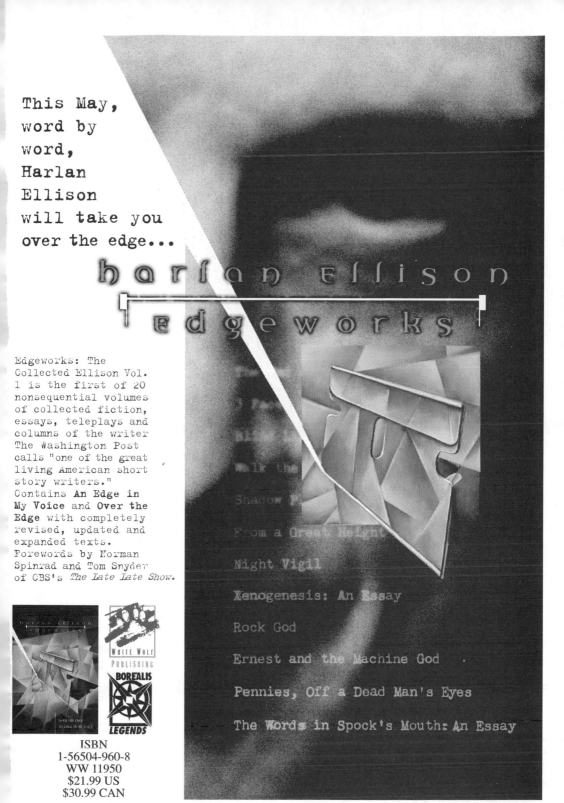

This May, word by word, Harlan Ellison will take you over the edge...

harlan ellison
edgeworks

Edgeworks: The Collected Ellison Vol. 1 is the first of 20 nonsequential volumes of collected fiction, essays, teleplays and columns of the writer The Washington Post calls "one of the great living American short story writers." Contains **An Edge in My Voice** and **Over the Edge** with completely revised, updated and expanded texts. Forewords by Norman Spinrad and Tom Snyder of CBS's *The Late Late Show*.

WHITE WOLF
PUBLISHING

BOREALIS
LEGENDS

ISBN
1-56504-960-8
WW 11950
$21.99 US
$30.99 CAN

Walk the

Shadow

From a Great Height

Night Vigil

Xenogenesis: An Essay

Rock God

Ernest and the Machine God

Pennies, Off a Dead Man's Eyes

The Words in Spock's Mouth: An Essay

Available at your favorite bookstore. For more information, call 1-800-454-WOLF.